Death of the Fox

Other Books by George Garrett

Death of the Fox

George Garrett

Quill
New York

Library of Congress Cataloging in Publication Data

Garrett, George P., 1929–
Death of the fox.

1. Raleigh, Walter, Sir, 1552?–1618, in fiction,
drama, poetry, etc. I. Title.
PS3557.A72D4   1985   813'.54   84-18060
ISBN 0-688-03464-0

Printed in the United States of America

First Quill edition

1 2 3 4 5 6 7 8 9 10

FOR SUSAN

Note

First of all, and finally I hope, this is a work of fiction. It is meant to be. It is not supposed to be in any sense a biography of Sir Walter Ralegh, although, naturally enough, there are a great many things about his life and many parts of it which are retold here. There are important and celebrated aspects of his life, true and false, but part of his fame and of our history, which are not so much as mentioned in this story.

There are any number of fine biographies of Ralegh, written by scholars of distinction. As far as we know now, most of the facts that can be gathered have been; and the biographies of Ralegh written in our time are excellent. I would especially recommend: Willard M. Wallace's *Sir Walter Raleigh* (1959), Margaret Irwin's *That Great Lucifer* (1960), A. L. Rowse's *Ralegh and the Throckmortons* (1962), Norman Lloyd Williams' *Sir Walter Raleigh* (1962), and, most recently, *The Shepherd of the Ocean* (1969) by J. H. Adamson and H. F. Holland. And there are many other books and studies of the man and his works and of those imagined times, some of them superb, done in our age by scholars without whose skill, dedication, and wisdom we should be left with only the dimmest recollections, faulty and distorted like the memory of a dream, of a great age and the people who lived brightly then.

I dislike prefatory notes as much as anyone else. That this is here at all is an admission of one kind of failure. I wanted to make a work of fiction, of the imagination, planted and rooted in fact. I wanted facts to feed and give strength to the truths of fiction. It seems wrong, then, not to be truthful at the outset even though, as in all free choices, there is a price to be paid for the privilege.

GEORGE GARRETT

Death of the Fox

Part One

My lost delights now cleane from sight of land,
Haue left me all alone in vnknowne waies:
My minde to woe, my life in fortunes hand,
Of all which past, the sorrow onely staies.

RALEGH—*Farewell to the Court*

1

Sir Henry Yelverton lies warm in a great curtained bed, half awake, hearing the sound of breathing, the rustling of his servant, Peter, who, just or unjust, can sleep like a dog at any time, content in the trundle bed set at the foot of his own. It is past one o'clock. He has heard the sound of chimes and bells, near and far, and in far from perfect agreement, announcing the new day. Bells and the hoarse barking of a dog in the court beyond his chambers.

Past one but not yet two o'clock. At two his servants will be up and about. At three he will be wakened.

Cold beginning of a day in October. Chilling outside, beyond these chambers. That time when even the most ancient stones seem alive with strange sweats and humors. Time when fog along the river gathers, musters, and begins to march, soundless and veiled, a slow, solemn procession into narrow streets and low places, claiming possession of both banks of the river and soon owning all of London, Southwark, Westminster, the fields, roads, and suburbs for miles around.

Past midnight and a day is new, but he cannot recall the

sound of the cockcrow. When would a cock crow on such a day? And without a chorus of crowing how would ghosts know when to breathe their last sighs, to shrug and go to ground?

Better, since he cannot sleep well, to lie easy and warm, and to think about the day to come.

The dying fire will be rekindled and refreshed, will spit and mutter and begin to dance an English country dance. Candles will brighten the chamber, driving the remnants of night into nooks and corners, casting new shadows on the ceiling's beams. By that dancing fire, on the hearth, ewer and basin of fresh water, lightly scented, will be waiting for his ablutions. And on the rack before the fire his clothing will rest dry and warm.

Later he must act his part as the King's Attorney General. Over the barrel-stave bulk of his body and the layered clothing he will wear against the cold, he will be clad in the robes of his office, black and of damasked silk, tricked out with decorative tufts, and worn open in front in the new style; and all overtopped (alas for a full round face and head) with a traditional bonnet—large and ample of brim. All these have been cleaned, sponged, and brushed. He will wear the robes of office with pride, not so much of vanity as out of respect for the office of service and for the honor of his dead father—Sir Christopher, "the silver-tongued," the poet of Parliament, once Reader here at Gray's Inn, Sergeant at Law for the late Queen, and toward the last of his long life serving the King as a judge for King's Bench. Sir Christopher was a man of greatness and an orator, never brief. One who did not cultivate the austere virtues of brevity.

The son, shadowed by the father's reputation, lacks his

[14]

father's brilliance. Caution has become his style out of necessity. He has taught himself; for each time he has allowed himself the luxury of fluency, he has paid a price for the indulgence. Because of some loose words not so long ago, it has cost him a pretty penny, more than the ordinary price, to circumvent the King's favorite, Buckingham, and gain title to this post he had earned the right to by good service. He paid heavy ransom for incautious words. But he has managed to salvage some honor; for he made his gift directly to the King and amused the King thereby. And thereby learned and proved at one and the same time that Buckingham is not without some limits in his influence.

And so on this morning Sir Henry will be wearing his honor and the honor of father and grandfather before, manifest in a black shiny silk robe. And, more than that, he shares in the abstract honor of the office of Attorney General, the true sense of which coming to him most strongly from the example of a predecessor, Sir Edward Coke. Coke scrupulously observes the ancient customs and ceremonies of the law, large and small alike. Coke makes much of the appearance of all the lawyers and officers of the courts. Coke is as strict in honoring the sumptuary traditions as in the observing of precedents. Coke loves the gnarled English law as no other living man, at times a blinded, smitten lover, but as faithful as he is ardent.

"Blessed with such a wife as Edward Coke has," says the voice of gossip, "what other choice would a man have?"

Well, there is some truth in that, sufficient to fuel the fires of idle tongues. If his wife were born to be neither faithful nor loving and obedient, still he could be all of these to his true love, the English law. They might smile behind his back or behind their lazy palms now that Coke has lost power and

[15]

luster. But though he cannot suppress an inward smiling, Yelverton will not be so incautious as these others, or, for that matter, so ungrateful. For high or low, wherever the creaking wheel of Fortune turns him, however blown or becalmed by winds of chance, Edward Coke *knows* the law as no other man. And he will be, as long as he may live, a man to be reckoned with.

Still, Edward Coke is not a man to be followed in all things. Not by any means. . . .

Great men rise above their peers like the tallest trees of the forest. Proud, but first to catch the eye, and therefore soonest to be cut down. And down they come with a groan and brief thunder. When they are gone there is only a rotten stump and an empty space of sky to prove they have ever been there.

Yelverton has learned to seek what is to be found, what is there for a man able to curb appetite and weakness and to school himself in virtues appropriate to himself. Others may find fault with him, name his caution cunning. Those upon whom fortune seldom smiles can call him merely fortunate and curse his luck. These vain opinions do not matter now. Such as these can do him no mischief or injury.

Slow and sure, like a crude, sturdy, high-wheeled baggage cart rattling along the English roads, the world's worst excepting Scotland's and barbarous Ireland's, he is moving forward with all his goods intact. Not those others, raging or lazy, struggling and straggling knee- and hip-deep in mud, pulling and tugging bulky swayback rented nags behind them, forever cursing foul weather and bad times, can trouble him awake or asleep.

But there is another sort to deal with now. These, bold and shimmering as midsummer gnats, call modesty a mask, define caution as weakness, and assign the cause of it to faint heart. It has been said in jest that Henry Yelverton responds to the least words of the King "as to a thunderbolt or the roaring of a lion." Which, true enough, amuses ambitious men. But Yelverton's solace against the echo of imaginary laughter is in this thought: he serves the King and the King is not displeased with him.

In the balance he has been well rewarded for his service. He has every reason to anticipate his good fortune will continue. And if he lacks the armor of that higher wisdom, prudence, he can always be worldly wise. Armor may shine, scoured and bright, in parades and tournaments, on feast days. But in the brute wars of the present age it is no proof against a mere musket ball the size of a grape.

Caution is his strength, then, and no cause for fear, but good proof against it. He need not be afraid.

And yet . . .

And yet he would blithely sell shares in all his future at a bargain, if he could someway be spared the necessity of performing his duty to the King on this one day.

Surely by now, Henry Yelverton is thinking, Walter Ralegh has discarded the luxury of hope. Or if not—for we live as much by hope as by faith and charity—he will at last have tossed aside his peddler's sack of tricks. Ralegh must see clear that his best hope for life lies in humble submission.

No matter, his dancing days are done. What possible harm can he do? His power to harm has been squandered with his hopes.

Yet there's some truth in that old saying—*any baited cat may turn into a lion.* . . .

At least Yelverton is well prepared for the man and for the business at hand. The latter being of no complexity, a simple

[17]

hearing, rehearsed and its ending already written down, beyond any blotting. There are some problems of law, certainly; for there is no precise precedent for this action. Or if there is, he knows of none and must rest in faith that Coke, who has been brought back to serve on the Commission, will determine the most expeditious means of managing the affair. Yes, Coke would know if there were precedent for or against the King's strategy.

Yelverton can deal with questions of the law and answer them. And as for the man, well, he has the fortunate advantage of Coke's example and experience years before to guide him. Not to follow the selfsame path made by Coke's large footprints, but to find an easier way of his own.

For weeks now he has kept near at hand, for study at any free or idle time, a careful fresh document copied by his clerk, in clear secretary hand, done from dusty notes made at the time—"The Trial of Sir Walter Ralegh, Knight, For High Treason, At Winchester. The 17th of November, 1603, 1 JAC. 1." Has read it and studied it, weighing each word as if he were an assayer of precious metals. And having weighed and valued, he has also glossed it, large and small, as once the ancient Fathers glossed texts of Scripture. He has seen things, made note of subtle turnings and shiftings, which Coke, being engaged in the combat of the trial, thrust and parry, could not properly have seen at the moment of happening. And clear enough Coke did not *foresee* . . .

Which speaks nothing of failure. If Coke could not have foreseen how the trial would change beyond strategy and expectation, then no man could. Coke knew his man well from the old days, especially in the last Parliaments of the Queen. And in those important trials of the first year of the King's reign he was meticulously prepared.

Prepared for everything. Except what in truth occurred.

Yelverton has not only gone deep into the record of the trial of fifteen years ago—and to satisfy himself has skimmed the words again this night before snuffing out his candles—he has also summoned up the times, the very days, blustery, wet and cold, the place and the people, so many of them dead and gone now. It is like a stage play he has seen many times, always performed by the same company. He can play any part in it by rote and, better than many players, with understanding.

He can at any time, as he does now, dozing, half dreaming, waiting for clocks to strike, hoping for cockcrow, close his eyes and bring back that time and place, and people it with ghosts . . .

Plague, worst in memory, raged in London. Stalked the streets like the drunken soldiery of a conquering army. Thousands dying and bells of their departure rang round the hours day and night without ceasing. Thousands dying and other thousands, all who could so do, fleeing the contagion.

The King was crowned with brief ceremony and left at once to find a healthier place.

A bad time and a bad omen for the new reign, some were saying. Others said it was punishment for sins of the past reign, a purging. What was beyond all debating was that London was on fire with sickness. The living lived as if the world were ending on the morrow. The sick and dying, maddened, sought to infect the living, to drag all into the darkness with them.

The Court was at Winchester, seat of old kings, and there Ralegh was brought to stand trial at Wolversey Castle.

[19]

The end was sure from the beginning. In a case of treason, given sufficient clues and evidence, and above all the will of the King, who hated and feared Ralegh enough to believe in his guilt, there could be only one verdict. A trial was necessary, but it was a play, a ceremonious ritual.

The ending was anticipated by most. The King could have asked for no better occasion to assert his authority. Ralegh had been close to the late Queen. She had used him and she had rewarded him splendidly. Hated and envied furtively before, Ralegh could now be hated openly. When he was being taken from London toward Winchester by coach, hadn't crowds gathered, risking contagion of plague, to curse Ralegh? They threw sticks and stones, mud and filth, and, appropriately, tobacco pipes at him. They surged against the guards, and his life was in hazard. In the face of which even his calm seemed arrogant. It was said he had smoked *his* pipe. Just as he had once leaned from a window puffing and content when the Earl of Essex freed spirit from flesh, parted company from his handsome head.

Perfection of that story: James loved Essex and hated tobacco.

Ralegh compared that crowd, people of London, to a pack of barking dogs. True or false, it sounded like the man.

Perhaps, it was rumored among superstitious rabble, the death of this man would serve as a sufficient sacrifice for the sins of the past age. The judgment of the plague might be lifted. Peace and plenty would follow.

So Ralegh had entered the hall in Winchester a hated man and a doomed one.

A place, town, high castle, cathedral, with, by image and association, half the history of England there. Haunted with memories of dead kings.

The hall had been built by the Conqueror. And at the western end, high on the wall for all to see, hung a round table—Arthur's table, in fact or fancy. No matter, no distinction between the one and the other, when common faith is given freely. It had been new-painted, restored and placed there by Henry VIII. It was not an extraordinary exercise of imagination to picture the ancient kings grouped around it, for once, in death, of equal power and precedence, like Arthur's legendary knights. And, staring down with an enigmatic scowl, Henry himself. Eager to see and to judge the power of the Stuarts.

A high-ceilinged hall, with a vaulting of wooden beams. A row of twin tall slender columns joined by pointed arches running down the length. Rich with shadows. And, from deep-set, painted, warlike windows, sudden and dramatic shafts of light.

The hall had been crowded since daylight by the Court and by such others as could find a place for themselves. The great men of England, including judges, the earls of Devon, Suffolk, and Salisbury, Sir Robert Cecil and Lord Henry Howard, were the commissioners. Lady Arabella Stuart, who might have been Queen had the alleged conspiracy succeeded, was present, accompanied by the Lord Admiral.

And the finest lawyer in England was Ralegh's adversary. Another man might have been intimidated by the presence and bearing of the accused. For Ralegh is a full head higher than most men and stands tall in any crowd. But Coke is tall too, handsome and big-boned. He wore a short beard then, pointed, and his eyes, large and dark, brimmed with inner light. If there were to be a struggle, it would be splendid.

[21]

Two stags, locked horn and antlers, shaking the forest with the thunder of hooves. . . .

But it was Coke who roared and thundered. His voice fell on the room, harsh as a town crier's. It was understood that he must speak for all to hear and for the King as well. The King, who was settled at Wilton, but who might be listening from some hidden place or even in the crowd, well disguised. Ralegh, however, spoke so soft that the crowd had to sink into silence to hear him. And for all his years at Court and in the large world, he still affected the broad accent of Devon. You had to listen carefully to hear him. In an open trial, no matter how hated or by whom, he must be heard. This put Coke at the disadvantage in any exchange. To change his own manner, to amend his style, would have seemed a concession to a traitor and, perhaps, a kind of condescension. Coke could not make light of conspiracy and treason against the King. He had no choice but to maintain a sonorous outrage against the accused. Against that soft voice he could only rail and raise his thunder and thus seem, for all his gravity and dedication, somehow foolish.

Why should a faithful servant of the King, strict in the performance of duty, seem foolish beside an arrogant traitor?

Still Coke could not have been surprised at that. He knew how Ralegh had often used the softness of his voice to hush the fractious Commons and be heard. And no surprise, either, in the bearing and demeanor of Ralegh in his courtier's clothing. Coke would have counted upon glitter of the finest cloth and jewels. Shimmer of a jewel box open to candlelight. The absurd fantastic elegance which the late Queen so loved. Costume bright and bold as an April butterfly. Which on another man, a man of lesser stature and reputation, would have seemed foppish, would have wakened anger in some, knowing smiles in others. Here designed to catch and hold the vagrant eye. While Coke, in the ancient robes of the Attorney General, would seem more like a steward or servant than an adversary.

Then Ralegh himself, with his high smooth forehead, his hair neatly combed; a wonderfully pointed beard which turned up naturally, to the envy of those who had to use hot curling irons on theirs; above all the eyes, small bright cold eyes, heavy-lidded, now veiled with sleepy languor, now opening as if from a sudden excess of light and fire. A countenance easy to hate, but still easier to remember.

Coke lost control only when, after a series of accumulating difficulties, he found himself forced into an unfamiliar posture, defending much in the law which he despised, his adversary lightly presuming to attack on Coke's own grounds. The finest lawyer of them all let his passions b come mutineers when this courtier, this sad butterfly living at the tag end of a daylong dream of sun, stepped onto the hallowed grounds of Coke's private garden—the law. Courtier became lawyer himself, citing old statutes and precedents, quibbling over points of procedure, even elaborating theory.

True enough, Ralegh had passed time, like other gentlemen of ambition, at the Inns of Court. They did not *study* law, though. A smattering was sufficient. They whiled away time, browsed and grazed like contented sheep, satisfied to learn enough to handle their own affairs, to act in the role of sheriff or justice of the peace in the country later, if need be; meantime happy with comradeship and ceremonies, masques and revels, enjoying the pleasures of the city to the measure of their purses and beyond that; with a swagger wearing a fortune in

[23]

debts on their backs, creatures of pretense for whom life was a play.

No, they did not study the law. No inky fingers and dusty parchments for them. Left that to those who had no better, knew no better. Left that to a man like Edward Coke. The law was a mere wench to them, an old whore known in youth, with even her name soon forgotten.

There at Winchester with all the world that mattered watching, Sir Walter Ralegh, once of the Middle Temple, once courtier, soldier, seaman and sometime poet, and now brought to stand judgment for high treason and doomed to die for it, on that day Walter Ralegh assumed the role of lawyer and with insolent grace. As if to know the law were no more than a change of cloak for him, a shrugging off or a putting on. As if the occasion of the trial were no more than his turn on the tennis court. He was not a good lawyer, to be sure, as he was the first to announce; but he was on that day a dangerous adversary for Edward Coke.

By law, the letter of the law, Ralegh was guilty and would die whether or not he had conspired with others against King James. Under law there was sufficient evidence against him. Ralegh did not have to be a lawyer to know that much. And knowing Edward Coke and, better by far, knowing the ways of this world, he knew that Coke was playing a role too, that of spokesman for a new king.

Did he know Edward Coke well enough to surmise what an offense, inward though it was, this duty was? Coke knew better than anyone in that hall how the letter of law, without the spirit, kills. And he must teach by demonstration to the new King the first letter of English law, its value to ruler and subjects alike. For, remember, not long after the King crossed over the border and began his progess to the throne, he had ordered a pickpocket hanged. Hanged, without a trial or hearing, upon the royal command. Perhaps things were ordered that way in Scotland, but not here. The King must learn the letter of English law, but more important he must learn that the law gave him more power, not less. The power of right and justice. Power derived from the trust of his people. This trial for treason could be an *exemplum* of precisely that. Not even a suspicion of a conspiracy against the throne should go unpunished, but public trials would make punishment acceptable and just.

If Coke was unhappy with the present condition of the law on the matter of treason, nevertheless the law was not on trial.

Before he was done, Ralegh made it so. Coke and the judges found themselves forced to defend the letter against the accusations of the spirit. Where was that more clear than in the exchange between Ralegh and Popham, the Lord Chief Justice of England?

RALEGH: I do not know how you conceive the law.

LORD CHIEF JUSTICE: Nay, we do not conceive the law. We *know* the law.

Ralegh's hope to save his life was to protest innocence, while acknowledging the justice of the law, and then to throw himself upon the mercy of the King. Which, indeed, he did in the end. But not until he indulged himself, in disregard of peril, in a tragicomic role which won the hearts of all who saw him. Before it was over the crowd, including so many of high place, muttered against Coke, *hissed* at him as if he were a villain in a bad play.

Could the King ever completely trust Coke after that?

[25]

See the ancient ceremonious procession. Judges in scarlet robes faced with miniver, wearing white coifs, lace pointed, with black coifs over them, and all this covered by the velvet corner cap, *pileus quadratus,* not to be removed even in the presence of royalty. The Chief Justice with his gleaming gold SS collar, a chain formed by and of the letter *S,* linked together with garter knots and in the center a rose with portcullis on each side. Sergeants at law in their parti-colored blue and green, in those days; the blue striped with white or pale yellow, the hoods being blue and green, lined with white fur. Clerks in gowns of black stuff without sleeves, and wearing round caps. Gentlemen in regalia of office, badges and staffs, according to their rank and precedence. Guards in playing-card colors. And then the prisoner a shimmering springtime garden, bedewed with jewels, outshining all.

Judges and commissioners took their places. Walter Ralegh was brought before them. The clerk rose and read the substance of the indictment against him and then, according to custom, asked him to raise his right hand, owning himself to be the person named in the indictment.

Ralegh raised his right hand.

"How say you," the clerk called out, "guilty or not guilty?"

"Not guilty."

"Culprit, how will you be tried?"

"By God and my country."

He was asked if he would take exceptions to any of the jury of twelve knights and gentlemen.

"I know none of them," Ralegh said. "They are all Christians and honest gentlemen. I except against none."

Politic and polite, but one might infer, from his relinquishment of ancient right, more arrogant indifference.

[26]

Then, a moment later, he asked for a favor which was no right. With the same calm politeness, he made a request. Professing a weakness of memory and the effects of a recent sickness, he asked that he might answer to the points as they were delivered rather than all at once.

Coke objected to this. It was not proper for the King's evidence to be broken to pieces. It must be presented whole and answered whole.

The judges ruled Ralegh might have his request.

Easy for them to be gracious and concede the point. Easy for them when they knew that no matter how the evidence was presented or answered Ralegh would be found guilty. At the outset they might appear magnanimous. It was not easy for Coke, though. He would have to make his case in bits and pieces, advancing by fits and starts, engaging his adversary in a ragged duel.

Ralegh, swordsman of wit, would draw some blood.

And in early sallies Ralegh pricked the Attorney General to anger. Even before the proofs were presented, Coke was forced to suffer the indignity of hearing the Lord Chief Justice of England attempt to justify the lawyer's outrage to Ralegh. As if in apology for Coke!

"Mr. Attorney speaks out of the zeal for his duty and for the service of the King," Popham said. "You speak for your life. Be valiant on both sides."

Be valiant on both sides. . . .

The presumed equality in the admonition was deeply insulting to Coke. Coke had hatched no treasons. Nor had Coke played upon the King's known fears until the King was persuaded there was a plot against him. There were those who had done so, and some were sitting with grave faces among the row of judges and commissioners. To compound hypocrisy, they now wished to appear courteous in the eyes of the crowd.

When the clerk finished reading from Lord Cobham's examination, Ralegh scoffed at it. Surely, he argued, a case for the King cannot be built upon such a weak foundation.

"Here, let me *see* the accusation so that I may make my answer to it," Ralegh said.

"But I have just read it to you," the clerk replied, unaccustomed to irony from felons. "I have shown you all the accusations."

Ralegh smiled to himself, as if embarrassed for the flimsy structure Coke must defend.

And here came the crux of it all, as Yelverton has come to see it. A point in the progress of the trial where nothing more than a general statement and denial would be anticipated. A broad answer to the broad and vague accusation. Almost a formality. A preliminary to the hard business ahead.

Yelverton can picture Coke turning away to his papers, missing much of it, and aiming by his disregard to show how inconsequential Ralegh's answer would soon prove to be.

Coke appearing indifferent. For he had the case and the evidence. Let the man have his say. No matter how nimble, Ralegh would soon be stumbling over his own words like a village clown.

Which, Yelverton has concluded, is precisely what Ralegh anticipated. Knew he had lulled Coke with quibbles and early playacting. Knew, too, that the crowd in the hall would soon be quiet and still to hear him. And knew they had come here for that purpose. Had come to see him in humiliation, true; but to savor that, they must listen.

Knew this was his best moment, perhaps his only chance

to turn their hearts to his advantage. For, no matter how they hated him, he was alone and vulnerable, all power ranged against him, the wide black-robed back of Coke turned away, indifferent to him . . . and thus to them as well. Here and now, if ever, he could engage his audience. Once engaged, they might be converted.

Again protesting innocence, Ralegh began to answer. He touched upon some petty details of the charges with vehemence, seeming confused himself. And so permitting the suspense of his hearers to mount as they grew more quiet to hear.

Then, adroit, dexterous as a dancer, he was into his true argument. The case of treason was built upon probability; therefore he must challenge the probability that he would ever enter into a conspiracy to advance the cause of his old enemy—Spain.

But it was not for the judges or the jury that he was truly speaking. Upon a page copied in the secretary hand of a young clerk who could not have known his hornbook when Ralegh said his say, the words still shine clear. Clear, and yet a subtle cordial of distilled spirits. And, Yelverton thinks, *there is the man at last.* . . .

"Is it not strange," Ralegh said, "for me to make myself Robin Hood, or a Kett, or a Cade? When I knew England to be in a better condition to defend itself than it ever was? I knew Scotland united, Ireland quieted, and Denmark, which was suspected earlier, now assured. And I knew that having lost a Lady whom time had surprised, we now had an active King, a lawful successor. The state of Spain was not unknown to me. . . . I knew the Spaniards had had six repulses, three in Ireland and three at sea, and once in 1588 at Calais by my Lord Admiral. I knew that Spain was discouraged and dishonored. I knew the King of Spain to be the proudest prince living. But now he comes creeping to the King, my master, for peace. I knew that whereas once the King of Spain had six or seven score of ships, he now has only six or seven. I knew that from twenty-five millions he had taken from the Indies, he scarcely had one million left. I knew the King of Spain to be so poor that the Jesuits, that used to have a large allowance, were now forced to beg at the church doors. Whoever read or heard of a prince disbursing so much money without some guarantee, a sufficient pawn? I knew that the Queen's own subjects, the citizens of London, would not lend Her Majesty money without lands in mortgage. And I knew that the Queen herself did not lend the Netherlands money without Flushing, Brill and other towns as a pawn. How can it be thought that the King of Spain would let Cobham have so great a sum?"

Attorney General Henry Yelverton, lying in bed and listening to a slow-dying night, knowing that he must rise and dress and ride to the hall at Westminster, now after fifteen years about to bring to a final period a long digressive sentence spun out on that day at Winchester, has to smile to himself.

Ralegh was always a poet. One must not forget that. Coke, for all his brilliance, is a man of solid prose.

Ralegh's argument was not complex. It had been anticipated by Coke. Besides which as argument it was obscured, clouded by the digression. He came to his point the long way around.

But when a man is as crafty as Ralegh, it is not likely he would discard craft at a crucial moment.

Ralegh was making music, not argument.

To look at those words and the order of them. To mark how he plays upon familiar chords in an orderly harmony;

while at the same time banging a small loud drum on the nerves of the King.

Robin Hood . . . Kett . . . Cade . . . Each an English outlaw, wicked, bold and storied characters. Each an outlaw, and two of them open rebels within memory. Old Robin Hood kept alive, as recent as the others, by ballads, in country tales. So, naming them, and grouping them together, he managed to summon up the English past and, for this court, memories of childhood and country. Moreover these allusions would strike the King with refreshed memory of the English traditions of outlawry and popular rebellion, of the violent past leading up to the present and, perhaps, to return in the future. . . .

England in a better condition to defend itself . . . A faith, a hope all shared with pride. Had they not endured the worst dangers already? They knew what they had done. They believed this, all of them except, of course, the King. Note well that Ralegh, stating belief in the power and strength of England, chose to express it in a conditional sense—"better able to defend itself." The word defend conjured up threats and real enemies. And called up, as if in reflection in a looking glass and, thus, reversed, the memory of beleaguered times.

Scotland united, Ireland quieted, Denmark assured . . . True enough. A picture, with three examples, of an improvement in foreign affairs. Undeniable and unexceptionable. Move a little closer, though.

The names of other powers, by their absence, are large. Scotland is the first link in a little chain, leads a list of troubles and dangers overcome. Truth in that. For the English, of whatever faith and persuasion, had feared a war with James if he had been denied the accession to the throne. They had feared war with Scotland and an English nation torn asunder,

[31]

ripped ragged, and hurled rudely back in time to the brutal past.

The old Queen, dying at Richmond Palace, had played her final game of triumph with Court and Council, withholding the highest trump almost until her last breath. Standing by her bed with members of the Privy Council close beside him, Nottingham, Lord Admiral, recalled a recent conversation on the succession. She had told him then that the English throne was a throne of kings, that only the nearest of blood should succeed her.

"I told you my seat has been the seat of kings," she said. "I will have no rascal to succeed. Who should succeed me but a king?"

It was Cecil, young Secretary of State, who dared to ask her to make her meaning clear.

"My meaning was a king shall succeed me," she said. "Who should that be but our cousin of Scotland?"

All that she gave them was a question, but it was enough to assure peace and a peaceful succession.

Ralegh linked Scotland to Ireland. Ireland . . . All the history of bloody troubles returned. Blood and troubles still. Scotland and Ireland. Scotland made more rude and barbarous by the analogy.

Denmark assured because James' Queen Anne was Danish. By implication England had triumphed over three troublesome enemies. Put in this fashion, it would seem that the accession of James VI of Scotland as James I of England was an English victory.

Having lost a Lady whom time had surprised . . . Graceful, gentle, courtly, this turn of phrase in the old chivalric manner. The Queen would have smiled to hear it. A small compliment which called up all the best of that lost time. The Queen had died old. She had reigned long, perhaps too long. The coming of James had been greeted with joy. Bells and bonfires celebrated the news. There would be change, but in that change was the hope for the future.

Now the slight turn of phrase must have touched them with shame. Awakened the memory of the grandeur of her reign, touched a pride and sadness in English hearts. There were many in the hall who had known her and served her in love, as few monarchs had been loved. True, there had been troubles and sadness. But it was not the picture portrait of the old Queen of a troubled country, dying after living and reigning long, that he bodied forth. No, it was the ghost of the young Elizabeth, and the proud figure, even when old, in her wig and jewels and one of her thousands of dazzling dresses.

And so she came to enter the hall to join the kings at the round table.

Mention of her in a fitting style reminded them of an odd coincidence. That the day of this trial was the anniversary of the Queen's accession to the throne. For nearly half a century this day had always been an English holiday. Occasion for bells, bonfires, parades, and feasting. That this was the first time that her holiday would not be celebrated, and in this year, the very year of her death. Had she lived there would be no proceedings in Winchester. Had she lived, plague or no plague, there would have been public rejoicing across the land. And the Court would be gathered somewhere, wherever she chose, grumbling no doubt, but ready to be entertained extravagantly.

The Queen gone less than a year and already mourned and missed. A present twitch of shame increased by this reckoning, by the memory, still fresh, of the eager joy which had greeted the coming of James.

And for the King the scarcely subtle reminder that his reign, therefore all his power, was still in infancy.

We now had an active King, a lawful successor. . . . The King could not take offense. It was a compliment on his behalf, a further example of England's "better position." Except that the King was, thus, *set against* the memory of the Queen. She was described in poetry, he in prose. Active? Yes, he was already busy with affairs. And Ralegh called him a *lawful* successor. A matter the English had agreed to agree upon. Yet the English law was doubtful. In this hall was the Lady Arabella Stuart, on whose behalf, though all unknown to her, Cobham's plot of treason was hatched. The probability of the plot depended upon the strength of her right to the throne. Though the King enjoyed priority of blood, the Lady Arabella was English by birth. And under the letter of the law there was that old statute, 25 Edward III, which stated that no one born outside England could inherit land within the realm. And there was also the last will of Henry VIII, which would have barred both the Lady Arabella and King James.

By asserting the lawfulness of the King's throne, Ralegh reminded one and all that there were at least some doubts.

The state of Spain was not unknown to me. . . .

Ralegh had often played cards with the Queen. Here was his trump. He had held off naming the true enemy, the most urgent danger, until now. He stood accused of entering into a conspiracy on behalf of Spain. Very well, he would picture the present state of Spain in the world. He counted off English victories, ending his count with the defeat of the Armada in '88. And here he was, one of those soldiers and seamen who

[34]

had beaten the Spaniards back again and again. He pictured proud Spain from the popular English view—dishonored and discouraged. The pressure of Spain for a settlement with the new King was seen as "creeping to the King, my master, for peace." The fortunate King was reaping a bountiful harvest which others had planted and cultivated. Even the peace he so desired with Spain could be seen as inherited, a gift of the late Queen and the English.

Another quick thrust at the King. Peace, the King's ideal and noble aim, coupled with "creeping." Who goes the extra mile for peace, goes it on his hands and knees.

Whoever read or heard of a prince disbursing so much money without some guarantee, a sufficient pawn? The unlikelihood of the Spanish King gambling wealth on a conspiracy.

Ralegh had cited the example of the Jesuits in Spain reduced to mendicants at the church door. A picture that pleased his hearers, Catholic and Protestant alike. Yet it was the intelligence of Spanish Jesuits against the English Catholics which had given the King his first clues of this treason.

And even though Spain might not squander money on the dubious prospect of an English conspiracy, to be managed in large part by old enemies of Spain, still there had been many conspiracies and plots fueled by Spanish gold in the last reign. He recalled them, even in protestation. Spain was not to be trusted, in peace or war.

He gave example of the practice of princes by referring to Elizabeth again. He reminded them how the rich citizens of London had required mortgages from her. The old quarrel between the Court and prosperous London began again. And with that the memory of how faithfully and rigorously the Queen had repaid her debts, a fine profit accruing to the lenders.

Thus Ralegh called their gratitude into question.

The Lord Mayor had closed the gates of London and armed the militia when the Queen died. He refused entrance to the Council to announce the succession until he was certain James would be named King. The citizens of London were strong for James, and they were already receiving their rewards from the King. Pictured as demanding and receiving mortgages from the Queen, they did not appear to best advantage.

Another slight feint with a metaphorical dagger. In Scotland the King had been poor and hard-pressed. Here he saw riches, rich houses and lands, many palaces and more money than he had ever hoped for. Yet the Queen had been frugal and had devised tricks to keep taxes down and to prevent unhappy confrontations with her Parliament. At once overwhelmed with riches and aware of the limitations of his new estate, already anxious for hard money in his coffers, James was here reminded that the Queen had often been forced to borrow from merchants of London.

A digressive discourse on probability. Ralegh would not go free. No chance of that. But from that point on it was a different kind of trial. It was the King and the Law who were on the defensive. Details of the treason plot seemed trivial. Points of law seemed inconclusive.

The trial disintegrated into charge and countercharge, clash of conflicting evidence.

It was amid all this that Ralegh most deeply wounded Coke.

Professing ignorance, he asked only for two things: that there should be more than the testimony of one witness to prove a man guilty of treason and that he should have the right to question Cobham face to face. He cited statutes from the reigns of Edward and Elizabeth to support his requests.

[36]

It fell upon Coke, then, and the judges as well, to explain how the old laws had now been repealed or changed, that his citations no longer applied. Which was all true. Point by point. Yet Ralegh seemed entirely reasonable. Ralegh's arguments were clear; the law, devious and equivocal.

For Coke it was especially galling. Ralegh had stood for traditions, embodied in old statutes, of the English common law. Coke honored common law as the breath and soul of the law. And, in truth, the traditions of common law supported Ralegh firmly in both his arguments. To answer him, and answer him he must, Coke was made to turn around, to stand on his head, to defend the letter of recent statutes against the spirit of English common law.

It would have been less humiliating had Ralegh hurled dung and stable straw at him.

And so, before the conclusion of the trial, the King's justice was strongly challenged. Coke was left shamed and frothing with fury. And Ralegh, though convicted by the jury in less than a quarter of an hour, was triumphant in disgrace.

After a perfunctory protest against the verdict, he was brief in his acceptance of it.

RALEGH: I submit myself to the King's mercy. I know his mercy is greater than my offense. I recommend my wife, and my son of tender years to his compassion.

Before passing sentence, Lord Chief Justice Popham felt compelled to give Ralegh a lecture. Not on legality, for the law had a bitter taste by that time of the afternoon. But, of all things, to lecture the Fox on the subject of worldly wisdom —"It is best for man not to seek to climb too high, lest he fall; nor yet to creep too low, lest he be trodden on." He

[37]

laid on hard, stressing Ralegh's wealth, power, and his ambitions. And chastised him for the rumor, once bruited about, that Ralegh had held "most heathenish and blasphemous opinions."

Something must be salvaged from all this for the King. All that the Lord Chief Justice could do was to try to erase the trial and to return it to its beginning, to recreate Ralegh as the best-hated man in the realm, and then to pass sentence on him.

Again the advantage was with Ralegh. He stood, tall, head up, silently bearing the redundant and unnecessary chastisement.

Finally the sentence: *"That you shall be had from hence to the place whence you came, there to remain until the day of execution, and from thence you shall be drawn upon a hurdle, through the open streets, to the place of execution, there to be hanged and cut down alive, and your body shall be opened, your heart and bowels plucked out, and your privy-members cut off and thrown into the fire before your eyes, then your head to be strucken off from your body, which shall be divided into four quarters, to be disposed of at the King's pleasure. And God have mercy upon your soul."*

The traditional and symbolic execution of a traitor. Drawn on a hurdle, backwards at the tail of a horse, unfit to tread the earth and, upside down, to breathe the air. Strangled by being hanged between heaven and earth, unworthy of either. Castrated as unworthy of leaving any seed behind him. His bowels and heart ripped out and burned, for they, too, were guilty—the secret places where he had kept his treason. His head, the schemer and imaginer of mischief, to be cut off. His body to be cut into quarters, a disgust to men and food for carrion birds.

[38]

The Lord Chief Justice took the white wand of authority and broke it, ending the proceedings. The guards, breastplates and shiny halberds, red velvet doublets, swords and short cloaks, moved around the prisoner and marched him from the hall.

If the King had hoped to rally support around the disgrace of Ralegh, he had already failed when Ralegh was led away by guards he had once commanded, to climb to a high tower cell overlooking the yard.

Two of the King's courtiers, one an Englishman and one a trusted Scot, brought him a prompt report on the trial. Roger Ashton spoke to the King with some courage and honesty, though not directly to the point.

"No man ever spoke so well in the past," he said. "And I doubt any will do so in times to come."

But it was not Ralegh's rhetoric that concerned the King. James Hay, the Scotsman, once a favorite and always to be trusted, told him what he had to hear, like it or not.

"When I saw him first today, I shared the common hatred of the man. And I thought I would have gone a hundred miles to watch him hang. But before he left the hall, I knew I would go a thousand to save his life. And so would others who were there today."

But that was long ago, longer than the span of years between. A lifetime long, and the world has changed as if by flood or fire, washed or burned, and now renewed.

Only, through odd circumstance, this affair of the last age must be settled now. And Sir Henry Yelverton is the King's man and the man to settle it. All things are ready. He cannot be better prepared.

[39]

And, most comforting of all, he knows his man. Oh, there are limits to readiness. No doubt in the world the Fox will try a trick or two. But he's an old fox now, stiffened with age, and there can be no new tricks. Let him come in all his dazzling finery. Let him have his full say, play with wit and poetry. It will be wasted. If never born to be called a silver tongue, Sir Henry will treat him with respect and honor. His modest simplicity will make the man's mime of bravado ring counterfeit.

And if Ralegh can whisper up a multitude of famous ghosts, who will remember them? Who will know their names and faces?

Yelverton is confident and can find no cause for apprehension. Yet he cannot sleep.

He supped well enough. Had good appetite. His bowels are not bound, and his head is clear. He went to bed at the customary stroke of nine. Here he lies, in good health, in warmth and comfort. And deeply uneasy. . . .

He waits, impatient, for the sound of a cock, for the vague music of chiming bells, and for the noises of his servants.

He cannot find any source for his nagging doubts. Cannot find a cure against a feeling that something, unknown, nameless, utterly unforeseen, is threatening him.

He can only lie in his bed, keep still and wait, hoping that, after all's said and done, the King will not be displeased.

You who would know something of the truth of kings, who stir dust and peruse the leaves of faded documents, seeking to retail the chronicle of dead kings and queens—yes, especially you who meddle with the dead, must first strip and simplify yourselves, becoming as the basest subjects who are content to love, honor, and obey their rulers.

You who would begin to conceive of kings, living or dead, must change yourselves to do so. Must unlearn all to learn again. And then perhaps you may come to some dim understanding —like that of an infant in a cradle of the tall alien world of faces which lean hugely close, then vanish without rhyme or reason—not of kings or the mysteries of kingship, but of the dream of kings.

The King of England thinks these words, framing them in mind as if he were putting them in ink upon a parchment. He is awake, not wishing to dream. If he could sleep without dreaming, he would set his mind free and do so. But to sleep is to be at the mercy of dreams.

The dream of kings is not so strange that it cannot be

[41]

shared. All men have known it, if only in memory of the past. So Adam dreamed of the one true King, who was his maker.

To dream of kings you must imagine a world to contain them. Imagining that world makes it so. . . .

The bed in which James I, King of England, lies is much like that of Sir Henry Yelverton. He, too, lies curtained within a larger chamber. Floating high above hard bedboards upon layers of stuffed woolen mattresses, and atop all those, a softness from France, a down feather bed. He, too, feeling the texture of the huge sheets, large as sails, and enjoying their odor of fresh-laundered cleanliness and the delicate scents of herbs and flowers used to sweeten them. His body, too, so weightless for the time being that he can believe himself free of its burden. He, too, warm under wool blankets, with a fine-wrought coverlet over all. His royal head rests upon pillows made of down and edged and bordered with an elegant stitchery of lacework.

The king's bed is grander, its posts more intricately carved and polished, its headboard a marvel of beasts and nymphs and satyrs, leaves, flowers and fruits worked into the wood until, in the light from many candles in niches, all these plants and creatures are alive.

Candles burn, as upon a Popish altar, on the headboard. Standing candles and tapers throughout the chamber make a continual, soft light. And the fire burns high.

No evil can come from the dark where there is none.

He is safe and secure, at the center of the inmost maze of a great house. Before he entered the bed and drew the hangings together all around it, guards searched the bed and the covers, crawled under it; one even bounced upon it and felt every inch for any threatening thing. Now all around the bed stands a barricade of propped mattresses, and outside the only door to this chamber, locked and bolted from within, two armed men stand guard. Which must be sufficient. Since, after all, only two men stand guard at the gate of the Tower of London at this hour.

Was there ever a king born without a witnessing of signs and portents? Has one king died without the signs of nature mourning or rejoicing?

Mourning and rejoicing accompany the demise of kings. For kings are ritual and sacrificial beings, born and called to live and to die in celebration of both life and death, relinquishing their claim to common humanity for the sake of celebrating all that is worthy in mankind. Receiving, at the moment of that relinquishment, an invisible but palpable inspiration, a fiery gust of the original divine breath which transformed dust into the first man. Kings are coupled to divinity, but not so much in wedlock as by rude rape. And ever after, so long as a king lives, he is at the mercy of his Ruler, subject to each blessing and each curse bestowed upon him.

And it is for this cause, and not for any visible pomp and glory or power, that a king is worthy. Worthy to be loved, to be honored, to be obeyed, and yet also to be pitied and prayed for.

To deny the divinity of kings would be to deny the print and seal of the divine upon the human soul.

Who denies the divine power of a king denies divinity within himself. And thus he denies God. And in so doing he surrenders all claim, all privilege to be called human.

Within the chamber are trusted servants. One is wrapped in a blanket and lies dozing on a pallet by the hearth, his duty to feed the fire with logs through the night.

[43]

The other is a handsome young nobleman, not more than a boy really, splendid in white silk. He sits on one of the new chairs, a Farthingale chair of oak, upholstered in dark velvet, a chair without arms, designed for the ladies' fashion in skirts. It serves his purpose well, for the young man can curl his slender legs beneath him on the chair and read a book.

Probably a play or some romance. There is no way to protect the young from their own folly. Idle and inwardly insolent in their bloom, they dawdle time away. Well, it is part of their everlasting charm, that they are so aware of their gifts yet somehow shielded from the knowledge of mutability. They do not dream that all gifts are loans made at high interest, to be repaid on demand. It is well that they do not take the wisdom of the ancients seriously. For the young and the beautiful, words, wise or foolish, are mere sounds, music, occasion for a dance. Then let them dance while they are able, dance and be beautiful as flowers. Spoil them now, for time will spoil them soon enough.

And should the time come to die, now or the next night, this young man in white silk will die for the man in the bed. For how can a bright flower, which has known nothing of the world save the glory of itself, fear the cold cutting edge of the scythe?

In safety, in comfort, and (sweetly, sadly) in love, the king should be asleep. He must go hunting at daylight. Which is why he has come here to Theobalds in Hertfordshire. He is weary from the tedious weight of affairs at Whitehall. And his body is sore from the tooth-rattling trip by coach to the country. He should be sleeping like any common workman. He has supped late and well. And afterwards he sat in the privy chamber in the company of well-favored young men and drank deep of one of his favorite Greek wines, thick and sweet, and strong enough to stun the brain like a cudgel blow. Indeed one young English courtier, a mere lad, matched the king sip and swallow until his eyes rolled up and his legs turned twigs and he lay on the floor, snuffling and snoring like a hound bitch.

The king laughed and drank more, and the talk was easy, of hunting and horses and dogs, until at last he found himself yawning royally, yawns worthy of a contented, well-fed lion.

To bed then, but not to sleep. Since bidding good night to the last and most favored young man, he has remained propped up by pillows, reading from the Bible. He has been preparing a book of meditations upon the Lord's Prayer. So much to study and to weigh, and so little time for meditation. But tonight his eyes did not serve him well. The printed text seemed to fade away as he pondered it. Words in a foreign language. And even if he had been able to steel himself to reading the words one by one, he felt too weary to gloss the simplest text.

Meditation failed him. Thinking of the Kingdom of Heaven he thought once again of the mysteries of kingship and was lost in riddles and contrary paths.

Nevertheless he continues to hold the Bible in both hands, would seem to be reading though he clutches the book as a child in a strange bed clutches a familiar doll.

Since he cannot sleep and cannot let his mind run free like a hoop or a loose carriage wheel, he can try to think on something pleasant.

He can think of the coming morning, the feel of the saddle, where he is most at ease and, for once, the equal of any man alive. Can think on the prospect of hunting, tame here at Theobalds, but offering good hawking and fat deer in plenty. He can hunt here, two hours by horseback from the hurly-burly, can enjoy the pleasures of Theobalds, yet follow events and affairs at London and Westminster. And can think more clearly thanks to the distance from clamor and distractions.

He knows the events and affairs of both London and Westminster for the next few days, as well as if he had authored them himself. Knows all that in likelihood can happen, come good or bad weather, inevitable and irrevocable except the Lord shall decide to declare for His Last Judgment.

Why think of the future then?

More pleasure in this present moment. And most solace in the present for remembering. Here he comes often to restore himself and his spirits, to this place which delighted him from the beginning and can delight him only more because of memories.

The brightest of which remains clear and pure to this time.

A warm day in early May of '03, a month after he had bade his Scottish people farewell and begun his journey to accept the crown of a new kingdom, to see England for the first time. Crossed over at Berwick, leaving the sharp weathers of Scotland behind, advancing, grandly, leisurely, into and against the current of an English springtime. Slowly swimming against a tide of new and fresh blossoming, of clean air scented by multitudes of flowers, now rain-rinsed, now bright blue and breezy, ever warmer and alive with bells and chimes of bird-song.

In pomp and ceremony welcomed and entertained in each shire and in all the manor houses, each to his eyes a palace and more splendid than the last. A strange dream likely to vanish, at the rubbing of his eyes. To wake to such a dream, beyond even his long daydreaming, anxious years of waiting and uncertainty, made all of that past time become a delusive dream and this future the only truth. As if scales had fallen from his eyes. As if he had suffered long only to be at one touch restored and reborn.

Did the lepers our Lord healed remember the horror of their sores when flesh was clear and clean as a maid's? Did the halt and the lame, delighting in the dance, recall the bitter bondage of shriveled limbs? If so, did they doubt the wonder of newness, fear that it was false and would fade?

James feared that, out of long habit and custom, but he had come to live with his fears as a man lives with old scars. Come to acknowledge, then, that sometimes the slight tremor of fearing and doubting adds spice to the wine of astonished pleasure. And he could banish the past, its pains and fears, with a shrug.

Still nothing in all that wondrous first month prepared him for the day, beginning at Brockebourne when he and his retinue were greeted by Howard, Lord Admiral, by Ellesmere, Lord Keeper, and Dorset, Lord Treasurer, and all their men. These all joined his company. And bravely escorted by Edward Denny, sheriff of Essex, and his company of a hundred and fifty men, clad in yellow and red, they set out upon the journey, a few short miles, to Theobalds, home of the man who would serve him, well or ill, as his chief counselor. He had already met and talked with Sir Robert Cecil at York. And long before that knew him from secret correspondence, from the reports of his special ambassadors and from private intelligencers. Knew him, however different in body and aspect, however young and untried he might be, to be his father's

[47]

chosen son, cast in mind and mold after the model of the father, Lord Burghley. Had known Burghley as well as the celebrated discretion of Burghley would permit.

The King had spent three days, over the feast of Easter Sunday, at Burghley House, entertained there by the elder brother, Thomas Cecil. From its order and beauty and grandeur, he had conceived a picture of what he would find at Theobalds. Old Burghley had spent twenty-four years and incredible sums of money building the house as a fitting place to entertain his Queen.

Therefore King James expected a fine manor house, perhaps a little finer than any he had seen, commodious and graceful and well ordered. Ample enough to have offered comfort for the Queen and all her Court upon a progress.

Yet though each step southward had been a surprise just beyond the limits of imagining and anticipation, still and all, he was not ready for Theobalds.

Facing northward, a splendid prospect of brickwork and shimmering glass, upon a hill overseeing the road to and from London, the house was enormous in the earliest afternoon sun.

From that highway to London rose a smoke of dust. Crowds of Londoners, on foot and by horseback, had come out from the city to press around for a view of the King. Cecil, anticipating this pilgrimage and knowing the King's dread of close crowds, had provided a new road for this occasion, a circuitous diversion from the route, leading around and about the grounds before meeting the broad avenue, itself finer than any highway, which led, straight and wide, bordered and dappled with the shade of ash and elm trees, toward a magnificent gateway.

Up the avenue the company came with heralds sounding

trumpets. And through the ornamented gateway entered into the forecourt of the house. There the stone and brickwork and the glass of the three-story façade loomed over them, suddenly much larger than it had been in the distance. Four square towers, evenly spaced and balanced; each with four turrets upon which gold lion weather vanes glittered to mark the turnings of whimsical breezes. Four large square towers and twenty-four towerets. And at the center of all, the entrance and a broad sweep of stairs below it, was an enormous turret made to resemble the shape of a lantern and hung with twelve bells, each of a different size and pitch and tone, which, by a cunning mechanical contrivance, tolled the hours of the day. Mullioned windows of the best glass, swelling outward, as large as sails bulged with wind, from great bays. High up, along cornice and line of roof, were patterns of surprising pleasure, obelisks and pendants. And highest of all, groupings of slender, round chimneys, contrived to look like the columns of ancient times.

With that glowing, sunlit fantasy behind him, Sir Robert Cecil stood waiting to welcome him, with other members of the Council and Court, all attired in a blaze of colors, dressed in richest and most fragile of silks, satins, taffetas, velvet and laces. Each pair of doublet and hose, each loose-slung decorative cloak or delicate jerkin being worthy of the wardrobe of an Oriental potentate. They seemed for an instant as if they were wearing the English springtime.

From within came a noise of solemn music, and, after obeisance and greetings, the King was escorted inside to dine in state. To dine upon such dainties, first to last, as he had never before tasted. Using plate, the finest in England, it was said, for old Burghley knew and loved good plate. To use, for the first time, slender Italian forks of gold—if it pleased him to. To drink wines from silver or gold or agate or crystal.

And this for a King whose entire stock of plate had once been valued at one hundred pounds.

But to dine is to dine. Once full and finished, the pleasures vanish as the melting of snow. More than the elegance of dinner, he marveled at the hall where they sat. For pillars around the hall, there were carved stone trees, each clad in real bark with branches, limbs, and leaves of the season artfully placed. So like trees that birds made nests there.

In the midst of the hall a fountain tossed its jet almost to the ceiling. From a motley base of precious stones of every color and shade, the fountain, now purest water, now red or white wine, leapt improbably for heaven, danced at the peak of desire, then fell away to be caught in a stone basin held by two savage men made of rough stone.

And looking upward to the delicate plasterwork of the ceiling, puffed like shapes of clouds around an imaginary sky. A sky with the planets and chief stars there and the signs of the zodiac. Glowing with light and moving, precisely mysterious, in strict accordance with the movement of the heavens. At night they shone brightly and the moon rose and glowed. By day they glittered dim and faint, as the burning sun followed its appointed path.

Amid the plasterwork were set stones of divers sizes, painted and gilded with many colors so as to seize and return the light of tapers and candles.

After dinner, upon his request, he was led on a tour of the house. Through five inner courtyards with fountains playing water dances. With suites of rooms and chambers and cloisters leading from one to another against the weather. Then inside through a labyrinth of rooms and suites and formal chambers. The walls, every inch it seemed, covered with tapestries, velvet curtains, hanging pictures and portraits, curtained with stuff so delicate it could have served as veil for a queen. In the halls, large or small, were murals, brilliant on the walls; a map of England showing every shire and town worth naming, upon which were set out the trees of the leading families together with the heraldic devices of the nobility; the Kings of England, their battles and triumphs, a picture history of the land; views of the principal cities of the world.

Led finally to the wonder of the gallery, walled outside, it seemed, with glass, and so long a man could practice archery with a longbow there if he pleased. Upon the walls were depicted in glory all the kings and rulers of Christendom in appropriate costumes, together with scenes of the history and customs of other lands.

For furniture there were covered chairs, well padded; a crowd of clocks, no two alike, all so exact as to chime together like a choir. Tables and cabinets of rare woods, elaborately worked and carved and decorated. Some covered with turkey carpets. Others left bare to show inlays of many-colored marbles and rare stones. Tall cabinets with shelves of drawers open for the viewing of coins and jewels and curiosities of fantastic virtuosity, wrought by the most crafty artisans of silver and gold, decorated by every kind and form of jewel.

And everywhere, throughout the gallery and the mansion, the warm steady glowing of old Burghley's plate. Sufficient to require the entire Spanish *flota* to move it.

Outside the gardens and parks were as much a waking fantasy as the house. To the east a garden where, by tender care, oranges and lemons and other fruit trees, strange to the country

and climate, grew. To the south the garden contrived by Burghley for pleasure and surprise and executed with all the skill
famous herbalists could bring to the task. Encompassed by water,
as by a moat, deep and wide enough to float a rowing barge,
the garden was many mazes and paths, some graveled, some
planted with herbs for scent at the crush of every step, fountains, some silver, some stone, hidden *jets d'eau* to play jests
with the ladies, and with troughs and pools for all kinds of
fish. So extensive, a man could walk two miles without re-
tracing a step or reviewing the same vista.

Deep in the garden stood a stone pavilion, the banquet house.
Where guests could gather around an enormous table, all one
piece of black basalt, and dine while hidden musicians played.
Or, should it strike their fancy, climb to an upper chamber to
bathe and float like the fish in the garden, in huge leaden vats
of pure rainwater.

To think upon that, floating in water on a warm May
evening, then when his kingdom was new and the world renewed, should be weightless enough to let a man, even a king,
fall into a sleep. To go to sleep remembering the fulfillment
of dreams should be assurance against the shudders and sorrows
of nightmares.

This is his house now. He had given his heart to that day's
fantasy of stone and brick, gold and silver, timber and plaster,
trees, herbs, and flowers. He wanted all that, which dazzled
and humbled him, for his own.

Which was not a difficult trick to turn. Cecil was eager
to please. And the King was beholden to him for the ease of
his accession. Something could be arranged. If Burghley spent
a fortune building Theobalds, it would require more to maintain it. Demanding more than Robert Cecil had or could

honestly expect to gain. And soon the King learned that Cecil was on close rations, having saddled himself with a burden of debts at large interest in a dozen scattered ventures. Though it would be less than wise to free Cecil completely from his burden, it might be prudent to ease his mind somewhat, if only to free him to practice a more devoted service.

In return for the old seat of Hatfields and for all the lands and leases, upon which Cecil could promptly begin to rebuild his fortune, Cecil gave Theobalds to King James in 1607.

Since then it has been both his pleasure and his refuge from many sad misfortunes and vexing troubles.

Still, in the memory of pleasure the King cannot find the keys to sleep.

He blames it upon the supper he wolfed after his uncomfortable journey. Coaches are becoming the fashion, but none of the roads of this realm are made for them. As soon as he had gained possession of Theobalds, he set pioneers to mending and repairing the highway from London. So the King could follow his preferred route from Whitehall—through the Strand, up Drury Lane into Holborn, Kingsgate Street, and at last upon the road now called Theobalds Road. The road mended to Theobalds and later on beyond to Royston, Newmarket, and soon, he hopes, all the way to Thetford. As decent a stretch of road as lies in the kingdom. Yet, still, not made for coach or carriage. Or, to place the fault squarely, neither coach nor carriage is contrived for comfort of travel. He prefers horseback, yet cannot ride without attracting crowds all along the way. They cackle like corbies, and some always manage to slip past guards to kneel by his stirrups and press a suit or plea or, worse by far, to touch him. Lousy, diseased, ragged lunatic fools. Not one to be trusted. Any rogue who can touch his boot with a hand can easily find his heart with a bare blade.

James chooses the safety of a coach with curtains drawn and horsemen close around. Even then the rabble cheers and yells and presses forward. But if the coachman does not spare the whip, the King rolls by and feeds them dust. Small matter if he must rattle like a dry pea in a pod.

He blames the late Queen for this trouble with the rabble. For her own reasons that woman was ever on display. She permitted them, those who could press close enough, to offer gifts, to kneel and tender petitions. And she did not discourage the old belief that she might heal, cure them with a Sovereign Touch. Indeed, in her great age, in the last years, she seemed eager for these encounters. To what good purpose? The risks were grave. Perhaps it was all female vanity, which is boundless beyond measuring, deeper than the ocean and higher than clouds.

No, the old Queen never doubted or denied the truth of her divinity, a truth so certain to her that she need not speak of it. Moved easy among her subjects, enjoying their love while it lasted. And they in ignorance, an ignorance now doubled by false memory, never began to surmise that which is most clear to the King: that the truth of her common humanity, of her flesh and blood, was no more than a dream to her until death awoke and claimed her, stunned her into silence.

God knows and so does any man who will trouble to look upon her tomb or her wax effigy in the Abbey of Westminster or any of her other monuments or portraits she was not beautiful. Oh, she could *wear* beauty, face a mask of powders and unguents and false colors, hair a wig, clothing so extraordinary and bejeweled that an angel would consider the sin of pride

[54]

before donning such light-riddled robes. And no doubt this playacting diverted the multitudes, though it cannot have deceived them much. Still, what value, what gain in the pleasure and diversion of that beast with many heads—the crowd? To her, perhaps, a sense of being loved. Most beloved Queen . . . Yet even a vain old woman must know that the affection and approval of the crowd are dearly bought and brief as the moment of a spark. Are more fickle than ever Fortune and more changing than winds and weathers. Those who clapped their hands raw and called God's blessing for her in the morning might, between dinner and supper, come to applaud and cheer to see her wrinkled head upon the end of a pike.

To buy the mob's love is to invest it with value. To strike a bargain. To imply that the negative power of hatred or even the absence of love, simple indifference are unacceptable to a prince, are therefore a threat to the prince. Which seed, planted in the minds of the thoughtless and unthinking, can ripen to make them overbold. And in good minds, not blinded out of thought by childish shows, would be an offense. For they would know her aim to be deception. And thus if her desire were for popularity, it was ordained to be frustrated.

Safety in numbers? Witness her life, ever threatened. It is not the mob with dirty hands and stinking breath that kills a prince, though if foul breath and stink of bodies could kill, no prince could live long in England. No, it is the single bright-eyed Bedlamite, a crazed one with a loaded dag or a sword or a stilleto—God's wounds, a table knife will do!—whose face is lost in the field of faces, who can send the prince's soul to eternity in an instant. Or it is the cold-blooded plotter, coming out of the darkness where plots are hatched, like a serpent after the sleep of winter, warmed by the fire of occasion, concealed among a flock of sheep in his sheep's clothing, who strikes for the throat like a wolf.

There is something we have forgotten.

(No, I have not forgotten. I have allowed myself to imagine I had suppressed the rebellious memory of it when, in truth, I have failed.)

We ride again up the tree-lined roadway to Theobalds, the procession moving at a walk through flashes of sunlight and leaf-dappled shadow toward the high archway. Drums and trumpets. Our many hooves make a powder of dust.

Light blasts like silent cannon firing at us. It is the explosion of light against the glass of Theobalds.

Our eyes begin to smart and water. Or is it tears that cleanse dusty cheeks?

The King wipes his eyes with the back of his hand. He wipes them dry and holds up his head proudly as they ride through the arch.

On the broad stairs they stand waiting, these noblemen and great men of England. They are servants now, not enemies. We have nothing to fear. They stand, a gaudy marvel grouped on the stairs, unarmed and smiling a welcome.

Supposing we had possessed the power of arms? Let us imagine that the alliance with France or with Spain had come to pass. And we have come at the head of a mighty Scots army. We have come this far, to Theobalds. And here stand these men of England to surrender to us.

Unarmed, defenseless against us, here is more power and more wealth than all our armies and ordnance.

We could accept the abject surrender and order this place razed to the ground. Just as we have commanded destruction of Fotheringay Castle, where the English tried and executed, nay, murdered the captive Queen of Scots. Where they killed the royal mother of the King.

The King could command that this place be razed and burned, even the ashes scattered in the wind. Or he could accept it as his new possession, dumb with admiration.

Either way the King would weep.

We dismount awkwardly, even with assistance of skilled servants. Someone with an ewer of scented water and warm towels helps the King to wipe the dust from his face.

Led by the pigmy, Cecil, the Englishmen kneel to greet their King.

Among them, bowed and kneeling, one head is higher than the others. One face, handsome, cruel, and composed, with veiled eyes and slight, ironic smile, startles the King. It seems to float above the others.

Presented to him, the King tries to ease an awkward moment with a mild jest, a pun as much at his own expense as the other's. "Upon my soul," the King declares. "I have heard rawly of you."

He says nothing in reply. His face is an unmoving mask. His satiric smile is painted there.

But the others laugh politely, and the next man is presented to the King.

He will not answer the King then. He waits for another time. He waits until after the feast and the tour of Theobalds, when the King, borne on the wings of high spirits, faces them all again in the presence chamber.

The King makes a compliment to the company. The King says that now he has seen this place and seen them assembled together, he is deeply grateful. The King thanks God that he

[57]

was not compelled by circumstance to try to gain the throne of this kingdom by force of arms.

"Would God you had done so," Walter Ralegh says aloud. And there is a prickling silence.

The King tries to speak, but his throat is choked with phlegm.

The King . . . no, it is not he, it is I, I alone in the face of that company, speaking in a hoarse, broken voice.

"Why? Why do you say such a thing?"

"Because," he answers, eyes brightening, smile white against his beard, "then the King could have known his true friends from his enemies."

I close my eyes.

No, I mean to say the King is able to laugh and lead the others in light, coughing laughter. The King does not shrink.

But I . . . I am naked and defenseless and . . . ridiculous. I leave the paper, playing-card King in my place there. I back away from him and their laughter—do they laugh at me?— covering my shame. I run.

I run, clumsy as always, through halls and chambers. Laughter pursues me like hounds.

The rooms are empty of anyone. Only myself and savage laughter.

When I look at objects they fade, wither, fray, and melt. The house is melting wax, and I burst outside running in the maze of the garden.

I have escaped laughter. I am safe here. I can hide at the center of the maze.

I stumble on paths. And as I go the garden changes as if touched by frost. Leaves fall, flowers die, no birds sing. Fountains cease to flow.

But it is not cold. It is hot as a kitchen. I am burning alive.

I come to the center. A defaced statue, ruined, holds an empty, leaf-stained basin. I fall on grass to weep, silent.

And then I hear the rustling of her dress. I cannot see her. But she is here, close by me. If I could see her I could touch her.

If I could touch her, I could seize her throat and stop her laughter.

She is laughing like a witch. I hear the laughter of witches.

"See, see, what I offer you," she says. "I give you the gift you have waited so long for."

I look and see nothing.

"Here is the crown," she says, this dead Queen who will not die. "But remember, every crown is a crown of thorns."

I cringe and wait for the fire and ice of the murderer's blade.

I want to die.

It is true, her gift is a crown of thorns.

Scent of the unseen river, odor of the moat in the close chamber. But there is a fire and a drowsy servant to keep it alive through the night. His quarters on the *Destiny* were smaller and closer by far. Lord, how he pitched and rolled there with guts all awiggle like snakes in a fire.

Here in the walls of the Tower the earth stands still.

Sometimes, though, a whiff of the river's air brings with it the feeling of the tide running, comes into clouds of fever and rouses him with a palpable belief that he is aboard ship somewhere, now or years ago.

He has lived in closer quarters with less comfort many times before. Has lived well enough out of a cedar chest that two men can lug. Has slept harder and rougher than on this narrow frame, slung with ropes and padded with thin mattresses. Has more than one time found a place for himself in straw, or upon cold ground and stones. To waken stiff—and thorn-jointed, heavy-limbed as a lead doll. Many a pallet and bed, made in length and breadth for men of ordinary stature, has been too small for him.

That was long ago. That was in youth. Youth, a time when without wishing, in spite of hard use and abuse, suppleness of joints and limbs returns, as easy over the body as the heat of spirits or strong wines will spread through the flesh. Like dawn in the Indies, freshening all, bright and fair, rich with promises and first breezes stirring, bearing faintly the scent of spices and blossoms.

Now any warmth which touches his flesh—when the warmth is not the inner fire of fever—is like the last red glowing of an autumn sunset.

It is right and proper, with the justice of poetry, that he should simplify himself. Being slowly, continually reduced of more baggage and encumbrances until, at last, flesh and bones shall come to simplicity, being reduced to nothing.

Naked we entered into this world. . . .

The matter of comfort. Comfort, as everything beneath sun and moon, has a paradoxical heart. Even in a great bed, in a house like Durham or Sherbourne, with not an enemy in this world, he would suffer now and suffer much the same.

When a man grows old . . .

When a man grows old, pains come home to roost. Sad tough fowl not fit for stewing. When a man first feels the gripping fist of age and acknowledges that such fierce clenching will never again slacken, not loosen until the soul is loosed, then, still innocent, he regrets the loss of comfort and good health. Would be a poor fool not to, no matter how foolish it may be to regret what is gone for good and to add to discomfort by chafing against necessity. The man regrets. Complains and rails against necessity. Yet comes to live with it, lawfully wedded. And comes, perhaps, to add the grace of some style to his complaints. Sternly suppresses rebellion of foolish wishes. Puts down the idle desire to be restored and to live wasted time again, or to suffer his losses and wounds twice over. Time offers neither pardon, mercy, nor reprieve. And to live dead time again would be to suffer the same gnawings, tossings, and turnings, if not worse.

Just so he must guard against that other unruly crowd: vain wishes for the future. For what may be or never be, but is not now. To live with his aches and pains is sufficient exercise without yoking himself to new dangers. A man can learn that much and then learn to move, to walk like an old man, yet still to hold up his head, keep shoulders square; and when he must offer complaint, in public or in his heart, learn to do so with style.

That is not the last, of course. Not by an ocean voyage it is not. There is yet another step or two to take to the top of the crumbling tower of himself. Another chamber to lie in before the last candle is snuffed out.

And one not often imagined; not known by many men. Not men like himself, who toss their lives and fortunes in one hand like a tennis ball. Most of these die young. Those who do not, who stumble into the bitterness of age, die never knowing what he has lived to learn. At the last, that rusty iron age of man, there is a stone of weariness cold and heavy where the heart was. And yet there is also a new light-headed indifference to all, to past and future, to present pains and folly. And there is thirst. Not a thirst for pleasures which have been drained and are sour dregs. Much simpler. Pure and simple as spring-water, dancing with light, sweet as the earth is sweet. Not that fountain of perpetual youth which Spaniards clanked in sweaty jungles and died in searching for. Nor a thirst for ever more subtle elixirs and cordials, though surely those exist, can be found or contrived, mysteriously, from what God has given us. No, rather something sweet and simple.

Imagine, after a long voyage, water in the casks dwindling, diminishing, foul and bitter, coming at last to landfall, quiet haven. Drop anchors. A boat of ragged men rows him through surf to nudge the shore. A white sandy beach. He walks across it alone toward a waxy clump of green where surely there is water, pausing to scoop a scallop shell from the sand, to brush and blow the grit away. Steps into the shade of green and into a clearing. And there is a spring, round as an eye, clear as a looking glass at the edges. He kneels at the edge, bends to dip water with the shell and to drink it, savoring the taste drop by drop, from the rim. It cools his tongue. Sweeter than wine is the water he takes from the shell. A toast then. Praise the shell and raise a salute in honor of the element of water. To water . . . And isn't that the name the Queen gave him? Who gave a name to all she loved. She called him *Water*. To water, then. . . .

Looking down to see himself reflected in the pool. And seeing . . . A wide blue sky with clouds. Clouds slow moving like a fleet of ships in a fair wind. Clouds and sky and then, sudden, darting, the wide-winged graceful shadow of a white seabird. But the man has vanished. Sky, clouds, the flashing shadow of one lovely bird, come and gone. But in the mirror of the pool no face or form returns his stare. Behind him a wild bird cries out. Cries once and then there is silence.

He is not afraid. Enormity of silence is his delight and instruction now. As if his five senses had changed places. As if what he had tasted was the essence of quiet. As if a blessed quiet

[63]

came to him like water made into music, the perfect music of silence.

He wakes up drenched in sweat, crawling with chills and fever. Calls to the servant to fetch a cup of wine and a candle and to build up the fire. The servant lights the candle from the fire. He brings wine in a silver cup and holds it while Walter Ralegh, whose hands tremble, drinks. Then he turns and heaps more faggots on the fire until the chamber glows.

The sweat-dampened bed begins to dry. Fire crackles and the fume of the wine warms. Ralegh smiles at the vanities of an old man. In the dream he drank from a scallop shell. Awake he sips wine from a cup his servant could not earn in ten years. Why not simple pewter or a beggar's tin cup? Because, he thinks, I am proud. Because I am not one of the blessed saints. Because, vain and proud and sorely in need of redemption as I am, I prefer to sip wine from a well-made cup. What matter, what waste, when that drink may be my last?

But no man is without paradox. Walter Ralegh blows out the candle because the fire gives light enough. Why waste a good wax candle?

Head to pillow now, soft groan of settling. Eyes closed. Not dreaming, not awake.

Rolling fog forms the shape of a man. A long-faced, horse-faced, sallow-colored little man, puffed up like a bladder in fat clothes. Large, soft, busy, suspicious eyes, arched by miserly brows. Lips soft and full as a woman's, pursed primly between his mustache and beard. And no wonder, for when he forgets his lips, the short lower jaw falls slack and loose, and behold, there lies a raw tongue, heavy enough to be served upon a plate, an enormous, surprising tongue which drools a dew of spittle

[64]

on his beard. Pale hands fidget and twitch to no purpose. Unless it be some secret stuttering hand talk of deaf-mute Spanish gypsies. Flutter like dying wings and say nothing. He seizes them to still them, as if they were not his, but were a pair of animals, each with a life of their own.

Out of fog he walks forward. Is he imploring or beseeching? The walk's a duck's waddle or the rolling gait of a dancing bear. The eyes are sad and troubled. They sometimes roll up and away like a clown's.

Ralegh would applaud if this were a monster from a masque. In the theater should such as he enter to parade the boards, Ralegh would join the groundlings and gentlemen in hoops of laughter. But this is neither an allegorical monster nor a clown with a pudding face.

Out of the fog of half dreaming comes James I of England, his king, the man who will have his head.

Yet Ralegh, face against pillow, grits teeth in a grin. If the encounter were real, he would show nothing. In a prison chamber he can turn to the wall and grin to himself. He would strike his servant a blow and knock him to his knees if that man shared his amusement.

There is a logic to the figures and images of these dreams and visions, which, though freed by fever, are authored by no one but himself. His secret smile is in part for the sad clown he has conjured up and now dismisses; for his amusement lies in the discovery that the separate figures of his visions are plucked out of the past as random strange objects lifted by sleight of hand from a mountebank's purse.

The dream is now, but is a full fifteen years old. It has taken this long to arrive. The truth of dreams, like an English army with an English general—Essex in Ireland?—will not be hurried.

[65]

Comes on to the slow beat of its own drums, ponderous and implacable, to arrive and proclaim the lifting of a siege long forgotten in a war long lost.

Fifteen years ago he left the hall at Winchester, flanked and guarded by the same yeomen he had once sworn into service and commanded as captain; until the new King, wisely, replaced them with men of his own. Left the hall, already a dead man by law, but, behind his proud composure, feeling almost drunk with joy. As if by magic his youth and strength—and he was past his prime then—had been restored to him. The crowd made way, stood aside and stared in awe and honor. He might have been a victorious conqueror at the head of his army.

But that was the folly, the delusion of his feelings. A young soldier's intoxicated joy after a battle to find himself alive and whole. What if the field is strewn with the stiff and stinking corpses of comrades? He is alive. He is Achilles, the invulnerable. Nothing can touch or harm him, the world is new and beautiful. He would laugh out loud if it were not unseemly. Yet that crazed mood will pass before he has pulled off his muddy boots, and, alone, the young soldier will turn cold, sweat, tremble like an aspen leaf, and weep in secret for fallen comrades. And, out of pain and gusts of fear, he will weep for himself and a world gone gray with age. His tongue will turn dry and thin as a leaf in November. Gulping, gagging, he will hold up a bucket of ditchwater, water for horses, and drink it like nectar. . . .

No longer young, he left the hall in youth and had not climbed three steps of the steep twisty way to the top cell of the ancient tower of Wolversey before age bent him with a cudgel blow and every bruise he had earned in a lifetime was new, each scar itched like a healing wound. Gagged then, but did not puke in the presence of comrades, his guards. Stumbled on the third step as the stiffness of his leg, the crippling wound from Cadiz, made him wince.

A heavy hand, firm and hard, helped him keep his balance. A rough beard brushing his ear, whisper of words, hoarse whisper.

"Easy now, Captain. 'Tis a high climb to the top and no hurry. Let's all go slow and save sweat."

Steep and round and around to that topmost cell. Wondering why the King would want him there with a bird's-eye view of the castle yard and all coming and going. For a safety? He could be secure and out of sight and seeing in the darkness, dank straw, and excremental stink of a lower dungeon. Wondering what the King had in mind by having him placed in adequate comfort with clean air and as much light as autumn could give any place there, with windows where he could see as far as the light allowed. And would be seen.

Perhaps, to the King, this was the greater punishment, to be so placed and preserved as to be tormented, not by common darkness and discomfort, but by a keen awareness of the life he must soon lose.

In time the aims of the King came clearer to him. And there was time to see much of it, to hear news of what he could not see, to weigh and to think it through.

Before any action, death or mercy, all of those in the alleged plots against the King, joined together, though separately named as the Main and the Bye Plots, must be tried. The two English Catholic priests, of whom Ralegh knew nothing, had already been tried and convicted. They suffered and waited elsewhere. Likely in chains in the deep dungeon. There were more to be tried before any blood or pardon was possible. Which left time

[67]

to think on his condition. Time, like a wild bird in a cage, to wear himself into a stony despair. Time, like the thrashing of wings against a cage, to write letters, to seek to rally support and petitions to save his skin, if not his soul. Time to write more than once, if only for the sake of his wife and son, pleading for the King's mercy.

Very well, if that was the stratagem of the King, Ralegh would not resist it. If the King desired to break his pride, to see him humbled, he would give the King that pleasure, taking on humility by free choice. As a man might don a cloak against the weather. Live or die, he could satisfy the King's desires in such a way that there would be no satisfaction.

Immediately he wrote to the King, pleading for his life, yet asking, if he must die, to die last. Embracing the King's stratagem blindly. Back came the answer. His request to die last was granted. And he knew he had surmised the King's purposes with some truth. Better, by craft he had made a change. He was no longer a pawn or a knight, but now a player, hard-pressed, but still free to move and to counter the moves of his opponent.

And meantime the two were equal and together in one thing. For the present both could only watch and wait upon events. King and condemned culprit must wait upon the other trials, one by one.

The King must have been disappointed at how things had turned against him at Ralegh's trial. But that was done with and the King would not cry like a country milkmaid over the spilling of one pail of milk.

Perhaps the trial of Cobham could restore some order. Henry Brooke, Earl of Cobham, Warden of the Cinque Ports by proud inheritance. A foolish, vain, fearful, extravagant man, a man of quick tongue and slow wit, true. But Cobham would want to save his life above all things. He must know that his best hope was to please the King by repairing the damage of Ralegh's trial.

But Cobham feared for his life too much to see things clear or to contain himself. He was abject, trembling, sniveling. He mumbled, he wept, he blamed Ralegh for everything. And so he was doubted and scorned as a fool.

So much for the Main Plot of Ralegh and Cobham.

Next came Lord Grey de Wilton, charged with the Bye. With the priests already tried and convicted, Lord Grey's trial was certain to be swift and simple. Lord Grey was a young man and likely to value his life more dearly than even Cobham. Lord Grey was proud. He would value his good name as much as his life.

Value life and good name he did, but, alas for the King's design, he did so as only the young can. Without one least concession or hint of compromise. At his trial Lord Grey showed high spirits, energy, pride, and condescension. He fought back, fruitlessly to be sure, but point by point and without discrimination among large and small. The trial lasted more than twelve hours, wore on into evening and the lighting of torches in the hall.

The last of the public trials ended with dull yawns and the murmur of empty stomachs.

The effect of both these trials was to strengthen Ralegh. If Cobham defined one extreme, cowardice, then Lord Grey's bravado was the other—rashness. The mean they defined, exemplary of true courage, became Ralegh.

A slight setback for the King. The trials had failed to achieve their purpose. But now events returned to the hands of the

King. His moves and no others to interfere. He could demonstrate the power of justice or mercy or both.

The King had given much thought to the exercise of justice and mercy, and he had published his thoughts some years before in *Basilikon Doron,* a book on the subject of kingship addressed to his heir, Prince Henry. Addressed to Henry and to his Scots kingdom, but *published,* most likely, to speak to the English as well, to prove himself worthy of the English crown long before it was to be given to him. He spoke out for stern and strict justice against certain crimes—"horrible crimes you are bound in conscience never to forgive, such as witchcraft, willful murder, incest (especially within the degrees of consanguinity), sodomy, poisoning, and false witness." No mercy possible in such cases, but his ideal king possessed great freedom in dealing with any crimes directed against himself: "As for offenses against your own person and authority, since the fault concerns yourself, I remit to your choice to punish or to pardon therein as your heart serves you and according to the circumstances and the quality of the committer."

This King was said to be, by nature, a merciful man, generous and gentle. In the execution of the sentences at Winchester was his first occasion to show his nature to his subjects. Likely he would show mercy to some. Just as likely some must die. For the example of kingly mercy to be efficacious, there must be contrast, some fear and trembling. For mercy to have meaning there must be an example of rigor.

The certain victims were the lesser fry in the net. The two priests, Clarke and Watson, dim-witted and unimportant, would have to die.

Watson was crazed and cracked by the ordeal. Suffering had left him lunatic. Watson was an awkward man, ridiculously short and ridiculous for his odd blinking, squinting eyes. It had been bruited about, and he had shown the folly of asserting it at his trial, that he had served as an agent for the King and that he had obtained certain promises, notably a promise to be more gentle with loyal English Catholics and to cease inflicting upon them the burden of recusancy fines. Possibly so, but for a king to limit his freedom by adherence to private assurances given to persons of no consequence, would be to be no king at all. Moreover, had the King found it practical and politic to keep those promises, he could not have done so. The Spanish Jesuits were clear. They wanted Watson dead.

So the execution of two priests served divers purposes. A demonstration of justice. A warning to discontented English Catholics not to depend upon the King for succor and, by the same token, against the futility of attempting mischief against him. A bone to the Jesuits, yet a bone they could share with the English Protestants and even with those who so feared and hated Spain that they conceived all Catholics to be of the Spanish faction. Finally, by paradox, having shown himself rigorous against Catholic discontent, the King gained freedom to be more lenient with them in the future, without apology, when and if he chose to be so.

The King underestimated the capacity of the English to follow the trail of his motives. And he did not know them well enough to imagine a singular paradox of the English character.

On a clear cold day Ralegh stood at the tower window and watched the priests dance the dance of empty air and bleed on the butcher's block. They died courageously, but in horrid agony as, for once, that full sentence was executed to the letter.

At whose command?

Traditionally English executioners did all their busy work of disemboweling, castrating, and quartering upon the bodies of dead men. The stunned crowd did not cry out. The victims behaved with neither unseemly arrogance nor cowardice. Surely the executioners acted upon instructions.

The priests died and their grimacing heads, frozen in pain, were stuck upon poles above the tower. The quarters of their flesh hung over Winchester's gates. Sides of raw meat. As if ancient Winchester were a butcher's stall.

The King had not learned that the English, for all the bombast and blood of their plays, for all their bloody sports and pastimes, are not so bloody-minded as to be either frightened or pleased by cruel executions.

Next came George Brooke, brother of Henry Brooke, Lord Cobham. Since he was the brother-in-law of Robert Cecil, he was to be spared the pains of hanging, drawing, and quartering. He was to be beheaded. But before he died he won over the crowd with his courage, and he had left the truth of the Bye conspiracy veiled in doubts.

"There is something still hidden in all this!" he cried out. "And it will appear one day for my justification."

Did he die for what he knew or what he had done?

According to the ancient tradition of heading, the executioner gripped the severed head tight by the hair and held it up for the crowd to see.

"God save King James!"

Only one voice, the sheriff's, echoed him. The throng stood silent and staring.

After that there were four men left to die—Cobham, Lord Grey, one Markham, a soldier, and Ralegh. Three would die on the same morning. Ralegh must see their fate settled, too, before his own would be resolved.

The morning for the three was dark and cold. The yard and the scaffold were rain-swept, blown by wet wind. Yet, foul weather or no, there was a press of people. Drenched, hooded, and mantled, staring toward the scaffold. Guards, cloaked, rain glistening in beads on their ridged helmets, clinging to the points and edges of their partizans. The hangman and his helpers had hung the ropes, each noose an idiot's yawn, and propped up the ladders. They had their covered kettles of steaming water, baskets stuffed with wet straw. The thick wood block lay stained, clean, and rain-slick. Sharp knife for the butcher's work of drawing, short-handled, heavy-bladed ax for quartering, were nearby, handy.

First from the castle into the yard came Sir Griffin Markham, soldier, friend and companion to the dead priests, a principal of the Bye Plot. Black of hair and beard, broad of face, his great nose broken in a struggle somewhere. If not in skirmish or battle, then in a tavern brawl. His left arm withered, the hand a claw, from wounds. He aroused interest, for malcontent and villain or no, in his lonely, bitter, battered toughness he was of a type from the last age.

But now, led or pushed toward the scaffold, he was clumsy, stumbled-footed, dazed. Shocked not so much by fear, as ambushed without warning.

It was believed that he did not dissemble, lacking the talent for subtlety. No, someone, upon authority, had told him he would not die. And he, upon good reason, had believed it.

At the scaffold he protested, pleading he had not prepared himself for death. Nevertheless he was forced to mount the scaffold. Once he stood there, he could draw upon a soldier's shrug of courage. Could compose his body, turn his face to

[73]

stone. He bade farewell to his friends and began to say his prayers.

As he said his prayers, the sheriff of Hampshire, Sir Benjamin Tichbourne, suddenly left the scaffold. He pushed through the crowd to speak to a young man at the far edge. This was John Gibb, groom of the King's bedchamber. Who had come late and, unable to push through the crowd, had been shouting into the wind and rain, trying to gain the attention of the sheriff.

After a time the sheriff returned and, without explanation, motioned to the guards. Markham was removed from the scaffold and marched across the yard to the hall.

He was told he had two hours to meditate and to prepare himself for death.

Next came young Lord Grey. Came forward in the same manner as he had stood trial. Came to the scaffold as to some diverting occasion. Surrounded by friends, blithe, apparently fearless.

But he reacted with surprise when he saw no sign of Markham's death. All three ropes in place. And even though it was the practice of executioners, particularly for the execution of a gentleman, to sluice scaffold and chopping block, to wipe the blades of knife and ax, and to replace fouled straw with fresh, still, no amount of care could disguise all the signs.

As soon as he stood on the scaffold, looked from the ropes to the wet straw at his feet, Grey knew Markham was still alive. But he could not know what his fate might be. And could not, out of honor, permit himself the luxury of hope. Therefore, he, too, said farewell to his friends. And, indifferent to how it might be taken, he knelt to say his prayers.

When he was finished and rose and stood ready, the sheriff ordered him removed and placed in the hall with Markham.

[74]

As Lord Grey de Wilton, still fastidious and arrogant, though unsmiling, descends the rude steps of the scaffold, step by step, a murmuring of voices runs through the crowd, the sound rising to Ralegh at the window. Hooded faces, blurred by rain, follow the guards and the ambling stiff-necked progress of Lord Grey toward the hall. As he vanishes within, one and another of those faces glances to the top of the tower and its three rotting heads. A glance becomes a stare. One points and says something aloud. Continues to point as more and more look up into the rain. More looking and the murmuring noise of voices rising to him in scraps, like pieces of a torn book, scraps of paper blowing, until even the executioners pause to look, too, and the sheriff, upon the scaffold, clamps one hand on the brim of his hat to hold it against the wind and tilts his head to see also.

They are looking at Ralegh. His room is lit with fat-dipped rushes and a fire. He needs no cover but his loose white shirt. Can picture how he appears to them, framed by the window, lit from the flames of his cell, high, small, white-shirted, and white-faced, a figure of fire and ice against the wet stone of the tower, whose crenellations, whose eyeless skulls on pikes seem the axle for the windy turning of a sky full of bruised clouds.

He returns their stare, motionless, except for a wide gritting of teeth. Which at that distance and in that light will be taken for a smile. Is taken so, for some wave their hands, a few doff caps. A woman calls out something he cannot hear.

It may be the King hopes yet for some gesture of public confession from Ralegh to save his life.

He gives them nothing except a show of teeth.

And here comes Lord Cobham, some measure of lost courage restored. He carries himself like a born nobleman, not the man who wept and implored pity at his trial.

[75]

The crowd turns attention to him. Ralegh draws and spends a deep breath and observes Cobham, old friend and new mortal enemy, relieved to be again unobserved.

They, as he, watch Cobham close and in silence. They note, even as he does, that not once does Cobham break stride or look up to the scaffold.

Does not every condemned man, as if by a habit beyond control, look first to the destination, the place where he must die? Even Lord Grey, in his swagger, kept looking toward the scaffold.

Cobham mounts the scaffold and notices nothing amiss. *It seems* . . . Reacts to nothing, if he sees the three empty nooses, clean straw, blades, block, and boards, the spotless executioners. Nods to the sheriff and turns, head high, to face the silent crowd. Begins to say his piece in a resonant calm voice.

For the first time Ralegh hears patches of words.

Loud and clear, not a catch in his throat or tremor of tongue, Cobham reaffirms Ralegh's chief part in the Main Plot, naming him author and architect of it all.

No halting pauses, no slips of tongue. It is a speech by rote. Is it also a speech by command?

Others already asking the same question. For the quiet of the crowd is broken by murmuring again. Where they stood still there is much shifting and moving. Unruffled, Cobham raises his voice to be heard.

True or false, not many there will ever be able to believe in such a remarkable transformation from effeminate cowardice to Roman courage.

Cobham finishes his speech, makes brief farewells to a few friends and kin on the scaffold. Then bows his head to pray. Sheriff Tichbourne halts his devotions before they have begun. Signals for silence from all the crowd. Cups his hands and calls to the yeomen guarding the entrance to the hall.

"Bring the prisoners forth to the scaffold!"

Cobham replaces his hat to keep dry in the rain and stands waiting beside the sheriff, grave-faced, but at ease. He says nothing to the sheriff, not even asking what this may mean or why his prayers have been interrupted.

The other two, each clearly baffled now, mount the scaffold and are placed to stand beside Cobham.

Now there is quiet in the press of people. The falling raindrops, splashing on the scaffold and the stones of the castle yard, sluicing down the walls in rivulets, are abruptly loud. But the sheriff has voice enough for his duty, though it has become a player's part to be recited.

Each of the three is asked to acknowledge the justice of his sentence. Markham nods, nervous; Lord Grey says something brief, inaudible but apparently affirmative; Cobham's voice is equal to the sheriff's as he acknowledges the perfect justice of the King.

Then, brisk as a bishop at prayer, the sheriff announces the mercy of the King. Their lives shall be spared. He nods and the guards quickly lead them back to the castle buildings, each to his separate cell.

Silent still—no cheers for the mercy of their monarch—the crowd turns away, breaks apart. Quickly, as if seizing upon the double-quick rhythm of the yeomen and the sheriff's men —or is it because the rain is falling harder than before?—they disperse. And only one or two pause long enough to look again through swimming air for the man in a fiery tower window. They glance and are gone, too.

He remains there, seeing it all to the end, observing the

[77]

hasty departure of the hangman and his crew. They pour away boiling water, cram the stuff of death and the wet, unbloodied straw into sacks and chests. And last climb the ladders, set against the crossbeam for the culprits to climb to hang, untying the three ropes and stuffing them away too. While his assistants bring up the heavy, high-wheeled cart and pack it, the hangman surveys the scaffold, the empty yard, then, just as he leaves the scaffold, looks to Walter Ralegh, waves a wide hand and, unmistakably, grins.

The hangman takes up the reins, cracks his whip, and the cart rattles out of the castle gate.

The lone man at the window stares at nothing. . . .

Except perhaps Cobham—how else to explain his pompous confidence?—the King must have told no one of his intended gesture of mercy. He kept strict counsel. And the fate of the three men rested wholly upon the King's groom, who was almost too late.

The circumstances of his clemency could not please the English. It was not fitting for the King to make a scaffold into a theater stage. His mercy was humiliating to those who received it. He gave them their lives but at the price of shame.

The trials and executions at Winchester went badly for the King—in many ways. Men of England, many courtiers and gentlemen, went their ways full of doubts, wondering if the King would ever learn to rule wisely and well.

No show, no spectacle for Ralegh. He, with the others, was transported to the Tower of London, to remain there at the King's pleasure. Which could be brief or forever. Which might, one day, be a full or limited pardon, or none at all.

Ralegh lived in the Tower for nearly fourteen years and is again confined there. But he has been fortunate.

No luck for Cobham. Having performed a service of self-humiliation, dragging Ralegh into the center of the stage with him, Cobham was duly repaid. His life was spared. As no doubt he had been promised. But Cobham's life was of no value to anyone but himself. His estate was plucked, cleaned, and gutted like a fat goose. When a cloud of legal words and the dust of documents cleared, it was plain that the principal beneficiary of Cobham's holdings was his brother-in-law—Cecil.

After some time in the Tower, modestly maintained by the King and harmless as a eunuch, Cobham was given freedom. Freedom to starve. The King was spared the price of maintaining a prisoner. Cobham set free to live until he died, half crazy and as lousy as a Scottish knight, in a hovel not much better than a farmer's pigpen. Climbed a rickety ladder to sleep in foul straw in a loft. In the Tower, at least, poor Cobham slept on a pallet. Someone, Cecil perhaps, may have wished to prove to Cobham the wisdom of an old saying—*He that lives in Court dies upon straw.*

The others were gone, too. Markham got his fill of poverty in banishment from England. Pawned the jewels on the hilt of his sword for food, but wisely kept the sword and hired out as a soldier on the Continent. He has vanished now, dead in some inconsequential skirmish or tavern brawl among strangers. Lord Grey died in the Tower in 1614. Of an illness, they said, though as time went along in this reign, people wondered if any man would die of a natural sickness.

And now Pigmy Cecil is dead and gone, too, after a long and lingering illness. His body hardly cooled and stiffened before the world he had hated and had known so well turned hatred on him, heaping ridicule in satire and slander, from those who had once brought him bribes in both hands and repeated a litany of flattery.

From the Tower Ralegh joined the yapping chorus at Cecil's death, writing a satirical epitaph in the classical style.

> Here lies Hobinall, our Pastor while ere,
> That once in a Quarter our Fleeces did share . . .

But he had earned the right to anger and scorn, owing less than nothing to Cecil, except, perhaps, his fall.

Cecil's cousin, Francis Bacon, was more cruel by far in his little essay "On Deformity," published after Cecil was safely dead. Some wisdom there. But Ralegh has lived long enough to see the flaw in Bacon's judgment of the man. Francis Bacon has somehow managed to forget that, ever since Adam fell, *all men are deformed,* to one degree or another. Though a man may be wonderfully cured of one deformity, yet the cure creates another. . . .

Why think of little Cecil now? God knows they are almost all gone now, good and evil, the men of the last age. They burned brief like summer's fireflies, and now their only light is recollected, borrowed. They live in flickering memories and for a little time. Soon they will be memories of memories, men caught between mirrors on both sides, all deformed, parceled out in a riddle of counterfeit images.

If they care, the best they can hope for is a yawning of unborn children at the mention of their names.

Perhaps Cecil has the last word, after all, having left his own laughter behind in a surprising answer to his fair-weather friends, freed by his death to announce themselves as enemies.

It is his tomb I think of; with his tomb he haunts us still. Do not look for him with his blood kin and family—father, mother, wife—whose bones rest in the Abbey of Westminster. He chose not to accept that honor. Must have known and accepted, though acceptance cost him a gnashing of teeth, that the sum of his honor would die with him. Dead, his honor would be stripped by fools whose only power and accomplishment was to live on after him. What value in brass or plaque, another tomb among the honored dead of the Abbey?

Look for Robert Cecil in the parish church near Hatfields. Find his astonishing tomb there. Wrought as he wished by Maximillian Colt, his own man, brought out of Arras and Utrecht, pensioned and patronized by Cecil for, perhaps, that one purpose alone, the creation of his tomb. For nowhere else has Colt, or anyone, done a piece of work like that one.

Calm and pale, in whitest marble, the First Earl of Salisbury rests upon a starkly plain black marble bier. There are neither columns nor canopy. At the four corners, kneeling, in classical robes but bare- and high-breasted are the Four Virtues mourning a sad loss.

Those with sharp eyes and cynical wit profess to recognize at sight each of the four ladies. They will say their virtues are, indeed, extraordinary, though hardly so much as Cecil's arrogance in assuming he could satisfy them all on earth or in heaven.

Black and white marble in clear and surprising contrast. Final satiric statement of a man who saw nothing in this world as pure or simple. Alive, he was black bones in white flesh, a gray man.

The tomb is a magnificent . . . jest.

But time turns even the jests of the dead against them.

The tombs of the ancients have vanished or are defaced beyond recognition.

[81]

A man can rest well and wait for the Last Judgment beneath even a deformed stone.

There is neither honor nor flattery in death, only silence and secrecy until all secrets are revealed.

Let Robert Cecil's tomb say what it will to any beholder. It cannot speak truth or falsehood.

Cannot equivocate either.

If the beholder grins, as I do now, that is proper.

All skulls offer the same grin and say nothing.

If the living could believe this, there would be no more loss of sleeping in this weary world. . . .

In this vexing matter the King has been prudent and patient. Now thanks to patience the affair is settled.

There will be no public show of a trial. No more of that folly.

Coke and Bacon, for once hand in glove, have urged a public trial upon the new charges of disobedience, of Ralegh's failure to keep his oath to the King. Together with other examiners, they are convinced that there is a just case under law.

Coke has urged the trial to be rid of Ralegh and to wipe clean the slate of the disaster at Winchester.

By God, the King once most graciously and freely consented, if not to affirm, then not to deny their ancient customs. And he has done so. But here are more weighty matters. He has ruled long enough to act as a King must act; and act as a King he has, too, as in '16, when he came down to sit on the throne in Star Chamber and preside. The first to do so since Henry VIII. Sat on the throne and laid down the Law of the King to judges and lawyers and (spare us, oh Lord!) the *Parliament* men.

"Kings are properly Judges," he told them, "and judgment properly belongs to them from God: for Kings sit in the throne of God, and from thence all judgment is derived."

And more: "The absolute prerogative of the Crown is no subject for the tongue of a lawyer, nor is lawful to be disputed. In your pleas, presume not to meddle with things against the King's prerogative and honor."

Judges wisely bent with the wind. All but Edward Coke. And his pride cost him dear. He lost his office as Lord Chief Justice, replaced by a more reliable man.

Perhaps he had learned his lesson. Coke can be of value in his proper place. Coke is a great man in their Parliament. Coke perhaps can yet serve him there. And he has needed the counsel of Coke in this affair. But some of that advice is unacceptable, if not untrustworthy. The trial in '03 brought the King much grief. The Overbury trials brought him more woe, and Coke, whether through excess of zeal or by cunning, brought forth far too many private things to public view. He is a meddlesome man, but is still able to learn a lesson when rapped with the schoolmaster's pliant rod.

Let him make an idol of the Law, then, but the King need not serve a strange god.

Bacon is more supple. As soon as he realized that it was the King's pleasure to rid himself of Ralegh without a trial, he offered sound advice. And he is even now at work on a statement of the King's case and justice which can be published if need be.

Early on this morning there will be a hearing before the King's Bench at Westminster Hall. Yelverton and the judges will take care of that. Ralegh will be dead and gone on the

[84]

following day, his execution as early and swift as his hearing.

And then there is Don Diego Sarmiento de Acuna, Count Gondomar, Ambassador of Spain. Who is called, by friends and enemies alike, "the crafty." He will have his satisfaction. After which they can proceed with the cobweb of negotiations for the marriage of Prince Charles to the Infanta of Spain. This long deferred, oft delayed, upsodown-and-back-again affair that they call the Spanish Match.

Which was first sown in the King's thoughts when James was still King of Scotland and Henry (blessings on his departed soul) was his heir. The idea has thrived, sturdy, but not flowering, ever since. To bind England and Spain together, as they have been before and within memory, though briefly and loosely, in holy wedlock. The knot of a royal marriage is better by far than any paper treaty. Bids fair to ensure peace for generations to come. Not only between two nations, but peace in the wider world. For who could be so foolish as to challenge the combined power and position of Britain and Spain? There need not be any more wars among the Continental nations. Against the perfection of this alliance all others will be dependents whether they wish it or no.

And he shall be named the father of this great change, the father of the Peace.

Blessed are the peacemakers . . .

Looking not so far forward, the Match will serve present purposes within this kingdom. Will win back for good the sorely taxed loyalty of his Catholic subjects. And will do so without throwing more than a slight instructive shadow of fear upon the fractious, numerous, and troublesome Protestants. With

[85]

a little care and cunning these can be told—and will believe —it is a victory for England and themselves.

Then trade and easy commerce between nations will fill up the coffers of merchants, stifle doubts and silence discontent. From these bulging, groaning coffers the monies will overflow, to be snatched up and passed from palm to palm, purse to purse. In peace and plenty, all his subjects, in every estate and condition, in contentment, must be more well disposed toward the author of their felicity. They will not then or ever again be so niggardly as to withhold from the King his rightful share of the wealth he has given them.

Look closer, though, to where what is possible becomes likely.

With the dowry to come with this Infanta from Spain, he will have less need to call upon the unruly Parliament, to be helpless in dependence upon their whims and grudging generosity. His burden of private debts, seven hundred thousand pounds and growing like a canker, will have dwindled to nothing.

Therefore it follows. With the marriage, a lasting time of peace; with fat in the land, present troubles will be forgotten like a dream. And so, too, will be forgotten that false dream of the glories of the last age. The King will, at last, be honored and loved while he lives. And it will be he who is well remembered, and that memory will be upon a foundation of truth. And Charles and all the Stuart line to come will sit upon a throne which is set upon that rock foundation. More mystic than the old Stone of Scone within the throne of England now.

A king as much as any man has the duty to build up his estate. Not to bury his talent in the earth like the foolish, faithless servant in the parable. To build his own estate, with God's help and under God's will, to the benefit of all the kingdom, is an exemplary action and an act of faith. No man can fault him for it.

To act out of duty and love is to be rewarded with duty and with love. And the mutual love of king and subjects will serve as an *exemplum,* too, of the duty and love all living creatures owe to God, not in exchange for His infinite Love, but in humble thanksgiving for the same.

Weighed in the balance against all these things, just how much can the old gray head of one man weigh?

Oh, the King is a more cunning and canny defender of the faith than his English counselors will ever know. That is their great weakness. They will not credit him with wit and wisdom equal to their own.

His accent, his manners, the fashion of his dress, his hunting and drinking, his sudden flashes of high temper or bawdy humor, these things have contrived a high invisible wall between them and the clockwork elegance of his mind. Coke once compared the Court to a clock with many wheels and many motions. Good, but you should have looked more closely, Edward Coke. All those wheels and motions move toward one great rhythm and purpose. And when the hour rings, it rings with the clarity of bells.

The King knows how to bait a trap, and when the trap springs iron teeth upon unwary ankles, he knows a greater trick—how to make the victim happy with the pain of it. As if to be trapped were an honor. As if the trap were of their own devising.

Long before Ralegh returned home from his fruitless voyage,

indeed before it was clear that the Fox might live to return or, alive, consider such a course, the King outraged them. As soon as he heard reports of Ralegh's crimes against the Spaniards, hearing this from a furious Gondomar, he published an angry declaration, disowning Ralegh's actions. And privily he insisted that Ralegh must be apprehended and given over to the Spaniards, to be disposed of at their pleasure. Since Ralegh had turned pirate, let him be treated like one. Let him be carried away, in chains on his own ship, to Spain. Let the Spanish make a spectacle of his punishment.

Let that prove the power of the King of England.

Gondomar had been instructed by his King to express fury and outrage, to demand justice and, thus, to test the King. But Gondomar was astounded at James' proposal. The King, then, bolder and eager to befuddle them further, took another step. Briskly circumnavigating the Ambassador and *directly* offering Ralegh to the King of Spain. Philip III declined his offer. As the King had known he would. But, more important, it gave James a glimpse of the cards in Philip's hand.

All shows and pretense aside, Spain does not wish to chance a loss of favor in England.

Therefore it follows that Philip III must desire the Match as much as the King of England.

Meanwhile a rash offer is as good as the performance of it. In truth it may be better. Whatever becomes of Walter Ralegh, Spain is now beholden to James and without discernible gain.

Gondomar has been pressing forward, urging the marriage as if it were to his advantage as much or more than in the interests of the two kings. This is a ruse. But now the King believes, as he has always hoped, that the Match is not a ruse.

[88]

And Gondomar must study more strictly the motives of the King of England. What a fine satirical stroke! Gondomar has been building cloud castles upon the belief that he is gifted with the power to influence and persuade James. On the one hand with threats and promises and upon the other with the oil which protects an expedient friendship from rust—money, gifts to the spendthrift King and his favorites. And James has made some show of being pliable, of listening to and sometimes acting upon Gondomar's suggestions. Even to the apparent disadvantage of the King in the eyes of his people and his Council.

Well, Gondomar is left with doubt. Either he has *more* influence and power over James than he imagined or James is more crafty than he knew. Either way, it is trouble for the Ambassador. The King knows Gondomar has told his master many times that he has managed so to ingratiate himself, to win James' favor, that his services to Spain are of inestimable value. Just so . . . And, just so, Philip, no fool, will have already considered the alternative that now troubles his Ambassador, but with a difference. It is the King of England Philip must deal with, not his own servant, the Ambassador. If Gondomar is as influential as he may be, then he is dangerous and not to be trusted. If Gondomar has been duped by King James, then Gondomar's a fool and of no use to Philip.

No wonder that Gondomar is off to Spain to wait out the uncertain weather of events, but also to report to his King and, perhaps, plead a case. And what will he do there? Clever, cautious, ever politic, he will suggest that James is attempting to throw them off guard. That James has no intention of doing more than chastising Walter Ralegh. Not saying this with too much certainty, but to divert attention from his own skin—

[89]

no doubt sweating drops as thick as Castilian olive oil. Philip will conclude he needs Gondomar in England. A man who may have guessed wrong, but who is close to the King, able with understanding and wariness and a new humility to keep watch upon him at a crucial time.

Imagine, then, when Gondomar learns that the King, after delays, has cut off Ralegh's head. Again astounded. Then more humbled. Then urgently needing *James'* favor to restore his own credit in Spain.

And so to save his skin in Spain, the Ambassador will sue for the favor of James. Philip may know this, but will weigh it against the delay which must follow if he chooses to send a new man to England. Philip will put the fear of God into Gondomar and send him back to England as he must, all the while wisely doubting him.

And this change will tip the odds for settling this Spanish Match to the advantage of James.

You must know your man, whether he knows you or not. Gondomar has the southern, the Mediterranean temper. Made a great to-do about nothing when he first landed in England at Portsmouth. Custom required that his ship, entering any English harbor where an English warship lay, should lower its ensign. The Spaniard refused. The English captain threatened to blow the Spaniard out of the water. It was left for the King to decide. He bowed to the Spaniards. Gondomar puffed up like a pheasant cock, drums in his breast. Concluded that the King feared giving offense to Spain above all things. Which was partly true. A great lie, to be swallowed, must have a tasty sauce of truth. In his pride, Gondomar would never have guessed that the English captain acted upon the King's instructions from the outset.

[90]

Gondomar has the twilight temper of the Spaniard, half jest and half earnest. He imagines, and the King is at no great pain to refute this conjecture, the King is still duped and puzzled by him.

Know your man: Gondomar has Latin weaknesses—one is lechery. A thin, meager man, he burns hot, a turning spit. In caverns and chambers of his skull English ladies, cool and pale and rosy, shed their stiff gowns to dance naked as witches. Gondomar has them in his power and at his mercy. They crawl and slither toward him, as to an Eastern emperor, hiding the fear in their eyes with their hair, covering him from toes to rearing rosy bishop's head with fat kisses. Now he is an Indian chief from the New World, naked and blameless, a cannibal king. They are brought before him in huge dishes of gold and he eats their sweetness to the bone. Next, in fury of guilt and frustration, he is a galley slave, with a ragged loincloth or breechcloth to cover his quivering shame, on a galley of Amazons with whips. They whip him till he howls —and shudders for joy . . .

A man who is a slave to desire, servant of his lusts, suffers the pains of the damned while he lives. We seek for opposites, true. Believing that we can somehow be made whole again. Little, and we lust for large; fat for thin; cruel for gentle. As if Adam, coupling with Eve, could regain his stolen rib. All men are wounded in that way.

The King knows the source of these failings. His own love for handsome favorites is a hunger for the beauty he was deprived of; their love for him, kindled by royal gifts and favor, makes him beautiful in his own eyes. It is satisfactory, for no man can live entirely without illusions. Your crippled, leprous beggar dreams himself beautiful. And why not? In

God's eyes all Creation is beautiful. These dreams, though false to the reason of the world, are true to a higher reason. By a little love the heavy soul is somewhat restored, regains a measure of its original lightness, that lightness which is the breath of God. . . .

The King has done royal duty by his Danish wife, sown royal seed. He has never, like many another, turned to women, been faithless to his wife and vows. He has never risked the intimacy of other women, for they have loose tongues and cannot be trusted. No fault of their own. It is the way God made them. The King has never been the victim of his hungers. He purges them when they mount. He leaves himself free to dream the great design of the future. Surely God, who knows all secrets and who is Justice itself, will forgive these slight failings.

Besides, in time of trouble, women can be of small comfort. There is something of the witch in all of them. They owe allegiance finally to themselves. But a *man,* one who has been favored and not in secret, must die for or with a king.

Let swarthy Gondomar snigger to himself. He dare not ask himself which of the two, himself or the King, is in truth effeminate. Effeminacy is a state of the soul. Gondomar, like many a Spaniard and many a so-called lusty Englishman, may tup and toss wenches until his eyeteeth fall out, but he has the weak soul of a woman.

It follows, sure as tides turn and stars follow courses, fantasy's the silver key to Gondomar. The least acorn planted there will afford more shade than a grove of real oak trees. So much for Gondomar. In him the King now has found a servant in the Court of Spain, all the more useful in that Gondomar believes himself to be the dancing master.

As for my English and in especial this Commission appointed to deal with Walter Ralegh.

When he raged and swore Ralegh must be handed over to Spain, they puffed and stiffened. They argued as much as they dared to.

He allowed them to cajole, plead, to try to persuade him of the obvious.

If he gave Ralegh to the Spaniards, he was counseled, such a deed would perplex and anger his subjects. Who, out of ignorance and misunderstanding, might somehow misconstrue this as a fawning gesture made out of fear of Spain.

The King refused to hear this.

Was he not the King, after all? This man, already once proved by law a traitor to King and country, had by the King's bountiful mercy been granted liberty. Only to break oath and faith to the King. The man was a villainous pirate and must be punished for it!

—Indeed, Your Majesty, it would seem to be most exactly as you have said. But may I humbly suggest it is more fitting that he be punished under English law?

—Your English law has given me much grief, he snapped. Law is no remedy.

—Your Majesty has some cause to think so, Bacon said. The Law often dances like an old fishwife in wooden shoes, with little grace and less dispatch. But pray let us remember the melody she dances to is old and pleasing to the many.

—Spare us figures of speech, Coke said, to himself, but audible.

—Many a tide has flowed under the bridge since the trials at Winchester, another says. The man is old and sick and touched by the death of his son. The Fox is mangy, stiff-jointed, slow of foot. He cannot work mischief now, may it please Your Majesty.

—It pleases us not. The wretch has already done mischief enough for a lifetime.

The Fox has been harmless since he lost his gnawing and biting teeth in '03. His design was always to spare Ralegh's life in '03. Spain wanted him dead, then, too. Part of the price for peace. The King was the better bargainer. Before the time came, Spain feared the results of Ralegh's death. Came pleading with the King for Ralegh's life with more conviction than his friends and with more urgency than the man himself. Ralegh in the Tower was like the lions of the royal menagerie, safe so long as caged. Perhaps they hoped he would die naturally. For certain they feared him alive. And with the passing of years even more so, for as long as he lived and did nothing, no act that could be tested, the legend of the man could only grow. To the Spaniards legend became truth. He was a giant, held in check by the whims of the English King. To the King he was a common, but increasingly valuable pawn for peace. There are others who died in the Tower when it suited the King. Ralegh bore a charmed life. And the Fox did not imagine it so.

Even his voyage had served well. Could not fail to. He could have died on the voyage. Which would have made a simple disposition of the matter. He could have found his improbable gold mine. In which case the King would have some gold. Could continue to press for the Spanish Match, but now as dealer of cards. Returning, Ralegh could have fled to France or to some other nation, his legend having spread wide. Fine; then let them learn that the legend was a man and an old

[94]

one too. Since he chose an unlikely course and returned to England, he could be useful one more time.

James was pleased to hear the English plead for Ralegh's life on honest grounds. The legend had died in England. Which made his resolution easier. Let him die quickly now that the time had come. There might be grumbling for a day or two. Good, better grumbling than pity. A little grumbling, a few ballads and broadsides, and in no time at all the man, half forgotten already, would be less than a memory.

Unless, of course, there should be any reason for the King to change his mind.

—Then, may it please Your Majesty, there is another way, says Francis Bacon . . .

Give him time enough to test the direction and force of the wind and Bacon is as wise as a wisp.

Patiently the King let them come to the place where he had been waiting for them. Let them, led by Bacon, spin out the plan of the King's own design, thinking it their own. The King, with a show of reluctance, agreed, placing responsibility upon them. In turn he signed the warrant and hired himself away to the country.

Ah, the English in all their native wit and wisdom! Between them they have as much true wit as three folks, two fools and a madman. Their wisdom is all in their beards, when it is not situated in their lower beards. It takes the patience of Job himself to rule them, to rule in such a fashion that they know it not. He has come to understand them well enough. Understanding has not always made him happy.

Though Walter Ralegh has, unwitting, more than one time been of use and service to King James, he has given the King no happiness. The King does not profess to understand him as well as he does these others.

Take the figure of a tennis ball. Ralegh was inordinately fond of that foolish French game, allowing him to use his strength, size, and agility to advantage. Consider a tennis ball, forced to be bounced and played back and forth according to the will of players. Yet imagine the ball as possessing an infinitely tiny degree of liberty, sufficient to deviate a hair or two from its prescribed course. Able to fall short, to take an odd bounce. Now, allowing that the players possess an almost even skill, it may be the tennis ball which decides the game and settles all wagers. . . .

How was it, except upon some knowledge of his own freedom, Ralegh not only lived, but thrived through those years in the Tower? And was able to trouble and to prick enemies, including the King?

Ralegh was wrong, after all, in his remark about true friends and foes. Friend or foe, the distinction is more subtle and secret than either fools or wise men know. It is a strict matter, in this politic world, of circumstance, expediency. Fools and wise men miss the meaning of many an ancient proverb.

Neither friend nor foe should ever know when your foot is asleep.

That friend who faints is your foe.

When friends are needed any wise man can make a friend of a foe.

Ralegh was able to make the King of England, if not a foe, the contest being unequal by circumstance, then an occasional antagonist. One who sometimes must acknowledge, however briefly, that he has been beset by an antagonist not unworthy, not entirely without power, like a blue buzzing horsefly, to sting a king.

The King conceives him to be worldy wise. The King, unlike the English, respects a clever fox. The English will not make sport of hunting the fox, considering that creature a varmint, base vermin. Not worth trouble of man or horse or dog. They will rather hunt the hare.

If Ralegh is foxy, why did he refuse to play the game at the beginning? Before the Queen died James' agents were everywhere, and among others, they sounded Ralegh out. Ralegh dismissed their overtures lightly, saying he could serve only one prince at a time.

To James that spells a shrugging indifference.

To the anxious James of those years, it seemed that Ralegh was bargaining. Would sell his services only for the highest price. If so, James concluded, Ralegh gambled and lost. The final price would be nothing at all.

Or, rather, say he did service at the highest price, himself the buyer. His payment was his life.

Yet shadows of doubt remain.

Suppose it is possible that Ralegh spoke the truth to his agents. May be that Ralegh was unable to live in the hope of the future. Or, if able, then would not allow himself to do so.

At the last, while so many others were turning away from a dying Queen and looking toward a new dawn, the Captain of the Guard stood in his place, tall and obscure, more shadowy as the shadows lengthened, until her last light was gone.

Perhaps the future never held much meaning for Ralegh.

Or perhaps Ralegh came to distrust the future and, in distrust, to deny it. Certain it is that all his investments in the future had failed him—hopes for plantations in Ireland and

Virginia, schemes for remote Guiana, plans for the estate at Sherbourne.

Perhaps his own downfall gave Ralegh some solace. Seeing hopes dashed and worst fears come true served to confirm his certainty that the future was to be distrusted.

Then, if that were so, how to explain his latest actions. He had achieved the goal of freedom. Only to turn freedom into new bondage. Paid a high price for freedom. Is like to pay the highest price now. For what? The right to gamble upon—the future. Rolled the dice, betting all, and lost everything.

Yet he has added more doubts with recent deeds.

Why, like an arrogant blundering fool, did Ralegh come back to England? Having broken his oath and the terms of his commission and knowing he must pay for that.

Why, the man had more choices than a rich widow!

Pirate that he always was and is, on land or sea, he could have settled for a life of piracy. Other Englishmen have done so and some, even now, are up to that mischief. None so well known as Ralegh. He might have succeeded in bringing them all together, rallying around him a navy of cutthroats. And with such a crew have come down upon the fat sheep of the Spanish Indies like a pack of starved wolves. And in so doing have ruined the King's peace with Spain beyond all repairing.

If it is honor that spurs him—and love of honor is the worst of English vanities—there were honorable choices aplenty for him. From his informers, the King knows of offers of safety coming to Ralegh from France and Venice and Denmark and the Netherlands.

Suppose he feared for the safety and welfare of Lady Ralegh and his son. Then why has he squandered the best part of their estate upon this voyage? Does Ralegh not know that under protection of a foreign power, he could assure the safety of wife and child?

Instead he came sailing boldly into Plymouth Harbor. Came home to his county of Devon. Left alone, for a time there, unwatched, he wasted every occasion to escape. Could have fled England, taking wife and child with him.

Perhaps his boldness was built upon belief that his old friend Winwood could check the King. Yet Ralegh, even before he sailed, knew the plans for the Spanish Match had changed the King's views and altered the power and influence of his faction. Knew, or should have known, that Winwood's influence was waning. Knew, before deciding to return, that his actions would have sorely tested Winwood at the least, at most have diminished his powers. And therefore could not, in reason, expect Winwood to risk becoming his advocate.

What he did not know, not until he landed, was that Winwood was dead. He could not have been depending upon Winwood. Else he would have fled to safety at once.

Unless, for some reason, he deemed such a flight would work injury to other friends and allies in the faction set against Spain.

Grant him that much. Then how to make sense of his next moves?

The King sent Ralegh's kinsman Stukely to place him under arrest. Stukely, a man Ralegh knew well enough neither to trust nor to fear. Then Ralegh playing a foolish game for time, feigning illness, counterfeiting madness, according to the outworn, theatrical customs of the past age. For what purpose? To gain time. To play for time. Well, since the King was upon his summer progress, the sum of time was already his without such devices.

[99]

To gain private time, then, to write his "Apology" and see that it reached the King before the King's mind had set.

If so, fallacious. This "Apology" would work, if at all, at a later time, the last possible occasion.

Ralegh had no evidence that any of his writings or arguments had ever pleased the King. On the contrary, knew the King to be hostile and suspicious. Why bank hope upon the composition of an "Apology"? One which depended upon the King believing him, taking him at his word. One which, even had the King thrown reason and caution away and chosen to believe it, is far from sufficiently humble or chastened in tone and substance. An "Apology" which admits next to no fault, leaves too many doubts and gaps.

God's wounds, the King could have made better arguments on Ralegh's behalf!

Perhaps the failure of the voyage has crazed him.

If mad, why feign madness?

No, all the "Apology" could do was to arouse the King's doubts and suspicions more.

Even the "Apology" was a device. A device for what? For more time? Time to do what? To hatch a plot? Not likely. Too late to begin a plot. If not to hatch a plot, then perhaps to cling to time, waiting for some plot already hatched to begin.

Or, perhaps not. Perhaps wishing to give that *impression,* to play upon the King's fears. And believing the King would at least wait upon the chance of a plot and keep Ralegh alive as the key to it.

If so, offensive and insulting as well as foolish.

Best, at the time, to wait and see. Be watchful. Leave him some measure of liberty but keep eyes on his use of it.

So Ralegh came to London. Where, instead of prison, he

found himself in his wife's house, comfortably lodged there, still in Stukely's keeping, but loosely guarded. With freedom to move about the city.

Did Ralegh not smell a dead rat in the wainscot?

Evidently not.

At last he agreed to follow the advice of Stukely. A man he knew he could not trust.

Nonetheless agreed to Stukely's plan, the scheme to flee to France. A scheme almost successful. But allowed himself to be foiled, prevented by a single barge and a few armed men. Made no resistance. Was sent to the Tower of London.

The King was astonished when news was brought of Ralegh's capture. The King was so struck that he laughed out loud and called Ralegh a coward.

Surely Ralegh would, could, should have resisted. Would either be killed in the brawl or make good his escape. Preferred not to. Even at the expense of being ridiculed.

Maybe the heart has gone out of the man. Maybe he has turned coward. Maybe has always been a coward and this occasion exposed him.

The King cannot accept these conclusions. Too wise and wary to allow himself to believe what's easy, what he most wishes to believe.

If wishes were thrushes, beggars would eat birds. . . .

No, the King called him coward and professed to believe it. But is not such a fool as that. Even the King's enemies allow him to be the wisest fool in Christendom.

There is some complex design in Ralegh's actions.

Or there is no design at all. Except to *imply* that there is or may be.

[101]

A commission was formed to examine him closely in the Tower. A special keeper set on him to watch and report.

The Commission determined nothing.

The keeper reported nothing new.

Perhaps he still believes the King will not dare to kill him.

Perhaps, upon landing at Plymouth and finding himself free, he misunderstood his position. Believing then, and clinging to it now, that the King is not truly offended.

Or believing the King wishes him out of the country and his hands for politic reasons.

Perhaps Ralegh wishes to force the King to end the game by killing him.

But why should any man wish for that?

The King of England sighs.

All malice, real and imagined, Ralegh's and the King's, will die upon the instant stroke of an ax. Be buried with him. His faith, then? Whatever remains will be parted. Some will go with the head and some with the headless body. Let them look for each other upon Judgment Day. Perhaps on that day, in the haste of it all, the bodies of traitors will have to settle for heads other than their own. Some inevitable mismatching of villains and rogues will take place. And one fine bony fellow will spy his skull upon another's body. Then another. And then maybe we shall be witness to the brawl and battle of the bones. . . .

The King nods. His spectacles slip off his nose. He feels them fall away and does not care. Now he can sleep at last. In a while they will wake him. At dawn, clad in hunter's green, he will raise a horn to his lips and blow a call as loud and clear and strong as any huntsman in England. He loves to shatter the

dim silence of dawn—and the stiff decorum of the English—
with that earsplitting blast. And he loves the belling, boiling
answer of the hounds, more faithful and useful than all his
Court. He loves to sit in the saddle and ride into dew and wind,
ride like the wind, toward the blood of the rising sun and the
blood of noble game.

The Bible slips from his fingers as he falls quiet at last.

He wakes with a sudden cry. Frightens the courtier in the
Farthingale chair. Rouses the servant by the hearth. Alerts the
guards outside the door of his chamber.

Where he has been, what he has dreamed, he cannot remember. Some part of it seems to have been at the Tower, that
fearful place whose first foundations were tempered by the
clotted blood of slaughtered beasts. In the dream Henry was
alive and well. Christian of Denmark was there too. The keeper
was baiting one of the lions with bear hounds. But it was a sad
lion that would not fight the dogs. The dogs were all snarls
and teeth like knives. The sad lion looked at him. A lion with
his own face . . .

Then he was somewhere else. He cannot remember where.
Only that, cold sweat on him, it was as dreadful as hell itself.

He curses the servant and the courtier. He shouts at the
guards outside and curses their rattles and muttering.

Then for a moment there is a blessed quiet again. He thanks
God for the candles burning in his chamber.

He will not sleep again. He will lie back against pillows and
wait for the morning.

Head resting on soft silk. But hands, poor troubled hands,
will not be still for him. They are still dreaming. He clenches
them into tight fists. A sound like a cracking nut. One hand is

falling to pieces, bones and all. Warm and damp. . . . He dares to open it and look. Laughs first at the sight of the spectacles crushed to slivers in his palm.

How foolish!

But his palm stings and he looks to see droplets of blood on palm and fingers. Drops as fine and small and round as rubies.

He gags.

"Steenie!" he calls. "For God's sake, Steenie! I have cut myself. I *bleed* . . . *l*"

Like a white shadow the young courtier is beside him, holding his hands, speaking words of comfort. Eased, the King feels lightheaded, drunk with emptiness.

If it were not for the warm salt of tears in his eyes, he would laugh out loud for joy.

Bells have tolled, some near, some distant. It is past two o'clock.

Faint stirrings, muffled voices, vague odor of smoke prove the servants are up, the fire in the kitchen is alive. It will soon be three and time for Henry Yelverton, as for any serious man, to wake and rise up to be about his business.

He hears the soft-footed stride, like the pad of a cat on the rush-strewn floor, of his servant, Peter, moving to the fireplace to stir embers and to kindle the fresh fire. Peter will never learn to walk on tiptoe like your Continental servant. No, he will pad as if his large feet were made of velvet. Yelverton smiles while Peter coughs a hacking, croaking, morning cough and the kindling wood, dropped, rattles on the hearth noisy as a bag of old bones. Peter will try to walk soft so as not to wake his sleeping master. But otherwise, save for the obeisance of his feet, he will always be himself. So much for your English servant. Peter, a countryman by birth, would have broken his fast and milked the cow by now, and he will never live long enough to approve of city ways. Trained at Court, he will do lip service to his station and your own. But, Lord bless him, he will cough when he has to and scratch when he itches.

Not many like him in these days, Yelverton allows. Not many who share, his views, his whims, his independence. He is left over, a beached and rotting hulk, a vessel of the last age. Peter will never admit that. In truth, he deems himself a man of the times, the more so because he can so clearly remember the bad times of the past. He will say if asked—and let us not ask him or there will be no silencing him betwixt now and dinner hour—that the times are not bad and are growing better. He is the living proof of that.

But . . .

But, in a trice, to prove his case, like a clumsy lawyer, he will turn prosecutor against himself. Will, as the old always do, rail against the restless young, who know nothing of where they come from, know only the keen dissatisfactions of the times, caring nothing for forgotten discontents. The young, who, in ignorance and impatience, not wishing to imagine the past, unable to imagine the future, grind their teeth in surly present time or, upon impulse or out of frustrate outrage, tear up their own roots. Leave farm and village or family craft for something, anything that's new and strange. Those who would work—many nowdays would rather beg or steal or catch a conny in a hundred ways—care little for skill and only for gain. They fill up jails and clinks. They swell the ranks of foreign armies. They go forth in rotten ships to the ends of the earth and the bottom of the sea.

Your new-fashioned servant, Peter will tell you, though he may dress neat and clean and smile to do his master's bidding, makes faces behind the master's back. Sells secrets for the highest price. Knows nothing of fidelity, but will ape the habits of servility, believing that because his service is falsely rendered, he does not humble himself.

Will fight for nothing save greed or to keep his life, which even a black rat will do. Knows nothing of honor or honest pride. Would as lief be a Frenchman or a Spaniard. Except that he is too lazy to learn another tongue.

In short, Peter, to prove these are good times, will demonstrate a most dismal future for England.

Of course, Yelverton thinks, I am past prime myself. He is a foolish old man, but my man. And, for all his faults, he's a comfort to me. Sometimes I suspect he may be right. Or that I, too, am stiffening with years. Even the baker's youngest apprentice is restless and ambitious. Busily seeking continual change, as a poet wrote. Well, Henry Yelverton thinks, we live in a time of change, when only change is constant, and who can blame a lad for rowing his boat with the tide? The old wheel goes up and down, round and around, and some go high and some go dashing low. Some wax fat and some are ground exceeding fine. Old Peter has at least spared himself a ride on Fortune's wheel.

He cannot make complaint against Peter. He is like an aged dog, with a few tricks and many bad habits. But, like a good dog, he will be faithful. If thieves in the night or, God save us, foreign enemies burst and batter into this chamber, Peter will put his body between them and Henry Yelverton, old as he is. He would be a comedian, a Will Kemp or a Tarleton, armed with a rapier or broadsword. But give him a knife or a stout cudgel and he fears no man alive.

Once riding a road together, daylight failing and the inn still a far piece ahead, they were set upon by some wild rogues, ragged and desperate men, who came out of a hedge like rats from rushes. Yelverton had his sword and dagger and a case of pistols. But it took a moment to get at those and fire them. He gained that moment when Peter rode straight at the rogues, laying at their randy heads with a short stick. His young law clerk, fresh minted from the Inns of Court, whinnied like a colt, and rode away. But Peter Rush made heads ring like a blacksmith's anvil and curses fly up like a covey of quail before Sir Henry could fire his pistols, and the rogues, howling, vanished into the briars they had come from as if carried by the puff of smoke.

"Oh, sir, we could have kilt the lot if you had but drawn sword and spurred!" Peter reproached him.

Peter has no trust in powder and shot. He would go forth against an arquebus, armed with his longbow and perfect confidence. He would fight when he had to and run when he had to.

Poor Peter, what need does he have of weapons now? If he opened the ruined gate of his mouth—as even now he blows heavy on the embers of the fire—with here and there a ruined leaning tower of tooth left, if he opened wide and breathed upon the enemy, they'd fall popeyed into a swoon of stone. Odor rich as an open tomb. Peter believes in the use of a sweetwood toothpick after a special feast; but not for him the daily ritual of tooth soap and a soft linen cloth. Nor any ablutions with warm water and soap sweetened with rosewater and violets. Let Henry Yelverton, lords and city merchants, primp and care for themselves, sweeten and brighten. Yet the worm will have them too. And after a season in earth, who can tell Sir Henry's skull from Peter's?

The kindling fire spits and crackles. Peter hawks and spits back at it. New light falls through the hangings of the bed and, glancing, Yelverton can see the shadow of Peter huffing and puffing, rimmed with an orange glow of fresh flames. Smoke and the odor of dry wood burning well. The fire begins growling like a mastiff on a chain.

Sleepy and comfortable, Henry Yelverton recalls the story he has heard from his latest clerk, one passing among lawyers who hover about at St. Paul's. Of some country gent whose fortune took a change, a high vault. Perhaps had mortgaged his land and risked all, buying himself shares in some privateering venture. Some fellow, for whom the coast of France was as far as the moon, risking his estate on a rotten ship and a cutthroat crew. Mortgaged land and bartered plate and the roof over his head. And then, *mirabilis!,* after lean and worried times, the ship returns, all of a piece and now rich-laden with foreign goods and the gains of a prize or two. And behold, our gent has his money back and ten times over. He who had been dining on dry peas and tough beef, on country ale and barley bread, finds himself, by sudden chance and change, a rich man.

Well, so this story goes, he decided he was too old to change his habits very much. Rich food ruined his digestion. Rich cloth on his back made him feel naked and womanish and gave him the itch. The one luxury he allowed himself was a bed, a fine bed like a lord's. And likewise he ordered a servant to wake him on the hour all through the night so he could have the pleasure of knowing he could sleep a little longer in that bed.

That pleased, but was not sufficient.

Then he hit upon a happy idea. He hired an old actor, broken down from years of bombast. And this man earned his keep as a sort of night watch, walking to and fro in the garden beneath the squire's bedchamber, not guarding anything, but talking to himself.

"Cold, cold, Lord, I am cold! I'm all a cold pudding. I'm cold

[109]

as a clock and cold as a key. Colder than clay on a whetstone or a dog's nose. Brrr . . . I'm cold as charity . . ."

Which our squire found gave him more comfort than a warming pan.

"Sir?"

He must have laughed out loud.

"I am awake, Peter," he says. "Light the candles and bring me my Bible."

"Yes, sir."

"And look to my great robe."

"It's as clean as a new kettle. I saw to it myself."

"See to it again," Henry Yelverton says.

Muttered assent from Peter. Who thinks that too much cleanliness is vanity.

Yelverton will be clean and well dressed today, though. It is only meet and right when your duty is to take the head of such a grand and glittering dandy as Ralegh.

In moments Sir Henry Yelverton will have his Bible in hand and candles lit in the niches of the headboard. He will read some from the Psalms, then rise to kneel at the edge of the bed and offer up morning prayers. He will wash himself and wash his teeth. With Peter's help he will be combed and dressed. Henry Yelverton is a sturdy, stout man, shortish and jowly. In the long robe of the Attorney General, feet hidden, he is said to float more than walk, as if set upon little wheels.

A man of sanguine humor and sound digestion, he will have a hearty, simple breakfast: bread and cheese, salt herring, some cold beef, all washed down with ale. He need not eat to last through a long day, however. With luck and wit he will be done and the whole affair settled by early afternoon.

Now there is a rapping on the door of his chamber. Peter padding no longer, shuffles to ask who is it and to unbolt the door. Yelverton hears the voice of his clerk, up and dressed early. No doubt that young man has slept lightly too.

Once comforted by his favorite, once he has swallowed tears and stifled laughter, the King of England acts upon an impulse as if he had weighed it by logic all night long. Thinking perhaps that is true. All his thoughts circled one decision and he did not know it until now.

Beautiful Theobalds will not do. The hunting is too tame. There are too many hangbys, because they are close to Westminster. If he cannot sleep here, if the hunting is no true pleasure, if there are too many in his company, then there's a simple solution.

Besides, he is amused imagining the confusion and difficulty, shouting and anger from steward down to scullion, his decision will create.

He tells the young man that he has changed his plans for this day.

The courtier, wrapping a fresh lace handkerchief around the King's lightly scratched hand, smiles and raises his neat-trimmed brows like a pair of wings. His lashes flutter. So long, so naturally fine. Any woman would envy him.

They will not hunt game at Theobalds, the King tells him. No, instead, with the smallest possible retinue and least baggage, they will travel north today to the lodge at Royston. He should never have left there to return to Westminster.

"But there were affairs of state," the young man tells him.

He is trying, gently, to reassure His Majesty that the uncomfortable journey to Whitehall to deal with irritating affairs, some of which could have been deferred, was not in vain.

"But we were content there," the King says. "Were you not happy at Royston, my boy?"

Cool fingers, gently rubbing, have calmed the King's trembling hands. The boy's eyes are half hidden by lovely lashes.

"Indeed," he says. "Yet I find my felicity in the presence of my King, and therefore anywhere."

Touched, the King snorts so as not to show his feelings. And, as well, so that the young man will not know how powerful a balm is flattery when one is flattered, not out of love—for true lovers need not flatter—but from the attentions of those most admirable, beautiful, and worthy of love.

"You shall yet learn some polish in this Court of mine," the King says.

"I'll be all shine and polish like a silver salt."

"We shall believe that when it is seen," the King says. "Enough. It is a mere scratch I have. No cause for a surgeon. Pass the word that we are pleased to proceed to Royston."

The young man, still smiling, steps gracefully back from the edge of the bed, bowing. Pauses.

"An' it please the King . . ."

"Speak up, man. I may yet sleep some before I breakfast."

"Royston is far from Westminster."

"Indeed? It is said old Burghley made the journey in a single day once. But I doubt it, considering his age and condition."

The young man, head tipped still in the beginning of a bow, edges of his lips pointed with the hint of a smile, waits.

"Royston is at some distance and Theobalds is closer by."

"Good boy! You shall learn our geography yet before you die. Now, be off about your bidding."

The hint of a smile is gone and a slight wrinkle creases his brow, even as he bows his head and steps backward.

"It grieves you, does it not?"

"Your Majesty?"

"You do not wish Walter Ralegh to die."

"I wish nothing," the young man says. "Except the health and felicity of the King. I wished only to remind the King that Royston may be too great a distance, should, for any account, the King desire to change his mind."

"There is no distance so great, the length and breadth of this whole land, that can frustrate the will of the King. Remember that. Weigh it. Rest assured that Royston is near enough for us to change our mind a dozen times, if that is our will."

Bows again. Then, tall and slender, lean-hipped, broad-shouldered, so graceful at times he seems to be dancing to unheard music, he unlocks and unbolts the door. Slips outside, a white silk shadow, closing that door softly behind him.

Soon a messenger will be off riding hard to Royston's lodge to rouse the keeper with the news that the King is returning to course the English hare. And, because the timbered lodge is small and the village nearby offers scant accommodations, he can leave more than half of his party here at Theobalds. Taking with him only the best of the lot. There is no such thing as a true privy chamber, as true privacy for a King.

The King draws the hangings again. And stretches, warm and content, before easing his head to the pillow.

The servant, awake, is building up the fire.

Poor boy, he thinks, poor Steenie. His beautiful simplicity. Here he acts out of loyalty, what he deems it to be. Loyal to those he thinks raised him up. Loyal to a man he knows little of. Who, by arrangement, paid him more than a thousand pounds for his assistance in obtaining release to make a foolish voyage.

Well, so long as it be simple, such loyalty is a good sign. Perhaps he may prove loyal to his King as well.

Unless . . .

Unless, of course, there is more money to be had for the King's pardon.

The King chuckles.

Ah, Steenie, if I only knew the sum and thought it might serve you, I should give you that pardon and feel better for it. But there's more than you can yet imagine cloaked in these matters. And a sum so large I am sure you cannot imagine it.

At least, I hope you have not yet conceived of such sums.

7

Still the damp chill, scent of the river. And he feels to the marrow of his bones the fog and chill of fever. Lying on his hard pallet. And, though he is now burning, now sweating drops cold as pearls and trembling like a dry leaf, he cannot feel much self-pity, or offer complaint against these conditions.

There's the paradox. Even these modest comforts, easing some aches and pains of flesh, come too late to matter.

Never upright like Job, he nevertheless knows something of how Job's restoration to felicity, a gift and blessing it is true, changed nothing much. Since, in rags, bright with sores, lank in poverty, Job had already endured all—even that thundering voice from the whirlwind. After hearing the voice of God, what difference could content, health, and prosperity have made?

Ralegh is thinking of how he has come to where he is, how he has endured years of disgrace, of imprisonment, and, by enduring, changed. By changing has somehow passed beyond even the pride of endurance.

At first acceptance of hard truth rewarded him with a newer, finer sense of caution in himself. Knowing himself more clearly, he need not degrade or despise himself. Nor distrust himself. But knowing himself and the boundaries of his reasoning and imagination, he need never again depend upon himself so much either, any more than a man should permit his estate and fortunes to depend completely upon the good will of his servants.

He need not again be ambushed by despair. Alert, he could not be ambushed by himself.

And then another step. Awareness that these things would also be true if he were chained to a wall or stretched on the rack or one of old Topcliffe's hideous engines. He could not be much changed so long as he lived. Upon the rack, until blinding pain of body wiped out the mind, he would not be alone. Alone in pain, yes. But nonetheless a partner with his tormentors. Thus, until mind and spirit broke and surrendered to pain of bone and joint, he would be a necessity to them. Even when it is the sole purpose of the tormentor to inflict the utmost of pain, the victim has one trump card: that once mind and spirit have broken, once pain is master, then he is no longer the same man that the tormentor desires to injure. The tormentor, frustrate, can continue to devise more horrid tortures, to inflict more pain, but the broken victim is a stranger even to himself. Mere suffering meat.

Such a thought not easing the pain, by any means. But perhaps it is the thought that has enabled some men, astonishingly, to bear much suffering without breaking. And others, who finally fell apart, to accept that condition without shame.

How fortunate he is that so many people for divers reasons, the King included, for such a long time have desired that he should live.

Knowledge he came to possess of himself also taught him

[117]

that most free men have no occasion to come to such truth. Therefore he had an advantage. As if he could see some, but not all, of his opponent's cards. Could wager, with odds in his favor, they did not know his mind as well as he did.

Thinking: *Thus we are all double-dealers always whether we know it or not.*

He has schooled himself to bear all things he can imagine. Forgetting that this strength came from acknowledging the enormity, wider than seas and continents, of the world beyond imagining. Freed from fear of known pains, he has continued to suffer wounds. Suffered because he is alive, and, more than the beating of heart or the ghost of breath upon a glass, the one irrefutable proof of living is the capacity to suffer and to be wounded.

Already he flinches, winces inwardly, feeling the presence, the nearness of a pain he cannot name.

Out of fog another shape appears. A form that is faceless, as yet, but instantly known. A bear of a young man. And the old man groans aloud. A light film of tears comes into his eyes. He wonders at these tears, wonders that after so much, after all has been said and done, any man alive, however old and wounded, can still shudder at the thrust of pain like a virgin at the thrust of love.

Because, he thinks, *wounds are not wisdom enough.*

A long-legged, broad-shouldered, swaggering bear of a boy, spit and image of himself, save that this image is chiseled more crudely. A parody of the original. Flushes quicker with the family's sudden choler. Is equally proud and is more rash, more daring, but not out of an educated disregard for risks. Rather out of the desire to prove himself the equal or better of his father.

[118]

So it is with fathers and sons.

The boy comes imitating each gesture of his father, borrowing, without discrimination, both bad habits and good. With one huge difference: this boy has a deep fine resounding voice —gift of his mother's Throckmorton blood. His words can be heard across open water in a stiff northern wind. As loud as Tom of Lincoln that boy was, when he wished to be.

Ah, then, here is Walter, son and heir, and once keystone of his estate and posterity.

Ah Wat, Wat, how did I fail you?

Sent to Oxford, where he was "addicted to strange company and violent exercise," or so his tutors said.

Sent to the Continent with the learned Ben Jonson for companion. To mend his manners. Surely that poet, who had come along rough roads, was man enough to hold the boy in check. Yet back from Paris came the story. How Wat drank Ben into a stupor, hired a cart and placed Ben on it, dead to the world, in the image of a man crucified, and showed him on the streets as "the living crucifix."

Went all the way over to Holland to settle a duel begun in England. Duels and brawls aplenty. . . .

Wore the favors of ladies stuffed in his codpiece. And they laughed and loved him. His mother laughed and loved him too. Spoiled him out of the memory of his young father.

And never to forget the story which made the rounds of London and the Court until it became a legend of father and son. How Ralegh and Wat had been invited to dinner at the house of some great man. How Ralegh wished to go alone.

"Thou art such a quarrelsome, affronting creature that I am ashamed to have such a bear in my company," Ralegh told him.

Wat blinked at that, but neither laughed nor swore nor protested. Humbly confessed past follies and begged to be given another chance to prove his reformation of character. Promising to display the best manners in England.

Sat next to his father in the company of great men, so correct and attentive he seemed to give the lie to every story coined in his name.

Ralegh, amazed and pleased, though, as ever, skeptical. His doubts bearing fruit when halfway through the meal, at a moment of quiet, Wat spoke up loud and clear.

"I woke this morning without the fear of God before my eyes," he began. "And at the instigation of the devil I went to a whore . . ."

His father stiff and staring at nothing. Like a corpse on trial for treason in Scotland.

"I was very eager," Wat continued. "I kissed her and embraced her. But when I came to enjoy her, she suddenly thrust me from her and vowed that I should not . . ."

Great Lord, where would the idiot boy go next with his satirical tale of courtly love?

"I asked her why and she refused. I persisted, demanding an answer. 'Tell me why,' says I. And at last she allows as how it is not proper or fitting, this most delicate of whores. She gave me no choice but to prick her pride—if nothing else. And then out of anger she confessed. 'It is not right,' says she, 'because your father lay with me only an hour ago!'"

A gust of laughter, fists on the table, rattle of plates and cups, knife and spoon. Interrupted by the flat sound of Ralegh's hand across the boy's face, a clap like the noise of a musket, a blow that lifted Wat's hat and sent it rolling in the rushes as if blown by a breeze. A blow that rattled Wat's head and blanked his eyes as, for him, the room was suddenly full of fireworks and falling stars.

Laughter cut off as if by an ax with one clean stroke. Then all at the table waiting to see what the wild boy would do next.

Wat threw back his head and laughed alone. He shrugged the shrug of a Dutch moneylender and turned from his father's fury. Turned to the gentleman next to him and fetched him a blow of the same force.

Gasps as another hat went tumbling on the floor.

"Pass it along!" Wat cried. "It will come back to my father anon."

And they all roared with laughter, even the gentleman who was the butt of his joke. And Ralegh shook his head and laughed too until his shoulders shook and tears of laughter fell into his plate.

How did I fail you, poor boy? Why in God's name do I fail you even now?

Chill grips him now, hair to toenail, leather tongue to limp crotch.

He cannot be certain if he suffers from fever here and now, or if it is the memory of that worse one. The fever of the troubled voyage which tossed him and turned him, pitched him and rolled him, shuddered and shivered his timbers and left him stranded helpless in the cabin on the *Destiny*. Fever that killed and weakened many of his crew. Fever indiscriminate between inept gentlemen adventurers and the rest he had called "the very scum of the world, drunkards, blasphemers, and other such as their fathers, brothers, and friends thought it an exceeding good gain to be discharged of." Fever that

[121]

killed so many and left the rest white and thin, bright-eyed, reeling, clumsy as new kittens, men in a trance.

Oh, we were all of us sick with fevers. Fevered in our dreams of mines and mountains of gold. Dreaming beyond that and through the interminable green hellfire of jungles to the gaudiest dream of all—the hidden secret city of legend, the ruined golden temples and pavilions of El Dorado . . .

Men possessed by fever of flesh whose minds and hearts were burning in a hotter higher flame. Men burned to ashes by dreams.

Ah, Wat, roaring boy, you come as if to a summons. I summoned you not. But here you are, alive and armed. I lie on my bed in the cabin on the *Destiny,* at anchor and rolling with the tides off Trinidad, while you and Keymis and the others . . .

O faithful—faithless Keymis! We were in the midst of the fever and knew not what we did. You and Keymis and a hundred others are moving in small boats up the treacherous river.

Be careful, be vigilant. Go careful and quiet as your Indian guides! You do not know that in the years which have gone by the Spaniards have moved the village of San Thomé. You do not know the King has betrayed our plans and our numbers to Gondomar and that the Spaniard is alert, expecting us.

Or is this true, any of it? A man in grips of fever, wrestling with himself as Jacob wrestled with an angel, a man afire with fever, all ice in chills, cannot tell much between sunshine and rain, wind or calm. Cannot trust anything except the sense of his own suffering. All the world's reduced to that, to hot and cold, to bone-dry or drenched with sweat, to pangs and

[122]

snarl of guts. A man with fever is reduced to condition of newborn infancy.

I did not allow for the fever, which would do more injury than a battle. And would lay me helpless on my back. Of course I allowed, as ever, for the chance of death. But did not allow for the bad fortune of not dying. Of being alive and helpless, mind and spirit beclouded.

Well, fortune is that which is beyond all allowance.

My greatest failure was with Keymis. Had come to trust him too much. Which trust was no fault or failing until I found myself unable to do otherwise than to add faith to trust. To depend blindly upon him.

In the end, through clouds of fever, I must learn all that had happened from Keymis. He had the first and last words, then was silent. And now, in fever or in health, I will never know the truth of it.

But in imagination I live it. God knows I have lived it again and over again.

God knows, Wat, though I lay in my cabin while you took my place, I have gone in your steps countless times since then.

At sundown you come ashore on the riverbank for the night. Later you are attacked, your encampment overrun by Spaniards. Could have all been killed then, every man jack of you, in the shouting dark. But Wat, you and the captains rallied your rogues and beat the Spaniards back.

Now you are awake and in order, but you do not know the numbers of enemy, where they have come from, when they might come again. You cannot stay where you are. You have a choice, to flee by water, which is likely what the Spaniard hopes; or you can muster and pursue them, making attack of your own. You urge the latter course, Wat, believing your father would.

Before the dawn you and others move off into the jungle. By first light you have found a trail, a footpath freshly stirred and trampled by Spanish boots. Eager, you go forward with pikemen, leaving the musketeers to catch up as they can.

The trail twists, the way begins to clear. And suddenly ahead there lies a village. It is very quiet. They have hidden the women and children and even the dogs. They have put out all the fires.

It may be they are fewer in number than you believed. It may be they have fled into the jungle and abandoned the village.

Quiet in the trees, among the vines and the long roots and the dripping leaves.

Be careful now, Wat. The Spaniard knows many tricks.

You will not. You and the others stumble forward toward the village. You rattle like a tinker's cart, sword in scabbard, helmet and breastplate.

A bird flies up and shrieks warning. You hear it not. You and your men, panting and fevered, sweating, run forward.

Damn you, Keymis! Why aren't you there? Stop them! Make them wait for the others!

Why won't you listen to me, Wat? Your father is not such a rash, bold, unthinking fool as you believe.

Listen to me, son! I cry out to you. But you do not hear me.

No, no, it is not so. Wat is not there. He lies safe in bed in England. And I am not sick in my cabin. Younger, my legs and arms full of springtime, as full of rich blood as a German sausage, I am there instead of Wat. I am leading this pack of fools.

[124]

Allow me . . .

Follow me, lads!

We race like a street mob toward the village.

Glint of metal in the leaves. Wink of metal, spark of fire, flash of flame, thunder in our faces and air full of black smoke, dry sweet odor of gunpowder. Now the sound we hear is the howling and cursing of a poor wretch, one of ours, rolling and writhing like a chopped snake, clothed in crimson of his blood, wreathed in gore, clutching a broken sack of entrails, holding guts like slippery eels. Cursing and howling. Begging God to spare him pain.

We scatter, scuttle like crabs for cover of tree trunk and brush. More thunder and shot singing in leaves. Plumes and feathers of dust along the trail. Where the wounded wretch is quiet now in the puddle of himself.

I lie at the base of a rotten stump, tongue of rough wool in a mouth of brass, pressing my face to mud. I am panting and my body twitches and heaves. Like a man with a woman, flat as a flounder, beneath him.

I am there, not you, Wat! I am the one!

They will kill us if we remain here. The lucky will be killed. Unlucky will sup with Spanish cruelty. Be smoked and cooked like meat. Be flayed alive. Be lutes and citherns of screaming.

I raise my head to peer around the tree. I see moving in the leaves. Squirrels in rustic armor. Only a few, though. Others will be hidden in the village waiting for us to come.

Behind I hear one man running away.

Why don't they come now, while we are scattered and surprised? They are waiting for us. Huddling as hidden and

[125]

fearful as we. Why? I know the Spaniard. When he does not press his advantage, he has reasons.

He is fewer in number than he would like to be. He does not like the odds.

Here they come now. Out of houses and from behind barricades, forming up ranks. Their officers shout at them. They fear us too.

Well, we can lie here and die one at a time. We can run for our lives and likely lose them too. But if we rush them suddenly, before they have been formed . . .

Their weapons are primed and ready. One movement and all will fire.

My heart a beating drum. Sweat crawling, like a procession of spiders and ants under the bowl of my morion. One movement, one target and the Spaniards will fire. And in smoke and the clumsy time of reloading we can take them.

I draw breath.

"Follow me, men!" I shout.

I spring to my feet to stand in the trail, solid on earth, pointing my sword like a compass needle to the village. I grin because at the first move I made the air was crackling with fire and smoke, the air was swarming with bees hiving home to the stump where I had been.

"Come on, hearts!"

I run now and hear others running behind me. I lunge forward at steel and a crowd of faces. I slash at the nearest and see light go out of his eyes before I feel a blow in my chest, such a blow and a heat of fire that I fall full length like a cut tree.

Head up, eyes open, I see a Spanish officer who saved his musket for me. I am half on my feet again in a lunge. Calm and slow, as in a dream, he aims the butt of his musket at my head. My head explodes inside. My brain is a pudding of pain and I am kissing earth again. Feet and shouts all around me.

Who said the earth's a cold hard bed? Earth's as soft as goose feathers. I lie floating on a soft bed.

Someone turning me over. I hear myself groaning. Dim as by horn lantern light I see a tower over me. A topless tower with feet and English boots. A giant holding a halberd dripping with blood. The halberd droops to earth. Tower crumbles away. The giant kneels. A face as huge as the bowl of the sky. Bees brush past us. A body falls near.

"Wat, Wat," the giant is saying. "Lord bless you and keep you . . ."

It is my father's face. Not shining upon me. His face is all dark. Father's turned nigger, a bloody blackamoor. I open my mouth to laugh and tell him. No laughter. Froth of my blood like froth on a pitcher of ale.

A pitcher of ale would cure me now. I'm drunk and flat on my ass in a deep Devon lane. Sweet odors of springtime. Will get up and go find me a bed. A good bed and a wench to warm it. Not now, though. Later will be soon enough. I lie in an English lane counting the stars and listening for a nightingale. And then I sleep . . .

Keymis, I could kill you now.

My son dead. The Spaniards driven off, but enough lived to tell the tale. You found no gold mine. Baubles and trash from the village of San Thomé.

In my fever and sorrow I cursed you and the day you were born.

"Then, sir, I know what I must do," you said.

[127]

I did not raise my hand to stop you. Closed my eyes and bit my tongue. I heard your feet go away. I lay there until I heard the shot and shouts.

Keymis had been cleaning his pistol and it fired, they told me.

You bungled that too, Keymis. Had to finish yourself with a knife.

God forgive me, I laughed, thinking Keymis could not even kill himself cleanly.

God can forgive me and will, I believe and trust.

Now I ask your forgiveness too, Keymis, my old faithless friend.

The man on the bed mutters something. The servant by the fire blinks and stirs.

"Sir?"

"Nothing, nothing at all."

Then: "Heap up the fire, Ralph, and brighten this room."

"We're low on firewood, sir. I doubt we'll last through the morning."

"Well, if we don't, we can burn my bed and chest."

"Sir?"

"Never mind, Ralph," the man on the bed says, sitting up, clutching his blanket around him like a cloak. "We won't be needing wood or coal for more fires here, I'll warrant."

"As you wish, sir."

The fire burns and the room glows.

He thinks: *And if we need more wood than my bed and sea chest, why here am I, a bundle of old dry sticks.*

Smiles to remember the proverb: *Two dry sticks will kindle a green one.*

So much for the wisdom of this world. Even Aristotle couldn't have said it better.

"Fetch me my pipe and tobacco," Ralegh says. "I have slept enough for an old man."

Part Two

But what of all this? And to what end do we
lay before the living the fall and fortunes of the
dead, seeing that the world is the same that it
hath been and the children of the present time
will still obey their parents? It is in the present
time that all the wits of the world are exercised.

RALEGH—*History of the World*

Having perused the documents three times over, word by word, weighing each one—a task not made easier by the haste with which the clerks scribbled them—Lord Lieutenant Apsley of the Tower descends from the upper chambers of his house to where the others are waiting, backs to the fire, cups of his ale, warmed against the weather, in their hands.

"Well . . . ?"

That is Wilson, Sir Thomas Wilson, the one who is smiling. The other two, young men, gentlemen officers of the Court of Westminster, are as strict-faced as playing-card knaves. They are dressed drably, nondescript, cloaked; plain texture of gray and brown cloaks, doublet and hose being almost part and parcel of the weather itself, as if tailored out of last night's fog. Their wide-brimmed, low-crowned hats are likewise plain, brightened with neither feather nor band. Only Wilson, shorter than either, a stumpy rooster of a man, is dressed for a public occasion. Not grandly, if the jewels were counted or cloth touched to test quality, but bright and bold enough. So that,

[133]

at a distance and the more so because of this company, he will be seen and will seem the picture of a gent of the Court.

He must not have come to the Tower with them, by water. For, as Apsley, coming down the steep stairs and crossing toward them, notices, it is their cloaks, not Wilson's, which steam by the fire, their hats which are still wet as if with a dew.

All three are armed, sword and dagger.

"Well now, Apsley," Wilson continues. "Do these instruments meet with your approval?"

Apsley wrinkles a frown. "It is not for me to approve or disapprove," he says. "It is for me to obey my orders when they are properly presented."

Wilson snorts. "You may be sure they are, sir. Anything from the King is proper."

"To be sure," Apsley begins, hesitant, "but I must be certain that all is in order . . ."

An answer wasted on Wilson, for he has turned to the fire, giving Apsley his back to talk to, and is sipping the last of his ale.

Apsley feels a flush on his cheeks. Is grateful for the beard which hides most of it.

"No man will question your care," one of the gentlemen begins. "It is true these papers were hastily drawn. There could be some flaw in them. You are to be commended."

"There is no flaw," Wilson says, over his shoulder. "If there is, leave it to the lawyers, who will scent it soon enough. A soldier is hardly a judge of these things."

"Nevertheless I must judge, Mr. Wilson," Apsley says, surprised at the curtness of the voice he hears. "And judge I shall. In the name of the King and for the King. I shall read through again, if I choose, to satisfy myself."

Now Wilson turns, his tight smile unchallenged, but his right hand resting easy on his hilt, his eyes hard.

"Then, God's wounds!, read on until you grasp the meaning, Apsley." To the others: "We may well spend tonight here while he studies."

At this Apsley, astonishing himself again, abruptly relaxes and laughs.

Wilson shrugs and laughs too, as if relieved. The other two are men with wooden masks. As befits their station and this duty.

"All is in order then?" one ventures.

"All but one thing," Apsley answers. "There must be a writ of *habeas corpus.* I must have it before I deliver him over."

"You shall have it at Westminster," Wilson says. "It shall be delivered to you there."

"I trust so," Apsley replies. "For without that writ I can give him over to no man. I dare not."

"Oh Lord," says Wilson, sighing. "Let one of the men of the Commission command you to and you'll jump through a hoop or dance like a clown. Do not be so brave about this thing. It does not become you."

Now it is Apsley who half turns away, biting his lip, pretending again to examine the papers. He bites his lip, tasting a salt of blood. He is not certain why, whether it is to check his anger or to hide his shame or both. . . .

"Have no fear, Lieutenant Aspley. You shall have your *habeas corpus* and the rest of your life to study it if you wish.

[135]

You are not of such consequence in this affair as to be in any danger.

"If you prefer," Wilson continues, "I shall take the man and deliver him up myself."

"You do not have the authority."

"That, sir, is a moot point."

Indeed it is.

Sir Allan Apsley knows it well enough. He could scarcely have anticipated this singular dilemma when, after a long service as a soldier and no small sacrifice—all his sons lie under Ireland's misty sod, killed in the wars there, he received this office in reward. He paid for it, of course, and a price he could not afford. But it is an office with opportunity for a man to feather, belatedly, a neglected nest, to end his days with something to show for himself and, he hopes, to pass on. Perhaps enough to make a decent dowry for his daughters. An office where a prudent man, in bits and pieces and without breaking the laws, may with good fortune, recoup his investment and turn a modest profit. Under ordinary circumstances. . . .

His predecessors have fared badly, not blameless to be sure, but caught in traps of extraordinary circumstance, Elwes —of course he was careless, but what could he have done, truly, beyond exercise prudence? and was that, carelessness, not his sole crime?—lost his life.

Now Lieutenant Allan Apsley must contend with Sir Walter Ralegh. It is almost too complex and devious for him to grasp. Nor would he try to grasp beyond what he can know. His only course, from the dawn when Ralegh was brought here by Stukely and the King's men until now, has been to be careful as he can. To seek to offend no man.

Sir Thomas Wilson has tested that resolve and has made the exercise, even of common carefulness, most difficult.

Ever since Ralegh emptied his purse by torchlight and became a prisoner, at the end of a warm summer night, Ralegh —and Apsley with him, then—has been turned and shifted like a weathercock. Apsley lodged him first here in the safety and comfort of his own house, still called the Queen's House. A trim and tidy place, though small, solid old brickwork and the heaviest of timbers turned iron-hard with aging, resting in the southwest corner of the inner court within the full shadow of the bell tower, where the Lady Arabella, herself in like fashion apprehended in flight by water and returned here, languished and died.

Aspley, though alert, kept Ralegh more as guest than prisoner. Ralegh ate at table with Apsley and his wife and daughters, sometimes joined by Bess and his own kin as well. He added to Apsley's larder most generously, to be sure.

Was visited by friends and servants. And from the Queen's House it was a slight walk and an easy climb to enjoy his old walking place on the walls. Where the crowds again gathered to watch him. Sometimes, preferring some privacy, the old man would turn instead to the green and make the circuit of the entire Inner Ward, stopping to talk with the yeoman warders and others he knew.

Bess Ralegh moved back from Broad Street to the house on Tower Hill close by.

Apsley was most courteous. He felt some pity for Ralegh. Some disapproval of the trickery which had placed him in the Tower again. But Apsley was not moved to act kindly either by pity or disapproval. Two luxuries, private feelings, he could not afford to act upon. He held in mind the scandal of the Overbury poisoning. He did not fancy the image of himself dying upon the scaffold like Sir Gervase Elwes. And, a hardened man who knew the wounds of this world, he took note that twice Ralegh had been lodged in the Tower and twice walked out by Lion Gate into London a free man. He would, therefore, endeavor to keep Ralegh's good will until he was free again or safely dead.

With small subtlety—what need for artful deception when power is beyond measure?—the King then appointed a man of his own choosing, Sir Thomas Wilson, to act as a second Lord Lieutenant. An equal, then, in rank, but without authority to command in the Tower, and so without responsibility. The King had his reasons. The Commission he appointed to examine Ralegh, ransacking the affair of his voyage and return and his attempt to escape, hearing every witness they could find, from steadfast Captain King down to the hired oarsmen of the wherry, was not moving to any resolution with dispatch. The King sent Wilson to act as Ralegh's close keeper. His presence to prod the Commission. Chosen to win Ralegh's confidence if that were possible. But chiefly to stick to him, a leech, next and near as a shadow. And to ferret out secrets, catch scent of plans or schemes which might elude the gentlemen of the Commission. Who were circumscribed by custom and procedure and, not least, caution of protecting their own interests.

So Wilson had come to the Tower to take the keys and the keeping of Ralegh away from Apsley.

Wilson might find a way to poison him, Apsley surmised. Ralegh could not be gulled by a spy. The King must know it too. If the Commission could not find grounds to punish him, if Wilson could not find or fabricate some other cause, then it would be a convenience if Ralegh died in the Tower. Perhaps even to Ralegh himself. A solution with advantages to many.

Except, of course, to the Lord Lieutenant, who might have to die for it.

Wilson might be a good intelligencer, but seemed less than gifted with extraordinary intelligence. Sounding the depths of him, Apsley has concluded that Wilson took on this task either at full value or as a man gambling recklessly for everything . . . or nothing. In either case a fool. In either case compelled to act in much the same fashion. Somehow convinced that he was capable, where betters had failed, of working a delicate foist and taking possession of Ralegh's purse of secrets.

Never mind motive then, if the actions that followed from it were to be identical. Wilson would fail. Failing, he might become desperate. Would turn from craft into an artless nip, a common cutpurse. Would fail in that too. Then, thoroughly frightened, he would be subject to suggestion from any quarter, including his own inner promptings. And then he might try poison.

What Wilson, it seemed, would never come to face, at least until he, too, might stand shivering in his shirt upon a scaffold, was that the King had duped him. No matter what Wilson knew, Apsley knew that if Wilson murdered Ralegh, it would be both of them who would pay the price for the King's convenience.

All who dance must pay the piper. . . .

After Wilson arrived, he ordered Ralegh moved to a small old cell, rich with pitiful inscriptions on the walls, in Constable Tower on the eastern side of the Inner Ward. Aptly chosen, for here in the time of Elizabeth many Catholic priests had been held. There Ralegh would be out of sight if not of mind.

Wilson could not have imagined, unless he forgot the man's whole history, that discomfort would overmaster Ralegh's spirit. Or that Ralegh, who knew by heart every inch and niche of this tower, would be frightened by the words of men who had suffered here. Or that, fox defending life and den, he would feel any shame, having played a part in placing some of them here. Or that, being of a satiric turn of mind, Ralegh would credit Wilson with wit.

Ralegh formally petitioned Star Chamber for better quarters. His situation became a matter of public record and could not be ignored. He was ordered moved to Brick Tower, north and east, quarters of the Master of Ordnance, and Ralegh's first lodging in the Tower when Elizabeth had sent him there. From these casements he could see the Inner Ward and patches of the river and London coming up to its wall, Tower Hill, Aldgate, the raw shacks and suburbs, unlawful but irremediable, just beyond. And, beyond that, the wide fields, where women, following the old custom, spread out swaths of cloth for bleaching.

Wilson countered. Wrote to the Council, pleading his prisoner was not secure. He would not object to the prisoner's comfort and health. But Ralegh should have a safer, higher lodging. Somewhere, as Wilson put it, *a little nearer to heaven and yet from which there could be no escape—save to hell.*

And once more he was transplanted, this time the old twig appropriately planted in the innermost, first, and final bastion of the fortress.

The satirical thrust: here was where Sir Thomas Overbury took his sweet slow time dying of the poisoned tarts. Whose irony and to what purpose? Perhaps the Council, speaking finality. Possibly the Commission for the expedience of using the high old presence chamber for deliberations. Even, it may be, the King, to speak to them one and all and especially to Ralegh, saying: *Let this man of history settle his fate in the Tower's oldest place amid a fit company of English ghosts.* . . .

The White Tower at the center of the fort. Keep of the castle built by the Conqueror upon the very spot where an old timber tower of the Saxons stood. And both of these placed upon the ground and foundations, built of and out of the ruins, of an ancient bastion of Julius Caesar. A mighty tower, solid, with fifteen feet of wall.

And there he lies now in one of the chambers, once used by monks and even the royal Court when this was the chief palace of London, near to the Chapel of St. John. A chamber decent enough for comfort. And far better for anything human than the places for wretches of no consequence who must try to live in the dark vaults of the chapel and the crypt. Why, on a rare morning not long ago, one of the last rinsed days of autumn, Apsley and Ralegh climbed to the high roof. Could see as far as Greenwich, as if through a spyglass. There the sun gilded the stones of palace buildings and the windows were shattered points and puffs of brightness. And breeze filled the sails of incoming ships.

"Since our Lord Lieutenant is satisfied that the King's clerks and lawyers know their trade, let us proceed with this business," Wilson says.

And so, accompanied by a yeoman warder, they go out across the green toward White Tower.

Apsley wonders if Ralegh will have had some warning. Like all the great men, he has a crew of intelligencers. Can, at dinner, delight and amaze with pictures of things to come soon, as much as any mountebank or prophet, but needing no inspiration for his prognostications. It will not surprise Apsley to find Ralegh dressed and ready, all aglitter, smoking his pipe and waiting for them.

Though Ralegh has been courteous to him, Apsley is not deceived. Perhaps Ralegh likes him well enough, indeed wishes him well. But he has been used, set over and against Wilson by Ralegh. Encouraged—he is ashamed but not too blind to confess it to himself—in his fears of Wilson. To fear Wilson and his rashness and folly. Ashamed, but not too proud to see there is wisdom in Ralegh's method. For just so long as the two, each contending with and suspicious of the other, were at odds, then Ralegh, though caught between two keepers, well kept, possessed the greatest degree of freedom and safety.

He might die of fever or boredom, but not from any poison Wilson could procure. For from the learned Dr. John Dee, now gone to eternal reward or punishment, and from his own experiments, some performed here in the Tower, Ralegh knows as much of poisons and their remedies as any man in England. Perhaps even in Italy. Should it have suited his purposes, he could have poisoned Wilson, or indeed Apsley, and so that no man would have been wiser. Should it have served him, he could have poisoned himself and left the two of them behind to stew like a couple of Irish cows cooked in their own hides.

Here again, now as they singly climb the flimsy outside stairs to the White Tower's high chambers, Apsley wonders about Wilson. A spy, to be sure. And there are many of those of many stations and degrees. Some worth their wages, some worthless, pure extravagance; some skilled masters, some, who though they may be lucky and live long and die quiet, will remain forever prentices in the shadowy craft. But Sir Thomas Wilson is not an ordinary spy. He is the King's man, specially chosen for this task by the King. Must, therefore, have skill or craft to catch the eye of the King from among all those the King could have, snapping his fingers one time. Just so . . .

Then how shall we explicate Wilson's fear that Ralegh would take his own life? Can Wilson, has he imagined yet what Apsley first sensed, then was certain of—that not then and not now will Ralegh take his own life? Apsley has made inquiry and found that not once, but twice in this tower long ago, it is recorded that Walter Ralegh attempted to kill himself. Both times without much harm. Once it was when he was imprisoned because of his marriage. A theatrical gesture from which he was restrained by a number of gentlemen witnesses. But which, for what it may have been worth to him, was reported to the Queen. And once since, when he was taken to Winchester to be tried. The latter may or may not have been a genuine impulse, though sudden, rash, and against the grain of his character. The former was clearly, to Apsley, a belated apology, a ceremonious salute to the Queen. Perhaps the latter attempt was too. To try old stratagems on a new King. Yet from documents, which Apsley has never trusted, a man might conclude that Walter Ralegh is inclined toward self-murder. Some of his enemies, past and present, have stated this conclusion. Whether they believe it or no, who knows?

There is other evidence, cloudy and contradictory. It is recorded in papers of the Tower and of the Council that not long after the trial at Winchester Ralegh was denied use of a razor to trim his beard. He wrote to assure his keepers and the Council that to take his own life he needed no razor. When he chose, he had said, he would ram his head against a wall and crack it like an eggshell. They must have believed him. His razor was promptly restored.

Consider also his private chronicle. Time and again in war and adventures Ralegh has risked life. Apsley, the soldier, can understand that well enough. If you will call a good soldier, a courageous man whose survival, though often a testimonial to Fortune or Providence, is nevertheless the best and irrefutable witness to the wisdom of his choices, a self-murderer at heart, then what distinction between Ralegh—or himself for that matter—and any wretch who will cut his own throat, ear to ear?

Surely the troublesome Wilson—who, as a spy, must also risk life upon the strength of wit and cunning—knew this. Yet he was, from the day he came to the Tower until now, continually concerned, watchful. Spoke of his fear that Ralegh would outwit them by self-murder.

Perhaps, Apsley has surmised, Wilson's fears have been grounded in something more firm—knowledge or suspicion of the true intent of the King.

It would have been and might yet be expedient if Walter Ralegh died and spared the King the trouble of disposing of him. Perhaps the King has to believe that Ralegh will do that. Will be driven, by doubt and uncertainties and despair, to take his own life. If only to deprive the King of his royal prerogative. A last made rebellious gesture.

But outwardly, by sign or gesture, Ralegh has never suggested any feeling toward his monarch other than respect and the ritual love a servant owes his master. Apsley knows better, or believes he does. For it is this unruffled evenness, never broken even in rage, which betrays the frost-blooded control Ralegh exercises.

No, Apsley has thought, and thinks now as they reach the last

[144]

precarious high landing and enter the shadowy tower—Ralegh hates the King of England so deeply and so well that he will not die but will rather live to spite him.

This disloyalty, deepest and most dangerous, Apsley deplores, even as he respects the courage of the man who harbors it. Apsley, as soldier, learned not to waste imagination upon the perils of others. They must stand or fall as they will, as God wills. A man has more than enough occupation dealing with his own perils, contending, as best he can, against his own fears.

Much as he fears that something in this affair may turn against himself, Apsley will be relieved to arrive at the ending. Allowing that he will, in truth, deliver up this prisoner today upon a proper writ of *habeas corpus,* he will sleep better with the old man gone from his keeping.

Let him live or die as he will, but let it be out of the hands and sight of the Lord Lieutenant.

Heavy footfalls, their own, in the chambers. Then the yeoman warder raps heavy-handed upon a huge door, unlocked, and, hearing the muffled reply from within, pulls it open, hinges groaning, holds it for the gentlemen to enter.

A smoky chamber, smoke of the fire, smoke of a pipe, as Ralegh, rising from his pallet, greets them.

Lord Lieutenant Apsley is astonished. But says nothing. Leaves it to Wilson to riffle documents and to announce the news of this morning. Apsley stands open-mouthed. For, though Ralegh is as calm and unrevealing as ever, he is unprepared. Perhaps it is the fever. . . .

To Sir Thomas Wilson's announcement Ralegh only nods. Apsley realizing that so far he has only spoken a word of greeting to the yeoman, now standing, gripping his gilt partizan, inside the doorway. Nods and knocks out his pipe in the fireplace. Turns—Apsley watching those cool veiled eyes—and stares at their boots. Sees they wear no spurs.

"Well, then, gentlemen," he says. "The tide will have just turned. If we must go by water, let us go now."

Apsley, out of the corner of his eyes, sees that the two wooden-faced men from Court cannot control their own astonishment either. Only Wilson seems the same.

Behind Ralegh his two servants (rich Devon accents) protest he must not go until he is prepared. He is sharp with them. Orders them to pack and to be ready to come to him when he sends for them.

"God save your scruffy skins if you drink the last of my Canary!"

Now Apsley finds some words: "No need for unseemly haste. You have ample time to dress yourself."

"Surely," one of the gentlemen suggests, "since you must appear before King's Bench, you will wish to be . . . yourself."

"Ah, if I thought that were true, I should do so and thank you for permitting me the time," Ralegh says. "But since I know it cannot be so . . ."

Wilson rattles the papers. "But I have read these to you. It is so ordered."

Ralegh shrugs. "You are mistaken, gentlemen. Look to your calendars. There are no courts of law today."

"Calendar or no, you must go to King's Bench this morning," Wilson says.

"Perhaps," the gentleman begins again, "you may wish to fortify yourself with breakfast."

"Is this, then, to be my last meal?"

"I fear we have not made our meaning clear," Wilson says.

[146]

"Do not deceive yourself. You are as clear as my lady's looking glass."

Ralegh turns then to Apsley, close, touching his arm. He looks into his eyes. And Apsley reads the dry hard brightness of a man not so old or infirm that he has mortgaged reason or surrendered possession of the present.

"Believe me, I am grateful for your courtesy," Ralegh says. "But I have suffered all night from a burning fever. There's no disguising that. And I could not keep food down if I swallowed it."

"You could take some of your medicines," Wilson says.

"Pray be silent, Mr. Wilson. I am almost done with your care and have no need for medicines."

"There is no need for unseemly haste," one of the gentlemen says.

"You talk like a parrot, young man, repeating yourself. No haste when a prisoner is called before King's Bench! Surely the habits of judges and lawyers have changed wonderfully. I never knew a judge who could be cheerful while waiting for a tardy culprit."

"I only mean to say, sir, that we have come about our business early."

"Early indeed, and with small ceremony."

"You may have as much time as you wish," the other gentleman adds.

"As much time as I wish. . . ."

Ralegh begins to laugh. Laughs until he is checked by coughing.

"Are you ill, sir?"

"How much time does a dying man wish for? Can you answer that riddle?"

"My meaning is that you may have as much time as is need-ful."

"See, Apsley, this man eludes my question with equivocation. I say he will go far in this world where men must equivo-cate to prosper. I have myself been said to practice the craft of equivocation, do you know that?"

No answer, though one of the gentlemen suppresses a slight smile.

"As much time as may be needful. Just so . . ." Ralegh con-tinues. "God himself gives no man more than that."

"We have all heard of your skeptical opinions," Wilson says.

"Indeed, Mr. Wilson, you have news of everything except what you were sent to hear," Ralegh says. "You should not strive to be impudent or over-bold. I may forget to pity you."

Stung, Wilson puffs and touches the hilt of his sword.

Apsley steps between the men, turning his back to Wilson. "You might do well to reconsider," he says.

"Many's the cold morning I have been up before cock-crow . . ." Ralegh begins. Then abruptly checks himself.

"And I am as ready as I shall ever be," he says. "Lead on, gentlemen."

He seizes a knotty walking stick, hefty as a cudgel, straight-ens his shoulders, lifts his head, and takes a long stride toward the door.

The yeoman warder backs toward the low door, banging the point of his partizan, then gripping it to steady himself. The officers swinging about face to face in near collision. Wilson hanging back, an unhappy dog.

Apsley steps forward, motioning with his arm. As if inviting Ralegh to join him on a stroll.

"Your cane, sir."

That is Ralph, the servant. It is Ralph's walking stick Ralegh has taken.

"Yours suits me better," Ralegh says. "You keep mine."

At the door he stops and turns back to them.

"Be ready to come at once. And mind you, not a drop of my Canary!"

Past Wilson's face, all clouds like a man in need of physic, the faces of two servants identically and purely wrinkled with puzzlement. They nodding as if puppet heads were jerked by a single string.

"Go and eat. Find yourselves some comfort and a quart of sack."

Tossing a coin to them as he turns away, lowers head and shoulders to go through the doorway.

The coin glitters in candlelit, fire-colored air. Like a huge spark. Falls to the stone, rings matin, rolls.

Ralph, younger, snatching it up. Holds it close to the light of a candle squinting. Pinches, then bites it.

Smiles now. The coin like a bitten wafer still touching the edge of his lower lip.

"It's gold."

"The old man has lost his wits," the other mutters.

"Thanks be to God for the blessing of that."

"How do you say so, Ralph?"

"Why, it will make the work of the headsman that much easier. One or two good strokes, and he who was master shall be in eternal service. A proper servant of the Lord."

"Watch your tongue—for your own sake, lad."

"God's tooth! That is the proper wish of every Christian,

is not? To be taken up into Paradise and be a servant of the Lord?"

"And so?"

"And so it seems to me that in precedence it must surely fall upon those who have most skill and practice at service to be closest to high table in heaven."

"Shame on you!"

"I believe we shall be Stewards and Carvers there. While many who were high and mighty shall be placed in the kitchen to scour the pots. 'Tis said so in Scripture."

"Lad, you shall be lucky to be a turnspit in hell."

Ralph shrugs. "Better the cook than meat on a fire."

"Amen to that."

"I know the keeper of a tavern, sign of A Running Hare, not far from here."

"But, lad, that's almost as far as All Hallows Barking."

"A walk will settle your humors."

"Or kill me. I'm cold as a church key."

"Then we should both have a swallow or two of good medicine. To wit, our master's precious Canary."

Ralph winks. The older man will not wink back, but cannot prevent a ragged, motley smile of black and yellow. And he nods. They drink.

From his cell among the old royal chambers Ralegh walks with Apsley and they pass through St. John's Chapel. The Norman chapel, massive as if the house of God should be a fortress place to endure in this world. Huge, squat, round columns in a file upholding arches like horseshoes. Hints of first light from rounded, deep-set windows. Ceiling still lost in shadow. But, dark or light, the pavement, curling in a geometry, as if stone could be a turkey carpet, of colored stones. A simple and beautiful place where once kings and queens, great men and their ladies, in joy and in despair, offered up their prayers.

Gripping the cudgel for support, Ralegh lowers himself to kneel on those stones. The others wait while he says the Lord's Prayer.

Apsley knows they do not approve of kneeling and will misconstrue it. Smacks too much of old ways and customs. So be it, then. A man of any faith and persuasion would feel an urge to kneel in this place.

Clinging to the cudgel, he rises. All move in quickstep through the presence chamber and, following the yeoman, through the long council chamber and down the turning inner stairs.

Feeling his way more carefully now. Needing the staff to steady himself.

It would have been quicker to descend by the scaffold of wooden stairs outside. But they go down the old stairway.

Past the armory, where useless armor rusts and cannon from the time of Henry VIII—Great Harry, Long Meg, Seymour's Gun—lie idle, oddly comic in repose.

Down and across the hall and at last outside.

Dawn air chill, ghosting breath, but sweet after the sorrows of old stone. Breathing it. Taste and odor, in keen chill, of October's falling, dying leaves, of woodsmoke and coalsmoke from houses and towers. And always faint salt of the river and the sea. All around the yard is sprinkled, leaved with October blood. From houses and walls and in the yard there are watchers. Who have turned to stone.

Apsley wonders why the yeoman has chosen this way. Since that soldier has been at the Tower many years, Apsley saw no need to instruct him how to lead to Traitor's Gate. They could have gone the covered way, less exposed to the common view. Perhaps he, too, is in Ralegh's service. For certain the trip by water was ordered to spare them the crowds and delays of the city and to keep some measure of secrecy. Well, with half the people of the Tower observing, the news may reach Westminster before they do.

Apsley eyes Ralegh. His stiff leg, with its old wound, still thorn-jointed, wincing from the weight of him, staff or no. Ralegh breathes deep and holds the air. Not wishing, Apsley thinks, to show a shortness of breath.

Walking south across the yard, skirting early shadows. Aiming to pass by Garden Tower. Aiming to walk through the tunnel, Wakefield Tower, then, and cross the moat at Traitor's Gate. Creak of leather boots. Light rattle of sword and harness.

Here's a warder in their path. Guiding two people. Up so early to see all the sights of London. For a penny here and a penny there they'll have a tour of the Tower and even perhaps be shown the lions and beasts of the King's menagerie. Where once there have been rare beasts indeed. Leopards and curious apes, apes with beards like old men, apes who bark like dogs and flash their red-colored arses, an ostrich or two, sleek cats from the Indies. Gray native wolves and one white hart. Bears from Muscovy. White dogs, or wolves, from the snowy Samoyed. Many a fine beast gone. Now some few lions, bears, and dogs. Save for the sleepy lions, more a common kennel than a menagerie.

He's a wide-hatted yeoman farmer of middle age, wide of beam, horn-handed. Rough clean kersey and heavy walking boots. The woman beside him in Sunday best, holding her hands demurely folded beneath a lacy apron. They stop to step aside for the group coming down the path. The farmer raises his hat.

[152]

Wind and sun-wrinkled face. Jowls of good food and prosperity, and shrewdness about the eyes.

Ralegh stops, leaning on his staff.

"You have a Westcountry face," he says. "Have you come here from Devon?"

"Yes, sir, an' it please you."

"And where in Devon would that be?"

"Near Chadwick, sir."

"A pretty place there, but a mile or so too far from the sea," he says. "Did you have a good harvest?"

"Not for many a year," the farmer says. "We raise sheep now."

Ralegh turns to the warder, draws a coin from the purse chained to his waist.

"Show them all the sights that may be seen."

"Yes, sir."

"And not another penny from them, do you hear?"

"Yes, sir."

"When you return home, you may say you were guests of Sir Walter Ralegh in the Tower."

Off again, limping, but less so now on scant grass and raw earth. Crackling leathery sound as over across the yard toward St. Peter's a startled fountain of black ravens rises.

Apsley glances, following the spray of flight, seeing faces pressed to leaded glass of upper windows of the houses nestling along the western side of the Inner Ward.

Ralegh stops short, turns and grips Apsley's arm.

"I have changed my mind."

"Sir?"

"I cannot eat food this morning. But I need a cup of wine to settle my stomach."

"Very well," Apsley says. "I shall send for it."

"I was thinking I might warm my hands by your fire."

Apsley clears his throat, studies the man. Learns nothing from set of lips, from the eyes.

"It might be wiser to wait until we arrive at Westminster."

"Surely you'll not begrudge me such a thing," Ralegh says. "It will delay us less time than I might have required to dress."

"I am not sure it is wise. . . ."

"Are you so very much afraid?" Ralegh speaks in a whisper as the others wait for them.

Apsley flushes and knows his beard does not hide it.

"Never mind, then," Ralegh says. "I took you for a better man than God made you."

"I assure you, sir, I have no desire to be uncivil. . . ."

"Name of God, Apsley, who can hurt you now?" Jerks his thumb at the three curious gentlemen, the impassive warder. "Those two are mere lackeys. They do not even have names and never will. And as for yonder keeper, Wilson, he can do you no injury now or later. Believe me, you have nothing to fear."

"He is the King's man."

"So are we all."

Apsley lowers his eyes.

Ralegh speaks to the others, tone of command.

"Gentlemen, the Lord Lieutenant has offered me the kindness of a cup of wine and a few private words in his dwelling. Pray wait here for us. It will be a short time, not even long enough to catch a cold."

And with that he is off toward the Queen's House, limping. Apsley has no choice but to follow or be left with the others. Catches a glimpse of Wilson's puzzled frown (lost his smile at last!) before he hurries to catch up with Ralegh and, shortly, to open the door for him.

Into a chamber with beamed high ceiling, the hall, where they pause by the fireplace. Ralegh extends his arms, flexes long fingers close to the flames.

Apsley calls for a servant to bring spirits to the upper chamber.

Ralegh, turning his back to the fire, looks at his hands, clenching and unclenching them.

"I feel stark naked without a ring for my fingers."

"If you will pardon me the liberty," Apsley says. "It might be wisdom to dress yourself with more care."

"You are much concerned with the wisdom of this world, Apsley. It is not to be despised, mind you, but it does not become you to offer counsel to those who have studied it more."

"I only spoke in your interest."

"Well, you are right, Apsley. And I am glad you did so. For unless I am in my dotage already, they will all expect me to demonstrate just such wisdom and to appear before them like a waxwork courtier of the last age.

"I have often acted imprudently, with little wisdom. So I suppose I must continue, for the sake of custom. Old customs are as slow to die as the widows of kings. I sometimes think it is our climate, our wretched weather, that keeps custom alive here. Just as the same weather preserves the red and white of a lady's flesh."

He looks up, smiling now, at Apsley and beyond and behind him. Aspsley turns to see what has caught his stare.

Set in iron brackets on the wall rests the ceremonial ax of the Tower. Which, according to custom, is to be borne by the Lord Lieutenant, to and from Westminster in a case of high treason. Gilded, it shines against the wall.

"Is it heavy to carry?" he asks.

"What's that, sir?" Apsley asks.

"Your ax, man. What we are looking at."

"Ah . . ."

Apsley turns away from it.

"Not so much as a fearful heart," he says. "Let us go up now." Touches Ralegh's arm to direct him toward the stairs.

"It's a pretty thing," Ralegh says. "But I'll wager could not cut a Cheddar cheese."

The upper chamber is more private and more amiable, having been repaired in recent times. They move to stand by the fireplace. Which is also remade to fit with new fashions. Set back deep and narrow and the hearth now bricked over, concealed and disguised by an ornamental chimney piece.

From a servant they accept delicate long-stemmed Venetian glasses, Apsley's best, filled with seeming smoke.

Ralegh looks at the little memorial set on the wall by Sir William Waad, once among his judges on the commission at Winchester and later his quarrelsome keeper here for a time, to honor the King's Providential Escape from the Gunpowder Plot. A wooden bust of the King. On tablets the names of the conspirators together with a Latin inscription composed by Waad. His lips move as he translates: ". . . illustrious for piety, justice, foresight, learning, hardihood, and other royal virtues . . . author most subtle, most august and auspicious . . . apple of the eye . . . Roman Jesuits of perfidious, Catholic serpent-like ungodliness . . . William Waad . . . his great and everlasting thanks."

Next to the memorial a painted portrait of the King, done in Dutch style. The King with cock feathers, brave and smart, worn on his hat. The hat worn square set on the head. As if it grew there. No ruff, but, instead, a wide delicate falling band.

[156]

And the King was full-bearded then, his sad, slightly bulging eyes saying nothing.

"He wears a somewhat pained expression."

"Sir?"

"I say," Ralegh continues, "that our King is here most justly portrayed as a man of contradictory feelings."

"I am bound His Majesty's loyal servant . . ." Apsley begins.

"I am not jesting at His Majesty's expense," Ralegh says. "Far from it. But I understand his feelings. Who would not be pleased, even a king, to have a servant erect a memorial in his honor? Yet to mangle it with wretched Latin, corrupt in grammar and confused in the sense!"

"Sir William never made claim to be a scholar."

"Ah, but Lieutenant Apsley, the King does. And therein lies the source of his expression."

Ralegh twists the stem of the glass in his fingers, raises it to sniff.

"Scotch *aqua vitae*," he says.

"It is strong stuff, good against the cold."

"Then let us drink it in honor of the King who came down to us from Scotland. And to his good health."

Ralegh swallows it in a gulp.

"Will it please you to refill your glass?"

Walter Ralegh shakes his head. "I thank you for it, and for the comfort of your fire, but that is not why I asked for these moments with you."

Apsley nods and waits.

"I have nothing but respect and warm feelings toward you," Ralegh says. "My words out there . . . I saw I must prick your

[157]

pride to have this privacy. If I imagined you were a coward, I should not have wasted time upon you."

Soft voice and light smile. Crafty deceiver. Master of equivocation and of sly and oblique flattery. This angers Apsley, but he struggles to check anger.

"I know the truth of myself," Apsley says. "I do not need the confirmation of praise or blame, sir."

"Don't be a fool," Ralegh snaps back at him. "Why should I trouble to flatter you? You flatter yourself to think so."

"I meant no disrespect . . ."

"Pray be silent. I am too old and too tired for a lengthy prologue. Let me be simple. I have a favor to ask you. Not a grand one, nothing uncommon. But it may take a backbone more sturdy than silk ribbon. It may require a spice of courage."

"What do you wish me to do?"

"Our friend Wilson has shown a considerable interest in my books and instruments. He will have them if he can, if I lose the power to keep them myself. I wish that you would see that he does not take them."

"I cannot stop him if he has a proper writ."

"He will have no writ. He will have no paper to show you."

"But if he has the King's command . . ."

"He will not have that either, though you can wager your daughter's dowry he will say he does."

"I have no wish to offend Sir Thomas Wilson any more than I have already."

"You would prefer the risk of offending me?"

"I did not say so."

"Mark this, Apsley. There is no way Wilson can harm you. That is the truth. But if I live, and that is possible, I can work harm you'll remember."

"I do not doubt that."

"And, alive or dead, I can do you some service. You have a daughter . . ."

"So you mentioned."

"If you will stand firm about my books and papers and the instruments I have here, there are those who will reward you for it in my name. The choice is simple enough. You have nothing to lose."

"I shall think on it," Apsley says slowly. "But I can promise you nothing."

"There is no danger from Wilson."

"So you say."

"Very well," Ralegh says. "Think on it. That is enough. But also remember that once I am delivered out of your keeping, the power of Wilson's commission is gone. When he comes to you again—and he will come here if things go as he wishes—he will have no more rights in this place than that Chadwick farmer we met on the path. Though he struts and blusters, he'll be no more than a penny visitor."

The servant takes the glasses from them. Slowly Walter Ralegh descends the stairs, speaking as he goes down.

"It is true. I look for all the world like some poor knave who first lost his pride and then his wits. I believe I could set out upon the highway and make my bread as an Abraham man. . . . And in a sense I am only a poor comedian. But though I begin this day like old Will Kemp—and by heaven I'd dance all the way to Norwich myself if I had my freedom and a pipe and drum . . . ! Though I begin this way, I shall soon enough be a darker sort of fool. Like the player Robert Armin. He will run with a quick jest to the very edge and rim of the grave, and teeter there, able to fall either way. . . ."

[159]

They are now in the lower hall again. Ralegh looking once more at the fire.

"I will most gladly give you a hat to wear," Apsley says. Ralegh shakes his head.

"Answer me this, Apsley. Am I not now known to be the vainest strutting peacock ever penned within these walls?"

"You have a style, sir, and are admired for it."

"Vanity! It is mere vanity. Yet grant me this much. Though I am old and troubled enough, I am as clear and sound of mind at this moment as I have ever been."

"I do not doubt it."

"When you and the others entered my chamber, I had not yet fixed upon the costume I would wear. Seeing this business is to be brief and with little ceremony, I made my choice. I am now most properly attired for the spirit of the occasion."

"As you will, sir."

Apsley moves to open the door.

"The ax," Ralegh says. "Won't you need the great ax?"

"I have no instructions on that."

"A good sign," Ralegh says. "Let us both go lighthearted, then."

Outside they join the others and walk to the gate of square St. Thomas Tower, facing the river. The gate is up and river water flowing into the moat.

Moving on under the low archway, a long flat arch without an apparent keystone. Like the hood of a huge fireplace. The walls within with loopholes where some may watch all comings and goings in secret.

A loyal heart may be landed at Traitor's Gate.

A plain unmarked barge, low, long, and lean, waiting for them, moored and bobbing. Bargemen, eight oarsmen, and a coxswain, wearing no blue uniforms, but dressed in the manner of London's watermen. A rented barge? Perhaps, but these have the look of men in costumes, ill at ease. In unison, the group approaching, they raise their oars. Blades shining, dripping.

The two officers step aside. Argue something between themselves. Ralegh ignores them, looking across the wharf to where a small ship is taking on barrels of powder from the Tower stores. Above the wharf and the masts of the ship gulls soar and cry. One rises higher than the others, sails in a circle above the towers, riding easy on the level air.

Light fog lifting. A weak sun coming. Pale gull in pale sun.

Apsley touches his arm to direct him toward the barge. A quick glance back. The yeoman, returning to the Tower by way of St. Thomas Tower. Exactly . . . They are then under instructions to bring him to Westminster as quietly as possible.

Stepping careful, a helping hand from the coxswain, into the stern. To stand near the small covered place for passengers. Padded chairs for comfort. Stands while the others board. Looking toward the lightening sky eastward downriver. Seeing a delicate forest of mast tops, masts, nests, and geometry of rigging. Leafless trees, against that sky. No sails, for there's less breeze now than the breath of a kitten. Movement, though, the incoming tide slowly overwhelming the flow of the river. But water calm as oil. Masts tilt and bob as ships are tugging at line and anchor.

They push off and ease out of the inlet of the water gate.

Now nearby along the wharf a clustering of boats. Boats to hire. At your service the celebrated watermen of London. Watermen wearing their tough linen blouses, canvas sailor's doublet and puffed baggy short breeches to match. And mostly these days the high-crowned wide-brimmed hats. Set squarely on the head, pulled down to the ears. His Majesty the King can look no better.

Hard-faced, scar-faced, sun- and wind-burned faces watching. Not deceived by a plain barge or an odd crew of oarsmen. Eyes colder than mirror glass, glinting no questions, telling no secrets. Skeptical hard eyes of Southwark. Prideful tip and tilt of chin. Lips drawn tight, but ever ready to purse and spit in contempt or to savor the salty telling of outrageous lies. Ready to brawl for a fare and to bawl for a tip above the established fare with the raucous clamor of Old Testament prophets crying for justice, calling down grief and woe.

Surly, proud, bold, and tougher than tanned leather. Scum of the earth, but beholden to no man. Not fearing to charge full fare and to expect a gratuity from the devil himself with hooves and horns, and his spiky tail.

Full of more gossip than a street of fishwives and widow women. More tales and wonders to tell than any town crier. To be delivered with more authority than a royal herald. Timber of their voices brassy enough to serve for trumpet calls in absence of musicians.

Proud and rude and as armored in arrogance as the barons of old. And well may they be so. For no one place in England, save the city of London herself, has furnished more soldiers for the wars than rowdy Southwark. But these watermen are mostly old sailors. Men who have seen the Indies, the coasts of Africa, or even Muscovy. Men who have sailed once or more with Drake and Hawkins and Frobisher and Sir Humphrey Gilbert. Some who sailed in the season of '88 or have been with Ralegh and Essex at Cadiz and the Azores.

Observing all, expressionless as blackbirds on a limb. For

once silent. Staring at the barge, its crew, and an old man standing astern as the barge eases into the flow of the tide.

Ralegh cups his hands.

"Heave and ho and rumble-o!" he calls.

Some grinning and a thorny crackle, like kindling twigs, of laughter from them. One fellow, wearing an old woolen statute cap, rises up to stand in his boat.

"I sailed with you before, sir, and by God, I would do it again for one word."

"Bless you, but we are both of us too old for open ocean now," Ralegh answers.

He opens his purse for another gold coin. Lofts it against the light of the rising sun. Well thrown, and the old waterman can catch it by clapping his hands.

Solemn-faced the sailor pulls off his woolen cap. And now the others are rising and lift their hats too. He waves to them and turns to his companions.

"Give me a jury of Southwark watermen and I'll be free as a gull before dinnertime."

Apsley and the others are still half standing by their seats.

"Pray be seated, gentlemen. I will stand awhile and see the sights once more."

Apsley nods and they sit down.

Ralegh moves forward, braces himself by an oarsman's bench, one hand resting lightly on the young man's shoulder.

2

Above the river veils of fog are parting. There will be no blue today, but the sky and the day will brighten.

And, subtle and gentle, a scuffling ruffle of scales along the calm water, the first hint of breeze. There will be more breeze and later hauling and hoisting, unfurling of square sails to catch it, among the crowd of ships, Englishmen, Dutch, and Danes, Swedish, Genovese, Venetian, Frenchmen, also from Hamburg and Spain and even Sicily. A leafless forest of idle masts will spring into white bloom like pear trees. Flags and pennants will flutter.

Pulling away now from the Tower walls, its shadowy line of turrets and bastions and cannon. Yeomen on the walls stand watching.

Looking back and upward at them on the walls of the Outer Ward.

Farewell, then, to my home and estate. For I have lived there, spent a sum of more time than any other place I have ever owned, built upon, called my own. Money and time and labor and love wasted on the dream of Sherbourne in Dorset.

Better I had spent even a tithe of that sum preparing trim chambers in the Tower of London.

There my last, now only, child, young enough to be a grand-child, was conceived, first drew breath, and saw light, was christened in the old Chapel of St. Peter in Chains. There he, too, was almost taken from me when the Plague came prowling in the chambers and snuffed out lives as near as the thickness of one wall.

How much of the dolor of the Tower has entered your soul, poor boy? How much of the weight of sad years falls on your shoulders? Quiet child, you do not smile often, never have laughed much. We gave you silver spoons at your christening. But you took on an invisible yoke of cast iron.

Behold the old Tower of London, my son, a mighty fortress of kings gone and kings yet to come. And yet rightly you may call it your father's home. That's the legacy I leave you, Carew, child so quiet, so solemn, and so small. The shadow of the Tower is in your soul. Ancient cold and dust have entered your blood.

Let not your heart be troubled. Some men leave estates and some men leave the shine of honor to their sons. I leave you the Tower of London and, God willing, a good name to wear while you live.

Sad and serious boy, Carew. Whom I scarcely know at all. I could wish it different. I pray it as I look back now. Will look back no more.

Looks forward at the river and London.

What need to look behind, since in mind's eye and a winking he can picture the river all the way past Gravesend and into the sea?

A soft touch of breeze teases beard and hair. His eyes narrow.

He is hungry to see and to feast upon this banquet—Jerusalem or Babel and Babylon—of London awakened and coming to life.

City of sturdy wall, of stout gates, narrow streets, and long memories. Ever changing and rearranging, repairing and razing, ripping and tearing down, with license and abandon, to build out of your ruins and rubble anew. Spading up the skulls and old coins and broken shards to make room for more.

With all your history, untroubled by memory. Unhaunted by the savage ghosts of old men who wish you no joy. Believing you shall bloom and prosper with or without them.

Bubbling, fermenting, all yeasty, cloudy as strong ale.

Bursting at sleeves and button points with press of people. Multitude which even plague cannot conquer.

Filling and spilling over the wall and across the ditch. Overflowing like your countless wells and springs (some clear and clean, some foul as streams of hell) to spread in a slow tide ever outward into fields, suburbs, and villages.

Slow, sure, with timber and brick and stone, mortar and plaster, with conduit and cobblestone, seizing and choking the last life of the fields and spaces within and without the walls.

But your half-hidden gardens are splendid. Your trees, now bloody or minted in autumn gold, stand high and tall. In April and early May they toss fair heads of brightest green. Cast ponds and pools of shade in midsummer.

Slow, sure, houses growing taller over narrow, thronged, clamorous streets, as if to join hands and shut out the sky. Like the old houses of merchants up on London Bridge.

Noisy, bustling, crying, laughing, boldest city in the world. Proud of your savage music. Deafening noise of thousands of voices speaking all at once, from the muttering of lawyers at

St. Paul's to the hundred musical cries of the street vendors. Cartwheels straining, crying for grease. Carriages nudging for space. Crack of whip and shouts to make way. Clatter of hooves, ringing of bells, clear ring of hammer, song of saws. Bells and the cling and clang of coins like a multitude of little bells.

Rude and clamorous beyond believing. Rich and busy beyond believing too.

A strange many-colored flower, but flower of English towns. Let others bloom and prosper, dry and wither, London is blooming, ever growing. Foremost of cities, set down in glory and beauty beside and now astride the still clear-flowing waters of the Thames with its snowflake clusters of swans proudly riding.

Phoenix of cities, forever consuming itself in fire and energy, forever from ashes rising again, newborn. Even before the ashes cool.

London the largest and finest jewel in the Crown. Yet unpolished, uncut, flawed, as if rudely ripped from bowels of earth. And still, all that said, shining always and always more precious than perfect stones. Its fire not a gift of art and stolen light, but the glow cast by an excess of inner burning. Not a diamond, but what the diamond aspires to be: a thing made of light as if light were frozen.

Came here first a boy. Half-man, bigger than most men.

Westcountry proud and poor. All overgrown, hands and feet and heavy muscles, and awkward. Disguising this behind a slow, thoughtful way he hoped might be misconstrued as lazy gracefulness.

His head cram-full of the family stories and the chronicles of Devon. Yet eager and most willing to be rid of that baggage. Hall and chambers of his brain all bedecked and decor-

[167]

ated with loot, imaginary trophies from books and, richer and stranger by far, the painted cloths and tapestries wrought from the echoing tales of Devon seamen. Who, having seen the ends, the nooks and corners and closets of the world and lived to come home, were not shy or loath to share some news of that with a lad who would listen.

Came to London happy to be away from all he had seen and known and been. Glad to be eased of a burden. And yet sad to be far from the familiar places, all shapes and sounds, odors and colors, the feelings of home. Glad to be young and free, yet within himself ashamed to feel so blithe. Sad and yet ashamed of that feeling too. For it seemed so childish. For once, he hoped, he had left the child he had been behind him.

Came then inwardly trembling with the shock and clash of opposing feelings. Believing that life would always be this way. Not knowing then that he was in the midst of the war any boy must wage within himself if he is to become a man.

Not able to comprehend that the power of change is absolute.

But it was more than the war a boy must wage to seek the triumph of manhood. Was one particular battle as well. For even his pride of family, his love for the place of his birth, were confused and paradoxical.

Proud of his father, his name, and the names of kin. His hive of kinfolk in Devon. Yet also ashamed; for why were they now left clinging to memories or dreaming of other futures? Proud and ashamed and ashamed of being so. Love for the Westcountry, its places and people. Yet hating them, too, knowing them too well. Their passionate factions in religion. Cutting each other cruelly and, even more so, those who stood quiet in faith, sharing passions of neither the old or the new. His father, before he was born, had been abused, during the Rising and other broils, first by one faith, then the other.

Young Ralegh contemptuous of both even as he might lump them in one pudding. Resentful of the rich, rising merchants his family must deal with; yet already knowing their prosperity was close-linked to his own. Loving the lay of the land; yet his heart with his family and friends, the seamen, who shook dust of Devon from their feet for love of something else. Despising the placid villagers, the farmers content to be chained to acres as to a plow. Admiring most the seafarer, who would brawl in the taverns with the landsmen between voyages. And then, if Fortune allowed this mariner an old age, forced to chop wood, feed the hogs, and empty jakes for some yeoman to whom he must raise his cap as if to a trueborn gentleman.

Came to London first with all this and more bubbling inside. Like a blackened pot of beggars' soup. Boiling above a dry crackling of sticks and thorns.

In the solitude of being young, he was unable to know that the boiling within him was as nothing compared to the cauldron of the city. That his little fires would go unnoticed amid the flames and heat and blinking coals of that continual forge.

Came to London, suffering more in youth and health than he ever would in age and sickness. And partly out of pride and part for shame, determined to keep his secret to himself with the lofty demeanor, the frozen composure of a card-playing tavern man.

Prepared to be unimpressed by London. Or Jerusalem either if that had been the city. His attitude reflecting what he deemed the truth: that nothing he would see, then or ever, could come to equal the secret glory of his imagining. Compared to which all life must be a shrugging disappointment. He would have denied this even on the rack called "Little Ease," lest he be taken for what he thought he was and wished most not to be: an ignorant, unpolished, untested, untried, unfinished, uneasy, discontented inexperienced boy.

Came first time along the old Roman road to Canterbury *from* Canterbury he would have said then, walking tall and proud and slow as he could.

Though Hayes Barton, Budleigh, meant nothing to these people, they would know Exeter. Which was close and familiar to him.

London could claim no more history. Exeter, Citadel of the West, knew Roman and Saxon and Dane and Norman as well. Athelstan, first king of all the English, built the walls and tower.

London's Tower? Let them come and see Rougemont Castle.

Churches? Exeter has so many of those that half are never used. And speak to me nothing of bells if you have never heard the bell of St. Pancras.

Your Guildhall? Exeter has the oldest standing in England, its gilt beams resting upon carved bears with staffs. And the roll call of our lord mayors is longer than London's. Ask anyone who knows.

Brag of the riches of London, the baubles and bubbles, pouring into your shops as from a conduit in ceaseless flow. Then hear me when I tell you we of Devon are makers as well as takers. And *you* must take from us and pay for it too. The stuffs we grow in our fields. Best husbandry in England, for our wool and hides, our stout English cloth. Our tin—together with that out of Cornwall—and other metals. Jangle your purses and talk of the plenitude. And I'll not answer in kind with the bells of silver crowns and half crowns, half groats, and pennies, but try that trick in Exeter city and such a response in golden sovereigns, ryals, and angels you'll receive as will ring a curfew upon arrogance.

London may well bloom bright, like fruit trees in springtime. But Exeter blooms lofty like the ancient English oak.

Prate no more of your merchants' houses. Let me show you High Street, Exeter.

You have Thames. We have the Exe, with ships and cargoes, some *diverted* from their intended destinations, it is true, from all over the world.

Don't move me to pity and terror with tales of martyrs of Smithfield. We burned many a good heretic in Southernhay. And I'll wager among all your cornucopia of heresies and sects and atheisms you never saw the like of the one called The Family of Love. And I'll wager there's nothing in all of London to equal the Bishop's Brass Clock in Exeter. It is said—do you doubt it?—to be the oldest clock in all England, as old as time, and it keeps good time. With a wondrous dial which shows the movements of the earth and the sun and the moon.

Cathedrals . . . See Exeter Cathedral and let your eyes pop and your jaw fall slack. Such carving work and stonework as you have never dreamed. And all of it, sir, first stone to last, done by Devon men. Strangers came to learn the craft from us.

For palaces and gardens, you shall have to show me anything as fine as the Bishop's in Exeter. For number of books, I doubt you can equal his library, and nothing so rare and fine here as the *Codex Exonienis,* all written out in the language of the Saxons. While London, no doubt, was a ford and a watering place for scruffy, sour-milked cows.

Before he was halfway across London Bridge, forever twilight

[171]

from the high houses coming together overhead, hearing the rush and thunder of waters, unseen, beneath the piers, Ralegh forgot all of this and more.

And tossed away his posture of pride, like a moth-eaten old cape, without a tremor of regret. Thinking, in that moment, like love at first look and the arrow of Cupid in the old romances, that he was surrendering nothing at all.

When he crossed and before he was near half over the span, he knew he was a perfect *exemplum* of the country clown in his modest-cut, well-made clothing of Devon broadcloth and kersey. Why, here even a common prentice lad looked fine as a gentleman with bright buttons to decorate his blue and a smart hat worn like a tilted halo, half shading the eyes, the smirk of the lips. No need to imagine he could conceal country ways. Might as well have been naked.

No occasion to plead for the honor of Devonshire when these folk could not have cared a groatsworth.

Feeling he might as well have fallen from the moon. Which they, these citizens and such of London, would think of, if at all, as London's lantern.

Halfway across the Bridge he was content to forget even that and gape at everything. Let them think whatever they pleased. If they pleased to notice him at all.

Thinking he had renounced forever the old and embraced forever the shining new.

Not knowing or imagining it was all new only to his eyes.

As, for example, a lusty lad, out of a lusty imagination and small experience, might embrace and fondle a widow old enough to be his mother, but by dress and style, diversions of jewels, invitation of perfumes and concealment of cosmetics, seeming to him as young and fair as a maid.

[172]

And the wisdom of this widow woman being the wisdom of all womanhood. She knowing that so long as fancy burns and fantasy is not glutted, he will honor fancy first. So long as he is caught in the net of lecher, poor fish, he will call that net love.

No use blaming woman. Eve may have been deceitful, but Adam allowed himself to be deceived.

How the wheel comes around. How, beyond reason, the design of things works as it will.

Paradox lies here. Much that a man may imagine he chooses has been long chosen for him. And much that seems no more choice than sailing downwind in a gale wind, seeing he cannot sail against it, blown away from intended landfall, nevertheless does lead straight toward that haven. So a man may conclude that either the harbor or the wind, and the compass needle, sun and stars, charts and cross-staff, either one or all were fantasy. Or may consider the possibility that all were, are, ever shall be equal fantasies. To live is to stand parceled out in innumerable fantasies as a man in a room wainscoted all around with mirror glass.

Yet this is incomplete. Consider that by some mathematic rule, the sum of equal fantasies becomes the truth.

There is a pattern and design in any man's actions, in the chronicle of his words, thoughts and deeds, which is an image, apelike, of the larger sum and total of the acts, the thoughts and deeds of all men. Which we call history. What was, is, will be. And its secret design is Providence. Which we can come to know only by and through contraries and paradoxes.

Intricate beyond comprehending, it speaks of a beautiful simplicity.

Nothing we touch that we do not decorate in this age. We

[173]

paint and plaster. We carve and shape wood and stone. We beat and twist metal, until it seems that all are as one, subject and servant to imagination and whims, of man, the maker. Imagining we imitate Creation in our manifold creations. And thereby do seem to celebrate the Imagination of God.

But with this difference. Though we may take a raw limb of walnut and round it and polish it smooth and convert it, by carving, into a wonder of living emblems and faces, flowers and dolphins and nymphs and satyrs, still and withal it shall serve as a mere post to hold up a bed. And still and withal, whatever our art and ingenuity shall work upon it, it remains a piece of a walnut tree.

Though a goldsmith takes gold and fashions it into stem and leaf and petal of flowers and with enamel so paints this bouquet that bees may come buzzing to bruise against it, still it is gold of such-and-such a purity and weight. Which selfsame qualities it possessed as a rock in the earth.

Take another figure. Clothed in all his finery, a naked king is invisible. Even unto himself. Clothed only in bare flesh and hair, the anatomy of bones is unknown. But the body beneath clothes and the bones beneath flesh are always there. And after clothing has rotted and flesh in corruption has shredded away, there, intricate enough, yet simple, stands the design of the man who lived. And no robes he wears, royal or rogue's, no form of flesh, clean or filthy, healthy or sick, can work a change upon that in most architecture.

Just so, the layers of a man's thought and deeds. Bodied forth, clothed as the times permit and require.

See this as a satirical paradox of myself: how, youthful, I cast aside the contraries of my past like a pair of worn boots. Loved London (thus my life) for the newness and strangeness of it.

For which reason and later for my own politic interests at Court, that is, for advancement and for the sake of the new, I became a patron of the old.

All, merchants and great men alike, who were able, were building new with old stones torn up from their proper places to make the new.

Against the grain of fashion was the scholarship of antiquarians. Those who, out of old bones and coins and broken pots and memory, would erect and so preserve, even as it vanished, a timeless edifice, the chronicles, surveys, and descriptions of this kingdom.

In truth this was a new thing to be doing. Expedient also, for it served the policy of the Queen: to make a troubled kingdom see itself anew, one nation and not without pride.

And therefore, surprising even myself, one day, years later, I found myself joining with old Bishop Parker in patronage of the new-formed society of fellowship among antiquarians. To meet with such as William Camden, Sir Robert Cotton, good John Stow and many others. To advance their cause.

Even then, later, as I imagined myself a lover of all things new, here because the enterprise was new, I was bound over to the recovery and preservation of the old.

And thus, paradoxically, returning in a disguise so clever and subtle I could not recognize myself in a mirror.

To become again the same boy from Devon.

Who, as he crossed London Bridge, imagined he discarded all past things for the new. A lightening that seemed no loss. Cast aside like the sack of a rag-and-bone man.

That same sack becoming later a bag of gold.

Now mark another turning, a new paradox:

In the Tower of London, I myself became a proper explorer

of history. To what purpose? Why, man, among others, to find keys to freedom, the freedom to make ventures, to set forth on new voyages, to restore my fortunes.

Now see how the turning of the wheel may work. See how the design of a garden maze may be contrived to return a man where he began.

Sailing to find El Dorado, I found my haven in Plymouth Harbor, first port of farewell.

And now voyages and ventures are of no more value to me than that sack of rags and bones. Myself rags and bones. And all the gold I looked for became a handful of dust.

But now the dust of old books and manuscripts was—I see it clear and bitter now—dust of finest gold. . . .

The boy on London Bridge, he saved a penny.

For they had not yet been moved to the southern gatehouse tower, so that the first welcome would be, as it is now, a savage bouquet of shriveled, peeling, pickled, eyeless, shrinking heads, skulls of traitors and felons on the points of rusty pikes staring south at nothing. Saved himself the penny it would cost him now to rent the use of a spyglass and look closer.

Slept light, waiting for daylight to come, in an inn called the Mitre, in Cheapside. Heard Bow Bells toll nine o'clock. Heard bells from St. Martin's-le-Grand call curfew and the shutting of the city gates. Listened to music and singing, laughter and voices, and one wretch puking in the night, from below. Then hearing the calls of the watch, and bells, some near, some far and faint, marking the hours. Two giants came out of the clock at St. Dunstan's and would waken any but a native-born citizen of London. And from far off in Westminster, from the clock tower of Edward I, Great Tom boomed royal solemnity.

Rose early, ate a countryman's breakfast, and waited, impatient, until the morning was half gone, for his kinsman, a scholar at the Inns of Court, to come and show the sights of London. His cousin elegantly dressed beneath a loose gown. And he more ashamed than before in his country-plain and -sturdy doublet and hose, his old-fashioned flat cap, his walking boots heavy as Irish brogues.

Paid a warder too many pennies to see the sights of the Tower. Not imagining the leisure to see those things again.

Next a walk along the thronging of Tower Street, East Cheap, Watling, west toward Ludgate and the loom of St. Paul's. Walking brisk as they could in the crowds; for his cousin had small time to spend on this idleness. Pausing near the church of St. Swithin's to show him the London Stone. From which stone, set by Romans, all distances from London are measured. The center, hub of the wheel of roads those Romans built.

Paid more pennies for them both to climb to the top of the spireless tower of St. Paul's. Where he could look over and around the whole city laid out as if upon a living chart. From there, highest place on Ludgate Hill, able to look down upon the clusters of the other two chief hills—Cornhill and Tower Hill. Could see the way he had come, halfway toward Canterbury it seemed, and the south bank of the river and the river frothing white as it went beneath the Bridge.

In one turning able to encompass the city within the line of the Wall. More than two miles of wall and the raw wound of the ditch without.

Descended partway and paid another penny to give a tug to the bell. While his cousin went ahead to wait for him in the cathedral, pleading an aversion to noise. And therefore Ralegh gave it a memorable tug with all his strength to rattle eyeteeth for a mile around.

Permitted upon descending, a swift craning look at the shadowed grandeur of the cathedral, with its sculptured tombs for illustrious men. His cousin, with an annoying, all-knowing smirk, taking him by the arm for a turn up and down the wide center nave. To enjoy no hush, no signs of awe and piety, but such a clamor as it might as well have been an exchange, a Whitsun fair, a shambles and marketplace, and all in one. Up and back again, slow, shouldering and elbowing their way, upon what might have been, except for absence of horses and carts, as busy a street as is in London. Criers selling anything and everything. And amid such a collection of rogues and vagabonds and candy fellows, tricked out to look gentlemen born and bred, the lawyers in their various gowns cracking jokes and walnuts, spitting seeds and contempt for their clients; all this in the aisle called Paul's Walk. . . .

"Be they Jews and money changers?" Ralegh asked.

His grand kinsman laughed.

"There are no Jews in London now. And if they are here, you shall never guess it, for they will spend more time in devotions than the monks ever did and will swear upon the wounds of Our Savior one hundred times a day."

Adding: "Now you may consider yourself christened for London. And if any man should ask you who you are and what is your business here, why you may tell him you are an honorable member of the Company of Paul Walkers."

Soon a brisk turn, all too hasty, among the outer courts and buildings and the churchyard. Where, more than by anything within the cathedral, he was struck silent by the row of booksellers. So many printed books all in one place, and all for sale if a man had the price in his purse.

After that he was led, a hard trot on foot now, racing against

[178]

the bells of the hour, through Newgate and beyond the walls. Passing the gatehouse of Newgate, where from the prison, asquirm and crowded together like salt herring in a barrel, the prisoners at windows cried out. A profane choir, begging for alms and food.

To his question, his cousin stopped long enough to smile and reply.

"Why, lad, it is a wonderful place! It is a prison common to all men, open and free for all."

"Free?"

"Any man alive is free to walk in, be he ever so humble, and free to beg out of Newgate till he starve to death or die from fever."

Then went westward on Holborn, crossing the River Fleet, going past palaces and churches his cousin did not name and inns he did not have to, for Ralegh could, like any fellow without even his alphabet, know them by their signs—Red Lion, Blue Boar, Dolphin, Pelican, Three Ravens, White Fox. . . .

Turned north along Gray's Inn Lane to enter at the gate and into a bricky pink-red court, ringed round with a steep-roofed building and the walls a wealth of windows, multiplied into innumerable small panes, so as to glitter even in faint light. To dine, then, in the new-built hall, built since his own birth, of Gray's Inn in the company of gentlemen and scholars and in the presence of judges and great men who sat among the Benchers.

Had to take off his boots for a pair of his cousin's mules—soft and light but not a fit; must curl up his toes to walk—and to borrow a plain gown as well. They were strict in observance of the sumptuary rules.

The hall was half of silver from abundance of plate and cups. After the ceremonial sitting and the saying of the grace, he whispered to his cousin that here was enough silver to sink a fleet.

"You may have it all, every piece. There is a tradition that any who wants to may have our plate for the asking. If he will promise to furnish the necessary glass and the earthenware to replace it."

"What sort of bargain is that? A man could furnish that for an hundredth part of the value of the plate."

"True," his cousin answered, "but there's more to the bargain. He must *keep* the Inn so furnished, replacing all that breaks. Who's rich enough in England to do that?"

Saying little himself. Swallowing hard, though dinner seemed like a banquet feast. Listening to the young gentlemen at table whose wit was more nimble than a Morris dancer's feet, as swift as the blade of a fencing master. Drinking too much of their good Spanish wines. Though a walk through the quadrangles and in the shade and sun of the garden cleared his head. "We are much celebrated for our walks," his cousin told him.

"Now then, country cousin," his kinsman told him. "You have seen all of the chief sights of London, excepting Westminster. Which you may visit as you go on your way toward Oxford."

"I thank you for your kindness."

"Pray remember me to your family." He offered his hand. "Now be off to your college and see if they can teach you something."

But, though he bade his cousin a formal farewell, he did not go on toward Oxford then, not yet. Stayed on in London, pinching his pennies for a fortnight.

To wander the streets of the wards and liberties. To look

upon many a decaying tower, palace, and priory. And to peek into churches.

Old John Stow, I would have given a good arm to have your "Annals" and "Survey" then. . . .

Incredible shining elegance of Goldsmith's Row. Where merchants could live grander and finer, side by side, than country noblemen. Where master artisans with delicate tools could turn gold from lumps and bars, old coin or broken jewel, into whatever shape or form heart might desire and imagination contrive. And the wonders, not believed until seen, of the plate displayed at the hall of their company.

And many the halls of guilds and companies, grand enough, but all overtopped by Guildhall of the Lord Mayor and all the companies. The hall overseen by the images of the giants said to have fought for London, Gog and Magog, carved from fir. Giants told of in pagan stories, and in Scripture existing after the Flood in the Land of Giants, ruled by King Og of Basan.

These merchants of London are the giants of the present age. Power of their money and trade made them mighty.

It was in that Guildhall that Sir Nicholas Throckmorton stood trial for treason and, *mirabilis,* was acquitted by a jury of his peers. His defense was eloquent they said. And he walked out free. Then the jury suffered for it.

It may be some expected me to follow that example in '03. If so, they may have concluded that I lacked the man's eloquence. I concluded, before I stood trial, Sir Nicholas indeed set a precedent: never again would any jury be foolish enough to acquit a man on a treason charge.

He could not yet see the greatest show of the power of London money, though he walked near Pissing Conduit where it would soon stand, Sir Thomas Gresham's Royal Exchange. He did see Gresham's shop on Lombard Street. And he saw the house called Timber House where Whittington lived. And at Mercer's Hall saw a portrait of Sir Richard with his curious cat; Dick Whittington, runaway prentice boy, who turned back to be Lord Mayor of London four times and a knight. To leave almshouses behind in his name and his name as a legend. Who once at dinner with a King of England calmly set fire to and burned to ashes a bond of sixty thousand pounds which the King owed him. . . .

Our King James may hope the same from Sir Paul Pindar of Bishopsgate, with whom he will dine. But Pindar is not Dick Whittington. He will have his one for ten and full payment, too.

Saw the markets and the fairs of Southwark, and Bartholomew, near Smithfields, where so many martyrs were well done. And the old church there, where bishops had worn full armor under vestments.

Wandered everywhere trying to see it all at once and once and for all.

Toured the Abbey at Westminster and in and out of the hall of the Old Palace, now settling into sleep. But he could not have gone through these more swiftly on horseback. Courts and tombs and such caught his interest not at all. What fired him was the sight of the Queen's courtiers and a few ladies. All clad in stuffs and colors so fine they would have turned Joseph in his coat as fierce with green-eyed envy as his brothers were.

Ralegh looked with envy too, but kept it hidden from himself. Never thinking, even as he wished, like a maid upon St. Agnes' Eve, to be one among them.

Saw settlements of strangers from other lands: Cloth Fair,

where French and Flemish clothworkers lived and sold their work; Austin Friars, belonging to the Dutch to hold their own services, all but such fanatic radical rogues as Anabaptists and the like; and out in Spitalfields he saw houses of the French and Walloons, silk weavers, with high glazed windows for attics where they worked and cages of birds hanging along the roofs. And bought a singing bird from them. Which he sold to an alewife, later, for half the price he paid.

And he walked the lanes of old Jewry. His cousin was correct. If there were any Jews here, they were well disguised behind common Christian names and every sign of sober Christian piety.

Stood awhile to hear a sermon preached from the stone steps of canopied St. Paul's Cross. But found more pleasure standing to see a pantomime and a puppet show of London and Nineveh, and two plays, one a crude comedy of puns and farce, the other a corruption of Seneca, all blood and thunder and bombast stuffing, at Shoreditch and Newington Butts.

Oh, and everywhere were minstrels and jugglers, dancers and ropewalkers, musicians and tumblers to do tricks and pass a cap or bowl for coins. Not yet the wonder of a talking horse. But dancing bears and monkeys. And parrots who had learned to say "God bless the Queen," among other things.

At Newington Butts he tried strength and skill with a longbow and won a wager. Another at Islington, where he walked to see the brick kilns and found plenty of sturdy rogues to bet against. In Finnsbury Fields increased his earnings by wagering with gentler folk at the archery butts. And looked on the practice of the artillery there.

And once while walking in St. Nicholas Shambles, where butchers work and gutters are clotted with offal—Londoners call it Stinking Lane—heard the bells of St. Pulchre toll news of an execution. Ran and came in time to see a fellow given his nosegay in front of that church, then followed the crowd all the way to Tyburn, with a stop at St. Giles, where the prisoner drank his last cup of cheer, to see him ride upon the Three-Legged Mare, as they called the gallows there.

Watching that fellow die, he saw a lank shadow cut a purse, as clean and neat with a knife as a barber surgeon and less painful by far. For the victim never felt his loss and the cutpurse vanished.

For more of blood and courage there were the cockpits and the bear and bull baiting. Where a man could make a wager too. But he was no match for the Londoners, who knew the names and histories and the pedigree of every animal.

Money dwindling, and he could not wisely return to those places to wager on his archery, Ralegh crossed over from The Mitre to its neighbor inn, The Mermaid. And found that a Devon lad with a country look and quick hands could turn a trick or two with dice. Then, Fortune favoring him, he haunted taverns, and alehouses with their painted lattices of red or green. For a time his only losses came from tapster's arithmetic.

Until at last he met a fellow, a Westcountry seafaring man, fresh out of "Sailor's Town," east of the Tower. Met the man at Devil Tavern, sign of St. Martin and the Devil, on Fleet Street, close by the places of the moneylenders.

Seeing the boy's skill at dice and cards, the seafarer proposed a joint-stock venture.

"Boy," he told him, "you have skill and a good head for remembering odds. But it is not enough in this wicked town, where there are guilds of cardsters and dicers and haunters of even gentlemen's bowl yards and tennis courts. They have as many tricks as any lawyer or dancing bear. And they speak in canting tongue and pedlar's French to each other. You are no match for them."

The fellow prated on, parading a great knowledge of Barnard's Law and Vincent's Law, of Setters, Versers, Rutters, Markers, Scrippers, and Oaks, all of them in league against some ignorant Martin like him. And then proposed that two good Westcountry men have more wit than all these put together and how, using the blunt end of London arrogance against them, the two might proceed, playing the fat conny, to catch some conny-catchers and be gone before any man was wiser.

Young and foolish and homesick for the sound of Devon speech, Ralegh agreed. And they played that dangerous game all over the city, and were even so bold as to try their luck and lives at Turnmill Street and Pickt-hatch, where the houses had turning doors with spikes and every man and boy above knee-high was a roaring boy who would fight over the cut of his hair or the cast of his eyes.

And all went well until—oh, the satires of Fortune!—they found themselves caught in the midst of a brawl in Bible Tavern, close to the Devil, where they had begun. A bone-breaking, eye-gouging, table-smashing battle having nothing to do with cards or dice, or any cause he ever knew of. But once it began it was every man for himself and to hell with the hindmost. Just before the constables burst in with the watch, it had come down to knives and death. Ralegh went out, following others, through a trap door and a passage.

And never saw the Devon sailor again. Who either ran all the way back to his ship without one backward look or else lay on the floor of the Bible in a bed of blood, making two grins from ear to ear.

Could as well have been himself lying there to greet the lanterns of the watch.

A night or two later in Southwark he followed a woman up to a high chamber and let her instruct him in the world's oldest dance for two. Then, light-headed, blithe-hearted, he went to play at dice once more in a tavern. Lost the last of his coins, but cared not at all. Sang old songs and laughed with a one-eyed soldier, a vagrom man for sure, with a patch over his bad eye and a scar like a crescent moon across his cheek. And afterwards they fought each other in an alley and, feeling his young strength for certain, Ralegh hugged that soldier till his ribs cracked and then hurled him across the alley in the air.

Ran from voices and guttering torches, through a rat's nest of muddy alleys and lanes, past barks and snapping dogs and many a curse from high windows. Ran swift, laughing like a moon-man, until he found himself, heavy-footed and breathless, in an open field under a sky full of spinning stars. Spread his arms like a scarecrow and, looking into the diamond-spattered sky, laughing his breath away, turned round and around, a top spun off a string, until string broke and sky melted and stars came down to fill his head and slam to the lids of his eyes.

Woke with rain in his face. St. George's Fields for his bed and a forlorn windmill for companion. Woke with his skull a beating bass drum and his tongue made of fresh-sheared greasy wool and each bone a rotten timber, creaking when he tried to move. Lay in rain, too weak and dizzy to dig a grave and climb into it. Finally, by prayer and wishing, got to his feet and stumbled through mud toward Southwark. Found a ditch by the road and lay beside it vomiting up London's pleasures. While a wild-haired, savage-looking beast of a man (a gypsy?) with a cudgel crouched nearby and watched him. Lying there puking, Ralegh drew his dagger and showed the fellow the blade. But the man made no move at all, still crouched there, when Ralegh set off on the road for London again.

It was not the blade that saved my head a cracking. The fellow could see I had no purse or jewel. What a fool I was! The knife was all I had worth the trouble of stealing and I showed him that. Perhaps he pitied me. . . .

His cousin of Gray's Inn was not so charitable, though he laughed till his eyes were cloudy with tears.

"First, young sir, I must show you the Chapel of the Temple. I'll not be seen with you in our own and there is something I want you to see there."

So down they walked to the round church of the Knights Templar, made in the fashion of the Holy Sepulcher in Jerusalem, church for the scholars and lawyers of Inner and Middle Temple.

Rain slacked and sky clearing, but the streets were rivers of mud. This time his cousin took the honor of the wall. He had the honor of mud from horses and carts.

Entered that ancient chapel, under the Norman arch of the western porch, humbly flanked by polished rows of Purbeck marble columns, to see two churches. Then on into the round church, where eight armed knights lay in solemn stone upon the pavement, unsmiling.

He thought he would change places with any of them but none of them stirred.

His cousin took him past tombs to the stairs leading to the triforium and showed him the penitential cell, opening onto the stairway. Where once a knight could lie naked in a sort of coffin, too small by half for Ralegh, of stone and hear the saying of Mass while he starved. And be led forth every Monday to be flogged naked in public by a priest.

"Now then, Wat Ralegh, go down and say your prayers. You may kneel if you wish to, for we are alone here."

Knelt indeed and bowed his head and moved his lips. But if he prayed, it was not in proper contrition. He gave thanks that he was still alive, and then quietly prayed his cousin would see fit to be generous to him.

Back they went to his cousin's chambers at Gray's. Where he was ready to kneel too, if he had to.

"What an excellent beginning!" his cousin told him. "And now you will make a scholar. Master of the arts of the tavern, of drinking and whoring and alley brawling. With especial skills—as witness your empty purse, nay, you have lost *it* too— in the subjects of dicing and cards."

"I am ashamed already," he replied.

"For the good of your soul I ought to send you off to Oxford as you are—a Westcountry vagabond with an empty stomach and not a penny to your name. Perhaps you can fall in with a tribe of gypsies and live a happy life.

"But you seem somewhat humbled by your adventures. And we are, you and I, alas, of the same stock and blood, however distant. And perhaps they can make a semblance of a gentleman out of you at Oriel, if never a scholar. And, above all, you will be *there*. My conscience need trouble me no longer. Therefore give thanks that you have a most charitable cousin."

He gave him money in an old purse. Not enough for renting a horse or riding a baggage cart ("You walked here—no doubt to save money for the city—but walking nonetheless.

[188]

Walking you came in, and walking you shall go out!") and only enough to spare for a modest chamber ("What need a feather-bed for a stout fellow who sleeps in open fields?") and the simple ordinary at the inns ("Eat plain and hearty fare and your stomach will thank you for it.").

"I thank you kindly."

"Be off with you now and allow me the pleasure of forgetting you."

He nodded and turned to leave.

"Wait," his cousin said.

And when he turned back his cousin threw him a penny he had to stoop for.

"You may wonder what that is for. Well, sir, walk over to Bethlehem Hospital, which the vulgar call Bedlam. And there for a penny they will let you wander about among the lunatics and see the worst of them chained to the walls. Which is where you will be if you don't mend your ways. Which I doubt upon the grounds of Scripture—the leopard cannot change his spots."

"Our Savior did heal the mad," Ralegh said softly. "He cast out demons more than once. Do you recall the incident in the country of the Gadarenes?"

"The demons were turned into pigs, were they not? and leapt to their deaths."

"Not all of them," Ralegh said. "Some lived to propagate and multiply. And over the ages have turned back into a semblance of human form."

"What proof of that nonsense?"

"I did not believe it myself," Ralegh answered. "But now I will bear witness under oath that I have seen the living proof of it in London—a pig in a gown at Gray's Inn who calls himself a cousin."

And he hurled the penny at his cousin's face. Turned heels and walked out across the courtyard, his cousin shouting after him.

"Pride, Wat Ralegh! Your damned pride will undo you. Mark my words."

Pompous fool was right of course. He came to nothing good, but nothing evil either. Lived quiet enough, a gentleman and justice of the peace in Devon. Lived to die quiet in his bed.

Walked out proud enough and direct to a barber. From which, patched up and brushed clean, he went forth to find rain and clouds gone and sunlight making a balmy day. Set out walking down Fleet to Temple Bar. But the way was crowded with sober, decent folk, and he turned to the river and took the ragged lane called the Strand, running past the gatehouses of bishops and great men, then going up and on to Charing Cross. Past St. Martin's-in-the-Fields and fine houses (one of Burghley's) and the sign of the inn of The Swan. Where a drink would have soothed him, but cost too much.

By then he was sweating in the sun and his muscles and bones were new again. So he could laugh at his own folly and his kinsman's shocked furious final face, as he swung north from St. Martin's, stopping for a drink of water from the old well at St. Giles in the fields. A mean, poor, dirty little village it was. A few shops and sagging houses clustered close around the dissolved and decaying hospital for lepers. Fearing that all his doings were written on his flesh and announced by a bell which would call folks out of their houses to shout "Unclean!", he muttered a prayer to St. Giles, especial patron of lepers and cripples.

Perhaps his good cousin (damn his eyes!) was right. Pride would be his lameness.

Well, St. Giles, help me get from here to Oxford. Though you were not much comfort to Sir John Oldcastle, when that poor knight was slow-roasted in chains here. And, since he had time while they cooked him, I wager he called upon every other saint he had ever heard of. No, Saint Giles, thank you for the drink of cool water and that is all I ask. Though I confess a Smithfield saloop would be better medicine for what ails me. Better a beggar with a clapper than a cellar in St. Giles, Londoners say, to mark the lowest ebb of poverty. Well, Saint, I thank you, but I shall not tarry here. Amen. . . .

Off again until the road crossed the highroad to Oxford. And turned west on it. Stepping lively, to the rhythm of tunes he learned in London and could now whistle against loneliness.

A poor scholar he was, but poor he would always be, Master of Arts or no. For that boy was feeling shrunk to the size of a dwarf, after the extraordinary shine of London. Feeling good to have seen it and known it once, feeling good to be young and strong. Keeping his pride, but feeling no hints of promise as he walked toward a place where he would be too poor to buy or even to rent his own gown.

Smarting in love and pride and shame for the old name he bore, for his Westcountry home and accent and ways. Not daring to dream much. Not caring much yet.

Not knowing how much he cared. . . .

An ignorant boy came to London and caught the fever of it, though he knew it not.

Will not say farewell to city or fever now. Too many farewells already. Too many times. None final, excepting as every farewell is final.

Came to love this city as I have loved my home in Devon. Have seen her all in grandeur and all naked and bare. But I am not a boy now. Or, rather, since I bear the boy I was within me, I am more than that boy.

Am also an old man with a new sack of rags and bones, each one a regret.

I regret the loss of a London I never truly possessed.

Better and wiser I had followed John Stow with his measuring stick and his spade.

Poor Stow, he followed me, at a distance and not at expense of study, and my fortunes. This man who has made London forever new by charting it old. Up and down. By 1580 we were called Collegium Antiquariorum. *And by favor of the Queen we met at Herald's College. Were we not like heralds bringing news and true reports? Bishop Parker, upon whose power and favor the thing commenced, was dead and gone. Thus not able to taste the first fruits of his planting.*

And the paradox of the merchant tailor—Stow. Thus favored, he gave his time and substance to his task. To what purpose? The new King favored neither the enterprise nor him. To keep old English embers glowing, giving off heat, was not the intent of the King.

And it may be—I can conceive it—Stow and some others, too, of that little band, suffered from the King's suspicions because I had been one among them. They were forbidden to meet again, though they could not be prevented from happening upon the Boar's Head Tavern upon the same evening.

Could not prevent some of these from coming to the Tower as visitors to me. But the sun was not shining on them.

Poor Stow, now truly poor, and weary from labors, received in reward neither aid nor pension, but, satirically, a patent from the King—a license to be a beggar.

Died within a year. Scarcely time for a man of four score years to learn a new trade.

Yet, thanks be to God and to John Stow, his Survey of London *restored the freedom of the city to me even as I was penned in the Tower. Thanks to his pen, I could walk those streets again.*

I could wish you were with me, old man of Three-Needle Street, my companion here and now. To brighten a brief moment with the long-burning light of the past. Could wish you here and this boat a proud and decorated barge, myself having come to fetch you to the Queen. Who shall this day honor and reward you. I am her Captain again, and all the boats and wherries must give way for us. Watermen and citizens raise their hats and cheer. Ships at anchor and tied to wharfs fly flags, fire cannon salutes, and the crews climb ratlines to see you. You stand in honor, uneasy not to be walking, tall and lean.

John Stow, I am no prophet, no prognosticator. But I will tell you this. The King is a scholar and he writes books, a rare thing for any king. Still, reason tells me your words will live when his, and mine, too, no doubt, are feeding the insatiable worms that love most those books least read.

—Why so? you ask. I never sought to write wisdom.

—John Stow, wisdom and folly are close kin and time will make one common tomb for both of them. Your pains and care were for simple truth. Which is most precious, the brightest of all things in this dark dream of a world. . . .

In time measured by sands in a glass or by clocks, time passing has been too short for measuring. A few grains of sand, a stutter of the clock hand, a blink of the eyes. Time for a few strokes of the oars of the barge, a call from the coxswain, as she eases into the river and the incoming tide, straightens and steadies to go.

If sun were shining, sky were blue, and water calm, they would still be floating in the shimmering image of the Tower. Having moved less space than a stone's throw.

Such is the time of memory, though memory may be long.

Time of tides is otherwise, rising and falling to the whims of the moon. Rising and falling to the stirring and shifting of the vast sea, engirdling the landsman's world. The sea owes fidelity and obedience to the moon; yet the sea and the winds are free to blow and rage together from all quarters, and free also to be deadly calm. The tide of the Thames, then, servant to the sea, rising and falling to a great command, within an ordered scheme.

Yet the simple truth, and any fisherman or waterman can tell you so: no two rivers or harbors have the same scheme of time, rising and falling. Each with its own rhythm and order. And even within that ordering much change according to the seasons and the moon.

And the fat or thin of the moon comes from the sun, as the moon on its own rhythm and set in its path as strict as the river must follow its banks. That moon, ever the same, is ever changing, new to old to new again, and thus forever different.

Tides of the sea will sometimes rise high, lap over bank and wharf, flood low places and then withdraw again.

Against those tides, steady and undeterred, is the river's flowing. Which, according to clouds and sky and rain, according to the wealth or poverty of well and freshet and spring, will flow, now swift, cloudy as a horse trough with a cargo of earth, now slow, a thin clear trickling. And more than once in a lifetime has turned into an ice as thick as stone pavement.

Each thing, all things sublunary, being bound in obedience to the other, yet each in bondage separate and free to be and become itself. By letter of natural law condemned to constancy. Yet, by the terms and spirit of the same law, pardoned and free to be forever changing, thus ever inconstant. . . .

Standing, his hand light upon the shoulder of an oarsman, who has dipped and pulled his oar a few strokes only, breathing the river, Ralegh can picture in the same tumbling time as a shuffling cascade of cards the journey of the river toward this place. A passage to here and beyond.

Arising, some say, from the seven clear cold bubbling springs, called Seven Sisters, near Cheltenham. Others name other sources; no matter. For certain this river flows two hundred crooked miles to London. Longest and largest of English rivers, swallowing other rivers, freshets, streams, rills, and these all fed by the waters of wells and springs beyond counting.

[195]

Flowing toward London and the sea. Past many places he has known.

Past Oxford, where gentlemen and scholars can boat but are not supposed to swim. But where on warm nights without too much moon he shucked clothing and played and splashed like a dolphin. And once on a bitter starless night when the river was all thinly frozen, he slipped out of chambers, climbed silent over the wall, and went alone to break the sheen of ice and feel the breathtaking cold as he plunged in to test his manhood. As a boy will do.

Flowing past Oxford, walls and towers of colleges. Where the river is called Isis.

Beginning a taut loop, a bending, like a pulled bow, as it runs past the ruined Benedictine abbey at Abingdon, once nearly dying into nothing with the monks gone, but now reviving on the power of malt.

Past Dorchester, where the Augustinians were. Here where the first West Saxon Christian king was baptized in the river. And where no snake or adder may dwell within the sound of the bell of the abbey church of Peter and Paul.

Below here Isis and River Thame join in matrimony, the holy mystic copulation of waters, to become one—the Thames.

Subject worthy of celebration by his friend, the poet Spenser. And, indeed, Spenser was planning such a poem once—*Epithalamion Thamesis*. In which not only Thame and Isis were to be wed, but every river and stream in England would come as wedding guests.

Past Wallingford, named for Saxon crossings, where the cock crows and hens lay eggs in the ruins of the abbey and the duchy castle still stands proud, though harmless now.

See how the river, renewed, now begins to wander idly, as if more sure of its destination, certain and unhurried, south of the chalk and the tall beeches of Chiltern Hills. Going gentle past farms and villages, and half-timbered houses.

Grows stronger and deeper, drinking the waters of the Kennet at Reading. Where stones of the abbey have served to make a royal lodge, the Queen's House, and been dispersed to many purposes.

Then turns again to uncoil in a shivering of loops and slack knots like a tossed length of line.

Passing by Sonning and Henley. Bending up and around and down again to run beneath the gray freestone battlements of Windsor Castle, lofty on one bank, and the school of Eton upon the other.

Windsor, a proper royal castle, sited splendid upon a chalk hill to view the woods and fields and the river.

Windsor, once perfection of and still a wonder for hunting. Especially for the red deer. With sixty and more parks for this purpose, each enclosed, but by gates opening into another.

Arthur is said to have built the first fortress tower here, where now the central keep, like the drum of a giant, stands. And there are those who multiply the myth beyond the powers of imagination, saying: long before Arthur it was Arviragus, son of Cymbeline, who built here.

Well, even a man who is skeptically inclined will confess the original to be old. Someone before the dawn of English memory built there. And all kings thereafter built upon the place anew or repaired the old.

Three courts, each one within the other. Chapel of St. George there, saint of the Knights of the Garter. Where hang that order's shields and helmets and banners. Where is a most remarkable organ able to mimic the noise of any musical instrument. Tombs and towers. Residences and apartments furnished with hangings of gold and silver and precious stones. Some chambers all ceilinged and walled with mirror glass. A high open-timbered gallery from which the ladies can watch the hunting.

And for a conny of quality, native or stronger, who is willing to believe, there are such treasures as the horn of a unicorn, nine spans long. Or the magnificent Bird of Paradise, bird which never pecked or flew nor had to be gutted and stuffed, being artfully contrived out of air and feathers and whole cloth.

Let false birds and mystic horns, fancies of wood and jewels called joinery and hangings and glass mirrors repeating the image of a man beyond counting be emblems for Windsor. Remembering that all these can be easy enough packed and removed and rearranged in another place, for another time. As in the theater. For theater it was and remains though the old stones are true.

And the river, no trick of scenery, flows by, indifferent to both truth and illusion.

The river flows on, in a while dividing round the sparse island of Runnymede. Where a king of England, bowing his head to parchment, in the iron presence of his barons, did, with no more than a whisk, a scribbling, scratching flourish of the end of his pen, change the chronicles of England forever.

Now moving, a lazy snake in the first warmth of spring, as towns and villages press closer to each other—Egham, Staines, of the old London Stone, Chertsey, Walton, Hampton, Molesey. . . .

Now and next, and properly called an Honor of the Crown, is Cardinal Wolsey's elephant of folly, which serves the Crown

[198]

better—Hampton Court. Close by the bank of the river and made of red brick.

Enter the gate, above which remains the late Queen's golden rose and her device, *Dieu et mon Droit,* into a puzzles game of ten courts. With, outside the walls, two parks, one for the deer and the other for coursing hare. Enter into a plenitude of chambers, residences, apartments. The chapel and hall, high-vaulted with Irish oak which forbids spiders and cobwebs and will stand off any insect or gnawing vermin.

And here most especially the strangers who visit—princes, nobility, ambassadors, and such—are bedazzled by the richness and abundance of things—hangings, tapestries, paintings, the wonders of the Paradise Room. But if dazzled by the opulence, they are delighted by contrivances and curiosities: the machine of the fountains in courtyard and garden, permitting the water to be played upon as a musical instrument, from towering jets and columns, to drops as light as a lady's tears; the twelve Caesars done lifelike in plaster; spheres and astrolabes; exact portrayals of the native man, woman, and child Sir Martin Frobisher brought home with him from the Northwest, together with their curious clothing and the costumes of others from far lands; musical instruments made of gold and silver and glass; the head of the spear which was thrust into the side of our Lord and Savior.

The river goes on without awe or servility. Lazy and indifferent to the wonders and follies of man's making. . . .

Here at Hampton our King assembles the full Court in early September. And his Court has grown so large with new offices and appointments and hordes of hangbys, that even the King must read the *Book of Offices* to know one from the other. And not all the apartments of Hampton can house them, but fields and courts of tents are needed.

The river needs no book to make distinctions between fool and wise men, all being equal. . . .

The river needs no accommodations, being surely bound for home. . . .

Hampton is most pleasant for that courtier with a full purse of unworried time to spend. Great Henry left cockpits, bowling alleys, tennis courts, and tiltyards enough to keep them so busy in idleness as to be unable to meddle in affairs of state or to sweat too much while waiting for advancement.

Here will be Anne of Denmark, wife to James and friend to Walter Ralegh. Unless, in her illness, she is still at Oatlands.

Now comes Kingston, where in dim days Saxon kings were crowned.

Widening, deeper, the river passes the palace of Richmond. A favorite of the late Queen, though not so much for pleasure as Nonsuch or Greenwich. Most remembered as the chief seat of her grandfather, Henry VII.

Place where, still a princess, she was reconciled with Mary, the Queen. Together they came from London in midsummer on barges covered with fresh flowers so that each seemed a floating garden. Came to feast in the banquet house upon a miracle of sweetness, a huge cake made to appear like a pomegranate tree and bedecked in colored sweets to show the arms of Spain.

Place where we came from London on torchlight barges, to the noise of musicians and under a canopy of fireworks, for a night of revels—masques and dancing, perhaps a play.

Place where Elizabeth took much delight in her grandfather's cunning secret passages.

Place where it pleased the late Queen to permit her godson, Sir John Harrington, to build and install his wondrous new invention, the Ajax, a machine designed to replace the privy and the Jordan pot of the chamber. Calling him her saucy poet of the laystow, the Queen allowed it. But also allowed as how the galloping rush of waters which followed upon the pulling of a chain near frightened her out of her wits and like to have bound her innards for a week. Saying: "Go to, Sir Jakes, your jest will be the ruin of my bowels and is unfit for all but savages. Take a patent upon it and sell it to Irish or blackamoors. But not in my kingdom!"

Richmond, the place where Henry VIII, young, made entertainments for the Venetians. And where, after many years and near to the end of her reign, when the Venetian Ambassador, Scarmelli, came to complain of English pirates, the Queen received him grandly and graciously chided him for long years of silence from Venice. All in his native tongue. And after he had bowed and departed, the Queen turned laughing to her Court, half in wonder herself, for she had not spoken the Italian tongue in half a century.

Place for such curiosities as the chamber where Henry VII died, the walls sprinkled and dotted with his blood according to his wishes. Where can be seen the round mystic mirror wherein that king could see all things presently passing in the world, on land and on sea. Which mirror broke at the instant of his death. An inconvenience for all future kings of England.

Place for the library of Henry VII, an abundance of printed books and manuscripts. Some forbidden, dealing with magic and black arts.

Where a visitor may be shown a vellum scroll of twenty feet

in length, demonstrating the genealogy of the English kings from Adam onwards.

Where one Henry died and where King James' son, Henry, Prince of Wales, spent his final summer. A place of too many deaths to please our living King.

Except the one death which pleased him. For here at Richmond, alas, the late Queen suffered her illness, dying upon the eve of Lady Day.

Beyond Richmond and coming to the curving turn at Lambeth Marsh. Passing the old manor house of Copped Hall, where the Lady Arabella, eager as James, waited for the Queen's choice.

Now at the turning, tall upon the south bank, a sprawling of brick and stone, high-topped by towers, is Lambeth Palace, seat of the archbishops of Canterbury.

Highest above the outer court walls, overlooking the river and half of London, that small tower built a century and a half before by Archbishop Chicheley, for his convenience in the leisurely torture of the Lollard heretics.

Across the river stands Westminster, with the hall, old palace, the abbey, and Whitehall.

And now at last, deeper, still running clear, the river swallows up the waters of London, gulping the Fleet without hesitation. And taking thereby much that is foul from London, darkening its clarity.

Taking London's waters and waste, but leaving a blessing for fishermen, fishmongers, and tables, a treasure of trout, perch, smelt, shrimps, bream, flounder, haddock, and many others. Sometimes, though rarely, a catch of carp. And upon occasion the fat salmon, though never so sweet as the salmon of Exe and the Devon rivers.

Flowing past London, now eagerly dreaming the sea ahead.

Perhaps one last regret, a moment of hesitation, a bulge and loop, like a gut, at the Isle of Dogs, with Greenwich and noble buildings across the way.

Salute to Greenwich, then, and off and away, wider and deeper and swifter, running easterly past Beckton, Woolwich, Grays, Tilbury—where the greatest English army gathered and dispersed in triumph and without a fight—and Gravesend.

Until, like a huge jaw yawning with astonishment, the river goes to sea.

Waves shrug ermine shoulders. Shrieking gulls claim possession of blustering air.

There with wind to fill sails and belly them out like a woman with child, strange chords plucked from lines and halyards, the rig strummed by mad fingers, a cithern accompanying the crying of the gulls, who wish us no good luck; there to sail south down the British Sea toward Westcountry ports.

And from there on a day of favoring winds to set forth to far southern islands.

Where, at last, we turn westward with the trade winds and follow the sun, to sail on into the burning water and gold of the sky. . . .

But he is not on any rolling, pitching, wind-teased vessel now. The breeze on this river is not more yet than his own breath. He sighs for the shimmering, evanescent, butterfly's wing of the present moment. Which reason again reminds him is his most precious possession. That moment, in purity, always threatened by memory and wishes. Or is that true? Why not call the present the sum of all?

The trick of time lies in its deceptions. Pea in the pod, shell game, past, present, future, shift place in one instant and who can say which is which and be sure?

Oars of the bargemen rise and dip and pull together, light and easy, wet with fresh drops as they feather, then swing to pull again. They hold the slim barge straight, riding clean in the water toward the arches of London Bridge.

Ralegh sits down, taking a place beside Apsley. His legs are tired.

The watermen and passengers in boats and wherries have seen him and guessed the purpose of this journey.

They will have told his name a thousand times before twilight. Indeed, before midday dinner his name will be bruited the length of the town.

So much value, then, for the precautions taken by these gentlemen from King's Bench.

There are more virgins than there are secrets in London.

And there are more black swans than virgins.

Seeing now, in dawnlight hodgepodge, hurly-burly, hugger-mugger of the rooftops and gables, spires and bell towers, all shapes and sizes. Across a slant of distance, rising above everything, the bulk of St. Paul's. Taller than all even without its spire. Shape of a lazy giant, half asleep, sprawled, propped high upon one elbow, heavy-lidded, overseeing all.

The inlet at Billingsgate. They pass close by a weather-worn merchant vessel, her ordnance bristling. Watermen are off-loading cargo to the wharf.

Back from the Baltic run, with rough furs and straight Polish timber lashed on deck.

London Bridge growing sudden and hugely ahead. With noise of water running through arches. With dim clatter of traffic overhead. Twenty-one stone piers to hold up twenty arches. Water narrowing, blocked by corn mills and waterworks on the south side and by heavy-timbered starlings built out to protect each pier. Narrowing so strict it makes waterfalls at the peak and the turn of the tide; when shooting the bridge takes all of the skill of the best of the watermen and allows an unwary passenger to taste his heart.

Did that also young and green with another whose name I cannot remember. Upon a wager and too drunk to fear the devil. And the waterman prayed like a Turk atop a temple howling when we steered his boat clumsy and laughing through thunder of white water to drop and spin around like a chip in a whirlpool. Yet not so much as a drop splashed our clothes.

London Bridge was built for wise men to go over and fools to go under.

Fool or wise, I have walked over and around more times by far than I have gone under. For ever since I first crossed over, I have rejoiced to walk in the crowded savage streets. Savage? It seems so to the stranger. Friend Spenser, reared and schooled here, calls it "merry London." Our King calls it "a foul town."

Though famine and plague may scatter the crowds—not *silence* them, mind you, for they are as noisy in disaster as in triumph and festival—they return. Coming leaping back to spawn again.

And such a rage of color and textures. Granite stone from Cornwall and Devon, sandstone brought from York, freestone and, chiefly, Caen stone from Normandy. Marble from the Isle of Purbeck. Brickwork, glazed or plain, every age and shade, from blood and rose to rose pink. Plaster and timber, oak from Shropshire and Sussex, Lancashire and Cheshire, dark as ebony from time, or tricked out with gilding and painted dec-

[205]

oration. Roofs of slate or lead and sometimes, against all common sense and regulation, of plain timber and even thatch.

Such colors in the streets—flowering of signs and banners and pennants.

And swirling street crowds. As if each dirty roadway, street, and alley were a river of flowers and flesh. No, not of flesh. Flesh not often seen except when some rogue or mort is stripped to reveal it. And it, too, is colorful soon with stripes of blood.

Only faces are seen, and faces of strangers are paper masks, their bodies clad, even the poor, in such various colors you can believe the shards and fragments of all the broken stained glass of England were seeds. Took root here by the river in the bone-rich earth. From which these living flowers bloomed.

Here the figure fails. Who'd sniff the scent without a strong nosegay in one hand, a pomander in the other, and a bag of sweet herbs around the neck? Whoever heard of flowers who can bawl more noise than a battlefield?

Though it may be if our ears were rightly tuned we might hear garden flowers shriek or squeal like butchered beasts when the cold knife cuts them off at stem or they are yanked by the roots to slow death. . . .

A head-tilting look, straight at the roofs of the high houses on the bridge. There toward Southwark side stands that new buffoonery some wag calls Nonsuch House, a drunkard's fancy in timber, made by Dutchmen and shipped over to be pieced together here, crowned with crazed gilt domes and a clutter of gilded weather vanes to rival the pickled heads on the gate.

I will not picture how my head might look, no man being

[206]

at best advantage bodiless, unbarbered, grinning on the end of a pike. . . .

And, going under, craning to see the tower of the Chapel of Thomas built upon the central pier of the bridge.

The crypt, they say, has a secret flight of stairs to the river. For a man in danger to go down. Better it were for a man to go up, I say. . . .

Smoking chimneys of houses. Each year the chimneys multiply, not going forth, but standing in one place. Multiply and grow taller to belch more smoke of sea coal and wood.

Under the bridge and look to the left now. To Southwark and tower of St. Mary Overy. Which some call St. Savior.

Many a marriage, many a christening, and funeral there. Many the tombs. And lately it is again the fashion to be placed there.

There lies the tomb of the moral Gower, greatest of all the old poets excepting Chaucer. A painted effigy beneath a canopy of carved stone. His head resting upon his three most celebrated volumes for eternal pillows.

And an inscription reading: "Whosoever prayeth for the soul of John Gower, he shall, so oft as he doth, have an M and a D days of pardon."

Then let us all pray for John Gower's soul until all England is pardoned forever. . . .

Out of sight, down the road to Canterbury, stands Old Tabbard Inn. From whence the finest English poet before our Spenser, and Spenser's master and better, set forth with nine and twenty others on an April pilgrimage.

All their pilgrimages are done with, both Geoffrey Chaucer and Edmund Spenser now lying in a corner of the Abbey of Westminster, hard by the Chapel of Henry VII. Chaucer, the

Flower of Poets, and Spenser, named Prince of the same breed, close together. Setting a new ambition and fashion for our poets. Ben Jonson praying he shall be buried there too. Not only for ambition but, ever the satiric wit, for the poet's justice of it. Saying: "By God, when I was a bricklayer, I laid half the new brick and repaired half the old that is there. It is only right I should be allowed to rest there too."

Oh, old Southwark has many fine taverns and inns now, and a cluster of no less than five jails. None of them vacant or idle. No scarcity of that sort of pilgrim.

Now Bankside. Where the wise, going up- and downriver, disembark to walk around to the other side of London Bridge.

Bankside, proud with the Bishop of Winchester's old palace.

And beyond there seeing the rising up of the familiar shapes of the playhouses, the Rose and the Globe. The Globe new built again since that time when he watched from the Tower to see it burn, an unplanned part of the show of *Henry VIII* by William Shakespeare.

And also, standing taller than either of these, the triple-tiered, many-galleried shape of our English Circus Maximus—the Beargarden. Where, though you can see neither Jesuit nor Puritan fed to lions, you will see native English dogs test courage against the bear and bull.

Or an ape with a whip ride a pony like a man, round and around, shouting in an incomprehensible tongue, fleeing a pack of wild dogs.

Or a blind bear chained to a stake fighting off dogs and ripping them gutless as cleaned fish.

All this and more if blood is your pleasure.

Your hard-shell snail of a Puritan rails against it. Just so calls the playhouse the house of the devil. Being able to speak with the most righteous vehemence because he has never been to either.

Tell him there are many worse things to see in this world if he will open his eyes. And he need not travel far, not beyond the limits of his own ward, to see them.

Go ask some drooling, poxed wretch, with a ruined rotten flap of a nose, to tell you of the pleasures of the stews in Southwark. And he will hawk and spit at your face.

Nothing special in that, though. For a man can acquire rosy emblems of the French disease in any ward or liberty of London. And for a modest price. Even, indeed, in stately shadows of Westminster. Though a man must pay more dearly for a lady's favors there.

Passing now the inlet of Queenhithe on the London Bank. So soon? His looking at Southwark and Bankside costing him more time than he knew. Has gone past Ebbgate and Dowgate, with barges loading and unloading, already.

Here lies a middling-size Spanish vessel, of too much draught to ease into the inlet. Therefore anchored, fore and aft. Off-loading cargo to watermen. No love lost there between them, amid the shouts, as oranges and lemons go ashore and casks of Spanish wine. The Spaniards certain the watermen will dawdle and loaf time away, costing them tide and breeze. The watermen thinking what the returning cargo to Spain will be. Thinking good powder and English ordnance, on-loaded at Tower Wharf. Thinking: *We are not galley slaves yet, so mind your sharp voices, you blackbeard bastards!*

Just ahead lies Puddle Lane Wharf, overseen by the towers of Baynard's Castle, as old as the Tower and built by a lord who served the Conqueror, to match the Tower and to end the old wall of London.

Baynard's Castle now wasting and crumbling away. Though Great Henry came there often and troubled to rebuild it. And there most proudly lived the Earl of Pembroke, who proclaimed Queen Mary, and upon occasion of her first Parliament paraded to Baynard's Castle with two thousand men and sixty of his gentlemen, men in velvet coats with chains of gold, gentlemen in blue coats and each wearing the Earl's badge of the green dragon.

And once the old Earl held a banquet for Queen Elizabeth and afterwards they climbed a tower to see a display of fireworks, the river afire with reflection of falling stars.

Three towers face the river and an ancient gate with portcullis. From which a stone bridge leads down direct to the wharf.

But this morning no carts rumble under the gate. They are busy at Puddle Wharf, loading barrels of beer and returning to the new-built brewhouse nearby with barley and malt and hops. To be brewed with sweet healing waters from the well at St. Bride's.

If you prefer our old English ale, sir, I say we should turn back to Southwark. For Southwark ale is so snappy and strong it will keep a man from church. . . .

Now Blackfriars and the wharf, a free landing place. And once, before the Dissolution, the sprawling seat of nine acres of the Preaching Friars. Where Parliaments once met. Where Charles V, Holy Roman Emperor, was lodged.

Here Cardinal Wolsey was tried. And here, too, ecclesiastics gathered to hear a cause of matrimony between Henry VIII and his lawful wife. Which, unforeseen then, was to be the end of Blackfriars.

The old parish church of St. Anne is a stable for horses. There are tennis courts and places to let and lease to gentlefolk.

[210]

Here Henry Brooke, Lord Cobham, kept chambers in the porter's lodge, and had his garden. Ralegh dined there once too often.

Here, in the larger precinct, Ben Jonson lived.

And Robert Carr, Earl of Somerset, and his lady lived there too, before they were imprisoned.

In '76 the old Parliament Chamber was rebuilt into a private playhouse, smaller than the suburb theaters, and with seats in the pit. And there he saw by candlelight, in the company of others from Court, Jonson's *The Case Is Altered,* and many a comedy acted by the Children of the Chapel Royal.

When that theater closed—he could still go to see the Children of Queens Revels at Whitefriars—he tried his skill with Rocco Bonetti or his son, Italian fencing masters who kept school there. Bonetti was quick and nimble. Give him a chance and he'd take your buttons one by one with so delicate a flick that he would neither scratch the skin nor tear clothing. All bravado and dexterity he was. But not so well versed in the rough and tumble of plain swordplay. As witness the scars he wore from choosing to cross blades with that stout London master, albeit a loudmouth bragging rogue, Austin Bagger of Warwick Lane.

To dance and to capture buttons is good exercise for eye and hand, but has not much to do with the craft of carving and killing.

In the last years of our Queen, after shrewd Burbage rebuilt the playhouse in an extraordinary grand style and brought the Children of the Chapel to play there, Ralegh came often to see them perform the plays of Jonson and Chapman and Marston.

And in '17, fresh from the Tower but forbidden the Court, he could be where the Court often was. Came there to witness work of new men like Massinger, Beaumont and Fletcher. It was only then, when it would serve him to be seen, that he paid the high price and sat among gallants on the stage.

Plays were better seen in the suburb playhouses. But if you wish to see a play in the city—and how proper Londoners, those few, hate the stage!—you must settle for children. Who can sing and dance well, and be observed in comfort, with an intermission between the acts. And there at Blackfriars is the machinery for any kind of scenery and for daring celestial flights. But you must go back to Bankside for cannon fire and fireworks and booming of bass voices.

The end of London's wall at the bank, River Fleet pouring sluggish water into the Thames.

Next Bridewell Palace, whose stones include those of Montfichet's Norman castle. Bridewell rebuilt by Henry to house Charles V in splendor. But the Emperor preferred Blackfriars, and put his company and retainers in Bridewell. Its two court-yards and apartments now serving as a hospital, workhouse, prison, and a little Bedlam for fools and mad. So many these days that Bedlam will burst like a windy corpse wrapped in tight lead.

Almost a tavern for the district; for with the ancient sanctuary rights still reserved at Blackfriars and Whitefriars on either side, the place would soon be a new Bedlam if bishops and judges still lived there. Sign of the Stark Bedlamite, Bare-Arsed. . . .

It was this wildness and the stink of muddy lanes and the river rising by the moon in January and February (you could float a fair-size wherry in the hall, then plant a crop in the mud left behind when the river withdrew to its course) made Kings Henry and Edward give over Bridewell and Savoy Palace as well to charity.

Look left and south now to see, already behind as we cling close to the north bank, the landing of Paris Garden stairs leading up from the river. And near there the theater called The Swan.

Then, as the bank begins to bend south and west, that wide space of low ground, Lambeth Marsh, crossed by the track of the Roman road to New Haven. Tops and towers of Lambeth Palace.

Nearer to hand, rowing close by the bank now, is Whitefriars. Once friary of Carmelites, the brick now broken and repaired into lodgings for gentlemen of the Court. And the private playhouse, as in Blackfriars, there for pleasure.

Pleasures of Whitefriars are dimmed by the site. Lower and just below the terraces of Temple Garden, Whitefriars suffers from damp and fog and flooding. And in the press and crowd of old buildings the privilege of sanctuary has gathered an assembly of rogues of every kind. There are more alehouses and taverns than dwellings. By pitch dark the shouting and singing and tumult can guide a man here as safe as any burning beacon.

From one of these taverns, in the early days of James' rule, two servants of the Scots Lord Sanquhar waited to follow the English fencing master, John Turner, to his house and to waylay him. Not with sword and dagger. For John Turner, though drunk as a wheelbarrow, could have carved them up like capons. No, they murdered him with pistols.

They were quickly found and taken. Confessed they were paid by Sanquhar. Who had by accident lost an eye, and with it, he imagined, his honor, in practice with Turner.

A great scandal, then; for the English were much outraged at the swarm of Scots nobility who had come down, like a flock of hungry corbies, upon them.

"The beggars have come to town," the London rhyme went. "Some in rags and some in tags. And some in velvet gowns."

And all the skeptical-minded, meaning every man jack and knave in London and Westminster, waiting to see what action the King would take.

The King, weary of the Scotsman and needing a bone to throw to English pride, gave Sanquhar over to English law. Whereupon all learned a thing or two.

Lord Sanquhar learned he might hold title in Scotland, but none in England. He stood trial as Robert Crichton, to hang as a common felon.

And the King learned that his gesture was not taken as a generous gift but a right.

And the English learned that the King would let a man of his own hang if the death served a turn.

What James had not learned then—and who could learn it unless it was already part of the marrow of his bones?—was the paradoxical nature of Englishmen. Who would not, will not, cannot be reasonably pleased. They might have been half pleased by clemency. For no man but a savage brute is a steadfast opponent to mercy, the more so since mercy is the King's right. And, curious, though muttering against his mercy, they might have begun to love him more. For he would have confirmed their doubts and skepticism.

To flatter a man's worst opinion of yourself may be an end to distrust, if not the beginning of friendship.

They might have honored, even as they professed contempt for it, the common humanity which will sometimes permit a man to ignore principles and policy out of loyalty to old friends.

The English are most difficult for strangers to understand.

The trick being that at bare-arse bottom they are single- and simple-minded.

Poor James, he will die without knowing the English are easy to please. . . .

Now here are Temple Gardens, sloping down toward the bank. With the water gate of Temple Stairs ahead. Where a few scholars in gowns are calling for watermen.

Why, come aboard this barge, young gentlemen. We are for Westminster, where you may learn some law not taught in readings and moots. Come join us at Westminster Hall, where a suit may hang for half a year before a half-hour's hanging at Tyburn will end it. . . .

Temple Stairs, where so many times he has stepped to shore to walk up the lane to Middle Temple. Where, for a time, scholar or no, he kept commons regular, even attended readings and moots when he could not avoid it. But was never called by the benchers to be a barrister.

Now thinks he would willingly bid his present companions farewell to walk up that lane and turn in at the gate with the arms of Cardinal Wolsey above it and, on the sides, the arms of Middle Temple, a red cross on a white ground with an image of the Paschal Lamb center. Arms of the Knights Templars.

The Christmas revels, commencing with learned benchers and judges and the Lord Chancellor of England himself, are led by the Master of Revels, to dance three times around a smoky sea coal fire.

And we drank deep, and at Middle Temple there was more playing at dice than any tavern in London. With London on the one side and the Court upon the other a young man need not stir far to divert himself.

A most pleasant place to be for a time. Unless, like Edward

Coke, of Inner Temple, you must chain yourself to a seat, as rarest volumes are locked and chained, and squint yourself half blind in study.

Wonder now, those years ago at Winchester, whether Coke was lightly pricked by one oblique dart—"Is it not strange for me to make myself Robin Hood or Kett or Jack Cade?" Coke must have cursed Jack Cade one thousand times over. Having found the trace of his crude hand in many blank spaces. For that traitor hated all lawyers. And when his men came to London they prowled the Temple and the lawyers' chambers and houses, burning every piece of paper they could find.

Old Coke in his studying must forever picture flames and fountains of smoke rising up to the sky. And, hidden in that smoke, a multitude of lost words.

Was it Cade or Wat Tyler? No matter. All traitors play mischief with the law. Yet, Sir Edward, the law is always the victor. Finding a precedent for even these.

Arms rightly taken by Middle Temple, for we alone of the Inns preserve the order of those military monks and dine, as they did, with the benchers at the raised table like knights, barristers ranked as brothers, and those who merely keep commons as novices. Their ancient cow horn still calls to dinner. And we gather to dine in the hall, newest and finest of all the Inns. High and wide, all strutted with beams of best oak and gilded pendants. Oak paneling all around, and those panels glittering with arms and devices of famous men. Four large windows all around, glazed and decorated and one larger one stained, as it were, with the arms of men from here who have been Chief Justices of England.

Not so rich, nor so crowded, as Inner Temple. And, Lord,

we were strict with rules and fines and observances! Must never fail in attendance at chapel. Must not wear more than three weeks of beard. Must ever be seen in the sad-colored gown with more pleats in the back than the wrinkles of Medusa. Must wear no silver buckles or velvet caps, boots or spurs, silk or furs or great ruffs and such. Though at Middle Temple we were permitted both sword and dagger.

I would willingly walk there now. Though I fear the porter would not admit me, not even to serve as a washpot.

If strict in observance of rules, we were equally exact in our pleasures. Especially in customs of revels at All Hallow's Eve, Ascension, Candlemass, and, most fully, every night from Christmas Eve to Twelfth Night.

Now they have passed by unseen Temple Bar and are alongside the liberty of the duchy of Lancaster.

Here begins a splendid row of palaces, built along the river. Each with landing place and water gate, high-arched and ornamented. Each with gardens and muster of buildings and outbuildings. Each holding space between the strand and the river.

First Essex House—once Leicester House and before that the place of the Bishop of Exeter; now called after the rash Earl who rallied his men to go forth from here, then sadly returned to end this farce of rebellion. All in a day's work.

Next comes Arundel House, built of and upon the palace of the bishops of Bath. Much repaired and amended by the young Earl as a place to contain his treasure of paintings and strange sculptured figures of unpainted stone.

Has he returned from Italy yet? He was a friend and may be yet, though he has lost his investment in the Guiana venture. . . .

[217]

Newer built, in trim, symmetrical Italian fashion, the stones of Somerset House. Not so high—the odd old towers of Burghley House behind it seem to sit upon the roof of this one—it is spacious enough to have needed the grounds once accorded to two bishops, Chester and Worcester. Its prospect is toward the river and the south, not being built Janus-faced like the others of this row.

The King has given it to Queen Anne, and all are commanded now to call it Denmark House. But many forget the new name. The Queen herself, out of forgetfulness or modesty or both, calls it by the old name.

And here's the Savoy, the hospital built into the shell and ruins of the palace of John of Gaunt, once looted and pillaged and burnt by Wat Tyler's men.

At Ivy Bridge is Robert Cecil's house, which some call Salisbury for his title, newest built of all along this row. Fine brickwork and timber and a wonder of windows.

And each and all of these, excepting, of course, the Savoy, if not new-built, then all rebuilt and repaired and furnished in the finest fashion. With tapestry for the walls, paintings and portraits and carved figures. Kingly displays of plate and jewels and curiosities. All furniture of fine wood and veneer and inlay; turkey carpets enough to clothe half of London's poor. Plastered ceilings and painted and gilded timbers. With least sunlight or lighting of candles, these rooms spring to life and dance with color as if to music, composed not of notes and harmonies, but of the colors of the rainbow.

Wide stairways made for easy, proud walking. Heavy and solid as ship timbers with their rich-carved banisters and newel posts.

Floors strewn with clean fresh rushes and the rushes scented with herbs—saffron, rosemary, meadowsweet—to sweeten the air.

Places created for feasts and dancing, music and singing, and late hours with cards and nuts and fruits and good wine.

Each made to represent the image of earthly paradise, salute to, symbol of lost Eden. In keeping with which image, each has its enclosed garden with the trees and flowers, fruits and herbs of all England and half the world growing, well tended there. Each with paths and mazes of hedges, its sundials and figures and fountains and ponds, secret *jets d'eau* for laughter's sake.

Stroke by stroke, even and steady, the oars rise, dip, pull, rise, and feather again. Moving in concord together. Moving to another music of time.

Two times are a counterpoint. His own, a lifetime in little, a walk and a turn in the gallery of his mind. And the future sits silent beside him, written upon the faces, set like masks, of Apsley and Wilson.

And even as oars mark time, there is the sum of the time of the bargemen, looking past him, back toward the dwindling tops of the Tower and the shrinking bridge. Pulling strong together as they ride with the still rising time of the tide and against the time of the river's flowing. As they stroke and pull they are the inhabitants of past and future. Or perhaps they think nothing at all, feeling only strain of sinew and muscle, fresh sweat on their faces.

Stroke by stroke they are easing past the water gate and Durham House. Which—and *that's* another time indeed—was his.

Outwardly built in the fashion of castles, for the Bishop, with round towers, turrets, and battlemented plain walls of gray stone. And Ralegh kept it that way. His concession to fashion being the marble arch in bastard Italian style at the water gate. Kept the face and expression of Durham House as he found it.

Because it pleased him. And also because he enjoyed the contrast with the others along the row. At a great distance, from any direction, his house, just within bounds of Westminster, would, by contrast, catch the eye.

And kept it so, as well, for the sake of increasing the pleasures of surprise. For behind those walls he ripped out and gutted the innards and spent a fortune in building and furnishing until, in truth, nothing except the chambers of the Queen shone so bright or bold.

Outside a kind of disguise. Within the secret was revealed with stunning surprise and delight. Those stones of Durham House told nothing. Just as an oak or cedar chest, locked and dusty, tells nothing of what it may contain—a king's ransom in treasure, or rags and tatters and broken things.

Likewise the garden. Where he planted and kept strange fruits and flowers, shrubs and trees from all the world. His covered and carefully tended orange trees gave good fruit. And one was a marvel, a single tree growing oranges and lemons and limes and all their sweet kin, hanging like many-colored baubles there.

Bess never liked Durham House. Too damp for her there. Too close to Court, from which she was barred.

Yet he spent happy hours alone in the small turret which he had remade into a kind of shore cabin, with books and charts, paper and pen and instruments, and a powerful eye-glass to enjoy a long view of the river and a closer look at the heavens by night.

Perhaps that was the reason Durham House made Bess unhappy. With one sweep of a glass from the turret he could see the ships coming and going. She would feel him catching a seafarer's itch to be off again.

In his best days he lived there lordly, with a host of good-weather friends, and some true ones as well. Had forty serving men to wear his colors and arms. Which was more men, twice over, than the warders of the Tower.

Well, thanks to the wheel of Fortune and the King's whim, it belongs to the bishops of Durham again. Thanks to Robert Cecil's speculations, the New Exchange now stands on part of the grounds.

Comes now York House, home of lord keepers and lord chancellors. And again the residence, after a sojourn in the wilderness, of Sir Francis Bacon.

At last, here is Whitehall. Spacious palace and buildings. Splendid tower of the chapel rising. Largest of palaces in Christendom, they say. And it will be larger by far if Mr. Inigo Jones has his way and the King finds the money to humor the builder.

The late Queen loved this place in its season. There were festive times here all through her reign. Even into the fading twilight.

Sound the trumpets to announce the feast. For she loved the tones of the trumpet. Games in the gardens. And some of them were innocent enough. Sport in the afternoon—bowling and fencing, fortunes wagered on the bounce of a tennis ball. Masques and pageants, feasts in the old banquet house. Coming and going, with flourish and ruffles, great ones from all the world. Cards and dancing and music and long walking in the gallery in the evening and in times of bad weather. What a wonder it had been!

Memory of Christmas Revels there, like a string of prayer beads, waking dreams interrupted only by real ones. And a young man seldom need sleep alone.

Giving of gifts to the Queen upon Twelfth Night. All in the Court, from Lord Chancellor and Keeper of the Great Seal to lowliest servant, striving to catch her eye and win approval with the finest gift they could, each exceeding his means. Tables groaning with the weight of gifts and the Queen, like a child, laughing and touching and counting. Never forgetting the giver, for good or ill.

The Queen recovered her fire that Twelfth Night at the end of the century. Twelfth Night was the last night of Revels in those days. James, they say, will one day soon have to abolish Lent to prolong Revels until Easter.

Twelfth Night in Whitehall Palace the whole Court was there and likewise two most distinguished strangers. A befurred and thick-bearded Muscovite lord, a man disguised as a bear, come to be the new Ambassador. The other, young and trim, slim of waist, broad of shoulder, tuned and well-turned of leg, dressed like a prince and perfectly tailored, an Italian, the Duke of Bracciano. He brought some light back into her eyes.

After a feast, they gathered in the hall to see a play by William Shakespeare. Who, if he lacked the learning and thunder of Kit Marlowe or the careful, calloused hands of Ben Jonson, had sweetness in his lines, could make a scene fit like a shoe or a glove, and could always turn a phrase as easy as he turned a profit. He could shake the platform with clowns and heroes and villains. Mr. Shakespeare, though solemn and correct, was ambitious. When he walked the boards as an actor, he played kings.

Twelfth Night, the comedy was called, and the Queen was much pleased by the quick turns of plot and the satirical thrusts. She led the laughter and applause.

A year later and the dark began to reclaim title to her eyes. World turned and dimmed too. Laughter that leaves a bitter aftertaste was the fashion. Ralegh returned to Middle Temple for the Revels and saw another play by Shakespeare. Ever a vane to the winds of fashion, the poet gave the scholars a feast of the fare they enjoyed, a play called *Troilus and Cressida,* all composed of follies of war and lechery.

And they laughed at the chaos and barbarism just beyond them, howling outside walls as thin and frail as an eggshell. . . .

Now at last a cluster of houses, cheek by jowl along the smooth bank, behind whose roofs tower the shadowy buildings of the Abbey and the palace of Westminster. And there . . . there is the incomparable high roof of Westminster Hall.

At the landing there are a pair of royal bargemen, clad in proper blue, waiting to take hold and tie the barge fast there. Behind and above them, on the flight of stairs which leads from the landing to the gate in the wall of houses, there are two armed yeomen of the Guard. These are not so tall as the yeomen were when he was their Captain and his size was the measure for the Guard.

They had to scour all England then for giants and, rarest, for graceful giants who would not tangle their feet or trip over each other's partizans. . . .

"We are here," Wilson says.

[223]

And Apsley touches his arm lightly, repeating: "We are here, sir."

"Such a short time," Ralegh says. "My brain was busy with idle thoughts. I scarcely noticed."

"May I ask what you were thinking of?" Apsley still touches his arm as if to direct him, to keep him from falling when he stands.

"I was thinking of the light in our late Queen's eyes, how light her eyes were, even to the last, when something made her happy. . . . You see how mad the thoughts of an old man may be."

"And why not remember that if it pleases you?"

"Because we deceive ourselves," Ralegh says to him. "The last of that light is gone."

The coxswain eases the barge alongside the landing. Not so much as a rocking of it as oars go up high and blue-clad bargemen loop lines to make it fast. The yeomen begin to descend the stairs, coming toward them.

Ralegh stands up, so quick that Apsley's hand falls away. "I shall lead on. I know the way."

One hop and he's over the benches of the oarsmen and stands on the stones of the landing, eyeing the advancing yeomen, then turning back to the barge, leaning upon the walking stick, offering his hands as the gentlemen scramble out of the barge.

As if he were there to welcome them.

Across the landing, flanked by the brace of yeomen, they begin to climb marble stairs. Moving slow to keep to the rhythm of a limping man, while faces at the windows of houses and others behind them, riding the Thames, watch all this. And going under an archway, its figures and words of stone blurred by seasons, and into the large bare stretch of yard leading toward Westminster Hall.

Symmetrical, the hall guarded by two square-shaped towers and the roof rising steep above all, reaching a peak in a pendant where a weather vane turns in search of the breeze, the entrance-way and above it the huge arched window, wait for them.

From the clock tower Great Tom booms the hour. Announcing nine o'clock of a Wednesday morning in the Michaelmas Term of the Law, and, as it happens, the feast day of Saints Simon and Jude.

None of the courts of Westminster will be in session. Not the usual crowd of lawyers and clients, witnesses, servants, the idle and curious, to witness the session at King's Bench.

Someone has planned it so, but there is a flaw in the planning.

[225]

Everyone knows there will be no sessions in the courts today. And so an assembling of judges, lawyers, clerks, servants, and others for King's Bench will have wakened curiosity.

Easier for a fair woman to go stark naked and unnoticed at Bartholomew Fair than for such a secret to be preserved. There is already a little crowd off the streets near the entrance to the hall.

Peter Rush has been waiting, standing just within the entrance. He has seen to the care of the horses and he has assisted Yelverton to robe himself in an upper tiring chamber. Went down then to the porch and planted himself to be sure of a place. Knowing that once Walter Ralegh is seen disembarking at the landing, word will flare like flame in kindling.

But it is late and nothing has happened. He sees two yeomen and some officers coming. Whoever it may be he does not recognize. An old felon, no doubt, a man bent with a walking stick, wild white hair, gray beard. Some country man who has seen better days. Judging by his heavy wrinkled mud-stained hose, old-fashioned breeches of faded tawny, ill-fitting doublet with gaps and with buttons missing, brown leather jerkin and no cloak and no cover for his head. Some poor fellow whom Fortune has ill used.

Peter Rush almost turns away before he sees the eyes of the man. Then he cannot believe his own.

Peter Rush, once a servant in the Court of the Queen, who has seen so many come and go, knows this is the man he has been waiting for. But how sadly altered. . . .

Ralegh has paused a moment, breathing, leaning on his stick. He looks into the eyes of Peter Rush and smiles.

Peter fumbles in the leather purse clipped to his waist. Steps past the yeoman, holding a comb.

[226]

"Oh, Sir Walter," he says. "Let me comb your hair."

"Let them comb it that mean to have it!" Ralegh snaps, brushing away his hands.

Someone behind them at the entrance murmurs the name. Then it is shouted in the yard.

"It is Sir Walter Ralegh, brought from the Tower!"

Running feet on the gravel. A growing ring of staring faces. The yeomen and the officers move closer.

Ralegh puts his hand on Peter Rush's shoulder.

"Peter Rush," he says, "I remember you well."

"We have both seen better days, sir."

"Do you know, Peter, if there is any plaster which will put on a man's head again once he's lost it?"

Peter Rush removes his own woolen cloak and places it around Ralegh's shoulders.

"It's bitter cold in the hall."

"I thank you. . . ."

They move on, followed by a crowd, leaving Peter Rush standing there thinking. Suddenly he laughs out loud.

"What ails thee, Peter?"

That is John Greene, servant to one of the judges. A big bluff fellow nibbling from a basket of hot chestnuts.

"I can't help laughing, John," Peter says. "I spent a full hour this morning helping my master dress up for this occasion."

"And?"

"And the old Fox has foxed them again."

"Devil take them all!" John says, offering him chestnuts.

They enter the port of the hall, passing beneath clock and bell over the entry. Pause there a moment while Ralegh rests, catching his breath and exchanging words with a servant who recognizes him.

[227]

They stand waiting upon Ralegh while he speaks with the servant, the servant looking every inch his superior. On each side of the entrance port are stairways ascending, one to the Court of Exchequer, the other to the Duchy Chamber and Star Chamber.

Now they are moving again into and down the length of the oldest, largest hall of this kingdom. Begun by the son of the Conqueror, but built by Richard II. Who then lived to be deposed here. Once, long ago, the pride of kings. Where Christmas feasts and the Revels were held. Where often there was dancing and, upon occasion, even tennis. And once in a flood lords and courtiers played at rowing boats in this place.

Now used for feasts and such no more except at Coronation.

Now the palace and apartments around it are in much neglect; the Great Hall is reserved for practical affairs of state. Above are the places for the Parliament, Lords and Commons—the Commons meets in cramped St. Stephen's Chapel—and various courts of law. Below lies the cellar, called "Hell." But the hall is wholly given over, during four terms, to the law. Chancery and Common Pleas on either side near the port and entry.

They go down the length of the hall. Nearly a hundred yards in length and full twenty yards across. And so high that the celebrated oaken ceiling is lost in gloom.

Down the length of the hall, crackling over dry, tired rushes as they move toward the partly screened southeast corner and its shining marker—a wide white marble bench. Which is used by kings at the feast of Coronation and gives to this court of law its name.

Going past the ascending stairway that leads up to St. Stephen's.

[228]

Going past the stairs that rise to the White Hall and to the Court of Wards and Liveries and to the Court of Requests.

Halting to face the marble bench. Heavy trestle tables for the judges and lawyers. They wear their outdoor hats, and cloaks and furs are worn over their robes against the cold. Some sniff at nosegays to stifle the stink of rushes.

Ralegh stands facing the judges, leaning on his staff, silent, expressionless, as Lord Lieutenant Apsley, upon receipt of the writ of *habeas corpus,* which he studies with care, formally delivers over his charge. Ralegh stands not listening but, with hooded eyes, studying the names and faces before him.

The King's in the country. Hunting again and with such passion for the chase that he may yet rid England of game before he dies.

Ralegh sees no one here who might be the King in any costume, behind any beard.

Sir Henry Yelverton, King's Attorney General. Stout, bluff and forthright. Eager for the King's favor. More caution than tact. A man in his early fifties, some ten years younger than Ralegh. Cambridge man and a scholar from Gray's Inn. Will be a judge one day, if he continues to please. If he learns to oil joints and curb tongue. His father was a good Parliament man. . . .

Sir Thomas Coventry, Solicitor General. A man of forty, friend to Yelverton. More moderation than zeal, more mercy than thunder. A good lawyer and a fair one. Plain speaker, but forceful and persuasive. Likely to be Attorney General soon. An Oxford man and member of Inner Temple.

And there are three puisne judges of King's Bench.

Only three? There should be four and also the Chief Justice if this hearing is to be valid.

Sir Robert Houghton, Norfolk man, a few years older than

[229]

Ralegh. In Parliament he stood for Norwich. Lincoln's Inn his school. Some say he is a good judge—prudent, learned, temperate. Bacon calls him a soft man, malleable, and easily persuaded to follow with the majority.

Sir John Croke, of Ralegh's age almost to the year. From Buckinghamshire and to law by way of Inner Temple. Ralegh remembers him from Parliament. He was Speaker of the House in '01. Dark-haired—it must be dyed now—heavy-browed, black-bearded, dark-complexioned. Known all his life as "a very black man."

Sir John Doderidge, close to his own age. *These lawyers live long!* A Westcountry man from Exeter. Oxford and Middle Temple, studying there when Ralegh did. Knew him there and in Parliament also. Bacon has said he pleads a case straight and well "like a good archer." Strong supporter of the King and ready and willing, unlike many judges, to give opinions in secret. They call him "The Sleeping Judge" because he closes his eyes when hearing a case.

Sir Henry Montagu, Chief Justice of King's Bench. His grandfather, Sir Edward, was Chief Justice also. Henry Montagu's a Cambridge man, studied at Middle Temple. Ten years younger than Ralegh. Knighted, together with the multitudes, by James in the first year of his reign. Resolute and vigorous, yet at ease. Replaced Coke when Coke fell in '16. He holds the key to what will happen here.

Among other worthies present Ralegh spies George Abbot, whom James made Bishop of London and then to the amazement of all—most especially to elegant Lancelot Andrews, who thought himself sure to be chosen—Archbishop of Canterbury. Holds an uneasy favor with James. A man of not much moderation and less tact. Has opposed the Spanish Match too persuasively.

Spots also James Hay, Viscount Doncaster. Scotsman who came down to England as the King's favorite. But always his own man. Lavish in taste and dress, he nevertheless has shown no signs of gnawing ambition. Has served the King well and honestly, though often at variance with policy and willing to say so. He is as strong opposed to Spain as Ralegh. Hay will give the King a true report of these proceedings.

Someone has brought a stool. He nods and, as he sits, sees Francis Bacon, Lord Chancellor, taking his place on the King's marble bench. Where, except for the King, only the Lord Chancellor may sit.

Sir Henry Yelverton is on his feet to speak for the Crown. Gripping his stick, Ralegh swallows an urge to smile. Beneath his loose flowing robes Yelverton shines, barbered and dressed for dancing and a masque. Somehow foolish in all his splendor. Seems troubled as well. His round face wrinkled with a frown.

"I shall call upon the clerk of the Crown, Mr. Fanshaw, to read from the conviction delivered against Sir Walter Ralegh at Winchester. It has been fifteen years since then and this man, the prisoner, has been for fifteen years convicted of treason and sentenced to death. The King, His Majesty, out of his abundant grace, has been pleased to show mercy to him until now. Now justice calls to him for execution."

Yelverton has moved closer. Stands silent a moment, eyeing him. One hand nervously touches links of the heavy gold chain and medallion the Attorney General wears. He shakes his head and turns back to face the judges of the court, raising his voice.

"Sir Walter Ralegh has been a statesman and a man who, in

[231]

regard to his parts and quality, is much to be pitied now. He has been as a star at which all the world has gazed. But stars may fall. . . . Nay, they *must* fall when they trouble the sphere wherein they abide!"

He pauses again, gestures toward Ralegh. Then steps to the judges at the table. His voice lower now, words quick, flat, routine.

"It is therefore His Majesty's pleasure now to call for the execution of this former judgment against this prisoner. And I now ask order for the same."

Not looking back at Ralegh, he returns to his place. The clerk reads the words of the judgment at Winchester.

Chief Justice Montagu asks the prisoner to hold up his right hand, signifying that he had heard and understood the judgment. He does so.

"Now then," Montagu continues, "what says the prisoner why the execution of this judgment should not be awarded against him?"

Ralegh rises and limps toward the table. Halts and leans on his stick.

"My lords, my voice has grown weak from illness and on account of the ague that troubles me even now. Therefore, I should like to ask you for the relief of pen and ink so that I may answer."

Montagu shakes his head.

"You are audible enough. We can hear you."

"Very well."

"Proceed, if you please."

"My lords, I hope and trust that this judgment of death I received many years ago will not now be strained to take away my life. In His Majesty's commission for my late voyage, my life was implied to be restored. I was given the power of life and death over others. Surely under law my pardon and restoration was implicit. I undertook that voyage to the honor of the King to enrich this kingdom with gold. If the voyage miscarried . . ."

"Whatever you say concerning the voyage is not to the purpose of this hearing," Montagu says.

They wait for him to speak. For a time, brief enough but silence is long, he stands and stares at them, moving his head slowly to look into the eyes of each of the judges, coming back then to rest a stare upon Montagu. His left hand ruffles his white hair. Someone coughs.

"So be it, then," Ralegh says.

"I shall, however, speak touching upon your commission from His Majesty," Montagu says.

Ralegh waits silent.

"The King's commission can be of no service to you," Montagu continues. "For treason can never be pardoned by implication. That is the law. You must, then, say something else to the purpose. Otherwise we shall have to proceed with the order for execution."

"It is apparent, my lords, that nothing whatever I can offer in my own justification will be to the purpose. Therefore I submit myself to the judgment and put myself wholly upon the King's mercy."

There is a stirring at the table. No one expected this to come so swiftly.

"There is wisdom in your submission," Montagu says, after a moment.

"Yet I do honestly hope," Ralegh adds, "that the King will take compassion upon me, concerning this judgment rendered so long ago. His Majesty was of the opinion that I received more

[233]

hard usage than justice that day. And there are some here present who could bear witness to the truth of that."

"You have been as a dead man to law for fifteen years," Montagu answers. "The King, in his mercy, has spared you all that time. And it might seem heavy if now, without some reason or provocation, the sentence of death is to be exercised in cold blood. But this is not so. You understand full well how your new offenses have stirred up and wakened His Majesty's justice to revive the former sentence."

Ralegh nods and waits for Montagu to continue.

"I know that you have been valiant and wise in the past," he says. "And I doubt not that you retain those virtues. Now you shall have occasion to use them. In the past your faith was questioned, but I am resolved that you are a good Christian. Your *History of the World,* an admirable work, is the witness to that."

Nevertheless, in spite of his intentions, Chief Justice Montagu finds himself proceeding to lecture Ralegh upon the subjects of sorrow and the fear of death. Ralegh stands listening, attentive, humble, but stonefaced.

It is Sir Henry Yelverton who is wondering what it is about Ralegh which can make an otherwise intelligent and politic judge turn into a tendentious, tongue-wagging fool. It is as if the judges spoke to relieve themselves. As men snatched and saved from peril may babble nonsense, the sound of their voices serving to prove to doubtful mind and body that peril is past. Exactly . . . But what peril had old Popham felt? True enough, on his deathbed he asked forgiveness for his part in that first trial.

Montagu, however, has no such feeling. This hearing has been brief beyond anticipation. The others must be as surprised as

[234]

Henry Yelverton. Must feel, too, a slight sense of disappointment. Like him, they prepared themselves, were ready for everything. Except what has happened. . . .

Therefore—Yelverton's mind impatient to grasp at a conclusion—there is a similarity in difference. Both times Ralegh astonished his antagonists. Each time may be thought of as a victory for him. The execution of judgment, the passing of sentence, which ought to be the triumph of the law, becoming someway diminished in importance, an irrelevant epilogue to a play of which he, the prisoner, is author.

What else can a judge do, stunned by the feeling of impotence, but plead his own case?

Ralegh stands and listens without expression. Patient and knowing. Like a kind father hearing out a tedious story told by a child.

Yelverton bends his head as if to examine papers and covers a smile with his hand.

For he thinks he sees the grotesque beauty of it. The Fox has tricked them again and especially the King. In this, the last act, he has made his entrance in most pitiable condition—shabby, ill, and old. No one who has seen him today can fail to pity him. No one can but wonder what purpose the death of this man can serve to either state or King. All the weight and power, glory and pomp of the kingdom are ranged against one frail old man. Were he guilty of a thousand heinous crimes, it would be difficult to rejoice at the victory of justice.

Perhaps the word of this, or some sense of it, will go to the King at his hunting. Lord Chancellor Bacon will no doubt send report. It would be like James Hay to leave this hall and mount a horse and ride to the King.

It is possible, Yelverton thinks, that this is Ralegh's stratagem.

[235]

Report of the hearing, together with appeals from friends in high places, might cajole or frighten the King into another act of mercy. Yelverton has already learned of petitions sent from Lord Carew, from the Bishop of Winchester, from the Spanish Dominicans, who fear any Jesuitical triumph, and from Queen Anne. There will be others.

Ralegh will lose his life or he will not. Let us assume the King is unmoved. Then he will go to his death as he is now, a poor harmless wretch. And it will do the King no credit.

Ralegh pleads a case much like a lawyer, Yelverton thinks. But not with words this time so much as with his life, with his body and soul. And here is a dimension of freedom which staggers the mind. It is, indeed, as if he were a star, moving to a different music, ruled by other laws than ours.

Quite suddenly Henry Yelverton is pleased with himself, for he believes at last that he has found the keys to the man.

Montagu has finished his peroration, urging wisdom and courage. He has stated that execution is granted.

Ralegh moves to speak, but before he does, Lord Chancellor Bacon is on his feet, coming down from the marble bench, two of his young servants assisting him with his robes. He carries parchment, the seal of the kingdom showing on it. He bends close to Montagu to whisper. Montagu examines the papers, then passes them to the clerk. Mr. Fanshaw reads them before rising. Judges and worthies whisper together.

Ralegh stands erect and expressionless. No longer leans on the walking stick.

"Hear what our gracious majesty does command," Mr. Fanshaw intones. "Herein, signed, and sealed on this date at Westminster, His Majesty, dispensing of the manner of execution according to the former judgment and releasing the prisoner of

[236]

same, that is, to be hanged, drawn, and quartered, says: 'Our pleasure is, instead thereof, to have the head only of the said Sir Walter Ralegh cut off, at or within our palace of Westminster, commanding the Chancellor hereupon to direct two several writs under the great seal; one to the Lieutenant of the Tower, or his deputy, for the delivery of the said Sir Walter Ralegh to the sheriffs of Middlesex at the said palace of Westminster; and the other to the said sheriffs for the receiving of the said Sir Walter Ralegh from the said Lieutenant, and for executing him there; for which this is to be his warrant and discharge, against us, our heirs and successors forever.'"

Chief Justice Montagu asks the prisoner if he has understood.

Yelverton thinking that the King's clerks were in such a haste to write this down for the King's signature before he departed that it is a wonder that any man could understand it.

Ralegh raises his right hand.

"Let the record show that the said Sir Walter Ralegh has heard and understood the pleasure of His Majesty," he says.

Some at the table, and others who have gathered around to hear, chuckle at this sally, but Montagu silences them with a cold glare.

"My lords," Ralegh says, his voice stronger now. "I have some requests to make and something more to say, if I may be heard."

"You may speak."

"I shall be as brief as can be, for I assume that many here present intend to go their several ways to dinner. And indeed I confess that I look forward to my dinner today, since it seems likely to be my last one."

"Take as much time as you need."

"I hope and trust and most earnestly desire that this execution shall not take place suddenly today. For I have something

[237]

yet to do, something in the discharge of my own conscience, something to satisfy His Majesty, and something in which to satisfy the world."

"It would appear to be the King's pleasure that you shall die tomorrow," Montagu says. "For this document is so dated."

"I thank your lordships, then. For I need time before my execution to settle both my affairs and my mind more than they are at this moment. For, as I say, I have much to do for the sake of my reputation, my conscience, and my loyalty. And I beseech the favor of pen and ink and paper, so that I may express myself and, as well, that I may discharge myself of some trust of worldly matters that were put in me. . . ."

Yelverton thinking that all this is intended for the King. He need not have asked the judges for the privilege of pen and ink and paper. He wants the King to know he will be busy between now and the time of his death.

"My lords, I crave not to gain one minute of life, for now that I am old, sickly, and in disgrace, and certain to go to my death, life is wearisome to me. . . ."

That the King may further know that what he takes away is of small value to its owner and therefore this punishment is light. . . .

"And I do lastly humbly beseech your lordships that when I come to die, I may have leave to speak freely at my farewell, to satisfy the world only in this, that I was ever loyal to the King and ever a true lover of the commonwealth. For this I will seal with my blood. . . ."

That the King may be reminded that a man upon the scaffold always has the last word before the ax falls. . . .

"I thank your lordships and His Majesty that I shall die here

[238]

in the open air of Westminster and not within the walls of the Tower. . . ."

That the King may be aware that, Lord Mayor's Day or no, an execution at Westminster will be public. . . .

"My lords, I bid you farewell, craving your prayers for the mercy of God."

He bows his head, his lips moving as if in silent prayer. Then turns and moves toward Lieutenant Apsley.

"It appears, Lieutenant Apsley, that you are now free and clear of the burden of me," he says. "Since I am not to return to the Tower with you, will it please you to dine with me here?"

Apsley is hesitant. "I thank you . . . I fear that I . . ."

"Be my guest as I have been yours. A man must eat dinner. I promise you the best fare I can provide."

"I am grateful, sir, but . . ."

"Good then. Show your gratitude by joining me and eating hearty."

He turns his back to Apsley, calling out, "Now then, where are the good sheriffs of Middlesex?"

Judges and worthies are mounting the stairs to the upper chambers. Yelverton starts to follow them, hesitates, then pushes through the crowd to where Ralegh stands talking with Apsley and the sheriffs. He must say something, if only to pray his forgiveness and to wish him the mercy and love of God.

Before he can speak, Ralegh faces him and is talking.

"That was a nice figure of speech, Mr. Attorney, the simile of a falling star. For a moment I thought I heard the silver voice of your late father."

Yelverton flushes, clears his throat. Before he can answer anything, Ralegh continues.

"I would add something," he says. "A star in the firmament,

however bright it may be, is but one of many. We look and behold it in its proper place, and that is sufficient. But mark this: whenever a star falls, it burns so bright it dazzles the eyes of the world."

"I wish you well, sir," Yelverton says. "May God and His Majesty have mercy."

"Amen to that."

Ralegh strips off the woolen cloak and hands it to Yelverton.

"Pray return this to your man, Peter, and thank him for the use of it."

Yelverton nods and takes it. Together with the walking stick which Ralegh gives him.

"Farewell, Mr. Attorney. And may God and His Majesty show mercy to you, too."

Ralegh turns to Apsley and the sheriffs, leaving Sir Henry Yelverton burdened with a cloak and a crude walking stick. Yelverton looks at the stick a moment, then looks up again to see the tall man striding out of the hall with the officers. Not the least sign of a limp now.

Sir Henry Yelverton shakes his head and smiles.

He is thinking that in this strange year of three comets, signs which have people talking of the end of the world, he could not, indeed, have found a more telling figure of speech.

They are leading him toward the old gatehouse. As he expected. Indeed, moments after the judgment, he hired messengers to carry the news to Bess, to servants, and friends.

He has invited Apsley and the sheriffs to join him at dinner. Poor gentlemen, the King has added to their burdens. For this is their last day in office. Tomorrow, upon Lord Mayor's Day, two new gentlemen selected as sheriffs will be sworn in here at

Westminster. There must be some doubt as to which of the four will legitimately hold the office when and if he is to be executed. They must prepare a scaffold in Old Palace Yard in haste. And be prepared to contend with a large crowd of people.

The King has been ill advised. Apparently his stratagem is for the pageants, processions, and festivities in the city to be honey to divert the flies. He must have forgotten that the ceremonies require the new Lord Mayor of London to come here to Westminster in the morning. And that event, even without the prologue of a state execution to attract them, will gather crowds in Old Palace Yard.

Coming out of the hall Ralegh sees a small crowd gathered outside already, and spies an old friend, Sir Hugh Beeston.

"Will you be there tomorrow morning?" Ralegh asks.

"You can count on it."

"Well," Ralegh says, glancing at the crowd, "you may be hard put to find a place. I fear you will have to shift for yourself. Thank God, I am sure of one."

Moving on then, taking his time, talking with Apsley and the sheriffs while the yeomen make way for them.

Here is a kinsman, Francis Thynne, a kind-hearted man with the shadow of a Puritan.

Ralegh greets his kinsman and invites him to dinner too.

"I promise you the best dinner that my money can buy," he says. "And money can work magic. No miracles, of course. If I could perform a miracle I would invite everyone here to share a basket of loaves and fishes."

Others laugh, but Francis looks pained.

"Do not try to carry it with too much bravery," Francis whispers. "Your enemies will take exception."

Ralegh puts his arm on his shoulder.

[241]

"Ah, Francis," he says, "this may be my last mirth in this world. Pray do not begrudge it to me. When I come to the sad parting you will see me grave enough."

Walking away, head high, not needing a walking stick. Has left it in the hands of Sir Henry Yelverton to do with what he will. A token, just as Yelverton gave him one—the figure of a falling star.

He will not think of Yelverton or figures of speech or the walking stick now. He is preoccupied with arrangements to be made for his quarters in the gatehouse, for dinner to be ordered for his guests. For everything that can be done to pass through this time with composure.

After that, after he has composed himself, there will be time for other things. There will be time. . . .

Not thinking of Yelverton now. But he did so during the hearing. Listening and not listening.

Could read Henry Yelverton's face. Yelverton was astonished. What Yelverton saw was a ragged, disheveled, sickly, pitiable man. Who had been always, even in disgrace, among the brightest, and now was diminished to least luster.

Men of the world, the judges and lawyers and other worthies present, could not be certain whether this was only another stratagem of the Fox. Since they could not determine this, they would do what they were compelled to, accepting it both ways at once. His appearance being, then, both crafty device and truth.

Truth or craft or both, he forced them to perform their duty with a reluctance, a muted reticence. Has any man ever been so quietly condemned?

In a larger sense, the cornered Fox was asserting the last

freedom left to him. He was left with a choice of style. He exercised that choice and caught them unaware.

In acting freely, he took nothing from them. No part of the plot, the fable, of which all, including himself, were a part. Excepting one thing: he took away the right to possess what they did not have any claim to except by his volition—the right to choose the manner in which he would meet judgment and bear defeat.

This is a small exception. But there are times when something just so small can render the astounded beholder speechless. Times when the simplest exercise of liberty can dazzle those who witness it.

So it was, then, with that man of the world, Sir Henry Yelverton.

Yelverton was forced to grasp for an appropriate convention. For lawyers as well as poets know there are moments of truth whose only true expression is in the conventional. And so he expressed himself, on behalf of the King and the law, with the figure of a falling star.

An image, it is true, from the old astronomy, already much questioned. No matter, though, about the science of the night. The truth of the figure is not in natural philosophy.

Sir Walter Ralegh has been as a star at which all the world has gazed. . . .

Indeed? That figure might have better suited the lamented Essex. Who sought and coveted admiration. And who died for it.

Yet Yelverton, seizing the handhold of convention, meant more than that. Meant also, by similitude, an alien and admirable creation, a nature of different fire, moving in time to tunes beyond reach and pitch of mortal ears. A dancer moving in

[243]

graceful motions to a music of concord and harmony. Dance and the harmony of the music being beyond common understanding. Subject to the same law which governs sticks and stones, snowflakes and raindrops, snails and whales, earth, air, fire, and water. Subject to the same law, yet likewise ruled by another law, much like that law which governs the motions and brightness of stars.

In one rhetorical stroke Yelverton placed the case of the King before this court. Saying, in effect, that though the common law of this nation was not easy to invoke to work Ralegh's ruin, the law of the sun could be summoned. The King, being the sun, brightest of stars.

Saying not that injustice is justified, but rather calling upon a justice above and beyond the power of the Court of King's Bench, though the exercise of it must come through the judgment of that court.

And thereby ending all argument and contention. Leaving the matter entirely in the hands of the King.

But, live or die, Ralegh has gained a marvelous new thing.

Sitting to hear the argument, standing to hear the judgment, Ralegh felt free as a falcon sent aloft. Though belled and bound to return to the wrist of his keeper, he was for that moment free and high-flying, sailing in the easy rolling sea of the air.

Thinking then: let these and all the world judge as they are able. To some a lunatic. To some pathetic. To some a fool. To some ridiculous, depending on a simple, foolish device to save himself. To some too subtle, a rebel against right order. For he has managed to make his death—if it comes—a sort of murder. To make his life—if mercy should be granted—a just reward.

Perhaps a few, if not Henry Yelverton, have moved beyond commonplace conclusions. Ralegh outfoxed enemies and surprised friends. Now the King is forced to act. If the King has planned this game to its very last trick, saving one final trump to be turned up and played, Ralegh has deprived him of the pleasure of playing that trump.

Live or die, he has deprived the King of some freedom.

To be a king in bondage is to be no king at all, even though those bonds are frail as a spider web.

Something else he has gained at the hearing. He came before them not in humility, but the image of a dishonored man. Seeming to welcome and embrace dishonor.

It is the eyes of this world which award honor or dishonor. The world can bestow honor or dishonor, or, can be indifferent to a man, but cannot control the indifference of the man himself. A single man's indifference shatters the power of the world to pass judgment.

Therefore, if the world is not to melt away in self-contempt, it, too, must act. Knowing, even as it does so, that any demonstration of spurned powers is ridiculous, the world must bestow honor or dishonor upon a man who has challenged both.

Just when Ralegh was able to renounce both honor and dishonor equally, false idols and strange gods, Sir Henry Yelverton, fumbling and finding an old figure of speech, awarded him more honor than he had ever held.

has been as a star at which all the world has gazed. . . .

Spoken in past tense to describe a lost condition. To make the most of his present condition of dishonor. In short, an equivocation by a good lawyer and a reasonable, politic man.

As if to say: *If he will have neither honor nor dishonor, then, by Almighty God in heaven, we shall award him here a measure of both. Let him live or die with that.*

But here is a satirical touch which pleases Ralegh. In a twinkling and a trice, all his spent life is brightened again with honor. As Christ on the Cross could, with a sentence, turn a thief into a saint, so with a few words Walter Ralegh could become a man of honor.

He can leave Bess and Carew that legacy of honor, not given when he sought for it, earned when he had renounced it.

As to the disgrace of his present condition, that is seemingly awarded too. But perhaps prematurely. For this—*a man much to be pitied now*—is within his power to build upon. Though honor is a castle in the clouds, it has been given to him and is his to do with as he pleases.

He walks away to be a prisoner in the gatehouse of Westminster, possessing at this moment more freedom than he has had in years.

He felt warmth, some gratitude toward Henry Yelverton. Therefore on impulse gave him the one thing he had to give—a servant's crude walking stick. Perhaps it will bring Yelverton luck, too.

He gave him a stout walking stick, feeling not so much that he did not need it as that Yelverton had forced *him* to walk out of the hall with all the swagger he could manage.

He has enjoyed a triumph over men and their schemes. Entered the hall as a sick old man. Has left, and in time for dinner.

Meanwhile, as Scripture says, a merry heart can work good medicine.

Part Three

For I have been a soldier, a courtier, and a seafaring man. And the temptations of the least of
these are able to overthrow a good mind and
a good man.

RALEGH—*Speech upon 29 October 1618*

1

Weather has turned foul. Pins and needles of rain. Wind
sweeps across Old Palace Yard to beat on the tiny panes of
the porter's lodge. Where Ralegh has been placed in the upper
chamber. Here he has more space and comfort than in either
of the prisons which flank the gatehouse, the one ecclesiastical
and the other common. Though neither of those is crowded
now. For he saw not one face, heard not one call or jeer
from the high, slit, barred windows as he came toward the
gatehouse. Came knowing he would not lie upon damp straw
in either of those places. For he still had a purse, with coins
saved as a squirrel hoards nuts, against this day. And the porter
would have occasion to supplement his meager wages, and such
pennies and farthings as he can glean from other prisoners in
his care, with gold.

He was ready to rattle and ring that purse like village church
bells at a Whitsun Ale. But the porter was prepared, having
known of his own good fortune before the ink of the King's
signature had been powdered dry on the documents.

Greeted Ralegh like an innkeeper meeting a guest. Led the

[249]

gentlemen all up to a large, low upper chamber, mumbling apologies for the accommodations. Which Ralegh saw at a glance were the best that could be arranged. With solid old oaken furniture, with a trestle table. With a fire on the hearth, having burned a good while, too, for the room was well warmed. And plenty of firewood and faggots. With the room clean and dusted.

Best of all, an adequate bed. Not elegant, but comfortable enough.

Where he lies now, dozing, in the hour after dinner and farewells to the officers and gentlemen who had joined him.

Had decided, never mind expense and trouble, to do well by these guests. Even though this meant sending messengers and boys on errands as far as the city. The affable obsequious porter was prepared for that as well. The trestle table was soon set with pewter plates and knives and spoons, a side table displaying more pewter and earthenware. The porter announced he had two pieces of meat roasting and whiteflour bread fresh baked by his wife. Had two servants—perhaps hired from an inn, for they displayed some modest skill—for carving and serving and boys enough to form a choir, to run and fetch what Ralegh might require. With meantime a cask of good oysters and both sack and ale for the gentlemen while they waited.

Ralegh rattled his purse and gave of it freely. More than the dinner and all arrangements might cost, though not so much as to satisfy the porter beyond future expectation or into a slovenly disregard. Enough to establish Ralegh was the master, though prisoner, and his keeper, a servant, not host. Enough to send the boys scurrying. Enough to furnish dinner for his guests.

And, despite the rude chamber and common furnishings,

it was a satisfactory dinner. Ample enough and with plenty remaining for the servants and hangbys and the porter's larder. The wines were good and the gentlemen joined in his light-heartedness. Not a solemn word was said until farewell.

Now alone, except for his brace of servants from the Tower, who arrived, somewhat sobered by cold rain, coming by cart with his chests, he is content to rest on the bed for an hour, no more, before he must rise and untangle the last knots of his worldly affairs.

Content to allow dinner to settle, the wine to clear from his head, and the weight of his heart to return.

Resting quiet and easy alone as a man can be—*in prison is the only privacy,* they say—upon the shores of sleep.

Time outside of time, the time of dreams when soul proves itself by leaving the body.

He rests content. It is a time to summon up imaginary ghosts. He will not be angered by the presumption.

From childhood he has known the common beliefs about the spirits of the dead. From a country childhood into the reign of a king who truly believes in ghosts and demons and witches, and not as merely preying upon the delusions of the poor and ignorant, but as the servants of the devil.

The King's beliefs, made public by his published writings, have given old follies new stature. And given more than one of his Court a cause for secret smiling. And given small comfort to common folk who share those beliefs. At least in the time of the Queen they had the solace of doubting, even while, out of the stubborn liberty of believing what they pleased, they clung to country myths as old as time.

How the coming of death is bodied in the cry of an owl,

or a raven's croaking, or the howl of a wolf, long after none could recall the sound of a wolf in Devon.

How—and they swore they had seen it—at the moment of death a pale flame appeared, dancing outside the window. Then danced away to the churchyard. And you must follow exactly the path of that flame when you marched with the corpse. Or the ghost would return to haunt you.

Indeed? Must follow the charted course of a dancing flame? No doubt over walls, into wells and ponds and bogs, through haystacks and somebody's bed chamber. Or are we permitted to go around these things? And what of the fellow who permits no procession of mourners to tramp through his garden?

Ralegh has seen funerals and walked in them too. To the solemn ringing of the passing bell in each church, by law, to the funeral wake. Which in the country has such abundance of ale and *natural* spirits as to make ghosts and wonders a probability.

Has known great men who might have known better, to haunt their living heirs with wills calling for magnificent funerals, extravagant tombs, and splendid inscriptions and effigies, not noteworthy for lifelike portrayal of the dead. Designed in hope of fooling God as well as the devil.

Knows the ways of ghosts. How they appear at midnight, in living form, and with substance no weapon can wound. How crowing of cocks will drive them back to churchyards. Which is why the cock crows all night on Christmas Eve. . . .

Why, then, I think a fellow should have a cock that will crow upon command. And keep him ever on his shoulder like a talking bird or my lady's pet squirrel. And what shall we do on a Christmas Eve when the cocks, ignoring the calendar, are quiet? *Shall the sexton flap his arms and cry out cockadoodle-doo all night?*

In wild Ireland has heard how the Irish can turn themselves into wolves. How Ireland is half populated with ghosts.

Well, they fight like wolves and lay an ambush so stealthy a ghost might envy them.

In the playhouse ghosts are more often seen than anywhere else.

And why not? It offers the designers and artificers a chance to demonstrate their craft. It presents an actor occasion to speak in a squeaky voice and to trouble to learn few lines. For ghosts are most particular to whom they speak and not known for wit and idle chatter.

How you can speak to a ghost in Latin and even drive him away with its power.

A good inducement for a lazy lad to study his Caesar, Virgil and Ovid. Though a clever lad may well ask what will happen if the ghost is some ill-educated lout who could not tell Latin from Welsh or the Canting Tongue? Or is it that the very sound of it, recalling the miseries of school days, will drive even the dead out of their wits?

And the Church has prayers for exorcism and its bell, book, and candle for cursing.

Walk softly. Say only the Church must contend with many beliefs, and for the sake of the true faith show itself master over strange faiths.

And Walter Ralegh has been rumored to be a sort of an atheistical necromancer. Keeping company with men like the Earl of Northumberland, Dr. John Dee, and Thomas Hariot.

If study of mathematics and the motions of the stars, of qualities of plants and herbs and minerals, all natural philoso-

[253]

*phy—is magic, then it is magic of God the Creator—if this
is more outrageous than drawing a circle in sand to forbid
the devil—a circle which will not keep out a mouse—so be it.
At least fools will not dare disturb the privacy of study and
experiment.*

In short, Walter Ralegh has not much interest in ghosts.
Believing that this absence of interest is mutual. He stands
upon the Father of Church Fathers, who said it plain and
without equivocation. Ralegh wrote in his *History:* "For when
our spirits immortal shall be once separate from our mortal
bodies and disposed by God, there remains in them no other
joy of their posterity which does succeed than there does of
pride in the stone which sleepeth in the wall of a king's palace.
Nor any other shame for their poverty than there does shame in
that stone which bears up a beggar's cottage. For (as St. Augus-
tine has written): 'The dead, though holy, know nothing of the
living. No, not even of their own children. For the souls of the
departed are not conversant with the affairs of those who remain.'"

Time, while the old man dozes, to summon up ghosts, imagined
and imaginary. Nameless except for their roles and stations.

Perhaps he will not be offended if they are to be considered
characters in the fashion of the types of Englishmen drawn
by Sir Thomas Overbury. Who showed more wit in his book
of *Characters* than he did in his appetite for sweet tarts.

Perhaps Ralegh may ignore an interlude with imaginary
ghosts, since they are nameless and of no more dimension
than figures in tapestry or stained cloth.

If therefore it be demanded whether the Macedonian or the Roman were the better warrior, I shall answer—the Englishman. For it will soon appear to any that shall examine the noble acts of our nation in war that they were performed by no advantage of weapon, against no savage or unmanly people; the enemy being far superior unto us in numbers and all needful provisions, yes, and as well trained as we, or commonly better, in the exercise of war.

RALEGH—*History of the World*

2

Scars on the soldier's face are partly concealed by his beard.
He hides stiffness of one leg by a slow, rolling swagger and,
when he stands still, with a wide-footed solid stance. Come
closer, note the fatness of lips, often split and healed. Wide flat
nose and the little scars at his eyelids camouflaged by heavy
brows and more at the corners, lost in a network of wrinkles.

Heavy brows and heavy lids above the eyes. The eyes which
now seem light and clear as water in sunlight, now dark and
cold as wet stone.

Clothes of rough cloth and several foreign fashions in one,
but cut to fit him. Patched and shiny, but brushed neat and
clean. Sword and dagger hung from a stout leather belt. Not
shiny in dented scabbards, but smooth at the hilt and no fleck
of rust from hilt to point. And point filed bright and edges
honed keen. Sword and dagger as much a part of his body
as his four limbs, fingers, and toes. For in service it would have
cost him his life, by regulations, to go outdoors without them.

Calls himself Captain now. Though more than once he has

carried all the weapons of the infantry. And served longest as sergeant.

Knows more ways to lie than a Venetian, but cannot be blamed when the world values any counterfeit above all sweaty, worn-smooth, hard-earned coins of truth.

Patience and silence are not his guiding stars.

Best let him speak before he spits on the ground, turns heel, and vanishes.

Speaks in a voice as rough as oak bark, and he affects a number of styles, high and low, whatever suits him, as the chameleon can change its coat to suit the leaf it lands on.

Best give him his head. Let him head for the barn at his own pace and choosing the way. . . .

Well, now, I'll talk to you the same as I would to any man. Out of the pure milk of human kindness in me, I'll allow as how you can't be as stupid and ignorant as you look. You can probably find your way to the privy and back without messing your clothes or getting lost. And if you can't, don't expect me to draw you a chart or hold your hand.

No matter what your mother told you, there are some things a man must do for himself.

I'll treat you with the same respect I would any green, whey-faced, knock-kneed, rope-backed bumpkin fresh from a country muster; or some pale-faced, weasel-eyed sneak of a rogue pressed out of prison to be a soldier. You'll find me more fair and just than any justice of the peace. Treat me with respect and try no tricks, for I've seen them all so many times I yawn at mention of them, and I'll treat you the same. Which is more than you deserve.

If it gives you comfort, think on undeniable and unequivocal and immutable truth: the life of a soldier's better than what you have ever had—and don't tell me otherwise—or will have again. Enjoy it while you can—until some hairy bastard gives you what you're good for. Which is the point of a pike straight up your arsehole.

And when that happens, and it most likely will unless you're a better man than you look, take consolation that you're finally rid of me. Your immortal soul is free as a bird. I claim no power there. Ask the company preacher, if you can find him and if he's sober.

Your soul belongs to the preacher and God. It's the skin of your ass that's all mine. . . .

A mere demonstration, sir, no offense meant. To prove you my first point. Which is plain enough.

All soldiering's the same.

Though I've never had time or inclination to read Ralegh's *History,* I don't need a book to make my points.

Has there ever been any man on the face of the earth, since Cain and Abel—which is far enough back to begin, you'll agree? —in any country whatsoever, any climate or age of time, who has not had to *imagine* his life and death as a soldier?

Peace is so high prized because there's damn little of it. In truth there is none and never has been. Not since we were drummed out of Eden.

Even in peacetime there's always murder and war in men's hearts.

Add up the number who have lived the life of a soldier.

Millions and millions of ghosts—and if I didn't believe in ghosts, I wouldn't be talking to you now, would I?—from all the wars and causes, hover over our heads. Look around you, and odds are favorable you'll find some of the maimed and the crippled and scarred. And many more, though masked in health, unmarked and whole, who are as inward wounded as any with scars to show.

Weigh it a moment, and you'll agree that when it comes to the life of a soldier, you possess all necessary knowledge of it at your fingertips.

Even killing has not changed much since Cain. One way is much the same as the other. And there's no good way to die. Except in your sleep in a feather bed. Agreed?

So I say you'll have no sweating and straining to imagine any soldier who ever lived.

But any who have been soldiers know it is imagining more than fear, which will come when it comes anyway, that turns the guts to sour pickles and soft jelly, that will take life out of him quicker than a musket ball between the eyes. And so to endure, to live until he dies, a soldier must learn to live, as much as he's able, here and now. No thought of the sufficient evil of yesterday or regrets for the good of it. No wincing for the wounds and pains of tomorrow.

Take away a man's past and his future and he's left with the present. And then it seems the whole of Creation has been treated with a coat of paint.

To be a good soldier is to be drunk on what's here—a pair of dry socks, birdcalls from a bush, clear water, a bottle of wine, the body of a woman.

No wonder you can't trust any old soldier. I include myself in the proposition. For if he lives to be old, he will look back to even the worst times as good, when all things were naked and simple.

[259]

Those who have never known that time can imagine every-thing else—pain and discomfort, waste of time, injustice, rage, fear, and horror. Can imagine everything—except what it is to be a soldier.

Here's a prime example: *Item*. The world with all its his-tory, knowledge, and contrary evidence, has always believed that men fight and die best for a good cause and do not die well in the service of wickedness.

Allow me—and any old soldiers who may be listening—to laugh out loud.

The cause for being where he is, that's the first thing a soldier discards to lighten his marching load. His only cause is to live as long as he can. And sometimes he must fight very well for that cause.

Soldiers know there was, is, never shall be any cause or purpose worth dying for.

They die when they have to and as well as they can.

And that's the first secret of the soldier's craft.

All wars and fights are the same and all soldiers the same. Agreed? But here comes a turning.

The aim of soldiering is war. But, war or peace, his fighting times are few and far between. Every soldier, living or dead, is blood kin to every other in the experience of fighting. But by the same rule, every soldier is single and unique. For the life of a soldier is most a matter of what he has eaten, pleasure or pain of his boots and uniform, the weight and quality of his gear.

So, while saluting you as a brother at arms, I am entitled to say and bound to believe that if you have never trailed a pike, then you don't know your arse from a kettle bottom.

Do you follow me this far? God's blood and sweat you ought to!

You want to know some things about being a soldier.

Well, you have come to a man who can tell you. There are many around and about—I will mention no names—who would tell you a Jordan pot full of lies.

If that's what you want, go elsewhere to find it. I'll flatter no man—unless he has a dagger's point at my throat. In which case I'll fawn like a puppy dog. At least until I have gained an advantage of *him*. At which time, sir, though he lick my boots till they shine like brass, and he swear I am the Hector of the English, though he offer me money and use of his wife and daughters, I shall have his heart parboiled and served upon a treen platter and feed the rest of him from a bucket to my hogs.

I'm a kind-hearted man. But I would be no man at all if I had lived by less than my full wit and for more return upon my investments than eye for an eye.

There's many a man who needs schooling. I count you among them. So, head up, eyes front, pay attention and listen well.

If you have anything to ask or say, you shall have your chance.

We now have a season of peacetime. Now while Sir Walter Ralegh naps on a bed in the gatehouse. Peace ever since, in 1604, the King and his clever little man, Robert Cecil, settled the war with Spain. Fourteen years for what it may be worth. A long time in the history of this nation or any I know of.

Making peace between England and Spain, that was King James' first purpose when he came to the throne. All his life the King has been strong for peace. And no wonder, with Scotland so often torn by risings and wars among the lairds, with Scotland, alone, a short march and an easy campaign for the English when they had a mind and a reason to fight. To survive he had to bolster himself with alliances, in truth and illusion, with France and Spain, especially Spain. Fearing war so much, and hating it too—though never a soldier himself, fearing and hating from hard experience—he deemed he could know power when he saw it. On paper, that is. Power of the Spanish Army, power of the *flota,* power of wealth and resolute, ruthless kings. He added the sum of that power and trembled. He weighed that power against what he knew of English strength and shuddered at the thought of what would become of us.

It was said, when the Armada came against us in '88, that, once the Spaniard had cleared the British Sea and put their army from the Netherlands ashore, down would come James with an army from Scotland to finish us off and take the throne. And that might have happened except that the winds and the sea made slops of the Spanish strategy.

Do you know what the Queen did then, sir? On the face of it, it's hard to believe. From her spies—best in the world and worth ten thousand men in the field—she knew what James was thinking. So the Queen did what he least expected. She withdrew all but a token force, a few guards, from the only garrison on the Scots border at Berwick. And she sent the musters from the northern counties south to the army at Tilbury, leaving all the North an open door to the Scots if they came. No doubt James took her to be a lunatic woman, crazed with unwarranted confidence; but however he took it, he did not move against us.

Because, to him, it might have been a trap. Supposing she knew something he did not. Supposing she was not crazed with fear or arrogance either. . . .

If the Spaniards failed—as they did—he would be caught at

[262]

war with England, would lose his army, likely his kingdom, maybe his life, and for certain any chance to gain the throne.

He could only fret and wait. When the Armada came to nothing, he could breathe easy at first, conceiving himself wise in his fearful delay. Then later he learned the truth of it—how it was not the English, by land or sea, who dispersed the power of Spain, but bad fortune and bad weather; and he knew that the failure of the Armada was not the end of anything, for, where there's wealth and power and resolution, new fleets can be built, new men mustered; how he had been tricked by a woman and had failed in all things; how he now had ruined the chance of an open alliance with Spain, for all the succor he could offer was to fish out some few half-drowned Spanish seamen and send them safe home.

After that and in the years that followed until the Queen died, all he could do was to pray for the fortunes of the foolish English and hope that when he was their King—if he *were* to gain the throne—he could find a way to make peace with Spain. Robert Cecil, who could make a treaty with the devil, did it for him.

No wonder, though, when you think on it, Ralegh was a thorn in his side. And Ralegh did not ease his fears by offering the King, on his arrival into England, powerful arguments against peace and all for more war with Spain. . . .

Well, we are at peace now and have been for a time. Too long a time to be true, if you ask me. More of a calm than a peace. A stagnant calm with wind and weather building black castles all around the sky. A peace which only a fool can imagine will be prolonged forever.

But let me speak of the times before, when there was no peace worth mentioning, in the reign of the late Queen.

[263]

When Queen Elizabeth came to the throne in '58, lucky to have a head on her shoulders to put a crown on, she came to rule in a kingdom as ringed with troubles as the seas around us. Beset, too, with dangers within.

Under King Edward there had been rebellions in '49, Kett's Rebellion, and the Western Rising. Put down, true enough, and in bloody battles. But the backbone of the King's forces were mercenary soldiers from foreign countries. Well-trained in killing and more than a match for our yeomen.

Though, please to remember, those yeomen were decent armed. More arquebuses than longbows, even in those days.

Soon after came Queen Mary, whom some call the Spanish Tudor and some Bloody Mary. Her aim was peace abroad and surety at home—aim of all princes.

She failed in both by the end.

Surety at home. . . .

Her reign commenced with doubt and with rebellion. Lady Jane Grey named Queen in the Tower. Which for nine days served her as palace, and for the rest of her days as home. Anyway she was spared the inconvenience in the moving of bag and baggage.

No great shakes of war there, but making the throne of England a shaky chair to sit upon.

And soon as she was settled enough to marry the Spanish King, Philip, troubles were real enough. They were able to nip in the bud a large stratagem which would have overturned her easy enough. For only one small part of that plot, the rising in Kent under Wyatt, came as close as the thickness of Ludgate to victory.

The long and the short: Wyatt took Rochester. Down came the Queen's men, two hundred of the Guard and six hundred whitecoats of London city bands and a couple of companies of loyal Kentish men. When the time to fight came, the Queen's forces went over to Wyatt. And their commander, the Duke of Norfolk, rode away to save his life, leaving a litter of his armor behind.

On toward London comes Wyatt and, before he enters Southwark, the last of the Queen's Guard are already close to mutiny. True to her blood, the Queen goes down to the Guildhall of the city. Makes her plea and makes many promises. London stands with her, the gates are closed, and the bands mustered. Then much confusion, false rumors, tricks, and counters. A little fighting and Wyatt yields.

Now, unlike your sleeping Ralegh there, I have never stood guard beside a Queen. Never so much as entered a presence chamber. I know nothing of these things. But I know a little of leading fractious men. Have seen a mutiny or two among our own men and those of other nations. When a mutiny's spent or crushed, there's only one choice to be made. The man in command can come down like Jehovah upon Gomorrah. Fire and brimstone and holy terror. And I've seen that done and work for a time. But now, sir, that leader has spent his choice forever. Must therefore continue to maintain authority by terror. Must thereafter, unless he's a fool, live in fear that the same will happen again.

By hard experience I learned to take another choice. Justice for a few of the worst malefactors, mercy for all the others. And some consideration of the causes. Which, if they cannot be cured, can be blunted by a willingness to try. Do you see?

Under Philip and Mary we had our time of Spanish discipline. And cruelty, too, for we were likewise enemies. But not so much of either as to leave us as we did Munster in Ireland. Too short a time before Queen Mary died.

But in that time English power fell into decay. We lost Calais, our stronghold in France—whose gates for two centuries carried the inscription: "Then shall the Frenchman Calais win/ When iron and lead like cork shall swin."—in a siege of a week.

Queen Elizabeth came to the throne with the kingdom poor, wounded within, and with more danger from enemies abroad than ever before.

Scotland on the border, hostile and suspicious, close kin to France.

Ireland hostile, in open rebellion, and, truly, never having been subdued. Ireland close kin to Spain.

Neither France nor Spain friendly, each a threat and together overwhelming.

And what was her power? Her Guard and pensioners, the file of warders at the Tower, some crumbling garrisons of soldiers, few in number, mostly at Berwick and Dover. And the militia, men of the musters of counties and cities. And these having chiefly proved they could rise up and work mischief.

The walls and cities with their fortifications and the old strongpoints were useless beyond repair and too costly to consider repairing.

The Navy, small as it had been, having wasted and declined further.

Say, then, that she began her reign with no power at all.

Now, that can be reduced to the bare-shank terms that a common soldier can understand. From the beginning, outnumbered and outgunned everywhere, she could take only one

[266]

tactic—delay. A soldier might surrender, gambling on his life. But surrender of a nation ends its life.

I believe the Queen at heart was a good English captain. Of all her generals and marshals of armies, there wasn't any, except the last one, Charles Blount, the Lord Mountjoy, worth the tailfeathers off an Irish crow. Call the roll of pompous fools, who could kill more men by ignorance, folly, and rash stupidity than plague and famine together, and scratch your head to recollect a victory by any of them: William Grey, Lord Grey; Robert Dudley, Earl of Leicester; Henry Carey, Lord Hunsdon; Edward de Fiennes, Lord Clinton; Thomas Radcliffe, Earl of Sussex; Peregrine Bertie, Lord Willoughby; Ambrose Dudley, Earl of Warwick; Robert Devereux, Earl of Essex; Sir Henry Bagenal; Sir Francis Vere; Sir John Norreys, and some others whose names even I, mercifully, have clean forgotten.

Masters of proud musters, and able to present a procession of troops marching out and away in time to the beat of the drum. They were also mighty skilled in arranging that armies would not have an excess of food to waste upon themselves, nor too much powder and shot to injure the enemy, nor such regular payment as to make their purses heavy. Those soldiers who, by luck and by God, escaped the fevers and starvation, were given occasion to escape this mortal coil, this wicked world, by being sent out upon ill-conceived skirmishes and impossible assaults.

Christ, is it any wonder she hastened first to repair the tilt-yards of her palaces and castles? So these men could *play* at war and hurt only each other. Let them throw snot about, by which I mean weeping, for the noble death of Sir Philip Sidney at Zutphen, but waste no tears for many thousands gone.

Take Essex, who had every chance to prove his mettle matched his mouthing. At Cadiz he raced ahead of everyone to scale the wall and got stuck there while others smashed the gates and entered the town. At Lisbon he stood before the fortress and issued the old-fashioned challenge for single combat with their champion. And shook his fist at answering laughter from the walls. He never served so low as a captain. Had small use for captains and none for common soldiers, whom he called artificers and clowns who apprehend nothing but what they see before them.

Well, sir, there are many sorts of clowns. Give me one who sees what's in front of his eyes instead of that clown with a general's baton who sees Agincourt wherever he is.

The Queen was our captain. But when the time came we most needed a general, she was there.

The English Army at Tilbury never had to fight. And that's the best tribute to a general.

It was more than mere show when she donned silver armor in '88, while the Armada was still in the sea, and rode bareheaded, jewels in her hair, on a white horse before the troops at Tilbury. And there was hard sense in her words to them.

"I know I have the body of a weak and feeble woman, but I have the heart and stomach of a king, and King of England too, and think foul scorn that Parma or Spain, or any prince of Europe should dare to invade the borders of my realm; to which, rather than any dishonor shall grow by me, I myself will take up arms. I myself will be your general, judge, and rewarded of every one of your virtues in the field."

Our little wars were in Scotland and Ireland, in France and in Spain and Portugal, in bits and pieces, and scattered across years.

Many musters and alarms in England. Some, I think, to practice the business of mustering and to bring people together against a common danger. But only one at home that might be truly called war—the rising of the Northern Earls in '69. A sad, foolish, vainglorious affair, settled between October and Christmas, in that miserable country up beyond the Trent, all pasture and moor, forest, bogs, and rock-strewn uplands. Old castles and poor crumbling towns. The earls in their old armor and lacking artillery, raising much dust, but accomplishing little. It was settled for good by musters from the South. Who picked them as clean as the Spaniards would have. And when the dust settled, we hanged more men by martial law than we killed in the fighting.

Many—Essex for one—were strong pleaders for a standing Army, like other nations. Something secure for the soldier. And men well trained, not clumsy farm boys who must be taught and blooded anew each time. And they argued that already there were too many rogues and vagabonds about, masterless men; and the poor, cast out of old crafts by the new or pushed off of the farms by enclosures, wandering the roads, suffering themselves and causing mischief to others.

When you add to this the number of men from armies, discharged and sent home to shift for themselves, there was even more danger. Men with nothing to show for their service but scars and the holes in their clothes and shoes. Men who had skill in use of weapons and the habit of using them.

But truth is standing armies cause more danger. Spain, with the largest and proudest of armies, had many desertions and mutinies. Witness the Fury of Antwerp in '76, when the King of Spain could not pay his men.

[269]

Better separate vagabonds in England than battalions and regiments of them.

And it was either too late or too early for England to forge a fighting Army. In Europe, where land wars took place, they were ahead of us in equipment and tactics. We still had fools extolling the virtues of longbow against arquebus, musket, and caliver; who believed armor was manly and useful; who would rather die by the broadsword blow than a thrust from a rapier.

Some thought of using mercenary soldiers. All other nations, from France to far Turkey, had mercenaries. But we had seen them here in England. They were hated here, and are always dangerous and costly. We have used them sometimes in Europe, but not with much success.

On the other hand, it was useful to have Englishmen serving as mercenaries for others. Those who wished to could fight elsewhere at the expense of someone else. If they lived to return, they could become what we lacked—veterans around which an Army can always be made. So Englishmen fought in all the wars, and often on both sides.

From these came our veterans and captains, including myself. And if we could not whip green mustered boys into such shape as to match Spanish foot or German light horse, why, we could put the fear of God into them and lead them as well as men can be led.

You should know, too, something that is too seldom said. There is a point at which a green, but drilled soldier has an edge of advantage over the veteran. The fear of the green soldier can serve to advantage. He will obey commands in faith and go careful, by the book. He fears, but does not yet know how much he has to fear. Your old soldier knows all dangers and has long since concluded his life is a matter of luck. Has no faith in commanders. He may break and run if he feels he's lost the last of his luck. Or he may become careless, a ghost of a man, whose only safety, he conceives, is that he has shrugged off his life in advance.

We had captains, who had been to other wars, to lead companies in ours. Some, I am sad to report, took time out to write books. When every country gent who's trooped a line at a muster can publish the final word on the art of fighting, my view is the ones that *know* should ignore books and stick to their business.

I'll mention two men and be done with the subject.

One is Sir Roger Williams. Now, Williams was a Welshman, a hardass weasel with a head like a dented burgonet. Was as bitter and sharp as a pulled leek with earth still clinging to it. Sour as last season's cider. He was half outrage and the other half pure exasperation.

But he saw a lot of service in his time. Fought in the Netherlands for Spain, for the States, and even, at last, for the English. Was at Tilbury when the Armada came. Made the voyage to Portugal and back. In the nineties served in France. Commanded the port of Dieppe and greeted Essex when the Earl landed there with his men. I have my doubts he was ever in Scotland or Ireland, but I can't be sure.

When I knew him, he had seen and suffered so much folly that nothing would ever surprise him again. Except, perhaps, an example of common sense. Drank too much and loved wenching. But he wrote brief and to the point. Allowed himself only few occasions to lie. And he was tough as a bear and intended to keep alive as long as he could. You could call him a good captain to follow unless a better one came along.

The other I call to mind wrote more words than many a poet and fancied himself the supreme scholar of war. Sir John Smythe, all blood and iron, iron of his armor and blood of our wounds! Praise be, he never was a general. He had the makings for that. But he wrote himself out of all chances.

Might have known better. Saw his first action and killing in '49, fighting against rebels of Kett's Rebellion, and in the Western Rising. On the Continent saw more battles and warfare than most, as far away as Hungary and Turkey. But always with *books,* Caesar and Sallust, handy. Came back to England to make a name for himself.

As in '87 he was to assist in the muster of Essex and Hertford. Tried to teach clod-footed bands such things as what he called "the order of marching of a semicircle of two ranks oblique according to the Hungarian and Turkey manner."

At Tilbury he was a bleeding colonel. Captain General Leicester found him amusing until the day he inspected Smythe's troops. Of which the Earl reported: "After the muster, he entered into such strange cries for ordering of men and for fight with the weapon as made me think he was not well. God forbid he should have charge of men who know as little as I dare pronounce he does."

Leicester relieved him and sent him home to write more books.

Smythe discovered the English longbow. It must have been new to him. The Council was eager to keep archery alive. It was a matter of statute. Not for warfare, mind you, but for general health and welfare and to discourage folks from less healthy ways of spending leisure; and to keep our English craftsmen, the bow makers, from starving. But Smythe had to attack the Privy Council on such subjects as supply and recruiting, organization, arms and equipment. Adding his groatsworth of opinion on the subject of the recent failures of the English Army, and, especially, the Earl of Leicester's expedition to the Netherlands.

His book was suppressed and he was fined.

In '96 he found his hard head in the Tower. For, two days drunk, he came to a muster in Essex and tried to lead a rising. Lucky for him, he was too drunk to be understood and fell from his saddle.

He never ceased offering advice to Council and anyone he could collar in an alehouse.

Smythe was one of the *best* of the pudding-headed fools. He died poor enough. Even had to pawn his armor. But the best of that kind will get you killed or leave you one-legged or crippled to prove that Euclid or Pythagoras were right or wrong; and shipped home to beg at the edge of towns and fairs, wrapped in bandages like a babe in swaddling. Leaning on a stick like a stork on one leg.

Christ on the Cross, deliver me from them all! They have made the sod of half the world grow greener over bones of Englishmen.

Smythe, that windy fart, he was a mighty scholar when it comes to vanwards and rearwards, sleeves and wings and forlorn hopes, trenches with half-rounds indents, traverses, quadrants and angles of fire. But, do you know, he barely touches on the subject of the siege? The siege, that's half of warfare. Digging and sweating and waiting.

I've got the calluses to prove a soldier's got more use for a pick and shovel than a pike.

[273]

Any damn fool can see at a glance that the captain is the key to the English Army.

Now, many a man who's served his time will tell you hair-raising tales of captains. I've heard them all myself more than once. And there were some bad ones just as the world always has room for wicked scroyles. Otherwise how would we know virtue when we meet it? Do you see?

But seeing I've served as a captain myself, I ought to say a few words in defense of my fellows.

Ask yourself this: why would a man want to be a soldier? Never mind musters and press gangs and such. There are ways to avoid them. Once bitten may not be the beginning of wisdom, but it teaches a man something about dogs. And a soldier can always run away and many did that too. There were times when even I, myself, took leave on my own. I'll admit it. My four limbs and the head on my shoulders are proof of it. When Gabriel sounds his trumpet, I can report to that final muster all in one piece and won't have to hunt all over half of Europe and Ireland for leftovers. I'm sorry for the ones who will, but that's their medicine to swallow, not mine.

But why would a sane man ever choose to be a soldier? No future in it, sir, no future at all. Exactly. . . . But a soldier has no future and no past. And therefore, it's as logical as any schoolmaster could ask, he isn't thinking of a future at all. Hard as it can often be, the life of a soldier can also be merry. There are times when he's in good health and out of danger, when his clothes are clean and dry and the rations are good, when women are free with favors and wine and ale are strong and cheap, when his luck is running with cards and dice. Times when a soldier can laugh at the plowboy stumbling behind a plow and the prentice fumbling to learn a craft. Times when gentlemen, merchants, lords, seem like clowns of Fortune with so much to regret and fret over. And a man who farms his own plot of land can starve to death on it or work a lifetime and lose it.

Nobody starves a soldier on purpose. And if he's got half wit he needn't starve anywhere I know of. Except in Ireland, where starving is the way of life.

A soldier has nothing to lose but his life. And that's a good thing to know as long as he can believe it.

Back to the captain. He wears a different pair of shoes. He is least likely to be killed and, further, can fix the odds in his favor. He has to think somewhat of the future, and if he thinks it through, he'll see it's a shabby one. Lucky the captain who ends his service with enough in his purse to give him a decent old age. He makes do with dead pays and a muster roll that lists dead men and deserters as alive and on duty. He's a merchant when it comes to the buying and selling of provisions and clothing. And some, not of the best, have been tempted to deal with the enemy. Especially in Ireland, where the kerns and gallowglasses would give all they had for an ordinary English arquebus.

What harm? Say the arquebus of a dead man. It's no use to him now. Better for someone to have it than rusting in an armory. The Irishman still has to find means to feed it with powder and shot. And sooner or later he'll get one anyhow off a corpse. He'll kill for it. Why not save a life and make a profit at the same time?

Not that I engaged in such traffic myself, of course. You have my word on it.

But there's a check on how far a foolish or wicked captain can go. His company will stand for only so much. And there are more ways of disposing of a captain than mutiny. The captain knows this better than the men.

There is always a chance that a captain doing well enough may find one foot on the ladder of preferment. There are many examples of that—Ralegh, for one.

For a man with no fortune and small future, there's not much to lose and always at least a chance of a change for the better. . . .

It is true we had a good issue of uniform, all in all. But the use and comfort of clothing depend on where you wear them. Ours might have been adequate for England. But in France and Portugal we sweated and fainted from heat. Dutch cold stiffened our joints and shivered us to the bone. In Ireland we might as well have been swimmers in wet air. In Scotland, where God has turned his back and witches dance bareass with the devil, if the cold does not kill you, you'll drown in the damp.

The wet is worst, for English cloth will shrink around your frame. Picture a march of a dozen miles, a fair day's march, in the rain and mud, clothes as heavy as armor. Then the sun comes out for a peep, long enough to dry us, and everything shrinks to fit as tight as a new glove.

In Ireland our clothes were rags in no time. Shoes of English leather rotted away, and everything metal rusted. I doubt that St. Patrick had trouble persuading the snakes to leave. No trick to that. Birds and beasts are scarce enough, too, and I've seen the Irish, half-naked, wrapped in a piece of cowhide, men and women alike, eating grass and leaves and nuts off the ground.

We wore Irish brogues and breeches when we could find

them. Even if it meant sending some Irishman on his way barefoot and baldass.

Ireland was the hardest service with nothing worth stealing and even our friends couldn't feed us full. The weather was misery, winter or summer. And no proper war at all, but an ambush here on the road, a skirmish there at a ford, or a cattle raid. The drums would call *To Arms* and *To March* and away we'd go through mud a goose would disdain and rocks that would take the breath of a goat. To catch a few, hang them, bring back some heads on the ends of pikes. No beginning and no end to it, with nothing improving no matter what we did, or if we did nothing.

It had a beginning for the soldier, though: a puking voyage on a stinking ship, like riding a wild mare on waves, stinking rations and foul straw to sleep on if you could sleep; and all that to remember, to endure again if and when your time was up.

A wet, dirty, bloody war where you would never learn which was your enemy and who was a friend, if they knew themselves. And the least you'd get out of it was Irish ague for life.

That was a school that taught a man nothing but declensions of misery and prepared him for nothing except the pains of hell.

But hell's bells and the devil's clanging balls! That was not all the truth. For even in this telling, I can recall good times.

Men have said your Irishman is a savage. I have heard (in one ear and out the other) preachers tell why. The Irish are a lost and outcast tribe of Israel. Sometimes they are the last of the branded offspring of Cain, etc. And I have heard tavern

[277]

tales of old mariners, who will tell you that the black African or the red Indian is a better man by far and puts an Irishman to shame.

Well, I know less of Holy Scripture than I should and believe less than I admit. I wouldn't waste a small fart in a high wind worrying where the Irish came from. And though I have seen both black and red in London, I've never yet been to Africa or the New World. All I can say is I doubt I would have been any different if I had been born an Irishman. And I'll say the same for you.

After all's said and done. . . . And why not say it? The Irish are cunning and treacherous, cowardly and cruel when it suits them, lazy and idle, ignorant and dirty, arrogant and proud, and all crazed—a nation of Abraham men. But they can be as brave as any who ever lived. And when it suits them they can be as free and generous as if they own the world to the horizon and have never heard of tomorrow.

You'll hear more than one Englishman, some dainty lad pressed out of the clink in Southwark, rail against their rude shamrock manners. Curse dirty oatcakes and sour milk and lice as thick as the freckles of Sir Francis Drake. They'll tell you how the ignorant Irish still plow by the tail and sleep bare naked by the fire, toasting first one side and then the other. They'll tell of dirt and stink and how one Irishman clings to more foolish country beliefs—of haunts and faeries and spirits and such—than all the Welsh and Scotch put together. They'll tell you, too, how an Irishman will explode in blackfaced choler and draw knife against you if you fart in front of him, lacking even the first understanding of civil behavior.

I confess this last is true and I don't understand it at all.

[278]

But farting does enrage them, and so it's best to humor them. Hold it if you can. Walk away if you can't.

Not an Englishman, though, unless he is a liar to the marrow of his bones, but will tell you the Irishman's courageous. He can live on roots and grass and march for miles and make a stand and fight to the last and never cry quarter or mercy.

More than once when I was a captain there, I found myself at the feast of some seneschal. All served outdoors at a log table or on the ground. And devil take weather, wind or rain. For a feast they'll eat the last cow they own. And once you are accustomed, you can learn to hunger for their food. It warms both heart and bowels. It sticks to the ribs. A chunk of butter with oatmeal and fresh blood and plenty of meat. They won't touch fish or wildfowl even when there's plenty of both.

Some Englishmen cannot swallow meat of a beast that's been skinned and cooked in its own hide, sewn up and strung over a hot fire. It's a different taste, true, but savory with juices.

Best of all and the finest medicine against cold and damp is *usquebaugh,* as they call their spirits. Drink it straight and full like ale, or mix it with a little milk, and you'll fear not the devil or any man alive. And before the feast is done you'll be drunker than Noah and will see the whole world in pairs as he did.

At a feast there would be singing and dancing. Always boys playing pipes to match the piping of your blood. And a poet with an Irish harp at the last. To sing old stories and sorrows while everyone keeps silence and beards glisten with tears like raindrops in a holly bush.

On the morrow they may slip six inches of steel between your ribs. But at an Irish feast a man can believe in brotherhood.

Will you believe this? When I was mustered out the last

time, home from France, I offered myself as a common soldier. I would have carried arquebus for eight pence a day, to get back to Ireland.

It wasn't just fighting or feasting either. There is something about an Irish woman. . . . Not only that her favors are for sale at bargain price. There are always women where soldiers are. And we all know, being sons of Adam, that there's none of it a man can ignore and pass by except at the price of regret. A Bishop in a bush is pure pleasure in any language, call it what you will.

An Irish woman has something different and pleasing beyond all the others. I never saw such comely sturdy flesh—even on the poor. With their long dark hair and their color all over, head to toe, of fresh cream. And something wild as a witch about them, sparks of hell in their eyes. She may join you in a feather bed or behind a hedge—all the same to her—and for no price at all save the joy of it. And never ask your name or tell you hers.

Once I was riding alone, carrying a message through forlorn lonesome country. Cold wind blowing and rain falling steady. I lost the trail and then lost my way and direction. The wind was blowing up more fierce, rain in my eyes, dark coming on and no recollection of north and south. Not a tree or a bush for miles, it seemed, or even a rock for shelter.

I came over a rise and there below was one of those round stone towers they like to live in. A fenced yard with wet cattle standing. Light from ports of the tower and the top of the tower smoking like a chimney. Not a soul in sight and no man challenged me. I kept my hand on the hilt of my sword and would not unsaddle, though I fed my mare some oats. Rain was coming down harder and not a star in the sky or the memory of a moon. I was as wet as a flounder and cold as a cod.

So there was nothing else but to hike back my shoulders and go up to the door and rap my knuckles black and blue against it.

After a time I heard bolts squeaking loose. I gripped the hilt of my sword, ready to cut and fight and make a run for the mare. The door swung in and there in the light was a woman, not much more than a girl, standing there smiling at me. She was wearing a shift that came down to her knees, a thin shift as soft as a bandage. And the light behind revealed all secrets.

Before I could say a word, she beckoned me to come, and I stepped in and she slammed the door to and shot the bolts home again. She motioned to follow and I followed her up a creaky circle of stairs to the top. Where she opened a door and we came into a round hall with a fire burning and smoking in the middle and the rain from the smoke hole spitting into the fire.

And there around the fire, as white and rosy as angels, were nine more like her, of divers shapes and sizes and all dressed the same. They stood up and smiled and I smiled too.

Then a young man came in, a comely lad, and he welcomed me and bade me be his guest for the night. For a moment I would not trust my eyes, for there he stood, all smiling and polite, a gentleman to be sure, and as naked as a newborn babe.

I mumbled gratitude and he spoke to the women in the Irish tongue. And they laughed and ran to me and seized me like a prisoner. I wrestled and they wrestled back and he told me they meant no harm, only to take my clothes to dry. And take them they did, every last stitch, and laid them near the fire. Then two of them rubbed me dry with a soft cloth and another brought me a wooden bowl of Irish spirits and one to my host. He nodded and raised it and drank it down in a swallow or two and I followed suit. And then here was another one, full to the brim, handed to me.

The women took carpets from a chest and spread them in a ring around the fire. The young man motioned me to take my place by the fire. The women slipped out of their shifts and came and lay down too. Astonished I was, to be sure, and suspicious as well. But not completely defenseless; for the dagger at the fork of my legs was well nigh a pike by that time. Which seemed to amuse them all a great deal. They brought some bread and cheese and more *usquebaugh*. And we lay on soft carpets and toasted ourselves pink on both sides till the fire began to dwindle and the hall to darken and we had to huddle close to warm each other.

I kept warm enough that night, I'll tell you. And, neither asleep nor awake, I did my duty as an Englishman. Until I conceived it might be a cunning plot to kill me with excess.

Then I shrugged my shoulders and I thought to myself: *If it is a plot for murder, they will find this victim cheerful and willing to the last breath. And if I die let me go, Lord, to the Turkish heaven. . . .*

In the morning, weak as a kitten, I set out following directions they gave me. The sun was shining and the day was fair. My host bade me stay on for more hospitality. And when (damn fool!) I said I could not, he told me I would be welcome any time.

I confess as soon as I was able I set out to find that place again. But there had been raids and fighting in all that section.

I never found the tower, though there were ruins that could have marked the spot.

One night like that in a lifetime, sir, is worth one thousand nights with a nagging wife in a thatched cottage with all comforts. And I reckon it's worth all the trouble of being a soldier, too. . . .

But I see you are impatient. You did not imagine me out of the darkness to hear the chronicle of my life or my privy opinions.

It is Walter Ralegh you are seeking. He eludes you as he lies there snoozing. You say half asleep. Not so, sir. He sleeps now, well enough, but he sleeps like a soldier or a cat. Light enough for a change in the wind or the dying of a fire or another man's snoring—if the other be a sentinel on the watch—to wake him as quick as lightning and thunder.

The old saying goes: *A captain must not sleep a full whole night.*

Rightly so, for Walter Ralegh is a soldier. And if he saw no future in soldiering and left it, do not forget that he found a future by soldiering.

But he was a special kind of a soldier. I do not mean your candy soldier out of London and Westminster. Nor your tavern bully or brawling courtier, ready to cross swords over a slight; though record shows he did not fear a tavern brawl with rowdies or a duel with a swordsman either. It shows, too, he sought neither brawls nor duels. In truth—read his own words, sir, and match them with and against what you know—he had contempt for dueling and such deadly games. Was not easily provoked into quarrels of that kind.

Need I tell you—for surely the world in its age has not

[283]

grown so ignorant of the nature and humors of man—that because he was not quick to fight he was the greater challenge? And that sooner or later, especially when he was young, he would be pushed into a wall with his back to it, and then would fight as well as any.

To a soldier a sword is not a toy or a decoration. When he draws sword, he means to kill with it and stands ready to be killed.

Another mark against Ralegh from the beginning in the ledger book of King James.

The world knows he will not permit an unsheathed blade, sword or dagger, in his presence. Knows, too, the padded bulk of the King's clothing comes from the heavy sort of waistcoat, leather and links, he wears always next to his skin. 'Tis said to be proof against any blade or pistol. There are many who will tell you his fear of blades began in his mother's womb, for she was large with him when his father and a band of the lairds took swords and daggers to David Rizzio, her secretary—and some say her lover—directly before her eyes. And he was a child when he saw his uncle sliced to fillets in swordplay. His life was in close danger many times in that land where even the noblemen are cutthroat ruffians. We now celebrate as a holiday his deliverance from the hands of Gowrie. Lord, no wonder he fears brawling and blades!

No wonder he feared Ralegh, swordsman for the Queen, her Captain ever ready to kill in a moment or at a sign.

No surprise he would believe that Ralegh conspired against him in '03 and that Ralegh was chosen to carve up the King, his Queen and all the children. . . .

Ralegh was a soldier but not a kitchen garden sort of soldier. Was off to France first, a boy, in a gentleman's troop of horse

[284]

from the Westcountry to serve the Huguenots. Few of them well-to-do. And himself with a name, a horse, his trooper's gear, and not much else. An ordinary horse soldier, then, with not a pisspot to call his own and to fear to lose. A difference from many another young gentleman. Starting not an ensign bearer with eyes up on a captaincy.

Beginning in ignorance and innocence. No doubt he was trained in use of his weapons and a good horseman too. He would not have been there otherwise. And no doubt he must have heard many a story from old fellows much like me. He had kinsmen who had ventured far to fight the Turk. They would tell him what they could. But all that is nothing until you take the knowledge to you like a woman. There is no training known can ready a man for his first time in battle. When someone, near or far, seen or unseen, is carefully trying to kill—*him*. A man is never the same after that dawning. He's as startled by not having imagined it before, by the lost innocence, as he is by the naked ambush of truth.

If he lives through that first encounter, he's a soldier then, for better or worse. Whatever he was before is dead and gone.

Now, the way they used horse was to support the infantry. No more charges as of old. Horsemen worked as wings of the infantry, guarding flanks on the march and in battle. And they served as the Forlorn Hope, working ahead in the point and behind in retreat as a screen. And they scouted and skirmished and set up ambushes. And they reconnoitered and carried dispatches and messages.

It was lonesome duty, liable to be deadly any time. Their chief enemy would be the enemy's horse soldiers, up to the same things. Killing was done with pistols and caliver or, when thick and close together, with bare swords. Two groups of men must come close to deliver fire, each close enough for the other to hit them. Pistols fired at fifty feet, calivers at a hundred yards, and usually dismounted. Not blocks of men in mob and melee, confusion of shot and shell, with screams and cries and drums beating the orders. But meeting a face you can see and remember. Cool craft of murder required.

Ralegh learned with dispatch or he would not have lived long enough to matter.

And all the while he soldiered like any other, except that a horseman has more to worry about: his mount, whose health is his own, and woe to the man who loses a mount. It was custom to degrade him down to the pick and shovel pioneers. Then all that saddle and bridle and gear to care for. And finding food for two.

All this in a strange country in the service of a foreign Army nearly as hostile as the enemy. And all in a war of religion. Which is the worst kind. For then there is no cruelty. That it cannot be justified.

The boy who went as a horseman to fight in those wars received an education in the art of war, which, if it didn't kill him or cure him, was likely to last.

Proof of which comes later when he went to Ireland as a captain of infantry.

You know some of the stories from that time.

How once alone he held off a seneschal and twenty men with a pistol at the edge of a ford to rescue a comrade who had fallen off horse in the stream. Risking, wagering neither the seneschal nor any of his horsemen would *volunteer* to be the one man killed by his pistol.

A good cavalry wager. . . .

How once when an English army was on the march, he hid

his company and remained behind when camp broke to march on. Waiting until the Irish appeared to poke in the ashes of campfires, to scavenge for what they could find. Ambushed them there, in their own style of warfare. Took prisoners. One of them carrying a bunch of willow withies.

Captain Ralegh asks him what they are for. "To hang English churls," he replies. "Then," says Ralegh, "they will serve as well for an Irish kern." And orders the fellow hanged with his own withies from the nearest branch.

A soldier's sense of jest. Without false pity or imaginary fear.

How he marched his company all night across hostile country-side and captured a town and seized the castle by a ruse. Then marched them back with the lord of the castle as prisoner. And all at the cost of one life, a man who fell in a bog.

Might have made it without harm to any if one fellow had watched where his feet were taking him.

Damn fools can't and won't be saved in peace or war. Will choke to death on roast beef or drown in a brass bathing tun. So shovel him under, poor boy, and God rest his foolish soul. . . .

How one day at Smerwick . . .

Here we had best pause to consider. For the story of that day's work is well known. If James of Scotland heard it or learned of it later as an English king, he would have nightmares and would be confirmed beyond question to keep Sir Walter Ralegh forever far away and out of sight, dead or alive. Because he has always been thick and close to Spain, I've no doubt that he's heard it, maybe many times.

It was Italians, soldiers of the Pope of Rome, who landed there, threw up an earth and timber fort, and began to prepare a permanent one. Some say it was Spaniards, and there may have been a few of them there among that motley band. But for certain it was not the Spanish Army. How do I know? Because Spaniards would never have yielded. Proof of that? Look how the Spaniard, less than four hundred in a similar fort at Crozon, guarding Brest, held long and fast against Sir John Norreys' whole army in '94. The Spaniards fought and died to the man.

Down to Smerwick, perched on the windy southeast cheek of the arse of Ireland, came Lord Grey with an English army. Forced marching in hellish haste, for they left behind much undefended country; and there was already news of an Irish army gathering against them. Why leave the country undefended to march across Ireland and take a little fort? Because there was every reason to believe this Fort del Oro, as they called it, was designed to be the handhold for landing a large expedition of the Pope's soldiers or Spain's or both, who were already thought to be at sea. If they waited to see, they could be caught between the Irish and a foreign expedition like a walnut in a cracker.

With the weather miserable and bound to get worse, they arrived at Smerwick, bone-weary and on short rations; and they mounted an attack on the fort. Which, being well set on high ground and with the sea at its back, proved more than they had bargained for. After Lord Grey had killed off sufficient of his number to prove the fort could not be taken without ordnance, they settled in to wait for an English fleet. The last of the rations were vanishing and the weather was only worse. Then up sailed a patrol of English ships to blockade the fort and off-load cannon. Fort del Oro was so nicely placed that the ships could not come close to bring their fire to bear upon it. And even as the cannon began to do their work on the earthworks and timber, the ships pulled in anchors, hoisted canvas, and sailed away on new, urgent orders. Leaving the soldiers, even in victory, with the prospect of a march back at double pace and with next to no rations.

The English spared no powder and pounded the fort with cannonballs until a white flag appeared and the Italians parleyed for terms. Now, Lord Grey was not among the best of even *our* generals, but he was not such a fool as to embark upon a forced march with six hundred prisoners to guard and feed and prod along. He demanded an unconditional surrender and promised them nothing. The poet Spenser, serving as his secretary there, has borne witness to this. Some say that neither the Italians nor the English understood each other in the parleys, but there were a goodly number of Irish and English renegades in the Pope's forces.

Consider the ways of warfare. Even when all the old rules of chivalry are invoked—of which I doubt the knights of old heeded one—any man who surrenders to the enemy is gambling skin and bones unless there are the strictest conditions and the means to enforce them. In Ireland the luckiest prisoners on both sides were those hanged or beheaded on the spot.

Most likely neither the English nor the Pope's men were plain or clear with each other. It smacks of double-dealing, but there can be advantages both ways in ambiguity. Lord Grey may have hoped to persuade the last ships to take on prisoners and carry them home to be held for ransom. If so, they were unable or unwilling. The last ships sailed away.

The garrison yielded, laid down weapons and took its chances. Maybe hoping the English could not stomach the slaughter of so many. But Lord Grey gave the order that they should all die and quickly. He orders two captains, Ralegh and another, to take their companies and to do the work. To hang the Irish and English renegades, breaking their arms and legs first. To put the rest, every living soul, to the sword. There were women and children among them. No matter.

They killed them swift and sure while the rest of the army packed and prepared to leave. Then the two companies, without taking time to clean the clotted blood, packed bag and baggage, adding weapons and sparse loot, stripping corpses of anything worth keeping, and marched away.

Until they found time and water to wash themselves, his company must have looked more like a gathering of barber-surgeons then soldiers.

Most interesting is why Lord Grey chose Ralegh for the duty. I can think of reasons.

Ralegh had already proved a good soldier. Though not always perfect for obedience, he would do what he was told. And his men would follow him.

News of Ralegh's other adventures, having reached the Court and Council in dispatches, captured the interest of men in high places. And Captain Ralegh was now taking time to write letters to these men. Letters concerning the state of things in Ireland. Letters in which he did not hesitate to be critical of Lord Grey. And more sure than if it was sealed in butter, Grey would know about this. For Ralegh, following notions of his half brother, Sir Humphrey Gilbert, and all his Carew kinsmen, favored the rule of Ireland by blood and iron. And then repopulation with Englishmen.

I see Lord Grey say to himself: *Here's an impudent man who can lay an ambush and seize a castle, who can kill in battle and is not afraid. He knows something of war and soldiering. Blood and iron? Well, here's an inescapable occasion for both. Let us see if he has stomach for it.*

And Ralegh, knowing his commander, taking the order

without raising an eyebrow. Performing it without losing his appetite.

Perhaps, too, who knows? Lord Grey rightly feared the displeasure of the Queen at the thought of all that ransom money wasted on blood-soaked earth. Let Captain Ralegh take a share of blame.

Ralegh was a good horse soldier and hard as they come. But wars are not won by the cavalry on the wings or in skirmishes or ambush. Wars are won by the plodding infantry square. He commanded his company as he had ridden his horse. And no doubt loved his company in much the same way. If he had ever fought much in close ranks with pike or black bill in the common sweat and slaughter, he would have learned a different sort of lesson.

I do not know what he learned at Smerwick.

His story and the stories they tell of him show he always remained the sort of leader of men he had been in Ireland. By land or by sea. At Cadiz, sailing the *Warspite* into the harbor. And is he different at Fayal in the Azores, limping along with his cane, bareheaded and a large white scarf tied to his arm for all to see, leading a ragtag and bobtail crew up a narrow exposed rocky trail under a beehive of Spanish bullets, his cape as full of holes as a piece of Geneva cheese, to storm and take the Spanish fort there? I think it is the same man.

No doubt he knew what he was doing and the reasons why. Believed circumstances called for the gamble. For though he might and did often take risks, he was never a rash—and vainglorious in my humble opinion—man like Essex.

I think if he had not been on his back, wrestling fever for his life, he would have taken the Spaniards at San Thomé and maybe have found his gold mine there.

[291]

Still, I believe he learned a lesson in Ireland. And maybe at Smerwick. Learned that it was already too late to unlearn old habits. Too late for him to change the cavalry style. Learning that war stark naked is more than the canter of cavalry. For after that time in Ireland, he never favored the use of large English armies on land. He fought by sea and sometimes on shore when a landing must be made; and he only soldiered in defense of the realm.

Ride hard, hit fast, and run was his style, the only style he knew. Well, he could have it that way on a ship, I'd reckon. But not for him to lead armies. He let Essex do that and fail and fail again. He watched Mountjoy do it and succeed.

No, he did not lose his appetite for fighting at Smerwick. But I'll wager he lost his stomach for the tedious butcher's work of blood and iron.

And he saw Lord Grey carry that idea of blood and iron to the extremity in Munster. Lay waste to all, denuding the land and leaving a wealth of bones, some living on as walking bags of bones, it is true, behind. Where the only thing, man or plant or beast, left thriving and fat was the wide-winged, slow-soaring, insatiable kite in the sky.

After Ireland, he was chiefly in and of the Court. In and out of favor with the Queen.

She took a threadbare knave of a soldier and made him one of the richest men in the kingdom. Showered gold and honors on his head.

Let me not pretend to understand all the why's and the wherefore's. But, casting aside envy, I have some opinions.

I note that in a very short time the Queen made him from nothing to a great man, almost overburdened with the weight of riches. I note, too, that even when he was in disgrace because of a secret marriage out of necessity to one of her maids of honor in '91, even then she did not deprive him of what she had given —estates, perquisites, offices.

For the whole time that he was forbidden the Court, he retained and she left vacant—a very strange thing it seems to me —his post as Captain of the Guard.

And I note, too, sir, that although in her reign he held many offices, his chief and only office *of the Court* was always that— the Captain of the Guard. Never, in spite of intriguing, was he elevated to the Council.

All this whets my interest. A little puzzle game. Childish it may seem to those who know the ways of Courts, but for me it is a knot to untangle.

I say these things to myself:

She who was Captain of England chose one of the best of her military captains to be her own.

She, who the world knows was frugal as a poor farmer's wife, nevertheless was fantastical in her rewards to this man. More than to any, directly, if you consider it. For she may or may not have given more to other favorites, but he was given most, because changed most. From nothing to great wealth is more and means more than any addition to the man who possesses an estate.

She, who was fierce in retribution to all who betrayed her confidence and trust, let him off with a punishment so light it was, in the ways of the Court, I imagine, no more than a frown. It was Bess Throckmorton who suffered most.

Now, sir, much has been said of the Queen's fondness for her favorites and her womanly jealousy and suchlike. I'll not deny that, since I don't know enough to affirm or deny.

What I do know is what can be easily known and proved.

That, allowing for misjudgments, the late Queen had a marvelous habit of choosing the right man for the proper office. I cannot imagine Court or Council which contained so many good servants. True, they were often opposed to one another and their advice and counsel was contradictory. Just so. I understand this. When I was a captain I listened to my lieutenant, my green ensign, my sergeants and corporals. Indeed, I would listen to a pikeman if he had something to tell me. Listened and weighed all, then made my own free choice and issued my orders. In the nature of things, each speaking out of his own view, from his own vantage, their counsel would be different. Which is fine. God help me if they had ever agreed in perfect harmony.

The Queen could, likewise, listen to Ralegh and listen to Essex. Hear Burghley and Leicester, Throckmorton, Sir Nicholas Bacon, Walsingham, Gresham. Oh, name a hundred more. Could, as one of her mottoes says, see everything and say nothing.

Very well, I have wandered afield.

My question is: Considering all I know and can judge by, beginning and end, what caught her eye and kept her favor toward Walter Ralegh? Why this one instead of a dozen or more of the others hanging by, men who were living on promises, patiently waiting upon and serving her until their patience finally vanished with their wits and the substance of their estates?

Say this: She marked him for what he was, a man with nothing to lose—a soldier. A man who had gambled his life for no reward many times.

Just as she had. Just as she must.

A man who acted like a veteran captain. She, who had lived with danger since childhood and more danger as Queen of a threatened kingdom, needed such a man close by.

Then, my guess is, she tested him, with lavish rewards. The

[294]

best of men can be corrupted by an excess of good fortune. The hardest resolve can be softened by too much sweetness.

Outwardly he changed not at all. Or better, since his swagger and appearance outraged so many, say that though he changed his vestments, he gave every sign of being the same beneath them.

Misfortune settled the matter. When still a soldier, though in the privy chamber and beyond, he found one of the Queen's maids of honor swelling up with his seed, he married her in secret. And the two tried to brazen it out. They failed, of course.

Here, someone will say, he failed the Queen's testing.

Another will add that Ralegh proved his limits, how far and how well he could be trusted.

I would argue that to find the limits of trustworthiness and fidelity—and all creatures, even a good dog, have limits to these—had been her aim all along. She may have been secretly happy upon two counts. First that his actions served to confirm her original judgment of him. And all those who lead men need some confirmation of their judgments.

Second, relieved she had not been so enchanted as to raise him higher, where he could work real harm.

He proved himself not quite fit for the Council. Not by greed, for she made good use of greedy men. Not by lechery either or, for that matter, folly or infidelity. Those failings can be taken into account.

Not by any of these so much as by—*indifference*. In a final corner of himself, he did not care. The Queen could go and stand on her head.

I think, sir, the Queen may have been pleased. Now she knew her man by heart.

Do you see?

In certain conditions, in the grip of uncertain events, Ralegh would throw away his future like feed for chickens.

Now she knew that his finest moments would come at those times when a future seems no longer possible. His most shining times would be those, like a soldier's, of pure and perfect present time.

She could hope such a time would never come for her or the kingdom. Yet if it should happen that all things fell away, in adversity and dreadful misfortune, and all things and all hopes were lost, he would still be there and then he would surely live or die for her. His life and body would shield hers. And not out of love or fidelity or ambition or honor or virtue, but out of the joy and the style of it and because that time would truly be his home.

Thus none of her favors had been wasted. She could wish him well and look on him always with love and confidence.

Well, so do I wish him well. Though if I wake him from his snooze to tell him so, he'll curse me for a meddlesome fool. And we would come to blows soon enough, I'll bet you.

There he dozes. Who else but an old soldier could nap in the shadow of the heading ax?

Why not? He has lived a long time and far beyond the use of king and kingdom. His time was really done when the King made peace. For a soldier in peace is a chimney in summertime.

One thing more and then I am done.

Somewhere in the fields of France a stranger wheeled horse and fired at the lad from a dozen paces and the wind and heat of the bullet singed his ear. Then the lad fired his pistol and saw a man gasp, go white-eyed, and topple out of saddle to lie spurting blood on grass while the riderless horse galloped away. Somewhere, then and there, Walter Ralegh gave up his ghost with a shudder. And as a good hunter honors the fallen stag, so he, looking down at a dying stranger, partook of death himself.

A man can only die once. A soldier dies early, and he lives, if he lives, on time that is given him, nothing he ever earned.

Every soldier is the ghost of the man he was. He can never shed fear until he sheds flesh and bones. But he need not be fearful.

What does a ghost have to be afraid of?

Take it all, wars and glory and riches and fame, and stuff it down the privy.

I'll settle for one more night in a certain Irish tower by the burning fire.

Say to the Court it glowes and shines like
rotten wood . . .

RALEGH—*The Lie*

For whoso reaps renown above the rest,
With heaps of hate shall surely be opprest.

RALEGH—*dedicatory poem
for Gascoigne's* The Steele Glass

3

Comes forward now, slouched, faint smile, eyebrows arched to engrave a smooth clear forehead with thin delicate lines which may mean annoyance or merely signal mild tedium, so composed, from the blink of the lone diamond in the center of the ribbon-flower rosette upon the high-heeled velvet slippers, pinked at the toes to show glimpses of the lining of contrasting satin, to the crisped curls and ringlets of his hair, he seems to have been created all at once as he is. By a portrait painter perhaps. Limned upon wood or canvas cloth and fixed in a decorative gilt frame to hang upon the wall among others of his kind.

Could be one among hundreds who played out their spring-time in performance of vague service, living on abundance of hope, only to depart from Court, sooner or later, older, im-pecunious, and embittered, if no wiser.

He could be just such a one, a likely type, though not likely to speak across time offering anything more than the worldly wisdom of wounded pride and thwarted ambition.

Whatever truth he might tell would be tinctured by failure, an honorable experience, but one many men have shared.

Besides he would have been at a distance, though in and of the Court. Sometimes in the presence chamber, he can never have been admitted to the privy chamber. He could offer long views, through, over, around the heads of a crowd. A bird's view of ceremonies, processions, pageants. Tag ends of gossip. Color, noise of music, voices raised together in psalms or in concord counterpoint in madrigal and motet; rich resonance of viols; exquisite echoing of lute and cithern; birdcalls of recorders and woodwinds; bold bell-ringing brass of trumpets and, deeper, the long hautboy; pulse, shiver, and throb of drums; heraldic splendor of the organ and the light wine-sparkle of the virginal; of pippety-pop, slither, and slide of dancing slippers moving to the latest corantos, pavanes and galliards; discreet crackle and rustle of stiff expensive cloths, tinkle of chains, snap and stretch of leather; outdoors shouts and cries and laughter, prancing rhythm of hooves on stone and hard earth. Moments of abrupt hush to hear through a press of bodies, over the garden of heads, the announcements of heralds and officers, or, soft and clear, the voice of the Queen. Or that same voice and others, and then a burst of male laughter, with all the chitter-chatter of the maid of honor and Court ladies, too distant to be distinct.

Odors: scent of perfumes and herbs and powders and unguents from body and clothing and nosegay, rich as incense, thick as smoke of burning leaves, yet all invisible, and all together not quite disguising the odor of the sweat of bodies too often unwashed; of dying rushes strewn against the cold of halls; crisp lightwood burning in fireplaces and the smell of sea coal; sweetened candles casting a sky of little stars; or the fat torch in its socket sparkling, smelling of the country; dank, damp, and sour, the odor of privies and stables; sour and stale, despite herbs and perfumes, the odor of bedsheets.

Odor and taste of the score and more of dishes served at noon dinner. Meats and fowl spiced and sweetened. Candied fruits and marzipan. Wines fuming in silver and glass. Ale like the heart of grain at harvest time, dry and musty.

Oh, they ate well, and he might be happy to remember that.

He could tell of lazy afternoons at cards and dice, where he had small luck; bowling or tennis and wagering. Of walks in the glory of garden paths in good weather. Strolls along galleries in grayer light, where portraits watched the coming and going, pieces of joinery polished and shining, locks and handles of best brass and silver.

Tell of days at the theater or an evening masque in the banquet house. And what the clown said that made the Queen laugh or frown. What a dying hero, sore distressed, put into noble words which made them dab at tears with handkerchiefs as lacy as their ruffs and cuffs.

Speak of brawls in spinning crowded taverns and how, laughing, they outran the London Watch.

Tell, with a sigh, of cold hours and interminable sermons in churches; flutter and feathers and blood of the cockpit; and wagers there too.

All off together, young and unimportant, to Tyburn to hear a wretch make the one speech of a lifetime, then dance his capriole on air. Or watch a vagabond or a whore whipped naked through the streets.

At night alone in a small chamber. Too small for more than one servant and lucky if that. To prime pump with wine and to waste costly paper, powder, and ink on verses written to a

[301]

lady too grand to know his name. Crumpling paper and feeding it to the dying fire. Rising not steady, but steadily more aroused, to stagger and stumble in hat and muffled cloak toward some house, hand on hilt of sword and hat cocked with menace against any wretch with club or knife who might think he was defenseless. To enter that house and wait for his turn with someone who, if no lady, offering no idyllic garden, could share, bright as a summer hayfield, in the immemorial country of flesh and forgetfulness.

Yet knowing, even at peak pleasure, he would sleep late in the morning, eggshell head full of noises, drums and horsemen, dreams of another kind of rod across his backside at school long ago. Fears, too, of the first jewel, prime bloom of God-knows-what nameless French or Italian disease. And then a cure of strong waters, foul purges and medicines, chilling baths.

Might tell of the solemn frenzies in summer when the Queen made her progress in the country. Miles of wagons and horses; jolt and jar of roads. Saddlesore, sunburned, wind-wrinkled, sweat-bathed, and well powdered—with English dust. To arrive at last at some manor house, grand as a palace and newer than any, owned by a fellow no better than himself, only luckier.

"Well, we'll see about that, my great man, while we drink you dry, cellar and wells, gobble your fodder in stable, pick your meat to slick bones at table. Break glasses and filch a silver salt . . ."

Placed in a chamber small as a monk's cell, if not in a tent, a bed like a coffin to share with three others. But to turn out prompt and clean as a whistle, fresh as a May morn, to stand and hear interminable hexameter Latin verses and speeches delivered by bumpkins, officious merchants, mayors, and ministers and rusty old knights, full of fire and beer and braggadocio,

[302]

greeting the Queen. Music tortured by awkward musicians. With good luck, maybe a country dance of lightly clad, beflowered, sturdy-limbed country girls.

"Always a chance, my lad, in the darkness, while fireworks and colored fountains play for the Queen's pleasure, to slip away with some fine country lass and teach her the oldest of Court dances, to clothe her in green clover and show her a wondrous rocket of my own."

Up before daylight to hunt; not himself to kill, but to haloo and cry with valiant vigor though it lift the roof of his head, and to bear, with saintly grin, hunting horns screaming inside it. Seeing not much with red-rimmed, red-veined, and lid-lazy eyes. Holding tight rein and gripping saddle with trembling shanks lest he tumble and break a leg and have to lay a month in the country to mend. No better off than the parable's man in the ditch; and not one Samaritan this side of London.

Up at dawn in a roar of packing and leaving.

"And who stole my toothcream and toothpicks? By God, I'll have his liver in an Apostle spoon!"

More speeches to hear, farewells; and pray that the girl, over there, doesn't know your face by daylight; it's for sure you never told her your name.

And then off again, one of a string of fantastic beads, down a road of pure dust or pure mud, mouth full of wool and beard made of cobwebs, happy to doze and happier to sweat away ale and soreness of the nights before.

"Call it a poem and a pilgrimage. I call it a pain in the arse."

He could tell all that and more. With uncertain nostalgia and shrugging. Conceal any shame behind a taut grin of regret. For he was not raised up to or taught to love idleness. And that's what it was, what all added up to in the reckoning. A long accounting of wasted days, pleasant at the time, give or take, but sadly regretted now that none of his schemes took roots.

Better he had stayed home to become, maybe, a justice of the peace. Or taken a company to the wars to risk his neck and his health for small pay and dead men's wages and whatever he could scoop and scrounge; or gone to sea and risked fevers and drowning and the Spanish Inquisition in the hope of gold and other dry goods.

Better that than this; but he chose it once because—they told him at home and he believed them—he had good looks, quick wit, a nimble way about him, and an eye for advancement.

Now looks have gone, wits are weary, having never had much exercise; limbs are not nimble, and his eye rests on a fat country widow who smiles to prove the scarcity of good teeth in England. But she has a nice piece of land and a sturdy half-timbered thatch-roof house, and cattle and pigs, and not too many children. Bless her heart, fluttering beneath a sack of paps. For he'll still dress up in the patched ruins of his Court clothes —lucky to have kept clothes on his back—and strut like a peacock; as at Court he never could.

Ah, he saw the real peacocks, close enough to copy. Though he skulked and shrunk whenever they came by. Though slack of wit and weary of recollection, he can tell lies as well as a London tapster. And if his tales please her, and though her tail prove as tough as a Dutch saddle, he can live out his remaining days in modest comfort, and—who knows?—die a country knight who lived a fool.

But leave him, for this moment. Leave him to the English countryside.

For it is not he who has come to stand with an ambiguous smile and a loose-limbed satiric posture. Not he set free from the frame of a portrait or an oval miniature by Isaac Oliver or Nicholas Hilliard, fitted to one perfect gold locket; to hang upon a chain of thin gold and to rest warm and unseen—unless that fashion should change this season—between two perfect, gentle, milk-white, classic, rounded temples, pavilions of love, much worshiped in an excess of adoring kisses.

Not a finished picture. Not to be found in any gallery, or high attic festooned with cobwebs, or turned to the wall in a cellar. He has never posed for his own portrait; though he has sat in a stiff pose for another, a great man, after the features and lines of the true model were drawn from the quick. Such men are busy with affairs and cannot keep still for picture makers.

For a jest he wore his own new slippers wrought in frilly, fancy Paris style. But the gentleman he posed for cannot have troubled to notice this, and now sits in the portrait gallery of a manor house in all his splendor, wearing an incongruous pair of peach-colored, utterly foppish French slippers.

He will sit no more for others' pictures. Unless, of course, the King himself or a member of Council should ask him. And that will not happen. He will not, either, have his own portrait done.

No way to know if this ageless young man has come from manor house or ancient castle. Perhaps he is a younger son, cousin, or a nephew of modest means. A matter of no conse-_uence. Nor whether he idled at Cambridge or Oxford or which, if any, of the Inns of Court he calls his. He has read proper books and knows improper ones as well. And, rich or poor, son of an ambitious merchant or some stark-Bedlam knight of the pasture, he plays his part with such an ease that anyone must wish for him that his bloodline could be traced back to Brito-martis.

To wish is but a half step from believing it so.

Handsome, healthy, and well favored, much barbered, groomed, and beautifully dressed—even to the last gentle grace note to complete the harmony, a certain slight *negligence,* some signs of artful casualness, this man is unchanging. For him mutability's a word for poems and easy rhymes.

The other one kicking stones and clods in the meadow behind the cottage he first came from and has returned to, poorer than he planned, still daydreaming, a litigious daydream, the case for and against the widow; widow of the gap-toothed, irrepressible smile. Trying to discount a cynical, skeptical barrister's voice that tells him he knows, without further examination, what secrets lie hidden beneath apron, kirtle, gown, skirt, and shift. Denying that voice and trying to conjure up an inverse ciphering whereby her charms, at last exposed and tasted, will be sweeter and softer and uncloying exactly in opposite balance to her formidable front: ragged-sail, leaky; just as an old galleon may conceal chests of treasure, sacks of rare spices, bolts of silk; just so imagining her and hoping imagining will make it so and raise his ensign proudly and no retreat; fantasy being more than half the music, half the art.

This one changed, grew older, bade farewell to the Court silently, not in verses. Slipped away by dark of the moon on account of a misunderstanding with a certain greedy money-lender who had not given him half value on his best plate. Vowing never to return. Took passage homeward not by horse or coach, but propped in a rumbling baggage cart. Until, one day's journey from his village, he rented the best post horse at the inn. Changed into his finest, buckled harness and sword and set forth. Into a pouring rain, leading and tugging the horse through mud on a road that seemed to have vanished, and, indeed, did so before, far after nightfall, he sneaked up the village street and beyond it to a house where he waited, rain or no rain, a long time to knock and wake the servants, feeling, without having to see, his wet ruff and cuffs limp and sad, his hat shapeless as an oyster; muddy as a pig farmer; all soaked to the bone—one last lost survivor of the Armada.

Ready finally to rap on the door and hold up his head into the glare of a tallow candle, yellow in its horn lantern, unblinking in spite of the gasps which greeted him.

"I should have been here in time for supper. But I was set upon by a half-dozen idle rogues armed with cudgels."

"Lord God, are you hurt?"

"A few bruises. No matter, no matter. One of these gypsies had a pistol and he pointed it straight at my heart. . . .

"But rain had ruined the fellow's powder. He couldn't make flash or fire. So I skewered him clean with my sword. Danced him like a chunk of mutton on a spit and left him to feed kites.

"If a man points pistol at me and aims to kill, he must pay the price."

"And the others?"

"Well, now, when they saw this gypsy go to God, they dropped sticks and took off like a flock of bleating sheep. *Haloo!* says I. *I may be late for supper but damn me if I'll miss the sport!* So I ran them for miles, clean out of the county. And I doubt they've caught their wind yet. . . ."

Laughs and laughs until the old servant chuckles too.

A pause.

"Well?"

"Are you finished, sir?"

[307]

"What do you mean by that?"

"Only, sir, if it pleases you, I was thinking if you had done with your tale, you might like to come in out of the rain."

No, not that man. Who changed with the times without ever changing.

Ask him, and he'll define mutability without hesitation.

"Why, 'tis the wiggling of fingers and wagging of hands whereby the deaf and dumb make chatter with each other."

Take instead the other, the ageless young man.

Take him as young and unlined, save when he raises an eyebrow, or the laughing edges of his eyes, the corners of his lips; forever unchanging and unfading. He is the child of change. And all that can be outwardly seen of him, all that the changing world and Court could ever know, burning with change, his nature like the nature of flame, restless, ever swaying and dancing, dying down to flare up again with least encouragement of air.

If he is one man, he is also many. As all the cards together make a deck. . . .

And in that bunch every card's a one-eyed knavel

Voice of our disgruntled, discarded country gentleman, still outraged.

Listen! he calls out. *I know the fellow well, or else his twin brother. I sat at table playing cards with him. Played at Spanish primero and honest English trump. Played gleek and maw, post and pair, and Pope July, and never won so much as a clipped coin off him. Those young peacocks had rings upon their fingers with mirrors set amongst the jewels.*

—Console yourself, sir, the young man replies. Think: *Far from Court, far from care.* Think, in restored country wisdom:

A man must go old to Court and young to a cloister who wishes to go from thence to heaven.

Damn you, sir! (the other voice, fading, answering from safety of distance), *An ape is still an ape though he be clad in purple.*

—To which, sir, in the same spirit, permit me to reply: *You cannot make a whistle out of a pig's tail.* Be content, and remember before you spurn that well-fed village widow: *There is a virtue which poverty cannot destroy.* Go to and be content. You are out of the rain. You are eating bread and cheese and drinking the widow's cider from a stout wooden cup. And if the woman will believe half your tales, why you may yet be named the best liar in England.

There is no further answer from the other.

The young man turns to best advantage, to the light, to speak for himself.

—A poor country bumpkin, with little money and less charm. Though, perhaps, with a bare necessity of both, sufficient to lord it in some godforsaken village in a distant county where none of us knows anyone or wishes to. Some fellow whose grandfather was knighted by a dead king in a moment of drunkenness or fever. And on that alone, came bouncing into Court to make his fortune, to play the bright angel who tripped over the ledge of heaven and fell, ass over joint stool, down to common earth.

—Pity is wasted on the man. He is a sheep, fit for an age of sheep. And sheep are single-minded animals, solemn and stupid beyond believing. The last frisk of life goes out of them when they cease to be called lambs. Their happiest destiny is to be a joint of cold mutton in an alehouse.

—Believe me, I have no compassion for those fellows. The

worst are insufferable impudent rogues. The best are bodies to fill a chamber or swell a progress. And each and every one is a clown. Of course, the more the merrier. We plucked them, feathers and all, down to natural goosebumps, and then sent them home. Without them one might have been sore pressed, at times, for money and amusement.

—I recall one solemn fellow, fat as a pig and not half so fastidious, who besought us, with most touching simplicity, to teach him the ways and manners of the Court and how to advance himself.

—We laughed and were about to begin his education with the art of throwing dice, when Harrington, Sir John, the Queen's godson and a most amusing fellow, really, Harrington stopped us before we had begun.

"No, no!" quoth Harrington. "You idle, ignorant, lascivious, negligent, parasitical popinjays have forgotten the first principle of the Gospel according to Castiglione."

"A sinister and wicked Italian, as I recall," someone said. "A devious writer bent upon corrupting youth."

"And, devoting yourselves to wholly frivolous pastimes when you could be reading *The Book of Martyrs* or hearing a sermon in the city."

"But, Harrington," says another, "I *am* a sort of martyr, don't you see? I've taken on poverty, chastity, and obedience, all in the service of the Queen. And now I offer my life and example, a martyr to eternal tedium."

"Be still," Harrington says. "You were born to die at the end of a rope. It's written in the stars."

"I never look at the stars. They are too perfect. Perfection is tedious too."

"You are so debauched, so vicious with deadly sloth and the

other six, whatever they may be, you have forgotten all you learned in school, if you learned anything but to count the strokes of the master's cane on your backside. Have you forgotten Ovid? This world is nothing but continual change and transformation. And I propose to prove the poet was right. I intend to turn this into a silk purse."

"Oh, thank you, sir," says the fat boy. "And I promise to share with you anything that Fortune may send to fill that silk purse."

—Followed by our laughter, a pack of hounds at their heels, Harrington and the fellow left our chamber arm in arm.

—Rumor was bruited about that Harrington was dead earnest in his pedagogy. And, sure enough, he might have been a Jesuit for all we saw of him for a month or so. We heard he was teaching the fellow, in brief, of course, according to Castiglione. He was seen hopping about like a trained seal, while Sir John shouted hoarse encouragement, at an Italian fencing school. Someone passed beneath a window and heard a lute, terribly tuned, tortured, and a voice singing what might have been "Greensleeves," if sung by a drunken Muscovite.

—It was widely believed in our circle that Harrington would try to pass the fellow off as a foreigner. Or perhaps with a cloak of feathers and stain of walnut juice he could play an Indian. In rags he would be a perfect Irishman.

—Not so. . . .

—At last Harrington placed him in the care of his own tailor. Then brought him forth, a very elegant satirical model of the finest men of the Court. Perfect to the last details tailor and barber could contrive.

—Being the Queen's godson and amusing to Her Majesty at all but most serious moments, Sir John had no difficulty arranging occasion to present his pupil to the Queen. It was, as I recall, in the large presence chamber at Whitehall. There were many of the Court there, for the news had traveled the corridors on greased wheels.

—The two were summoned and brought forward to kneel before Her Majesty. They must have rehearsed it a thousand times. For the pupil dropped to his knees before the Queen as graceful as if he had been doing so for all his years.

—Unfortunately, as he did so, he farted.

—It was not, I should venture, a decorous fart. Some say it was a trumpet fart. Others, because of the rich resonance, insist that it was more like the deep blast of an hautboy. It reminded me of nothing so much as a large cannon fired in a small room.

—At that moment all the candles flickered and burned blue. Portraits went aslant on the walls. A pensioner or two may have fainted. I swear I heard a halberd fall and clatter on the floor before the echo had died away. There was so great a quiet you could have heard whispers behind a lady's fan at a hundred yards.

"Which one of you did that?" Her Majesty demanded.

"I confess it was I," Harrington, ever unruffled, replied. "I've been somewhat windy all day."

—The Queen said nothing for a moment, staring at the two of them.

—And very slowly, as if fire had been kindled behind his eyes, the round face of the pupil began to glow, first maiden-blushing pink as dawn, then brighter and deeper, until, having run through a full day in less time than it requires to snap your fingers, his face was a truly magnificent sunset painted in scarlet.

"Damn you Jakes Harrington, you tell more lies than the

Pope's epitaph!" the Queen said. "It was that fat boy who let fly the fart. Begone, both of you. My eyes are burning and I think I may go blind."

The young man smiles again, tilts his head and seems to lean back against nothing, as he might be resting against a wall or a column. A trick, no doubt, he learned at Court.

Come closer and see him change, transformed without moving muscle or adding a cubit to his stature. Except, of course, as fashion in heels and in thickness of soles causes him to rise and fall.

First, he's beardless as a boy, short-haired, flat soft slanting cap with a burst of downy feathers over one ear. Long, high-collared doublet, short hose, and over all a long gown with hanging sleeves, fur-trimmed; heavy shoes with square, blunted toes.

Next he wears a beard, long and full, merging with a thick, downturning mustache; paned and sleeveless jerkin, embroidered shirt beneath; a jewel or two, thin rim of white at the collar; and where he once wore an ornamental dagger, he wears one sharp enough to carve meat; and wears also a large-handled, heavy, one-handed sword.

Look again. . . . Well before the Armada sailed you find him—a little awkward now—in padded and stiffened short doublet with many buttons and peascod belly (like a pregnant wench). Puffed sleeves with wings, short hose and bright garters; flat lacework collar overtopped by the high rising of a white shirt collar. Long hair, cut even below the ears, and beard and mustache short and pointed and tamed.

—Truly, he interrupts, that was a bad time, brief as it was, for any man with decent conformation. It was a plot, a con-

[313]

spiracy of certain wicked old men, rough seagoing types and suchlike who were then close to Her Majesty. Or perhaps it was Her Majesty's stratagem to make these salty dogs at home in the Court. And an attempt, wasted of course, to make the rest of us, her perennial honeybees, ashamed of being such idle fops. The Queen was very moral at times about such things. She offered us occasional opportunities to feel some shame for our shallow lives and idle pastimes. But I am happy to report that none of my acquaintance ever took advantage of the occasion. Nor, I suppose, did she expect us to.

—May I say with all modesty that upon one occasion I was kneeling nearby in attendance, and I overheard Her Majesty jesting with the Earl of Leicester. Who, as her favorite then, set the fashions.

"If we women were half as vain and inconstant in our clothing," she said, "we would ruin our lovers and husbands and plunge the kingdom into poverty."

—Leicester grumbled and pretended to take offense. He assured the Queen that he took no more thought about matters of appearance than a scarecrow in a field; for she of all people should know that his heart and mind were wholly given over to the service of Her Majesty. She looked into his earnest face where he knelt next to her, the portrait of an aged choirboy. And then she laughed out loud. "Go to, go to!" she cried out. So heads turned from a distance and the corners of the chamber quieted to hear.

"You foolish man, I'll wager a jewel if you come here for dinner tomorrow, barefoot and naked as Adam, with only an empty fish cask to hide your shame, why, before supper every man in Court, except my Guard, will be clad in wooden staves and smelling of flounder."

[314]

"If I did that," the Earl said, "I would want time to discuss the matter with my friends in the fish market."

"You would, indeed," she said, pinching the jowl of his cheek. "A proper cask would be worth its weight in silver before you put it on."

"Well," says he, " a well-made cask is worth a lot to a fishmonger."

"You'd extoll the virtues of wicker baskets and then buy casks for half what they're worth."

"I fear you don't know the shrewd practices and sharp wit of London fishmongers," he says. "An empty cask in and of itself is one thing. A pure fish barrel, as it were. There are very few of those, Your Majesty."

"Do you speak from experience or rumor, Robin?"

"From speculation, ma'am. You know I am a Puritan at heart."

"Go on, then. Tell us your fantasy."

"I say that an empty fish cask, pristine and unsullied, is rare as the unicorn in this kingdom."

"Then you shall have to buy full casks. What will you do with the fish?"

"When the watch is sound asleep, I'll steal through the streets of London and leave heaps and mounds of fish at every corner. And for years after it will be a holiday, proclaimed by the Lord Mayor himself, the Day of the Earl of Leicester's Miracle. He produced no loaves at all, but there were fishes in God's plenty."

"Why, man, the whole of London will stink of dead fish."

"It will not be noticed, ma'am."

"It is a miracle that I do not box your ears in the presence of this company."

"Why then, I could not wear a fish barrel. Nothing but sackcloth and ashes would serve me."

"Ah, Robin, not even you could bring sackcloth and ashes into fashion in my Court. But I still wager a jewel you won't appear tomorrow in a fishmonger's cask. You are too vain."

"Your Majesty knows me well, chapter and verse. You shall have your jewel. But I am not so certain that vanity is the spring of my fears."

"What then?"

"Allow me a little Christian compassion," he says. "Some of these fine fellows are as slender and delicate as a willow wand . . . (*Pointing directly at me where I knelt and she nodding and smiling.*)

"And might shiver to death in Adam's costume."

"I suppose," she said, still glancing at me, "it would be a trick to kneel in a cask."

"Perhaps he could manage a fig leaf gracefully."

"Go to, you naughty man!"

—Where were we? Ah, yes, we were digressing upon the theme of the padded doublet, if anyone could possibly care. Of course, God's truth, there were times when I cared about nothing else but fashion. And, considering all, those times were, if I may say so, among my most memorable.

It is possible to believe him.

—Pray do not fall into that common error. Nothing good can come from too much trust between strangers—friends either. Excess leads to ruination. The rule of moderation holds true for everything save laughter. There can never be enough of that. Without the gift of laughter we should surely enjoy a second Deluge, for this world would be drowned in tears. . . .

The faint smile never flickers, but the eyes are tired and sad. In a moment he might weep, if ghosts can shed tears. Perhaps, like a player, he can summon tears for any performance.

—Let us return to the high thin air of Courts, thinner and colder than winds of the Alps.

No doubt he has visited Italy.

—Every Englishman of any quality has made a tour there. Has traveled in spirit if flesh were willing, but purse too thin.

—Now then, let us be done with the peascod doublet once and for all.

—I do here solemnly confess that I, too, wore it when that was the fashion, ridiculous as a puppet, Punch or Judy, no matter which. But there were other choices. When I could, despite its overt military air, I wore a pinked sleeveless jerkin, pinched in tight at the waist, with a high standing collar, chin up like any fearless soldier, and only a thin line of puffed lace along the edge. It suited me well, except for a flare at the hips and the loose short breeches. Which implied that I was proud possessor of a beam as broad as a Devonshire milkmaid.

Now see him in the glorious eighties, wearing a short doublet, knee breeches, long trunk hose, short, elegantly embroidered doublet fitting naturally; a cloak worn loose with a swagger, held by hidden laces; the collar gone, replaced by starched white folds of ruff, slanting from beneath the ears down to the point of the beard; rings on his fingers, and jewels join the feathers of his cap. For his feet he wears soft felt or velvet, backless mules; high boots for outdoors.

—Let the record show that I courageously ignored the prevailing fashion of the high-crowned sugarloaf hat. I owned one like everyone else; and, I admit I wore it once. But my friends told me that I most resembled a chimney looking for a fire.

At the time of the Armada see him in matching doublet and Venetians, soft slippers with backs, and an astounding cartwheel ruff of lace, held out half a yard by wire or bone, and making his head, the hair a little longer and brushed back behind the ears, seem set upon a white platter.

Before the century has turned, he is in better form in tight-fitting doublet, short, the shoulders widened and padded with wings; much intricate small decoration and embroidery against sober colors; the ruff diminished to more modest proportion, but now aided and abetted by a lace collar, or a falling band, beneath it; of the same material, delicate to transparency, an inch or so of lace cuff turned back at the ends of the sleeves.

In the Court of King James the ruff will grow marvelous again, then mysteriously vanish forever, replaced by a wide starched collar; short doublet coming to a point; a length of stocking for the showing off of a fine leg—thin ones could be deftly padded, but woe to a fat man; seldom sword and harness; pointed shoes with high cork heels, roses and ribbons or jewels on the shoe; and, like it or not, a tall crowned hat, wide or narrow of brim, with a colorful band and one or more feathers drooping low. Hair longer, sometimes to shoulder length; beard no more than a well-trained point of the chin; mustache, however, full and wide and waxed.

—May I add something to this protean picture? Please remember that any part of any one fashion might be worn with an alloy of others, according to taste and preference. Allow, too, that a man could settle his choice upon one style that pleased him most and wear it without regard to fashion.

—Travel has been mentioned, both in uncomfortable fact and contented imagination. Some brought the bits and pieces of foreign fashions home with them. Others—some who had never stepped beyond the counties of their birth—would borrow a whim or notion, transformed by English tailors.

—Consider that all the turns and counterturns, wars and troubles on the Continent cast up foreigners to live in England. They came from the Netherlands, from Germany, France, and Portugal, bringing their styles and their crafts of making and dyeing; new ways of weaving and coloring and cutting; starch and colored starch.

—There was the jest in a common play, an English play, how an Englishman acquired his doublet in Italy, hose in France, bonnet in Germany, and his behavior everywhere.

Taking such for granted, he does not mention the uniforms, gowns, and badges of office, of clerks and scholars, officers of government, offices of the Court, the clergy with ordered ranks and vestments, orders of knighthood and nobility. And the habitual clothing of the crafts and guilds, prentice, journeyman, and master. And servants clad according to the master's wishes, the whole intricate ladder of ranks and stations, from turnspit and scullion to secretary and steward.

—Compound it more by considering regulations and sumptuary laws, statutes designed to preserve some kind of order amid this confusion, requiring that citizens dress according to their stations. Needless to say, these laws changed with the music of fashion and were largely unenforced, being unenforceable. A freeborn Englishman has always deemed it a part of his natural liberty to dress as he pleases.

—At Court, however, whims of the Queen were law. Woe to the lady who appeared there in anything more resplendent than the Queen!

He is not interested in religious distinctions: the Puritan who railed against sumptuous apparel and affected, as his badge of honor, sober dress of plainest stuffs. The Jesuit, risking his life to bring his ministry to the faithful, therefore carefully disguised.

And this is less than one half of the chronicle of costume. For the women, as ever, and especially in England, where their freedom forever astonished foreigners, were more elaborate and various in their fashions.

—You have not troubled to mention the materials from which our costumes were wrought. From our native cloth makers came wool and other yarns: fustian, kerseys, broadcloths, and cottons. From the instruction of foreigners came variations such as grogram, bays and says, and mockado. And a wealth of the finer things: silk, damask, brocade, taffeta, sarcenet, satin, velvet, fine lawn, and cambric.

—And the colors! All colors of nature and shades of the rainbow, together with a hundred subtle distinctions of each, each with a proper name: Popinjay Green, Peachflower, Maiden's Blush, Russet Red, Horseflesh, Peas Porridge Tawny, Flame, Gingerline, Ash, Maidenhair Brown, Drake's Color, Dead Spaniard, Devil-in-the-Hedge, Marigold, Kendal Green, Isabel, Bloodred, Gooseturd Green, etc.

—Picture every kind of fur, from beaver and otter to ermine. Every kind of leather, kidskin, suede. Handkerchiefs of rarest silk. Lacework adorning, and that lace made as fine as ferns. And all but the plainest garments embroidered inch by inch with rich threads, sometimes gold and silver. Tiny perfect jewels and gems sewn into cloth. The linings of all things made equally fine and then garments slashed and pinked and paned to show that beauty.

—Not extraordinary to see a close row of buttons, ten, fourteen, or twenty-four, with each button a piece of gold, a small cut diamond in the center.

[320]

—Hats of every kind and shape made of velvet or silk or beaver or ermine, adorned with ribbons and jewels, and with such bursts of the feathers of rare birds that we were called "the most feather-headed folk in the world."

—With gloves and shoes and girdles delicately scented.

—Men and women wearing golden chains for their purses and watches and mirrors and penknives. The women carrying their masks and fans, all jeweled; busks, muffs, periwigs and bodkins. And whether wearing wigs or their own hair, dusting it with bits of jewels, flecks of the dust of gold.

—All wearing jewels. Earrings of pearl and precious stones. Jewels upon scabbard and hilt of sword and dagger. The women with long rows of heavy bracelets over their sleeves. Necklaces with cameos of ivory or whale tooth, pendant jewels and jeweled watches. And bracelet watches to keep the pulse of time upon the wrist.

—And at a cost beyond calculation. An embroidered waistcoat could cost as much as a small merchant ship. Short Spanish cloaks were worth several waistcoats.

—If Walter Ralegh indeed spread a cloak for the Queen at a splashy place, ·the Queen then walked across a good year's living for an ordinary gentleman.

—In the reign of the Queen a pair of silk stockings cost more than an entire costume of her grandfather's time.

—Strangers, even from the rich countries, were baffled by our light extraordinary costumes. Which were worn with a blithe disregard for their fragility, and a perfect indifference to weather.

—Costumes, worn as if all were actors in a play. And indeed these were true revelers, playing parts in the masques and joining the dancing afterwards with the Queen.

—Fantasies out of a dream of chivalry, created for the surprising entrance of some man and his attendants before the Queen. Pleasing her or displeasing her—*upon one occasion, one day, one time. . . .*

—No playhouse could offer such a scene as that one on Accession Day, 1598, when a tournament was prepared in honor of the Queen. For her pleasure, Sir Walter Ralegh gave the yeomen of the Guard plumes of orange tawny to wear. Whereupon, the Earl of Essex suddenly appeared, fresh from Wansted, where he had been in a fit of pouting and sulking, with more than two thousand men, knights and retainers, ten times the number of her Guard all wearing the same plumes. The populace was delighted by the Earl's crude wit.

—The Queen was not diverted by the sight of the Earl arriving with an army, like a baron of long ago, and, even in jest against a rival, willing to insult her honor, and, more dangerous, playing to the people, a show of wit and force and indifference, for *their* favor, their delight.

—The Queen waited and watched and said nothing. Until Essex, all eyes on him, performed poorly at the tilt. At which moment she chose to cancel the celebration. As if to spare herself the sight of Essex's disgrace.

—There you have it, but not the full beauty. For, you see, the Queen knew Essex was no champion of the tiltyard. Knew there were a dozen men who could make a clown of him. Therefore she sat in her place and let that occur. Then, out of a gesture of seeming pity, called off the tournament and departed. Leaving those who had applauded him to laugh. The final rosette of irony being that she did, in truth, pity him and sought to school him in the craft of survival.

Well then, disguise laid upon disguise. Life like a butterfly, a bee's brief springtime of gathering honey. All things changing shape and form. All things afire with change. And yet, beneath all changes and disguises, was the forked, pale, hairy pelt of flesh shared by all alive. And, in fact, all that flowering clothing, fruit and blossom, was grafted upon one trunk. The multitude of changes catches the eye and disguises the deeper, more essential truth: that the one model of clothing never truly changed. Doublet, hose, jerkin, these were the three elements of costume of all Englishmen for a century and more. Farmer and blacksmith, beggar and barrister, mariner and merchant, child and man, all wore essentially the same clothing. No matter what differences in quality or kind of cloth. A way of dressing in functional purity, well fitting, made for action, for graceful and quick movement and for hard labor too, for riding, climbing, running, fighting, working. . . .

—And for dancing and merely idling about. Though half the English nation might seek to imitate the Court, while the other half was railing against us, the Court was always the same and true to its original form; unchanging though it seemed to be the theater of change.

—Clothing tells the story in small compass. Our clothing only seemed to change, the true design being maintained within disguises of decoration, embroidery, accessories, and whims of fashion, and all we cheerfully aped from foreign nations. Which amused strangers well enough, but served some purpose. One being show, the spectacle of power. Conquest, as it were. We seemed able to take whatever we chose from foreign nations for ourselves. To loot and pillage without war. What we took up could seem like a tribute offered. Adding up to create an imaginary empire served by all nations, friendly and hostile, with England at the center. Which is a fable as unlikely as Aesop's moralities of talking, reasoning lions and ravens and foxes and geese. But a fable can inspire a dream that it is true.

—Consider also that, as in all double-edged things, the discontent of Puritan, Jesuit, or proud old-fashioned Englishman against fashions of Court served a beneficial purpose. All railed against our *apparel,* each for his own reasons. It was a diverting subject, an object for satire and contempt. They were not only diverted, but beguiled. For they would have made complaint in any case. Better, therefore, they should squander wrath upon fragile illusions.

—And their complaining served somewhat to check extraordinary excesses by the Court.

—And do not forget that the celebration of the old, which had not been so celebrated when it was new, became a part of the same fable, implying a unity, an honor of the chronicle of England.

—Not least, all could unite in complaint against the Queen's gaudy Court and most against those supreme peacocks—her favorites.

—Better satiric arrows, of those who swore all our virtue was gone with the longbow, should be aimed at them than at the Queen.

—For all its beauty, our clothing lasted not much longer than the fashion of it. Materials made for the present, not to last. Gone like the autumn leaves. Just so. . . . Gone with the tottering banquet houses where once we danced. Gone with the jewels she had pawned by the end; so that the new King found much cunning paste and glass. Gone, at the last, with the Queen herself, her policy, her great men, and her favorites. . . .

—Sir Walter Ralegh served two Courts, the one long, the other briefly. In the former he was called a fortunate upstart knave.

In the latter, though never a presence, he has been, like the ghost of himself, a long and vexing memory.

—The letter of all courts is much the same, but the spirit comes from the prince, first set, then maintained according to the purposes, character, and power of the ruler.

—You must imagine the Court of the Queen before you picture him there.

—When she came to London for her coronation, at one of the magnificent arches where spectacles were presented in her honor, she took especial note of a player who was tricked out as an ancient man armed with a scythe and an hourglass, representing Father Time.

"Time . . ." she said. "Time hath brought me here."

—Which was all she could gloss from the text of the past. Last and least likely to wear the Tudor crown, indeed lucky to be alive, to have a head to hold a crown, she came to rule when all choices had been made and spent, all means of ruling tried. Disregarding the Lady Jane Grey, Queen for nine uncertain days, there were in one century five Tudor princes; and the chief purpose of each was the same—the renewal and revival of the kingdom. Each sought to break and to end a long winter, to announce and display a season of springtime. The first, Henry VII, sought this in the literal sense, rising to rule from the blood of Bosworth Field. For the other four—Great Henry, Edward, Mary, Elizabeth—the task became multifoliate, no less literal but partaking of allegory as well. They became sowers of seeds as in the parable. Only the last, Elizabeth, sowed seed on fertile ground. Only the barren Queen reaped a bountiful harvest.

—But she could not have imagined that any more than she could have dreamed that one day, by Providence or the satirical whims of Dame Fortune, she would be Queen of England. She

[325]

came all unprepared and thus, by paradox, was the one Tudor perfectly prepared to rule. The future was beyond knowing. She could build no castles there. The past had been spoken in a language beyond translating. And so she was left with the changing and inconstant present, whose common language is Mutability. She could possess the present, but only a day at a time. Who but a woman, masked with woman's inconstancy, was so suited to preside over the present?

—It is true that what she accomplished was out of necessity, but to perceive necessity—that was her wisdom.

—From the beginning she lacked wealth. All the wealth her grandfather had carefully garnered, her father had spent twice over. The reigns of Edward and Mary became, in accounting, a sum of debts. She had no chance to increase the wealth of the kingdom except by careful conservation and by the artful and deceptive distribution of it.

—She had some means, to be sure. She held the power of customs duties, poundage and tunnage, the monopolies, royal wards, attainders of property and estates of traitors, and indeed the Privy Seal, which could be pointed like a cannon at some rich lord. And she could call upon her Parliament for subsidies.

—She could not consider arranging royal marriages for their double-stringed advantage—peace and profit. She had only one marriage, her own, with which to bargain.

—Nor could she consider war an investment, the merchant-adventuring of princes. The price was impossible. There could be no profit from even the smallest war. Only a few princes, already rich, already endowed with military power, could consider war in the old way. And these deceived themselves. Philip of Spain, with the wealth of an empire and the New World in his hands, possessing the most powerful forces by land and sea in the world, was hard pressed. When he was not spending his wealth, he was accumulating debts, forced to pawn and to borrow. The truth, evident to the Queen and a few others, was that she could not afford the most limited defensive wars. And at the end, forced into war, even her victories proved to be as she must have known they would, disasters.

—In each of the means of increasing wealth, she had a strong bit, a sharp snaffle in the mouth restraining her. She must be exceeding careful. To meddle too much with the customs, for example, could destroy the trade it sought to encourage. Monopolies and perquisites could be sold to advantage. But she must not permit these to work ruin upon trade or to increase doubt and distrust among her people. The estates and marriages of royal wards might yield something, but nothing in proportion to her needs. The ancient Parliament of England could levy taxes and make subsidies. But they could also bargain with the prince, giving a subsidy in return for things they desire—including, of course, more power, more liberty. And England was the lowest taxed nation in the world. Her Parliament could change that forever, being liberal with the wealth of others. As for the attainders of the properties of traitors, she was willing to take advantage of this means whenever a plot was discovered and treasons were proved. But she had seen how the temptation could—witness her father—untune a mind with the discord of imaginary plots.

—She had come to the throne with a weary people, willing to trust her because they had no choice, until she proved herself unworthy. This was her greatest credit. She must not dissipate this trust even for the general good. And she must reciprocate by demonstrating trust in them.

[327]

—She must, therefore, seek new ways to earn wealth. No choice but to be frugal in all things. Yet she must not seem to be as poor as she was and thus reflect to the kingdom and a hostile world the poverty and weakness of this nation.

—A most economical woman, our Queen. She knew prices to the penny and could have outbargained a fishwife. She could squeeze a gold half angel coin until the angel dropped his spear and fell like the groaning dragon at his feet.

—Yet she knew how to seem spendthrift when the gesture was worth a fortune. As when upon a progress, the baggage all loaded and ready, word came to unload and unpack. The Queen had changed her mind. And a burly carter, not knowing the Queen stood at the window above him, roared with laughter and said how, by God, now he knew the Queen to be a woman exactly like his wife.

"Who is the villain who says so?" she shouted from the window.

—And the poor man humbly knelt.

—Then she laughed and threw him three gold angels and wished him well.

—A gesture worth three hundred angels to her by the time the story had been told and retold.

—One tongue is a flame and can burn down a forest.

—Another example: how she always managed to lose something—glove, garter, jewel off her dress, etc.—whenever she appeared in public. This thing to be snatched up at once and kept like some saint's relic by the finder. Yet she counted and recounted everything she possessed. And everything she lost was carefully recorded. The profit from her carelessness far exceeded the sum of all her losses. She never lost anything of much value. A careful carelessness, to say the least.

—And she was well advised by men skilled at trade and all the tricks and sleights of hand with money. Sir Thomas Gresham, for example, who saved her fortunes; who milked Antwerp, Fleming and Spaniard alike, dry, for England and his own hungry purse; then, in effect, moved Antwerp to London when he built the magnificent Royal Exchange with its gilt grasshopper proudly surmounting all. And he spared no money in the setting up of charities, schools, and almshouses, either. If he filled his purse in her service, his services were worth double that price.

—Her Court cost her, thus the nation, only one third what it had cost Queen Mary. She had an annual allowance of forty thousand pounds for the Court at the beginning of her reign. Half a century later, though prices had trebled and troubles had multiplied like hares, she refused to ask for more allowance for the Court.

—She would summon Parliament for a subsidy she believed would be granted in the interest of all, but not in the matter of her own maintenance or the expenses of the Court.

—She must have money of her own, that was clear enough. Though she insisted upon every economy, her demands were impossible to satisfy without a corresponding reduction of the size and the functions of the Court. Which she would not allow.

—Consider she must maintain her royal palaces and other royal residences in good order. She built no new ones—surprising in such an age of building—but she must preserve what had been given to her. And clustered around each of these palaces was its own community, its life deriving from the presence of the palace. She must not stint, then, or permit the environs to wither away. Must hold residence in each and all—some were favorites, some housed bitter memories. With Coun-

[329]

cil and Court, she had a household of almost two thousand, not counting servants and hangbys. Who must be fed at groaning tables, in ostentatious abundance.

—Her menus were joyous. Even the most fastidious strangers, who never failed to mutter at our English cooking, admitted that the foods at Court were a marvel. Her table was laid to the sound of trumpets. Then, dish by dish, some lucky yeoman of the Guard tasting all for her safety's sake. But she seldom ate in public. This ceremony was for her Court. She dined most simply in her chambers.

—Servants of high and low degrees must be paid for their services.

—Though she kept a sharp eye on accounts, she turned away from corruption of her servants, high and low, thus permitting, indeed encouraging, them to fatten meager earnings with gifts and bribes, according to degree and need. Judging them by work accomplished, not by means. And expecting some share of their wealth to come to her, directly or indirectly. Finally knowing that because all were guilty, all could be dispensed with, should that become expedient.

—If great men sold middling offices, her concern was that the affairs of bought offices should be executed with loyal dispatch. If not, another buyer could always be found. There are always more seekers of office than offices. She transmuted ambitious men, turning their weakness to strength. There would always be factions. Nothing could change that. But by setting each of these men on his own, able to reward and punish, able to reap for himself, she could prevent even those of the same faction and persuasion from joining too closely together. Thus men like Burghley, Walsingham, Knollys, Sir Nicholas Bacon, Leicester, etc., though all might be strong Protestants and inclined to favor the Puritans above the bishops of her church, still they could seldom effect any unity of purpose; each being a man of strong character, each ambitious beyond ordinary hopes and appetites. So long as their ambitions were neither entirely frustrated nor satisfied, she could play them like chessmen.

—She wrangled with merchants for bargains and kept expenses modest by means of her purveyors, hated like vermin by many, but less hated than higher taxes would have been.

—Unable to gain a bargain for wines, she outraged native vintners by buying wines more cheaply abroad. The vintners soon came around. Unable to supply the Court with the rivers of beer it consumed, she permitted the show of a Royal Brewery being built at Whitehall. The brewers saw the light.

—She invested in seafaring ventures, modestly so as to reduce her risk; but, for the sake of the Queen's support, which ventures, without her support, might have been named piracy, she received a queen's share of any profits.

— *Item:* the *Madre de Dios,* taken by Ralegh's men as a prize, yielded her eighty thousand pounds return on an investment of eighteen hundred pounds and the loan of two old ships.

—Her custom of receiving and carefully cataloguing New Year's gifts grew to be a practical kind of annual subsidy.

—Her father had been famous for his entertainments. So was the Queen, but she preferred *to be entertained.* Ambitious men were willing to oblige her. And nothing will equal the splendor of those masques and revels, dances and performances of plays, tournaments and celebrations. For which she furnished the royal setting, the Court, and herself.

—More often than any prince in memory, she would go forth to grace the entertainments of the Inns of Court or, carried upon a litter by her knights, to the wedding festivities of the daughter or son of some servant or friend. She was godmother to scores of the children of the gentry. In all these appearances she and the Court were seen by the populace. A very inexpensive thing to do and for good return.

—She made her royal presence felt on all the native holidays and festivals, not only the feast days of the church, but also the old English May games, Midsummer Watch and so forth, adding her Accession Day, and later, on St. Elizabeth's Day, a festival to honor the defeat of the Spanish Armada.

—It is true that the masques of King James are more surprising in many ways. They are written by the finest of our poets, though they scarcely need the poetry of words, having the poetry of the designs, the scenes, and machinery of England's new Merlin, Inigo Jones. He raises a curtain to such a glory of painted scenes, lit by hundreds of tiny glass lamps in the Italian fashion, as must be seen to be imagined. And there are cloud machines, wave machines, aerial devices, fountains and costumes for the masquers as never were seen in the last age. Some costumes, worn by both ladies and gentlemen, as the late Queen would never have permitted except in a painting or an arras. But the cost of the King's marvels outweighs their grandeur. The Queen was much stronger for imagination, for richness of words to work the magic. Her banquet house at White-hall was a tentative thing, propped up, repaired, useful for her reign and not much longer. Now the King must have the ingenious Mr. Jones to build him a new one of stone, costly as a royal palace.

—And now the anti-masque is all the fashion since the King favors the drollery of satyrs and mermaids, bawds and furies, wild men, baboons, the magpie, crow and kite. Now a gentleman does better to portray an ass or a hog and a fine lady to be

[332]

all feathers to her navel and all naked flesh above, if either would gain the applause of the King. The old virtues slowly vanish from the masque. And with them the spirit.

—Queen Elizabeth built no palaces, no churches, no forts; though after the Armada with the money of a grateful—and frightened—Parliament, she shored up and repaired some old fortifications against a second coming of Spaniards. Even the spire of St. Paul's was not restored.

—But she disposed of old lands and houses freely to her favorites. For one price or another. By the fashion and example set early in her reign, these lands were put to work, and old places refurbished to fit new styles. And they were well scattered across the counties. Whether she ever visited them or not, they must be prepared for her visit. So, large or small, grand or modest, the houses of the favored must be built not only to appear palatial, but, if need be, to serve as palaces for her. Each with its orderly arrangement of presence chamber, privy chamber, coffer chamber, etc.

—Again, in return for the income of the lands and the estates, a man must spend a fortune on keeping a great house. This leaving him, still, not entirely free of necessity. Not too satisfied or too comfortable.

—This device, more valuable and cheaper than many showy palaces of her own, brought to the English land a bright and bold appearance of grandeur and prosperity; the great who owned them becoming like ambassadors to the counties. Required to spend freely, then out of necessity to develop and make use of lands and holdings or else become poor. And great houses became centers for charity, as the palaces were and castles had been. Except that these were not built for defense like the castles. Were, rather, indefensible. Which, besides advantage to herself, brought a sense, by appearance, of peace to the land. For who would build a grand palace with no walls—except windows—if he feared danger?

—Never mind that the dangers were real enough and were most feared by the very men who brought the scenery of peace and prosperity to the land. Allow, though, that whether these men began to believe the illusions they lived in or not, they were thereafter in self-interest required to protect those illusions from crumbling.

—All of which leads, as if by a winding stair, to the subject of her favorites. . . .

—Though she could not shower gold upon many, she could reward a few grandly. These in turn—especially if young and ambitious—were compelled to spend also, to distribute wealth, to build up a following, to gain support. They must make a show of affluence commensurate with her favor. For most had nothing else except the favor of the Queen. This being true, they never doubted where their wealth and power came from. They must be both loyal and grateful out of necessity. *See how she shared thereby her own condition with them.* Likewise all who came to serve the favored man, to cling to his cloak, knew the origin of his fortune and the conditions of it. So a man favored by the Queen became the merchant of her favors. The Queen, not the favorite, was credited with largesse. Therefore—and all save foolish Essex knew this—their own allies, servants, and supporters were beholden first of all to her. Loyalty to the patron existed only so long as he remained in favor. A favorite's disgrace could empty his house overnight.

—Moreover, she could be credited far beyond any accounting of her generosity. For there were few who were favored in

Court who did not wish to seem more so. Affairs of a man who seemed to be in favor could prosper. The man whose affairs prospered because he was presumed to be in favor would, by this token, owe his additional prosperity to the Queen. For it was inspired by her. Through these she gained credit for generosity far exceeding the truth. An occasional great giving, for all the world to marvel at, to see and envy, and this coupled with a boon here and a bone there, together with some bits and pieces of possibility, these gestures made a little money go a long way in her Court.

—She, herself, was never loath to accept gifts or service from almost anyone of the Court or outside it, always reserving the right to examine each suit upon its merits. If they chose to see her as corruptible, conceiving her according to themselves, they could attribute injustice, when they failed to achieve their ends, to the unreasonable whims of a woman. For which she could hardly be blamed. When they succeeded, perhaps because the cause was just or their aims reasonable, they could attribute success to their own cleverness.

—So much to be done with so little. England was ringed with enemies, hard pressed, almost powerless when she came to the throne. She could not build military power. She might have increased her safety somewhat, but at the risk of ruining the kingdom. And, doing so, she would have lost the favor of the people, who cannot conceive of enemies until they appear in armor at the gates. Instead of armies she created a show of peace and plenty, illusory but confident; permitting thereby, within England at least and for a time, peace and prosperity to bloom like flowers in a glass house. Her people had been saddened and dazed by the inexplicable turns of Fortune. In that

[335]

final season of the Tudors, which ought to have been a leafless winter, she made an artificial springtime out of thin air.

—From those who served her the Queen demanded the outward and visible signs of love and loyalty. She insisted upon ceremony and flattery, as a sign of sane and reasonable behavior. Her favorites must be ardent in professions of love and loyalty; not because she was gulled, but because it was proper and becoming. It is said that a scholar may be gulled three times. The Queen, like a soldier, could be gulled only once.

—From the first of her reign the Queen had her favorites, cast in no single mold, having not much in common with each other except that each was a remarkable man. Placed in one chamber, each given simultaneous youth, health, and vigor, restored to the condition which first captured her attention, they would appear to contradict one another. Ciphers in an old account book, balanced once and discarded, they cancel each other out, becoming, in sum and balance, nothing at all.

—It seems possible that she imagined them and that they existed only there, in the Queen's imagination.

—Thus any one of them could be chosen as a type for all.

—Why not Ralegh? He shows the qualities of contradiction she favored. And he came to favor neither at the beginning nor the end of the reign. He could never be so close to her as Leicester, never so pure and abstract in distance as Leicester's stepson—Essex.

—He was not as the braggart captain would have him. Nor as he seems now—an old man, sick and tired, in disgrace and danger, a gray shadow of himself. We must take him as he was, in that lost time, when he was in and out of the Court, from his beginnings; seeking by imagination to see what she saw, what pleased her, what allowed her to turn to him with favor.

[336]

—I cannot, with the confidence of that captain, spitting out his small wisdom as if it were the core and seeds of the Original apple, speak of anything except the world I know and what was known of Ralegh there. I do not allow myself the simplicity of imagining that this or that thing, which may or may not have happened, irrevocably marked his soul like an executioner's branding iron. I know this, though. That for all its easy shining, the Court is as fierce a field to test the mettle of a man, to give him his share of wounds and blessings, as any other.

—True, Ralegh came, like others beyond counting, to seek a place at Court. True, he managed in due time to catch her eye. And when she looked at him, she could read in him qualities she favored. He was valiant, intelligent, diverting, proud, flawed, and enigmatic. He was still young enough, singularly handsome, correct in fashion and manners. And, perhaps, she could appreciate a lonely reticence which was in harmony with her own.

—His beginning was by rote. For it has been said by some wag that a man must come to Court like Job and then abide there like Ulysses. Which, in part, is Ralegh's story.

—He came first to Court in the seventies. Another young man, a soldier back from a foreign war. One who had passed through the polishing of Lyon's Inn of Chancery and the Middle Temple.

—At Middle Temple he was among friends and kin, even if he lacked means beyond what little of a much divided estate might be his and whatever he might have scrounged and looted while playing soldier in sunny Languedoc.

—And, as well, within his little world of Devon, means or no, he came from an honorable family, whose honor went back to times before the Conquest. Whose distinction, however, was a matter of cloudy memory. The truth for him being that he was the youngest son of Walter Ralegh of Fardel, youngest son by the third wife. His mother was of some distinction. She was Elizabeth Champernoun, daughter of Sir Philip Champernoun and the widow of a man of note in those parts, Otho Gilbert. By whom she had borne three sons, Ralegh's half brothers, Adrian, John, and Humphrey Gilbert. There is also an older brother with the Ralegh name—Carew.

He was last in a family of honorable name and slight means. His best inheritance, his hope, lay in blood and kinship. For by blood and marriages he was kin to good Westcountry names—Carew, Granville, Tremayne, Courtenay, Saintleger, Russell, Drake, of course the Champernouns and Gilbert, and others.

—There was small chance in the Court for such a man. Except for having some good kin in Devon, he was on his own to stand or to fall. He had his looks, his wits, his courage, and such shows of appearance as he could beg, borrow, or steal to give him a beginning. Further, he wore the yoke of pride. Pride which could mean nothing to most young men on the edges of the Court, his satirical, cynical, urgently ambitious peers. Others at the center, including the Queen herself, might have knowledge or recollection of his name and kin. And, true enough, the Gilberts were a little above the common pit and press of groundlings. But they could not be expected to raise him up much. At Court a man must look to his own advancement first.

—Walter Ralegh, of Hayes Barton in the parish of East Budleigh, Devonshire, had no advantage over an army of young men coming to the Court.

—Not much is known or remembered of those first fruitless years, and no wonder. For no one takes notice of a new man until after he has come to some good or grief. He must have done the usual things. For certain he wrote verses, and in 1576 some hard satirical lines of his were published to recommend George Gascoigne's *The Steele Glass*. Which is enough to speculate upon.

—There was a friendship on several grounds. Gascoigne, a few years younger than Ralegh, was a soldier too. Had come earlier to Court from Gray's Inn. And here's an irony: George Gascoigne's first patron at Gray's Inn was that distinguished bencher, Sir Christopher Yelverton.

—Ralegh would know something of Gascoigne's soldiering, for Gascoigne had served under Sir Humphrey Gilbert in the Netherlands in '72. Served twice there before he was captured by the Spaniards and sent back to England. Gascoigne had proved himself a man of courage, and would prove it again at the Spanish Fury of Antwerp, when he drew his sword and saved English lives from the mutinous Spaniards who invaded English House.

—But later in '76 Gascoigne was on the edge of the Court, publishing poems, seeking to make a name. And, give or take a button or a breath, he must have been ahead of Ralegh in the footrace toward the slippery ladder of preferment. At least he had been given more occasion for advancement. In the summer of '75 Gascoigne was Leicester's man and was put to work in the creation of the festivities presented for the Queen to honor her visit to Kenilworth. He wrote parts of the spectacles and, as a player, appeared before Her Majesty, first in the part of A Savage Man and, at her farewells, as Sylvanus. And he managed to find some favor from Lord Grey. With favor from Leicester and Grey, having been noticed by the Queen, Gascoigne should have cleared idle harbor and have begun to sail with fair winds. Burghley and Walsingham took note of him. He did service for them as an agent on the Continent.

[339]

—But in 1577 George Gascoigne was dead.

—Gascoigne's story ended when he died. The friendship with Ralegh must have been deep and true, however; for after Gascoigne's death, Ralegh took over the other man's motto, proclaiming himself divided between two gods—*Tam Marti Quam Mercuris*. Half of peace, half of war, of healing and of force, of eloquence and action, of strength and of cunning. A proclamation, then, of bold contrarities to be resolved.

—And Ralegh had gained, perhaps through Gascoigne, some notice of both Leicester and Grey. Both of whom he later served.

—In 1577 Ralegh could list himself, as many with and without office did, as being "of the Court," when he stood bail for two rowdy Devon men, his servants. He was living in the suburb of Islington. And there were already some stories of tavern brawls of his own. In one, which went the rounds, he tied the long ends of a fellow's mustache into a knot, then stuffed it in his mouth.

—In the summer of 1578 Sir Humphrey Gilbert received a patent to settle with Englishmen any lands in the New World "not actually possessed of any Christian prince or people," allowing him six years to find and to settle lands overseas. Sir Humphrey drew into this adventure his brothers, Adrian and Sir John, and to assist him his half brothers Carew and Walter Ralegh. Gascoigne had also invested before he died.

—One partner in the venture, Sir Humphrey's chief support, Henry Knollys, was son of Sir Francis Knollys, the Queen's Treasurer of the Household. But before they had well begun, Knollys deserted this for privateering in closer waters.

—At the end of November of '78, just the worst time for a crossing, Sir Humphrey Gilbert set out with seven ships. One of them, old and leaky, was the *Falcon,* commanded by Walter Ralegh and mastered by Simon Fernandez, the Portuguese pilot. Storms and other troubles caused Gilbert's venture to fail. His ships were scattered and returned to port. Ralegh, however, went on alone in the *Falcon* to try his luck at privateering. Did not return to England until May of '79.

—I know nothing of his nautical affairs and care less, except as they illuminate his shadowy early life at the Court; but there is some urgency in the man who will take an old ship, his first command, alone for six months, risking everything on the venture. There must have been nothing tugging him back to Court. And he could not afford to have the adventure come to nothing. Perhaps on his voyage he gained something, enough to offset his losses, but it could not have been much. He was fortunate to bring back the *Falcon* afloat and to be alive.

—By early 1580 he was making his mark in another way— and the worst way to please the Queen. Was called before Council and committed to Fleet prison, for a week, for coming to swords with Sir Thomas Perrot. Not long after he was again in a brawl at the tennis court and was packed off to cool his humors at the Marshalsea.

—Nothing unusual, except that he was able to survive an unhappy reputation. There were many in the Court who foolishly looked for renown as ruffians. It is always easy to pick a quarrel or begin a brawl. And these rogues of Court, those who lived long enough, vanished forever. Both Queen and Council were adamant against permitting her Court to become a cockpit.

—Most curious is why Walter Ralegh fell to playing this game. In his writings he has ridiculed the courtier's habit of dueling. And later he proved himself able to exercise restraint

[341]

in the face of provocation. It may be he had given up all hope at Court by then. A younger crop of courtiers was already blooming. His chances had passed him by.

—By the summer of 1580 he was gone. Back to the craft of warfare. Off to Ireland as the captain of a company of foot soldiers.

—There his fortunes took a turn for the better, for when he came back to Court it was as one of Leicester's men, and given a nod of approval by Walsingham as well. He returned in time for the Christmas Revels of '81.

—No doubt in the world but William Cecil, Lord Burghley, had an eye upon him too. Which was Cecil's duty and self-interest. But it was the eye of quiet suspicion. Like a good clerk, he was aware of Ralegh's motley record and the signs of contradiction in him. Would be alert, but far too careful to interfere yet with a young man of tentative promise, especially before the man had gained anything. Wisdom and experience taught Burghley, who endured like a willow, by bending, through the times of Edward and Mary, to stand tall and transformed now, like an oak, that to sound premature alarms is a waste of time. Young men, even if they did happen to catch the Queen's eye and please her, came and went, blossomed, then faded like May's meadow flowers.

Burghley knew that if Ralegh did not capture the Queen's interest, Leicester and Walsingham would drop him like a loose coin. There were always others. And he judged that neither Leicester nor Walsingham would advance any man they had any reason to fear themselves. Their separate interest in Ralegh was, therefore, reassuring.

—Suppose he did attract the attention of the Queen? He would gain a rung or two upon that slippery Jacob's ladder at

Court. Chances were he would be left there to hang on for as long as he was able.

—All misjudged him, Walsingham, Leicester, and Burghley. More important, they misjudged the Queen.

—Within a few weeks after his return, Ralegh had been noticed by the Queen. She singled him out of a crowd for a moment of recognition during one of her Sunday processions.

—A public notice of his existence and a few words . . .

—A sign that she found him pleasing and that he might be watched. No great shakes of a lamb's tail. Many men labored long at schemes and good works, spending themselves poor in service to gain nothing more than that. An honor, to be sure, and more than he could have expected. And, in justice, had he never received another sign of favor from the Queen, it would have been sufficient. Not to his ambitions, of course, but in the scale of things at Court.

—All misjudged Walter Ralegh. They misjudged the Queen also. Not perceiving that she had now ruled for nearly twenty years. And what that meant.

—Her early favorites were older. Beginning of stiffness in the joints of nimble Sir Christopher Hatton. Who had danced into favor when dancing was her best cordial. All were older; though she would not, could not hold up a mirror glass for them to see it. She, too, would be caught in that cold reflection.

—As Queen she could justify her impulse to find a new favorite. Besides which she was a woman, and she could not soothe her mixed feelings, of content and discontent, of thanksgiving and vague dread, like any milkmaid who can buy a new bonnet at the fair. Yet she could find a new favorite if she wished to.

[343]

—Here was a full-grown man, a proud soldier, being put forward by her counselors. Worth looking at.

—In a short time, by spring of 1582, there was no doubt that Walter Ralegh had stepped into the charmed, inmost circle close to the Queen. The next bestowal was a nickname. Walter Ralegh became Water, and sometimes Wit or Oracle.

—Old favorites itched with anxiety. Which flattered her.

—And now the world was suddenly all promises for Ralegh, of everything or nothing. His deep-grained satirical sense let him bear uncertainty. He could make light of it, and she would understand that and take it for a compliment.

—About that time, on a spring day, the Queen and a party were walking in the gallery of the palace.

—He stopped walking and went to a window, where he busied himself by writing on a pane with a diamond. He wrote: "Fain would I climb, yet fear I to fall."

—Turned to find the Queen standing behind him. He knelt, then, and she took the diamond from him. She wrote the second line in answer: "If thy heart fail thee, climb not at all."

—Without a word she turned and rejoined her group, leaving him kneeling, smiling to himself.

—The Queen kept the diamond.

—For the next ten years he was showered with rewards and favor. And even after the disgrace of his marriage and his time in the wilderness, there were more.

—In a marvelous short time Walter Ralegh was a man of wealth. Among the rewards she bestowed upon him were two estates from All Souls College; the monopoly patent to license the selling of wines and to exact fines in this capacity; other monopolies, including, aptly, one upon the traffic in playing cards; a license to export woolen broadcloth; Durham House on the river; the whole estate of Sherbourne in Dorset; forty-two thousand acres of land in Ireland along the River Black-water, in Cork and Waterford—and at that time by statute law no man was allowed to hold seigniory over more than twelve thousand acres there—including nine castles, properties in and around the town of Youghal, and Lismore Castle; a license to export any and all commodities from Munster whether or not there were legal restrictions; and when Anthony Babington died for his plot against the Queen and forfeited his estate, Babington's lands and property in Nottingham, Lincoln, and Derby went to Ralegh. Ralegh also received a patent to explore and to make colonies in any part of the New World not already in the possession of a Christian kingdom and the rights to control all access to any settlement he should found there.

—He was knighted by the Queen, who was frugal with this honor.

—Among offices and titles Ralegh held were these: Captain of the Guard, Lord Warden of the Stanneries, Lord Lieutenant of Cornwall, Vice-Admiral of Devon and Cornwall, Ranger of Gillingham Forest, Captain of Portland Castle, and Governor of the Island of Jersey.

—He was possessed of the wealth and power of many of the nobility and with the possibility of using it to accumulate even more. He could, if he wished, like a dog with a bone, settle for the present satisfaction and defend it. Which satisfaction was, in truth, more than even a child's falcon-free imagination could comprehend.

—Pain and poverty and thwarted ambition, which are the lot of most creatures, whether they live at Court or a barn, can break the virtues like brittle bones. But it is also true that good fortune can jar and shake a man's soul. For, most remarkable of

[345]

all, he was free. Changed or not, he was, upon the whim of another, freed of all he had imagined himself to be.

—Consider that for the favorite, even as the head-whirling intoxication of favor released him from many bondages, it forged new fetters. For what had been given to him could, in like fashion, with the same absence of warning or justice, be— *The Lord giveth and the Lord taketh away. Blessed be the name of the Lord*—withdrawn.

—Now he was studied by the court. Observed like any fish in a garden pool. Every word and action noted, glossed for hidden meaning. Raised above others, he must pay a dear price; lonely when most public; rich, yet belonging to others: all others who, clinging to the figure of justice, as sailors, they say, will hang on for life to a gloating chest or broken spar, examine him for any signs of virtue which might justify his fortune. Likewise, more close and intent, solemn as a jeweler searching a stone for flaws, yet calm, too, like poised cats studying the antics of a wounded bird they watched and waited for signs of weakness which might betray him.

Walter Ralegh proved no miserly guardian of new fortunes. He was willing to risk it all upon adventures. He spent of his wealth as if, like the deepest well, it could never run dry.

—This was a secular act of faith in which the Queen was well pleased. It pleased others at Court for other reasons. By his blithe disregard he was most vulnerable, able to fall in an instant and to fall as far as he had been raised.

—Yet, as if sharing a secret with the Queen, as if in league and conspiracy with her, he knew these things, and they did not trouble him. Vulnerability never taught him to be humble. Rather it increased his indifference, up to the edge of impudence.

—He seldom pressed suit for himself, but he took pleasure

[346]

in seeking favor for others, high and low; especial pleasure, no doubt, in making suit for his onetime master and better—the Earl of Leicester.

—Once in the presence of a crowd he knelt before the Queen and asked some favor for a friend.

"When, Sir Walter, will you cease to be a beggar?" the Queen demanded.

"When Your Gracious Majesty ceases to be a benefactor," he said.

—She laughed and granted the suit.

—On another occasion, that sassy little Mr. Richard Tarlton, the celebrated comedian, was performing. And, noticing Ralegh beside the Queen whispering into the Queen's ear and the Queen nodding, he clapped his hands as loud as an arquebus and leveled an accusing finger at Ralegh.

"See!" he cried out. "See how the knave commands the Queen!"

—Ralegh laughed out loud. And the Queen corrected Tarlton with a gentle frown.

—And all the while Ralegh was spending his wealth upon ventures and the voyages he could not make, being required to remain at Court. He became an equal and generous patron to the new learning and to our antiquarians. He gave comfort to scholars and artisans and limners. A gentleman of means is known by these things. The books which are dedicated to him are the witnesses of affluence. Printed books acknowledge Ralegh's patronage and interest in history, geography and cartography, medicine, antiquities, and the natural philosophies such as chemistry. He was a patron of music and even John Case's *Praise of Music* calls him a lover of good music and a skilled musician. His portraits, from a proper early miniature by Nicholas Hilliard to the final one, made before his last Guiana voyage, show he was much interested in and knowing of fashions in painting. He hired the artist John White to join with Thomas Harriot in depicting, by words and pictures, the new world of Virginia. He spent a lavish sum to support the English publication of the drawings of James Morgues.

—Two great natural philosophers, Harriot and Dr. John Dee, were more friends than servants, and assisted him in his studies of chemistry, astronomy, mathematics, geography, shipbuilding and navigation.

—A poet himself, he was recognized as one of the finest of the gentlemen poets, whose work was seldom published but widely known in manuscripts. As early as 1589 his repute was sufficient for him to be singled out by George Puttenham in *The Arte of English Poesie*: "For dittie and amorous Ode I finde Sir Walter Rawleyghs vayne most loftie, insolent and passionate."

—But if he was known and respected for his verses among the poets of Court, from Sidney to Harrington, he was surprising for the divers poets he patronized, men as various and variously gifted as Edmund Spenser, Christopher Marlowe, Ben Jonson, George Chapman, Francis Beaumont, and John Fletcher. More than patron, he mingled with poets and scribblers, taking as much pleasure in an evening at the Mermaid as a night at Court. By circumstance he can never have been close to Mr. William Shakespeare, who was servant to both Essex and Southampton, but he must have known him at the Mermaid and elsewhere, for Ralegh haunted the playhouses. Was closest of all to Edmund Spenser, whose holdings at Kilcolman were near to Ralegh's Irish estates. Spenser wrote of Ralegh in "Colin Clout's Come Home Again" and allegorically in *The Faerie Queene*. For which great work Ralegh produced a dedicatory

[348]

poem. It was Ralegh who first introduced Spenser at Court and managed to secure a pension for him.

—Curious, whenever Ralegh found himself unable to patronize these men, he found other patrons for them including some among his enemies.

—It was not difficult for enemies to turn this patronage and friendship with learned men, poets, artisans and such, against him. Like the others, he sometimes made use of poets to serve his turn, to promote enterprises or to satirize rivals. These things could be answered, thrust and counterthrust. But his friendships with these men, especially the nature of their discussions and disputations, his experiments with new instruments and theories in natural philosphy, were to prove more dangerous. Easy for the envious to conceive that their privacy was secrecy. Easy enough to trouble the superstitious and the unlearned with rumors of their doings.

—So long as he was in the Queen's favor, he was secure. Yet his indifference to Court opinion and popular gossip made him a fine standing target for satire.

—Though he never set new styles of dress or affected foppish fashions, his clothing was priceless. Every courtier wore his fortune on his back, like a gaudy snail, and so did Ralegh. When he had no fortune, this was common enough to be ignored; but when he was rich, his show of pearls and jewels was taken to be proud and arrogant. He seemed to be biting his thumb at them all.

—Once he appeared in a splendid and original costume of black and white only, sprinkled with countless pearls. It was so like, as if cut from the same magic bolt of cloth, a gown the Queen was wearing, that they appeared like twins together. When he first astonished her with this costume, she laughed and embraced him. Any woman who had dared such a thing would have been boxed about the ears in a trice. And most men, even among their favorites, would have been sent off to enjoy a long season of English country life. His impudence differs from that gesture of Essex at the tiltyard. Essex's jest was for the crowd; Ralegh's, though public, was more like a secret shared with the Queen. He courted no favor but hers.

—There was always some self-satire in his mirth. Once, another time of the tiltyard, when rumor was he had suffered some misfortune or disgrace, Ralegh came riding out of the gate of Durham House and down the Strand toward Whitehall, not, like Essex, making a show of the number of his retainers, but himself clad entirely in armor made of silver.

—From these occasions and many others I conclude the Queen was willing to permit him to play the conny-catcher to the world of connies, to gull his rivals, to equivocate, to take on almost any role or pose he fancied. What she demanded in return was an absolute, unflagging loyalty and trust.

—If so, then he was bound, sooner or later, to betray himself and fail her.

—Later in 1591 he secretly married Elizabeth Throckmorton, one of the Queen's maids of honor. In March of '92, while Ralegh was elsewhere, freed from the confines of Court by the war with Spain, preparing an expedition to strike the Spanish Indies *flota* and the Isthmus of Panama, his firstborn son, Damerei, was christened, the Earl of Essex serving as godfather. Within a month Bess Throckmorton returned to Court and resumed her duties. By May Ralegh had been recalled and committed to the keeping of Robert Cecil. Otherwise no action was taken against him.

—It was not until August that the Queen acted, ordering

Ralegh and his wife committed to the Tower. The rumor of the marriage had been bruited about Court for some time, and Ralegh had denied it to his friends, succeeding only in arousing more speculation. The Queen must have known the truth for a long time.

—Never mind that at Court there was much outward wise nodding and inward rejoicing at his fall. All that mattered, in truth, was the Queen's action. She had waited, it seems, for him to confess the truth, to submit to her justice, to beg her pardon. Others, even proud Essex, had done so, and had received the Queen's forgiveness.

—Ralegh knew this, but he did not, would not play the part required of him. Months before he had been only a step away from being sworn to the Council and close to receiving a title to nobility. Now he was in the Tower, having lost all that and likely to lose everything. He would play roles, but he would not perform the one which would save him from disgrace.

—Much was made then, while she lived, and ever since, about the Queen's jealousy of her favorites. And no doubt, like any woman, she could be jealous, even though by that time in her life—she was nearing her sixtieth year—jealousy was a familiar experience to her. As Queen, however, her reaction must be shock, disbelief, followed by anger and disappointment.

—Her half dozen maids of honor were young ladies of distinction, her closest and most intimate companions. She had them dressed, usually, all in white, and they were with her everywhere, like the nymphs of Diana. In due time she found them husbands, attended their weddings, was godmother for their children, etc. But until that time came, they were duty-bound to her, in chastity and obedience. And they were, as if they were her own daughers, required to have her permission to marry.

—The Queen was responsible for the welfare of her maids while they served her. Their failures were her own.

—Bess Throckmorton meant something more to her. She was the daughter of Sir Nicholas Throckmorton, who had died in the Queen's service in 1571. He had known Elizabeth since she was a young girl, a princess of ambiguous status in the household of Catherine Parr. When, in the clouds of confused suspicion following Wyatt's Rebellion, the Princess Elizabeth was sent to the Tower, so was Throckmorton. When Elizabeth came to the throne, Sir Nicholas became one of her men, serving her in peculiarly delicate duties and offices, especially in diplomatic missions to France and Scotland. He was one of the first of her master intelligencers, creating a network of agents and spies, one which both Walsingham and Burghley could not only use, but refine into England's first line of defense. When Sir Nicholas had died, Sir Francis Walsingham wrote of him: "For be it spoken without offense to any, for council in peace and for conduct in war, he has not left of like sufficiency his successor that I know."

—The Queen was sensible of her obligations to the Throckmortons and that she had failed them. More to the point, she was aware that two people close to her had broken faith, and, worse, had been able, for a time at least, to keep their secret; and then to imagine they could keep it longer. Breaking of faith is grave enough. For therein lies the gravest danger to all kingdoms, long before enemies arrive upon shores and borders. But, even so, the Queen had cause to believe that she knew Ralegh. Chastened, sufficiently frightened, he might learn something out of failure, perhaps a clearer definition of loyalty.

If the prodigal returned, seeking pardon, he would be welcomed.

—On the other hand, England was at war, more threatened than ever before. The life of the Queen depended upon knowledge, imagination, cunning, and faith in herself. Now she must question her own judgment. Self-doubt was compounded when Bess returned to serve her, pretending nothing had happened, and apparently believing she could deceive the Queen. And Ralegh, a man of forty years wise in worldly matters, made no move to repent or to avert the Queen's anger. Either he had, indeed, lost his wits, or he no longer cared what the Queen thought, what she might do, or what he might lose.

—To the astonishment of all, Ralegh was confined only a brief time in the Tower, then freed to go and do as he pleased, though banished from Court. Her punishment was strangely mild. He had not lost his offices and perquisites, not even the captaincy of the Guard, which she kept vacant.

—Deprived of none of his blessings, though cut off from advancement, Ralegh continued his various activities, spent as free and lived as grand as before.

—He built up his estates in England and Ireland. Made of his new seat at Sherbourne not only a most profitable holding —five thousand a year it earned him though very few, even to this day, know that—but a grand manor worthy of comparison with any.

—He made the voyage of exploration to Guiana in '95, claiming it for the Queen. And wrote a popular book about that adventure—*The Discoverie of the Large, Rich and Bewtiful Empyre of Guiana,* published in '96.

—He served, with the outspoken independence which was his consistent stance before and after, in the vexing Parliament of '93. Speaking out for the Queen's interests in such matters as the subsidy, but most eloquently arguing against the repressive acts which Archbishop Whitgift—thus the Queen, who called Whitgift her "black husband" and raised him to the Council—was determined to impose upon both Catholic recusants and rebellious Puritans. Though he was no longer Senior Knight of Devon in Commons, having no more distinction than to represent the Cornish borough of St. Michaels, he was a powerful presence in that Parliament. The Commons in '93 was more than half composed of new men. Chaotic, troublesome, threatened and browbeaten, subjected to many pressures and dangers, most originating from Whitgift, it was in this Parliament that a small number of men distinguished themselves by resistance to the proposed excesses and by a defense of the hard-earned rights and privileges of the Commons. Walter Ralegh was one of the leaders, as was the Speaker, Solicitor General Edward Coke. . . .

—As a result, he came under the suspicion of atheism, together with some friends and servants. The most vulnerable, Christopher Marlowe, was killed in a tavern brawl by two agents of the Archbishop. No doubt a warning to the others. And an ecclesiastical High Commission was formed to examine the suspicion of Ralegh's atheism. Ralegh did not deign to attend their sessions. Nothing came of the charges, except laughter at the expense of some pompion-headed preachers. And he was so little frightened that he made a mockery of false piety by making a great show of the same himself. When he returned from Guiana in '95, he announced to the world that he had "seen the wonders of the Lord in the ocean deep." And he went daily into London to listen to dull, interminable sermons at St. Paul's, the very model of outward humility.

[354]

—And this gesture proved—to Queen, Court, and the Archbishop, if not to the populace—that he had not changed a whit. Good fortune or bad, he would be himself, no other.

—In June of '97 he was accepted back at Court, resuming his captaincy, much as if five years had never happened. And though he was unlikely to advance much higher, he was again to be feared and distrusted, therefore hated. As much as before.

—Other favorites rose higher, but none were luckier or more trusted by the Queen.

—For those who looked for justice, it did not fall on Ralegh. Strict justice was reserved for his wife.

—Elizabeth Throckmorton, tall, blond, fair of skin, handsome in a strong and asymmetrical way, trim of figure and shapely of limb, could have done much worse by herself from among the men of Court. The Queen understood the attraction the older man held for her. Could not blame her for that, though, like a woman, she charged her with any seduction. What did this young woman know of anything? She was too young, too spoiled and safe to imagine the knave beneath silk and jewels. She might have him naked in her arms, as the Queen could never do, but she could live forever and never know him truly, truly naked, as the Queen did. The Queen might even have pitied her.

—Except that Elizabeth Throckmorton, having had her pleasure, and keeping her secret, returned to the service of the Queen as if nothing had happened.

—Which meant that Elizabeth Throckmorton believed or allowed herself to hope that Elizabeth, the Queen, was only a stupid old woman.

—Elizabeth Throckmorton could never be forgiven for this assumption. And—it pleased the Queen to know this—she would never know why. She was too vain to admit the truth to herself.

—Angry, disappointed, jealous, hurt, yes; for the Queen was a woman. But she managed to transcend that. To be what she was, for better or worse. First and always, Queen of England.

—After five years out of the center, Ralegh returned to serve the Queen for the rest of her reign.

—Within weeks of the death of the Queen, Ralegh was rudely stripped of his offices, perquisites, monopolies. Within a few months he was a convicted traitor, a plot beyond testing for truth or falsehood. His Court was the Tower, where he should have been out of sight and out of mind. But for fourteen years, from those walled acres, he managed to trouble the King. Famous men from England and abroad, even Indian chieftains from the New World, visited him. Crowds came to watch silently when he walked the walls for exercise. He won the friendship of Queen Anne and the young Prince Henry, who would have freed him if the prince had lived. "Who but my father would keep such a bird in a cage!" the young Prince exclaimed. And Henry had planned to restore Ralegh's lost estate of Sherbourne, perhaps a more suitable place than the Tower to wait for pardon or freedom. Sherbourne, which had been taken by a legal trick, devised by Cecil, so that the King could give it to his current favorite—Robert Carr. And all through those years Ralegh nettled and needled the King with his writings—*The History of the World,* written for Prince Henry, and which the King wanted suppressed because it was "too sawcy with kings," together with a rash of pamphlets in manuscript on subjects from the art of shipbuilding to "The Prerogative of Parliaments," each and all offensive to His Majesty's views.

—Finally Ralegh was freed to prepare and make his voyage

to Guiana. Ralegh was set free earlier than had been planned so his apartments could be used for the culprits in the Overbury poisoning. He left upon a sudden warrant, so swiftly, or conveniently, that he had to come back to gather the last of his books and papers. And thus met, briefly, face to face, the foolish, vain, and marvelously ignorant Robert Carr, now Viscount Rochester, Earl of Somerset, and now no longer the King's favorite, but a felon, charged in the scandalous poisoning of Sir Thomas Overbury. Carr, who had taken Sherbourne from Ralegh and had spurned even to answer Ralegh's measured and humble letter pleading for it. Met Robert Carr at last in the Tower, himself the free man and Carr the prisoner. Surely he did not really need to return for his books and papers. He could have sent his servants. But he went back to fetch them himself, making it clear even to cloudy-witted Carr.

—Ralegh was a figure of cold courtesy, soft-spoken, sad-faced, indeed almost apologetic for intruding upon Carr's misfortune. Which could not fail to drive Carr into a fit of rage. Ralegh accomplished that with ease, assuming the satiric role of the former owner of these grounds at the Tower, instructing Carr in ways and means to make life there more tolerable.

"You shall find it comfortable enough as soon as you become, like any caught bird, accustomed to your jess and hood and bells," he told Carr. "Indeed, should it be your misfortune to remain here as long as I have, or for the rest of your natural life, you will find many blessings to be thankful for."—Carr said nothing, but his eyes blinked and there was a dark cloud on his face. Which, of course, led Ralegh to continue offering good advice.

"Above all, sir, you must not squander thoughts or good spirits upon what might have been. Nor regret what you have lost. If

[357]

you must think of the past, as we all must do, think upon those who, in this selfsame place, have suffered so much more and lingered long."

"I need no counsel from you!" Carr said, not able to contain himself longer.

"Perhaps not," Ralegh said. "Then consider that you are free to ignore my counsel, as any man is so free. Have you not offered counsel which was ignored? And there must have been times when you yourself have ignored the counsel of others. For example, I am certain you cannot always have concurred with your late lamented secretary, Sir Thomas . . ."

"God's blood and wounds!" Carr roared, raising the heads of servants in the room and catching the ears of the many others who were curious about the encounter. "Christ on the Cross! I'd kill you if I could!"

"Oh, sir," Ralegh answered, "you must not curse and think of murder any more. Rather be thankful. In the olden times in England they would have boiled you alive for poisoning, you and your handsome Lady Frances too."

"By God, I *will* kill you with my bare hands!"

"Would you strike an old man? Shame!"

"If I were free—and mark you, old Fox, I may be free one day soon enough," Carr said, still so choked with rage he was not able to stop himself from shouting, "I'd have my honor at swords' points."

—Very softly then: "Which is the only place, sir, you shall have honor, as a rogue with a weapon."

"Damn your black heart to hell, old man!"

—And soft still: "Old it is true. But mark you, sir, I shall never be so old or frail that I could not spit the likes of you on the point

[358]

of a rapier like a poor sparrow. I would cut you clean from your high beard to your lower one, where all your brains dangle. . . ."

"Begone, you upstart rogue and beggar! Begone and may you die soon!"

—Carr turning away, black as a Moor, an ebony face on the edge of apoplexy.

—And Ralegh: "One word and no more," speaking to his back. "In my study of history, I could find no precedent for our altered status. Where in the world has the world seen the like? A King's prisoner able to purchase his freedom while the favorite of his bosom stands in the wreath of the halter. But now I have remembered an example—Mordecai and Haman. Look up the story. You shall have ample time to read. I did. . . ."

—Ralegh turned, smiling, and left at the head of his servants. Hearing, as he did so, the shift of Carr's feet on the stone, the swish and whisper of his clothing, as he too turned. Unable to curse. Unable to run away from torment. Forced to turn and watch the back of Ralegh's head as he left him. And Ralegh not needing to look back again for the proof of what mind's eye showed him clear as a portrait. A fierce face, lined with outrage, but strangely weak and harmless, almost pitiable for the bright welling-up of tears in the eyes.

—To whip Robert Carr naked from Tower to Westminster Hall could have given Ralegh less satisfaction.

—The Court of the Queen was bright and brilliant, but frivolous enough to be demanding. That much, at least, was our discipline. Those rituals became our purpose. And we were all actors in a quiet play, like one of John Lily's, performing for ourselves, our only audience. Elsewhere seed was sown, grain grew and was harvested. Elsewhere ships swallowed the wind and sailed over the edges of the world. Elsewhere merchants waxed fat and rich or died in debt. Poor rogues roamed the roads and slept beneath hedges. Elsewhere, as ever, sheep were fleeced and slaughtered for tables.

—It might be said, and not entirely as satire, that we practiced for the leisure of eternity by enjoying a portion of it here and now.

—The Court of the King is more extravagant and correspondingly rude. Blame it, as they do, on his hungry flea- and louse-bitten Scottish lords who came down like a flock of raucous crows; nevertheless the way of the Court is largely our own doing. With suddenly rewards beyond imagining or asking there for the plucking and taking, with the truth of the dwindling treasury known to everyone except possibly the King, there is a piquant urgency to our fleecing; now or never, it seems; with many of the old formalities and rituals which served the Queen discarded to be replaced by grander pageants and gaudier games; with the King by his tippling setting the literal example while we stumble foolish drunk and besotted, if not in flesh then in spirit; the old center is gone, vanishing so easily it might never have been, and no man can know how long the present humming and whirling will endure.

—Just at a time when many good servants were gone, the plain fact of service fell upon us, who had lost even the charm of our indifference. The King takes the *sense* of the Court he was given without ever learning the hidden *sentence*. He knows the letter, but he cannot read it. The spirit is a mystery to him.

—To publish the letter of the Queen's Court is to report nothing of the truth. Lacking an inner spirit, either to be disguised or exposed, the Court of the King is exactly what it seems to be.

—You will have heard of banquets turning into riot, where

[360]

the rush and press of crowds causes tables and silver and glasses to be overthrown. Foods and sauces and wines, bread and wasted salt, mingling in a rich paste, to splatter our clothes, until we look like weary travelers from the country of Gluttony. It is true. . . .

—Read report of the King crudely butchering a fallen stag, his doublet clotted with gore and excrement.

—Perhaps you know the account which Harrington once gave of the visit to England of Christian of Denmark. When the two kings vomited at table and were carried off snoring to bed. When the three Court ladies, as Faith, Hope, and Charity in the masque, were too dazed and drunk to stand and deliver their lines.

—What this means and signifies is—itself. We rush to the banquet table, pigs in silk and satin, destroying as much as we swill and devour. As if the late Queen in her last act ceased to be Diana and became Circe instead and turned our whole crew to swine. Faith, Hope, and Charity are knock-kneed and sweating drunk and cannot recall their lines. A peace-loving King has innocent blood up to both elbows. Idleness is now deadly serious. Men die of it and the good—Prince Henry, for example— die young.

—The Court the Queen left behind her was an apple, red and ripe, polished to a high luster. Down came the King from Scotland, hungry as a wolf. Bit into that apple with joy. To taste no sweetness, only dust and rot and worms. If he has never fully recovered, well, few men do so when the dreams of a lifetime prove false.

—But all of that, even this—the old man sleeping in the upper chamber of Westminster's gatehouse—is epilogue to a play which

[361]

ended long ago. Ralegh's last glory, his final triumph came in the last years of the Queen.

—To speak of the last times of the Queen, I must become a divided man. Half Egyptian upon one bank, the other among the fleeing Jews; the former outraged and dismayed, shaking mailed fists; the latter dancing for joy, biting their thumbs at erstwhile masters. Safely separated by a sea which first miraculously divided for the scampering mob, then closed again to drown Pharaoh's army.

—This figure applies well to a single man, divided from himself by a sea of time.

—Would the Jews have rejoiced and followed their prophet had they dreamed of the forty years of wandering in wilderness that lay before them?

—And the Egyptians, all worldly power and glory and pure frustration on the shore. Perhaps a vision of the harsh future of the Jews would have offered some solace, but was at that instant supremely irrelevant. I do conceive, however, that they might have sighed in mighty relief if they had known that with those Jews went also all the plagues and troubles they had suffered, that, in truth, their own power and glory would remain untarnished. At the loss of an army, it could have been called a bargain.

—My meaning is contained in that figure. All history is a sort of recollection, but between us and the things remembered flows a division of time, once crossed over blithely, but now unfordable. So it is with the life of a man, his chronicle of recollection. As you imagine me, so I must imagine myself.

—After the death of the Queen, something occurred in this kingdom which now seems final, so absolute it is a sea which divides us forever from ourselves. But then it was a cause for

[362]

celebration; no ending but a new beginning; a birth, disguised as death, whose name would be hope.

—To speak of the last times now is to be janus-faced. And the truth of it is lost in something deeper than the sea. . . .

—In those days the problem seemed simple. The Queen had lived and reigned too long.

—After a high tide of glory, the defeat of the Spanish Armada in a year of wonders, all things began a slow changing for the worse.

—In the war with Spain we pressed to no advantage, and the war went on, piecemeal nibbling the wealth, substance, and will of the kingdom. There were small actions of no apparent value or consequence. There were false flares of hope, like the sacking of Cadiz in '96, great stratagems which failed. Meanwhile there were ceaseless musters and alarms. Englishmen died in France, the Netherlands, Ireland, and at sea. They returned, maimed or whole, to swell the ranks of vagrant, masterless men. Or they deserted in droves at the ports even before they embarked.

—Spain was growing ever more powerful and was on all sides against us: stirring rebels in Ireland; supporting the Catholic League in France, and occupying ports there; in Scotland plotting and conniving; causing disruption of trade with the German cities and even with Poland; working as well within England by secret agents, her Jesuits, to stir up discontents and to keep hope alive among hard-pressed Papists.

—The orderly trade of our merchants was much disturbed. There were crop failures and rising prices, times of near famine; there were outbreaks and riots as grievances grew. And then the Plague came to England.

—The Queen was old and still the question of her succession was unsettled.

—The Queen was harsh in her age, seizing the circumstances of war and troubles at home as occasion for severity. She gave her Whitgift free rein to ride roughshod over opposition to the established church, to the equal injury and dismay of Puritan and Papist alike.

—All the men who had once led and guided were either dead —Leicester, Walsingham, Hatton—or dying, like Burghley. With them went the memory of the times we had come from and come through.

—When Ralegh returned to Court, there were many new men in power. Not only Whitgift and his faction, but Burghley's secretive son, Robert Cecil, and the Lord Cobham of whom little was known, but enough to be distrustful. The one hope of the Court and Council was young Essex.

—And now he was checked, by the return of that clever schemer, our English Machiavelli, Sir Walter Ralegh.

—True, Essex might be rash, but he was open and wonderfully generous to all who served him. And he courted popularity, which Ralegh, in confident arrogance, disdained.

—From the date of Ralegh's return the frustrations of Essex began. Those Essex favored and put forward were ignored. And Cecil, Ralegh, and Cobham seemed to have most influence with the Queen.

—Meanwhile the Queen and her counselors were seeking and finding sedition everywhere: in plays, poems, broadsides, and ballads. The more they sought to stamp these out, the more they flourished.

—Sedition is rooted in discontent, but it grows and spreads mighty when pruned by repression.

—Essex led a mighty army into Ireland. Failed there and, his version being popularly taken at full value, the failure was

[364]

blamed on the Queen and her favorites. When Essex returned, leaving Ireland to plead his case direct to the Queen in '99, he was disciplined. Shortly he was forbidden the Court, and his lucrative monopoly on sweet wines was taken away, leaving him pressed for money. He became ill. To many at Court and to many of the people who hoped well for him, his troubles were a senseless injustice, not only to him but against all.

—The gaudy Court continued, but never before had the courtiers been so ridiculed in satires. The history of Richard II was revived and applied to the Queen. Richard, too, had permitted himself to be blinded by false favorites. He had been deposed for the good health of the kingdom.

—In whispers some began to think upon Essex as our last hope. Perhaps he could act boldly and save the old Queen from the parasites. Perhaps, it was suggested, Essex might settle the matter of the succession once and for all.

—Meanwhile the Queen pondered what to do about this. Or, true to her habits, she waited for Essex to act and make decision unnecessary.

—Essex House became a headquarters for his friends and for malcontents of all persuasions. If he could bring Papists and Puritans together under one roof in a common cause, perhaps he could do so with this divided kingdom.

—There were all the outward signs of a conspiracy. Even in this Essex was without guile.

—One of the conspirators was Sir Ferdinando Gorges, Ralegh's kinsman and his subordinate in Devon. A meeting between Ralegh and Gorges was arranged. Ralegh rowed alone out to the middle of the Thames. He ordered Gorges back to his post at Plymouth Castle. Gorges refused and warned Ralegh to get to *his* post at Court.

[365]

"You are likely to have a bloody day of it," Gorges told him.

—Someone on the bank at Essex House fired a weapon four times at Ralegh, missing every shot. . . .

—Ralegh broke off the meeting and hurried back to Court.

—Essex's rising began with those shots.

—Essex and his band rode through the streets of the city, crying a plot against his life and pleading with the citizens to join with him for the sake of the Queen.

—They did not stir.

—There was a brief clash of arms at Ludgate, and he fled back to Essex House.

—He was besieged there. From his high roof he shouted proud defiance against Ralegh and Cobham, that his death would be worthwhile if only he could rid the kingdom of such caterpillars and atheists. But shortly he surrendered.

—He was tried and convicted of treason, proclaiming his innocence and denouncing his enemies. And he bore up proudly as many friends and fellow conspirators, from nobles to the ambitious Francis Bacon, gave evidence against him.

—On February 25, 1601, Essex was beheaded in the Tower Yard.

—Ralegh witnessed the execution from the Armory.

—It was reported he smoked his pipe, contented, as Essex died.

—Ralegh and the others remaining in favor were linked together in many an angry ballad and broadside.

—Ralegh continued at Court, serving the Queen for the two years she lived, now conniving and scheming openly for a place on the Council, for even more favor. Meanwhile ignoring his chance to ingratiate himself with James of Scotland. Contented,

[366]

it seemed, to be the favorite of a dying Queen, to play the courtier in her Court, whose gaiety now seemed a coarse parody of itself, until her final silence.

—When Cobham's plot against James was exposed, there was much rejoicing in that news. At least until Ralegh had his day at Winchester. . . .

—Plot or no, it seemed justice to wipe the old slate clean.

—But in the passage of time much has changed, and, with the changing of the present, the past has changed as well. There have been discoveries of hidden truths which alter the appearance of that past.

—Of the war with Spain: We know the Queen feared it greatly and avoided it so long as she was able. Then what an irony! When the Armada failed both England and Spain were committed to a war which neither was capable of sustaining. As the new King was to learn, sadly enough, even the little that we did to resolve the war exhausted our treasury and resources, wiped out the Queen's wealth, and in the end caused the burden of taxes and subsidies to become almost intolerable.

—She permitted the popular notion that her funds were being squandered upon favorites. Allowed that as less dangerous than the harsher truth, that we could do no more than was being done without ending the frail illusions of peace and prosperity at home.

—We know now, too, that the new habit of good times made the signs of poverty more evident.

—We know what our King had to learn for himself—that the power of Spain, also, was taxed to its limits. That the best hope for a true peace lay in the policy of the Queen. Which was, simply, to conserve as much of England's strength as she could, by any means, while Spain's wealth and power were dissipated.

—When Philip died at last, she allowed herself to hope that his son would stop the attrition. But the new Philip was frightened and uncertain. He pursued his father's policies with renewed vigor and at greater expense.

—We see now that the question of the succession, so long as it remained a question—just as the question of her marriage had been in the early years—was a formidable weapon.

—Harrington has described the condition of the last years well enough: "a time when malcontents abound in city and country, when in the Court the common phrase of old servants is that there is no commiseration of any man's distressed estate, that a few favorites get all, that the Nobility is depressed, the Clergy pilled and condemned, foreign invasions expected, the treasure at home exhausted, the coin of Ireland embased and the gold of England transported, exactions doubled and trebled, and all honest hearts troubled."

—Yet he soon knew how much the Queen had given, was giving up to preserve this much. Holding out, holding on, maintaining her illusion.

—Harrington served with Essex and came home with him from Ireland, a champion of the Earl. But Harrington was soon after disenchanted. And now we see, his brightness having diminished, some of the truth of Essex. Who failed in everything except in his self-deceptions.

—He squandered his wealth upon friends and servants. Not spending it as Ralegh had done, but in the folly of believing he was purchasing invulnerability.

—Time and again, with all things propitious, he failed at war. And though each time his eager servants rushed into print to justify him at the expense of others and though the populace took him for the hero of England, Queen and Council knew better. Again, there was no harm in permitting the people to have a hero if they wished to. There were few enough. His reputation became part of the illusion.

—But his failure in Ireland was a huge disaster. Not only did he fail to achieve any of his assigned duties, but now, taking advantage of confusion, there was a Spanish army in Ireland for the first time. Mountjoy, coming after him, finally succeeded, and against even greater odds.

—On the Council, it had been hoped that Essex would be strong and forceful. Strong enough to do what his sponsor, Leicester, and others of the old Protestant faction had done, and to check and restrain the excesses of Whitgift; and Essex in turn was to be checked by young Robert Cecil. But he was no match for Cecil.

—The Queen needed Walter Ralegh in between them and to watch over both. Indeed, she used him even in his absence, keeping his old post open at Court, in hope that the possibility of his return might serve to educate Essex and Cecil.

—Cobham was insignificant, a joke, too vain and dense to know it. Not dangerous to anyone but himself.

—Weary as she was, the Queen called upon Ralegh to play bear keeper in her behalf.

—At the end any sane man would have seen that Essex was surrounded not with loyal friends, but with fanatics on the one hand and intelligencers on the other. The Queen cut off his ready money from the monopolies so that he might learn to distinguish between true friends and false. She gave him time and liberty to learn, and at a serious risk to herself.

—But he killed himself as surely as if he were his own executioner. Essex was never wholly sane until he stood on the

[369]

scaffold. As Harrington has said, "the man's soul seemed tossed to and fro like the waves of a troubled sea."

—Sir Walter Ralegh may name himself a courtier and most would agree. Yet I think he was more anti-masquer than courtier. He was ever his own man until the last, when he made the finest courtly gesture of anyone in our time, itself a kind of anti-masque, if you will. On the one hand as noble as any, on the other more rash than even Essex. For by his actions Ralegh sealed his ruin.

—Consider that in those troubled last years it seemed to the Queen that after all things, after outliving all other monarchs— she had seen the passing of many kings and queens and of six Popes as well—steering through troubles and dangers, the tide of time turned against her. She was condemned to taste the ashes of regret. She was forced to entertain the ironic possibility that all of her years had been a long season of self-deception. To free herself from the Tudor curse, she had rejected both past and future, believing in only the present, keeping the faith, and trusting in Providence. But as Providence would have it— or was this only Fortune?—she lived and reigned so long that she had *acquired* a past, only to lose it. . . . And because it was ending badly. and nothing could be done, she had sad apprehensions for the future.

—Her Court was full of strangers. Her last progresses were thinly manned. The old ceremonies and observances, which once had lifted and lighted the Court so that literal and allegorical were one and the same, were now wearisome at best, at worst a grotesque dance of death, performed not by ghosts or anatomies of bones but by the pale children of the dead. . . .

—Even youth, Essex, on whom she had so doted and devoted herself, proved false and died.

[370]

—She felt the strangeness of her grandfather stirring in her. Thinking on how, at the last, that first Tudor withdrew into a long dream, staring into his magic looking glass. The magic glass broke when he died. *Or did the glass break first?*

—It was then Ralegh served her best. Bestirred himself with new vigor. Rejecting all occasions to sue for the favor of James or any other possible successor. Reverting to his old ways, scheming for advancement, for place on the Council, for new favors, titles, and honors. It was a wild mad course to take. For all these things would be without significance when she died. If he were cautious, he might have preserved something in the reign to come. If he were subtle or prudent, one half as clever as he was thought to be, he might gain much from a new prince.

—Like a fool, he acted as if his Queen would live forever. As if he would live forever too.

—His enemies laughed to see a man forfeiting the future. Here he was, past his prime, behaving like a young, somewhat clumsy, profoundly ambitious courtier.

—The Queen was annoyed; for she wished no more quarrels and squabbles than she had already known.

—And the old do not take much pleasure in being taught again the lessons of mutability, finding that those whose enchantment was youth are now old, only a few tottering steps behind them.

—I now conclude that Ralegh was not a fool. He weighed all these things, even the pain it might cause her; and all these were outweighed by his duty.

—He cannot have imagined that she would be deceived, even at the last, when she watched so silently.

—Cannot have been so presumptuous as to believe he could cure her melancholy.

—He was forfeiting his future and she knew it. Which may have pained her, too, the more so because he knew what he was doing. He knew that this compliment to her unfading knowledge of men could not please her. If anything, she could only wish him well disposed in an untroubled twilight of his own. Again, wishing her favorites to live by proxy for her, as she might have lived. Here was Ralegh rejecting her wishes, almost turning against her, chaining himself to a drowning woman. . . .

—It was more a duel between them than a last dancing.

—With time I conclude it was a mysterious gesture, yet altogether fitting and proper, a new and beautiful and wholly absurd model for the courtier, one that was never imagined by Castiglione or Sidney or Spenser either. For once someone other than the Queen could make a gesture whose meaning, sense, and allegory were one and the same.

—To Ralegh his actions had some secret meaning. Perhaps it was a testing, a self-inquisition to determine if he still possessed the spirit of the man he had been. Seeking to find if anything had been well preserved through the ravages of time, as a wife will keep last summer's fruit in sugar syrup through a long winter. . . .

—To the Queen, in her pain and deep discontent, all his last actions simplified into a single gesture, were as words written on a parchment, saying: *As I have been beholden to you, madame, for my life and being, so is our entire age. I give you to understand that the age was and is yours. I throw away my present honor and future hope, not as things of no value, but to bear witness to what I believe is truth: that to have lived in the age, your age, madame, is sufficient unto itself. With you the age dies. With you, madame, goes all that was finest in us. Thus, truly, we die with you. In the last moment of your light*

[372]

*will be all that matters of past, present, future. Go easy, then,
and go with no regrets.*

—And she died quiet as a cut rose.

—And so, a most satirical courtier became the distillation of
all the Court had wished to be.

This ghost, an ageless young man, ever idle and restless, courteous
and cruel, unchanging child of change, this man will say no
more. He touches his lips to signal silence. He smiles and, miming
the blowing out of a candle, he takes a thief's farewell, first the
color fading, then the sad cold light of his eyes gone, and one
last blinking of something—a jewel, a ring, a coin cupped in his
palm, and darkness comes between us and is final.

To seeke new worlds, for golde, for prayse, for glory,
To try desire, to try loue seuered farr,
When I was gonn shee sent her memory
More stronge than weare ten thowsand shipps of warr.

RALEGH—The Ocean to Scinthia

. . . Well now, I call that a voyage around the world and halfway back again. Beating the sea up and down even though it was all calm sailing. All for show with flags and pennants, drums and trumpets, cannon salutes, velvet rigging and tackle and painted sails of silk. Going nowhere and back again. With all the overcharged swagger you can muster but not enough to frighten away a Dutch fluyt. All for idle show as if time in the glass weren't sand but was gold coins and cut diamonds for my lady's fingers. . . .

. . . And why not? For that idle fellow, the one who was speaking his piece, he looks to be a lost Mayfly or maybe a salad looking for a dish to sit in. All his dainty colors and delicate stuffs! Why that silly scroyle could not cross the Thames in a wherry on a windless summer's day! Could not cross the river without the heaves.

. . . Oh, I'll grant he never did deny it. He was open enough. Open and shameless like the legs of a Bristol whore.

. . . But he would try to gull anyone. Smiles and lies like a Barbary pirate with every man he meets. Excepting those he knows to be his betters. His betters . . . Why, for the promise of favor he will kneel down and lick boots like a spaniel.

. . . And I'll never doubt he has succeeded in the art of the Court. That is (to wit and to woo), to gull himself most of all men. Learning to live with shame and idleness by pretending. And, as all the world knows, from the great Capes to farthest Muscovy, pretending is the father of that cheeful bastard—*believing.* Coming to believe, he with his goat dancing and high leaping, like a goosed milkmaid, his lute playing, sword crossing, reading and writing, riding and playgoing, and like accomplishments, *believing,* mind you, he has managed to do anything at all.

. . . I marvel at the wonder of it, ignorance wider and deeper than a Newfoundland landing, arrogance, strut of a rooster like a peacock in a barnyard, of these glowworms of Court.

. . . And yet I thank God Almighty the wretch never got bee in his ear or splinter in his arse that inclined him to going to sea to seek, adventure, high deeds, good name, bags of gold, and so forth and so on. For I have sailed more than once too often with gentlemen like him. And if I ever had time on my hands to ponder it, time to think, say when all wind was scant enough to be called naught and tasks and chores were done for the moment and a seafaring man can sit on deck to enjoy a pipe and drink his beer, I have been as mixed in my feelings as any salad. Chiefly divided between pity and contempt.

. . . Pity for any wretch who's seasick while riding anchors in harbor, before we have so much as raised a pennon, let alone heaved-ho to hoist a sheet. He, green-faced as a bullfrog, and knowing his guts will have more knots than our lines and will turn more flipflops than a flying fish in the bilge of a cock boat, before we have broke ground and cleared harbor. He knowing that the first fresh gale to fill sail and the steady pitch and roll will have him lightening cargo and ballast from every port of his body. A high hollow sea will send him below to black bilge. And if we should spew a little oakum from the seams and begin to gulp salt water, why, he shall open his prayer book to say the last prayers. Will give up his ghost three times over before we can furl canvas and bear up into wind to hull. Whereupon we shall be as dry and safe as a duck in a pool.

. . . Contempt for him because he is much too fine and soft-palmed to lend a hand with hauling and hoisting. Christ on the water! They will not take their turns at pumping even to save their own worthless bones.

. . . No matter if captain and master are good men and order the gentlemen to pull and work with every man aboard. No matter either if the crew is so thin and sparse from fever and flux or wounds that every breathing soul must labor day and night to keep us afloat. No matter, this fellow will be of less value than the youngest ship's boy on his first voyage out. Though the gent can read Latin and name Hebrew kings from Saul to Herod and backwards again, can tally numbers as swift and sure as a merchant of Levant and always to his own advantage, he will never live long enough to name the lines of a ship. Whereas that ship's boy, a fortnight out, will know the names and proper places and uses of three hundred odd ropes and lines, know how to do and undo the knots of them too, and can find them in pitch starless dark of a misling night. And if that ship's boy does not and until he does, by God, he shall learn not by his slow brain but by his quick bare arse, instructed by the very thing, a knotted rope in the hands of the boatswain on Monday morning.

. . . In a crowd, even aboard a yare ship, well mannered and

[377]

well mastered, these gentlemen flowers can turn a bone good voyage into a stickle disaster.

. . . Ask the fellow. Where does he think he came by any of these things he loves so much and lives for? Where did he get his silk and satin stuffs, gold and silver for his purse, spices and condiments to flavor his food and give him a thirst, the wines that make him thick-tongued, walleyed, and merry? I have shed a pint of sweat for every thread he wears to Court.

. . . Not pride says that, but truth. For there is nothing that I know of to equal hard labor of sailing a great ship.

. . . No matter, though. It is better for all that the likes of him live long and safe and comfortable—ashore. For thereby, among other benefits, many an ordinary English mariner shall live the longer and safer afloat.

. . . But pray do not believe him without some salt of doubt. He can talk as sweet as a sucket. And I would not take the word, unquestioned, of that lewd rogue who came out to speak first, rusty crowbait calling himself a captain. Neither of them knows much and the both of them together would have to confess on the rack of true judgment that they have settled nothing of great shakes in their time.

. . . It was the best men of England, the best men in the world I'll venture, your English seafaring man far from home who kept home secure and hearth burning. He put plate on the table and half the food to fill it. Put goods and stuffs in markets. Fought the wars, for the sake of peace at home, in both peace and war. While others, like Yorkshire pigs at trough, swilled down profits and grew fat and sleek. They fed the flesh that hangs on their bones, by his hard labor. Dressed and adorned themselves in brave rags and rare cloths he brought home. Likely then to go forth and tup the sweetheart, wife, and daughter of an honest seafaring man. For the sport of it. His thanks left behind, fruit of the womb, a child to mock the seafarer's old age. If he lives to have an old age.

. . . And nowadays, in the reign of the King, they will call us traitors and felons if we sail with France or Venice or the Dutch or Moors—who have of late come this far and to Ireland, too, searching for fair-skinned women for the markets, and with renegade Englishmen to pilot them. They will call us not Englishmen. Forgetting all we did before. Believing that we should go beg for our bread—and without a license to spare the whip and jail—instead of doing the honest work we know and do well.

. . . Nowadays they will have us join a throng of pressed men, hopeless rogues and criminals, and try to keep their rotten, leaky, ill-kept, short-rationed stink-timbered coffins, that they call the King's Navy Royal, afloat. And will have us to do this for wages which would not keep one of the King's beagle pups fed.

. . . Sail out with rigging, courses, and tackle as old as the Armada. Some say the biscuits and the beer in the casks were barreled then, too. And every mariner must have a *file* for his teeth like some Gold Coast cannibal to chew the King's rations. And if, say, the captain and the crew will take an honest prize or two and divide shares among them, according to custom, why, they will be named *pirates* and end up hanging in chains through six tides of the Thames.

. . . No, by the wounds of bloody Christ on the Cross, I would as lief pilot a ship of Barbary Moors to take on a squealing white-fleshed cargo, be they English or any other kind, as to beg on a public highway or rot my brains in the taverns,

[379]

where, with good fortune, I may hoard one cup of watery ale for half a night.

. . . Devil take them all, the courtier, the soldier, and the merchant too! He with his face as round and ruddy as a pompion, counting profits I earned for him at the price of my best years.

A voice, hoarse as the cry of a winter crow or a jay in springtime leaves. Rough as the lick of a cow's tongue. With a lifelong habit of speaking loud and clear to be heard above wind and slapping waves, heard in wind and weather, amid the slow groans and creaks of timbers and flapping of sails and whining chords of wind-fingering lines and shivering mast and crossbar, heard once, and understood once, or not at all.

A tavern or alehouse full of such voices would be louder than a clash of infantry, and sometimes as dangerous to life and limb.

Out of the darkness of dreaming comes first the voice. Next comes an odor. Oh, you can smell him before you see him. Not only the sour odor of flesh much sweat-soaked and rarely washed clean, for that scent could as well be the ghost of many a man in England, except the most fortunate and fastidious. Nor the sweet, sour, and dry odor of rough and ready clothing, tough as shoe leather but so worn and weathered, so sunned upon, misted, rained on, frozen stiff as body armor, that now it hangs loose and patched and faded, half rotten, shredding away like the flesh of a fugitive from an old lazar house. Nor even the lingering presence, shadowy odor of bilge water. An odor of dark foul stuff at deep bottom of hull, black sand and black water where garbage and scraps and refuse find refuge, together with the excremental humors of those on board who slip below rather than dare to perch, high and bare-arsed, on the rolling, ducking, pitching, spray-splashed beak and head before the bow. All this corruption distilled in sand of the ballast, becoming a liquor darker than ink, horrid as witches' brew, until even the captain on his high poop astern can smell and breathe nothing else. And then that ship must be cleaned and rummaged entirely. Not only the odor of bilge water, though a trace of that will follow him to the grave. But most, beyond all the others, the thick-sweet odor of pitch and tar. Coming from his ceaseless work. Tar that gives him a name. Tar that has colored his hands and arms and gone so deep it will never be gone until the marrow of his bones has turned to powdery earth again.

. . . St. Paul in the storm! You tell more lies than any Dutchman I ever knew! Though ignorance pardons you for it. But I cannot keep silent, with all due respect. True, we never had fine bathing tuns fit for a lady to scrub in. Nor wasted fresh water on such things. But we washed with salt water as often as able, in fair weather and calm. And we washed our clothing as well. And picked it clean of lice and vermin. And looked to our mates, picking each other's vermin where we could not reach or see. And in foul weather, why the rain and wind did a scouring job, right down to the slick of the bones, on every man.

. . . And when we went ashore, in a town or a strange place—sometimes even on hostile shore, with guards set about us and boats and oars handy—we filled our casks with water from stream or creek, and then, given time, we stripped down and bathed and scrubbed our garments.

. . . Not to be sweet as roses and rosewater, mind you. But for the sake of health, and to rid ourselves of the vermin you find on every ship, be she ever so clean, those pests which

[381]

swell up as big as peas and beans. Will drink a man dry of his blood, without a regular rummaging of himself fore and aft.

. . . And even in worst weathers, when there is nothing to do but work or sink, the sea coming over the bow and the waves on deck, the rain and the sleet and snow will keep a man washed down, clean as a lord, if he's working above or between decks. And if he must go below as naked as old Adam to man pumps, though he may be splashed by black bilge, he'll soon be washed clean with seawater.

. . . No, I say, a seafaring man, like it or not, is bound to be washed by water more than any other man in England, be he a farmer or a great man in a manor house.

. . . If I give off some faint smell in the dark in my seagoing garments, then it must be the pitch and tar. But when I go ashore to spend my money and take my pleasure, it will be good strong ale, cider, and spirits a dainty nose will mark. Together, I hope, and hope until I die, with the powders and sweet perfumes of a good respectable whore.

. . . Here I stand, a voice only. And here I shall stand until you have at least looked upon my home—the ship I spent my life on. I will be invisible until you have some picture of the ships we sailed, lived in, and died on. I am no fool. I have no expectation any man alive can come to picture her truly. I know you cannot, any more than I can sail myself into the future. But take one look and let yourself think on the simple things.

. . . Picture a good stout ship, yare and well found. And while you look remember we sailed her to Newfoundland, Virginia, Panama, Guiana, the farthest Capes, made the icy ports of Muscovy, Aleppo and Basra, even Java and the coast of China. We hauled up our anchors, hoisted courses and sailed out of

English harbors. And then, most of us and most of our ships, sailed everywhere and back again. Came home sometimes empty, light- and high-riding, and sometimes fat as a female rat, full to hatch covers and overflowing the deck with cargo and prizes.

. . . Picture her in harbor or river, anchor lines out fore and aft, bobbing gentle on calm water.

. . . And not to worry about the proper names of this and that—our jeers and carthapins, knavelines and all the like. I'm not the boatswain to beat you black and blue. You shall never know my craft and I'll never know yours. Which is fair exchange, I say.

High-charged, high-riding, made of solid English oak. From Devon, if possible, though more and more made from the timbers of Ireland, from the Baltic, bought from Poland and even Muscovy. Made from oak timbers, each from a whole tree and the trunks of the trees worked into planks in the shipbuilder's yard. But properly seasoned first. Then fastened with stout wooden spikes and treenails.

Small and squat to the eyes (though she is lean compared to the old vessels they call the round ships), with the length of her keel about three times the measure of the beam. Divided in three parts, forecastle, waist, and aftercastle. Beyond the bow and the sharp beak, is the bowsprit, a thin mast for a single square corse—the spritsail. Forecastle, set back from the beak, is small and low and for storing of cables and tackle. There are no cabins for the mariner; he'll sleep wherever and whenever he can; on open deck when weather allows. Aftercastle looms over the waist with a high poop deck, and has cabins for the officers.

The rigging is three masts, sometimes four in the largest

[383]

ships: foremast, with foresail and topsail, stepped up from the forecastle; mainmast with mainsail and topsail set in the waist; and a mizzen, aft at the aftercastle, lateen, for steering and maneuvering. Together with the spritsail, there are six sails to work with. Some larger ships will have top gallant corses for foremast and mainmast, and sometimes a second slanted lateen rig, aft of the lateen mizzen and called the bonaventure mizzen.

This ship is steered with a whipstaff below, attached to the rudder. Steered by compass and commands. Lookouts are top-mast in large crows' nests, and when wind is fair a man perched or lashed on the bowsprit.

Masts are slender, delicate to the eye. With light, slim spars of not much more length than the width of the canvas they hold. Sails furled and spars aslant, the rigging is a row of winter trees to a landsman's eye. All draped and webbed, the shrouds and tacklings, stays and braces, ratlines for climbing; and ropes from thinnest ratlines to huge cables for the anchors are hemp cordage.

Slender masts and light spars; for the spars, which have no footlines, can be lowered and raised by muscle in weather too rough to sit high astraddle there. Topmasts may be struck. And in the worst storms a whole mast can be chopped away to ease the roll. Can be replaced by cutting and rounding off a tall tree thousands of miles from home.

The ship is so simply made that any part of her can be made anew, if necessary.

Come close and she is higher and smaller yet, a smooth-sided, fat hull, bulging wide at waterline, then tapering, curving upward and thinner, with at least one row of painted ports, red and black, for guns. Often with more gunports than guns. And some are not ports at all, only painted squares. The planked

[384]

hull is not painted from the water to the wale, but dark from thick staining; for it is paid with coatings of tar and oil and resin and turpentine. Dark-stained and smooth, rising to sudden brilliance at the wale; the upper and outer works are bright-painted in designs of red, blue, yellow, and green. But no fine carving or gilding there. And at the peaks of masts and at stern, flags, pennants and pennons, the arms of the owner, the flag for the nation, cross of St. George for England . . .

. . . If you are speaking for me, you are wasting your living breath. And what's more precious than that? I cannot comprehend the good of it unless the huge glass of time is reversed and the living must once again become square-rig, galleon sailors.

. . . We had our craft and our reasons. Our vessels handled well for the men who knew the craft and obeyed the ways of wind and water.

. . . It's true, strong winds made trouble. We could beat up and down, tacking, for days at a time in a fresh gale and finally arrive nowhere for all our pains. And, running with wind, we must let out and belly corses like great sacks of air. Losing thereby, some swiftness. But not losing our rigging.

. . . And sailing too swift could cause trouble also. Often we were in uncharted waters. Needing time to sound the depths and feel the way.

. . . In a true storm we would come up into the wind and try or hull. But a good vessel rode well that way. And, strange as it may seem, it was the *only* time when a man could go below and be as dry aboard as a dog's buried bone. Our ships were wet sailors in good weather, but dry and quiet below when black storms raged.

. . . She rolled and pitched aplenty. For she sailed more *on* the water than *in* it. Floating like a bobbing cork. But, weighing, and considering all, I'd rather be ever rolled and pitched —providing her rib timbers are sound and solid—than cracked up and sent down to the bottom.

. . . It is true she was no good sailer in foul weather, though she could bear the worst by lying ahull. And true that too often—especially getting clear of England—contrary winds could keep us lodged in harbor, waiting there until our victuals were half spent and gone, and every man aboard as pained as a rotten tooth. But when it came to long voyages, it was never a tempest we feared so much as the terrible calms.

. . . To be becalmed in the midst of the ocean sea is far more fearful than to weather the worst storms.

. . . And the rig and tackle, the design of our ships was such that the least faint ghost's sigh of breeze could make us sail.

. . . A man cannot shoot a bow in opposite directions at one and the same time. We feared calms more than storms. So we built to sail by a breeze so faint and light that you could scarcely feel it. Flags and pennants might droop but our canvas could catch it and could set a high-riding galleon to moving again.

. . . But enough of ships. Whether they are new and yare or rotten and leaky as a fishnet, graceful as a dolphin or clumsy as a Yorkshire sow in May mud, ships are no better or worse than the men who handle them.

High time to think of the men who sailed and handled the ships, hauling ropes and lines and spars, furling and unfurling corses, handling the helm at the whipstaff, pulling oars, eating rations, curling upon the covers of hatches or the packed, stacked cargo to sleep when and where they could. Men who died of fever and diseases and sometimes of starvation and black thirst. Or lived to fight at sea and by land. Perhaps to die then, or be crippled and maimed. Or to be taken by enemies. Then to be whipped, well tortured, hanged. Or, perhaps, clad in the Fool's Coat of S. Benitos, yellow with red crosses fore and aft, chest and back, and a high-pointed cap like a dunce schoolboy's, and each man carrying a fat green wax candle, to be tried before the Holy Inquisition. Then burned to ashes at a stake. Or, more fortunate, their naked backs opened up raw and dripping slick with blood from public lashing. From which chastisement, if they survived, they were then sent off to a decade in the galleys.

Perhaps they lived through all, escaping all dangers, hale and hearty, to come home at last for good and to try to tell some truth of it in taverns. To die in bed like their neighbors and find a place in a churchyard or space in the church to be shared with others dead long before or after them.

Each vessel, large or small, on a voyage beyond land and horizon, was a place to itself—a village afloat. Except they could grow no crops of food though the sea might offer a bounty harvest of fish, and must find fresh water ashore when they went dry. Carried victuals for six months to a year. And hoping, praying these foods were well packed and preserved, kept tight in casks of seasoned wood with sound hoops to hold the seams against wet and vermin. Not forgetting that the most mortal blow against the Armada was Drake's expedition to Cadiz. Not for the sinking of ships or the singeing of metaphorical beards, but destruction of the well-seasoned wood gathered for casks. Forcing the Spaniards to sail with inferior casks. And to suffer for it.

Carrying also firewood for cooking when they were able

[387]

to have fire. And they preferred food cooked and hot and managed to cook it most of the time.

Carrying all other stores and equipment they needed, from the gunpowder to sandglasses to keep the half hours. And allowing for breakage and spoilage. Allowing, too, for the ceaseless tasks of maintaining and repairing. With a carpenter, a cooper, and a caulker aboard, and likely a blacksmith and a barber-surgeon.

There was neither a cook nor a sailmaker. All must be able to cook. Any good sailor must be able to sew and mend sails.

The carpenter charged with the care and keeping of the hull, the masts, and spars.

The caulker forever busy. All wooden ships have leaks, but he must try to keep her watertight and direct all pumping.

Cooper charged with care and keeping of all casks. The cargo and all the food and water aboard. An unenviable charge, judging by endless complaints about the spoiling of goods and food, the loss or ruin of priceless water.

All repairs were carried out by the crew. When they had to, they cut trees and made new masts and spars. When ropes and cables wore out, they made new ones from raw hemp. Building of new boats and longboats was usual. Repaired or replaced lost rudders at sea.

And many times must clean the ship's bottom of barnacles and weed and growth. Would find a shore and careen the ship, tilting her first to one side then the other, scraping her clean, caulking her, paying a fresh coat to protect the wood and discourage the teredo worm.

And at the same time they would rummage the ship. Pump out sewage and garbage of the bilges, shovel the stinking sand of the ballast, scrubbing bilges clean, sprinkling all with vinegar, *and then shoveling in a new and carefully balanced ballast of sand and stones.*

Patching up their own wounds and injuries as best they could and living with them.

Sailing from here to there. The final destination, often known only by rumor or hearsay, or by a memory from years before. Using charts which were at best grandiose portolani, whose coastwise pilotage directions extended outward, and, beyond known waters and near distances, more decorative than useful. Or maps done in the Medieval manner, valuable for cosmographers, but inaccurate for the navigator. Depending on dead reckoning, and with so many variables and unknowns as to make this seem impossible. But knowing what these variables were and aware of the unknowns. Passing along word of mouth and through books knowledge from the Portuguese and Spanish schools of navigation.

Working with instruments they were able to bring aboard and use. And working always out of the necessity of following the known winds and not shortest nautical distances.

Finding their way by means of a crude and uncorrected compass; by an elementary quadrant; by backstaff and crossstaff; by an imperfectly understood and only partially useful small astrolabe; telling hours with a sandglass turned every half hour by ship's boys who sang out announcement as they turned the glass; estimating speed of the ship by a length of rope with knots.

Feeling their way, in all but the deep, with frequent soundings of lead and line; working within sight of land whenever possible for the sake of the pilot's art of caping from one known promontory or landfall, often at great risk with land to leeward.

Remembering strengths and currents of the tides of harbors and calculating tides from the age of the moon in the month.

Mistaking the tides, even in familiar harbors, being the most common cause for distress.

Yet sailing off on the longest voyages. Often with an agreed rendezvous halfway across the world. And, amazing, making that rendezvous. Finding a spot in the ocean, more often than not. Failure to reach a destination was seldom the fault of navigation.

Now the men and the order of the crew:

The captain, most often a gentleman and sometimes the owner. Commanding all and charged with everything.

A lieutenant to be his legs, voice, translator of wishes into orders. Few good words have been wasted on lieutenants.

The master, chief navigator, pilot, and master seaman of the ship.

Master gunner, charged with all ordnance, powder and shot, and weapons, readiness, care, practice and use.

And besides carpenter, caulker, cooper, blacksmith, and barber there are junior sailing officers:

Boatswain for ropes, rigging, sails and flags and care of the longboat; also for punishments.

Coxswain, keeper of the ship's boat, lowest rank to carry a pipe and whistle for commands.

Purser, the clerk of records and keeper of money.

Quartermaster, responsible for victuals and the ship's hold; he cons the ship from the deck.

Swabber, to keep the ship clean; it's common punishment to be sent to serve under him.

Four kinds of seamen: the ship's boys, nine years old and up, for service and errands and high work on the masts; youn-

kers, the ordinary seamen; mariners, able-bodied, experienced, and skilled; sailors, older with much experience and the lightest duties.

Wages, not to be lower than the Navy Royal's ten shillings a month.

Rations: a gallon of beer a day and a pound of sea biscuit; two pounds of beef (or pork or peas) four days a week; on other days fish and butter and cheese. Most captains carried oranges and limes and dried fruit for the men. There was flour, but heavily sotted to discourage rats. Hooks and fishing lines were ship's equipment, for catching fresh fish when they could. Sometimes chickens were kept aboard, but seldom live sheep or cattle.

Though regulation stores were ample, they were often depleted by waiting for wind or spoiled on a voyage.

So a seaman's food could be described as being "shrunken ration of moldy cheese, rancid butter, weevily biscuit, putrid beef and sour beer. . . ."

. . . Amen to that. It is the God's truth.

And now he is more than his voice, coming out of the dark and into a twilight shadow.

A tanned man, his face a map, a chart of wrinkles, well- and often-plowed courses. A lithe, lean, smallish, small-boned man. Conveying sure quickness and balance, nimbleness, though he stands relaxed. Size of a boy. A boy made of leather and, when he chooses, of light-footed, graceful, sure-handed movements, easy, with no waste of motion or strength. Can vanish with a dart into the dark again if it pleases him. Can disappear forever in response to a threatening move. Not betraying *fear, though, in his spread-legged, shoulder-slumped stance, his head ducked, chin tucked down toward his chest, pale eyes raised, light-rinsed and unblinking, short-bearded, beard and trimmed short hair sun-bleached. A skeptical smile on chapped lips.*

Who would have imagined such a mighty voice from him?

Though alert and suspicious as a spring bird pecking in grass, looks harmless enough. Except for his hands. The left on hip, crooking an elbow, the right loose and open, palm down, across a taut belly. The right hand a few inches away from the hilt of his knife. And, even sheathed as it is, its plain bone sheath solid to grip and almost colorless, that blade can be imagined. Thick and clean and bright, keen of point and honed along edge until it will cut through a hair dropped across it.

What that blade can do to the carcass of a man, so quick he would see only a flashing before he felt the heat of pain and ice upon flesh from the cold of the blade. He considers himself well armed for anything he might meet on shore.

But the hands . . . Large, bulked and dark as if he wears gloves. The fingers long, square-ended, nails clipped close, one of them blue; yet these large, relaxed hands, grown so from years of gripping and pulling, with long, square, blunt-shaped fingers, imply much dexterity. Not for lute or viol or virginal. He would not have time or patience to tune a lute. But for the swift, sure, subtle tasks. A tailor or lacemaker might envy those hands and fingers at sight. A fool would ignore them.

The palms unseen but calloused, layer upon layer. Gloves cannot serve him better.

You can tell him by his clothing at a distance. He has canvas breeches, or tarpaulin, baggy and loose with many folds, a doublet or jerkin of the same; a white, tough linen shirt, to which he may add a short ruff for a ceremonial occasion, greasy-wool stockings for his calves, shoes of lightest, thinnest, toughest leather, with a metal buckle to tighten and loosen them. And he wears the old-fashioned thrummed cap. No doubt disdains the newer Monmouth cap.

. . . I will have neither when harbor is cleared and we are at our business. If I need a cap to cover my head in wind and spray or the rain, why, I'll wear one of my own making, cut from the wool of an old pair of socks where the toes wiggle in a naked dance and will not be darned.

. . . Well now, there are things I want to tell. That for heavy work, dirty work, wet or cold work, we had our long gowns if we pleased to wear them, to spare both body and clothing. And that canvas gown, though it might bag and luff like a sail—and we have sewn sails of them of necessity, will keep a man warm and dry if he knows how to wear it. 'Tis too clumsy to be used aloft—excepting in crow's nest or topmost —but is good service to a seaman on deck or under hatches when we are taking in water. And it serves well for a blanket to roll in too, if it has been kept dry.

. . . Though our clothing was scant enough (one shirt was all a good seaman could afford for a voyage and enough if he looked to the care of it), it served for our kinds of labor. Light and sturdy with nothing to catch or snag, and loose to leave limbs and body free. But I tell you, seamen nowadays, in the reign of the King, are a disgrace. A shame to England, to the King, and in truth, to themselves. I swear I have seen savage men in Africa, Ireland, and the Indies more bravely clad than poor wretches of the King's Navy Royal. In southern waters I have seen an English ship manned by a crew of naked men. Perhaps in the cold North they cover themselves with their gowns. Or else shiver like bones on a gibbet. They die for lack of proper clothing. And, barefoot in the cold northern routes, they will lose toes as easy as if by an ax.

. . . Well, things are not what they once were, I'll be a witness to that.

. . . And speaking of victuals; evil as they may sound to some landsman, even moldy cheese, stale bread, and sour beer are a feast when the choice is those or an empty gut all twisting like a dying snake and the black weight of the tongue when there's nothing to drink.

. . . Let them laugh and call a seafaring man a fool, ignorant and foolish. Most likely he knew little of reading and writing, words and ciphers. If he could read, he would read nothing much but the Psalms and some verses of Holy Scripture. No Latin or Greek, it's true. But bear in mind that after he'd sailed a voyage or two, he could buy and sell, curse and make love, order food and drink and ask direction in the Spanish, Dutch, French, Italian, and Portuguese tongues. Which, I'll wager, is more than many a gentleman at home. And there were plenty who could bargain and make talk with all kinds of black Africans and savages of the New World; could talk with the Turks and Lapps and Moors. And I, myself, after a perilous and icy voyage, have talked sweetly with a broad-beamed Muscovite girl.

. . . Except when a ship is direct commissioned on navy service or, say, upon a short merchant voyage, a seaman is not likely to be living off his wages. On a proper voyage, where prizes are taken along the way, the crew has the lawful right and custom of dividing among them one third of all profit when time comes for breaking of bulk and the disposing of it. One third of the value of prize and the cargo. And this comes together with the rights of pillage. Meaning that, excepting for a captured ship's instruments, charts, and the captain's chest, all goods and valuables not part of the cargo are fair pillage for the crew. And that would mean, too, the belongings and clothing of all of their crew, living or dead, and any passengers on board. Including even every shred on their bodies and backs. Unless, of course, a captain should feel full of the fear of God and give order against stripping them bare-arsed.

. . . So, anyone can plainly see that on a voyage of privateering a man could make plenty, even down to the topmost boy of the crew, if it was a saving voyage.

. . . Now, back to our subject of victuals again. On that kind of voyage, victuals are charged against the cost of the voyage and count against profit. No man would want to stuff his gut with dainty fare. Even if he were so sea-seasoned and brass-gutted he could keep such things down. He can always spice up his rations ashore or on the victuals of a well-stocked prize.

. . . The crew on these voyages were like holders in a joint-stock company. A fair wind of incentive to pull and labor together. And by rights the crew had a say in matters. When you hear gossip of mutinies and suchlike, it is well to remember that, before you jump to judgment. A captain who will pass by a likely prize or will risk ship and crew for a longboat full of codfish, you can be sure he will be told about it soon after. If not before. . . . And if he is a wise captain, he will listen to right reason and follow the will of the crew.

. . . You'll hear of many a voyage that changed at sea from its purpose and destination. Study and weigh each tale. You'll see that sometimes the will of the crew prevailed, even against reason. But, as often as not, the captain never planned to follow the intended course. He would keep his plan to himself till he put enough leagues of water between him and home so a spy would have to swim to report his intelligence. Or sometimes over the horizon here comes a sail or two ripe for the picking. A man with a good ship and crew would be a fool not to give chase, though he must sometimes abandon his course to do so.

. . . Now, on a good fat prize, say a vessel out of Portugal or Spain, when there's plenty of wine and pillage to quarrel over, there can be trouble. Especially if it's been a lean voyage with thin pickings, and there's been bloody work and the loss of shipmates. Trouble for which a man cannot be blamed. A good stiff fight at sea will scare a brave man into flux. After close chances and the sight of mates being killed, after having to enter and settle it with blades and hard knocks (and sometimes a ship will slip her grappling and leave you on the other vessel while she tries to sail around and close again), after all that fear and bloody work, with blood still running on the decks and waist and clotting in lumps like fresh tar, bodies of friends and strangers lying about and some not dead yet, but moaning and weeping and praying for death, I have seen good-hearted shipmates break open the first cask of wine and gulp it down like water. I have seen them laughing and cursing and singing and dancing among the dead and the dying. Have seen them strip crew and passengers, women and children too, down to the skin. Heave the children over the side to drown or bash brains on the mast. And lower breeches to the knees to have the women, unashamed, before the eyes of all. Have seen men hold a woman down on a blood-soaked deck while each had his turn with her. And, sir, they will kill any man, the first, who chastises them, even their own officers and captain.

. . . One thing for certain. No woman I care for will go as a passenger on a ship. Unless she goes with the whole Spanish *flota.*

. . . One time I saw a fellow take a fat black-haired Spanish dame—she was a lady and might have earned us good profit by ransom—and had her to kneel and take it behind like a dog. Then he called her a bitch in heat and turned her upside down, all wiggling like a tunny fish and crying like a wounded weasel. And he lugged her over to a wine cask and drowned her in it upside down. And then, when she was drowned and limp, with her feet still standing up in the cask, he takes his cup and dips it full and says every man will damn well drink with him. If it's good enough for him, it's good enough for the whole scurvy lot. And by God, we drank that wine.

. . . Our captain, not the best I've known, but a good man, is walking the poop of our ship with the master, pretending to study clouds and waves for signs of weather.

. . . Next morning that same brute fellow stands up with the rest of us, bows his head and mumbles prayers as we heave our own dead, all wrapped in canvas, over the side.

. . . No doubt you'd like to hear how he fell into the hands of the Spaniards and is now pulling an oar with scars on his back. Or maybe, to make his justice perfect, was taken by Moors and transformed to a eunuch.

. . . But the fellow did well enough and saved his money. He owns a tavern near Dartmouth where mariners go. He married a widow, most religious herself, and they are great ones for listening to sermons.

. . . He's a good and cheerful man. Always greets me warm and serves up a pint of ale for sake of friendship.

. . . I doubt he remembers it at all. In truth, I had let slip of it myself until now. For—and any seaman will be my witness—there is so much labor and danger to sailing that a man forgets from one day to the next. What he remembers will come back long after.

. . . Once in a bad wind we lay too close to shore and waves off Virginia. And we like to have lost the ship. And all I recalled afterwards was coldsweat fear and working in a fever of hauling and furling according to the wretched wind, until my hands were bleeding. But long after in a tavern, feeling good, not drunk but glad at heart and far from my troubles, it all came back to me. None of the other, but a strangeness I had not even noticed then. How when the wind would turn around and spring off the land, the scent of it was sweeter than an English garden in springtime. Like the scent of flowers had been laden into the land breeze. So sweet that fume, it could put you to sleep. And all the while a leaky rotten ship, crammed with shouting men and the pipes and whistles of the officers screaming in the wind and all of us working and throwing our puny cargo overside to lighten her and pumping like wild beasts, was about to break apart into firewood and convert us into food for fish.

. . . Well, there is no such thing as a safe and sure voyage. A man on water is a child of Fortune. Not safe and sure even in a cock boat on an inland pond. Water and wind will have their way and always have the last word.

. . . I have made voyages that should have been as quiet as a ride on a hoy down the Thames in midsummer. And have seen such a voyage turn into a nightmare. When bloody

[398]

flux and pox and itch and fevers and pustules without names have wiped out half the crew and crazed the rest. When rats, as fat and sleek as judges at Westminster, outnumbered living men. And while rats and lice and maggots gorged upon them, the dead were being robbed and stripped by their living mates. Drank bilge water and ate boiled leather until the ship finally gave up her ghost and broke apart. Casting a few upon a rocky shore, where we grubbed and groveled for mussels and crabs until a vessel chanced to sail by and carry us home.

. . . And just so I have sailed out upon the certainty of nothing but tribulation. To return unscathed, unscarred, unmarked, my purse full of silver and gold, my seabag stuffed with fine things, and myself fatter and stouter by far than when I kissed the whores good-bye.

. . . Oh, some things are sure. If you sail by command of a green young man from Court, why it's only roll the dice and your life is wagered upon one roll. Those peacocks, they desire a ship cram-full to hatches with gold and rare spices. And, more than that, they look for a tale of wondrous honor that may be told at Court or printed in a book. Meaning many must die to bring it to pass. And yet there are mariners who have endured such Bedlamite voyages and who are now masters and even owners of ships.

. . . If you sail for the merchants, the risks of the sea are all the same, but you'll be confined to the carrying out and bringing home of bulk cargo. And to defending it. Taking no chances, though you may take a prize if you happen upon an easy one. Yet there are good voyages where these will add up to a decent sum. And even if you are somewhat connied in breaking of bulk and must sell what you have to the customer ashore for a childish part of its value,—as if we seamen knew no more of prices and value than a red Indian!—still, you come to walk on land again with the jingle of money to spend and to keep you happy and in health for a while. Until the time comes when you must either ship out again or starve.

. . . I'll not speak of pirates and corsairs. With no home port, no country, it's a rat's life. Hand to mouth and never much more than the scars to show for it. Raids by night on villages where the best plate is dented pewter. And if you are lucky you may get a ransom for the life of the sister of some under-sheriff, though most likely she's too ugly and shrewish to keep aboard, even in chains, for long enough to find out. If you are a lucky pirate, you'll die in a fight or a tavern brawl. The best odds are you shall hang in chains. A pity it is, too; for we are bound to see many a poor man so trussed up in iron, many and more than you may know.

. . . For now the sweet good cider is gone for good, has turned to vinegar. The life of a seafaring man nowadays is enough to turn your stomach inside out. . . .

Here the seaman hawks and spits, cutting his eyes away, looking down to spit a gob, well aimed, just beyond the tips of his shoes. Has lowered his voice to a sort of whisper, though audible enough. Lowered head and eyes, lowered voice to a whisper, and, expressionless, speaks out of the side of his mouth, his lips still half pursed as if to spit again.

And now the right hand has moved slightly. It touches lightly the handle of the knife.

. . . It's a bad time for English seafaring in the King's reign, I tell you. We have what they call peace. Which means that every honest privateer is now a pirate. And means, since all the world is out for prizes, we are the fattest, fairest, easiest game. A nation of fat floating connies.

[400]

. . . Living, if you can call it that even in a jest, by their wages alone, and, mark you, common wages have not changed since the times of the Queen, men will not go to sea as before. It is no wonder that now they must swoop down and press crews as they do soldiers. It makes any honest seaman swallow tears, to see those surly scarecrow men, one half out of the jails and the other from Bedlam, men who know and care nothing of lines and corses, who think a whipstaff is a thing a constable carries and will shit upon poop deck, as much from ignorance as insolence. Who will steal water and victuals and think it a jest when their mates go on short rations. Will laugh at others until a day when all must starve equal. Whereupon they will fall not on their knees and cry mercy and forgiveness of God, but more likely curse Him for their fates.

. . . Not that it matters who the seamen may be, considering the state our ships are in. Have you seen the ships of the Navy Royal? Rotten tackle and rig, planks and timbers no sea worm with self-respect would condescend to chew on. All rats with half wit have long since departed. A mongrel pup would shy away from the victuals. Ordnance has gone to rust and you could bake bread with the gunpowder. Or else it is deadly as a siege mine. I heard tell not long ago of a gunner who, upon entering Plymouth mole and by custom, let fly a blank salute. Blew up the whole ship, it did, and the sky was raining seamen, some whole, and some in butcher's portions. Yet they sell the best English ordnance and powder to anyone who can pay the price. Have you heard how the Devil of the Dungheap, that Gondomar, has purchased a huge quantity of powder and new cannon from the Tower? It was loaded as cargo on the same tub that took him back to Spain. I hear it was such a bargain you might as well call it a gift.

[401]

. . . Someone will be along soon and warn me to curb my tongue. Now, that's a most difficult thing to ask of a seafaring man when he's safe on shore and has trapped a live one who'll listen to him. Talk will be the ruination of me. Let us return to safe harbor and talk of seafaring in the last age.

. . . You can call a seafaring man a fool. Foolish to risk life and limb for small profit or none. More fool for coming ashore with money in his purse to enrich half the tavern keepers and poxy whores in England. And unless he has more luck and wit than Prester John, a seafaring man will live to be old with more patches in his clothes than a gypsy. An empty purse, tired bones, a tough palm to catch pennies when he can, and a heart as bitter as wormwood. No wife or good woman to care for him in his dotage, and no children bearing his name.

. . . Call him ignorant and foolish. But call him no fool in matters of life and death. If he fares badly or starves because of a thieving, conniving victualer or an addlebrained captain or a lazy wretch of a cooper, he'll know it. And he'll curse them and maybe kill them too. But if it's bad wind, bad weather, the fortunes of a voyage, then he'll eat a weevily biscuit like it was manna from heaven. Though he curse the taste of it, he'll chew it and keep it down.

. . . Now then, I will waste not many more words. It would take me a lifetime to teach the first things of our ships and sailing. And that would be true even if I knew the right words to teach by. Because, except for an idle word here and there, I would sound as strange as any Turk or a Cimarron if I talked in the language of seamen. We weren't much for words at sea. On land we laughed and told lies and talked until our throats ached and our tongues were raw, for the pleasure of it. .But with, God willing, wind in the tackling and sails as tight and smooth as the belly of a woman far gone with child, and the sigh and shiver of timbers as she pitched and rolled to the dance of the sea, splash of white water at beak and trailing aft, and the lap and slap and swish and slip-slop of water rushing past, cry of lookout, barks of quartermaster to the helm, boatswain's whistle shrieking, and both hands busy when you had the watch (dead asleep when you didn't), why, there wasn't much time for idle chatter.

. . . No, I'll tell no tales and I'll not pretend to teach a craft that took me a lifetime to learn.

. . . You may have heard from other folks that your English seaman was like a savage and had no discipline worthy to mention. You find, in books, that our rules were strict and punishments severe; but that we didn't hesitate to mutiny and so forth. Well, there is never an answer to something truly contrary, but there is more to it than meets the eye.

. . . There are many kinds of discipline. One is in a man's craft and skill. It took more than obedience to orders to raise anchors, hoist sails, and get under way. If we lacked the skill and if we failed to work together, every man jack, with trust and with true care for each other, then we would never have been able to get a ship out of harbor, let alone across the world and back. And once under way there can be no slacking off of either, not until the last anchor drops for good and our feet are firm on shore and pointed in all the directions of a compass rose. One man failing, through ignorance or stupidity or laziness, at any task, and, by God, every man *feels* it from the captain to the youngest boy.

. . . Now, that is the least of it, that everyone aboard can feel with his body what every other man does or does not do.

It is more. For a sum of little failures or follies will be a broken ship and death of us all. And the same is true as much of a boat with a half-dozen men at the oars as with a giant carrack and a hundred men aloft working canvas. Think of us chained together, then, like prisoners, though the chains are invisible and we are prisoners by free choice.

. . . What most people mean by discipline is something else. The obedience of a soldier who goes where he is told and does what he is told to do without asking why. Now, I don't think the soldier's a fool, either. He knows that there is no purpose in asking or wondering why. But a man on a ship knows why he is doing what he does and he knows what will happen if he does not. And he feels it then and there because the ship and the wind and the waves answer to him directly. No, he does not know much of courses or navigation. He is too busy for that. Leave that to the captain and the master. There will be no course to follow if the sailor has no skill.

. . . The ship and the winds and the weather, the waves and currents and the tides, they are our masters and teachers, rewarding skill and punishing folly, all of us equally. We could choose to disobey a captain, but we had no choice to disobey our true masters and live to tell it.

. . . And all skill does not lie in the invention of ways to do without skill. Meaning that men do their work with what they are given. And the skill is in using the tools well to do the job. Agreed? Well, sir, to many eyes we sailed a tubby, clumsy square-rigged little ship with much to say against her. But she was all that we had and all that we knew.

. . . And some do marvel that we sailed out on voyages with no certainty. Sailing into the "unknown." Since we couldn't be sure of anything, beginning with where on the earth we might be. I would remind them, sir, that the sea is always unknown. Ever changing and moving and never the same. If we had feared the unknown, we would never have stepped off land in the first place. Stepping on board, in the innocence of a ship's boy or the knowledge of a gray-beard sailor, no matter, is always the brave step into the unknown. A voyage around the world can prove nothing more, since it merely follows the first step. A man's life is always a voyage into unknown water from his first cry to the sounds of dirt falling on the lid of his coffin. A man lives until he dies and a man will live and be himself in a country cottage or on a ship.

. . . I could be more windy than a Florida squall in September on this and more, but I won't. Because no one will know the truth of it unless he believes in it already. And if he believes it, then my words will make no difference. I will say this much, though. More often than not, we made landfall where we intended.

. . . Now, the proper use of these things was beyond the learning and experience of a seaman. And beyond the old habits of many a master. Which was why we needed a man with more schooling. And such a man was most likely to be a gentleman. We needed his skill and he needed ours. And so we worked together. And the gentleman was tested and learned as much as the least of us. If he had no skill, it was no secret for long. He would never again find able seamen ready to sail with him.

. . . The great men—Drake, Hawkins, Gilbert, Grenville, Frobisher, Ralegh, and so forth—together with plenty more, remembered or forgotten, enough to make up the crew of a Portuguese India carrack, they never had trouble gathering a crew.

[405]

. . . Keeping a crew for a long time of waiting for winds and for orders to sail is another matter. For lying idle is not yet being a crew all together. There is still a chance and every good reason to change your mind. They were different men and each with different ways, but you can believe that each one was skilled.

. . . Scholars have made sport of some of these men. To their view of things, Sir Humphrey Gilbert, by refusing to leave the *Squirrel* in that storm coming back from Newfoundland, is the type of a fool. They should remember there was a crew of men on the *Squirrel,* and their one chance to live, slim as it was, lay in fighting that cold storm with all the skill and all the strength they could muster. A man who knows he is going to die (and there's no doubt about it) may be brave as a lion, but is likely, is he not? to spend his last moments of life in as much comfort as he can arrange. Not likely to climb icy ratlines or wrestle canvas and man the pumps with half-frozen hands unless there is some purpose to it. If the ship is sure to go down, he is better advised to pray for his soul, if he is religious; or drink the last of the wine and die laughing if he cannot care less. Sir Humphrey Gilbert, then, reading a book in the midst of a storm, as calm as if the ship were at anchor in harbor, was no kind of a fool. If he saved his own skin, and lost the *Squirrel* and her crew, his skin would not have been worth the trouble of saving. There was always a chance she might come through. He did his duty (and atoned for the follies of that voyage) by giving his men one chance to live or die well.

. . . True enough, the Queen said Sir Humphrey Gilbert was a man who never had much good hap at sea. He was a soldier and a schemer. Too choleric in temperament to captain a voyage. But say this for him. When luck has vanished, when old Dame Fortune shows you only the mouth of her arse to kiss, then your best company is a man who knows the hairs of that same place by heart. Misfortune will bring out virtue in him.

. . . Or take Sir Richard Grenville, aboard the *Revenge* when she found herself all alone and surrounded by the Spanish fleet with less chance to live than Jack Calvin to be Pope of Rome. Reading of this in books some may think old Grenville was a lunatic fool, in love with his honor and good name. Who can trust a hero, having seen so many were really clowns in disguise? Can't say I blame them, but they miss some truth.

. . . Truth is, we cannot trust our lives to anyone but a man who values his honor and his good name. His honor and good name being bound, as much as our lives, to the fate of the ship. A man who values his safety more than his honor will kill us more quickly than the Black Plague. For a man who truly values honor wants to live to enjoy it. And if he can't live, then he will keep it if he can and leave a good name behind.

. . . Consider, for a moment, the truth of the *Revenge*. Alone, surrounded and caught by the Spanish fleet. No matter how that happened. No one knows for certain, and once you're in such trouble, it serves no one and proves nothing to pause and wonder why it is so. They were there and so were the Spaniards. So they fought all day until the masts were gone and the ship was down to the wales in water. And most were dead and Grenville was half dead with wounds. And at the end, rather than surrender, he ordered the last of his men to blow up the ship. They refused and carried him aboard a Spanish ship which was grappled to the *Revenge*.

[407]

. . . And there are always those who smile at that and with a wink say Grenville was a raving Bedlamite who lost his ship and killed off most of his crew.

. . . But Sir Richard Grenville was a sea captain. Consider what choices he had. He could surrender the ship and perhaps save his life as a prisoner, and, if he was lucky, be sent home for ransom. Then the ship would be saved to sail against England and to kill Englishmen.

. . . But I doubt he considered that. He and his crew knew that if he surrendered, the best that they could look forward to was the brutish life pulling the sweeps of a Spanish galley in chains. And the best they could pray for was that life would be short. He might have saved himself, but not a man of them.

. . . So they fought the Spaniards, and hurt them too, until the last gun was under water and only the decks were afloat.

. . . And he amazed the Spaniards and won their praise. All of his crew who lived were decent-treated and were returned to England safe.

. . . Some say that Sir Richard took his own life when it seemed he might recover. That may be so. If so, there's a reason for that. He had won over the Spaniards and saved the lives of some of his crew in the bargain, by fighting when reason demanded he must surrender. Seeing how he had won some favor for his men, he could not change his character to save his life.

. . . Foolish it may seem to any man who is so afraid to die he would rather live as a galley slave. It seemed foolish to the Spaniard too. They could have surrendered if the *Revenge* had been Spanish and the fleet had been English. But they could not imagine what it is to be English. The last fight of

[408]

Revenge gave the Spaniard something to think about. After that he would expect the worst. They had already learned to expect the impossible from Sir Francis Drake. From Grenville they learned to look for Bedlam courage, beyond all reason. They might not find that courage in all Englishmen, but they could never be sure, could they?

. . . Let some old scholar or a feisty young clerk who's in love with his own thoughts try that on for size like a new hat. Consider Grenville's defeat may have done more to save England than even the winds which broke up the Armada. And afterwards the Spaniard could picture a whole squadron of Grenvilles, each vessel a *Revenge,* and conceive that such a squadron could beat off all the navies of the world.

. . . Let scholars and ambitious clerks scoff and forget us. For if we are to be remembered, let it be as men of flesh and blood who suffered and rejoiced for their allotted time. Do not dismiss us as lying clowns for doing what is difficult to believe. It would be more charitable—and shouldn't we try to live in charity with the dead as well as the living?—to look through a fog of words and dusty thoughts and grant we lived like all men until we died.

. . . Some of our captains, who cared to write it down, have said we sailed for gold and glory. And there's some truth in that. You can wager the sum of your wife's nether hairs we did not sail out to find December roses. Nor to lower breeches and bare a puckered arse, clinging to the wild-riding head, because we took pleasure in crapping in cold-boiling waves. But you can believe that the prospect of all the gold in the history of this world could not be enough to warp us out of harbor.

. . . Some call us heroes. Well, I thank them. Flattery is the strongest drink I know of to turn a man's brain inside out. But truth is the cordial that purges and cures. There may have been heroes as in books and fables. I can only say I've never yet met one. Meantime I know that good men make best shipmates.

. . . A good man has his craft and takes an honest pride in that; and that pride need not be vanity. There was talking and dreaming of gold and glory, but our true labor was handling ships. And, God is my witness, we sailed our tall ships with as much pride and skill as any man can muster.

. . . None any taller or prouder than Sir Walter Ralegh. See it in him now, even now, sick and in disgrace in the gatehouse prison.

. . . Remember, and he was first to confess it, he never had much stomach for the sea. No shame there. Even the toughest mariner with guts of bronze must take his turn leaning over the wale to puke with the wind. There may be some jest in a seasick man. But there's no shame in suffering what you must suffer.

. . . Ralegh sailed out divers times after that first privateering voyage, when he commanded old *Falcon* and had the good fortune to have Simon Fernandez for master. Fernandez could teach him navigation and caping. There is some shadow of mystery about that voyage. Partly because it was a voyage of no great importance. Partly because Ralegh wished to keep it that way. He may not have returned rich with the booty of prizes. But he could not have come home empty hold and empty-handed. Six months' voyage with nothing to show for it would have finished him then and there.

. . . Success or failure of that voyage cannot be proved or disproved, anyway. Remember *Falcon* was an old, leaky ship, caused troubles and delays at the beginning. But once they

[410]

stood out to sea and the wind was shaking all the ships and the sea went high and the ships took to rolling and working, then it was the others who turned back. He took the *Falcon*, which he did not own and could not have paid for, out for six months and brought her safe home. And the least he learned was the captain's craft.

. . . Not much chance to put that craft to work again for a while or even to sail on a ship, excepting a passage or two to Ireland and across the narrow seas to the Continent. He was of the Court and not free to go voyaging. He saw Sir Humphrey Gilbert off on his last voyage. He spent his money sending out ships trying to plant a colony in Virginia.

. . . Myself, I don't believe his true purpose in Virginia, or Guiana either, was to raise up new English villages and counties. It looks to me he was aiming to make ports for English ships at both places and then bottlecork the Indies and the Main: Guiana at the end of the trade-winds crossing, Virginia where the Gulf Stream meets with the easterlies. Together they could have ruined the Spaniard.

. . . It takes peacetime to plant a true colony. Now that there's a kind of peace perhaps some colonies can take root.

. . . In the time between the voyage of the *Falcon* and the Armada, Ralegh was not idle. He schooled himself beyond the teaching of Fernandez. He put scholars and craftsmen to work at making better ship's instruments. He studied the ship-wright's craft. He built *Bark Ralegh*, of 800 tons, and sold it to the Queen. And that great ship, named *Ark Royal*, was the Lord Admiral's flagship in '88.

. . . Charged to defend the coasts of Devon and Cornwall, Ralegh held no command in the fight in the Channel. But he joined a ship to see the last of it after the fire ships had scattered the Armada and wind drove them north. By the time they came south he held a command, patrolling the Irish coast.

. . . In '95, a free man from the prison of Court, he could finally make a venture of his own. Made the first voyage of exploration to Guiana and back.

. . . In '96 he prevailed over bad planning and led the fleet into the harbor of Cadiz.

. . . The first plan was none of his doing. Ralegh commanded one squadron, not the fleet. They planned to bottle up the harbor from the sea, land soldiers to take the forts guarding the entrance to the harbor, and move on Cadiz. A fine plan, no doubt, when drawn on a chart, but most difficult under even the best conditions. Which they did not have. The fleet arrived by daylight and the Spaniards were alerted. A wind came up, stirred swells, and made off-loading of armed soldiers a disaster. Essex was sending soldiers toward shore and drowning them by the boatload when Ralegh persuaded him to desist. They called a council and agreed to Ralegh's plan; which was, like Drake's years before, to sail into the harbor, engage the Spanish galleons and oared galleys, and land the troops at the undefended quays. To do so they would have to sail the narrow channel between the Spanish forts and this time without Drake's advantage of surprise. And they had lost a day. Ralegh was given the honor of leading in the fleet with his vessel—the *Warspite.*

. . . At dawn the wind and sea were right; he pointed *Warspite* for the mouth of Cadiz and sailed. As they passed beneath the forts they got a greeting of heavy cannon fire. His crew—and who could blame them?—fearful and huddling with no place to hide, Ralegh stood tall on the open poop, an unruffled, perfect standing target. Instead of wasting powder and shot on the forts, he signaled his trumpeter to face the forts and blow a raucous blast, defiance and a fart at the Spanish gunners. Which bravado cheered and restored his crew, many sure to die or be crippled that morning. And the *Warspite* led the English ships to victory.

. . . It was on that day Ralegh himself was crippled, maimed his leg, and was carried half-dead ashore when the harbor and port were ours.

. . . Essex, of course, told another story. And his lackeys published it as truth. God save the Queen and Council, they did not give his story a moment's belief.

. . . In '97 Ralegh made the Islands voyage under command of Essex, who now was bound to prove he was a seaman and proved beyond doubt he was not. But Ralegh took and sacked Fayal. And, again, the cock-and-bull tales and excuses of Essex received—from all who counted, all but the landlocked city rabble—the acceptance they deserved. Which was none at all.

. . . There is a cloud of ill luck over Ralegh's ventures and voyages. He planned many, but could make few. Must be content to invest money and send out ships while landlocked himself. Others, kinsmen and friends, especially John Davis, who was as a brother to him in childhood, sailed more widely than he. And the fortunes of his plans and investments were poor. The luck of adventures he intended to join in, but could not, was disastrous. He was to go with Gilbert. He would have commanded *Revenge* if the Queen had allowed it. Grenville took his place. Still all his own voyages, excepting this last one, went well enough.

. . . Damnable pride has been named his great flaw. So named by courtiers and envious, better-born gents. But if pride was his canker on land, it was what won the respect of the seafaring men. They took off their caps and cheered him when he came down with Robert Cecil to end the pillage holiday aboard the *Madre de Dios*. Which he would have taken himself had the Queen set him free to sail. He had courage and all the craft of a good captain. He is entitled to pride.

. . . When no one else, not even Sir John Hawkins, could stop the looting and pillage of the *Madre de Dios,* Ralegh, sent from the Tower under Cecil's guard, came aboard and ordered an end to it. And was not only obeyed, but cheered by the men. And so he saved a fortune for the Queen from the richest prize taken in her reign, at next to no gain for himself. Even Robert Cecil, not an easy man to move to praise of another, was impressed and so reported to Queen and Council.

. . . Of the last voyage to Guiana, there is much that is unknown. Only one man knows the whole truth and he will not say. Others can only guess and imagine.

. . . Can do no more than share opinions why the voyage was made or what happened beyond the bare bones of reports and contradictions. But I know the way well enough. I can picture it, out of memory, from beginning to end. . . .

(. . . Take London and the towns around. For it was there he and Phineas Phett saw to the building of the *Destiny*. It was there he assembled ships and crews, took on stores and victuals. And down the Thames in early summer, he first set out.

(. . . Take the easy-flowing Thames and a breeze easterly, light, but fair. A fair day. Weigh anchors and ply slow downriver, the men clean in their best, walking the hatches or climbing shrouds to wave farewells to friends and strangers all the way past the palaces of Greenwich.

(. . . Coming, all in due time, into the gusts and hard chops of the Channel, those short, rough, ship-trying seas, where we can test our timbers, our ballast, and the balance of loading. Rough sea and changing winds. Then we beat down to Plymouth, enter, anchor, and wait. Tend to repairs and revictualing. Waiting for a fresh norther to lead us past Biscay and clear of Finisterre, to carry us southward to islands to greet the trade winds.

(. . . Then to sail westward with a good wind filling sail all the way toward the Indies. Blue sea, bluer than before, bluer than remembered, long swells, and the flying fish, porpoise and dolphin for company. Sailing westward toward flaming sunsets and dominions of sunlight.

(. . . If the first winds are piping east and northeast, they lead to the Azores. Islands of green with mist-wreathed mountains rising out of the blue swell. Come closer and see the rainbow-tinted towns with walls of gray stone, pale as the mist of the mountains, and white houses capped with red tile roofs. By night the dull glow of volcanoes offers the shine of doorways to hell. Sailing to islands of flowers. . . .

(. . . I've seen Fayal, where the women are hidden in sea-blue capes and hoods. On festivals and feast days they cover the cobbles of streets with carpets of fresh flowers. There they strap huge wine casks beneath their high-wheeled carts. Good wine, too, for the sweetness of the grapes and oranges grown there defies talking of it.

(. . . I've steered clear of Terceira and its deep wide oval bay. But come ashore at Pico, where the strongest, head-reeling wine is made, and they pull all carts with donkeys. At Pico you can see the whale fishermen. From a peak above the sea a lookout will call *"Baleia!"* And the men come running to

[415]

longboats to hunt and kill the great whale. You can buy whale's teeth there. And they will sell you fine carving from the pith of the fig tree.

(. . . If it's good water and fresh beef you want, then go to Flores. They have sweet water, and cattle graze there.

(. . . The Azores are not much use if it's ship timber you require. Their trees do not grow tall.

(. . . If, coming south, you ride a northwesterly wind and find no sign of freshening trades, you can sail on far, as far as the Cape Verde Islands. And there you shall find the trades for certain. Those islands ride rough, facing the winds like ships ahull in a gale. The winds blow hot and heavy. And the bilge makes such a stink you must pump and keep pumping as if in a storm. You come to landfall at the islands, fifteen large enough to be lived on, which the Portuguese named green. But they are dry and barren, short of water or timber, abundant with fevers. Mountainous islands, and the people, hostile and suspicious, live high, halfway up the mountains. There are few good landings, even for a ship's boat riding surf. Most bays and coves are open to the ceaseless trades. Bravo offers a shield and is the best place for anchorage. Santiago's the better, deeper harbor, but too easterly. They have some beef and hides and God's plenty of salt, some oranges to sell, mustard and strong distilled spirits. But water is scarce. Even the rainfall has a bitter taste.

(. . . Chiefly the islands of Cape Verde will reward you with fever and flux. No good place to land unless it's your purpose to trade with black Africans nearby to the east.

(. . . Best a northwesterly should take you to the Canaries, islands of pleasant weathers. Can be seen first from the glow of volcanoes, dim in the sky like lanterns hung on the poop of flying ships. Then, by day, the tall smoke. And rising hugely out of the sea, ruffed and capped with snow, is Tenerife, which some say is the highest mountain in the world. Not having seen *all* the world, I cannot say. In the Canaries you can find excellent sea timber, tall and strong, especially from the forests of Las Palmas. But water is scarce on all; for it rains seldom there, and they water everything they grow from their own wells.

(. . . No matter, their wines are a wonder. And they have little singing birds in cages, birds which can more please the ear than any piper I ever heard. Their fruit and fish are excellent. I have sat at table with them and dined upon a stew made of many fish, which they call *caldo de pescado*. And I also have drunk deep of the liquid flame they name *majo*.

(. . . They keep camels from Africa for beasts of burden. And there are strange and marvelous things to behold. Like the dragon trees, formed of as many trunks as a quiver of arrows.

(. . . And, ah, the women of the Canaries! They say of themselves and it is no lie, they are like their own mountains, tall with snow on the face, but wild burning within . . .)

. . . Thinking of Ralegh's voyage, which is a mystery, best to stick close to what is known.

. . . He was set free from the Tower to lead an expedition to Guiana and bring back gold for a spendthrift King. Had sailed there twenty odd years before to claim it for the Queen. And he had never lost touch, sending other ships and investing in voyages there even while in the Tower. He had been visited by some of the chiefs of that land, including the one they named Leonard.

. . . Set free to make an expedition to find and mine the

gold he said was there. With orders not to do battle with the Spaniards except in self-defense. Set free and soon enough found the money for it, his own and his wife's, and plenty of prudent men, too, for partners.

. . . All men are fools to one degree or another, just as all men have a streak of the rogue in their nature. But see how even a fool, all but those born foolish, will become the model of prudence, wise and thoughtful, when it comes to investing his money for a venture. Gamblers, men who bet gold on anything, from a game of bowls to a race between ship's rats, will pause before parting with money for adventures at sea. Yet those who came to join with Ralegh were rich merchants, well-respected gentlemen and nobles.

. . . There are some who say Ralegh was crazed by long confinement. Some say it was deluded memory and wishful fancy. An old fool, dreaming a fool's dream.

. . . Whatever his reasons, the King let him go. And not out of kindness or folly, shrewd men gave him money which, together with his own, was more than ample. And first he set out to build himself a proper ship. Hired the best of shipwrights, Phineas Phett. They conceived and built the *Destiny,* a ship of 500 tons; but for all size and weight, a yare ship, a bone sailer and swift. And most heavily armed. She had thirty-six pieces of heavy ordnance listed, as many of the best ships of the King's Navy Royal and no doubt superior to most, being new made.

. . . Some will turn that argument against me. Saying either that he could have rented or purchased one of the King's ships or some merchant vessel for much less cost; or that he only built the *Destiny* because there were no English ships able to make the voyage. And then, with a smile, they'll touch their temples with a finger. As if this was proof of folly. They can be ignored. No madman can design and build a stout sailing ship. Nor would Phineas Phett squander his time upon a mad notion. Not only, sir, that a shipwright of good repute cannot afford to risk work on building a poor ship for an ill-conceived voyage. But it is an honorable custom that the builder must make the first voyage of a new ship himself, if he is asked to. If Ralegh asked him, Master Phett would have gone to Guiana too, like it or not. So I'll warrant Phett considered carefully the building of *Destiny,* and weighed well the destination and purpose of the voyage he might have to make.

. . . Phett's not the only shipwright in England. But I have yet to hear him called a mad fool.

. . . Or some say Gondomar offered Ralegh a safe conduct if he would sail a small number of ships and, once arrived at Guiana, lead his men to the mine without arms, the Spanish promising protection. . . .

. . . Notice, I do not let go and laugh like a wild monkey. Nor laugh at alehouse philosophers who say he was a bigger fool for not accepting safe conduct, then, thousands of miles away, ignoring, if he chose to, the provision to disarm his men.

. . . I cannot conceive of a crew of Englishmen who would obey a captain who ordered them to go defenseless among Spaniards.

. . . As for the other, that clever stratagem dreamed up by alehouse admirals, well, whether well armed or naked as quimmy bitches on the block of a Barbary market, if he was to meet the Spaniard to wave his safe conduct like a battle flag, they must know when he is to arrive and the place of his coming. Half the ships and ordnance of England, all primed to fire, would do him little good if he sailed into harbor to find the fleet of Spain waiting to greet him and Spanish infantry upon the shore, pikes shining and their muskets primed for more than shots of courtesy.

. . . Not worth the mentioning, the Ambassador's offer, except to prove Ralegh was no fool. Gondomar may have deemed him old enough to dupe. But I never yet heard of a Spaniard, even a half-wit one, who would trouble himself to prepare a stratagem to frustrate a fool.

. . . Likewise they tell that Ralegh was too old and sick, unable to command. The power of a lie is in its threads of truth. Ralegh was old for seafaring when he came out of the Tower. No doubt, he never denied it, he had been ill and was not the man he had been. But he gave best proof of his own intent and belief, putting money of his estate into the voyage, not stinting so far as anyone could tell. More than that, though, I say it for Gospel that never a man in England, from master to ship's boy, will freely sail on a voyage that looks doomed. Nor serve under any man, be he ever so worthy, if that man looks likely to die on them. The truest friends will risk life and limb for each other. And they will do so blithely enough, but not to hasten the death of the friend or to push him into folly.

. . . No, the builder and investors took him in earnest. Also the King of England and his Council. Also the Spaniard. Also the masters, officers, and seamen. Likewise many of his kinsmen, the flower of Westcountry families linked to him by blood. If Ralegh was mad, then so were they all, and so was all of England.

. . . Which, I'll allow, may be the truth. But who shall be called mad in a nation of madmen?

. . . I think those who are so quick to judge weigh only

[420]

the evidence on his return. When fever and sorrow had wasted and aged him. When, it is told, he feigned madness, frothed and barked on all fours, to gain time to outwit the King and his enemies. And only this morning his appearance and demeanor at Westminster Hall confirms that.

. . . If he is mad now, has left his wits somewhere, no man can dare blame him. But the truth remains to be seen. Long before they called him fool, they named him Fox.

. . . For certain it was foxy, when he made a great show of the building and arming of the *Destiny* here on the river for the whole world to see. And next assembled a fleet of ships, well armed, victualed, and stored for a long voyage. Rumors flew about the city and all England, as thick as a sky full of larks. Many notions were suggested, the most likely being he would lead his ships to seize Genoa for Savoy. It was bruited about that once at sea he would turn pirate. A gossip he would not stifle, for when some man asked him what his course would be if he failed to find his gold mine, it is said he laughed and said perhaps he would seek another mine, meaning the Spanish plate fleet.

. . . It did no harm to let men think so. Would serve to keep the Spaniard doubtful and guessing. Doubt of enemies can preserve a voyage without a cannon being fired. Besides which he was gathering, as best he could, from what sort of able-bodied men we have in England nowadays, a crew. Who would be the more eager to join if they imagined such things.

. . . This much we could see with our own eyes. Could also read the orders he published in Plymouth in May of '17 for his whole fleet. For many these may be without great import, excepting that there are so many orders for ways of fighting an enemy if engaged at sea. But to any old seaman they are curious. The fullest orders he ever published. And including much that was, in our time common custom at sea. Though never so brief as, say, Sir John Hawkins, Ralegh had not before been so exact and full in his commands.

. . . This tells me something. Tells that before he was prepared to brave the open sea and before he had tried and tested his men, he knew full well the shabby quality of seamen nowadays. Knew they knew next to nothing. Knew that, as much as is ever possible, all things had to be anticipated. Not merely the unexpected, but the common as well. Knew that most of his men, whether worthless rogues or men of good will and intent, could not be left to act upon wisdom and experience.

. . . So, no matter who says so—and to defend his life he has said so himself—Ralegh cannot have been astonished that his men were not the best seamen he had sailed with.

. . . Likewise his orders tell something about his captains and his view of them: that he did not trust them and therefore would keep strict watch. He was to lead in everything, they to follow and obey.

. . . Not the signature of a timorous man, but the sign of a skeptical one.

. . . The published orders would be studied by many, both friendly and hostile. His friends and stockholders in the venture who, at the last, may have suffered second thoughts, could be reassured. They could comprehend that he was primed and cocked. King and Council could ponder too. See signs of care and planning. Be prickled by those orders for fighting, their doubts being kept sound and solid, intact. Knowing his plans were in all likelihood betrayed, he knew his greatest defense was the doubt of others. No need to discourage them from doubting. Likewise with Spain; oh, the Spaniard would peruse the orders, word by word, as if written in cipher, studying and sifting everything.

. . . And Ralegh knew that among his crew, at all ranks, would be intelligencers. Some in the service of stockholders. Some in the service of other nations, including Spain. Some agents of the King and Council. Even Sir Francis Drake could not escape it. The trick Ralegh knew by heart was to keep close-mouthed, though he might seem to babble like a brook. To preserve doubts and suspicion. To trust no man. And to use his own means for intelligence elsewhere. With so much at stake, he would have ways and means to learn the plans and secrets of others. He could not sail without this kind of surety, though he was too crafty to imagine his enemies were not as careful as himself.

. . . From London he sailed down the Thames with ceremony, *Destiny* leading his flock of ships, each carrying a full crew, together with gentlemen adventurers and some soldiers. Sailed in good time for the crossing, the middle of March. Beat about the Channel awhile, on account of weather, but also to train and try his men somewhat. Visited the Isle of Wight. Unhurried it seems. . . .

. . . From there to Plymouth for a final refitting, revictualing and repairs. There were delays and accidents, and he was forced to wait a fortnight or more for one Captain Bailey, who would later leave him. Lay idle at Plymouth until the middle of June, letting fair wind go wasted.

. . . Here begins more mystery. The route and dates of his voyage are record. But who shall know, now or in time to come, the reasons?

. . . Seven ships, four of them good-size galleons, left London in March. Among them they carried 138 pieces of heavy ordnance. A formidable fleet. At Plymouth he was joined by six more vessels. Thirteen sailed out of Plymouth with him. And there were rumors he would join forces with a squadron of French, that he planned to join with more English ships off Trinidad.

. . . Even without the French or more English ships, it was a large fleet of ships. Able to give battle to all but the greatest fleet, with the power to pick prizes like plums off a tree. Able to sack all but the strongest ports. Able to sweep up the Indies like a broom.

. . . The largest fleet he had ever commanded. Excepting that one day in Cadiz when he led on the *Warspite,* and then it was the Lord Admiral who was truly in command. Too large and unwieldy. For, I confess, the English have never worked well except in small packs.

. . . Yet Ralegh knew the risks. One guess is that he never intended to cross to Guiana with all; but, keeping all in doubt and chiefly Spain, he proposed to hold them together as long as he could until he caught the trades and went westward. He knew the Spaniards had sent out packet boats to the New World warning of his coming. This served his advantage, the more so if he delayed. For it placed Brazil, Guiana, the Indies, and Florida into a flurry of preparation and confusion. Each looking to protect his own. All seeking the most protection and defense, and devil take the others. This kept the main fleet of Spain tied to strings, like a puppet. They could not—not in direct offense to a friendly English king—come forth directly to intercept him. They must wait for him to move.

. . . And the more he delayed, the better. For there is no danger so great that time and the weariness of waiting will not blunt the fear of it. With enough time, he could, if he chose, have the advantage of surprise despite all warnings and preparation.

. . . He broke land at Plymouth on 12 June. Then encountered fierce contrary winds, storms, foul weather, and tall seas. The winds of June can do that. But what did he do? Most curious, he made a new course to his lost estates in Ireland, to port of Kinsale in County Cork. Where he lingered, visiting old friends and Lord Boyle, who holds title to Ralegh's estates there. Revictualed and managed to feed his men well while there. Lay idle for seven weeks. Waiting against unfavorable winds is his report.

. . . Please pardon me for doubting that. I have waited long for winds, but never so long as that. Never so long there was not a breeze a man could sail by, though it might not be the weather he would choose or the breeze he would blow himself. In short, he sailed out of Plymouth and vanished. Reappeared at the port of Kinsale, and there he sat quietly. While many pondered and worried.

. . . The record tells of no great losses, no major repairs done. There is always some refitting after a storm, but I've seldom heard of seven weeks of it except when a ship was near wrecked or broken apart in some distant land. If it was so terrible a storm, how comes it he did not lose one ship?

. . . No matter, in August he was off again, sailing south toward the islands. Off Cape St. Vincent Captain Bailey took French prizes. French pirates they were. But Ralegh made him pay them for all he took. Not pleasing Bailey, astonishing the Frenchmen, and further confusing all who would, soon enough, have news of it.

. . . In the first week of September he reached the Canaries. Sailed first to Lanzarote. Which, of all the islands, is poorest for provisions. All mountain and cinders. They make a fine wine there, but not much more. The natives refused to trade or sell anything. They ambushed his men on shore. Ralegh made no retaliation. Which must have surprised his own men as much as the people of the island. Instead, he sailed to the port of Gomera, exchanging shots of courtesy and all honors, dropped anchors, and proceeded to trade with the governor, paying the full price for everything. All was amiable and cordial between Ralegh and the Spanish governor and his English wife. The crew were given liberty of the town, though they, too, must be exemplary in behavior. Must pay for everything. His orders being that the man who stole so much as one orange, nay, one grape, would hang for it. There are no reports of complaints by the natives. And no one was hanged.

. . . All of which proves, if nothing else, his discipline was absolute and unquestioned. So far it had been an idle, lazy voyage with no scarcity of victuals or water, with almost as much time on land as on sea. No prizes or profit, it is true, but beyond the complaint of Captain Bailey, there were no troubles. No fleet of ships was so fit for the crossing.

. . . Meanwhile, piece by piece, the reports had gone their ways. Report on Ralegh's slow sailing and scrupulous conduct. Outwardly pleasing the King of England and the King of Spain. Inwardly increasing doubts and suspicion. To ask themselves *why,* they must unpack a full chest of other quesions. Meanwhile those who had warned against the venture, like Gondomar, were left to gnash their teeth and hope he would do something to give weight to their warnings.

. . . Ralegh sailed out of Gomera and, again astounding, paid in full for some fresh fish he took off vessels near Grand Canary.

. . . From here on, it seems, the reins fell loose in Ralegh's hands. Wind and weather turned, and he was forced to sail southward. More serious, there was fever on his ships now. His men began to sicken and die. He made for the Cape Verde Islands, with difficulty, for he was being driven westward by the trades. Which was what he was seeking. Then why did he not go west and make a swift crossing? Came to Brava at last, a poor place with poor harbor, and heavy blown by the trades. He attempted to procure more provisions. For what purpose, seeing he was so recently victualed? Failing, he turned west with the winds and set course for Guiana. But by then he was sick himself with the fever. Many were sick and dying.

. . . In the end, then, after the longest prologue and preparation, it was an unlucky voyage and came to no good. Captains deserted, taking their ships. Fever swept through his men more fierce and final than any battle. And he was first nearly dead, then weak and out of mind—the head and mind which kept the truth of his purpose, which had kept the secret, until it was too late to tell, then kitten-weak, helpless to lead his men at San Thomé.

. . . In the end he lost friends and kinsman. His son and namesake, Wat, killed in a skirmish. His closest man, Keymis, killing himself. Keymis, who either failed him because of his fever or betrayed him. No matter which. Keymis failed him and all was over and done with, lost.

. . . Yet even after all this, Ralegh sailed the *Destiny* all the way north to Newfoundland. Where she could be cleaned and careened and made ready for the final voyage home.

. . . Began with power enough to so scourge the Spanish Main that they would think the ghosts of Drake and Hawkins had come back to haunt them. If they had ever joined with the French or gathered separate Englishmen under his command, they could have picked the Indies clean as a Christmas goose.

. . . Except for the clash at San Thomé he fought no Spaniards, but he was armed with ordnance, small arms, soldiers, and powder sufficient to be called a cargo for fighting. It was a mighty fleet to be looking for a gold mine, with more muskets than shovels on board. The long delays, the leisurely sailing seem deliberate, by choice. But to what end? There are a dozen and more good explanations, not counting lunatic ones.

. . . I have one guess myself, for what it may be worth. Taking him at his word. If he set off alone or, with little support, to Guiana, there was nothing to keep the Spaniards from taking him. The show of preparing his ships, the long slow voyage and visit to all the islands kept Spain in doubt and her ships and men tied down and busy preparing for . . . anything. It may be he intended, before fever took command, to break up the fleet of ships or to slip away suddenly on his own, to arrive at Guiana with an advantage of surprise and with the Spaniards there fearful of his whole force. That stratagem could have worked.

. . . But no man will know until Ralegh chooses to speak. And he gives no sign he will break his silence. Perhaps there are reasons for that. Perhaps it is more than his secret. *Think: if the King knew his plan from the beginning, if the King is partner to the secret . . .*

. . . Think no more about it. It is safer to take things as they seem to be.

. . . From Newfoundland he brought the *Destiny* home. And that baffled as many as anything he did on the voyage.

. . . He has said that his men made a mutiny against him, that he was forced to promise to bring them home. No surprise if they did so, but surprising they waited so long. So he sailed across, pausing in Ireland to let the chief mutineers go free. Then, lightly manned, he sailed the *Destiny* home to Plymouth Harbor. Strange, where the last place for safety for him was England. . . .

. . . Some call that pride and some say folly. Call it the pride of a seafaring man. He came home to port, as he said he would, brought his ship and his men to harbor. Which some call foolish, because his life was in the balance. But that may be no mystery.

. . . Ralegh's a seafaring man. To bring *Destiny* safe home was his seaman's pride and honor. Without both pride and honor he could never have gone to sea at all. Some men change their character in times of danger. But a sailor learns a different lesson. When he is caught in a storm, there is no place to go. The end is in the hands of God. Until that end he must trust in the ship, his mates, and his skill, and ride out the storm.

. . . As for that mutiny. No harm was done to him. He continued to command. He was merciful to the mutineers, and the rest of the crew sailed to Plymouth by his command. All of which leads an old sailor to suspicion the mutiny was a ruse. Perhaps his men hoped to help him save his life, to give him some excuse with the King.

. . . Who knows? There's no one living or dead who will tell.

. . . Others can think what they please and go and be hanged for all I care.

. . . And as for me, I have already lasted too long. The good days are gone. What I have in my mind is to go down to waterside and find myself an old oar. Then I'll set out inland with that oar on my shoulder. And I'll keep on walking until I come to a place where people can point and someone will say of my oar—"What's that?"

. . . And that is the place I shall settle down for good and call home.

Part Four

The world discernes it selfe, while I
    the world behold,
By me the longest yeares and other times
    are told.
I the world's eye.

RALEGH—*translation from Ovid's*
Metamorphoses

Light misting rain, fine lacework, swimming in gray air. Beading small lozenged panes. Blurring shapes of figures, bulky and bundled, going and coming across Old Palace Yard.

Ralegh cannot see where they are working, repairing the scaffold. Cannot hear the ring of hammers or the calls of the workmen. Awhile ago a cart heavy with timbers rattled this window like a wind, passing under the gate.

It could be timber for any of the structures which must be ready for Lord Mayor's Day.

He cannot see or hear the river. But he can picture it now. Wherries, lone cargo barges easing along with leather-colored damp sails. The watermen, dark shapes against rain-wrinkling gray of water and the darker gray of the afternoon sky. Shadowy watermen and boats limned against two shades of gray and for background the dwindling roofs and walls on the banks.

Rain on the river. And glistening on stones of palaces and houses. Rain over London, rain and chill and, for once, a stillness in mud-pudding streets and lanes, a quiet time in the shops.

Time to put a lazy prentice to his hornbook lessons.

But the taverns are bright and beery. Loud with the stolen sounds of the street, with voices, laughing and singing. Warm from the logs, lit by flames of many tapers and candles. Above countless chimneys smoke hangs low over the houses, soiling the sky.

Behind him a fire has been rebuilt. And now he is clean and combed, wearing a long loose gown and soft slippers.

He can hear faintly the voices of the boys in the choir school next by. Boys and musicians rehearsing perhaps for some event on Lord Mayor's Day, or for an occasion he may not have living ears to hear. But he hears them faint and yet clear now as they, believing in and hoping for the future, practice for it.

He has nothing to rehearse yet.

There are other doings of this afternoon and evening he must prepare for. Things which he must rehearse as well as any player. But just now there is nothing. Can stand with his back to a warm room, feel firelight behind him, hear the voices of the choirboys and stare out upon the fading prospect of the gray autumnal day.

He imagines others who have played a part in what has been this day and what may come to pass tomorrow. Not for any of them can there be a time precisely like this, a weighty, yet weightless moment.

Each, witness and actor, is involved. Wheels and weights of clocks turn to their work without ceasing. Sand sifts down in many a glass. Candles burn short beneath their single leaves of flame. Fires die to ash and are rekindled, flare and flourish anew.

For each of the others the time is now. But it is a mere moment passing. Something to be spent. They hoard what they will of the past, and their eyes are on the future. Which is, for each and all of these, a true estate. All their hope and all joy. All promise and all dread.

They share the chill weather of autumn England. Which brings them indoors by choice to chambers or halls or galleries, seeking the pleasures of warm and dry, finding such comfort as they can.

They share weather and time with the man in the gatehouse. But with a difference which is enormous. Still in possession of the future, though lacking least knowledge of what they possess, they can banish this weather with a dream of next springtime; in full and certain knowledge that another English spring will come—come with rinsed skies of the lightest blue, with clouds of larks and clouds as swift as larks or gulls, with whistling blackbirds, with nudge and earth-crumbling thrust of first buds in gardens and growing wild in the fields, with water shivering aglitter in springs and brooks, buds tight as fists on the tip ends of trees, and sun, sun not yet warm but brightly set in pale sky, smiling, it seems, over the waking, washed world and the awakened and dancing senses, five in a ring hand in hand; the world awake and scrubbed to newness; a young woman rising from gentlest froth of surf, doe eyes, innocent, ever expectant, shy, modest, yet dreaming to be known, exposed to the changeless festive ritual of the dancing five; who will ring around her and dance until she too dances in marvelous abandon, dancing on and on until the sun browns her like a berry, takes her inch by inch, every secret place and portal, a patient perfect lover, takes her and leaves her at last spent, a single dead and fallen leaf; but once rising shy and modest, innocent and yet recalling all the world's story from the beginning, she is composed of fresh cream and wild honey, and she floats, glides

[435]

toward them in the dream of things to be, not upon sea but on a tide of light and air, seeking to renew, restore, repair them all, each and all, young or old.

Though he cannot imagine what their futures may be, having for this moment banished his own, he shares the present with them; those others who are not required to say a grace over a dwindling afternoon and to then drink it, sip and savor, like the last wine in a silver cup. To imagine that, to think upon them, is his prerogative. For to deny himself the pleasure of the future is not to stifle the voice of imagination. Which is beyond his power while he lives.

Sir Thomas Wilson, a man of courage, proved in the past, who serves the King in this matter, has gone to the house of the Lord Lieutenant of the Tower.

Sir Thomas did not join in the dinner at the gatehouse. He dined with a friend in a tavern and bided his time before taking a wherry with the tide to the Tower.

The waterman, though glad for a fare on such a day, would not show it. They will not shed their false pride, these sullen, fractious men. Would rather starve and die first. Well, all of us will die, and some will starve doing it.

No matter, Sir Thomas feels at peace with the world. An unpleasant, somewhat demeaning duty done. Good food and drink, well digested with laughter, riding warm inside. Let it rain and pour. Let the winds come and go.

"Tell me," Sir Thomas says, determined to make this wooden waterman speak, "what news goes around today?"

"News, sir?"

"The talk."

"Well, now, there is some talk of the weather."

"No doubt."

"There is hope it will change for the better by tomorrow."

"Tomorrow?"

"For the Lord Mayor's Day, sir. It would be a shame to dampen a holiday."

"Ah, half the Christian year is a holiday to you Londoners."

"Southwark, sir. Southwark is my town."

"Indeed? I would not have guessed it."

The waterman mumbles something and Sir Thomas Wilson smiles.

"Is there talk of anything else?"

"Let me see. . . . There is said to be a woman, a lady, sir, on Broad Street, give birth this morning to a two-headed boy. The child died."

"A pity."

"How is that, sir?"

"Every young gentleman in this age needs two faces to endure. But think, man, what good fortune it would be to have two heads."

"A man can lose two heads as easy as one. A man can lose the same head twice over."

"I miss the drift of your riddle."

"It is not a riddle. All the town knows Sir Walter Ralegh has been named to die a second time."

"Is that the truth?"

"You would know the truth of it better than I would, sir."

"What do you mean by that?" Sir Thomas' smile is fixed, but he feels the warmth of a flush on his cheeks.

"No insolence intended. I mean to say I was tied up at the Tower this morning. I saw you, sir, with the others and Sir Walter Ralegh when you came out in the King's boat."

"Oh . . . Well then, what do folks think?"

"I would not know."

"Come now, be open with me."

"I can tell you what folks say, sir. But I know nothing of what they may be thinking."

"What do you think?"

"I think this is a foul day in November and a poor time to be out on the river."

Nevertheless, his good spirits not to be dispelled by one surly waterman, Sir Thomas Wilson gives him a decent gratuity. If only to prove it is the privilege of a gentleman to give as he pleases and chooses.

Apsley, no doubt touched by the bravado of Sir Walter at their final dinner, has forgotten his manners. He is brusque in demanding Sir Thomas' business. Keeps him waiting, then standing. Offers neither refreshment nor comfort.

No matter. Apsley is to be pitied. All his sons (is it *seven?*) dead in the Irish Wars. And to be Lieutenant of the Tower. No chance to make much fortune there. A chance to survive with some measure of unearned dignity. Yet only by dancing like an ant in a hot saucepan.

"I have come to take possession of some few things."

"What things?"

Of course he will receive a reward for his time and troubles. But a man can never be sure in this service. Which is why he managed, adroit and circumspect, to exact the promise from the King. . . . Well, no, not a promise, to be sure. A servant exacts nothing from his master. But when he suggested the thing, the King did not change his demeanor. His face showed no change, no surprise. Shrewd, weary face, pursed lips. The King cleared his throat and nodded before he shifted in the chair and turned those soft moist eyes in appeal to Villiers, young dandy in chaste white silk and satin. *Like a maid of honor, by God, and pretty enough to be one in wig and farthingale; oh well, I've seen everything including one poor wretch who loved chickens.* Villiers, once a threadbare scholar boy, now a nobleman and ever rising. The King turned his sad eyes to the one he calls Steenie. And before young Lord of the Bedsheets could cough discreetly behind him, Wilson took his cue and bowed himself halfway to the door.

Not a promise, but near as one can be. Having reminded the King that Walter Ralegh possesses a load of books, old and new, and many of them well bound in leather and velvet, embossed with his arms, many in foreign tongues, in Latin, Greek, and Hebrew, and God knows what else too. Some of considerable value. And taken together, in a lump, a pair of cartloads, not without some value upon the market.

No value to the King, a true scholar and a learned man. But perhaps it would be wise for him to gather them together at the proper time to study them with an intelligencer's eye—modest scholarship to be sure, but expeditious, part of his duty only, sparing the King and others the time—for marginalia, notes, ciphers, and such. And to make a list of such items as could be named heretical or seditious, and to tender that list to the Council for their perusal.

Also, Ralegh being known for possessing curious instruments and such, he might collect these. As, for example, the glasses for stargazing or looking at jewels close, weights and measures and vials all specially prepared for him by divers makers of such things. These may have value too, but insignificant. For no learned man would desire to have them. Only the fools. Best

[440]

they should perhaps be destroyed, or anyway kept out of the hands of the unwary.

The King making no reply. But not frowning upon this either.

And he, Wilson, confident that though nothing would make him young or beautiful, he was, head to toe, clean and crisp, as the King insists his servants be. A good, stiff, clean, starched, modest ruff. A long, loose, flowing jerkin. Nice variety of colors. Trim neat shiny little shoes with gilt buckles. No harness and sword, by heaven! And nothing ostentatious, all correct.

His hair and beard fresh-barbered. Fingernails clean and clipped. This last an unfair demand, Wilson thinks, when the King will not wash *his* hands and *his* nails are dirty ragged new moons, some bitten to the quick. But no complaint, sir. When he is born a king, he, too, will preach one thing and practice what he pleases.

And all things gathered at little expense. Some borrowed, true. The jerkin, with its fine embroidery, taken off a base fellow who had been passing as one of the Court for some months. Not at the Court but in and among the idlers of St. Paul's Walls and the Yard.

Wilson noticed him first, reading a play in quarto at the bookstalls. Chewing a gold toothpick and, in form and physiognomy, every bit the equal of this white butterfly, waterbug, fop and flutter, young Steenie. But not so fortunate. No more a rogue, but less lucky. Unfortunately, the fellow was reading the play upside down.

Wilson and another man, separate at first, trailed him to a tavern. After some ale and tobacco, it was easy enough to become in the fellow's eyes a pair of shrewd and wicked fellows, wise in the craft of conny-catching, quick-tongued with canting talk. And home they went with him, he planning to show them a new way of clipping coins. Which was not new or clever, but nevertheless gave them occasion to frighten the piss out of him when they drew swords and arrested him in the name of the King. He weeping and pleading, and in the end most relieved he could outbargain the King's agents and spare himself the pains of felony in return for a promise to quit London forever. Picked him clean, they did. And saw him off in country kersey clothes on the back of a baggage cart bound for Bristol. The fellow barely to be distinguished from the heavy sacks he rode on.

Not that the lad had much worth the trouble. But the jerkin was handy, of proper size and fashion. Likewise the shoes, though a mite too large.

The King clearing his throat and Wilson adding that he would further make examination of things at the Tower and Lady Ralegh's house on Broad Street, and would ferret out other hiding places.

Not needing, with a man of this world like the King, to belabor the obvious like a blacksmith with a hammer: that to make examination means, *primo,* sir, to take possession of before examining. No one, not even the King, would know anything beyond Wilson's catalogue. Which could take some time to prepare. And some fine things, unlisted and no one the wiser, especially the charts and instruments, would fetch a fair price to sweeten this service.

Not needing to add that or hint at it. For the King's uneasy moist eyes rolled in appeal toward Sir Dandy Steenie, Lord Maidenhead, etc., etc. And Wilson, though neither young nor handsome to look upon, was as quick and subtle as this lamb of a lad in his fleeced gains of white silk and satin, Wilson bowing, then gone like a shadow. A smiling, humble shadow. . . .

The things Fortune will drive a man to do! He thought he

had done with his days as an intelligencer long ago. Not that he prepared for that sort of life. He began as a Cambridge scholar, and let no man deny it. A Bachelor of Arts at St. John's, a Master of Arts at Trinity Hall. Why, he had been friends with such as Sir Philip Sidney (*may he rest in peace*) and Mr. Arthur Golding. Once had gained repute for his own translation of De Montemayor's *Diana*. A promising gent not so long ago, and even Sir Walter Ralegh had sent for him and permitted him to invest in (*would God I had not done so!*) the Virginia venture.

Down on his luck, he worked for Cecil and Buckhurst as an intelligencer at home and in Europe. Most dangerously in Spain in 1604. . . .

Cecil made promises and, indeed, did find him the post of Keeper of the Records at Whitehall. From which nothing save trouble could be earned. But it was a place and an office. Without which a man is lost.

But Cecil died and he has slipped a little (*mark you, sir, never fallen*) since. At least he knows the King trusts him. As much as he can trust any man. Which may be defined as— somewhat, more or less.

The King has implied some profit from the close watch of Ralegh. Implication is enough. He'll have those books and charts and instruments. And somewhere among them he will find, he is sure, the clue to the chief unspoken thing—the Fox's jewels. Wilson will find them, if there are any to be found. Will satisfy the King with some good pieces and keep the rest as his own secret.

"What things, pray?" Apsley is asking him.

"Why, books, man! I'm speaking of books and papers and other pertinent items of evidence."

"I shall have to see your instructions in writing."

Wilson sighs to express his annoyance. It is a brisk gesture he has rehearsed, knowing, sure as the sun will rise and green apples turn red and gold, that would be Apsley's first response. It's fear, not pride, has turned Apsley into a textual pedant. And that fear will be Wilson's goad and Apsley's undoing.

"This is the King's affair," Wilson begins patiently explaining. "His Majesty has sent me here expressly to search and collect these things. It is the King's wish. And, Lieutenant Apsley, neither you nor I need question it further. Indeed, I suggest . . ."

"By what authority are you here?"

"The King's, as I have labored to make plain to you. Authority? My God, man, you have a copy of my commission in the matter."

"Your commission expired, Mr. Wilson, when I accepted the writs of King's Bench."

"The King will not be pleased by this pedantry."

"Perhaps not," Apsley says, and then smiles.

Smiles, damn his eyes! A condescending, knowing smile. . . . Do you suppose he does know something? Unlikely, nay, impossible. Apsley's head has been turned by Ralegh's wine; or the Fox has slipped a few drops of an elixir of courage in the drink; or Ralegh has bribed him, that's probable; or—why deny this until now?—the fool wants the things for himself.

A sigh, this time unrehearsed, is of relief. He manages a smile to answer Apsley's.

"I am sure the details can be arranged as soon as the King returns to Court," Wilson says. "Meantime, I am certain you and I, gentlemen together, can reach a satisfactory agreement."

"Agreement?"

"Arrangement then," he snaps. "I am sure an arrangement, which takes into account your interests, can be made."

"I do not understand what you are trying to say, Mr. Wilson."

Haughty, now, more than condescending, self-righteous, feigning insolent stupidity. By St. Dismas, Apsley will not deal. He wants it all! He is turning it upside down so I must bargain. That's his secret, then. Apsley is greedy as a Jew. Well, sir, Sir Thomas Wilson will not be bluffed by a lily-liver with maggots in the brain. The answer is Apsley shall have nothing. That will educate him to be . . . not less greedy, but more circumspect. He will profit from the lesson, though he's most unlikely to be grateful for it.

"No matter if my meaning passes you by," Wilson says curtly. "It is not the first time. It is enough for you to know I have my instructions and intend acting upon them."

Apsley shrugging: "But I have no instructions. And until I do . . ."

"These things have been promised to me."

"I doubt that. I very much doubt it."

Sir Thomas Wilson has endured much in one day. Out of natural patience and good will he has been generous to a fault, overlooking insult. But he is not a passive man by nature, and enough is enough.

He grabs and grips the hilt of his sword.

"Do you give me the lie? Do you dare?"

Apsley is not smiling, but composed. His eyes, fixed on Wilson's, are cold. His hands hang loose and easy, but he is ready to draw.

Why, the poor man has lost the last of his wits! That's the answer.

"I shall give you nothing, Mr. Wilson," he says, flat, voice cold as his eyes. "You shall have nothing here of Sir Walter's so long as it is mine to guard."

"They shall not be yours for long."

"We shall see about that," Apsley answers. "In the meanwhile, they and all things in this Tower are mine to hold."

"You are going to regret this," Wilson says.

And suddenly Apsley, for God knows what reasons (*does a Bedlamite need reason?*) laughs out loud.

"If I had a penny for every regret I have," he says, "I'd be the richest man in England."

Wilson leaves him laughing to himself, poor man. Walks out across the Yard. Poor Apsley will come to no good.

What now?

He cannot go to the King and make complaint. For, even if he could get to the King and gain his favorable attention, by that time all will have vanished. Or, the King may become more curious about these things. Let the King go chase English hares!

Perhaps he should have bribed Apsley. No, he, stubborn fool, would have refused. Let him die poor then. And let that be his consolation. Perhaps they will chisel "poor and virtuous gentleman" upon his gravestone. If he can afford a stone.

Speaking of which, what now?

Well, first a bowl of wine to lift the spirits, to drive away the damp. And then. . . .

And then, of course! He must try another tack. Perhaps to send a brief message to the Constable of the Tower, Thomas Howard, Lord Howard de Walden. Who will know nothing except the rumor and gossip. A cryptic message stirring Howard's curiosity. Then he will dress in his best and pawn a jewel to rent a coach, yes a coach, and a pack of mounted linkboys. And when, as it will, the summons from Howard comes, he'll roll stately there. And with never an unkind word against Apsley, mind you, only sympathy and respect, he will cook Apsley's goose, by God, and Ralegh's too.

Damned if he won't!

Wilson kicks a clod of mud and swears. It is an old story. The life of a servant of the King, one willing to do shameful work when need be, is ever a chronicle of vague promises, most of them broken.

Now *he* has to laugh.

By heaven, the King may be the greatest conny-catcher in the kingdom. Is it not so?

By the time he passes through Lion Gate and crosses the moat on the causeway, Sir Thomas Wilson has shrugged off disappointment and assumed the swagger of a man who can never permit himself the luxury of too much disappointment.

Stukely, kinsman and betrayer, is riding toward the Westcountry. Driven that way, as if by wind. He has been ill at ease in the city. Lonesome, restless, he rented a post horse and set forth a day or two before.

A hard journey this time of year, spurring his horse to pick a way through mud. Cloaked, he has pulled slant a wide-brimmed hat down against gusts of windy rain. But under that angular shadow his eyes are open, squinting ahead, his face drawn with the cold, his beard wet-beaded. He is alert, poised as a hare. Touches the hilt of his sword. Feels for the weight of the pair of pistols in a flat case, strapped beneath the cloak. He is prepared. A cold, wearisome tedious journey, in which each moment is a desperate risk.

For he is carrying a leather bag, wrapped in plain woolen cloth, strapped to his saddle. A red leather bag with rawhide drawstrings. Red leather and upon it, in gold, the arms of Walter Ralegh, Knight. In this bag there are a few jewels, given him by Ralegh for safekeeping at the time of his arrest. When, apparently, Ralegh took him at his suggestion, agreeing to let him play the keeper and so arrest him in the King's name. So that both would not be taken. Ralegh seemed to accept this stratagem, giving him the leather bag, and with it some rings off his fingers, some jewels from his purse.

Stukely listened to them drop among the coins in the bag. Torches were coming toward them.

Why, if he so readily agreed, did Ralegh wait until they had landed at Greenwich and then in the light say: "Sir Lewis, these actions will not turn out to your credit?"

Why, also, when Stukely was rid of his charge and able to open the bag—which took some doing; he with nervous fingers and Ralegh having knotted the rawhide strings into a dense sailor's knot—did he find what he did? Less than fifty pounds in coin, jewels of some value, but nothing remarkable. One ring having a value of sentiment, for the Queen may have given it to Ralegh. But, then, she had given him many jewels more valuable.

Ralegh could not have been planning to escape to France with so little. Yet when the King's men searched him, they found a few things to list still upon his person. The Fox was too crafty to pretend he was empty-handed. The greater part lay in Stukely's bag, untouched.

It must have been a ruse. One with two edges. On one hand, he could argue he could not have intended to escape to France with so little, no matter what French promises might be. Or, if that were not the best tack, why, come about and claim that what he had was all that remained of his wealth.

There must be more for the finding. If so, Stukely will find it and have it too. For he has time, a lifetime, and Walter Ralegh has some hours, a few days at most. Stukely has sweet time to savor. . . .

If the Fox has disposed of all or if he is, indeed, only a few coins away from being a beggar, then no matter. For Lewis Stukely has the King's promise of one thousand pounds for his services, to be paid for his expenses as keeper. And the possibility of more, sure to come with the King's favor. That favor will come soon enough. Stukely's fortune has changed after luckless years. And meanwhile he has fifty pounds and a few jewels as a gift. And if it is not the fortune he has imagined—and will have—it is more than he has ever carried on an open road. A gracious plenty to kill a man for.

The bag wrapped tight and dry in a plain piece of unwashed wool does not jingle, but is heavy with coins, and each coin is a little sun. None of them shining now. Eyes aching, limbs and joints stiff, haunch and crotch sore on saddle. And his slow horse picking her way through mud, fastidious and disdainful as a Court lady.

He has gone far. By this time today will have come to an inn near a village. Will have entered the gate and given over his horse to a boy in the yard, with stern instruction how to care for her. And then he will have gone inside, dripping wet, blinking against the sudden, dry, warmth.

Will have belied muddy first appearance with one gold sun, fished from hiding place and roundly rung like a little bell against the waxed surface of an oak table. One gold sun, and now he is no longer a wet traveler at an odd time of year, but instead a gentleman upon some business, affairs of the King perhaps, that will not wait for weather.

Gold brings him the best chamber in the inn, a pewter bowl of the best ale, and the promise of hot food. That coin brings a servant girl to take his dripping cloak and hang it near the kitchen fire. Brings into her sullen eyes an invitation, promises without a word.

He keeps sword and harness. Clings to the leather bag as mother to child, and seeing their eyes—innkeeper, his wife, servants, and a few travelers near the fire—seeing their eyes, though hooded, drawn toward the sword and the bag, he feels a chill of more than the cold and wet of autumn.

So plops down the bag with a muffled jangle on the table. A show of indifference. Sits at table, sipping ale as if all time were his servant. Makes idle talk, harsh laugh for punctuation, about foul English weather and such. Then, for all to see, he opens the case of pistols, examines them in the light. They are dry and safe and dangerous. . . .

The innkeeper stands nearby, smiling, exchanging platitudes, posies, and pleasantries, and joining his laugh with the traveler's in counterpoint, one note behind.

Odd music, two harsh crows whose laughter is accompanied by a young traveler near the fire who has taken up a cithern to pick some chords.

The servant girl, across the room, eyes him and licks her lips and brushes a strand of hair away from pale blank eyes. Eyes of blue and like an English springtime sky; she watches him, wet-lipped, pink and white, wild strawberry and fresh thick Devon cream, in firelight. And he can feel sap in his loins before the innkeeper's wife gives the girl a flat slap across the bottom to send her back to kitchen chores.

Behind him a tread on the stairway. He turns, his right hand releasing the pewter bowl and twitching, flexing on the table —like a crab on the sand by the sea.

It is a servant, an old, slow-moving man, who has carried his saddlebags up to the room and now announces, sepulchral and black-toothed, that the fire is burning, and his chamber is in readiness, if it pleases him.

Driven from London by loneliness, he must now, though lonely beyond the telling, go up and be alone.

Declines a second bowl of ale—perhaps later. Asks that his supper be sent upstairs. Rises, stretches, feigns a yawn.

"Well then, sir," says the innkeeper. "I shall send Margaret along to help with your boots."

"Margaret?"

"The serving girl, sir. She who took your cloak to dry."

Stukely, too, can feel the coming of springtime, envisioning the birth of glory from the sea. It shivers him. But fear in his bones is stronger. No, that will not be necessary. Tips a nod to the innkeeper and turns to the stairs, burdened with his bag and the case of pistols.

Halfway up the stairs, he hears part of a whispered question among the travelers by the fire; and he thinks he hears the young man's voice in a broad Devon tone say: "I think it must be Sir Judas Stukely with his bag of traitor's gold."

Did he hear that or not?

To turn back or not?

To risk his earnings and his life. For a word or two which he may have imagined?

He mounts the stairs to the chamber, hearing one final dissonant chord from the cithern, a raucous clownish noise bloom in the room, then wither into silence as he shuts the door behind him, locks and bolts it.

Scabbard and hanger on a wooden peg. Naked sword on bed. Pistol case on top of the chest nearby. Boots . . . His boots are glued to his feet.

Christ our Savior and Redeemer, what pleasure it would be

to have that dark-haired, blue-eyed, pink and white, lute-shaped
country girl, kneeling upon her haunches, warm as fresh-baked
wheaten bread, to help him out of his boots. Shining logs of
fire behind her as she kneels warming her wide soft bottom
and that downy nest, soft as fur of a blind mole, of private
places. . . .

A pitcher of ale, or, better, now that he is coming to Westcountry, of cider, warmed, no sweetening needed. Perhaps some
cinnamon to give the taste a teething edge.

Strong Westcountry cider. Fume and essence of apple. Nay,
more essence of earth distilled from the roots of the gnarled
candelabra of the apple tree. Earth and the sweet clean rain.
Branches, twisted, dark as thorns of a rose. Trunk and branches
year after year fruitful. And at the last to make a delicate aroma
when laid upon a fire. As if the element of fire could drink
up the history of an apple tree and then dance, drunk and
abandoned, in fiery costume, flames of orange edged and cen-
tered with blue. Alive and decked in blossom, how the bones
of that tree filled the air with perfume. Then came the bees,
tuning in several voices like a case of Italian viols. And in early
autumn from tight wens and fists the apples seized the essence
of sun, becoming four in one, earth and air and fire and water,
swelling to taut pouting satin finish. Within lies white packed
sweet of the fruit, even as the flesh of a brook trout, a fruit
compounded of all elements, to shiver a tongue with sweetness.
Sweet down to the center, bitter core with its five slick seeds,
so small, to be spat out on the earth. And each of those seeds
containing the mystery of all apple trees. Trees and many
seasons reduced to a tiny button, on the tongue. To be spat
out between the teeth.

Good cider is the spirit—as the high head of a fountain,

[453]

brief shimmering where air and water mingle together, is the visible voice of all waters—of many apples, many seasons, many trees. A man might be drinking smoke and swallowing flames as mountebanks do at the fairs.

How it all comes back to him as he comes closer to home. Comforts of an English inn. Visions of apples, nuts, and good cheese. Scent of roast on the spit in the kitchen. Idle consort of low voices and laughter. Someone singing and the fire lively.

Outside let it rain for forty days and nights and what care we, who live on the sides of a rainbow?

There was an apple tree beyond the window, high and small, in the chamber where he slept as a boy. When the last leaves, gone with sun and green memories of shade, had withered, and the branches stood glistening, then came the wind springing like a cat; and the tree thrashing, tormented; he shivered thinking of the gallows tree where wicked men died and dropped their last sweat, where flesh shredded away and eyes were sweetmeats for beaked birds; and bones groaned together, rubbing like dry sticks. It's a mad thing, and memory of it rises as it did then, but more baffling. For he has seen much of the world now, and need not fear dead earth beneath the bones of a hangman's tree where not even a mandrake root will grow.

A mad thing though: how that apple tree became in wind and rain a gallows; and then in a dissolving transformed into a thrashing, dying man, his face and tongue black, eyes bulging, pearls of sweat falling, foul stuff on his legs. Do not look. Do not! Looks. . . . Looks to see, huge and clear as a rising harvest moon, not body now, but the face of the dying man. Do not look to see whose strangling wild face! Looks to see it is his own face. Cries out.

[454]

Someone must come to comfort him with a lullaby. . . .

Christ's bloody wounds, not that! Let the servant girl come and comfort him out of old memory. For it's farewell country cider and welcome to the best wines in cups of alabaster rimmed with gold, or cups all in gold showing a frolic of naked nymphs to the pipes of a shepherd boy.

After lean years, here comes the time of fat harvest. And here's the first indisputable sign.

He unravels again the rawhide knot of the bag.

He has done well. Let no man deny it. He has served King and country. His kinsman will die or will not die. Which is none of his doing, according as God and the King will. He has done well and is going home. He has a bag of gold, seeds more rich and powerful than any apple's, from which a crop of golden grain will rise and shine in imitation of the sun. From which he can, if he so wills it, own a thousand apple trees. Let apples spoil on the limbs, fall and rot into earth. Let them live only to perfume the air.

He has his bag of gold, hard earned, well earned.

His kinsman, who in a time now gone, could plant a thousand kinds of trees, will die or not die.

If he dies, God rest his troubled soul.

If he lives . . .

Best not think of that. If he should live, should be pardoned for past service or out of pity, then what good will a whole sea chest of gold coins be? Life would not be worth a smudged penny.

He empties the bag upon the bed.

Faces of King and Queen; the King with laurel wreath, the Queen with small crown and stiff ruff. And on the other side the arms of England. Pure fire from bowels of earth, dug and set free by burning, poured molten in a glittering tongue to mold and form these images of glory.

Among the coins are a few jewels: a pearl, an emerald, some chips of diamond like fragments of frozen sunlight, and one small ruby like a single drop of blood.

Why, like a poor mumbling fool, has he been dreaming? There's not only this first installment, but the King's promise, good as gold and twenty times as much, and here is the *Destiny* still lying at Plymouth. Disposable goods there. After all, he is Vice-Admiral of Devon.

He will seek out the doddering, dazed Lord Admiral at his home before the news from London has arrived. *Can that old man still hear thunder?* With the influence of the Lord Admiral, he can proceed at once to selling cargo, fittings, and stores of *Destiny* before Bess Ralegh or other kinfolk have chained it down in links of litigation.

Why hadn't he planned this before?

No matter. Do not disparage inspiration. There is still time.

He will rise at midnight and ride away. Danger of the road will be less then, in truth, than proceeding by daylight. Someone at the inn will already have passed the word, and by dawn half the cutthroats of Devon will be laying their ambushes for him.

Well, though those bloody rogues rise up with the cock, he shall be long gone.

Home by daylight. Eat a country breakfast. Gather men and ride to call upon the old, slow-witted Lord Admiral. Before suppertime in Plymouth, he'll be done with it. And the devil take his Devon kin! He'll find another place to live in peace and leisure and call that home.

Lighthearted, he plunges his hands into the piled coins.

Winces and shivers, for the coins are cold.

A knock, soft on the door.

"Who is it? Who's there?"

"It is Margaret, sir. I have brought you your supper."

He reaches for lock and bolt, then checks his hand.

"Not now . . ." he mumbles.

"Shall I bring it back later?"

"Leave it outside the door. I will fetch it myself in a moment."

"As you wish, sir."

Sir Lewis Stukely turns, leaning his shoulders against the door. Looks at a clean and cheerful chamber, fire in fireplace and gold on the bed blinking with borrowed light.

He sighs a soft cat's whisper, then goes to the window. He hears the laughter from below, then voices singing, the tingling of the cithern.

Presses his face against cold panes. Rain blows against the window, runs down the pane. It is too dark to see the shapes of trees. All that is given to look at is his own face, pressed round against glass, stricken, tight, watery.

A man is drowning out there.

Rain runs down the panes, melting his face. Perhaps he imagines it is the rain. For his eyes are full of tears.

4

Ralegh at the window of the upper chamber of the gatehouse, looking out on the rain of the afternoon, has pictured all this, in a shiver of time.

For, as in a dream, truth and falsehood of imagination are of no consequence. They do not matter to each other, now rivals no more. He has pictured these two by choice. There is small malice in his vision, malice of sharp sight and strong memory. They can do him no good or ill. He can wish them no ill either, though he need not deceive himself by pretending to wish them well. Let them be. Let be what will be. He has squandered a few moments of time, an idle stroll in the imagination's market-place. He makes no claim for purity there, but it is a condition close enough to purity to permit truth and falsehood, equal, to lie down together like the lion and the lamb.

No difficulty to imagine them.

No trouble, either, to picture Francis Bacon, Lord Verulam, etc., Lord Chancellor of England, member of Council, second in precedence in all processions and ceremony only to the Archbishop of Canterbury, and one of the few men close enough *to the King to have advised upon Ralegh's present moment and, perhaps, to have had a hand in making his future.*

He need not allow himself to think of that future, but he can imagine Francis Bacon in his flow of time, his present, with a difference of degree from all others.

Lord Bacon in pomp of office . . . Was there ever a man, except a monarch, who wore robes and chains so splendid or raised ceremony from clumsy habit to the edge of a dance? Sat in Westminster Hall, above the court on the King's marble bench, observing, all unperturbed. His hazel eyes, changing according to the light, now sea-green, now nut-brown, seized everything without seeming to stare. A roving eye—"a viper's eye," some call it—never lingering on anything long, least of all on another man's eyes.

Throughout Ralegh's exchanges with the Commission in the Tower, even upon that occasion when it was Bacon who concluded the final session by advising him to prepare himself in case of death, he had not looked into Bacon's eyes.

Unlike Henry Yelverton and others, Francis Bacon was likely not surprised when Ralegh appeared looking like a pitiful scarecrow. Because long ago Bacon concluded that the chief strength of men of action and adventure, their weakness as well, was the stratagem of surprise. Bacon had been near, too near for comfort, to Essex. And Essex was so captured, enchanted by the endless *possibilities* of his part, that he continually surprised himself.

Bacon was not taken aback any more by Ralegh's appearance than if Ralegh had appeared as the Man in the Moon or pretended to be the King of Spain. Not needing to avoid Ralegh's eyes, for Ralegh did not stare at him.

[459]

Their eyes did not meet even when Ralegh in a perfunctory gesture of self-defense used an argument Bacon had used to reassure him. Once, not long before the last voyage, he and Bacon were walking in the gardens of Gray's Inn to settle a dinner. Bacon gave him the opinion that the King's commission of command, giving him both freedom and judicial authority over others, tacitly canceled out both conviction and sentence for treason of '03. A point in law, though shadowy and debatable. Ralegh had thanked him for his counsel.

"Of course, money's the knee timber of your voyage," Bacon said. "What will you do if you fail to find the gold mine?"

Ralegh laughed and shrugged. "Why, I shall lead my ships as an Armada against the Spanish *flota* and bring it all home, in tow, to England."

Words which had been remembered against him.

But when he raised the point at King's Bench, he did not look at Francis Bacon. There was more resignation than reproach in his tone of voice.

Only at the end, when the Lord Chief Justice read out the sentence, the court attentive and Bacon himself leaning forward slightly on the bench, did Ralegh look at Bacon. He raised his eyes as if in a silent prayer and appeal to heaven and caught the unguarded eyes of Bacon. Bacon looked away. Looked to heaven too. When he looked back, Ralegh was facing the judges, speaking again, no expression save one of grave attention, as if he were a judge himself weighing the merits of some argument.

When it was all done, in scuffle of rising, Bacon, slipping out with more alacrity than ceremony, was conscious of Ralegh smiling. Not at him. Nor at anyone. Unless it were at Henry

Yelverton, with whom he was speaking. Smiling nonetheless. . . .

An odd satisfied smile, which Bacon retained without a sign, like the memory of a melody, until he was secure and settled in his coach and could at last smile to himself.

Crack of whip. Creak of coach and wheels. Bumping forward then, his mounted retainers in livery, fierce boar emblazoned on their breasts. Rumbled off for the brief return to York House. So near that from certain high windows, over the wall, Bacon could see the Great Hall of Westminster as if it were a part of his own grounds.

Lives like a king in York House. Not *our* King, who lives like Francis Bacon if he were King, laughing at their common spendthrift bond and saying they will both surely die beggars. Lives as well as many a king in Christendom.

There was some satiric wisdom in the King's choice of Bacon as Regent when James journeyed back to Scotland. No man in the kingdom would enjoy more the pleasures of receiving and entertaining foreign ambassadors, emissaries, messengers, and visitors. And not even the King would do so with such extravagant display. And it would not cost the King one coin to allow Francis Bacon to represent him.

The King joked about it with Buckingham as they went north together. The King, after a little too much wine, in high spirits and good humor, suggested that perhaps a permanent arrangement could be made, whereby Bacon could continue to represent him in Court and company, with all the rabble and strangers, while the King could hunt and live the sweet life of scholar and lover.

"It would be sweet to be sure," Buckingham agreed, "but

[461]

short. Bacon would be among the crowd of beggars at your gate when the first feast day came around."

"Is he so thin, then?"

The King, never truly able to comprehend his own need for frugality, could not be expected to see truth concealed behind bold and glittering shows.

And Buckingham, too wise to tutor his royal teacher, smiled, enigmatic and charming, until the King continued to press the question.

"Lord Bacon is a worthy man who has waited long for justice," Buckingham said. "He will be a devoted servant so long as he serves."

York House, high-walled, fronting the river as the river makes its southward turn. Beyond those walls lies Durham House, toward London, and, to the west, Whitehall and old Westminster. Walled around, with celebrated gardens, sturdy small houses and outbuildings for his men, his stables, and the turreted stones of York House rising like an ancient castle. And all renewed, refurbished, refurnished, and rebuilt at a staggering expense.

Here Francis Bacon was born when his father, great-stomached Sir Nicholas, was Lord Keeper. From its precincts he had been turned out, together with his brother Anthony, after the death of his father. Always after that dreaming a return, fearing that, with slender inheritance, he should never rise so high again, unable to imagine that the dream would one day come to pass, though long deferred and delayed.

There was something marvelously satisfactory about his history. An emblem of the vagaries, the high unsearchable wonders of Fortune.

This one knowledge the two men shared.

Yet with a difference. For at his highest turn on the wheel, Francis Bacon cannot be blamed for clinging to a fool's delusion: that there is a justice of this world.

See how he has come, always by eagerness, spurred by impatience.

Though cast adrift by the death of Sir Nicholas, with three hundred pounds a year to build upon and no place to begin building except his father's chambers at Gray's Inn, Bacon still had reasons to hope. His uncle was Lord Burghley. His father had served the Queen well and had kept her affection. And his cousin, Robert Cecil, who had been as brother to him, stood, frail and bent, in the shadow of the father. Both close to the sun.

The Queen showed some favor to Bacon when she moved to admit him to the Bar as a barrister without the formal delay which custom required. The envy of his fellows at Gray's Inn was nothing to bear when balanced against the comfort of the Queen's favor.

Consider that he had not even had to contend with the rivalry of his well-loved brother. Anthony was off on the Continent, and, for obscure reasons, seemed likely to remain there.

Not knowing, then, that Anthony, though distant, was closer by far. Not knowing Anthony served Burghley and the Queen as a trusted intelligencer.

Bacon took his seat in Parliament in 1584, and, young though he was, he raised his voice clear and loud.

Alas . . . !

For he meddled. Meddled in matters of the subsidies the Queen sought, and in matters of religion, and at a time when his words could win only her disapproval. For which he can now blame youthful ambition. But must blame her for her failure to understand that these faults came not from an irrational flaw, but from youth, from ignorance of her true wishes. For which he should not be called ignorant; Burghley himself was often deep in doubt.

But she frowned and her frown lasted for her lifetime.

It was Jack Harrington who said that when she smiled it was the purest sunshine, but when she frowned it could be like a perilous black storm at sea.

Bacon never knew the Queen well. No man did, it is true. Francis Bacon was among the least knowing, but he should have known her better.

"He will sometimes stutter like a new-clipped crow," the Queen had said. "What does he *want?*"

Bacon was too impatient. And until it was clear not only to her, but also to Francis Bacon himself, what it was he was impatient for, there was no other course of action but for her to do nothing, to keep him waiting, and to doubt him very well.

And so his time did not come for thirty years. He was useless to her for the rest of her life.

No, not entirely so. He performed some service, when he served Essex. Again likely to have been seeking to advance his foundering cause, his own advancement, the advancement of Francis Bacon, by means of association with Essex. But, early or late, Bacon must have been in the service of Cecil. That would be the manner of Cecil, and not too difficult to arrange. By then, Anthony Bacon had come home, and Francis had learned the truth of his brother's vocation. Then Anthony died.

Bacon had come to blame Lord Burghley and his son for his bad fortune. Could blame the Queen, most secretly. Could blame her, but not so bitterly. For she was a woman. And

[464]

women were, as all the world knows . . . But Bacon knows nothing of women. He knew enough to assure himself that one word from Burghley or from crooked Robin could have vaulted him over any obstacle placed between him and his just deserts.

Bacon has ever been a man of quick mind and of depth, breadth and power, capable of enterprise, even, perhaps, greatness, if not frustrated too long until, like a wounded limb, he shriveled from disuse. Bacon possessing, with a difference, the mind of his kin, the Cecils. But Bacon could never muster all his forces to a single task. He could not harness himself and patiently plow one furrow, then the next, never doubting the harvest would be his.

He could discern the hand of the Cecils in his misfortunes. First father, then son held him back by refusing to question the Queen's judgment. But she had passed no judgment against him. She had suspended judgment, awaiting more evidence and proof. Still, she might as well have condemned him and consigned him to oblivion, when his own kin stood mute.

Before he moved into Essex's favor, Bacon distrusted them both. After Burghley's death he came to hate Robert Cecil.

What he cannot have considered was Robert Cecil's knowledge of him. Cecil knew him as a child knows the alphabet. Cecil reckoned all that Bacon was and might be. In one sense Bacon was inconsequential. Likely, without assistance, to trip and fall in impatience or panic. And his panic and fear growing; for he had twice been subjected to the indignity of being arrested for debts.

Yet Cecil knew his cousin possessed an ore which could be mined and smelted and, assayed, might prove the equal of his own. Before he was a man, Robert Cecil had learned there was no purpose in the luxury of doubting himself. Yet this made him keener, more alert, willing, patiently, prudently, to tax his powers to utmost limits. Let no man question the courage of Cecil. Trusting himself and his trust increasing as he grew in knowledge and experience, if not in wisdom and stature, which anyway do not serve any man at Court, he never feared to use any man, even an enemy, to advantage. Like his father, he hated waste. Was willing, then, to wager that he could defend himself from any dangers incurred by relying on another whom he did not trust.

Ralegh knew that Cecil had made good use of *him* in Essex's downfall. Too tedious to rehearse. Except in its similitude to the use of Bacon. Plotting not so much the downfall of Essex as the *possibility* of it, Cecil managed to commit Ralegh to make a peace between the two and then to bring all three together for a time. Simple and beautiful. Should Essex ever threaten Cecil, Ralegh stood between them. Should Essex succeed, then Essex was Cecil's friend. Should Essex fail, then Cecil would have earned the Queen's praise for diligence and still would not have forfeited the favor of James VI of Scotland. Whom he was already flattering, indeed serving.

But Robert Cecil was never one to rest content with less surety than he could obtain. Paradoxical, perhaps, for a man much addicted to gambling; willing to gamble recklessly upon schemes to make money. In imagination the paradox can be resolved. Gambling for recreation was comfort to a man who was as single and concentrated as a burning glass; a release from mind and from that weary, uncomfortable, unbeautiful body like the expense of his lusts upon healthy, well-fed, comfortable, perfumed bodies of Court ladies. As for Cecil's buying and selling of lands, his enclosures, strict rents, trials and errors, and investment ventures, to survive at all he had no choice, but to gamble on these things also.

Enter Francis Bacon, steaming with indignation, brought to boil by impatient years. The sort of man Essex would trust and need.

Cecil summoned Bacon to learn a first lesson in the *trivium* of politics. Cecil called for his cousin, demanded and won service from him.

In return for what? Promises, together with some palpable, slight signs of thaw from the Queen. To whet his appetite and to prove Cecil's power. In all of which the Queen may or may not have played a knowing part. An ignorance of some affairs was her protection, and her surety with Cecil. If one of his schemes came to disaster, he could suffer for it alone.

Within such bonds of understanding, trust is a luxury.

Moreover Cecil could demonstrate the folly of the common belief that Essex held the Queen enthralled, and that Essex's favor was a patent to hers.

It required no dexterity for Cecil to convert his cousin from an enemy into a servant.

See what he gained thereby:

Item. An intelligencer in the camp of Essex. Trusted by Essex. Cecil trusted none of his spies. He used them, weighed and sifted the news they offered, always reckoning that it might be false.

Item. Should Bacon prove useful, it would be Cecil who would profit most.

Item. As for James of Scotland, he could be diverted from Cecil, whom he needed, and therefore would be grateful for any reasonable occasion not to ascribe the fall of Essex to a trusted servant, diverted to others, including Francis Bacon, as false friend to Essex and intelligencer for the Queen.

Indeed Francis Bacon was singled out at the trial of Essex from among many double-dealers to be the very representative of clever double-dealing. And Bacon was forced to write a little book in self-defense—*Apology in certain imputations concerning the Earl of Essex*. Which may not have persuaded any man already convinced against him, but sold many copies in St. Paul's Yard.

Item. Should Essex succeed in a plot or restore himself in favor of the Queen, Bacon, having deceived Essex, would be a most likely sacrificial victim.

Item. For small rewards (*but to the hungry soul even bitter things are sweet*), Bacon would discover that he had compromised himself. Regardless of the chronicle of events or their ending. With the game over, all cards tossed on the table, one last grinning knave would stand out, despised by Essex, distrusted by the Queen, and doubted by the King of Scotland.

Thus, ever graceful and simple, Cecil gave succor to a needy cousin and finished, once and for all, it seemed, Bacon's hopes for future advancement.

To coat medicine with honey is an old device. A child will swallow it for the sake of the sweet. But for Robert Cecil it was more satisfactory that those to whom he gave the medicine of this world should know the taste of it truly as they swallowed it down. For one thing, they would never ask him for honey again.

So long as Robert Cecil lived Francis Bacon could not have prospered. And he did not.

Consider how in the fullness of his present felicity Francis Bacon still remains the pawn of his little cousin, gone to dust and corruption. No man is haunted save by himself. And yet a dead man may, indeed, triumph over a living.

Consider this: Bacon in the fullness of long-sought felicity is, without knowledge or assent, a triumphant creation of his cousin, Robertus Diabolus.

Item. Bacon's sudden rise to be more honored and powerful than Cecil was, could not take place until Cecil died. Thus, ironically, he owes it to Cecil.

Item. Francis Bacon is more vulnerable than Cecil ever was. Bacon has been left a legacy of dangerous delusion—belief in the justice of this world. How can he imagine otherwise? Surely the long seasons of famine and gnawing hope were unjust. If so, then the rewards, a feast beyond promise and expectation, must be just.

But if his reward is the working out of the justice of the world, then it follows there never was any true injustice. So the sweetness of the present is dulled by the compelling knowledge, taken for demonstrable and true, that he owes thanksgivings to the discontents of most of a lifetime. That he cannot, imperious as a conqueror, reject the man he was; for it is that man who has placed him, by suffering and sacrifice, where he is now. That man *must* be remembered. He is condemned to live again and again on discontents and doubt if only to believe in and preserve the man that he now is. At times the finest foods can have no more taste than a wooden bowl of boiled beans.

What profiteth it a man . . . ?

Item. That by these same terms, he is, then, required to remember *Cecil,* too, and to think at least somewhat kindly of him. Compelled to remember him not with the pleasures of revenge or triumph, but with ambiguous gratitude. As if he were deeply beholden to Cecil for all that Cecil did to delay, frustrate, and defer him until his true time had come. Small wonder that Mr. Bacon in his excellent *Essays* condemns the custom of revenge. Since he can have none, he calls it folly.

They say he goes nowhere, gallery or garden or chamber, nowhere except perhaps the privy—and who knows?—without his amanuensis in attendance, ready to write down for posterity Bacon's thoughts and observations. It must goad Lord Bacon to know he cannot speak of the things which he must, in truth, think on most. And what a mind the man has! What a pity that it must dance lame in chains.

Item. Cecil has done more. . . . Call it the world if you choose, but remember that it is Robertus, the world's amanuensis, who comes first to Bacon's mind whenever he considers justice or injustice. Cecil has not only spoiled the savor of the present for Lord Bacon (though nevertheless Bacon must dissemble, even to himself, and smack his lips and rejoice in evident pleasure at . . . *a plate of boiled beans!*), he also has taken away much of the joy of the future.

If a dying man forfeits his future and is, thus, freed of it, then a living man, upon a peak of eminence, standing and surveying the immensity of the unknown, of the unimagined and unimaginable, in awe and wonder—just so Sir Francis Drake in a high tree in Panama saw the vastness of that other ocean; and prayed thanksgiving; and vowed to live to sail across it; and being Francis Drake and no other, he did so—has every right to call the future his plantation. Much as Noah, when he opened the Ark to welcome the dove's return, claimed the kingdom of the world to come and named all mankind to be his sons. By rights, having endured and suffering all, having come to a new world colored with rainbows, Bacon should be able to cast aside his past like an old cloak, never to be worn again.

No man, impatient, eager, quick as a coursing greyhound in the mind, has loved the future, spent his substance so freely investing in the future, as Bacon. Possessed with the power of the new knowledge to restore this weary world—as much possessed as Kit Marlowe's German doctor, he dreamed the future when he had none, and, therefore, had no right to dream.

Now with eminence from which to see the vastness of the dream, with power to work upon the future and to leave his name and mark there, he finds that, in justice, he cannot do so. He must live in the comfort of present time, brief as any poor man's stinking candle, and he finds himself shadowed by a past he cannot ignore. Nothing has prepared him for this.

The future is stolen away, the past given back, but not as it was. All that was, is seen as an illusion, vanished scenery from an old play or masque.

Consider what this stunning knowledge can work upon a man whose power lies chiefly in the mind. To learn the mind has been a false servant, cheating him while seeming to serve him best. The mind has played him false, given him the lie before. He cannot be sure of himself again.

To live in a brilliant present, he cannot be content with his own powers. He must, therefore, call upon the example of Cecil.

Item. An old enemy, now safely dead, becomes a new model for his actions. Becomes in death more important than while he lived and held power. Ironically, in a past rehearsed, becomes Bacon's hope for the present.

Bacon must conjure the ghost then. He must open up the tomb in hope of finding Cecil there. He must sue once again for favor. Only to find, beneath marble, a grinning skull, dirt, a bundle of small bones.

Cecil would do him no favors then and can do him no service now.

Except in memory. And that is weak and watery as an old man's eyes. For while Cecil lived, Bacon hated Cecil too much to study him well. Indeed, he could not even have endured that time had he permitted himself to think too deeply on his cousin. Would have driven himself into melancholy and perhaps madness.

Item. In death as in life, the crippled cousin grins and refuses to assist him.

Item. Nonetheless Bacon must seek in some way to imitate his cousin if he is to survive and prosper.

Example: Bacon's final triumph over his rival, Edward Coke. Coke had been Speaker of the House; Coke had been Attorney General while Bacon still served the Queen without patent. But neither had been knighted when James first came to the throne. Came blithely, generously dispensing all kinds of titles. Unfortunately, for a price. Which Bacon could not afford. When he could, he was galled—gulled, if you wish—to be among some three hundred knighted by the King at once. Coke was one of six.

Coke always bettered him. Until at last he permitted that habit to become Coke's punishment. Bacon was instrumental in raising Coke to the position of powerless eminence, and against both Coke's will and wishes, to Lord Chief Justice. From which he toppled to disgrace. Toppled through his own doings, by his own nature. There is the sign of Robert Cecil triumphant.

But if Robert the Devil is proved right, then Bacon cannot be secure in his trust in justice. The fall of Coke need not be a demonstration of justice. Can be viewed as proving the power of injustice. More, this success over Coke hints that there is neither justice nor injustice, but only the whimsical, irrational, impulsive ways of Fortune.

Does the Queen live on, too, enthroned more powerful than before, as Dame Fortune herself? Surely, when Francis Bacon calls up the portrait of Fortune, the Queen is his model.

Bacon has cause to be uneasy. Though still in disgrace, Coke was called back by the King to join with the Commission, and to deal with Ralegh—himself like a risen ghost. Meet and right that Coke should be called back, for had Coke done his duty as he should have in Winchester in '03, Ralegh would be less than memory now. Coke's tactics failed. Therefore it is fitting that whatever the conclusion must be, Coke must bear a fair share in the responsibility for it.

But Coke is a man of mind too. In a different and deeper fashion than Bacon. For Edward Coke has formed his mind like a fine glass to capture the rays of the sun and bring them into the intense heat of a single beam.

Irony contained in the figure of speech. Coke, though made of different cloth than the Cecils, more than Bacon, has a mind which could match theirs. Ways and means are different, but the power is of high degree. His may be a simpler mind than Bacon's, but with the enormous power of simplicity.

Coke serves the Law of England; thus he serves England always. And he who truly serves England, serves the future. And he who serves the future, owns shares of it. Therefore Coke has more shareholds in the colony of future time than Bacon can hope for.

It is no humiliation to Coke to be called back to finish the affair of Ralegh. For he was thereby given an unexpected occasion to right wrongs done long ago. To make his peace with Ralegh without apology, by performing his duty to the King. Which he has done. Leaving Ralegh with no cause for quarrel with Coke, if any rancor remains.

So be it, Mr. Coke. You have finished. We are at quits. You need not ever think of Walter Ralegh, whether he dies tomorrow or lives to be one hundred years.

Bacon may believe he has a pawn against the King's displeasure if things should turn against the counsel of the Commission. Coke is the likely victim. And if all goes well, Coke does not stand to gain anything.

Bacon may believe that Robert Cecil would approve of his latest stratagem—persuading Coke to write the King from York House counseling a second public trial. That counsel was sure to displease the King. Bacon was willing to risk an implied endorsement of Coke's argument. Which would be necessary if only to dupe Coke. Coming from York House, bearing unmistakable signs of Bacon's style, the letter would prove to the King that Bacon was in agreement with Coke for once.

Precisely Bacon's intent. Should something untoward follow, then he has the proof that he advised against the present course. Again Coke gaining no credit. Should all things go well, Bacon need only remind the King that this letter is signed not by him but by Coke, and, swelling the scene, embellishing the tablature of simple music, he can cause the King to laugh by confessing he has played a trick, no more than a jest really, upon old Coke, that he left some clear signs of himself so that the King, excellent scholar, could see the deception.

Not knowing that Edward Coke assumed all this before he dipped pen in ink. Coke would know and be indifferent, enjoying an occasion to trouble the King with some impunity.

[474]

Bacon not knowing the King fears Edward Coke far more than he fears or needs Lord Bacon.

Not knowing that if the King should see the ghost of Cecil's hand in the stratagem, he will not be pleased. The King feared Robert Cecil living. The specter of Cecil haunting his tractable Lord Chancellor will cause the King to waken to a swarm of doubts.

Bacon not knowing that Robert Cecil would grin and shake his head.

Cecil would know that the fate of Walter Ralegh, at this time and place, is not so simple that it can be soon recorded as having gone well or ill. He would see that no man alive can foresee all the consequences. That if it is the will of the King that Ralegh must die, then die he will. But the intelligent man's best surety against whatever comes to pass lies, as always, in patient, watchful, wakeful waiting.

Francis Bacon, ever impatient and forever something of a fool in a world of knaves, has demonstrated once again the flaws of his nature.

Bacon not knowing that in the eyes of a living Robert Cecil he would earn credit for nothing.

Not reading rightly the meaning of the grin of the skull of Cecil under the marble tomb.

Yet despite discontent, Bacon's smile fades not at all as the coach, equipped for comfort and show within and without, but almost as rough on a man's bones as the flat-runnered hurdles which draw wretches to Tyburn, rattles, bounces, and bumps a brief journey along the Strand.

He could have come and returned by barge; for he has a barge as splendid as the King's and his own crew of liveried watermen ready upon his whim to push out from what is the finest water gate along the river. . . .

Canopied against the weather, the watermen on their benches with oars raised, waxed and glistening, in salute, the barge waited for him this morning as he passed under the classic marble arch and descended the flight of steps from water gate to wharf.

Bacon paused to look at the rain-flecked river. Close by two lean fishermen, ill clad and weather-soaked, were working their net and had cast out hooks and lines as well. Catching his stare, they looked up and returned his look, unsmiling. Cut his eyes away to scan larger distance. Rain and cold or no, there was much traffic on the river, and, he suspected, some of it composed already of the idle and curious taking in the sights of London.

Well, he had no intention of adding to their catalogue of wonders.

He turned back to mount the stairs without a word. Behind him some whispered voices, muffled scurrying.

His young clerk, taking quick steps, came close enough to speak.

"What is your pleasure, my lord?"

Bacon stopped, turning abruptly. The young man stumbled on rain-slick stone. Blushed with embarrassment and Lord Bacon smiled.

"I shall go to the hall by coach," he said.

"By coach, sir?" The young man echoing his voice, so others could hear.

"I fancied this weather would clear the river," Bacon replied. "But I think only the end of the world will empty the Thames."

"Indeed, my lord," the young man, his poise recovered, began. . . .

And Francis Bacon's quick eyes catching all the discreet motion around him. As servants slipped away, seeming to vanish. For coach and all horses must be made ready and seem to have been standing there always.

"Indeed, my lord," the young man, last traces of the blush vanishing, saying: "I fear to contradict your fancy, but I think Judgment Day will not improve our crowded river."

"How so?"

Moving at a slow pace to permit his harried servants time to deceive him. Probably he should have more servants. To gratify his whims and their deceptions. But, God's wounds! he has, how many?—more than a hundred already.

"Why, my lord," the young man saying, "your charitable disposition toward men deludes you. You overlook two plain truths of London."

"And what may they be, these plain truths I so charitably ignore?"

"Of all the people of the world, my lord, there is no creature so brazenly curious as your Londoner. London will as lief come crowding to the sounds of bagpipe, drum, and penny whistles, announcing some juggler or mountebank rogue, as to the call to alarm by the Lord Mayor himself. Indeed, sir, they will come sooner for a juggler."

Thinking: *And where were they all that day when Essex called for them? Judging their account books?*

But saying: "Well then, curiosity. I must admit the citizens of London, spoiled children all, are curious of everything, especially the new."

"Exactly as you say, sir. Allowing for one exception, if it please you; that though they tire sooner of the old and familiar than jaded emperors or potentates, still they can never have

[477]

their fill of common blood and thunder, be it at Tyburn or the Beargarden, or upon the stage."

"But I recollect you said that there was something else I overlooked."

"The tenacious venality of our watermen. Why, they would ferry Death himself, scythe and all, and shoot the bridge at ebb tide, if the price were right."

"No need to fear anything, young man, when Death is your passenger."

"Pardon the extravagance of my figure of speech."

"It is too early, God willing, for you to study death. Youth is the time for extravagance. . . . But tell me what is missing in your complaint against the city? You owe me some rousing conclusion."

"Sir?"

"We were speaking, I believe, of Judgment Day in London."

"Ah, yes, my lord. Picture it if you will, then: the Angel Gabriel, all history for practice and rehearsal, puts angelic lips to a heavenly trumpet and blows across the sky a flock of shining notes purer and cleaner than any music ever heard yet by human ears. . . ."

"And damnable loud, too. Don't forget that. It may be that the dead shall think it is clean and pure. But it will rattle in the skulls of the living."

"And out they all come, the merchants and prentices, servants and sailors, bawds and wives, all of London on the streets, jostling and pressing down to the banks, crying out for watermen—and they shall not be scarce that day or hard to find, having in all likelihood received advance notice of the event—to carry them out to the middle of the Thames, so they may

[478]

have best places to view and to criticize the performance of the prophecy of St. John."

Lord Bacon laughs. For all this, trivial and innocent, has kept his mind from wrestling with itself.

"What pleases me most," Bacon says, "is what you have touched on by implication—that of all God's creatures only citizens of London will believe themselves entitled to be spectators on that day."

"The Apocalypse, my lord, will be their final entertainment. Mark my word, they will find some fault with God's performance, though they may condescend to applaud as the blessed and the damned depart their separate ways."

"Your coach, sir. . . ."

A gesture and there stands the coach as if by magic.

"One more word."

"My lord?"

"What will become of the swans?"

"I confess I had not considered them."

"Think of the swans, young man. They have an evil temper, it is true, in keeping with our dismal climate and these wicked times. But still, our swans are beautiful. They offer much grace and purity to the eye. I sometimes doubt angels will prove to be quite so graceful.

"What will become of them, my boy? I can conceive of your Judgment Day in London. For like the Londoner, I, too, am insatiably curious. And I can picture this place, York House, Westminster, the City, all England unpeopled forever. I can view that prospect with a certain pleasure, even though perforce it entails my absence from the scene as well. But . . ."

"Sir?"

"But the picture of our river without swans is a cold thing

near my heart. What desolation! A river with no swans and no man left to name them and call them beautiful."

"I fear I have led you up the wrong path of the garden, my lord. It was not my intention to call up melancholy."

"But I am, as God made me, a melancholy man. And I have now a melancholy duty to perform."

He mounts the coach and settles on the soft leather seat, as a footman wraps a turkey carpet about his legs.

The young clerk stands attentive beside the coach. Raindrops, like dew of May flowers, are rich in his curls. His face is frowning, perplexed.

"I go to Westminster to see the last of one of our swans," Bacon calls out. "A black swan, it is true. But, then, black swans are very rare."

All that is behind him now in time. Melancholy is memory. He is returning to York House, relieved that it was so easy.

Lord Bacon prefers to dine in the latest fashion, in one of the smaller chambers rather than in the vast hall. But he must surrender to necessity. Almost every dinner at York House is a feast. Such comings and goings of the great and those hungry for greatness at his water gate and gatehouse. And most of them accompanied by a retinue of servants, clerks, and others. And all with suits to press, favors to seek. And each, according to custom, with something to offer in return for Bacon's consideration.

Never, even in the tall memories of his childhood, has York House seen such thronging. It is in keeping with the times. Bacon, unlike His Majesty, insists upon more ceremony and decorum from these suitors; his own little court becoming, as it were, a more elegant and suave shadow of the gaudy and uncontrollable Court of the King. Who—keep this a secret —may enjoy reassurance, a restoration of his oft threatened kingly esteem, by observing gentlemen and ladies turn into pigs before his eyes; who, if they cannot be ruled, can be shown to themselves to be the unruly victims of gross appetite. But Bacon's little court at York House defends old customs. A conscience to the realm, like a Puritan conscience, though clothed in a surpassing brilliance and never disguised in sober blacks.

Shadow and conscience; yet more substantial than the Court itself. For it is here where men of affairs must come now.

When Bacon feels need of recreation and sweeter air he's off to St. Albans, a score of miles northwest in Hertfordshire. Repairs to one of two houses on his father's land: Gorhambury, which Sir Nicholas raised up and then added to extravagantly after the late Queen observed it was well situated and delightful, but too small for such a large man. And Francis Bacon's smaller, new place, separate by a mile, Verulam House. There are oak groves, parks, and gardens. Ponds and pools, atingle with ripple and color of fish and waterfowl. Themes of shade, mazes in gardens, and the poetry of water. Sweet water comes, as his father wished, by pipes to each chamber of Gorhambury and Verulam. Gorhambury for fall and winter, Verulam for summer. Gorhambury as his father's monument, not so grand or curious as Burghley House, to be sure, but magnificent with its win-dowed portico, its tall, slender, separate clock tower, richness of furnishings and hangings, the small perfect banquet house in the garden, where the theme of the frescoes celebrates the Liberal Arts; its gallery with colored glass depicting the flowers, birds, and beasts of India. No, not so imposing as Burghley House, just as Verulam is overtopped by both Theobalds and Hatfields. But neither place is so liable to catch the eye or spark the envy of the King or one of his favorites. Important men with suits to press are suitably impressed. Arriving at Gorhambury they may come and go on any of three parallel roads he has built from the highroad to Verulam, seven coaches abreast if need be.

But now the world comes to York House. To enter an ancient doorway, where, as upon the doors at Gorhambury, Bacon has fixed polished mirrors. Not merely extravagance and delight. But so all who enter may experience a recognition of themselves. A moment which can be of advantage; for Bacon insists upon not only elegance of appearance, but also an honest cleanliness. He will purse his lips and wrinkle nostrils at the least indication of slovenly indifference.

A last look at the door to be sure that all—seam of hose, line of doublet, lacing of sleeves, starched rigor of ruff and cuff, composition of curls, head, and beard—is correct and clean.

But Lord Bacon is more subtle. Mirrors serve to divert them to the inspection of themselves. So that at their entrance they may be filled with a sense of themselves reflected, seen by others, not as they imagine themselves to be. Not, in truth, as they may be, in naked body, quintessential soul, but in appearance only. Mere appearances, decorative figures from a painting, an arras, a painted ceiling. . . .

None so lacking in vanity that he (or she; for the ladies come also to seek favor or redress) will not be pleased at the image. Pleased and reassured. Yet even as they smile to greet themselves, they are touched by a cold, inward sinking.

A lesson in humility at the threshold, Bacon thinks, seeing himself in his fine robes, in his own mirrors.

There is no good lesson in humility to be learned by hair

shirts, in sackcloth and ashes. Job in his nakedness, albeit blessed with a decorative pattern of boils and sores to relieve the uniform tallow of old flesh, naked amid ashes and potsherds, studied still to make himself perfect and was not humbled until at last a voice in the wind roared out the truth that the Almighty found no pleasure in his study. No, humility can easier be learned by and through indulgences of vanity. To see, and know in seeing, that nothing, not even literal perfection, is sufficient to merit anything beyond the brief attention of a powerfully busy man.

This truth underscored by the haughty usher, tallest servant of the household, clad in splendid livery, his Spanish boots six times scented in the making and scented daily in cleaning and polishing, his spotless gloves, with exquisite Flemish lace worked at the wrists, one hand casually, languidly beckoning, the other holding a white delicate ash wand. And not, as now, smiling and bowing, obsequious and deferential in greeting his master, who enters; but then a cold mask, a schoolmaster's, reserved for them. Exactly—a schoolmaster's. Making them small children in terror of having forgotten hard lessons committed to memory, feeling tardy, no matter how punctual. As with that languid glove in a practiced gesture he directs them to tiring rooms where they may hang coats and mantles on hooks and change from their boots or cork-soled shoes to soft slippers of velvet and ribbon before entering the hall and being directed to wait there or sent up the stairway to do a penance of patience in the gallery or in the isolation of some chamber. Until his lordship can see them, or, perhaps, send some clerk or servant, to hear them out in his behalf.

Bacon is neither much given to vanity, except the vanities of the mind, nor feels superior to all of these suitors. But he has been schooled by adverse Fortune into believing that, large or small, granted, denied, or deferred, suits must be heard in a theater of proper grandeur, in which they must whisper shyly like children at church; for their own satisfaction. It is not so much the outcome of suit, plea, petition, or cause that matters, though it may seem so to them. Nor, indeed, is it only the sense that they must be taken seriously. Rather the opposite, if the truth be known. They must be reassured that their suits are delivered at the proper place. As once men had spent the wealth, sweat, and half the stones of England to raise huge cathedrals, still standing, so that God Almighty could be properly housed. So that prayers might rise either to be heard or ignored, but always in a fitting and proper setting.

As the King is God's Viceroy, so is Bacon the viceroy of the King. The King himself lacks stature and grandeur. Because of that Bacon must strive the more to increase his own; doing so in behalf of the King. Just so Mother Church long ago had embraced grandeur, with stained glasses and images and precious metals and odor of incense, seeking thereby to convey hints of grandeur of Paradise.

To what purpose and with what hope would anyone offer his prayers up to a carpenter, penniless, ne'er-do-well, who ended his days on a wooden cross so rudely made that any carpenter would disdain it?

It is not pride alone, but duty which demands that York House be worthy. Not for Bacon's pleasure; for his deepest pleasure is in the company of men with quick minds and tongues to match, and, most of all, with books and the wonder of his own thoughts. It is little ease to dine at the raised table in the hall, tables packed with suitors, their servants, and his own, eager to be served a feast.

Though there is a design of pleasure in his choice, not quite an afterthought. Bacon loves music. And he has his musicians playing quiet accompaniment to his thoughts when he withdraws to his most private chambers, here or in the country, for meditation. Since he must have a daily feast at York House, he might as well do so in the hall, where he can hear musicians playing from the minstrels' gallery, screened above the stairway.

Good music is much solace. Medicine against the sight of knaves feeding off his abundance as if it has no end. Music's a cordial against the thought of that abundance ever imperiled by more debts. Music can empty his mind from grievous consideration of ravenous mouths, of the greed with which the world seeks to devour itself.

No unseemly haste. Bacon's dinner will not be hurried. Will last beyond two hours, possibly three.

Musicians are playing in the minstrels' gallery. The larger number of guests and his own retinue are standing in an easy gathering, talking idly, separate from the hall by the fixed wooden screen: fine-carved, rich-worked, fit for nothing less than a cathedral, if its designs—conventional dolphins and other sea beasts, mermaids and Neptune, story of Jonah and the whale, our Lord walking upon water, and all embellished with scrolls and classical figures—are somewhat different. Candlebranches throw patterns of light, scrolls of shadow upon these carvings, the work of Italians. Whose craft, to his taste, though exceedingly dear, has more delicacy than Dutch work, which has been too much copied and become too commonplace.

There must be a wealth of light, twice the candles the King would require. For Lord Bacon cannot bear much shadow. When the moon is darkened, or that rarer thing, the sun, he is taken with fainting fits.

[485]

Near the foot of the stairway, separate from the lesser herd, shepherded by the usher, stand the favored few who will join him at his raised table.

Music fit for light dancing—though no dancing here—plays. Odors rise over the top of the screen to whet appetite and curiosity.

And who are the favored guests today waiting at the foot of the stairs? A group only Bacon can have joined together: one country Bishop, known for sermons, together with his canon; the Ambassador of a German duchy, together with the younger half brother of the Duke himself, a Spaniard; an old scholar from Cambridge, in academic robes; an herbalist from France of much repute, though as yet untranslated, here to see Lord Bacon's planting; a knight born in Yorkshire and back from a year's travel in the Levant, odd with his squat bluff figure, his seamed and sunburned Yorkshire face, a beetroot from alien air and sun, clad in a motley of English and Persian fashions; a young Venetian, dark and thin, his brave silks and jewels proclaiming him a bravo, said to be of the nobility, though traveling incognito here, said also to know much of music and musicians on the Continent; a portly London merchant with his wife, fat from his dealings in Flemish lace, German stoneware, Norwegian timber, Russian furs, Azores wines, the modest sobriety of their clothing belied by the few expensive stones she wears, the coif of her curls, the rings on his large hands—and he may not know it, but will perhaps one day pay the reckoning for this occasion, even others to which he was not invited. . . .

Through the narrow entrance of the screen, impeccable, most immaculate of all servants, clean as a virgin bride, the butler appears. He has seen to the setting of places, the linen and napery, the bread and salt. With utmost care he has set Lord Bacon's table.

The crowd, apart from the few at the foot of the stairs who cannot see him, quiets as the butler tips a nod to the imperious and, by an hierarchical hair, inferior usher. What the usher does, then, no one can see, but the music fades away. And now the voices of those by the stairs seem loud. They glance at each other, then speak in whispers. The city merchant, with whom the French herbalist has been trying to converse in a bastard tongue of French and mispronounced English, coughs and catches the eyes of his wife, her round face, partly veiled and perfectly placid, and shrugs. And he tugs a chain to reveal a gold watch, half the size of a coconut shell.

The others who have seen this and the mild annoyance in the purse of his lips, gasp. The late Queen, who loved watches and clocks of all kinds, had nothing so grand. Perhaps it has chimes. . . . But if the chimes ring now, they will be wasted; for the sound of brass horns comes from the gallery, ripple of drums, and then in broken consort the musicians begin to play a pavane, stately and solemn.

There at the first landing, as if created by the usher's pointing wand, stands Bacon. He has put aside robes of office. He is a surprising delight in a matching jerkin, winged with limp-hanging sham sleeves, and the new-style cloak-bag breeches, fringes hanging at the knee. All made of richest stuffs, and though sober of hue, shot and shimmering with patterns of gold and silver. The sleeves of his doublet beneath the jerkin are a startling tawny satin; behind the cuffs are a rank of tiny pearl buttons, and the cuffs wide and loose; and his falling ruff is snowy below the ends of his beard. The shoes are velvet mules, fur-trimmed, tawny rosettes of the same satin, each set in a flower

[487]

pattern with a star of silver at the center. His hat is high-crowned, of narrow brim. Silk bands of ribbon brighten it above the brim, and an exquisite thing of feathers, made of a peacock's tail, falls casually away, drooping with excess, behind his right ear.

For one moment he seems still as a picture portrait, but now descends, fixed smile, eyes shifting to the crowd by the door in greeting, as hats are doffed.

Behind him on the landing comes his steward and the steward's wife, a secretary with a brace of pretty young ladies to make more pleasure and variety at table, and last of all his master of horse.

Bacon greets the favored guests, but his words are lost in the music. Turns then and leading the Bishop and Ambassador, the others following respectfully, moves toward the screen, and enters the hall.

His chief ewer steps forward, and liveried prentice boys assist him. They offer silver basins of scented hot and cold water and gleaming white cloths. Lord Bacon dips, carefully washes his hands, and wipes them dry. His guests follow suit. Lesser servants bear large basins of burnished brass and coarser cloths for the crowd of others who enter now behind Lord Bacon and his group. Who, strolling in time to the music as if idle in an April garden, move toward the raised table, where, nearest to the fire, they will face the others.

Deftly the usher guides each to his place.

Bacon stands before the salt, Florentine silver a foot high, set before his place. Eyes all in easy inspection. The tablecloth is a field of fresh snow in which, glittering in many-colored threads, has been worked the mythic story of Venus and Adonis. For the satiric sake of the huge boar, thus honoring his crest.

Napkins are neat folded. Knives and spoons and, amazing, forks, polished like new-minted. No smudge or fingerprint upon them, no fleck of tarnish on the great salt. Likewise the silver plate. At this table each guest has one small loaf of the finest manchet bread, the crust scraped smooth and brown, not a fly-size burnt spot on any loaf.

Bacon sits down and the others follow. He turns to the Bishop on his right and speaks to him. The music eases out of hearing. The room is silent. Lord Bacon doffs his hat as does every man in the hall. The Bishop, nodding, as if speaking directly to the silver salt, says a grace:

"O Lord, who hast given us this day to enjoy the full abundance and bounty of harvest, the riches of Thy Creation, hear now our humble thanksgiving. Let the brightness and order of this ancient room, the light we here see brightly by . . .

not much light from windows of colored stained glass today save reflection of fire a multitude of silver candlesticks on lesser tables candlesticks (which even the King reserves for himself preferring wall candles and chandelier for general lighting) and oil lamps of sweet oil and bright flames brought from Italy

". . . the untarnished richness of plate and glass . . .

behind him on buffets banked gleaming pieces of plate delicate gold rimmed Venetian glass and cups wrought of agate like seashells

". . . all serve to remind us of the sweet order and brightness and the ineffable richness of Thy heavenly Kingdom.

above the mantel of the fireplace Bacon's arms cunningly done in plaster and painted huge behind the praying Bishop's head

[489]

"Let us, ever mindful of Thy Love and everlasting goodness, giving special thanks for this day named in honor and celebration of the Apostles Simon and Jude, to whom all honor and glory in Paradise is due in Thy name; let us take comfort and spiritual sustenance even with our earthly nourishment, remembering that, as we feed flesh, we feed corruption to feed worms; but as we feed the famished spirit so do we grow tall toward eternity. For these, Thy corruptible gifts we are humbly grateful, O Lord, but most deeply for Thine own everlasting Love, the bread and wine of Thy body and Thy blood, salt of Thy Gospel, which shall never lose savor. We offer thanks and pray forgiveness for our manifold sins, trusting forever in our advocate and mediator, Jesus Christ. Amen . . ."

Before the muttered echoes of *Amen* have died the butler approaches Bacon's chair, bows deep, uncovers Bacon's loaf of bread and sets it beside the salt. Bacon breaks bread. Then a company of servants enters with the salads.

Noise of music, soft now, a lute or two, a viol, a virginal. . . .

Bacon turns to the Bishop.

"I must confess that my duties have distracted me. Until your prayer I had clean forgotten today is the feast of Simon and Jude."

"I'll wager that with your turn of mind, it is only the fixed feasts that slip the leash of memory."

"It is true," Bacon says with a laugh. "I can name you each movable feast for ten years to come."

"Let us pray we shall both be here to enjoy them."

"I'll say Amen to that."

"Tell me, what is the wine for today?"

"A Spanish red, a kind of Alicante. We have added to it a certain recipe of our own, spices, sugar, and ambergris."

The Bishop is given an agate cup, holds it admiringly and sniffs the light aroma of spiced wine.

"When I was a boy we still drank from a wooden cup passed round the table."

"And so do many who are not bishops," Bacon says. "Taste it."

The bishop takes two swallows and returns the cup to the servant.

"Magnificent!"

"You exaggerate. But your exaggeration always pleases."

The servant boy goes back to the buffet, pours the remains of the cup into a bowl. Beggars at the gate will drink from that bowl in the late afternoon. Wipes the cup clean and places it back where it belongs. Glancing right and left, not an eye on him, he dips two fingers into the beggars' bowl and licks them clean. Then looks up just in time to catch a signal from the butler and to hurry to bring cups of the wine to the city merchant and his wife.

See them now in the long gallery of York House. A high-ceilinged room running almost the whole northeast length of the palace, affording a handsome view of the Thames. New-made by Bacon for such days as this, when there can be no walking in the gardens; though even now the Frenchman stalks there, guided by one of Bacon's young men, whose *politesse* is being tested by wind and rain.

See the gallery fresh, for the first time, through the eyes of the merchant from London.

Who was impressed, in all five senses, by the opulence of dinner in the hall. He was duly impressed, but not awed. The halls of the Guilds, many of them, are finer. And he has been

[491]

present at other feasts in halls of manor houses, in England and abroad. Has enjoyed the pleasures of an equal fare, every kind of dainty and delight. Moreover, he was prepared to be impressed. He has heard much of Bacon's affectations, and he knows more than a little of his dealings.

Indeed, he was present at the ceremony of marriage at Marylebone Chapel, a little over ten years ago, when Sir Francis Bacon married Alice Barnham, the fourteen-year-old daughter of a city alderman and a draper. On that occasion Sir Francis was clad, head to toe, in purple, like royalty. And he furnished his young bride with a gown like a lady. At least, unlike some ladies of this age, she did not have to steal away with her new husband, disguised as a page. Though if gossip be true, which will be so when the Thames runs backwards and the seas go dry, she might have done better to pretend to be a page. These June and January weddings, though they may thaw the winter with one false spring, cannot bring back spent Maytime. . . .

At table he asked about Alice, and Bacon assured him she is most healthy and content in the country. Knowing the Barnham women, the merchant thinks she can be neither, but at least she can be safer there than here.

If the value of all things, from burnished weapons on the walls to silver spoons, from the plate and glass gleaming on the buffets to the stuffed velvet cushion of his chair—no simple stools for the high table—if the value is high, he could estimate it, within a mark or two, without troubling his mind with mathematics. A fortune in the sum of these things, true. But a fortune which was not beyond his own means, should he indulge himself in great luxury and greater debts. For no man, not even the Lord Chancellor of England, can afford such luxury long. It is a show, a stage play of wealth. He knows

[492]

that, at present, new to power, Lord Bacon is skimming upon the thinnest ice. He lacks, as yet, even the inherited land of a first son. Anthony Bacon's dead, but Lady Bacon owns the estate at St. Albans. And she bids fair to live long. Given time, Bacon can bring the coffers of truth into some balance with these expensive shows. There is his gamble. And this stolid merchant, with a thousand ears to hear with, has heard that Buckingham, the King's young favorite, has set his heart upon the possession of York House as soon as Lord Bacon has finished all repairs and rebuilding. If so, then Buckingham will have it. Unless, of course, another favorite comes upon the scene.

Meanwhile a stage show, appearance of wealth, will draw wealth to it. As honey draws hungry flies.

And meanwhile these things have value regardless of who may possess them. They remain rich whether paid for or owned, or, like the robes and properties of rogue players of stage plays, are only borrowed or rented.

Great men have advantage of the merchant. He must hive, harvest, and spoon out his own money with caution. While they are permitted to play a game of higher stakes. But their stakes are borrowed and the risks compounded. Always a chance —else why play such games?—of gains far beyond the means of other men. But the possibility of profit upon a scale commensurate with the wager they must make is in proportion to the risk. In short, to make any gain they must do so by risking the most which raises the odds against them.

The fortunate are those who manage to end their offices no worse off than they were when they received them. Extraordinary are the few who accumulate sufficient to offset their losses. A merchant of means can grow more, gather more wealth in a lifetime than the sum and average of these.

[493]

The merchant, dining in the hall, could enjoy the pleasure of many fine things without envy. For in a sense they were his to enjoy, whether or not he shall lend any money to Lord Bacon, as much as they were Bacon's.

Here in the gallery, however, is something new and strange for him. Calculation can be dismissed in favor of wonder and open admiration.

Only the few have been led here. The crowd at the lower tables is now dispersed. Some to the presence chamber, waiting, waiting. Some to the privy chamber, these with some reasonable assurance of seeing Bacon or one of his servants. Others, singly or in small groups, with certainty of presenting their suits to Bacon, though no surety as to *when*, this day or the next, led to a dozen chambers in the house. All waiting upon Bacon. Waiting upon his pleasure.

His pleasure is to entertain favored guests in the gallery. For, in a palpable sense, it is he who is pressing suit upon each of them. Though he need not do so overtly, can recline on his daybed of rosewood, covered with red damask silk, near the window, a wrought bronze brazier, red-hot with coals, warming him.

The room is as long as an open field. You could shoot a bow here. You could run a footrace. Indeed at the far end the two young ladies and the Germans, Ambassador and the brother of the Duke, are playing a game of shuttlecock.

There are one dozen windows—outdoing by one the windows Queen Elizabeth set into the gallery at Hampton Court, and these more perfectly symmetrical and larger too. And four of these are bay windows, each with covered seats and cushions, facing four large fireplaces all aglow with the flames and colored smokes of scented woods, each a different composition upon the theme of fire. The fire well framed in the fireplaces, wrought with figures and emblems to represent the four seasons of the year, the four humors of man, with entablatures of swirling plaster and fine woods, all painted and gilded to complement the color of flames.

Upon the twelve windows are etched and colored the signs of the zodiac. The floor's a chessboard of gleaming marble, lightly covered with matting and at least a dozen turkey carpets, flung there instead of placed upon chests and tables. These depict scenes from the lives of the Apostles. The ceiling's an airy masterpiece of plasterwork designs, gilded with spaces for the painted boar to be displayed.

When they entered, Lord Bacon led them on a turn and tour for digestion's sake, unveiling the chief theme, the paintings of Dutch and Italian masters—the Twelve Caesars of Rome; moving on without comment by the new tapestries which offer as much beauty of the flesh as instruction of spirit: Venus and Adonis, Diana and Actaeon, David and Bathsheba, Susanna and the Elders. . . .

With some eagerness he pulled aside a curtain, damask and cloth of gold, covering the centerpiece of all: a portrait in oil of King James, shown as a hunter, all in green.

Bacon then left them to inspect things at their leisure. Which the merchant finds most pleasant.

There are fine chests and tables, of course. Along the wall stand cabinets of rosewood and walnut and cherry, polished and scented, brightened with patterns of marquetry or inlaid with rare, different-colored woods and bits of marble and precious stones. And here are displayed, the cabinets open wide, all shelves of drawers pulled open, extraordinary objects: rare gems and precious stones, ancient coins, medals and medallions,

[495]

maps and charts and instruments of the new learning. All expected; for the merchant is familiar with Bacon's essays, his *Advancement of Learning,* and knows something of his bent and interests.

It is not so much these as others, more elaborate, frivolous, and fantastic, which astonish him. Bacon in his works makes strong arguments for the plain and pure and practical. How, then, could the merchant ever have anticipated such things as these which he now is drawn to look to, fascinated?

A ship made of silver, beaten gold for corses, rigging of gold threads, silver mariners, and figures of Bacon and his wife in gold standing tall at the stern.

Rare volumes and manuscripts bound in thick velvet, hinges of gold, his crest set upon the velvet in crystal, ebony, and ivory.

A golden machine to show the principle of Archimedes Screw, which raises by lowering itself; the head of the screw is of diamond.

An emerald frog with rubies for eyes poised to catch some jeweled flies.

Curious glasses which make the viewer fat or thin, distant or close, the glasses contained in velvet set with pearls, gold, and silver.

Lily pots of gold with tiny gold flowers, stems and petals brilliantly enameled. Flies of agate or set in amber. A butterfly of gold with jewels for colors.

Small nude figures of men and women, made of gold, eyes of jewels, each with a jewel at the navel.

Lockets, miniatures, all with a painting, watches of many sizes and shapes. His own watch, heavy and grand as it is, seeming suddenly nothing.

Curiosities—rocks found in form of hands or feet. Plants seeming to have human faces. The bones of a two-headed cat. Fossils of unknown fishes, gigantic footprints, much like a man's, frozen into stone. . . .

He feels more delighted than diminished. To be here is to be alive, within a musical jewel box. His back to the fire, he observes the Italian playing the virginal. One of Bacon's musicians has joined him, making accompaniment with a pandora lute.

The merchant's wife is playing at cards with the wife of the chief steward. No doubt he will have dealings with the steward soon enough. . . .

Servants pass among them offering sweets. He may choose from marzipan or candied nutmeg or ginger in silver bowls. Even preserved green ginger. He can take comfits from gold and silver comfit boxes shaped like seashells, walnuts, hearts. He may, if he wishes, have whole candied oranges or lemons.

But he declines these, accepting instead the ivory pipe and sweet tobacco one servant offers while a second holds a long match flame for him to light it.

Puffs and wonders why he feels no envy, only admiration.

He drinks the smoke and thinks: *Perhaps it is because I have never until now imagined such things, frivolous rich things without use or purpose, save leisure on a cold wet day, and cannot therefore conceive myself the possessor of any. The threshold of this marvel of a room, this little simulation of Paradise itself, being an invisible boundary and border which will always separate me from nobility.*

He is relieved. He feels as warm toward Bacon as the fire on his back. He has no desire to possess the gallery or anything in it, but he can be content, knowing such beautiful things exist. He will not be displeased to lend Lord Bacon some money.

He moves toward a group around the daybed. A servant seats him in an armchair next to the Bishop.

"Your tobacco pipe reminds me," the Bishop says. "What is to become of Ralegh?"

Bacon smiles and shrugs. "It is now in the hands of the King," he says. "I venture, however, that he shall die on the morrow. Swift and quiet in the Palace Yard."

"Swiftly, no doubt," the merchant says. "But I cannot imagine it will be a quiet occasion."

"Indeed?" Bacon frowns.

"I mean that tomorrow being Lord Mayor's Day and the procession beginning early and at that very place, it seems there will be a large crowd of people."

Bacon laughs now, swinging his legs around to sit up, touching the Bishop's arm.

"Lord preserve me!" Bacon exclaims. "Do you see now where so much busyness can carry a man? Until you said the grace I had forgotten today was the day of Simon and Jude. And I'll wager that no one paused to remember that tomorrow is Lord Mayor's Day."

"No one except the new Lord Mayor himself and all the people of London," the merchant says.

"Excepting, as well, the Fox himself," the Bishop says.

Bacon cannot contain his laughter.

"Well, I fear the King will surprise himself in this matter."

"And the Fox?"

"We can never be certain of anything about him."

Just then there is a soft tentative chiming noise. The mer-

[498]

chant sighs and produces his watch, opening it as one would open the hinged section of a pomander, to check the hour.

He is startled by the sound of a louder bell. Turns to see that he has missed the most extraordinary object in this gallery. A wooden chiming clock, half as high as a man, on the wall. Bells in a miniature belfry toll, chimes announce the hour. On a platform of the clock, beneath the face, two painted mechanical knights come forth. One's a Crusader with a red cross on his breast, the other a dark Saracen. They smite each other three mighty blows with broadswords.

Delighted, Bacon's guests cry out and applaud. He rises, signals all to hush. Moves to the cabinet where the silver ship with sails of gold, and himself and young bride sailing, rests. Touches a hidden spring.

The ship begins to move. Cannon ports open. Three cannon fire each with a different colored smoke.

Now they can applaud to their hearts' content.

He smiles, bows, and excuses himself to be about the King's affairs and his own.

The picture, two knights of the clock striking each other with broadswords to toll the time, a silver ship and puffs of colored cannon smoke, fades, and he returns to himself at the window of the gatehouse. He is staring at a tree across the yard. A lone tree, bare to the bones, small birds roosting there, riding out the weather on twisted branches. Under the tree a guardsman passes, wet glinting the blade of his halberd, held down, aslant.

Ralegh turns from the window and says something to a servant.

There are things that must be done now. No more time for thought of others and elsewhere.

He will not think of his own future. Cannot allow that liberty now lest it should paralyze his will. Not considering his own future, at this time, he will not imagine the future of these others. Not Yelverton, Stukely, Wilson, certainly. Nor will he imagine the future of Francis Bacon.

Yet with Bacon he could do so without violation of will.

For he has thought on Bacon's present estate deep enough, and he sees how it is threatened.

What can happen is already here and now.

Just as the Kingdom of Heaven, though alien to any kingdom of earth, is eternal and therefore changeless, while we are wholly possessed by the powers of change, the Kingdom of Heaven is nevertheless here and now also, printed in each part and piece of the aging, changing, temporal Creation. But who can read that text? The Kingdom of Heaven is here and now within him and has always been so, his body a colony of a distant empire, his soul an ambassador or viceroy of the true King; unknowable, unsearchable, ineffable, here and now, that Kingdom will be not always alien but, brightly and suddenly, home, not a place dimly remembered and returned to; for we shall most assuredly discover that all our journeys elsewhere, our voyages and explorations, pilgrimages and crusades, all these were imagined and imaginary, unreal and unsubstantial; that we never left home but only dreamed a dream of faring forth and returning; that we shall not be welcomed as returning, but rather greeted as if waking from a sleep and a dream; and that we shall be greeted in a language we understand, having always known it.

Just so, the future of a man, in time and of this earth, is carried in him from his first breath, his first cries; though there has never yet been a wise man, not even Solomon, who could translate so much as a phrase of this unknown tongue. A few chosen ones have seen the signs and ciphers of eternal language, and these alone, but sufficient proof that it is all written down.

Not Solomon or Joseph or Daniel would be taxed, however, to discern the most likely future of Francis Bacon.

[501]

Bacon is most threatened not because he has already lost it, but because he cannot bear to face the future.

His present time, for all its satisfaction, is, as he is, most vulnerable. He can sense that acutely. There is—has always been —a deep strain of melancholy in his humor. And there is also a sense of dread, more painful because he cannot name it.

Who knows Bacon somewhat, as Ralegh does, will have discerned that his melancholy is never more dominant, his dread never more apparent, than at those moments when he seems most smiled upon by Fortune.

Who lives with dread has some cause to. For the secret lies in this: that, whatever the cause of dread, that dread becomes the cause and occasion of its own fulfillment. Thus a man might argue, if he chose to, that the source of dread is the knowledge of its fulfillment.

A dog biting its tail and whirling in a circle . . .

A circle, a wheel within Fortune's wheel . . .

From this present time of comfort and security, power and eminence, never forgetting melancholy, dread and dreams, there is a pilot's chart on which to trace Bacon's course.

His extravagance, there lies a key to it.

And there is nothing new in that, for he has always lived beyond his means, always been in debt, even when his fortune added up to a sum of misfortunes. This is not without some wisdom. Fortune never smiles much upon a careful man. Fortune looks smiling upon that suitor who is most indifferent to her favors.

Or seems to be . . .

Or so it seems . . .

But Francis Bacon has never been indifferent to Fortune's favors. He is well equipped to feign indifference, to confirm this seeming indifference by permitting carelessness to settle into custom. Hoping that Fortune, if not deceived, will at least be pleased by this self-sacrifice.

He has made of Fortune a god, an idol. False gods or true will not be mocked. Upon those grounds alone, he dreads what Fortune has in store for him. All the more so because, being of sound mind, he is not a true believer. He knows Fortune is a false god. Knows Fortune is a crude similitude, something wrought by men to represent in their own image something else they fear to name or think upon.

Which is Providence.

He turns to Fortune, then, fearing Providence more, thus doubling his fears.

Meanwhile it is a simple story of this world, an *exemplum* of the justice of this world. His new wealth is without meaning because the habit of extravagance has increased.

Blessed with more than he ever hoped for, he finds it is not enough. Will never be enough. All the wealth of the world would only serve to make him spend more than the world's value.

Therefore everything has changed. And nothing has changed.

Small wonder if his wines have the savor of wormwood and all his meats still taste like boiled beans.

When care or prudence might serve to defend him, he must be most careless. As careless as saints who live by faith alone.

He, too, must live by faith. But it is a faith of this world, faith in the King he serves and in those who serve him.

There is no faith left for himself.

Grin, Robert Cecil, at that. For Cecil of all men could tell him how in the courts of this world, faith and trust are to be most secretly hoarded.

Bacon is, then, as spendthrift in things spiritual as temporal.

Because faith is blind, he must be blind to the King. Blind to the truth that Bacon's faith, though rendered in touching innocence, at best is meaningless, at worst is imitation; for it touches the conscience of the King. The King is not free to accept the gift of blind faith. The King needs neither faith nor love from his politic servants.

The King demands pure service. If service is rendered by someone faithful, loyal, and loving, good and well enough. But the King must preserve his freedom. To reward or punish strictly according to the service rendered. And, at the last, must keep the power to bless or damn without regard either to faith or good works. The King must preserve this power to preserve himself. If and when he is threatened, he must always have another, like the taster at his banquets, to take the poison for him.

Bacon, in all his eminence, is singularly appropriate for this service. An entirely satisfactory victim, should any victim be needed. But because his precious felicity depends, for him, upon his faith in the King, he cannot believe this.

Francis Bacon is a restless man, a light sleeper. Not as Ralegh is, by design and purpose. Bacon sleeps lightly because he cannot sleep deep and well. Because his deep sleeps are troubled by bad dreams. Awake or asleep, he is vulnerable.

It does not take an oracle to see the probability of Bacon's fall. For Edward Coke, though old, is alive and well; and in disgrace, with little to lose, and grows more formidable than before. Bacon cannot see clear what any clever courtier can, that, besides all other reasons, the King, by placing Coke upon the Commission to deal with Ralegh, is keeping Coke near at hand, a trump card in his hand. And more—a twinge of royal conscience?—he has made this manifest to Francis Bacon, has given him all warning he will ever receive.

Bacon's other folly, of placing trust in those who serve only for their own gain, this would not take a Robert Cecil to teach. They will serve him well only so long as it serves them. When weather turns bad, they will vanish like birds in winter. And they are not to be blamed for this. From stable groom to the high steward, they are all men and free-born Englishmen. Service can be readily purchased, but a man's love is not for sale.

Bacon knows this too, but he cannot believe it.

To ask for their love is to be more than a fool. It is to insult the deepest essence of the man. Not even kings can afford such arrogance.

To be given what seems to be love and to accept it, is to be deceived. It is to be surrounded by false and dissembling servants who are no servants at all.

Bacon must know this, but he cannot believe it. In desperate hope, he can only increase his offerings; and his extravagances correspondingly increase the duplicity of all who serve him.

There is a story which has lately made the rounds. It has much sad truth in its kernel, more than gossips can know.

It is told how some distinguished visitor was waiting upon Bacon. He sat in a chamber and waited his turn. After a while a servant entered, ignoring him, and crossed the room and opened a chest without bolt or lock on it. The chest was cram-full of money. The servant scooped up a handful of coins, filled his purse, and departed.

After a while there came another and another, and the last of these was so indifferent and careless that he left the lid of the chest open.

When the gentleman finally met with Bacon, he told him what he had seen.

Bacon shrugged. "I know, I know," he said.

"God's wounds!" the gentleman exclaimed. "Why do you not put a stop to such a practice?"

"Because . . ." replied Francis Bacon, Lord Verulam, Lord Chancellor of England. "Because I cannot help myself."

Part Five

Marke well deare boy whilest theise assemble not,
Green springs the tree, hempe growes, the wagg is wilde,
But when they meet, it makes the timber rott,
It fretts the halter, and it choakes the childe.
  Then bless thee, and beware, and let vs praye,
  Wee part not with the at this meeting day.

—*Sir Walter ravleigh to his sonne*

When darkness has fallen, Bess will come. And they will have supper together. His son will not come with her. The boy must not be too much tested until the affair is settled one way or the other.

Carew is much on his mind. Poor son of old age, he has never really known his father or a father's love. Not for him as for Wat, wild Wat, upon whom all love and hope had been laid—thus placed in hazard.

Wat was almost the same age as Carew is now when, in 1603, Ralegh said farewell to all joys and sorrows. Wat, however, was even then half raised to be his father's heir. He had stood by his father's side, imitating his pose, for a portrait. Until Ralegh's fall, Wat had known his father only as one of those to whom many doffed hats or made suits and for whom all doors opened. Wat knew this as his birthright.

His father's fall was inexplicable, a riddle to his unformed mind. Then, equally without rhyme or reason, Ralegh's life was spared. And even in disgrace, in prison, some brightness and power remained. Enough remaining so that the boy, though he found certain doors—including ones which had been his own, Durham House, Sherbourne—closed, felt no harsh pinch of need. He had been prepared to be fatherless and poor. And then with less cause than the flipping of a coin, he found himself neither. In truth found he was, ironically, despite the closing of those certain doors, more specially chosen, blessed as it were, by a father's love and, indeed, by blood kin on both sides, by his father's friends and even some of his father's enemies.

All of which, while pleasing and surprisng, seemed ridiculous.

For how could Wat know, even dimly surmise, that with his life, his father had also regained one hope—his son? That, snatching at the world again, Ralegh vowed to himself that, live in the Tower or die there, he would see Wat given all love, care, and education befitting the son and heir of a man who had stood once near the bright center of this kingdom. That in that ashen hope, though sworn to in sorrow and love, were the unquenchable embers of his father's ambitions.

No, it seemed all a strange game to young Wat, pointless and foolish, save that he never learned, until perhaps the last moment of his life, that he could, too, lose it.

He could not know why those who had not wished the father good, next sought the son's favor and good will. Unable yet to grasp the amenities of the struggle for power and honor. His father might curse Cecil for duplicities, and, indeed, it was that little man who, for want of a single word in a legal document, took from Wat, even before he held it, the estate of Sherbourne. But that same hunchback offered Wat many kindnesses. Wat had grown up close as a cousin to Cecil's son. He could not accept any of this with heavy solemnity. He was banned from a Court he had never attended, but he soon made a friendship with young Prince Henry. He lacked nothing much.

And because he was the son of a man now legally dead, beyond help or harm, he found himself free, outside conventions of expectation. His privileges were so vague as to be almost without limit.

Given the best education that England could offer. Given a Continental tour, in company with Ben Jonson. Raised as a proper courtier's son. Raised to lead and to command, when and if Ralegh's fortunes turned.

Given all his father's care and cunning could devise. Given the love of an indulgent mother. Who spoiled by cherishing him too much.

But none of this, none of it mattered. Wat was formed not by tutors and old books, not by any words of wisdom. Nor by sports and exercise at games—though he grew strong and was expert with weapons and a masterful horseman. Nor by the amenities of fashion, though like his father, he wore only the finest and best-fitting clothes. Nor by mathematics, though he could plot a course at sea by the sun and the Pole Star before he ever stepped aboard a ship. Nor by music, though his fingers, though not so graceful as his father's, could pluck and strum clean chords, clear notes from lute and cithern and a family of the viols, and he could raise a deep voice to sing a part at sight.

Not trivium or quadrivium, not tags of the ancients or mysteries of sciences shaped Wat Ralegh. Within the roaring boy was always the child who had learned once and for all that this world—time, mutability, fortune, honor, or disgrace— is nothing more than a jest, an aside by a clown who has captured the laughter of spectators at an otherwise flawed and yawn-provoking play.

From that belief Wat could have gone on in any number

of directions. He might have turned his heart toward religion. Let all who knew Wat laugh out loud, but still he might have grown into a grave divine. But since he had health and strength and growing good fortune, he did not grow out of childhood. He was the child of this world, no other. And yet because the world was ridiculous (a boy who had yet to be truly wounded was thinking this), a theater of knaves and fools, what cared he?

So he became a kind of careless martyr to this world.

Ralegh did not know this, deceived, seeing the boy through some charlatan's illusive spectacles. The charlatan was himself and his revived, undying hopes.

Well, perhaps that should be an epitaph for every father since Adam.

Yet he sensed that though Wat moved in and through this world like a proud horseman in a crowd of walkers, he did not know the world. Wat was, in truth, unworldly. Thus Ralegh's manuscript of "Instructions to his son," a manuscript wide copied and passed about. Coldly reasonable, not in extolling the wisdom of old verities, but as a chart to guide him. News of how it is possible to endure and thrive, not by impulse, but by design. Not by fortune, but through freedom. Not by chance, but by choice.

A distillation, a cordial of his own experience in the world. An old world, sick to death, for which there is no good medicine, however honeyed and spiced, that does not have a bitter taste.

Medicine it was, though, to help an unworldly worldling. Advice for the building up of his estate. His estate most of all. And in so doing to marry out of sane worldly wisdom and not out of fantasy and desire. To seek and keep good friends, ones who could help but never harm him. To shun the flattery of others and self-praise, which is flattery of self. *For flattery is the beast that biteth smiling.* To keep a close mouth and bite his tongue rather than reveal himself. To shun the weakness of poverty, and to seek riches not for their own value, but for the freedom wealth can buy. How to treat servants. How to avoid excess in fashion. To be careful of drunkenness; this specially for Wat, who possessed a mighty thirst. And only at the end, in brief sentences, Ralegh reminded him to serve God in faith and obedience.

Oh, there were those who laughed, remarking that therein lay all the vaunted wisdom of Walter Ralegh. Never mind the formal glitter of the poems. Nor the solemn, sonorous dignity of his *History of the World.* Nor the practical rhetoric of one document or the other. No, they said, see how he advises his son to live, and you shall know him plain.

And perhaps their posterity will come to the same self-pleasing conclusion from the manuscript—if any copy survive the worm.

No matter. He had not sought the opinion of other men. Let them think as they please. It was for Wat he wrote his advice. And the paradox was that it was wasted on Wat. Who never knew the world or believed in it until he tasted the living truth of death at San Thomé. And then, lacking both wisdom and experience, he could only have been . . . hugely surprised. Confirmed in his own poor wisdom. In death a witness to it.

Son teaching the father by dying. And unhinging the father, already half mad from fever. He was, until the fever left him, almost a disciple of the son. Tempted to take his own life. To let go of his suffering body and die. Not so much withstood temptation as outlived it. His flesh would not let him die.

[513]

And in the end, from Newfoundland, with what was left of his men, sailed home in the high cold bracing winds of northern seas, steady on course, to keep all appointments.

Which gesture Wat had not lived long enough to understand. Wat would have been baffled, though he would have tilted his head back and laughed at the bravado of it.

Ralegh invested his hopes in Wat and failed. Knows how he had been doomed to fail even though Wat had not fallen and should live long.

And all the while his sole claim to any posterity was Carew, the child of the Tower, still only a child. A child he hardly knows at all.

So much for the wisdom of fathers . . .

And Ralegh turns from the rain-beaded windows and a shattered view of Old Palace Yard, back to chamber and fire. Calls to a servant and moves to sit himself at a table. Where, according to his wishes there are paper, ink, sand, and feathered quills. And a penknife to sharpen the quills to the point that most pleases him. A mere toy, a lady's penknife of silver. Yet sharp enough to hold a keen edge.

Sharp enough to slash a wrist or cut a man's throat from ear to ear.

He sharpens quills to write, taking his time. His gown, shiny silk and with silver threads, hangs loose from bent shoulders. He puts aside penknife and quill to accept with a nod a cup of wine the servant places beside him. To sip, for the warmth of it. The servant has now lit fresh candles for him. Nearby a fire glows to fat embers. Soon the servant will heave another log and set it to growling and smoking.

He sips wine, liquid firelight tilting and reflecting itself in the cup, and wonders what he can say to his young son.

[514]

Long before, waiting his first appointment with an executioner, he wrote a rash of last letters and verses. Had written farewell to his wife. Through the ironies of time and chance, the letters were dispatched fifteen years too early. Nothing more to be written to Bess now.

No, he can talk to her this evening when she comes.

But to Carew, he must make an accounting. Must leave some words, somehow framed so as to be sustaining.

Any father would be tempted to be well remembered and loved by an only son, even though that memory and love should cost the son crippling pain. Any father would be tempted to lay up at least that much claim to immortality. Dying, to leave a ghostly memory, emblem of himself to haunt the living. And how many fathers since Adam must have done so? Have dreamed to triumph over death and time in that literal fashion.

He does not wish that to be his own folly. He has written again and again of the folly of men who seize the last occasion for immortality. And he has derided them for it. Not wishing to deform truth to leave behind false memory.

Alexander the Great, of whom he wrote in his *History,* had done that at the outer edge of his conquests, his farmost camp on the banks of the Indus. There, before withdrawing, he ordered artificers to build huts and furniture and implements and even arms and armor hugely beyond any human size. To leave a camp which, to others, would seem a habitation for giants.

A folly which Ralegh had ridiculed for its simplicity, but also as a grotesque emblem of the folly of all aspiring men.

He hopes his son will never imagine he was sired by a giant.

My son, it is the prerogative of the old to inflict upon the
young a tedious celebration of the past, spent seasons, festivals,
and holidays of lost time. And as the world goes, it falls the
duty of the young to hear them out or to seem to; and remains the privilege of the old to practice that prerogative,
though the exercise serve only to prove the folly thereof. For
the old hold no patent, license, or monopoly on wisdom, which,
being mysterious and, all reasonable men will agree, invaluable,
is beyond the possession of one man or another, one station
or one age. For youth, though bound to ignorance out of
inexperience, is not likewise condemned to be foolish. For if
the purpose of the old be to transmit such wisdom as they
deem they have come into, together with a history of themselves and their experience, judiciously framed and arranged
in quiet afterthought, and thereby to preserve for the young
the best of what has been, and so to defend them from the
repetition of many errors and follies of the past, then their
intent is surely foolish. It is doomed and fated to fail. The
young will either listen, nodding assent and masking an honest
indifference, thus learning chiefly the fine art of duplicity at

a tender age, or they will listen truly, but without full understanding; as newly arrived in a foreign country, one listens out of courtesy, with much frowning concentration, to a strange tongue, the grammar of which is less than half mastered. Or, should a young man be fortunate enough to be free from need to listen to elders or heed the clucking of old ganders, whose chief claim to excellence is to have lived long enough to be unfit for anything except a stewing pot, he will stop his ears or walk away in insolence, leaving an old man to mutter at his own shadow by the fire.

Nonetheless, with knowledge of the vanity of my purpose and some foreknowledge of its likely failure, I would seek . . .

I would seek . . . what?

A clumsy exercise in an antiquated style, lacking the time for revision and polish; so that even if I were not to be credited for any substance whatsoever, I might win grudging approval for virtuosity.

Time will bleed away, an inward wound, until I truly bleed.

If time were blood and the executioner struck off my head now, there would be nothing left in me for a crowd to see. A drained and cured carcass only. For I have been gutted and cleaned and hung up by time like a pig in the cellar. They say—do they not?—that I have the pig's eye. Just so. . . . I can find no fault now with that. What is gossip may sometimes be poetry.

"Old men are twice children," the proverb says. Perhaps he will bear with me for the sake of my second childhood.

He rubs his eyes. Outside autumnal light is fading. Fog rising in the air. Fine-pointed rain in the fog. Pressing his eyes closed, he can still see that single, dark-boned tree with small birds, nameless, huddled there. Can open his eyes to see a sunset in the rude fireplace. Near, the candle flames are burnished blades with honed edges; the quills are sharp; the crested paper clean and crisp. In a silver cup Madeira wine flashes its own fire, color not of sunset in England or the Indies, but of sun upon a windy sea among the southern islands. There where the ships turn westward to follow trade winds. . . .

Fire, not fever now, warms the man's veins. His fingers, steady, grip the quill. In his heart, center of the fire, he wrestles tall shining angels of memory and desire.

His mind is still wedded to this world, but ever aware of the imperfections of that wife. He loves life most, doubting that he has ever loved the world as much, even when he has embraced it most eagerly.

Must make accounting to his son.

No wonder that old men, wishing to preserve a last shred of dignity while they live, shutter their senses, lock the gates and doors of heart and mind, and settle for silence.

Let the boy read the *History* when he's able to. Let him read the other works in prose and the verses as well. If he chooses to and can lay hands on them. Let him read them all, realizing they are addressed to strangers and not to him.

And Ralegh cannot succumb to the temptation to present himself naked, as in a statue. For he is too inconstant to write the true chronicle of himself. Yesterday his words would have been the work of a man captured by a fever, anxious and uncertain. Now he can write out of a sense of relief, of comfort with himself. And if, by the will of God or the King, he will live to return to this chamber for dinner tomorrow, he will be yet again another man. That's certain.

Yet this is no reason not to follow the heart's desire to render to his son a form of accounting, a part of his invisible estate.

It is much the same as the paradox put in the Preface to the *History*. Following an appraisal of the peculiar follies of ambitious worldly men, based upon authority, reason, and experience; demolishing the idols of riches and honor. Only to take a turn, as if to reconstruct something else from the jagged shards he had made:

"Shall we therefore value honor and riches at nothing, and neglect them as unnecessary and vain? Certainly not. For that the infinite wisdom of God, which hath distinguished his angels by degrees; which hath given greater and less light to heavenly bodies; which hath made differences between beasts and birds; created the eagle and the fly, the cedar and the shrub; and among stones given the fairest tincture to the ruby and the quickest light to the diamond; hath also ordained kings, dukes, or leaders of the people, magistrates, judges, and other degrees among men. And as honor is left to posterity for a mark and ensign of the virtue and understanding of their ancestors, so, seeing Siracides preferreth death before beggary; and that titles, without proportionable estates, fall under the miserable succor of other men's pity, I account it foolishness to condemn such a care; provided that worldly goods be well gotten and that we raise not our own buildings out of other men's ruins."

Just so. And provided the father shall not raise up the memory of himself out of the ruins of his son. Provided he check his expectations with an awareness of his pride and vanity. The impulse and desire, however ambitious, to leave something of himself for his son, ought not to be denied.

That, too, could be called foolishness.

The young man, ignorant as Adam, takes possession of the

[519]

world as it is given to him. Never dreaming or imagining any more than Adam could, anything lives before him. He may love or despise what he is given, but never knows what has been before; and, not knowing, cares even less. Therefore all change startles him equally.

For the new generation the former one was always old.

For each generation there is a naming day. All things of this world are discovered and are named anew.

It is only the old who know (with a yawn) the names will be the same.

What can be spoken of, written, shared, then, is neither experience nor wisdom. But only a kind of news. A sense of the recent times, the passing world which the young man has never known to be and will never know of unless he is told.

Not that he will believe it. For it will all be as vague as a half-forgotten dream. But to have dreamed it at all is something.

In telling what he can of the dream, the father can, by oblique courses, tacking against wind, eventually arrive at his original destination.

He must exercise his own stiffened and weary imagination. Remembering·always what it was like to have been young once.

And then perhaps he will be worthy to be believed, whether he is believed or not.

Ralegh crumples the paper he has written on into a loose ball and tosses it into the fire. Where it rests for a moment, riding like a white frail cockle boat, then opens like a summer rose, blooms bright, and dies into ashes.

To begin again . . .

My son, there was a gentleman in London who commissioned a picture maker to paint an extraordinary portrait of himself. Himself in large, seated at a writing desk with pen and paper—as I am now—while all about him, in miniature, as if the scenes were his thoughts and memories, were depicted the chronicles of his life, from the chamber where his mother holds him, an infant, in her arms, to a stately funeral procession moving toward a well-wrought tomb. We see him at the wars and in his travels. We see him feasting, at council table, seated with friends around a virginal, joining together, flute, viol, bass, and lute, to make music. . . .

He was a gentleman who served his country well in peace and war. And yet how we laughed at his vanity!

"He lies, he lies! I give him the lie!" Sir John Harrington said. "He professes to have shown everything, but he lies."

"What, then, is missing?"

"Look and see for yourself. I see everything depicted, eating, sleeping, dancing, reading, writing, dying. . . ."

"God's death, would you have the man show himself naked,

coupling his wife, or, more likely, a whore?" said the Earl of Southampton.

"There are limits to candor and confession," Harrington said, "though I suppose they shall have to be bended if you choose to follow his suit and have your own life painted."

Southampton flushed red-faced as a Dutch burgher. And Essex laughed and gave him a slap on the back that rattled his teeth.

"If you don't order the thing done, I shall do so myself. And I shall see it hangs in the gallery at Whitehall as fair warning to all chaste Court ladies."

"Harrington always smiles so nicely," Southampton grumbled. "Except for that smile, I would box his ears."

Essex said, "You will not box his ears, because you fear he'll pull out your curls and snip off your beard."

"What, then, is missing, Sir John?"

"Do you see a privy anywhere? You do not. Yet a man spends more time there, at the absolute mercy of his bowels, than he shall ever spend at feasting or at music. His groans and sighs, the trumpets and whispers of an infinite variety of farts, these are the music a man knows best."

"But who can paint a groan or a sigh?"

"Find me a man who can paint a fart," the Earl of Essex said, "and I'll give him a pension for life."

Oh, we laughed at the man's folly; for that is the way of the world with every man's reputation. The dead answer no challenges. But the laughter is not malice, not truly, for the dead are also beyond injury and insult.

Even as I smile now, recalling the painting, I understand his wish to preserve some of what he had been. And if I had time aplenty to spare to waste, I would be tempted to seek out that painter and order one much like it for myself.

The picture is not wholly true. It does, indeed, conceal and equivocate. But it tells no outright lies. And it leaves all inference and judgment to the beholder.

Still and all, it seems to me painting is more innocent of guile than words; less liable to end in misunderstanding. Yet likewise lacking the power of words to ring like chimes and bells and to echo long after.

I speak of the value of words, my son, because you are such a quiet child, keeping your secrets.

Your brother, Wat, had a tongue that flapped like a banner in a fair wind, and the voice of a herald at the gates. Words were sparrows in the eaves, larks in the sky, blackbirds in a bush, a falcon in the clouds.

Poor lad, he has God's plenty of silence now.

Try to remember your tall brother sometimes and remember to pray for him too.

I would not try to persuade you to turn against your natural humors and seek to be like him or like your father. But much as I often felt the need to caution Wat against giving his tongue too much license, so I caution you against too much silence. Words fail and falter often, but they are the best servants we have. Do not neglect them. Certainly do not ever fear them.

Old men are citizens of the kingdom of what has been, ambassadors from far places. They frame tales in a light of wonder like travelers home from India and Persia.

They are not to be completely believed, no matter how eloquent, or how marvelous their adventures may have been.

When I was a boy in Devon, I listened to the stories of the shipmen, believing half and loving all. And dreaming, without hope or promise, to sail wide seas and see the wonders of the world myself.

After my lessons, which I loved no more than any other boy, I turned to certain books and cut my mind's teeth on the adventures of the explorers of new worlds and especially the shining, fearful *conquistadors*—Cortez, Pizarro, and Balboa. . . .

Strange now to think the first heroes I had were Spaniards.

I believe the child who changes, grows, and vanishes into the man, does not die so long as the man lives. I think that after all accounting of experience, good reason, common sense, my rage against the Spaniard had within it the small voice of a child, disappointed, who saw these mortals as the degenerate heirs of heroes.

Some have said this last voyage of mine to Guiana was a child's play, an old man playing out a child's dream, to come upon a secret kingdom as Cortez came upon and conquered Mexico.

I deny that. But I affirm there is a measure of truth in it.

If I had never dreamed of Cortez as a child, I could never have gone so far and risked so much.

But I will not trouble you with apology for the things done or left undone. You will come to your own judgment and understanding in due time. Most of all I would hope to be judged as one who loved you. Leave the subtleties of guilt and innocence to time and to strangers.

I speak of my dreams as a child because I do not know your dreams or what may waken the drumbeats of your heart. What you love now you will love until you die, through many changes and disguises.

What you dream now will somehow, in surprising shapes and forms you cannot yet imagine, come to pass.

[524]

There was a world before you and will be after. And both are your inheritance.

All I can do with small time remaining is speak as an old man (which I am) of the world, as I recall it. So that you can make that part of your history too.

Judge for yourself in the fullness of time. I trust that my own surmises will not be restraints, but will free you to find your way. What we do not know is what we fear most. I pray that you can face the future with only fears which you can master. It may be some comfort to face the future without fearing the past.

There is talk now, much talk of the golden days of the late Queen. I imagine the young are weary of that and able to doubt it.

And no wonder, judging by the evidence at hand. Even a fool knows that we had wars and perils, times of much famine and sickness, disorder and anguish. And the same fool knows the present time, vexed as it may be, if not a feast, is likewise not a famine.

And we are still at peace as I write this.

And thus it may seem perverse for the old to cling to a memory of something that never was.

Think on this: when I look into a mirror glass, I see what my eyes see of myself, but I can never see what you see. I can think of you and what you see, remembering that you have never known me without gray in hair and beard, have always known me as a man with one stiff leg. You have no reason to imagine I was not born with the wounds and scars I received. To me the gray and the deepening lines of my face are late intrusions upon my property, impositions enforced against me. I see them, but cannot credit them wholly. And each wound is from a date and a time. Before I felt pain and fire and the cracking of my bone, I could run and dance as well as most men. And sometimes my stiffened leg can seem to remember its former liberty.

The truth of mirrors, then, is more than meets the eye.

Thinking of mirrors, I remember the late Queen. She, as a young and beautiful woman, whom I knew not, began our age and she lived to end it.

At the last there was melancholy in her secret heart. In common (I know now) with all who live to see the strange ends so many bright and fair things come to. There were hard times in this kingdom, reflecting, as it were, her inward sorrows. And she was required to be not herself, but much like a player, like any boy actor with a high voice. For she must wear a wig and cover her wrinkles with thick powders, flush her cheeks with rouge, brighten her lips with paint, not smile for fear of showing her last few blackened teeth; must perfume away the stink of aging, wear many jewels and stiff padded farthingale dresses to divert the eyes from frail flesh and bones.

I tell you this so you can know things you will never understand until you live to be old yourself. Body decays and fails and flesh disgusts. Yet there is no man so deformed or so ugly that he believes himself to be beyond love or admiration. Easy enough to regret what one has once been, to curse the young with shine on their flesh and green sap in their limbs, and to wish them a long life too, and the same bitter fruits at the end of it. Easy, as well, to huddle in shame and wish only to be dead.

Still in all, I think no man is so loathsome that, even in self-disgust, he cannot cleave to the belief that in some way, magical, as in some myth or child's tale of transformation, toad into prince, sow's ear into silk purse and the like, that in some way he is far more beautiful than he seems or knows. I venture there is a hidden truth veiled behind this illusion. We are said to be in the image of God—which we take to be the soul eternal and not the corrupted and corruptible flesh—and to be in the image of God, is, therefore, to be beautiful. And therefore the naked truth of us, veiled though it is, is beautiful, and would be most beautiful if we could behold it. This illusion, then, though it be denied by every wrinkle and deformity of flesh, may be the one true apprehension of our true condition. It is a sad wish that is more than a wish, because what it asks for has already been granted.

Yet even without thinking of mysteries beyond understanding, we see how those whom we love are transformed. And being loved by another, we find that we ourselves have been somehow remade and restored. Indeed, through the power of love, we feel the surety of this in the lover's eyes. Who is to say that this fantasy of human love is not true for as long as love lasts? If human love is a weak reflection, a wavering image of the light of infinite and eternal Love (to the extent that it is *caritas* and not the fevered fancy of our lust), then it may be that in the transformation of lovers, each one to the other, we are given a sign of hidden truth. No, more than that, are seeing true and clear for the first time. In love not deluded, but the scales of our eyes fallen away.

An old and arrogant man, no mood and little time left for argument, I say experience teaches that the same happens with all the creatures and all the things we love. If so, then love has within it the power to transform all of creation, though none of us will ever live to see it, until Judgment Day brings us to life again.

Return to the Queen. . . . Consider a woman with more than a woman's will and all of woman's vanity. Consider that she had a woman's harsh and ruthless eye for the truth of herself. For women, in proportion as they are sensitive, know their appearance as well as the finest players.

In the myth Narcissus is depicted as a man. And rightly so. Only a man can fall in love with his own appearance. For it is a stranger to him. The woman at her looking glass sees what she sees and knows it. And therefore, I do think, women justly demand a slight subterfuge of flattery from us.

The Queen ordered the mirrors in her palaces removed or covered up in the last years. And this has been taken by some as a sign of her vanity and self-deceit. They do not know, or do not remember, that her inmost bathing chambers, where she was alone with herself, as naked as God made her, were made of mirrors—walls, floors, and ceiling. To see herself. And not in delusion or vanity or self-love. But naked from all sides, as no one sees himself, so that she would know and never forget the truth of herself.

She knew her appearance as well as any who make a life's study of themselves. Yet she took that aging body, that withering face, and she painted and daubed and costumed and disguised it until, at a proper distance, she was the very picture of a queen. Not out of the wish to deceive, but out of the compelling necessity to be what she must be to rule, and never to permit the expectations and the pride of her subjects or this kingdom to be diminished.

She was willing, then, to sacrifice even her own integrity of person in the name of her office and for the good of the kingdom.

I think it was too much to ask her to look upon herself

in the disguises of public mirrors and to beam approval and signify thereby a total self-delusion.

We deprived her of her youth, forbade her from the natural life and joy of a woman, and in the end denied her even the privilege to be old.

That she loved us and this kingdom I find remarkable. Yet she did love us and even at the last when so few loved her.

And it is that love, my son, all these years afterwards, which has the power to transform our memory of her, of the age, and therefore of ourselves. So that we view those times gone with and through the transforming power of love. And none of us who were witnesses in flesh, will ever again have the power to give true testimony.

We are all false witnesses. Yet the sum of our witnessing may be true.

When I was a scholar at Middle Temple, there was a type of rascal who would haunt the porch and hall at Westminster when the courts were in session. For a sum he would bear false witness in any case. And the sign of his trade, for he might be dressed as a gentleman or vagabond, was bits of straw set in the soles of his shoes.

I pray that if I am a false witness of my time, the transforming power of love will turn that dirty straw to gold.

I have managed to leave you some kind of estate, by fair means and by sly. All this will be clear to you in due time. I shall not leave you penniless, to be a yoke to your mother and trouble to your kin. But, much as I regret it, I cannot leave you a tithe of the wealth which I have gambled, spent, and lost.

I restore my esteem of myself with the hope that I may leave you a compensatory sum of imaginary gold, the gold of my love.

But I proposed to tell you of the world I knew which was new to me once. As this world, though older than memory, is now new to you.

New it seemed to us, then, all things shining with newness. And that was the magic of the Queen. She dazzled and delighted with seeming changes, as if to deny all our past and to celebrate the future. To those who were young it seemed as though, touched by the wand of her scepter, the world was freshly gilded and beginning again.

A false garden it may have been, after all. But God knows it was rich and cunning.

My son, my child, it will be difficult for you to believe all the changes wrought in this land, and worked upon the face of the land in a lifetime.

Look to the land. Imagine a hawk's view of it, the rolling pattern of forests, fields, and fens. Even the pattern and cut of the land has much altered. For now in the South you shall see an irregular motley for grazing and growing, enclosed with briary quickset hedges. This where once and still into my time, there were the common fields, champion fields, in long narrow strips like fat German bacon. The rule is now severality.

And so your yeoman farmer, like your town merchant or tradesman, has come to be a kind of gentleman. Differing in distinction, at times, in that he has not yet earned arms or title and he has less debt outstanding than most gentlemen in England.

The very color and the costume of the land has changed. Rich gold of wheat and grain where once a dozen crops grew in strips and patches. Sheep graze on fields of close green where unlucky men plowed and tilled and lived poor off the land.

Foreigners who come here speak well of many things, but hardly ever find pleasure in our roads, our marshes and fens, and our forests.

Our roads and paths are still barbarous. A native-born Englishman can lose his way within his own country. To know the roads of England is to wish devoutly to avoid them. Perhaps one day this will change, too.

It did not suit the Queen or her government to encourage easy idle travel in those times. Nor to offer any more broad Roman roads to invading armies.

Our marshes and fens are many, but they were many times more then, before the Dutchmen came, fleeing from wars, and taught us how to drain them.

The forests dwindled much in my times. Picked for the masts and timbers of ships. Plucked for the building of houses, for floors and panels, stairways and railings, and for the joinery to fill our rooms. Cut and hewn to make bracing for mines and to make machines. Burned to make charcoal. Consumed to ash in thousands of fireplaces where once there were only open hearths in halls. Gone up in the smoke of thousands of chimneys where once a hole in the roof served all but royal blood.

When I was young old men were saying that our smokeless halls and houses were exacting the price of English vigor. As if our strength came into being like the flavor of Westphalian ham. I'll only grant them that cloudy smoke may have spared them the odor of each other and of the animals that shared their houses with them.

From the forests look to the trees which grace this land,

offering a wonder of blossom in springtime and pools of shade in summer and harvest. When I was a lad we had an army of English trees—lime tree and holly, buckthorn, maple and wild pear, hawthorn and dogwood, elder and ash, the great oaks, the Cornish elm, birch, beech, willow and poplar, and not to forget, most English of all in its twistings upon itself, the yew tree.

All these remain.

But where you look now, growing as if they had been here from the first week of Creation, you will see, for instance, chestnut, tulip, walnut, horse chestnut, sycamore, cedar, laburnum, locust, the medlar and the bay, all of them new in my own times, each brought from foreign climes and planted here. Making this place their own. Yet the green of their leaves and the shape of the shade they cast is new to an old man.

And when you go to some great house in the country, or perhaps, with good fortune, come to hold one of your own, you will find growing there oranges and lemons, capers and wild olives, trees and herbs from the farthest places of the earth.

I am pleased to see the mulberry trees which the King has planted, not far from where I write now, are prospering. I think, though, that he planted them to feed worms and make silk. I fear the King will go naked if he gambles on English silk.

Now come closer to the houses. Look to their gardens. Not the marvelous gardens of Theobalds or Gorhambury or, yes, Sherbourne. But consider the common English gardens—kitchen garden, herb garden, flower garden.

I pray neither famine nor misfortune shall cause you to want for good English meat, that you shall always be able to answer the growls of your stomach with native beef, bread, and beer.

But fancy them or not, you shall find growing common here such newfangled things as the asparagus and artichoke, carrots, beetroots, French peas and beans, cabbages and watercress.

You know our English fruits and berries, the delights of our apples, cherries, pears, and plums. But you know as well the taste of the melons—the sugar melon, musk melon, pear melon. All new in my time.

I myself have introduced some things into this country. One of these is the pineapple. Which our King so relishes he says it is a fruit fit for kings alone. I wish he could have seen the naked Indians with paint on their faces eating it. Or our seamen, who stuffed it like bread.

You will eat the meat of the potato and the new potato. The new potato is adequate when roasted with good rich marrow and well spiced and sugared. Boiled it is an abomination!

But before you enter a yeoman's house, glance at the flower garden. Which his wife keeps for her salads, medicines, perfumes, and cordials, sweetening and savor of many things, and, indeed, more and more with these years for the pure bright useless pleasure of them. And ever among those flowers she grows and tends will be the invaders who now make much glory in our English springtime: daffodil, crocus, hyacinth, French cowslip, saffron flower, for examples.

Nearby, her plantings of new herbs would make a whole book unto themselves.

And if he is firm in prosperity, yeoman landholder or city merchant or tradesman, you shall find he has his pleasure garden for the idle time after dinner or after supper on a summer evening. He will have sweet, various hedges there, bowers made from twined branches of fair trees—lime tree, willow, whitethorn, maple, elm. Graveled walks to wander. Flowers growing beside them and not as before on raised beds of board or tiles or bones. He will have lavender and sage put there, camomile and rosemary. And he will turf a path or alley, putting down wild thyme, mints, and burnet, which, stepped upon, tincture the air with scents.

Come closer to his house. Built in the fashion and the stuff of his county. In Devon he will have neither stone nor timber to do much, but he will smooth over his old wattle and daub hive with a lime plaster. His door will be well made and carved, inviting, not defending. He will have windows squared off and wide, not narrow and pointed as they once were. And where he once looked out dimly, if at all, through thick sheets of horn, close latticework, or oiled linen, living within a lantern, as it were, now he lets in sunlight by day through windows of glass and brightens the early night with his own lights; tallow or wax candles now, seldom stinking and stuttering rush ends dipped in raw fat.

Enter and see where once he had one high room for the family and animals together, he has made a ceiling and partitions, and there are many rooms. And he has put his animals out into barn and sheds. He has covered earthen floor with stones or board. If he has no woven matting, you will find he has strewn the floor with rushes and his wife has sprinkled these with rosemary, sage, and saffron.

Our late Queen favored the scent of meadowsweet in her chambers. To remind her truly of the country.

You will see his walls are well plastered, brightened with painted or stained cloths, patterns painted there, and some pithy posy from a book, as proud as any nobleman's motto.

He invites you to share his dinner. Where there was once a place to put up the trestle table and chests to sit upon, he

[534]

has a standing table well made of good ash, elm, oak, or walnut. Your host has a chair at the head of the table, and you sit on a joint stool which, if it lacks bags or cushions to comfort your bottom, will at least have cloth or leather covering.

Look at the table. He has a knife at your place where not long ago even the richest gentleman expected you to bring your own. His old treen platters are gone. You are served off of pewter or even plate. His wooden spoons, once so carefully carved on winter nights by the fire, sitting on a chest where now he has the fine wainscot bench, are gone too. He eats with pewter and silver. Wooden bowls and earthenware crocks have all but vanished. His ewer and basin are brass. His salt cellar, over which he bends his head to say grace, is likely to be silver. His wine bowl, also silver, sits on the buffet nearby, winking bright, together with some pieces of good plate, and perhaps some glasses too, surely cups for wine and beer and ale where once he had horns to drink from.

If your drink is beer, you will call it English. But it is new enough. I have no trouble remembering when there was only ale and (so fine in Devon!) cider to drink. If he has wine to offer, it will be muscadel or malvesey, claret, Canary, Greek, or Italian whites of many kinds, bastard, with sweets and spices, or plain.

Here we are joined together. For you and I both take it for indisputable truth that all fit wine comes from other countries. And so it is; for there is scarcely one good vineyard in this kingdom. Yet when I was a boy your age, I yawned, listening to old men praise the virtues of the wines the English monks made before King Henry turned them out.

Where the yeoman ate bean bread and oat bread or, in bad times, a bread of acorns, he serves you fresh baked rye or barley bread in little loaves. And for an occasion may serve white wheaten bread.

Where once he filled himself and his guests with windy English broad beans, marrow, and oats and the drippings, you will have beef and mutton and veal in plenty, with chicken or the wildfowl, such as quail or partridge or pheasant, and oysters in season, and carp, trout, and perch; sometimes a brace or so of wild hare which he has coursed with his own greyhounds, swift and silent. Sometimes the sweet flesh of small birds taken by his own falcon.

You will have a salad of greens and herbs and fruits and flowers. And to finish there will be a sugarloaf and some kissing comfits and suckets his wife has made.

After dinner you may retire to his garden. Or in cold and rain you may sing together or pick at a cithern. He may read a book for pleasure and instruction and likewise his wife.

This man's grandfather could neither read nor write. His father read painfully slow, aloud from his Scripture and *Common Prayer,* following a blunt and calloused finger word by word across the page. Now he keeps books in a chest. He can write a letter on paper and keep his own accounts. His wife can read to herself. Already their children are pleased to correct their errors and to astonish them with the tags of Latin they have learned at school.

Once, even in prosperous times, leather, russet, and kersey were his costume. And still you will find him too shrewd to follow too close the model of the Court and go out in all weathers in silks and satins. Yet he is not ashamed that he owns some fine clothes of the best stuffs. And these he will wear for feast days, holidays, and fairs.

Also his wife, though she seems modest enough in foil to

any city lady, still must have her starched collars, her ruffs and cuffs, her proud and useless apron of Flemish lace, scented gloves of kid or suede, and little velvet shoes. Except for the sparks and embers of jewels, she's as grand as any lady of the age before.

Both will have hats of velvet, fur, or of Dutchwork felt. His brogues with a hundred hobnails have been discarded for boots of leather and fit for riding as well as walking. And so you will see him sitting an amble or a hard trot as well as any *chevalier,* riding not our scruffy little swayback native English horses, but one of the foreign horses, now as native as our own—the small swift Barbary; the Neapolitan, gentle and courageous; the proud Spanish jennet; the strong and enduring Almaine, the spirited Frieslander; the Hungarian of most expert hard trot; and lately the racing Galloway nag in honor of our King. To find an old English great horse you must go to the tilting yard at Westminster, where they are kept, together with other quaint customs of our barbarous knights of long ago.

This yeoman and his wife take their dalliance, ease, and sleep in a chamber with a feather bed, their sheets sweetened with fresh herbs and their cedar linen chests bulging, kept fresh with sachets and sweet bags made from her herbs and flowers. And she paints her face and reddens her lips and perfumes her flesh like a lady. Their chamber is clean enough, the Jordan pot emptied daily in the jakes, deep and distant from the house, where there was once an open steaming dungheap close by. And the jakes is kept clean and emptied by a laystow man and not by the master.

His father had a pallet on the floor. And his grandfather

jostled pigs for a place in a pile of straw and used a smooth log to pillow his head.

His grandfather sweated and toiled the whole year around, bent and stooped and old even before his prime. In summer he watered the land with his sweat. In winter became a snotty nose, with fingers and toes made of frozen turnip. Though he and his servants labor hard and long, he has a full tithe or more of the year now for feasts and holidays, fairs, and church ales. In spring he can pause in his labor and sniff the sweet new air and look upon the season with pleasure.

This very idleness, the leisure to pause from labor and enjoy some pleasure, is altogether new, my son.

The yeoman can while away hours hunting or fowling or angling. He can hunt the cunning hare as well, indeed with more freedom and ease, as the King. He can raise bassets and beagles and have his pack of hounds. Though he may follow old country custom and go out fowling with net or lime or pitfall, you will not find him armed for the sport, as he was in my youth, with a stone bow or bird-bolt. He carries a caliver and uses it as well as a soldier.

To speak of weapons: In my youth he was a sword and a buckler man. Now he will practice with rapier and pick his own style, as it pleases him, from a book, if not a fencing master. He can be a perfect French, Italian, or Spanish swordsman. And you, my son, if you desire to learn the old art of sword and buckler or the broadsword, must seek out a master in London and pay him well to teach you.

According to our law this yeoman keeps bows and arrows and must go to the butts and try his skill with the others. But this is a sport now, which, still in my youth, was called a weapon of war. He will obey the law, more or less, but only for pleasure and exercise and perhaps to set example for younger men who might otherwise find more solace in tavern ale, in dice and cards.

You will find some pairs of cards in his house, and he and his wife play with them, not primero perhaps, which requires the cultivated leisure of a Court, but surely triumph, gleek, mann and ruff and suchlike games. They may not play chess, but will be fierce at backgammon. Who, a little time ago, knew no such games and could not tell the jack of hearts from the king of diamonds.

They all play at bowls and quoits, nine holes, and shoveboard with their Edward shillings.

On holidays he will watch the young at their rowdy games of cudgel play, their wrestling and running and the riding of the quintain, where many a rustic will find his skull clouted and himself knocked arse over heels out of his thin saddle.

He can watch or join in the country dancing—the round, the hay, the trenchmore. Can clap his hands and shuffle his feet to the hornpipes and drums of Solomon's jig. Will return from fair with toys and trinkets for his little children. Toys which might once have pleased a prince and still amaze and delight the father, whose greatest childhood prize was a spinning top.

And when this yeoman dies, he will be placed in a wooden box, all draped in black, and buried with ceremony. Less than an age ago, his naked body was wrapped in a cloth and heaved like a side of bad meat into a hole while the parish priest muttered prayers.

All this, my son, has come to be in a lifetime. And it would amaze me no less if I had never left Devon and the house at Hayes Barton.

But many fair things are full false. And I would not, with praise for the changes, seek to disguise the scabs of failure. But I do not wish to indulge myself in thoughtless raillery either.

To be sure, the old have always railed against all things new. And you would find me guilty of that habit, too, I venture, if it were my fortune to live long and to see you grow into manhood. My consolation against the loss of that joy will be that I can spare you the shame of an old man's cackling.

The old railed all my young time. And the young made faces, out of sight, when good sense forbade them to jeer back. Saving jests and stones to hurl at strangers.

The old believing, not without some reason to be sure, that too much comfort is a sort of disease. That too much ease and safety can soften a man's soul just as they weaken the strength of his limbs. I have seen some men whom comfort, idleness, and sloth hastened to corruption of both spirit and flesh.

But I find small virtue in suffering. To bear it like a man, when there is no other choice, has some virtue. Suffering and pain you will know while you live. But to call these things the fountain of virtue is folly.

I never knew a soldier worth his pay who would march if he could ride a horse or find place on a baggage wagon.

I never knew a mariner worth stale beer who did not prefer calm anchorage in a safe harbor to the pitch and roll of a running sea.

Desire for ease only is not so much effeminate in a man as it is a lunatic folly.

I have felt too much pain and have known enough common

misery to believe there is any virtue in going forth in search of more suffering than it is our lot to endure. . . .

In my springtime the world was all on fire, burning with change. No spot of it untouched. All singed, crisped, scarred by flames.

And not all changes were for the good of all. As the plowman makes wounds in the earth with his plow, behind his pair of straining oxen, so with change overturning, even for the sake of new planting, there comes injury and suffering.

Men rendered masterless, jobless, even as others found themselves growing fat with prosperity. The number always growing, it seemed, of the dispossessed, the lost, the hopeless poor. And not only the old who had aged together with their crafts and ways, but the young and able as well. Their lives wasted. The wine of youth turned to vinegar before they had tasted it.

What can be said in answer? Especially by those at whose gates these beggars and paupers, swallowing their pride to appease the wolves of hunger, flocked like shabby fowl, crowded like packs of mangy curs to wait for crumbs and leavings? Paupers and beggars and, with them, mingling like goats in a flock of dirty sheep, true rogues and rascals, confirmed vagabonds. Who prey upon them and each other, living or dead.

God knows these ragged crows and scroyles are hard to love. God alone can love them all.

Our Lord Jesus Christ once told a rich man, who came to ask him, that he must give all of his substance to the poor, becoming most poor himself, if he wished to do some work in his lifetime in order to attain eternal life. And nothing less is commanded by the New Law.

[541]

But I do believe our Lord and Savior, being the one and only perfect Man, possessed also the perfection of human wit. Knowing full well it is far easier for a fisherman to leave his nets than for a rich man to leave his invisible, subtle nets of need.

Measured against the law all have failed, differing only in degree. None can be blameless.

Yet our work is in this world, no matter how the heart may long for home. And here and now we can offer only the inconsequential mitigation and extenuation (meaning less than nothing against the law) that we have not with malice and intent prospered upon the misery of others.

By which I would claim, and nothing more than that, that by a general rule we did much more than we might have done. More by far than ever in earlier times. More indeed than we might have wished to or intended, had not the Queen herself prodded us toward the custom of charity.

By her example, then, and to seek her favor, men dispensed with some of their largesse, if only in extravagant gestures to satisfy their self-importance.

I make no brief, can argue no case for the sufferings of my times or these times when the poor suffer still. When you look about you, you see suffering and misery aplenty. You will meet your share of beggars and rogues. But, even as you credit the reports of your senses, do not forget to temper that news with the judgment of your imagination.

Consider this, my son: That this imaginary English country yeoman, like his fellows of towns and cities, has in the time of one reign, come to live as well and better than many who lorded it over his grandfather.

Let him now learn to look to his conscience and see to the

needs of others, never forgetting that it was but a short time ago, as time of this world can be measured, when he would have been called most fortunate to keep himself clothed and fed from one day to the next.

There is another accusation against us. It is said that we spent our wealth and blood in wars, that it required the new King to make peace. Of the second proposition, time to come will tell the story and judge the King's wisdom. Of the first part, I cannot deny it. I would be the hypocrite to do so, having spent time in the wars myself and having counseled war more often than peace.

I would remind you that while all of Europe raged and bled, Christians butchering Christians in the name of Christ, England declared itself for Christian peace at home. We were never once free of the overbrimming of that strife, it is true. And Englishmen, Catholic and Puritan alike, died here on account of faith. But still, somehow, we rode out that storm secure and dry while others drowned in their own blood.

One reason was that there were men, and myself among them, who went and fought the wars. Peace at home was purchased by blood abroad.

Many a good man never returned. And many returned with their wounds. And you shall see these to this day, scarred, maimed, half-crazed, in every town and village.

When you see this, you will justly wonder how rulers could be so coldly cruel as to send men out to die or, worse, to live on like crippled dogs. You will judge, but try not to judge too harshly.

The rulers, Queen, Council, lords and captains, all who led, suffered too. The Queen was in no way dissembling when she spoke to her last Parliament, saying: "To be a King and wear a crown is a thing more glorious to them that see it than it is pleasant to them that bear it."

To rule well is to be wholly single-minded.

I have always envied the man who found one single role and played it, clung and grew to it like a barnacle on a ship.

Princes are given the greatest possibility to become the office they are invested with. But all who hold office and title, at some expense of liberty, gain another sort of liberty—to be what they seem. Simplified, they have occasion to do well or ill and to be judged by their actions. Purified, they have occasions to be happy.

I might call Lord Burghley such a one, though I cannot know if he was ever happy. There is small happiness in the management of great affairs, though there may be pleasure in the craft of it, joy in enterprises which can be judged successful.

Perhaps the purity I think of resides outside of all these affairs. Follows a mathematic law whereby as the worldly weight of the vocation diminishes, the possibility for happiness increases.

Who knows?

I know I have envied the plowman, the pikeman, the turn-spit servant, envied their simplicity. But not wished that life for myself.

I have envied craftsmen the joy of their skills—jeweler, gunsmith, woodworker, weaver, painter, sculptor, builder, miner, boatswain, charcoal burner, secretary, scribblers of stage plays, ballads and broadsides and fictions, tailor, fisherman, forester, gardner, wheelwright and cartwright and so forth and so on. Each with a craft worthy of a lifetime's labor. And there are always some in these crafts who earn a share of the world's rewards.

But though I could admire their skill, and envy the virtue of all work well done, I was too impatient with myself and the world ever to imagine myself in the blue coat and flat cap of a prentice.

I confess to some envy of the squire and his country life, tuned to the time and seasons of the English year.

But even when that was possible, when your mother and I were settled, for good and all it seemed, at Sherbourne, I was too restless in spirit to keep still. I admired the pleasures of peace, but in truth I was not made for them. Peace was always tedious to me.

I think in other circumstances I might have been a scholar. If you go to Oxford, which by affection I prefer to Cambridge, you will see that for the scholars, if not for the restless young, there can be a wedding of tranquillity with adventure. For adventures of the mind are sometimes wider, farther, more lonely, and dangerous than all of Drake's voyages.

But most scholars prefer comfort to the risk of voyaging. Most seem content to gloss and emend, to write the commentary and chronicle of dead men's adventures, and to look askance at the living.

Though I have had the courage to stand and fight in a skirmish and to sail across a sea, I think I could not have learned the courage to contend with fierce ideas or against the powers of ancient authority.

I felt then, too (and feel now), that so much of our learning was wasted, altogether inexpedient. Even what they called the new learning was dusty to me, divorced from the world beyond the walls of Oxford.

It was a scheme of Sir Humphrey Gilbert and myself, once,

to found a truly new kind of college in London, rebelliously devoted to practical affairs.

Some of this has changed in my lifetime, but not so that you will notice it.

I grant the universities a purpose I could not then concede. They are the preservers of other men's fruits and flowers. This first of all. They change little as the world changes, and they move to a slower time.

I lacked the courage and the patience to be a scholar, though I loved books and learning as much as many.

Most of all I admired and envied the men of law from the Inns of Court. For there the best of the contemplative life of a scholar could be joined to action. And of all the great judges and lawyers of my time I hold Edward Coke most in admiration, if not esteem.

But when I came to Middle Temple, it seemed too late and to no purpose to study the law.

I could never have imagined, in wildest dream, I should one day have to contend with Coke.

My son, I had no true craft, no honest vocation.

Who lacks a true vocation is left to play the jack of all suits.

I have possessed much wealth and lost much. And with wealth it has been my pleasure and privilege to hold, if not to keep, many beautiful things. Yet, except for pleasures I may have deprived others, I cannot mourn the loss. It was given to me. Time has reclaimed most of it. I owned many things, but I was never owned by them.

For wealth is neither a degree nor a condition. It is a sense of plenty which can be found, in measure, between extremes. The beggar, who finds a purse of coins when he had none, is a wealthy man.

Health is much the same, though more precious by far.

An old man calls good health that day when his tribe of pains afflicts him least.

But all this, a compound of tendentious worldly wisdom and the habit of aphorism, cannot tell you of the delight of being alive and close to the center of those times.

Out of the mud and ashes and excrement of war, I walked, all unwitting, into a chamber where the walls and ceilings burned with beauty. Where the ripe-pear-colored bodies of gods and heroes (from the Greeks and Romans, the Hebrews, from ancient and imaginary England) floated weightless and timeless as if in adoration. Kings and noblemen stared down, forever brilliant in oil on cloth and wood; where each and every hanging, carpet, polished piece of joinery was at once a celebration of itself and the virtuosity of its maker; where gentlemen and ladies seemed flowers, angels clad in flowers, jewels for dew, as they moved in leisurely service of the Queen; who was moon and sun, source and goal of all brightness; where every object no matter what its purpose, no matter if it had no purpose save pleasure, was so wrought and shining, so ingenious, it seemed that nothing there could be real, that all was a dream.

I woke from a nightmare into a new dream. When I looked into mirrors I saw the sad face of a stranger I need not believe in any more. He was not I, and I rejoiced to be free of him. To have died, as it were, and been raised again, bodiless, into a cunning paradise, fulfillment of lost dreams of conquest and the glow of gold dug from the tombs of ancient peoples. I was now a *conquistador* for certain. I walked light-footed, light-hearted, light-headed, fearless as Achilles. For had I not died, given up the ghost once and for all, to be so chosen? Now I was immortal.

And so it seemed until time reclaimed us from dreaming, each alone, not with a weapon of gold or silver gilt, but with a scythe, rust-ridden, but sharp as a surgeon's knife. . . .

I have been indifferent to my own wealth, for it has never seemed my own. I have been careless when I should have been prudent. But since it has been so, I can affirm I loved and love still all that multiplicity of things which were contrived for use, for brave decoration, for comfort and solace.

When I returned to London to live and make my way, fresh from my seasons of hell, I thought myself free-spirited, scornful of all the things of this world.

I remember I went once to the Hall of Barber-Surgeons just to see their anatomy there; a *skyleton* they called it, a man's bones hanging from a hook. I embraced and greeted this fellow as a brother. They thought I was drunk on sack.

I imagined then that, together with the last dregs of my innocence, I had lost a large part of my wits and most of my soul. But I had kept five senses. And though I scorned the world as the easiest thing to lose, the world laid claims upon me again through beauty.

I came to Court like a beggar on a feast day. Contemptuous, I was soon drunk on new wine. And I acknowledge that in that drunkenness, I might seem to have not only forgotten all I had painfully learned, but also to have lost sight of the truth that all things, and especially those most rare and beautiful, fall into ruin more swiftly than any man can believe.

So much, the greater part, of the wonders of those times, being perilously fragile, has already been lost, has crumbled away, becoming now no more than the memory of something which may never have been. New wonders rise up to replace them.

There lies the satiric touch to my chronicle, that I was permitted to live long enough to waken even from a dream of Paradise and find myself not immortal, but an old man.

Now your days are like a new-printed book where you may idly read, perusing first pages and words, slow and careful, unfamiliar with language and grammar. Yet always with the itch of impatience; for the book, a folio, is large and heavy in your hands and you fear you shall never have time to finish or learn much of its contents.

Yet should you, in good or ill fortune, live long, you will find an opposite condition to plague you. Old, and your days, each day a page, will flutter past, even in your hands will shuffle like cards, intermittent flashes, the pages blown away like fallen leaves. And like fallen leaves—once in spring as green as faith and signs of forever—your days and all the things you have seen and known and loved will not, mercifully, die until you die. They shall turn and flame yellow and red, splendid in their chiefest decay; then shrivel, wrinkle, turning brown as rust, fragile as ancient lace or parchment, and blow with each idle gust of wind, until you, rich or poor, in sickness or in health, will stand as empty-armed, empty-handed as a lone winter tree, naked to weather, joining your voice in the universal music of the trees, stiff groans and whispered unintelligible sighs.

All things, even the stones of palaces, fall to age and weariness and ruin.

Strip away all outward things and every man is the same raw creature, a beast as pale and dirty as a pulled root. A root full of hungers and fears, most hairy and hungry at the forked crotch where all separate lusts are joined together as in a wedding of rivers.

I knew this by heart, being old before my time. But I was unprepared for what I had not yet imagined.

Pleasure can undo a man as easy as suffering.

Even good Spenser's Red Cross Knight was powerfully dazzled by the Bower of Bliss.

Once drunk with admiration for the marvelous, we cannot be ruled by reason.

I have written of this in my *History:*

"But what examples have ever moved us? what persuasions reformed us or what threatenings made us afraid? We behold other men's tragedies played before us. We hear what is promised and threatened. But the world's bright glory has put out the eyes of our minds. And these betraying lights (with which we only see) do neither look up toward termless joys nor down toward endless sorrows until we neither know nor can look for anything else at the world's hands."

Yet I would not play a Puritan, then or now. It is true we must mourn our sinful, fallen estates. Without mourning we should be either too comfortable to leave this world when our time comes or too stiff-necked in suffering to yearn for a better condition.

Yet we are also required, it is our bounden duty, to rejoice at the good news of our salvation. To make a joyful noise in the name of our Redeemer. Isaiah has written that the oil of joy is for mourning. When God Himself restored all things double to Job, that signified the restoration of joy in the Creation.

God was not pleased by the sufferings of his servant Job, but rather by his faith.

[550]

We have been given beauty, and the power to make beautiful things from what we have been given, not that we should love these things alone, but that we should love them as the signs and figures of imperishable Beauty.

God has given us the sensual music of this world, not to enchant us, but that we may imagine the celestial harmony which is beyond the limits of mortal hearing.

He has given us dancing that we may feel in our flesh a likeness to the dancing of heaven.

A man is free to take these signs as he is able. He can imagine invisible harmony by the sensible concord of music. Or he can choose to be a deaf ass seated at a harp.

He can dance in joy. Or he can dance the oldest dance of flesh—which is death.

He can wear jewels for their cost and glitter. Or can wear them in full knowledge that they likewise betoken virtues: gold as the sign of wisdom; emerald for faith; sapphire shining for hope; and the red ruby is the color of charity; the topaz represents good works, etc., etc., etc.

To Puritans and Jesuits I say, God makes his residence neither in Rome nor Geneva, but in the hearts of all living men, and shines in all things of the world and in the world.

To condemn the beauty of the visible world is to deny the beauty of the invisible. Such denial is death.

I take it Job did not end his days in sackcloth and ashes to commemorate his sufferings.

As the old Fathers, reading the text of the world, did find some signification in each separate thing, each bird and beast, leaf and bole, the quiet stone and the crawling slug worms beneath it, until all of Creation, every grain of sand and blade of grass, became a living dictionary of the enigmatic language

[551]

of eternity, so it is, by simulation, with things made by art and craft of man. Which, however carved or melted and alloyed, beaten, wrought, twisted into cunning and curious shapes, gilded and painted and polished, retain their original character and essence.

Our imitations are celebrations of Creation. All that we have made or ever will make until time ends is proof that Creation is inimitable. Never before my lifetime in England had there been such music of all kinds to hear. Strangers called us the most musical people in the world. Whatever they meant by that, good or ill, I take it for a sign that our age was singing a new song.

Nevertheless there is a sense in which our music was enchanting and delusive; for none of us were angels.

This show, this masque for all to behold was (and remains in present memory) a digression, a diversion from the changeless naked truth of a man alone with himself and the eternal verities, the laws and theorems of change, which say to a man in possession of his mind that as in the life of a man, as in the seasons of a year, as in the times of a day, from dark to dark, so goes it with all things. With every tick of the clock the world grows older; and the finest chimes toll the death knell of another hour.

Right reason will teach even an ignorant savage that there can be nothing truly new under the sun.

Though strange men should descend upon us from unknown places as far as the moon, coming in flying ships and chariots, yet upon the breathless, wondrous moment of their arrival they should become our equals; and all of us would be subject to the same immutable laws of the world's mutability.

There is nothing new, undreamt of, under the sun. What

is under the sun comes under the power and majesty of Nature's laws, the sentence of which is continual change and decay.

If Providence has ordained for this kingdom or the common kingdom of the earth another thousand years to live, yet shall the earth be no better then, merely one thousand years older than it is now.

Meaning, my son, that the world cannot truly be renewed or restored. To stumble upon Eden now would be to discover that hallowed plot of ground is no younger than the yard beyond my windows here.

Yet, you will say, do we not have springtime every year, do we not see how the earth brings forth harvest in fall? Just so. Yet in all seasons, as in the life of man or the span of one day, all things grow and bloom in the sun and then go to darkness and cold. Our harvest here is winter, though the brave shows of springtime do always revive us.

A world continually revived, but never renewed or restored.

To the preachers who gloss the world, all our springtimes are similitudes and betoken, by their marvels, the marvel of eternal life, changeless and timeless. Revealing by these signs, as Holy Scripture does with words and signs, how out of death comes quickness, that if a man die, he shall live again.

And we can believe it to be so, holding firm to faith against the whispering witnesses of disbelief.

To the man of the world, pagan or skeptic, who will gloss the events of the world for the world's meaning, if he think deeply and truly, he will not look for any renewal or restoration. Which he can plainly see can never be. But rather he shall see that the law of Nature and the world is made with some wit and, as well, the craft of some juggler whose hands are quicker than eyes. It is the law of the world that we shall be revived, given occasion and courage to endure yet another turning of the seasons. Stoic, epicure, or cynic, he will find his solace in this truth, whether it be bitter or sweet to him.

The world deceives us, by this measure, though we remain free to deceive ourselves or no.

What then of this old age of beautiful things, the things made by and for man from the stuffs of the world? The pagan poets and philosophers, perceiving that the world can only grow older in time, divided all time into four ages, each of a baser metal than the last. And there is much truth in the figure. Yet it can never be truly apt while the world still lives. For if the history of man has its ages like the seasons, then, like the seasons, they must turn and return, be revived as well.

If my speculations have any truth, it lies in this: that we saw everything, *except these things,* while we floated on that time. I imagined a past too shabby to be remembered. And I believed I had succeeded in relinquishing all claims upon the future and was therefore free of it.

We lived in a false garden, forever new and changing. Of our own devising and the Queen's. A time of color and wonder in England from which even the poorest and most humble were not quite forbidden or spared. They crowded the gates and witnessed it too.

Time was as the tides of the river for us. We rode it, floated upon it like the Queen's barge. Her barge was a glorious thing with gleaming brightwork, awnings of cloth of gold, silken pillows and lacquered oars, and it was pulled steady and skilled by a crew in royal livery. Her barge moved down the river, fireworks fountaining explosions overhead, kettledrums beating, trumpets sounding proud and clear across the water. Her barge in moonlight, riding the Thames, that is a proper figure for our time.

And now that time seems to have been brief. And now that lost world seems idle and foolish. I could curse it for a false, illusory, chimerical, bewitched, enchanted lifetime. I could easily curse myself and my wasted days.

Except . . .

Except where I sit now I can still hear the faint lost echoes of the music, the broken consort that we danced to.

Except I can close my eyes and call up balmy spring evenings, light moon gilding roofs and spires and gables and towers in London and casting coins on the river. Moonlight on the river, where, smooth as in a dream, torchlit, brilliant, fireworks making new stars in heaven, the far pure call of trumpet and the kettle-drums like distant thunder, there (behold!) comes her barge—and ours. . . .

All memory is vain and foolish and all history compounded of many memories, therefore all the more vain and foolish. Yet a man could do worse than to remember such times.

True or false, it was a glorious springtime. True and false, the joys of springtime are sweet to know and sweeter to remember.

I am able to relinquish them now, but not without regrets. . . .

4

Quite suddenly Ralegh discovers that the afternoon is almost
spent. There is a faint intimation of distant sunset. The ship's
glass on his table has run out unnoticed.

He must hasten to finish a letter he has not yet really begun.
All he has managed so far is prologue. . . .

He feels a chill and sees that the fire has dwindled to dying
ashes.

Calls curtly to the servant. Who makes apology and goes
to fetch more wood.

Ralegh fears that chill. He fears that his fever and ague will
return. Will make him tremble on the scaffold. If he must
mount it in the morning . . .

Ague or not, he must not tremble, lest enemies take comfort
and friends should be ashamed.

Irritation, a single fear, and one deep concern. Concern how
to bring this letter to an end, properly and evenly, so that it
will work no harm on the child. Concern that no conclusion can
save it or spare the boy. Concern that, like any witness for

himself, even the guilty in confession of guilt, he has portrayed himself in a flattering false light.

Perhaps he should not leave the letter at all. Leave the boy to his mother's loving care and the love of God.

Perhaps he should give it to Bess and let her hold it until she judges him of an age to read it. Yet then she must read it herself. It could wound her more deeply than the child.

He cannot ask Bess not to read it.

Dear Bess, forever curious as puppy or magpie, she could never leave a sealed letter alone. If she promised, she would have to break that promise or have maggots on her brain. Better she should break the promise than try to exercise restraint and go half Bedlam. But if she breaks a last promise, dear Bess, good woman, she will make a giant of her guilt; then make a masque of her contrition. Spare her that. Spare me the thought of it.

Let the dying ask few things of the living. The dead can be remembered and sometimes honored, but are beyond credit and debts.

The servant returns and stoops to build up the flames with new logs. Ralegh rises, speaks to him more kindly and gains a smile in return. It does not matter, but he would hate to cause him sorrow for his failure to keep a fire alive on a man's last day.

Or is it that at all? Is it not, just as likely, more vanity? He does not wish this man, not quite a stranger, but not truly known, to remember him in any way but kindly. Perhaps . . .

If so, pure folly. The man has a life to live. If lucky, he will serve another, stoop and build up the fires of another master and forget this one as easily as he shrugs off his bad dreams.

Forget the first master as a dog does, and be happy, almost as happy as a dog can be. It would be better, less vain, more honorable to encourage the man to enjoy what may happen. Making it easy to forget this afternoon.

Thinking: Once when I was Captain of the Guard I saw a man who was about to be hanged curse his wife and children and even give his dog a stout kick in the ribs at the foot of the gallows. And the dog flew tail over head and howling into the crowd. And the crowd hated him for it and jeered and threw stones and rubbish. Even the hangman, who is too often the only charitable soul present at an execution, seemed to be angry. And the wretch refused to pray in public. When he was asked if he had any last words to say, he first cursed them one and all and damned their eyes. And then, as if to settle accounts, he said this: "My mother always said I would die with my boots on. So I now give her the lie!" Wherewith he pulled off his boots and threw them away into the crowd before he swung. . . .

The man was not only courageous, he was almost chivalric.
A dying man should leave no one saddled with his memory.

But having come this far, figuring his final vanities to be beyond cure while he lives, he must try to finish the letter. Holds his hands over the fire. Rubs them and flexes his long, stiffened fingers.

"There it is now, sir."

Looks to see his man standing at the window.

"What is that?"

"The sky is clearing, sir. And I can see the first star."

[558]

"May it give you good fortune," Ralegh says, "and bring us a clear day tomorrow."

"An' it please you, sir."

The servant leaves the chamber.

Now Ralegh stands at the window observing. True enough, the first jewel in the night sky, bright even though the day's light is not entirely gone. The last faint sign of sun is subtle, pure as the first flecks of ripeness on the skin of a peach.

What a color that would be to wear! A young and joyous color, the color of promises. He would wear it, if he could, and cut a fine figure on Lord Mayor's Day.

But on this day, seeing the sun dwindle, he must not imagine sunsets, but the sunrise of a morning world. For to think again of his son, to wrestle with words and to finish speaking to him, he must write literally by renewed firelight and candle-light, write from a sense of sunset, bearing always in mind, in imagination, the vision of remembered dawns.

He moves back to the table to sit and write again. To write swift and hurried. Time has claimed his consciousness. He is enthralled by dying light, by the chimes of Westminster's clock, and dim tones from the porter's lodge below—tones like birdsong (perhaps the porter's wife keeps caged birds in imitation of her husband)—unseen, as if in bush, copse, hedge, or tree, sudden and strange.

Time is a hard sound of hooves on a dry road in summer. . . .

He's young and poor again. Off from London to Oxford with a lifetime before him, and all the world's a dusty unread volume.

Hears a drumming sound, sudden and loud and near behind him. Leaps aside, staggers, falls into the ditch. Looks up (a head full of pinwheels) to see, huge and flecked with sweat and lather, leather flapping, glint and shine of bit and snaffle, spur and stirrup, eyes rolling, horse and armed rider, lean as a shadow or ghost; armed rider and galloping horse, dust-powdered, magnificent, huge against a turning sky (for he lies still in the ditch where he has fallen), as once the horse and the *conquistador* in shine of armor must have seemed, no, they *were,* in his dreams.

Sound on the hard-packed, sun-dried road as of distant drummers; a puff of dust like far cannon; a breathless leaping for life. And out of dust emerging, tall as trees or masts or towers, that lean apparitional rider and horse; here and then gone forever into the roil, an arras of dust.

He rising from the ditch, brushing his clothing, touching a stiffness which will soon be a bruise, and the dust still falling, fine as a cloud until he can see only dust, breathe only dust. The Sandman dusting his five senses to the sleep and dreams of a child.

"Even so is time . . ."

He bends and writes quickly, a hasty scribbling. Hoping perhaps this last will mean something to the boy. May salvage some portion of a father's good intentions.

Day is dying.

Bells call over London and Westminster to announce the triumph of time.

Feel of slick slender quill in my fingers. Color of ink and whiteness of paper. Color of fire and candles. From below muffled voices, odors of cooking in gatehouse kitchen. Footsteps, horse hooves, a slow walking below the window. Flicker of passing torchlight. Feel of rough wood at tips of fingers. Faint odor of last wine, dregs in silver cup. Light film of taste of wine

[560]

on my tongue. Scratch and rustle, light as hems of silk on stone floor—pen point on page . . .

I am awake and alert. I wait the arrival of my wife, your mother.

My son, be kind and loving to her. Once she wore cloak and mantle of beauty as fine as any you will ever live to see. She has suffered much and known many disappointments, but out of fires has come refined into that most precious thing—a true and good woman.

She shall have the cloak and mantle of all my mortal love and I pray God the memory of it shall be solace to her while she lives.

I'm awake and alert again.

I have lived long and never been more alive.

Day of St. Simon and St. Jude draws to close.

Music of this world dies and we dance on all, all, and each to echo and memory.

Old and mysterious saints, Simon and Jude.

Simon called the Zealous, so not to confuse him with Simon Peter.

Jude so-called to distinguish him, faceless as he is, and also by St. Mark once called Thaddaeus—a great-chested, stout-hearted man.

Martyred in far Persia, which I have never seen except on a map and by words of travelers.

I choose to believe it is there.

St. Jude who asked the question (which has no answer) of our Lord at the Last Supper: "Lord, how comes it Thou will only reveal Thyself to us and not to all the world?"

St. Simon patron invoked in desperate causes and cases.

St. Simon, bless me. Bless mother and son.

English proverb says drowning man will catch a twig. So be it. St. Simon, bless us three, father and mother and son.

In peril, as all who live must live in danger always, I turn to Scripture for the Festivals of all Martyred Saints.

To find first Job. Whose tribulations were great. But he bore them.

Job who out of suffering speaks to us here and now. Remember the words of God's good servant, Job. They may lift or shame you into that solace which is peace beyond understanding.

"Oh, that my words were now written, that they were printed in a book!" Job saith to us. "That they were graven with an iron pen and lead in the rock forever. For I know my redeemer liveth, and that he shall stand at the latter day upon the earth. Though after my skin shall worms destroy this body, yet in my flesh shall I see God. Whom I shall see for myself and mine eyes shall behold, and not any other, though all things shall be consumed within me."

Gospel lies in Luke in sixth chapter, where our Lord preaches beatitudes.

Terrible beauty and truth of.

Love that beauty, paradoxes of blessings and curses on the world.

Let us remember together.

"Judge not and you shall not be judged. Condemn not and ye shall not be condemned. Forgive and you shall be forgiven."

I shall pray for you later tonight, my son, and in the morning. When you read this later, I ask your prayers as well. Pray for me. Pray for your dead brothers, Wat and Damerei. Pray health and peace for your mother.

Pray for the dead and leave them to the Lord.

For the world, I leave you a small inheritance and less wisdom.

Do not think much on my own guilt or innocence or the justice of the world. Live and think only that justice is in the world. Believe that.

Small wisdom and that only in old words. Words no more than sweet comfits to lighten the taste of dust on the tongue.

Nothing stings like the serpent. No pain greater. Bear it.

If a bush should burn and the flames cry out, bow down.

If ever a stranger wrestle you, do not let go until you learn his name.

If after long voyages, tossing and fever, you find a new continent, plant your flags proudly. Stand tall. Send forth a dove.

Rarely the fruit you reach for shall return your love.

Written in love and for the sake of the fellowship that time has denied us, upon this holy feast day in the gatehouse of Westminster, year of our Lord 1618. . . .

Walter Ralegh, Knt.

Part Six

The thirsting Tantalus doth catch at streames that from him flee.
Why laughest thou? the name but changed, the tale is told of
thee.

RALEGH—*translation from Horace*

1

Bess Ralegh does not come to Westminster alone. Cramped in the coach with her are Thomas Hariot and a woman, a Throckmorton cousin named Mary, come to London not long ago from the village of Weston Underwood in Buckinghamshire. Mary is a tall and handsome young woman, as tall as Bess, and possesses everything she needs to win at the world's game except a proper dowry.

Ralegh expects Bess to be accompanied by one of her women, one of the older servants who could make her manners and then go below to sup with the coachman and the outsiders.

He has always valued some measure of privacy. Bess—perhaps more wise then he in her acceptance of the conditions of this world—has not. Ralegh long ago, youngest in the large family in the house at Hayes Barton, permitted himself the luxury of imagining being alone and without loneliness. As far from possibility as any dream, it came to be in the years of prison, but never for long or completely so. So that even as his longing was ironically satisfied, his hunger for the possibility increased.

Privacy. . . . Rare enough when every household is a village of itself, when all but the master of the house must share and wait turn for everything, from bed to Jordan pot. When the bones of the dead must have companions in corruption. Even in the honored vaults of kings and queens, bones must be pushed aside in heaps to make space for the new.

A man will live a lifetime and never be much alone except in his pains. Some privacy is luxury. Solitude is unobtainable at any price. The only true solitude is inward, where a man can cultivate his crop of secrets.

So, as much as he has been able, Ralegh has lived keeping odd and late hours to be in the company of a few chosen companions. And at each place he has owned he has created a smaller place there, where he could withdraw—the turret study at Durham House; the high chamber of the keep of Sherbourne Castle, and then the lodge at Sherbourne, built a quarter of a mile away from the castle, commodious enough but, by restrictions of space, reducing the number of those around him; the small perfect jewel of a house he planned and designed, but never could build, near Westminster; the time-and-again attempts to purchase and restore the house at Hayes Barton, so beautifully sited to catch light all through the day. . . .

Bess, knowing all this and knowing how the upper chamber at the gatehouse will seem crowded with one or two others there, chose to bring her young cousin, almost a stranger to him, with her. She will remain, cannot be properly sent below. Must sit down to share the late supper with them.

A stratagem typical of Bess, though she would deny there was any thought behind her choice, insisting upon her woman's prerogative to act on impulse and feeling without concern of consequences. A gesture so typical of Bess it proves that she can be true to herself even now, giving firm evidence that, come what will, she will endure.

Their lives together have been a series of farewells. If this must be the last, it will be awkward to be alone. She will have thought of that, sensing that to believe in each other and to be believed they will each have to pretend, playing an old familiar scene anew as actors do. To be like players is a merry game for young lovers arriving at first nakedness together. How fair blond Bess once shone by small candlelight! But he was not young then, not ever in the time he has known her. Knew even then that when a young woman will choose not youth, but a man who could almost be her father, either she's driven by strange need or fear, which Bess was not, or there is some calculation in her choice.

Grown older together, they have come to favor the dark. Out of love and respect, not vanity alone. And to open the ivory gates of imagination and to seek to recover, by fantasy, which is half the game of love, a reflection of the original shining of youth, some warmth from the almost forgotten fever of full desire.

Bess knows how he hates all clumsiness in himself. Believes that still to this time, in the portrait gallery of his mind, he sees himself as an overlarge, stumbling, shambling, clod-footed, heavy-handed, untutored, unfinished boy. Sees himself as she has never seen or imagined him.

And Bess will have weighed in balance his desire for some privacy against the heavier, unspoken urgency of keeping tight rein upon his feelings. Though it may annoy him to have the girl here, even disappointment will divert and distract him a little. Soon, Bess knows, he will become more lively, will call

[569]

up all the habits of enchantment to please the young woman. A brief diversion, to be sure, but it will ease him.

And perhaps, though she will not admit this even to herself, she has brought her cousin to represent herself, an ambassador of what she was once and what he has loved. Thinking that he will be able, once again, to play the courtier who once blinded her in love. And she, through her cousin, able to play her own part, to enjoy him as he was then.

In which case Mary, as much as any Aztec maiden, is a sacrificial victim.

Did not King David, grown old, ward off the stealthy coming of the cold in blood and bones with the bodies of young women? Not for lust alone, but for coverlet, blanket, and for the memory of being young.

Bess would be offended if he reminded her of David's wiles.

Nor will Bess have considered that there is more meaning to her gesture than she intends, that it is not only an act of loving kindness. She would deny, outraged, any suggestion that she must still remind him of her suffering long ago, the fortune which forbade her to enjoy the life at Court that she loved.

Since Bess will not have imagined such a thing, perhaps it is not true.

And for the sake of symmetry there is to be another player, his old friend, once his servant, Thomas Hariot. Who has served Ralegh and the Earl of Northumberland and the Earl of Derby, teaching them mathematics, astronomy, anatomy, chemistry, and the laws of plants and animals. It is he who led Walter Ralegh to the work and thoughts of such men as Galileo, Andreas Vesalius, Johann Kepler, Nicolaus Copernicus, Tycho Brahe, and Petrus Ramus. Hariot who went to Virginia for Ralegh and wrote of it in the book.

Magnificent in matters theoretical, Hariot does not disdain to turn knowledge to practical affairs. Assisted Ralegh in preparing charts, in navigation and the instruments for it, in smelting and assaying of ores and the making of chemical cordials, in gardening and the uses of herbs. He has been loyal and faithful. But more than all that, which also can be said of a good dog, he has shared much with Ralegh out of character and natural inclination. Is a proud man, too, outwardly indolent, outwardly indifferent to the praise or blame of fools and strangers. As Ralegh has avoided the beguilements of the active man, so Thomas Hariot has shunned the birdlime of reputation, which has caught the fantasy of many a scholar. Writing few things for the general. Content, it seems, in his correspondence with his peers abroad and with the friendship of a few men, in or out of favor. Content to know, glad to teach, and indifferent to reputation, true or false.

The two men complement each other in many ways, alike, yet each possessing something the other lacks. Of all his old friends and servants living now, Thomas is most likely to bring solace this evening.

2

Night has come and Ralegh is preparing himself, combing his hair and beard before a looking glass, propped on the open chest where he has rummaged to find a few jewels to brighten his appearance.

A shout at the gates. Creak of the gate slowly opening. Hooves and the rattle of a coach coming in. Hoarse challenge of guards at the door below.

Turning toward the window, Ralegh brushes against the open chest, and the looking glass falls and shatters into slivers on the floor.

His servant, startled by the noise, mumbles something, but Ralegh ignores him and the broken glass. Moves toward the window, knowing without seeing, the servant has now stooped to pick up the pieces.

In flickering lantern light the coach stands, rain like a fresh coat of gilding on it. The horses breathing foggy breath in the chill air. Shades drawn, and the coach without a sign or symbol on it. Two men on horseback as outriders, and these in plain clothing, wearing no livery.

One of the hooded guards stands at the door, offers his arm as Bess steps out.

Ralegh turns back to the room.

"Now then," he says. "See to the setting of the trestle table. And be quick."

The servant nods.

"I am sorry about the glass, sir."

"Oh, it is nothing."

"It is said that to break a looking glass will bring seven years of bad luck."

Footsteps now on the stairs coming up from below. Ralegh laughs.

"That is the best news of this day," he says. "If I live to enjoy the seven years, I shall be the most grateful man in England."

A rap on the door announces them. Two women and Thomas duck low under the sill (an ancient doorway made for ancestors who must have been small as half-grown children) and enter the chamber. The servant then assists them in removing their cloaks. And carries them away to dry by the fire in the kitchen.

Ralegh is pleased that though they have come cloaked, the clothing they wear is festive. Pleased, too, that he put on his pearl earring and some rings on his fingers, changing his old man's gown with a lightly comic, rakish touch of gold and the white of the perfect pearl.

Sees all in their faces and eyes: Bess determined to be courageous and cheerful, but most vulnerable.

Thomas, burdened with gifts of wine and tobacco, braving a faint smile, awkward and abstract in self-control.

Sees the sturdy, high-boned, roses-and-wheat-flour fairness of the girl's Throckmorton face, crowned with a sheen of golden hair, netted and lightly dusted, carefully simple, like a crown above eyes the blue of May skies, wide, large light-thrilled eyes too fine to be spoiled and reddened by weeping; and the puffy flower of her lips set in what she must imagine to be the expression of solemn gravity.

Assaulted by two ships (no help from Thomas here), he engages them at once, allowing neither respite nor occasion to join together.

"What news from the Bishop?" he asks Bess.

Her lips tremble slightly.

"Oh, Wat, I wish you had not asked me that. I have had word from the Bishop. He knows nothing certain, but he thinks His Majesty is adamant."

"Indeed?"

"It is his counsel that we should prepare outselves for the worst. And yet we should not abandon hope."

"Good news!" he cries. "A very good sign!"

And he claps his hands and shuffles his slippers in a sailor's jig, noting the amazement in two pairs of blue eyes. Noting that already Bess's lips have set into a purse of frowning disapproval.

So King David dancing with joy before the ark. . . .

"Why, Bess, can't you see the meaning? It is the Bishop's bounden duty to caution all his flock to prepare themselves for death, and most certainly he must be resolute in persuading this course to a *condemned* man."

Watching careful now beneath veiled eyes. Bess's frown having given away, retreated, replaced by puzzlement. Thomas relaxing, amused. Mary's eyes not so wide as before, more light also, covert beneath lashes. Her pout is not so easily converted, however. She more in control of herself, of course, than Bess, though

[574]

still blissfully, youthfully unaware of what the mask of her face conveys.

Oh, she is a juicy plum, this girl. By nature so, though now that he has gained her attention, he can see her face has been prepared with lotions and powders, her lips and cheeks subtly reddened, her eyebrows plucked, her eyes accented with the lightest hints of blue along the lids and at the edges. The latter concealing first faint prints of the crow of time. Either she is truly a country cousin, having spent as much time in sun and open weather as a milkmaid; or she is a little older than even Bess may know.

Mary is not nearly so simple and unworldly as she wishes to appear.

Ralegh continuing:

"Now, I know this Bishop well enough, though I need not. For all bishops are much the same. Except, of course, to each other. But not being bishops, we need not trouble ourselves with their secrets of distinction and degree, any more than we need to know which of two black bears is more like a man than a bear. No, ladies, let us allow that all bishops are cut from the selfsame cloth. They come in various sizes, to be sure, but in one fullsome shape—fat."

"Go to, Wat," Bess says. "You are babbling like a school-master."

"Nay, madame," Thomas says. "It is clear he has observed the animal in its habitat. I cannot question his conclusions, not having kept much company with bishops, thank God. But I have seen enough of them, waddling their way, to accept the truth of Sir Walter's observation."

Mary stifling a giggle with slightly clenched, gloved fingers of one hand.

[575]

"Not so, Bess. I am in high spirits, it is true, almost as merry as a Greek. But I must explain and justify my mood. For otherwise you and our pretty cousin will conclude I left all my wits at the Tower of London."

"Pray continue, then," Mary says. Voice of honey spiced with wine.

"The good Bishop, I say, being of the type of all bishops, that is, to wit, fat and comfortable enough to be compassionate, yet somewhat ashamed of how far afield he has, in his office, perquisites, and robes, strayed from the imitation of our Lord, the good Bishop will ever be cautionary to any poor soul. Will mouth the truth of the Gospel. . . ."

"Shame, Wat, you blaspheme."

"Not so, good lady," Thomas says. "He speaks by the book. Does not the Gospel tell us that we shall know the truth and the truth shall set us free?"

"Unfortunately," Ralegh adds, "our Lord was speaking allegorically. Otherwise we should be safe in some cheerful tavern instead of here. Now, pray permit me to conclude my lecture on the nature of that ecclesiastical beast we call bishop.

"He will preach the message excepting only when his natural compassion outweighs the shame of his worldly content. My meaning and interpretation is—for I have seen these, bishops and ministers alike, bring comfort to the dying and condemned a thousand times. . . . My judgment is that when there is no hope, they are, as the New Law instructs them, most hopeful, speaking not of dread and Almighty judgment, but of mercy vouchsafed by Jesus Christ."

"Amen," Bess adds.

And Mary, uncertain, starts to bow her head, then, upon second thought and a quick glance at Thomas, raises her rich

eyes toward heaven. Where if some holy saint upon the right
hand still has an ounce of animal humors left unrefined, he
will be much moved by her expression, though not deceived
by it.

"Therefore, good ladies and my friend Thomas, I perceive
that the Bishop is more concerned with the welfare of my
soul than any imminent peril to my flesh. He persuades me to
prepare myself, yet he cautions against dismissing hope."

"But he reports that the King is adamant."

"Certainly he does. And no doubt the King would so report
his own mood to the Bishop. For the King knows bishops even
better than I. And the King, like the equivocating Bishop,
knows that should he admit to the least weakening of resolve,
the Bishop will not seek to save my soul. The King is a frugal
man. He cannot permit one of his bishops an occasion to shirk
duty. They do little enough to earn their keep as it is."

"Shame on you, Wat."

"'Tis a shame, indeed, but truth. I conceive from your news
that the King has failed to convince my lord, the Bishop, that
he is strictly adamant. For if this were so, the Bishop first of all,
if only to remind us how close he stands to the throne, would
report not that he *thinks* the King is adamant, but that the
King *is* adamant. I know this fellow, the Bishop. I read him
like a broadside ballad."

"I hope and trust it is so, Lord willing," Bess says.

"Amen," echoes her newly pious kinswoman.

"I am certain of it. Certain now that we shall all dine together
tomorrow noon. My only regret is that you have come on a
night journey and steeled yourself against what will not be.
No, I must further confess I am now ashamed of my extravagance at noon dinner and in my modest plans for our supper.

[577]

Though God knows even my best laid plans could easily vanish in the clamor and confusion of my host's kitchen."

"I pray what you say will be true."

"I'll wager on it, Bess."

Then, turning to the young woman, he removes his earring and gives it to her. "If I do not dine with you three tomorrow noon, you may keep that pearl."

"I would not wager against your life."

"It is not a wager, daughter, understand that. I am inordinately fond of that jewel. I have no intention of losing it. But it is yours to keep until tomorrow noon, when I shall claim it and claim a kiss as well."

"I think it might be ill fortune. . . ."

"Go to! It is my life in the balance, and I conceive it to be a sure omen of misfortune if you do not keep the pearl for me."

"If it pleases you," with a graceful curtsy, tilted to show the elegant round bulge of her tits.

There's sweet perfume in the valley between them and I need not waste a wager that she's painted her pouty paps.

"Thomas, I am most pleased that you have come here tonight. And Bess, I thank you for bringing our cousin. I regret that I did not think to hire musicians to come and play for us while we dine. And afterwards we could all dance a little for the sake of the digestion."

"I do dearly enjoy to dance," Mary says.

Thinking: *I'll wager you do my milk and honey girl and any dance will do to show you to advantage and best of all dances you do is the dance of the eel when peeled down to silk and satin sweetness and sweet fire you shall writhe and dance that horizontal so well that a young man will flash fire and wilt proud ordnance before he's full grappled and boarded and*

[578]

an old man (oh, Lord!) will die of a seizure and in sad knowl-
edge of all the sweetness he leaves behind, honey for other
bees. . . .

But saying: "And so do we all, Mistress Mary. Yet we must
bow to the manners of the age. There are some who might
think it unseemly for a condemned man and his guests to be
dancing in prison. It would bespeak an insolent confidence. So
for their sake, I shall pretend to be very grave and solemn.
But perhaps you and Mr. Thomas Hariot will dance a little
later to please me."

"Just to please you, of course," Thomas says.

Turning, Ralegh sees that the table is set and ready, the
cloth spread, bread and salt, plate and silverware and napkins
all in place. He nods to his servant to go below and bring up
the supper.

"Come," he says, offering Mary his arm, "let us sit down. And
please to remember to keep a sad face."

"Why so?" Thomas says.

"Reputation, man."

"And who shall report our mood?"

"Thomas, for a scholar you are most wonderfully ignorant
of this world. You understand that all honor and reputation
are matters of report, true enough. And you ask the proper
question—who makes the report? To which I answer, for the
sake of your education, not spies, not scholars, not poets or
preachers. No, sir, reputation and honor are the prerogative of
carvers and servers, scullions and stable grooms. They decide
these things."

Thomas, laughing, replies: "How, then, can we ever gain their
favor?"

"I confess I do not know, Thomas. I have tried by every means, fair and foul, but my servants are imperious."

Now all are seated.

"And now," says Ralegh, "I must say an eloquent grace worthy of our friend, the absent Bishop."

"I think you might have been a fine figure of a bishop yourself," the girl says.

"Ha, girl! the Church is not my vocation."

"Perhaps a Pope of Rome," Hariot says.

"It is true that once or twice the idea of being an ecclesiastical shepherd crossed my mind. But then I met Bess and at the first sight of her I banished the thought forever. My own private bishop pointed to my true vocation as straight and proud as a soldier's pike."

"You will make the poor girl blush."

"That was my intention, Bess. And, see, she blushes sweetly in the Throckmorton manner," he says. "Now, good friends, pray bow your heads while I give thanks for all our many blessings."

It is almost midnight, hours since the coach came. The table is cleared away and taken down, though there are still sweets and nuts, a plate of cheeses and a choice of wines. Candles burn shorter and the fire is an even glow. The chamber is warm. A lone servant dozes, sitting on a joint stool near the door.

Thomas Hariot has taught Bess's kinswoman how to drink tobacco smoke from a pipe. And Thomas is sketching a likeness of the girl while she, her cheeks flushed from wine and her hair now in mild disarray, poses for him, puffing little clouds.

Propped up by pillows, Ralegh and Bess have made a sort of chair of the porter's bed, talking in low voices.

"I fear we are wasting our time," he tells her. "For I shall be pardoned and live to be a hundred."

"I pray you are right."

"Some old Roman—Seneca or Cicero, no matter—wrote that the best keepers of the vineyard are old men. A baldheaded lie if ever there was one. I promise you, Bess, that I shall grow ever more irascible, choleric, forgetful, long-winded, and foolish in my second childhood."

"And I shall grow ever more happy."

"No, you'll nag and complain. You'll drive me to sit in the chimney corner and pretend to be stone deaf."

"I will not be tricked. I will know when you are pretending, as I always have."

"After a while you shall ignore me there."

"Oh no. I'll watch you every moment like a cat and a mouse."

"What can an old man do that bears watching?"

"I shall be watching when you reach out to pat the bottom of the scullery girl."

"At one hundred years?"

"I know you."

"Pure flattery, but I thank you for it. And so for your sake I shall try to give our scullery girl such a pat and a squeeze that she'll squeal like a pig."

"Then you shall be treated to saltpeter in your broth and will mortify your flesh with rigorous cold baths. . . ."

No mortification of flesh tonight. It was a fine supper. Noon dinner, while somewhat ostentatious for the benefit of the sheriffs, good city gentlemen both, and the Lord Lieutenant, had been contrived upon the spur of the moment, depending upon extravagance to offset absence of ceremony and make-shift service. But there had been a little time to order the arrangement of the evening meal, at its odd, late hour. He had been most exact in instructions to his servants and to the willing porter, who was most eager to please, not only for the sake of whatever reward he would receive, but because the remains, certain to be ample, would end in his own larder. Would feed his family for some days. Indeed could make a feast of a dinner for Lord Mayor's Day. One to which he might invite some friends. So they might have proof that the station of porter has its special perquisites. There would even be enough leavings to pass on to the prisoners in the common jails brightening one day for them.

So goes the old chain of things which links us all together. A truth Walter Ralegh weighed when he ordered the food for his meal.

He knew he could not eat much himself. Of late he has thought there is much truth in the adage that has it that a man in his seventh age, under Saturn, time when food is the last of the world's pleasures left him, provided he's kept some teeth, will discover he can no longer distinguish the taste of meat and of bread, both becoming as bland and bald as beans boiled without bacon. Whereupon a man should shrug, sigh, and give up the world for good. But fears must have come and gone with fever; for the dinner was good and by the time Bess arrived, he had an appetite again. Still would not eat much, for fear of vapors and humors which might keep him awake or trouble his dreams.

The ladies also were sparing, having supped lightly at five o'clock.

Only Thomas awakened from thoughts to eat like a beggar on Easter.

Ralegh had arranged all well enough, allowing for the circumstances. A damask tablecloth was laid on the table, one worked and embroidered in illustration of the scriptural story of Susanna and the Elders. Napkins of linen worked with his crest, the Roebuck Proper.

Silver plate, plain, high-polished and smooth in the old fashion. For he does not fancy the fashion of engraved or enameled plate. One piece, however, for display, was enameled, bearing his arms—gules red with five lozenges cojoined in bend argent—and with it the martlet, the legless sparrow, signifying in heraldry's language that he is the fourth son of the family; arms unextravagant, unchanged since the day the Queen knighted him, though many others added to their arms or had them changed in this free and easy time.

Silver spoons and keen-honed knives set in ivory handles.

The salt, not so tall as many, was of silver, sculptured to show Virtue, shiny, nude, high and firm of breast, flat and smooth of belly and loins, rich and round of thigh, standing triumphantly graceful atop the cringing female form—only a shade less desirable than Virtue herself—of vanquished Vice. Once there had been jewels in the navels of these allegorical ladies, but these were gone.

A still jeweled pepper box of gold, taken from the *Madre de Dios*.

For spices he had saved and produced a toy. Not so grand as Leicester's silver ship, which is still the fashion, but specially made for him alone. A silver coach pulled by four horses and driven by a coachman, the reins and the whip of the coachman made of gold filament. By a cunning clockwork mechanism the wheels of the coach turn to send it along the table.

Bess never loved it, even when he had it made for her so many years before. She called it childish to spend such wealth on a mechanical jest. But he had kept it anyway, hidden it, even when he had been forced to put so much of his plate, his armor, and jewels in pawn.

And when at supper he set it running, showing how the coach could move the length of the table, even Bess had to laugh.

On top of a chest and on the plain table, whose cracks and

[584]

scars were covered with another damask cloth, a few pieces of plate, the ewers and covered serving dishes stood, together with a row of gold-stemmed, gold-rimmed Venetian glasses, delicate, made of light and air.

Resting on the several joint stools, impressed and put into unusual service, were shiny copper vessels of cool water, fresh from the keeper's rain barrel, to keep the wines chilled. The Canary was gone now. But he managed to provide an Italian white vernage, light and suited to his taste; a clary with honey and ginger and pepper; and for Bess, so English in her love of sweets, the rich raspberry wine called *raspes*. There was also a bowl of hippocras, a taste he favored for the end of a meal, though merely a taste, its strong distilled spirits of wine spiced and flavored with white ginger, nutmeg and cloves, a bit of boiled and candied orange, some grains of pepper, and ample cinnamon.

They could choose, pick at, taste, from cold meat, hot fish, and fowl. A shoulder of mutton and a beef rump. One fried rabbit for each. Sweet and spiced marrow on toast. A fat hen boiled with leeks and mushrooms. A gelded, sweet and gamy, peacock of the Ind, most for the brave show of its feathers. Some lobster, crayfish, and boiled shrimp. A pumpkin, sliced and baked with candied apples. And, most rare and ingenious at this season, a salad of motley herbs and greens, with seasonless hothouse flowers to color it and, in the eating, to make the mind glad.

In his salad and, indeed, in the sauces Ralegh insisted upon fine-chopped chives, assuring them that though chives might indeed make them thin if eaten in excess, he had found there was no truth at all in the tale that chives cause hot and gross vapors.

And if he could no longer enjoy the services of his own skilled gentleman usher, his yeoman usher, yeoman of ewry, yeoman of cellar, server, and carver, etc., still he could direct men how to lay a proper table and serve it well enough. And he, as he was proud to prove, could carve as well as any carver in England.

Bess, of course, frowned. Her first thoughts being that here was her reckless husband, spending far too much upon the occasion. And to no good, reasonable purpose. Perhaps in part for the porter, for the servants, and through them, for the world's vainglorious report that without any fear and trembling, he sat himself down to a sumptuous repast, somehow contrived, as if by the magic of old Merlin, here in a rude chamber which was, in truth, a prison.

Yet not, she would consider, in hope of good report. More likely its opposite. For he has always given that kind of offense. The pious would cluck their tongues and speak of Balthazar's feast and, eyes rolling toward heaven, recall the Last Supper in its perfect simplicity.

Yet they would be few. And perhaps that was not his purpose at all.

Maybe he intended a good report, but as a kind of legacy, an inheritance worth more than all his remaining estate for herself and Carew. Unlike his father, Carew seeks to please others even to his own disadvantage. She has chafed against Ralegh's stubborn lack of common tact. Which, she has sometimes felt strongly, added more faggots to the fires of the loneliness she had to endure. Had he courted favor more, she might have regained her right to rejoin the Court.

Perhaps this supper was a sort of *apologia* to her.

Yet she could not accept that proposition either. How many

times he had told her in his satiric, teasing way that his death would be their bill of divorcement. That women being what they are, and widows being especially restless, he would not be cool as the clay he was buried in before she found herself a new man. And laughed at her protestations.

No, most likely, she concluded, her logic leaping from bottom of stairway to top "like a witch on a broom," as he described her thinking, it meant none of these things. Rather it was demonstration, if any were needed, that he was the same insolent, swaggering boy of a man. Who knew no other way to live or to die. That he was even now unchanged from the man she loved first at a distance, then with an intimate mutual siege of chills and fever, in the Court of the Queen.

And this thought, the satisfaction of it was the assurance that if her choice had been foolish (if choice is ever a part of love), she had been right in her first understanding of the man.

Thus intuition of women put to shame all knots and gnarls and tangles of man's vaunted reasoning. She always believed that. But it was, always, a pleasure to have her beliefs confirmed.

And so Bess was soon all smiles and merry during suppertime.

The girl, meanwhile, having joined this household to seek her future at its bleakest time, having just now come from the Broad Street house where the servants tiptoed as if in mourning already, and, their faces like turtles, worried on their own futures; hushed voices and probably sometimes the sound of sobbing from Bess's chambers; the girl would have never seen or known him in such a mood as this. Would be eased that what had seemed certain to be a sad evening, a sadness she must share, was not to be so. Instead of the tedium of grief she found a festival. A glimpse of the life she longed for, not certain it existed outside of her imagination. Or if the sumptuous life which her country preacher, himself fallen from preferment at Court, had railed against so vividly as to plant roots in her fantasy, did exist, uncertain that she should ever so much as enjoy crumbs of that banquet.

Here in a prison chamber (so distant from her picture of rags, dirty straw, lice, and humiliations of jail, where sometimes in a warm bath of guilt she imagined herself paying for pleasures she had mostly imagined, the pain and shame a sort of pleasure to her soul, deliciously strong enough to shudder her flesh), here were only crumbs and leavings to be sure. But see how these things sparkled!

She could not, of course, seeing himself and Bess, imagine herself in their images. Being unable in youth, health, and ignorance to do so. Nor could she picture him as any more alive than old father Abraham. Could not picture them as ever having been full of green sap, clothed in the lovely bark of young flesh.

Could imagine almost anything else, imagination heightened by first taste and savor of good wines, of sauces strange to her tongue, colored with saffron, flavored by musk and ambergris and subtle receipts of spices. Almost anything except, of course, the truth. Or what he, in age and experience if not wisdom, took to be truth.

Seen by her, whether in steel glass of truth or tinted mirrors of fancy, he would always be an old man, scarecrow of old sticks and straw, clad in a fine dressing gown. She could not picture the truth of his wrinkled nakedness.

And thus could not conceive that *he,* old man, could see *her* as nude and shiny as the image of Virtue on the great salt or the embroidered Susanna of the tablecloth; could see all, though she wore more layers of clothing than Salome wore

[588]

veils, from pink piglet toes, past ankle, sturdy calf—from country walking—soft, round, solid, smooth thighs meeting at a cunning portal rich with light-flecked, rust-colored, softest grass, fit temple gate for an old bishop to enter unbending mitered head and proudly to march from nave to altar while, invisible, a choir cried out a frenzied anthem, from her other lips. . . .

She could not dream that picture. And when and if she (as eyes and lips and walk betrayed she must) pictured herself naked and sumptuous in another's eyes, then that other, whatever his form, would be like the similitude the clear water gave back to Narcissus. In truth merely herself rejoicing in being and possessing herself. . . .

Strange that I most old and purged, most weary, should feel the gnawings of desire. Perhaps as the fierce teeth of his frothing mad dogs tore flesh and tore from him screams of pain, poor Actaeon shivered with pleasure at the fading memory of Diana. . . .

He might have been ashamed. That the dying animal of flesh still tugged at leash and chain. But that would be another vanity. He found, rather, that he was lightly amused, enough for a smile, that even as he could still savor the pleasures of good food, so he could still imagine the pleasures of satisfied desire.

Must remember, he thought, to ask Thomas about this later. Thomas would know the natural truths of aging of body and mind. Though at the moment Thomas was wholly engrossed in no other study than the capacity of his belly. Probably had not eaten for a day or two. Not out of necessity, but forgetfulness. No one having sat him down to a table and put food before him.

Still, pleasures of company, food and wine, diversion of fine objects, even, amazing, the resurrection of the shabby ghost of desire, all these could only serve as the setting for the playing of a scene.

Let Ben Jonson and his collaborative rival, Inigo Jones, wrestle it out and settle whose craft is pre-eminent. Let them settle which one, poet or designer, should receive highest honor. Precedence aside, all things, costumes and decorations, winds and clouds, off-stage thunder and strokes of lightning, all these, and yes, all the words are well, are gossamer, ephemeral.

But, illusory or not, it remained for Ralegh to make a little play at dinner for them. And he was not able to do so like an English player, not able to speak the lines some poet had written, emended, decorated, and now vaguely remembered.

No, they must all play a scene more in the style of the traveling Italians. Whose art is to improvise words and actions according to one particular occasion and their own inclinations, directed only by mutual consent to a most general plot. Their little theater being, in an old man's view, closest to and most like the theater of life itself.

These Italians had delighted him once. Even though for deeper pleasure he preferred the English stage. They delighted him in memory; for he had not seen them performing in many years, not since the time of the Queen, when, in 1602, Flaminio Curtesse came to play at the Court.

Well now, he must be his own author and designer. And he almost alone must play the parts of the Zany, Pantaloon, and Harlakeen. Must also be, more suitable, Gratiano, the Doctor, and that other one (*what was he called? no matter now . . .*), the swaggering braggart Spanish captain, full of outward fire and fury and effeminate inward fear.

Captain Spavento, that was the name! Of the fearsome and

*fearful, furioso, braggadocio, cursing and cowardly captain of
Spain portrayed and well cudgeled by comic Italians who could
defeat a Spaniard on the stage though they would flee him by
land or by sea. Captain Spavento cut from stolen cloth of ancient Rome.*

*Curious workmanship of the mind. Which will allow a man
to recall an insignificant thing. The same mind of the man who
can sit by the muddy brook of memory, a very patient angler,
and seek with skill and bait to fish up the lost name of someone
once deeply loved or hated. And not so much as a tug or nibble
on his line. . . .*

Food, wine, idle divertissement of objects. Some artless tricks
of talk, harmless as the sleight of hands with a coin. The fanlike
flutter of polite, formal flirtation. All might serve for prologue.
But the soul of the scene—a scene where there were neither
ghosts nor confused alarms, no flags or brawls, not music or
grand processions, no leaps and skips and hops halfway across
the wide world, and no merciful swift passages of time by the
wishing and saying—a scene to be played in a chamber to a
rhythm of time as unhurried as the path of a snail in a dew-
sprinkled summer garden, the soul of the scene would be found
in its discourse. Not so much in the words as behind the words,
unspoken words within words. Which words he must use to
be like the wind to blow the three of them safely to harbor.
But it must not seem to be he who, cheeks bulging like a
trumpeter's at the corner of a chart, huffed and puffed them
home. He must, rather, be the wind while seeming also to be
blown by it. And they, meanwhile, each separately, must imagine themselves to be the source of the fair breeze that filled
their own sails. Each separately must follow the invisible lines
of a course of his plotting, arriving at last at the calm harbor of

his choosing. All the while imagining it was there they had intended to arrive and drop anchor from the first. . . .

Mary, knowing by rote the ways of English country life. Not wishing to hear more of that. Being ripe, poised to scramble, crawl like a cat (claw if need be), for any tossed coins, no matter how base their value, if they came from Court.

Against which Bess, trained to the Court, and once upon a time, time which has never yet dimmed for her, as close to the center as can be. And without least weight of anxious ambition. Save to be prompt and cheerful and modest in her service to the Queen. To listen when the Queen desired to indulge herself in woman's chatter. To be entertaining when it pleased the Queen to be entertained. To be decorative, yet decently inferior, when it suited Her Majesty to be set off by her maids of honor. To be one of a ring of jewels, lesser stones set around the one perfect-cut, flawless diamond.

To do these things, which she had done well.

And above all, to be faithful. Which she had not been. Never planning to be a country wife.

Who had done well enough her wifely duties, the endless management of servants, care of everything from rushes on floors to next winter's larder, from the planting of kitchen garden and herbs to the making of soap and dye, of ale, cordials, perfumes, and medicines. Who must minister to the sick and keep the healthy happy and well fed. To manage and direct more affairs each day than any sea captain, and all the while maintaining an ease and grace as if the doing were no chore at all. To be ever ready to smile upon gentlemen and ladies, coming and going; to be idle and merry with them at table; to make music on the virginal or the lute or in the singing, as if the mastery of these arts were no more trouble than the pulling on of a glove. In quiet hours to lead her own ladies and servants in works of sewing, embroidery, and needlepoint, by example, while, perhaps, someone read to them from a proper and properly tedious book. . . .

Bess having escaped from that when she came to Court to serve the Queen, then finding herself forced to return to the life of a country lady.

As in some child's fairy tale, the Queen had punished her most exactly for breach of faith. Bess, like some princess set to spinning and spinning in a tower, her time made more difficult to bear because there was always hope in her heart that she would be forgiven.

Yet because there was always hope, banishment would be bearable. For Bess could always reassure herself that she was a mere actor, playing the role of country wife, and that one day, any day now, it would end. Which hope gave her the freedom to play her role well.

And Ralegh was properly punished by the Queen by the same token, the more so when she again restored him his old station. For it was to him alone that Bess could turn to whisper complaints from her pillow coverlet. And he must reassure her, restore her hopes and false dreams, knowing them to be hopeless, for the sake of domestic peace.

As if the Queen had openly said to him: *So, Oracle, you would steal a fair rose from my garden. Well, then, welcome to it. Keep it with my blessings, being ever mindful that the thorns outlast bloom.*

Left to his choices at this supper he might have wished to talk of the pleasures of country life, hunting and hawking, planting and harvesting, glory and sadness of the turning seasons of an English year. Pleasures and sorrows of a life as old as

[593]

time in this changing world and likely to change little while kingdoms rose and fell. Not Edmund Spenser's allegorical pastoral vision. Nor Marlowe's painted picture which would turn country life into a masque. Yet something of both, together with the cry of the cuckoo in May and the sweat and weariness of a long day in the saddle, and of the unhooded falcon freed from wrist and climbing into a clear sky to fly in wide circles and dwindling music of its bells and to fall like a thunderbolt upon its prey.

And damp and smoky winter nights by a fire. A good book to read or a game of cards with friends. Nuts and dry fruit to nibble. Smoky ale to drink. . . .

It was a fable. He had chafed against the country, even as he relished its pleasures.

Thomas would not have heard a word of it. One place is the same as another to him.

Both ladies would wish to hear of the Court: one who has imagined it, the other who lived there, then spent years there in memory and in hope.

But above all and most deeply (and here he must gag his own feelings) he was concerned in love for Bess. For whom sorrows had multiplied. Concerned not that all sorrows could be lifted from her, but that she should continue to have the strength to bear them. Which she in truth possesses in full measure. But, a woman, she must be reminded of this, must be told that in his eyes she has shown fortitude and patience. And that against those virtues, her little follies, her complaints against the hundred darts of petty misfortune, weigh less than the downy tail feathers of a tame duck.

Her need now was to be reminded, though it be for the hundred hundredth time, how he had loved her young, loved

[594]

her well and lusty then; yet loved her still and more so because of those things which time cannot deface. Yet never implying that to this day he does not see her as he had in that first lusty light. And not to suggest, even as compliment, that she had not shown and he had not known even then the fine glow of her inner character. This last a respectful bow to the vanity of a woman whose vanity, in truth, is no more of her than the paint on her face, whose modesty is as much of her nature as her bones.

He had known nothing of her nature or her character then. Had taken her, as he had taken others, with no more thought than a ram tupping a ewe. Had taken her to be, like the others, more witch than woman, able to offer much harm and no good. When she swelled with his seed, he had taken her to be his lawful wife.

Later came to know her and to love her.

He could disregard Thomas for the time. Neither harm nor help from him until his belly rebelled and surrendered to satiety.

Wonderful wasted hours at playhouses might be summoned up to serve him.

John Lily was no help. His people were beautiful, but moonlight for blood. And there's no moon tonight.

Kit Marlowe would not have troubled to write this scene at all, not for love or money, unless it were indeed Balthazar's feast and could end with all the clamor and fury and rapine of the invading army. Kit must have a mighty subject for his grand, surprising lines. He had been the most gifted of them all. But had never trusted enough the power and magic of a simple wooden stage.

To be truthful Kit had not lived long enough to refine his

gift. Dead in a Deptford tavern brawl. Murdered by one of Whitgift's agents. And all of it—as always in these things—obscure, a tangle. It was part and parcel, though, of the same shadows they had raised against himself, the charge of atheism and "the school of night," etc. But he and the others were safe in the knowledge—even in disfavor with the Queen—that the Queen would not permit them to be touched. So they touched one and killed him, poor Kit Marlowe, who, a gentleman and proud, would stand behind no man for safety. And the truth of it so tangled that even when he returned to favor, Ralegh could do nothing to right the wrong. But the memory of it lies heavy in him to this night. For he must believe Marlowe was killed—because he was vulnerable—as a warning to himself and Northumberland and the others, even Thomas here, all of whom were safe. No point in warning them. And the greatest waste to kill a poet who could have brought much honor to England.

Once, in those days, William Shakespeare might have made such a scene, though it would have to be set in some distant and improbable kingdom. Swift, quick-handed, he could have pulled amazing toys from a fulsome peddler's pack. Concealing all brevity, all rude and rough places, behind a rainbow of words. Leaping past dumb silences with laughter. Would light upon the scene like a new-made butterfly, passing on to the next. Might have tried it and done it with facility once. But not for this age when tastes have changed.

Maybe Ben Jonson could do it, would do it now if the price was right. And he would set them where they are, the gatehouse of Westminster, and call it by name. Would have them speaking much like themselves, too.

But Ben, for all the humors of his comedy, would not let

the scene be comic if he knew what the end must be. Ben's a poet, true, and a bricklayer, soldier, and scholar. The latter by hard labor. But he will not mix laughter and tears. Honest artificer, he hates to cut against the grain of the wood.

If there are to be tears (says Ben) then let them flow, and let them be noble tears. Make sweet Bess, pretty Mary, hungry Thomas, and weary Walter Ralegh into four noble Romans. Set them upon the ancient, honorable pedestals of *gravitas* and *pietas*. Let them speak in well-laid verses with the measured sonority of Seneca.

And let them keep talking till the world falls asleep.

None of these poets could write the part for him now. But as these poets never refrained from nipping and foisting from the living and the dead, especially each other, so he would as lief cut their purses to take whatever he could use.

The picture of himself cutting their purses—Marlowe indifferent, he'll cut someone else's; Jonson outraged, ready to brawl; Shakespeare in anguish, echoing Job's lamentations—made him laugh out loud at table.

"What makes you so merry?" Bess asked.

"I was recollecting afternoons at the playhouse long ago."

"I have often thought Wat would have been happiest as a common player," Bess said. "In his youth he spent more time at the playhouse than in church."

"I have not yet seen a stage play in London," Mary said.

"You must go there for moral instruction," Ralegh said. "You can hear more good sermons at Bankside than St. Paul's Cross."

"The girl won't go to hear sermons," Thomas said. "What became of your good Canary?"

"I am sorry to tell you, Thomas, I drank it all. With some help from my servants."

[597]

"Well, the clary is not bad, if that fellow will fill my glass. . . ."

No one to write a scene for him. He must seize the subject by the ears. Ride on it like an ass. Summon up time and tide of youth. Waken Bess's memory of happy times, yet not to wound her. Delight the girl, but glut her hungers as he fed imagination's fuel.

Turning to paradox instead of the proud jog and trot of poetry.

Began then:

To converse upon shining but not to ask where are all the silks and brave things we loved

To rejoice in fragile delicate intricate pleasures shimmering like spiders' webs in light and air

To feed as once we fed on pure light and air like magical chameleons like Indian orchid flowers

No mention how we fed upon each other like cannibals until we were consumed by our own appetites

Call up beautiful brief daylong dream life of an April butterfly and song of the summer nightingale in velvet dark

Not say how silence wounds when song has dwindled and died

Celebrate stage plays and masques and triumphs and pageants and progresses by land and water

arrivals and departures and ceremonies and orations and songs and speeches and trumpets and cheering crowds

Not to ask who can remember now the words of last year's player kings and player queens or all the brave deeds of the playing-card knaves

Not needing to recall that the ending of each progress was a mock funeral all draped in black and mourning that each arrival prefigures a departure

that triumphal arches are torn down and where conduits flowed wine by miracle is water again

To praise costumes and clothing and to bathe the bodies of the dead and of our dead youth again in silks and satins and furs and gold chains and jewels

Not reminding what moth and rust and rot have spared can now be seen on the faded costume of a child's doll

or that the finest of those jewels are worn by strangers

To speak of clothing and so to call up nakedness

an old man made of dry sticks flesh of dry figs

from that unspoken emblem call forth the grin of the skull in the dark

How in dark no man can tell white mare of a Court lady from Southwark whore

To celebrate triumph and pomp and glory of the world in shared memory of happy times

Not to ask where haunts felicity now

Better seek to recover the song of summer's nightingale

More likely to live off the fruit of a cypress tree or scour a blackamoor clean as milk

than find consolation in things which once consoled

Bess through memory to make her smile and forget woes

For the girl a solace imagining while she is spared the loss of what she has never known

For Thomas the memory of talk more heady than wine and nights when stars moved with precision to his new-found laws

For himself some solace in pleasing them all and forgetting himself in present and future

Some solace in knowledge that the emblem of fame clad in gown of burning tongues is false

[599]

Those tongues burn with a fire of lies
Music is solace but silence is consolation
To celebrate the glory of the summer nightingale
To rejoice in the triumph of silence
To wake an old dream out of memory
To remember the joys of dreamless sleep

"But if you live to be a hundred, I shall be very old and ugly," Bess is saying.

"My eyes will be weak and my touch will be fine enough to distinguish flame from ice. If you are tough-skinned as old leather and have more lines than a pilot's chart, I'll never know it. I'll close my eyes and imagine you are young and smooth as ever. As much milk and honey as your cousin there."

"You can never make a compliment without being satiric."

"I would change my ways for you if I could, Bess. But I fear I am too old."

"I'll wager you never spoke in such a teasing fashion to the Queen."

"You can be sure of that, Bess."

"Then why to me? You loved the Queen and I think she loved you well enough."

"Perhaps. . . ."

The chimes of the clock ring and the bells begin to toll midnight. Unable to speak against the tolling, he lowers his lids a little to study her. At last she is—perhaps it is the wine—most deeply serious. Which must not be.

"It is true," he says, "I loved our Queen. But I took you, Bess Throckmorton, for my wife. And that was the wisest thing I ever did. I shall say the same thing in my hundredth year."

[600]

Bess smiles again. "Do not take credit for the actions of others."

"Why, what do you mean by that?"

"It was I who chose you, Wat, and long before you knew it."

"Well, then, I thank you for it. And I thank God."

Noise below. A cry from the guards. Sound of horses and a squeaking coach.

"Our kinsman Sir Nicholas Carew has sent his coach to fetch us home again."

"You must thank him for me. And tell him the wheels of his fancy coach need grease."

Rising, gathering together of things, brief preparations at the looking glass.

And here is a servant, sleepy-eyed, with their dry cloaks.

"Ladies," says Thomas Hariot, standing by the window, "it appears Sir Nicholas has half a squadron of mounted men to see you home. With your permission I shall remain and smoke another pipe before I leave."

"How will you go?"

"A walk will clear my head."

"In the night?"

"Lady Bess, nobody will rob a scholar by daylight or dark. Every rogue in London and Westminster knows me for what I am—a daft fellow with an empty purse."

"Lend him a sword and pistol, Wat."

"I would, if I had either."

"No need," Thomas says quickly, even before Bess can regret her mistake. "I have a fine old rusty blade I left with the guard below. It will not slice butter or wound a mouse, but it is something terrifying to behold."

The two ladies, cloaked against the weather, are ready now. He bids farewell to fair Mary.

"Remember, I will have my pearl back and a kiss to boot at dinner."

She does her little curtsy; her swelling breasts making the same sweet promise as before. And she descends the stairs.

Thomas is at the fireplace staring into the fire.

Ralegh stands a moment by the open door, smiling, holding Bess's hands.

"Pray for me if it will make you sleep better," he says. "And then sleep well."

"There is something I did not tell you, Wat. I have received a note from Council saying I have permission to bury your body."

The smile does not waver as he bends down close to kiss her.

"It is well, dear Bess, that you may dispose of it dead," he says. "You did not always have the disposing of it alive."

She starts as if to answer something, but as always, there is no answer to his irony, even when it is gentle and loving. So she smiles and shakes her head. Then turns away quickly so that he will not see her eyes fill up with tears.

He thinks he will call after her, say something more, give her the letter for the boy. But he watches the back of her hooded head disappear down the stairs.

Let her go now. Let it be. Bless her, she has suffered enough.

4

Close by the fire, Thomas Hariot watches him shut the door. Ralegh stands facing the door, not turning to look at the chamber or at Thomas until the last sound of the coach and horsemen has died out.

Then turns and limps toward Thomas, his face a mask set into a thin smile.

Thomas gives him a pipe and holds a hot coal on pincers so he can light it.

"I believe you could have walked out with the ladies," Thomas says. "You are lightly guarded."

"True," Ralegh answers. "Lightly guarded and closely watched. Indeed I am being watched this moment all the way from Theobalds or Royston or wherever the King is playing the English Nimrod."

"We could walk out together and be safe in France for our next supper."

"Perhaps the King would prefer it that way. Or perhaps to have me murdered out there. Who knows? I intend to sleep safely here tonight."

[603]

"I came tonight," Hariot says awkwardly, "because I cannot bear to come tomorrow."

"Thomas, I prefer your company now. And I share your distaste of crowds. I shall avoid it myself if I possibly can."

"I . . . do not think that will be possible."

"There will be no pardon then?"

"I cannot say. But it would seem not so. It seems you must die."

"How will Bess bear this?"

"She knows it. She will pray for you."

"And the boy? How is my son?"

"I believe he is . . . much like a man."

"Like a man. . . ."

Ralegh looks into the coals of the fire, blows a wreath of tobacco smoke.

"By God, I am much relieved. If the King should change his mind, I think it would vex me. I would not be happy to be beholden to him a second time."

"That's your damned pride speaking."

"Forgive me, then, Thomas. Since I have always lived a proud man, it would be an equivocation to die another way."

While Ralegh is looking into the fire Thomas tells him, awkwardly, that the arrangements for the worst have been made. And the worst is that Bess will not be given his body for burial. She said so, but knew better. Instead there has been a solicitous compromise, headless trunk and limbs will remain in possession of King and Council, to be disposed of by them. Bess will be given the severed head. . . .

"But she will not be here," Ralegh says. "She promised me that."

"No," Thomas says. "She will not come."

Ralegh spits in the fire and looks up into Thomas Hariot's eyes. The gown, loosened, has slipped away from Ralegh's shoulders. The reddish-brown tan of his face and neck are deepened by contrast with a thin, milk-colored line, color of his body's flesh, savagely clean-lined, marking the line of the collar. That sudden whiteness, softness of pale flesh, makes Hariot look down at the toes of his boots and the floor.

"Don't be afraid, Thomas," Ralegh says. "It is not proper."

"I am sorry."

"It is proper for you to wish me well, but it is unseemly for me to share my fear with you."

He raises his eyes to meet Ralegh's and finds that he has adjusted his gown so that the whiteness of his body is again covered. The eyes are no longer heavy-lidded. Catching candlelight, they seem almost to be smiling, though his lips are tight.

"Are you afraid?"

"God's name, Thomas, I have been with fear like a whore all day long. My bones feel it. They want to jangle like the keys of a virginal. And all of my hairs would like to stand up at once like the bristles of a boar. My blood is quicksilver and my bowels are a pack of beagles. Can't you tell?"

"I could not have guessed it."

"Good," he says. "It belongs to me, then. Will you have a last glass of wine?"

"I am too dry to drink," Thomas says, knocking out his pipe on the fireplace.

"I have a few notes and papers for my wife," Ralegh says, going toward the chest. "I should have remembered these while she was here. I shall be grateful if you will deliver them for me."

He has gathered up some sheets of paper, gives them to

Hariot, but keeps one bulky manuscript in his hands, not offering this to him too.

"Tell her that these are matters of business, simple enough and needing no explanation."

"Yes, sir."

"Are you certain you will not have a glass of wine?"

"My stomach has turned rebel. I could not keep it down."

"No matter," Ralegh says. "I shall drink your health later."

One hand light on Hariot's shoulder, leading, he steers him toward the door.

"God bless you."

"I am most pleased you came, Thomas. God be with you."

Nodding, slipping into his cloak, Thomas Hariot hesitates; then: "Do you wish me to take those papers also?"

Ralegh glances down at the sheaf of papers in his hands, as if he has forgotten holding them.

"You say Carew is much like a man these days."

"I believe it. You would be proud of him."

"Give him a father's love and blessings."

"And the papers?"

"Oh, these are mere stuff to fatten the fire," he says.

Thomas Hariot puts on his hat and, after a nod, slips out the door. Descending the stairs, he can hear the old man's soft voice calling for his servant to prepare the bed.

5

All the servants but one have been sent away to sleep below. And that man, curled by the fire, is snoring.

Weary, needing to sleep at least a little while, Ralegh has his Bible by the bed. There is wine and a cup. And ink, pens, sheets of paper are nearby, ready for any notes he may wish to make. He can think of nothing to write.

He is reading the Psalms of David.

His eyes blur and waver on the page. He has need of spectacles to read with and has long read printed words with difficulty. But, except for the King himself and such as are bishops and clerks and scholars, you will seldom find a gentleman of the Court, called, he would profess, to the business of the world in time, who will wear a set of spectacles, even though both words close by and the distant world shall dim out of sight. It is considered a folly and an affectation for men of the world to use these aids. Yet who named it so? The fashion of reading half-blind is surely the child of vanity.

Reading, restless and uneasy, turning pages at random, from the Psalms of David. Thinking, even as he glances at words he has said and read to himself so often that he need not any longer read more than a few to awaken the memory and echo of the whole, thinking of David. Of whom he wrote much in the *History*. Thinking of David the man and king, not similitude and prophet and precursor of Christ, though Christ came from the seed of David. David the youngest, least likely to be raised high, yet chosen.

I found David my servant and with my holy oil I have anointed him.

David, who first made his name with populace and public— and stirred the anger and malice of old Saul, who had turned from God—when he slew the Philistine champion, Goliath.

Good luck have thou with thine honor. Ride on, because of the word of truth, of meekness and righteousness. And thy right hand shall teach thee terrible things.

Standing between armies in array, he took a sword and cut off the head of the giant and grasping it, twining the curls at the roots in a fist of fingers, held it high for all to see.

O let the sorrowful sighing of the prisoners come before thee. According to the greatness of thy power, preserve thou them that are appointed to die.

David, coming to power with blood on his hands, and, mighty warrior, never to cleanse them and live in peace. To bring plenty, but not peace, to his kingdom. And to begin to rebuild the Temple of Jerusalem. But never, because of blood on his hands, to be permitted to touch the least stone of it.

So he, too, began his manhood with bloody, unclean hands. *My wounds stink and are corrupt through my foolishness.*

But consider also David the poet, more worthy than the most gifted of the pagans. How those same hands, those fingers which had snatched and snared the thick, sweat-flecked hair of Goliath, did play upon the harp and psaltery, making a joyful or a sorrowful noise, and setting to the music his words, his "dark speech on the harp."

Which we do ponder and where to this day do seek solace.

Made songs of sorrows and rejoicing until at the last, old, vexed, worn by tribulations, weary of himself and his sins, too slack even for love but needing the warmth of a young girl's body to preserve him from the creeping cold, at last he was silent.

As for our harps, we hanged them up upon the trees that are therein.

As his lost son, Absalom, his long hair knotted and snarled in a tree, met a bloody death. And David the king wept. Even as God may have wept for him.

How shall we sing the Lord's song in a strange land?

Lived and reigned long in triumph and tribulation, risen from youngest son to Shepherd of the Kingdom. As he, once a poor and youngest son, came to be called Shepherd of the Ocean.

Lived long and reigned in power and glory.

Who once had danced in joy before the ark and danced in the streets, died lonely and in silence.

O remember how short my time is. Wherefore hast Thou made all men for nought?

Lived to appoint and see anointed King, his bastard son, Solomon. But not to know that Solomon would be the greatest of the kings and the wisest of men, choosing the gift of wisdom above all things.

Yet as David ended days in sorrow, so did Solomon, wisest, fall to his knees and eat grass like a beast. Denied any vision of the glory of his son, David was also spared knowledge of his fall from glory.

What man is he that lusteth to live and would fain see good days?

If King David suffered so and also Solomon, the one as brave as Mars, the other wise and quick of wit as Mercury, neither of them able to imagine that he would be chosen to rise so high or, once in glory to fall into misery, who are we, even the kings, being lesser men of an older, baser time, to hope for more? We can take solace by example, it is true, that we share in their story, one and all. If their glory and honor was greater, so much so was their suffering.

Yet each man's suffering is entirely his own.

For I have eaten ashes as it were bread and mingled my drink with weeping.

For my life is waxen old with heaviness and my years with mourning.

But he must not, not now, he thinks, dwell on these things. Even though sorrow might be good medicine for his soul.

He rises from bed, sips wine, and moves to the window.

Somewhere in the huge yard, rude timbers, rain-slick, invisible to him, the scaffold waits.

But will not think on that now.

There are a few lights. Clouds and rain, again, obscure the stars. Faint reflections off the river from over toward White-hall and the row of houses.

No doubt coming and going continues, though diminished, vaguely furtive now, at York House; and will continue until Lord Bacon's late bedtime. No reason for Bacon to rise early on the morrow.

Reflection of torchlight from the gate and, closer, from the covered lanterns at the door of the gatehouse. Where two yeomen of the Guard stand watch, their crimson and gold concealed beneath hooded woolen cloaks. Which will keep them warm and dry for a time, perhaps until they are relieved. He hears the mutter of their voices, but not one word.

He remembers himself young, standing watch on many a wet night.

And so he wakes the servant and orders that they shall have some slices of the joint of veal and a bowl of warm ale, spiced with mace and ginger. It is likely they will have been forgotten here, at least until relieved.

After a time he hears the sound of a pebble light on the window pane. Squinting, he looks down to see a shape, young face white under the hood, standing in a pool of light cast by the lantern. The soldier raises the bowl in salute and thanks. Ralegh tips him the slightest nod. Watches as he raises the bowl and drinks deep, wipes his lips with his cloak, then steps out of sight.

Ralegh looks up at shape of Old Palace and its chambers. Only a few lights burning there. Some guttering lanterns outside.

The bed invites him. He yawns, moves toward it. But still it will be most difficult to go to sleep. Taking up a pen he writes down a poem in the flyleaf of his Bible, most of it by memory. For all but the last two lines a couplet newly added on, are lines of a staff from a poem written years before. Lines which have been playing along the edges of his mind all day. Now he knows why.

All those years the poem was unfinished. It has lacked a proper ending.

> Even such is time which takes in trust
> Our youth, our joys, our all we have
> And pays us but with age and dust;
> Who in the dark and silent grave

[611]

When we have wandered all our ways
Shuts up the story of our days.
But from this earth, this grave, this dust,
My God shall raise me up I trust.

One couplet, then, of faith and hope, to comment upon six old lines.

For he must sleep or not sleep soon. And if he sleeps, he must wake to live again, to die or not to die. He toys with the notion of snuffing out the candle by his bed. Takes up the silver snuffer in his hands and feels the light, cool, slick-smooth weight of it. Eyes the flame—one small burning tongue of flame in the dark. Considers the fat, squat, melting candle, consuming itself. Even as time and the elements consume the fat and fire of a man's life. Even as a man, like Samoyed or Indian cannibal, will consume himself. Until he is nothing. . . .

Considers for a moment lowering the hood or cowl of the snuffer over the flame. There will be sudden black after the bright meeting of silver and flame, and a faint dry odor of smoke, the scent brief and dwindling away. He will not see it, but can imagine the raw wick, poor and naked without its crown of flame, and the thin ghostly gray of the smoke vanishing like a tired sigh.

The snuffer, shiny as the edge of an ax (see how the shadow against the wall is shaped like the shadow of a headsman's ax), will fall and take away the flaming head and leave the used clownish pallid trunk of a spent candle, the raw wick stained. . . .

Lord, my imagination will not keep still!

The snuffer trembles in his hand. It is his hand that trembles.

[612]

By God and God's wounds, none of that now! If a shadow and a candle can make his fingers tremble for fear, then how shall he ever master his body?

To master fear he must make courage stand a muster. Call up courage to lead and scout for him, to cover the body of fear like the Forlorn Hope.

A young soldier of horse at the wars in France. And remembers riding down a twisty narrow path, turning to follow through gold and shade of some trees, a branch flicking the corner of one eye and bringing tears there, the horse stumbling, struggling, as they picked a way among the trees up a hill and the hill going steeper until, as he thought he would have to dismount and lead the nag behind him, they came out of the trees onto a high sloping pasture in sunlight. Below the ribbon strips of farms and a cluster of stone farmhouses.

A distant shout instantly echoed by a cry from one of their own horsemen. Then a sudden glitter of hard reflected light. In middle distance, packed into squares, flags flying, moving with pikes high, like a slow porcupine, the enemy infantry.

More shouts. Below and closer, much closr, horsemen are coming. Horses and riders appearing from concealment of the farmhouses and buildings. Coming into sight in a lean line like a snake in tall grass, moving at a trot. More shouting (and now he could hear steady drums of the shuffling infantry) and the file became a rank facing them. And the rank running toward them and shouting like hunters. Crying in animal voices like a pack of wild dogs.

And he sat frozen on his saddle, limbs of lead, ice in blood, tongue a brass farthing, and sweat in drops like pearls rolling down cheeks and slick on his palms.

[613]

His head heavy as a stone and the light horseman's helmet heavier even than that. Unable to keep it up. Lowers it down to the mane of the horse (*like kissing father with his beard*) and his fists tightening, gripping reins, pulling tight.

Knowing that in a moment, no matter what he will, his hands will command themselves, pull back sharp, twist. And, giving spur, he will turn and run away. Plunge blind into the trees in a lunge downhill and away.

And just then there was the old soldier who commanded the Forlorn Hope for that day. With one hand, gentle and firm, lifting his head up and twisting his face up to look into eyes above a grizzled beard. Speaking softly. Not in anger. Not like schoolmaster or drillmaster. But, his tight dry lips barely moving in the nest of the beard.

"Hold up your head, lad, and sit in your saddle. Hold up your head, sit tall and proud, and look at them. They are brave men and they deserve that much."

He, young Walter, his chin in the grip of the old soldier's hand, true tears in his eyes now, trying to nod his head. And shouts coming louder and nearer. The drums coming on steady, beating more slow than his heart.

"And hear this, lad. Now or in a hundred years you shall have but one chance to die. Don't waste your one chance to die like a man."

Nodding again. Free of the grip. Head free and light.

"Take up your pistol. Be ready to fire when I command and then wheel and ride like the wind."

He groped for his pistol, the horse shifty and unsteady beneath him, but horse and body obeying him. And tightening his knees, gripping the reins firm with a still sweaty palm.

[614]

Thinking only of the firing and wheeling and riding, and not of himself or his fear. . . .

Well then, back in the bed, candle snuffer in hand, eyeing a dying candle. It does not please him to snuff out the candle with a sigh. Nor to sleep all night long with lights—like the King of England.

He scribbles a couplet, hard and satiric, proudly complete in itself, in the flyleaf of the Bible.

> Cowards fear to die, but courage stout
> Rather than live in snuff will be put out.

He puts Bible, pen, and ink aside. He takes up the candle in his hand. Letting wax run warm on his fingers. Stares into the flame. Puffs his cheeks and blows it out in a gust.

Tosses the spent candle aside. Lowers his head to the pillow. And in a moment or two is deep and sound asleep.

Part Seven

Now for the rest: if we truly examine the difference of both conditions, to wit, of the rich and mighty whom we call fortunate, and of the poor and oppressed whom we account wretched, we shall find the happiness of the one and the miserable estate of the other so tied by God to the very instant, and both so subject to interchange (witness the sudden downfall of the greatest princes and the speedy uprising of the meanest persons) as the one hath nothing so certain whereof to boast, nor the other so uncertain whereof to bewail itself. For there is no man so assured of his honor, of his riches, health or life, but that he may be deprived of either or all at the very next hour or day to come.

RALEGH—Preface to
History of the World

1

A two-wheeled cart rattles windows. Riding on the driver's
rail are a boy and a man. The man is large and thick and square.
Crudely carved from a tree trunk. The boy's the image of
his father. Both are dressed in simple homespun black. Neat
and clean. Both are grave-faced, as solemn as preachers on Good
Friday afternoon. In the cart behind them is a bale of fresh
straw, some pots and buckets, and a long wooden chest like a
sailor's.

The boy shivers in the cold and shifts his limbs as an awkward,
growing boy will.

The man holds the reins as the old horse, a white nag, sway-
backed, walks along, clip and clop, head down, half asleep.
The man with his head up and his back straight. His neck
is so thick and corded it seems he has no neck at all. A square,
crude-clipped head set flat upon the shoulders. The face,
above a full beard, is hard as teakwood, calm and composed.
The eyes, alive though; dark eyes, liquid, calm, and curiously
gentle.

"Father," the boy asks, "do you think he will give us some reward?"

The man's expression does not change. He looks ahead along the narrow street. Nothing moves except his lips.

"It is the custom. And I know him to be a most gracious and generous gentleman, a true gentleman. . . ."

He means what he says, not being given to idle words. But the qualification, the second use of the word *gentleman*, has its edge. For this fellow is, by both law and the papers of William Segar, Garter King of Arms, a gent himself. By law and proper papers and at a price of twenty-two shillings paid to Segar, he has been awarded the arms of a gentleman.

Perhaps if he had had thirty pounds for the purpose (though the price is now forty, they say) he could also be a carpet knight, knighted by the King of England. There have been many, not all of them of any higher rank and many of less importance than he. After all, in the first year of his reign the King knighted a thousand men, including not only merchants, but a barber and a fellow whose one claim to honor was that he was married to the laundress of the late Queen. The King could hardly be blamed, of course. For the late Queen had left him a scant nobility and, likewise, so few knights that in many counties it was not possible to assemble enough to make a lawful jury.

Well, King James found one way to increase his wealth. Knighthood for sale. Noble titles less easy to acquire and more costly, but nevertheless upon the market. As early as his first year, in a stroke, James issued a summons to all the English whose lands yield more than forty pounds a year, to come and be knighted. Or else to make a lesser payment if they preferred not to purchase a title. And there were new titles, not only the costly English baronet, but all the titles of Scotland and even Ireland, some having precedence over English nobility. The King made a feast of nobility, creating sevenfold the number of English peers. And not neglecting his old kingdom, he invented the Order of Knights Baronet of Nova Scotia. For ten thousand pounds a gentleman could be named a baron and be called Lord.

Well, sir, no wonder that the heralds of the College of Arms, in imitation of the King, could make a fellow into a gentleman. The true heralds, of course. There are many counterfeit and crank heralds abroad who are also making good profit. And when the Garter King of Arms, established in Derby House, saw fit to grant arms to such as the son of a peddler, a soap maker, a plasterer, a fishmonger, a hosier, and even a common player, why, then, any man who could raise the price, even a cutpurse, had precedent for his ambitions.

The man on the rail of the two-wheeled cart paid his price and received arms, too, and was a certified English gentleman. But, through misfortune, there was a scandal concerning his case, not in the granting of arms, but an error of Segar in giving him arms still extant in France. For which the Garter King gained a respite from duty and a term in Marshalsea prison. For which the innocent man in the cart gained considerable embarrassment. And that embarrassment being more fuel heaped on a fire. For though his vocation and service is honorable and he performs it well, it is a vocation not much respected by common people.

He is resigned to that. And he is capable of making distinctions between gentlemen of this age and the last.

"Yes, lad," he says quietly. "He will abide by old custom. And we shall each receive an adequate reward."

They pass on. Only the creak of the old-fashioned wheels and the slow rhythm of hooves.

That pair is Mr. Gregory Brandon, Gent., hangman and executioner, together with his young son Richard, who is learning his father's trade.

2

For the first time in the week a canopy of stars. New clarity
of air and colder than the fog and gusts of rain on the feast
day of St. Simon and St. Jude. Stars, afire with continual overbrimming of inner light, in cold clear cloudless air, burning
steady and even. In foul weather, they are veiled from sight,
obscured and diminished, suddenly few and poor; and the tired
earth hunches to itself, lonely, a beggar without shelter. Ragged
creature, sore and stiff, shivering like the last oak leaves, gnawed
by hunger and without hope.

And then, upon a slight turning of wind, change of weather,
and there they are! Still shining though we have seen them
not; and therefore, o ye of little faith, ye have imagined them
gone for good, blown out like old candles and ourselves left,
hopeless, condemned, and self-condemning, to perpetual darkness.

Nay, there is more than breach of faith in this triumph over
right reason, which tells us otherwise, refutes fallacious imagination, but is not heard. For is it not true, brothers, that we not
only fear the future in the darkness of the present, but also in
fear and trembling deny the truth of the past? Ascribing the

[623]

memory of the sun and moon and all that multitudinous host of numbered but uncounted stars to our own fantasy?

What a foolish paradox is there, my foolish brothers! To permit imagination to rise above right reason in discord and untuning. And then, mark you, to deny the reports of five senses and all records of memory. To deny the works of reason in the name of idle imagination. Imagination, an upstart tyrant, having usurped the throne and scepter of the anagogical man, then empowered—by will, mind you, by our own free volition —to revise the chronicle of our lives and make it seem imagination has been always king and right reason only a Lord of Misrule.

How intricate the mind of man is at the craft of devising unhappiness!

How fierce is the spirit of man in the overthrow of felicity!

How weak is our power to withstand testing and travail!

In winter we fear spring will never come again. In springtime we shrug off memory of winter's barren time, as we toss aside our cloaks upon the first warm day, and in blithe forgetfulness take the wonders of blooming and blossoming to be eternal.

At harvest we gorge like grunting swine, stagger in a grinning similitude of ourselves, belly tight as a drumhead with church ale, more like an African ape or monkey than an image of God, our Father. We dance beneath the harvest moon like gypsies until we fall. On earth we reach out to possess each other, man and woman slithering together in spittle and juices of flesh like fish in a creel.

Waking one day to a world of bristle and stubble, leafless trees and earth turned to iron again. Waking to shame and famine, having made no provision for body or soul. Even the

[624]

pissant, the wren, and the squirrel shame us with industry. Waking to winter sprung upon us like an ambush. And yet instead of asking our Lord's forgiveness for follies, we curse ourselves, which is in no way similar to repentance or contrition. Curse the weather, and curse Fortune, and, indeed, may come to curse the Almighty in our hopelessness!

For absence of hope is achieved by the banishment of faith, and charity steals away with the other two. He without hope is near to despair, close to that unforgivable condition which we name the sin against the Holy Ghost.

O ye of little faith! Could ye not watch and wait one hour with me?

Consider sheep, oft cited in the Scripture, who have no immortal soul. The sheep, who of all our beasts is most ignorant, being unable to save itself from not only the ravenous wolf and the wiles of the goat, being also incapable of preserving itself against its own folly and ignorance without continual herding and safeguarding, prodding by crook and staff, barking and nipping by faithful sheepdogs. The sheep, I say, dirty and stupid, lacking not merely soul but half the wit of a mongrel cur, fit to be sheared naked of greasy pride, then to be cut and cooked in its own fat and carved upon a table, the bones for the dogs and the dung heap. Consider that this sheep can demonstrate more faith and reason than a man. For sheep will safely graze, never doubting the presence of the shepherd though they see him not and though that shepherd pipe not a sound.

Our Shepherd pipes without ceasing, his music being in and of the world and all the firmament and in the Holy Scripture and in the omnipresent promptings of the Holy Spirit.

[625]

We are most fortunate sheep and altogether undeserving. For when we do not see the Shepherd, we deny him. And when our waxy ears, deaf to all but the noise of our hungers, pleasures, and pains, when our useless, faithless ears, I say, do not respond to the threefold harmony of our Shepherd's pipe, we deny there is music anywhere.

And then, praise be His Name, there comes a slight change of wind, a turn of weather, and, lo and behold, the infinite majesty of starry heavens is revealed, a thousand thousand eyes forever watching over us; their luster undiminished and unfading; their music inaudible and ineffable but demonstrable by simplest intellection; holes and chinks in a crumbling wall of the darkness, revealing the promise of an immortal and infinite brightness which would blind mortal eyes; there are the stars innumerable as the tribes from the loins of Abraham. . . .

And then we rejoice in God's gifts and mercy. As is meet and right and our bounden duty. Yet in joy and celebration of the world restored, robed in borrowed light, we should fall to our knees and weep for shame at our restless unbelief, our doubts and denials and unfaithfulness. Should offer up tears of repentance, contrition, and resolve; our paltry tears, which stir God the Father with smiling mercy and forgiveness, which God, in infinite mercy and wisdom, does mysteriously value, counting as nothing His own tears wept for us. His tears which some poets say are these very stars which brighten the darkness. . . .

So goes the portion of the sermon, as yet unspoken, taking shape in the mind of Robert Tounson.

No more than forty and already the Dean of the Collegiate Church of St. Peter in Westminster, he stands before the gate of the future. Waiting upon an occasion to enter into the garden of greatness, he presides over a famous domain. Worthy of the power of a bishop. Indeed, in its time it was a bishopric. Until Queen Elizabeth placed all the Abbey and its environs under the rule of a dean, but one independent of the bishops, all save the Archbishop. Power of office and responsibility are his, though not, like the abbots of old times, the concomitant wealth from possession of a hundred towns, a score of villages, more than two hundred manor houses and all the revenues thereof. None of that now, not since 1559, when Queen Elizabeth put out John Feckenham and the last monks of St. Benedict and turned the Abbey into a collegiate church.

It is enough for a young man to preside over, including all but the ancient palace and hall; the huge church including its multitude of sanctuaries, large and small, and within its boundary chapels, bell towers, gatehouses, cloisters, and a train of outbuildings and residences. Presiding over a thousand years of history, here where royalty, kings and queens from the dim Saxon days to children of King James, lie buried and where kings since the Conqueror have received the crown in the service of Coronation. Presiding over the shadowy tombs and mysteries of the future, he rules twelve prebends, a schoolmaster, an usher, and their servants. He is charged with the education of forty young scholars in the school, and also the care of twelve almsmen.

From where he sits in Jerusalem chamber, he can hear, dimly, noise of young scholars in the hall. Who, having attended their waking devotions, are eating a breakfast on enormous tables, made of wood from the ill-fated Armada, and given by the Queen.

Earlier he rose and left the deanery to see to the church. Walked the length of the nave, on beyond, past the high altar and the ring of chapels, and into the chapel of Henry VII at the east end. This place, crowded with royal tombs and effigies, most recently constructed chapel of his church, delights him and lifts his spirit. Well lit with candles and tapers, the wrought stone—walls, niches, columns, and tracery—springs heavenward, lighthearted, so craftily chiseled that it has been magically robbed of weight, is as airy as the play of fountains. And so the waking heart, a cold and heavy stone, may be broken by joy and lifted spiritually to join the wish of stone, aspiring to the heights where the tracery of vaults—like splashed water frozen at the instant of splashing, like the miraculous fountain of St. Thomas in far India—disappears.

Restored, he returned briskly, turning from the church through the chapel of St. Faith and across the great cloisters to the deanery. In the cloisters he was first startled, then inspired by the change of weather. Sky suddenly alive, afire with stars. It took his breath and lifted him higher than his prayers.

With no guests to entertain here, he has come to the Jerusalem chamber to collect his mundane thoughts for the affairs of the day. It is a quiet chamber, warmer and more pleasant than the deanery, with a fire casting its color on the deep-set painted windows, the polished cedar of paneling, bringing a living movement, new luster to the tapestries which tell the history of Jerusalem.

This has been a busy week with no time for leisure or for the luxury of meditation. Now he has a few minutes, thanks to his early rising, to think on the stars. Which have wakened his sleeping thoughts like a hive of ringing bells. And from that silent ringing he has come upon the subject for a sermon. A sermon worthy of a bishop—apt and simple, faithful to Gospel, albeit less ingenious and not so rhopographical as some more learned than he.

Let them spin their tropes, parade learning. They may please courtiers and Court ladies, may enjoy the pleasures of London. But they will not wear the bishop's miter. For the bishop, shepherd of the flock, must be a humble man and wise in humility.

And Robert Tounson has been marked to be a bishop. He is a mere step away from the glory of his true vocation.

This has been a year for the death of old bishops and the investing of new ones.

There have been implicit promises, and these last months he has been on tenterhooks, as chairs and places fell vacant and were filled. Dr. John Jegon, Bishop of Norwich, died and there was much scrambling. When the tumult of gossip cleared, it was John Overall, Bishop of Lichfield and Coventry, who was *translated* to that place.

It annoys Tounson, as it does other ambitious young divines, that they must jostle against bishops, too, who can use wealth to find fatter pastures. How can the Dean, without sufficient estate to win favor from the King, bid for a place against even the poorest bishop, who is rich as any earl? But who was it went, then, to Lichfield and Coventry? Why, none other than Dr. Valentine Carey, Dean of St. Paul's. More power to him. It cost him a pretty penny.

It must have cost them both a goodly sum. For Overall had first to overcome the Bishop of Bristow, who was also hungry for Norwich. Then the subtle Valentine Carey passed by Felton, Bishop of Bristow, to vault into the seat at Coventry.

Some consolation there in the price it cost Carey. At first it was believed that Dr. Anthony Maxie, Dean of Windsor and

[629]

most pleasing to His Majesty, would gain a chair. And the bruit was that Valentine Carey edged him out with a fulsome five and twenty hundred thanks. For which thanks he received not Norwich, but Coventry.

Many places fell vacant in this year by the hand of the Lord. But they were filled by the open hands of the King and Council and sometimes surprisingly.

Item. The Bishopric of Chichester went to Thomas Morton, Bishop of Chester. And into his place came one John Bridgeman, a parson of Wigon.

Item. After much speculation Landaffe went to George Carleton.

Item. Most disappointing of all to Tounson was the elevation of Martin Fatherby, prebend at Canterbury, to the Bishopric of Salisbury. Which Tounson had some hopes for.

Item. Most recent the death of James Montague. Tounson has held no hopes in that direction. But he was as surprised as all others when Bishop Andrewes, the eloquent Lancelot Andrewes of Ely, and once Dean here, was made new Bishop of Winchester.

Still, in an odd year, with churchmen dying and the living playing at the game of chairs and music, there is possibility. Someone must take Lancelot Andrewes' place at Ely, if and when he relinquishes it. Then there is news that when John King, Bishop of London, last preached before the Court and King, he was tiresome and did not please.

But, though gossip feed imagination, it is not a meal of hope.

More to the point is the news that this Fatherby, so newly made Bishop of Salisbury, is heavy, ill with a dropsy and not long for this world.

[630]

Perhaps King and Council work with wisdom, after all. True, the King is hard pressed for money and therefore a bishopric can cost a fortune. Yet there is some justice in this; for by moving the older bishops about or elevating such types as Martin Fatherby, known to be in poor health, the King can be certain that there will always be places to offer. And here's irony too. For if Fatherby, for example, should die soon enough (pray for the health of his immortal soul; flesh is as grass that withers away), he shall not even have commenced to regain his investment. And still the diocese will be worth its weight and more. Why not earn it twice over, if one were a king?

The King is a shrewd merchant when it comes to the keeping of his church.

Why not, by the same token, the price having already been paid in full, use the Bishopric of Salisbury, a mere example mind you, as a reward for good service by a man who cannot pay such a large thanksgiving offering?

Yesterday afternoon the See of Salisbury ("a mere example, mind you," the Archbishop told him) had been planted in his head by George Abbot, Archbishop of Canterbury.

After the King's Bench hearing in the hall, Abbot dined with Tounson and some other churchmen. When Tounson complained that this unexpected matter added to the burden of a busy week, Abbot, ever crusty as seafarer's bread, allowed how it might add to his busyness, true enough, but that he could imagine no other affairs of this week, or any week, which stood as fair to add as well to Tounson's stature.

Abbot was always, it seemed, forthright, blunt, and direct; but it is unwise to take him so simply. Tounson politely asked him his meaning.

"Why," he said, "it is simple enough. The King is much

[631]

concerned in this matter, more so than he knows. But he shall know. Yes, he will know it soon enough. And, let me be plain and unequivocating, an affair which is of concern to the King and will come to concern him more, that affair, my good Dean, is of more concern to you than all other business. It does not often happen so, not often in one lifetime." Then: "On my word, your innocence does you some credit in heaven, but not in this world."

"It is not my innocence of the world," Tounson replied. "Allow my puzzlement to come from ignorance and from fear."

"A man's ignorance can be remedied if he is reasonable," Abbot said. "Fear is not so easy cured."

After dinner, as they walked in the cloisters, the Archbishop delayed his departure, to take Robert Tounson aside. It was then that he offered, as a mere example, mind you, the news of Martin Fatherby's decline in health and the prospect of Salisbury.

He must have had good reason for this. Abbot knows something more than he would or could openly declare. There is some surety in that. The explanation for his interest may be that already Abbot can see Robert Tounson as the Bishop of Salisbury. In which case Abbot will need his friendship; for Abbot, though high, is far from unshakable.

To be Bishop of Salisbury!

He has often imagined such a thing, but now has real cause to consider the prospect. And as if that were not enough, there is the prospect that at his age, with, Lord willing, with a long life before him, he may rise even higher.

"For, my young Dean," Abbot grumbled, "you stand in a favorable position in this matter. It must go well for the King.

Otherwise it shall go ill. There is no chance for something betwixt and between.

"Much that is outward and visible is not in the King's hands. He is at the mercy of weather, the hour, the disposition of the crowd. And Ralegh's behavior shall reflect upon him. No doubt of that. The report of all who behold it shall be most influential. Meaning—do you apprehend?—that though the King says the last word, the culprit shall *have* the last word nonetheless.

"Outward and visible, I have said. But you, sir, shall be the sole arbiter of inward and spiritual truth. And should the affair go ill for the King, it shall be within your power to turn it well by your accounting. In the matter of his faith, you, sir, shall be the judge, clerk, advocate, and jury. And so I say you shall render the verdict, which is the last and best report."

Bishop of Salisbury . . . I

"You are able, then, to render the King good service," Abbot continued. "For your own sake, I pray you shall be both honest and careful. . . ."

The rest, cautionary grumblings of the old man, he scarcely listened to.

The outward and visible Robert Tounson nodded and responded gravely.

Perhaps Abbot is afraid. Fears have overcome judgment. No matter. His views of the large meaning of this affair are theatrical and improbable. Not to be considered seriously. And even if true, still no concern of Tounson.

Ralegh, according to Abbot, is merely the goat. A sacrificial goat upon the altar of the Spanish Match. Gondomar, crafty *Gallego,* has demanded it. But Gondomar cannot have imagined the King would honor his demand. Clearly, it is the intent of the King to turn the tables, to render Gondomar and Spain speechless and beholden to him at the cheapest price.

Whether or not this stratagem will succeed, remains to be seen. And if it does, the results are far from clear, though the first effects may be gratifying to the King. For the stratagem is larger than this and the stakes are greater than they seem. We cannot see and know it all, but let us look to our own vineyard, the Church of England. Strange doings are afoot. Shifting winds and tricky tides. Upon the one hand it seems the King has lost patience with the recusant Catholics. So much so that it would appear he has cast his lot, or at least his favor and encouragement, in the other direction, toward the Puritans and eager pursuivants. Would seem, of late, his purpose is to punish the Catholics severely.

Yet . . .

Yet how does this match with the Spanish Match?

And where does this leave the Church of England? How explain the King's favor to certain particular churchmen who lean a long shadow toward Rome even while mouthing the articles of our faith?

Does the right hand know what the left is doing?

And so on and so on . . .

Abbot is old and troubled. For a man upon the threshold of something worthy of his gifts there is no cause to consider the fancies of an old man who has seen better days. Be polite and deferential, to be sure. But stand aside, just a little, in case he cracks and falls from his pedestal. . . .

"Are you the one that is to serve as chaplain?"

A rude, coarse, ill-mannered voice breaks his meditation. Tounson blinks in surprise at crimson and gold and a tall bluff yeoman of the Guard. Who has entered the Jerusalem chamber without a knock.

"I am the Bishop . . ." he begins. Then pauses, unable to check a slight smile at his own mistake, despite this fellow's impudence.

"I am Dr. Robert Tounson, Dean of Westminster," he says gravely.

The fellow must be daft. He is not in the least humbled.

"Well, you are late," he snaps. "If you plan to do any preaching or praying over Sir Walter Ralegh, you'd better be quick about it."

And then, without by-your-leave, turns heels and is gone.

Tounson can't believe this has happened. So startled he cannot remember the face of the soldier. Should make complaint of the man's lack of respect, but doubts he could recognize the culprit if they parade the whole Guard before him. Then why not act in Christian charity and forgiveness? These soldiers, bloody-minded men, lose whatever religion they may have had when they first learn to trail a pike. Might as well try to teach good manners to a wolf or a wild boar.

He will offer a prayer for the man's soul when he has the leisure to do so.

Meantime he has no leisure to think about it. He must quickly rouse his party of prebend, acolyte, and linkboys and be off to the gatehouse.

He comes through Jericho parlor and down the stairs into Dean's Court, shouting for them. Only to find his little party all there waiting for him, torches burning, and a servant with his hat and warm cloak ready.

His fault, of course. He has schooled them all against the offense of interrupting his meditations. For he can wield a

[635]

birch rod (in Christian charity) as well as any schoolmaster in England. But it is their souls he is concerned with, not the wincing cheeks of their fleshly backsides.

"You lazy lads!" he calls out, as he slips into the cloak. "What good are you standing about like mice? Be quick! Be quick! Lead the way! And God help you if you lead me through mud puddles!"

3

On this day, by coincidence, there are not the two, but four sheriffs for London and Middlesex.

The sheriffs for London and Middlesex are by tradition elected on June 24, Midsomer Day. They are sworn in early October, upon Michaelmas Even. The following day they appear at Westminster Hall, clad in scarlet and furred gowns, cut in the old fashion and still including a hood, though these days officers affect a fine hat of Spanish felt to cover their heads, accompanied each by their appointed men in parti-colored gowns, each with six clerks, sixteen sergeants, and each sergeant with his yeomen, all to be sworn. And to assume their duties for the new year.

Yet in a strict and literal sense of law the new sheriffs do not assume offices until after they have joined in yet another ceremonial oath-taking, together with the Lord Mayor of London, the aldermen and all their retinue, upon the morning of Lord Mayor's Day.

Which means that the sentence to be imposed upon Sir Walter Ralegh, should the King stand fast, is a problem for four men, two who have in truth already passed on their duties and perquisites to the others. The situation is exceptional. Indeed none can recall an execution on Lord Mayor's Day, at least not one of importance.

None of the four were happy about this. For the duties of the office of sheriff, especially of London and Middlesex, are demanding and expensive. And though the perquisites and means of offsetting expense are richer here than in other counties, it can easily be a purse-thinning office. Especially when the King has studied all possibilities of increasing revenues in extraordinary ways. In the country a gentleman may be expected to move adroitly to avoid the burdens of this office. Too many tasks have lately been imposed upon sheriffs, too many duties and responsibilities; the expenses growing and occasions for return small. In the country the gentlemen have shown themselves willing to pay a good price *not* to serve. King and Council, alert to this, have used it to advantage. Not only to gain gifts from a list of eligible gentlemen, but also to chasten this man or to diminish that ambitious man's estate. Moreover, he who is finally elected—that is, after being chosen by Council—is then encouraged to pay handsomely for the privilege to be named as an eligible gentleman when he would be so, anyway.

To be a sheriff of London and Middlesex is not a perilous calling. In good times a man can turn a profit. And it is one step toward becoming, later, Lord Mayor.

All well and good. But here is a difficult problem for these men. Who can be strictly by the letter, and the letter may prove vital to them all, called sheriffs of London and Middlesex in the early morning hours of Lord Mayor's Day? For whatever is the will of the King, be it mercy or rigor, he may come to regret it. Indeed it would be not unlike the King to regret action either way. The King may *intend* to regret his choice. And when a king has second thoughts, it is not he, but those who executed the first ones, who pay the regretful price.

These four remember how in '03 at Winchester, the page, a mere piping boy, bearing the King's clemency, could not push through the crowd and cried out until others with more voice echoed him and caught the attention of that sheriff in time to perform the King's stage play.

But (four men have thought) what if that boy had been delayed?

What if his cries had not been heard in that rain-swept crowd?

What if the sheriff had been too preoccupied to hear? For the poor man would have been busy enough with the hanging, drawing, and quartering of three men, one after the other.

Well, it could raise the hairs on the back of a man's neck to think on that.

Now when this hasty business of the *habeas corpus* writ, the delivering of Ralegh from custody of the Lord Lieutenant of the Tower to the sheriffs at King's Bench, had been told to them, the four met in a tavern on the eve of Simon and Jude.

The affair must be correct in each detail. And responsibility must be diffused among them so that none could bear blame entirely. A bargain made more complex because not one would dare to deal directly with the true subject—that all four feared the double-dealing of their own King. No, the discussion must be only how and in what fashion they might join together to work out His Majesty's wishes.

Oblique negotiation made the more tentative because the two sheriffs of 1617, William Hollyday and Richard Johnson, are gentlemen of means and distinction. Active in foreign trading and ventures, they are acquainted with Sir Walter Ralegh. The newly elected sheriffs are Sir Hugh Hammersley, a wealthy

[639]

member of the Haberdasher's Guild and one of King James' carpet knights, a man of repute in the Royal Artillery Company; the other, Master Richard Harne, a mystery to the others, who makes his home in London at The Blew Anchor, an inn in Cheapside. It is said that his wife, Alice, comes of gentle people in Cambridge and that they have no children.

Hammersley was polite, cautious, circumspect, and properly deferential to the other two gentlemen. Who, though not knights themselves, could afford to do without that distinction.

All three were equally, and separately, suspicious of Richard Harne. Who was a trifle too familiar when he was not openly indifferent to their reputations and the distinctions among them. Who drank too much ale while they sipped theirs. Who talked too loud when he did speak and laughed too much, often at nothing at all, some secret mirth. Who remained in the tavern when they parted company to go their ways. Last seen by them joining a group of roguish cutpurse types at the dicing table. Where, it seemed he was known, and not only as a new sheriff of London and Middlesex.

The fellow had not seemed to comprehend the difficulty. He had yawned in their faces.

"I know nothing of inkhorn law. And what's more, gentlemen, I do not care a rotten fig. Decide for yourselves what you wish to do and you'll find me agreeable. But let us not waste the best hours of the night. Decide for yourselves."

He played with a gold coin on the table and appeared to pay them no further heed until they had reached an agreement.

Yet, for all his sullen, ill-mannered unconcern, each of them accounted it likely he missed not a word they said. And in an hour or two might be able to write it all down verbatim.

They each allowed themselves to consider the possibility that

Master Richard Harne was not the man he seemed to be. He might dupe ordinary rogues and half-drunken cutpurse ruffians. But something about him, Master Richard Harne—if indeed that was the man's true name—was clipped, a counterfeit coin.

Hammersley knew him no better than the others.

Of course, this fellow might have acquired enough substance, never mind how, to purchase the office. And, considering the company he made familiar with, he might manage to turn a profit on his investment in a year's time. More so, in sum and total, than a gentleman sheriff. Who would not deign to cast their lines or nets to catch small fish.

Still they must each weigh another possibility, that Richard Harne smelled like a spy, an intelligencer.

Was it when they noticed that the gold coin he toyed with was *Spanish?* Or was the coin merely circumstantial? Afterwards, if asked, none of them could have told where reason and imagination first shook hands.

In the late years of the Queen, when there was discontent and when she seemed so influenced by Archbishop Whitgift to fear the dangers of Puritan and Papist equally, there was much use made of spies. Spies upon Englishmen. Spies to spy out other spies—Jesuits, Puritans, and these likewise spying upon each other. No one could know who might be a spy or spied upon. Well, the new King is even more fearful for his person than the late Queen. And there are believed to be more agents afoot now than then. So much so that it is a constant subject for ballads and broadsides and certain, if touched upon lightly, to raise laughter in the playhouses.

That may be an explanation. Richard Harne, intelligencer for the King or the Council, called to London after service elsewhere. Perhaps having finished his spying for good and all. And given a name and a modest pension and a reward—a year as sheriff to feather his nest.

In which event he has nothing to fear. Or like every snake of a spy, cold-blooded, he has lost the habit of fear. Lives by his wits from each moment to the next. And, as he put it, does not care a rotten fig.

Still, they must allow the possibility—that Master Richard Harne is still at this time an intelligencer. That the King or Council would place a spy in the honorable office of sheriff may seem strange. But there are many strange things these days. A reasonable man knows not what to credit and what to laugh at.

Very well, then ask why. One cannot deny the King's present irritation at the city of London. Perhaps he wishes to marshal information about them, if not evidence against them. But would that not be too simple? In his stratagems the King likes scatter shot, which can riddle more than one target.

Certainly to have his own man as a sheriff is one form of assurance in the matter of Walter Ralegh. And Richard Harne was chosen not long after Ralegh's return to Plymouth. . . .

The spinning Spanish gold coin tipped on its edge and spun in circle by . . . long slender tapering fingers. . . .

Clever fingers, not those of a common rogue. Hammersley, noticing the man's hands, felt his own, heavy and meaty as lamb chops.

All reason could do was to allow for possibilities and allow there was neither knowledge nor evidence yet of any.

They managed to reach an agreement. The two gentlemen soon to be retired for good, would go to King's Bench to

[642]

take custody of the culprit. And would place him in the gate-house and arrange for his security there. Sensible and strictly legal. Except, of course, for the whole begged question of the legality of *any* of these proceedings and actions. And nothing to be done about that.

Sensible, for since both these gentlemen are acquainted with Sir Walter Ralegh, they are in the best position to judge his mood and intent.

In the morning, then, Hammersley and Harne are to come early to Westminster for the execution. If it comes to that. Perhaps it will not, but should it be accomplished according to what they understood to be the King's wishes, then they must see it through.

"Who knows what the King's wishes are? Do any of you gentlemen?" Harne asked, without looking up from his coin. And evidently expected no answer, for he laughed to himself for his own reply.

There is, it must be admitted, another difficulty, the matter of time. Nine o'clock of the day or not long after that the Lord Mayor and the aldermen and all their men will be arriving at Westminster. If possible the execution must be over and done with before then, and the crowd diverted. By all rights, no other choice, Ralegh must be dead, if he must die, before nine o'clock.

Not to forget that both Harne and Hammersley must change into their formal robes for the ceremonies in the Hall.

Therefore Walter Ralegh must be upon the scaffold no later than eight o'clock.

"A pretty plan, gentlemen," Harne said. "But you make no allowance for the Fox. He has a part to play."

[643]

"What do you mean, sir?" Hammersley asked.

And now Harne palmed his coin and looked at them, smiling, leaning his arms on the table.

"The Fox can tell the time of day," he said. "Perhaps he will make an oration that will last until dinner time."

He must not be allowed to speak too long, they agreed. It is the prerogative of the sheriff to limit the speaking.

"Good, then," Harne said, rising first, returning the coin to his plain leather purse and standing over them. "If he will not stop his mouth, we'll stop it for him."

Then to Hammersley, with a wink: "Until we meet again, Mr. Sheriff. I shall greet you upon the scaffold."

He picked up his tankard of ale and left them to stare at his thin back as he walked away.

And now it is Sir Hugh Hammersley with a few of his men, carried under the stars on a small boat pulled by a pair of Southwark watermen. The only sounds are the splash of their oars. And of other oars as well. For there is traffic on the Thames already. Lights burn on both banks.

Hammersley is worried. Wondering how Harne will behave on the scaffold. And if his behavior becomes unseemly, how to manage him.

Hammersley has never been one of those men who enjoy the spectacle of public executions. At those few it has been his misfortune to witness, he has chosen to stand far back in the crowd and at the last to close his eyes.

It would be most embarrassing if the new sheriff of London and Middlesex should, on the scaffold in the presence of many, be forced to vomit.

He has taken a cordial prepared by an apothecary. But it

seems to be of no virtue. The light motion of a wherry on the Thames—or is it the idea of the execution?—has his bowels turning somersaults.

For his own sake, then, he offers a prayer that the King will be merciful this morning.

Spending the night in chambers in old palace at Westminster are certain of the nobility. They must rise earlier than is their custom to be barbered, dressed, and prepared for a public appearance.

William Compton, new-made, in August, Earl of Northampton, twenty years younger than Ralegh. Here to show himself in the splendor of his title. Here, more pertinently, because he invested money in the Guiana voyage and, what with the high cost of his title and other recent expenses, he wonders if he shall have any return on that. He is hoping that Ralegh may reveal something. Perhaps a clue to what has become of vanished jewels and other valuables. He might gain favor of the King and his kinsman, the King's present favorite, if he can give intelligence on this.

This new Earl thinks that a man about to die will not die with secrets in his heart and in the presence of a nobleman there to whom he is in debt.

There is young Henry de Vere, Earl of Oxford, well known in Court and London for drinking, brawling, whoring, and wenching, though he has only just returned from a tour of Italy. In Venice he offered to lead a band of volunteers in defense of that republic. And heard there that Sir Walter Ralegh might come to serve the Venetians as Admiral. It is reported that the Earl of Oxford has at last acquired some polish and refinement in his travels.

Greatest of the earls intending to be present is Thomas Howard, Earl of Arundel, proud, tall, and thin, now in his thirty-third year, though he seems stiff and grave, older than his years.

Already he has known such ups and downs of fortune as to be deeply disenchanted. His grandfather, Duke of Norfolk, was beheaded in the reign of Elizabeth in '72. His father died in the Tower in '95. And he lived his youth in close straits, near to poverty, seeing his own kin, the Howards, divide up estates and lands which should have been his. King James restored to him those portions which had been attained by the crown and made him Earl of Arundel. But two of his kinsmen, prodigal with his wealth and their own, remain in high office—the old Lord Admiral, now Earl of Nottingham, and the Earl of Suffolk, sitting on Council as the Lord High Treasurer.

The Earl of Arundel is a man of contradictions. He affects extreme simplicity of dress, perhaps out of the memory of times when simplicity was an enforced condition. Yet in his insistence upon ceremony, the old rules of etiquette and chivalry, in his examplary behavior, he has become, in contrast to a crude Court, the model of the ideal courtier.

James Hay has put it plainly, saying: "Here comes the Earl

[647]

of Arundel in his plain stuff and trunk hose and untrimmed beard in his teeth. And yet he looks more like a nobleman than any of us."

Arundel might be a Puritan by his appearance and rigidity, but was born a Catholic and continued steadfast in that faith until Archbishop Abbot brought him into the fold of the Church of England.

Though no one is likely to follow his style of dress, he has set one fashion—the collecting of pictures and statues from Europe, especially from Italy. Building upon the inheritance of a library and a gallery of pictures from his kinsman Lord Lumley, he has traveled the Continent in search of books and manuscripts, paintings and statues. And he keeps a network of agents there to buy for him. In travels to Italy, once in the company of Inigo Jones, together with his own company of thirty-six servants, he has brought home the strange ancient Roman statues and figures, all bare stone and unpainted, for the gardens and gallery of Arundel House. And the fashion has caught on with young Prince Charles and the rising men around him.

Arundel's wife, less interested in such things, has brought home a Venetian gondola for her passages on the Thames.

A disenchanted Earl, but never a wicked or malicious man. Exemplary, though rigid and severe; trustworthy and a man of honor.

Honor which has brought him here to Westminster. For just before sailing off to Guiana, Walter Ralegh promised Arundel, also an investor in the venture, to return to England come what would and might. And so he did, all rumors and reports to the contrary. Returned in disgrace, but in honor. The Earl understands that paradox well. If he had not returned, he might have saved his skin. And so it behooves the Earl of Arundel to lend some measure of dignity no matter what transpires.

There is a fourth nobleman, nearby in Westminster though not at old palace, who has come to witness the events of the morning.

Older than the three earls, he is Sir Edmund Sheffield, Third Baron Sheffield. Whose mother married the Earl of Leicester in '73. And he served under Leicester as a soldier in the Netherlands. He commanded a ship against the Armada in '88. But he was young and only one of many in the time of the Queen. Prosperity has come in the new reign. He serves presently as Lord Lieutenant of Yorkshire.

Has been acquainted with Walter Ralegh, from a certain distance, and indeed has shared in some of his interests, including the future of planting colonies of Englishmen in the New World.

But it is not old acquaintanceship or mutual interest which bring him to be present, to see and to be seen. Sheffield is caught on the horns of an old dilemma. Because he is married to a Catholic, he has incurred the suspicion of some of the Protestant faction at Court. Yet his vigorous actions, enforcing law to the letter, against Catholic recusants in Yorkshire, far from clearing away doubts, have brought him troubles from the other side. The execution of a Catholic priest a little over a year ago brought an angry complaint from the Spanish Ambassador and a reprimand, a cooling of favor from the King.

Today he is playing for both sides.

Let his presence be interpreted by the King and the Spanish faction as support of the King's actions.

[649]

Meanwhile let the Protestants read in sympathetic concern a proof he is not allied to the other faction.

If he keeps straight face and grave countenance, it will work. For a blank mask becomes the face of comedy or tragedy according to the wishes of the beholder.

Most important, he will be seen there, and can only be less vulnerable for it.

Four noble gentlemen of England, three of high estate, are awake and preparing to be seen at the occasion (death or life) of this morning.

None of them certain which way things may go. Knowing, then, no more than Walter Ralegh.

At least, though they may not imagine it, they truly share that much—the strict uncertainty of the condemned.

5

A man groans in bed. Where he lies awake, having slept little.

He is Sir Sebastian Harvey, a wealthy man, member of the Guild of Ironmongers. Today is to be the most important day of his life. But he has not yet recovered from yesterday.

Yesterday, on the feast of Simon and Jude, he gathered a host of friends, servants, and aides, masters of his guild, all tricked out in new livery, the gentlemen in fine new forty-shilling gowns, and all together with horses and shiny weapons and music, with members of the watch of the wards and the trained bands of the London militia carrying pikes and halberds, with even a whiffler crying out, going with a broadsword to clear the way for the procession, just as for the King when he moves in procession through the streets, all these and many more if you count kith and kin, friends and families, strangers and dignitaries from elsewhere, and a fair number of imposters, all to be entertained with food and drink, music and shows at his considerable expense; yesterday through the streets of London winding slowly, streets bedecked with a multitude of banners and pennants and huge gay-colored cloths

[651]

hanging down from the windows of houses, yesterday Sir Sebastian Harvey moved in triumphant procession to the magnificent Guildhall of London. Where in the presence of the members of all the ancient honored guilds (almost seventy now) and together with the twenty-six aldermen of each of the wards, he was given honor and authority to rule as Lord Mayor of London for a year. To rule and to represent this city and, within its walls and gates, to be second to no man living. The King himself, by ancient custom and privilege if not bald truth, being not superior to the Lord Mayor, once within the walls of London. Indeed the King must have the invitation and permission of the Lord Mayor to enter this privileged ground.

Amid pomp and ceremony was named Lord Mayor. Then the procession reformed and proceeded to the Ironmongers' Hall on Fenchurch Street. Where he and two score odd liverymen of the guild, together with the freemen and their wives and children and a crowd of guests, sat down to a feast in honor of his election; others who could not be accommodated in the hall being served dinner at that stone house, the Elephant Tavern, nearby.

At the foot of the stairs leading up to the hall, he saluted the old wooden statue of their patron, St. Lawrence, full of sympathy for that saint's martyrdom, as he considered the mounting costs of this day and the days to come.

Unwisely, though, he ignored the companion statue of the bird of the company, the mysterious ostrich. Which can digest iron.

But yesterday was small shakes of a lamb's tail, a prologue to the festivities of today. Which is his day. And yesterday, with coming and going of herds of clouds—a wan and seldom sun,

[652]

like a face pressed against a window, with whimsical gusts of wind and rain and, rain or no, a damp persistent chill pervading all—yesterday was as much disappointment as pleasure.

Disappointment that, due to fickle weather, crowds along the way were small, the banners and bright cloths sparse, the cheers thin, and the excitement literally dampened.

Pleasure not only in the award of the honor and power of the office, but also, he must confess in the thought that he was saving something with the much greater expense of Lord Mayor's Day to follow. That holiday when the water conduits and fountains must run adequate wines and all of London must be his guests. And an army from the various guilds must be his guests for a feast at the Guildhall; that day, come what prosperity or trouble the year ahead may bring, will leave him a good deal leaner than he begins it. The more so because it will all be dutifully, carefully chronicled by clerks, recorded and compared against the truth and legend of the festivities of Lord Mayors' Days, the long roll of Lord Mayors since the custom commenced, more than three centuries before Sir Sebastian Harvey. Each year becoming more expensive as prices rise, more extravagant as each man, for his honor and the honor of his guild, must outdo the last. Until he feels he must, in one short day, contend against three hundred years.

If an angel appeared at this moment to offer him the choice, he might most willingly exchange places with the knight in the gatehouse, off Tothill Road, leading into the yard at Westminster. Who can only lose, or not lose, his head on this day. Sir Sebastian Harvey's head, following the afternoon and evening of brave toasts, is as sore and twitchy as the bare back of a carted whore, as full of fires and clanging noises as a foundry. He would gladly remove it and rest it like a hat on a peg if he could.

[653]

Today will be longer and louder by far. Perhaps, the best he can hope for, wine will stifle his pains. Perhaps, he imagines, he will become lightheaded and his head will swell up like a bubble of soap and float away forever. Leaving only his wounded, fractious bowels to contend against.

Today for his honor and the honor of his family name, in respect of his recent knighthood, dearly bought, and in and for the honor of the office of Lord Mayor of London and all the dead Lord Mayors and all those yet to come (damn their eyes, the dead and the unborn!) he must offer a day to be remembered for at least a year. Not to mention or think of the seven or perhaps more fixed days of the calendar on which he must make a procession to St. Paul's. Or the ever increasing number of holidays, sacred and secular, where he must lend his presence.

In the morning he will go upriver on a richly decorated barge together with other barges bearing aldermen and dignitaries, and trailed by almost every piece of wood that will float on the river. Go up the river—*pray be calm, be gentle to my bowels*—clad in scarlet ceremonial robes. Land at the water gate of Westminster and proceed to enter the hall, where King's Exchequer will administer the oath to him and the aldermen and the sheriffs of London and Middlesex. Then back by water again to begin the progress through the streets. There will be triumphal arches for this occasion. Like a Coronation procession. Gifts and speeches and performances at the arches and other places. All built around some appropriate theme. For which he has paid dearly enough, for the services of one Anthony Munday, poet. Who has arranged the theme to be "Sidero—Thriambus, or, Iron and Steele Triumphing."

And after all that the procession will end at the Guildhall, where the banquet will begin.

[654]

There, by custom, the Sovereign should be his honored guest. Except the King is in the country chasing hares.

Except that even as Harvey arrives at Westminster for the solemn oath, there may be a public execution taking place in the yard. And the crowd will press around the scaffold. For, given a choice, who would not prefer a beheading to the sight of a plump and worthy ironmonger, tricked out in scarlet, come to take an oath.

Besides which, he has been told, there will be others besides Londoners, who are becoming as thick as maggots on a dead dog or fleas on a living, drawn to see a celebrated, disgraced knight pay the penalty for old treasons and new disobedience. Drawn from the nearby shires, to be sure. And he has intelligence there are some who have come all the way from the Westcountry, rough Devon seamen and even small miners from far Cornwall who can speak a strange tongue when they please to. These can cause trouble enough. If they do not interfere with the King's plans (*God, let them not riot against the King!*), they will likely make trouble for the city of London.

It does not take much at any time to cause riot and mayhem in London. But when the conduits are flowing wine and the streets are full of surly strangers, rubbing elbows and jostling for place with the unruly, ill-mannered Londoners, then . . .

Pray God in heaven my day will not go down in the chronicles as the Triumph of Broken Heads.

When he retired and tried to sleep, even his servants were drunk. And his best man, Arthur, puked his guts into the fireplace of the chamber; and that is an odor, frying vomit, which no perfume can dispel. Hearing Arthur heave, he would have joined him side by side if it had not been beneath his dignity; and then perhaps he might have slept and snored all night like

Arthur, instead of tossing and turning in the rolling room like a man atop a mast. He had hoped the foul weather might continue, even to his disadvantage.

But that hope was dispelled by a cheerful gap-toothed hulking lad, ugly as a donkey's rump and not half so symmetrical, who came staggering into his chamber with a huge armload of firewood—dropping half in an incredible rattle that waked Sir Sebastian's wife with a cry of "Thieves! Thieves!"—to announce, an' it pleased him, sir, that the wind had changed and the sky was clear as a bell and scoured clean of everything but stars and such, and wasn't that a marvel, now?

A marvel indeed for a wind to change as winds will.

If that boy should labor long and study like a Cambridge scholar, he may yet become a turnspit before he dies.

So he called for lights. And sought to calm his wife. Whom he kissed and she groaned at the blast of his breath. And she rolled over like a fat fish. Pulling pillow over head and soon snored in a counterpoint with Arthur. Whom a cannon would not waken.

There are no lights. *Are they all drunk and snoring save one idiot lad not to be trusted with a candle lest he burn down London?* And he lies in his bed, listening to the duet of snores. And, even as yesterday, only contrariwise, pleased and disappointed. Thinking upon a clear cold Lord Mayor's Day.

He allows himself to question the purposes of the King. Wonders why the King should absent himself from Lord Mayor's Day. Never mind all grand and glorious philosophy of kings, etc. It is no secret, every merchant in London, and no doubt every prentice and servant slut as well, knows the King has a mountain of debts. Well, Sir Sebastian, Ironmonger Knight, there shall be packed into the Guildhall for the banquet a

[656]

mountain of rich men with a mountain of money among them. More gold there, if truth be known, than all crazed Ralegh's chimerical golden mountains of Guiana. More gold than all the gain of the Spanish Match. Not that the King will get it or could find it if he rooted up all London like a pregnant sow. But it is there. Enough to buy a king free of debt and into felicity. And those members of the ancient guilds will take it to be an offense that he is too proud and too busy at hunting to attend.

Of course, the King has always feared crowds, even at Court, and lately has come to hate them more. He has never been pleased with London, crowds and clamor, its ever spreading warren of buildings and dwellings, law or no law. Some call it England's jewel. The King has called it—a wen. Would put a surgeon to that swelling if he could. But cannot. And that must rub him raw. For he needs London, prosperity of guilds and merchants. No doubt he would like to melt them one and all of riches like a gob of fat. But that would be to kill the magic goose. More-over, after the late Queen's example of promptly repaying all she borrowed and with full interest, he must do the same. With a difference: that his credit is not so sure as hers, and he must pay more interest and consider himself fortunate. Easy enough to see why the King might not love this city.

There is, to be truthful, a mutual distrust. Not so much dis-trust of the King and his judgment, as that in constant absences for hunting and pleasure, generosity to favorites, and evident in-difference to the knavish and rowdy behavior of so many of his Court, he is indifferent to the offense of the good citizens of London.

The King must have been angered considerably by the sa-tiric blasts coming out of London against the scrounging Scots-men he brought with him when he first came. Powerless, as also

[657]

the authorities of London were, to prevent this unless the guilty were caught. The Queen and her Court had endured much of this, yet ignored all but the most outrageous and blasphemous attacks.

Moreover, though decent citizens of London took offense against the idle living, the devilishly extravagant apparel, and some of the pastimes of the courtiers, like dicing, card playing, dancing, all games of chance, and going to plays in suburb theaters, they had not then one half the cause to complain that they do today.

The Court of the Queen, though frequently present and to be seen in formal and ceremonious affairs, was at a certain distance from the life of the citizen. Now the very opposite is true. There are few occasions when the splendor of Court is to be shared. But this larger, more cumbersome, undisciplined Court has spilled over into the city, and takes its pleasure and finds amusement there. You will find courtiers, noblemen of high birth and station, in London's taverns mingling with riffraff, and scarcely distinguished from them except by their fat purses, as they drink themselves sodden and stupid, engage in brawls and frays, make.sport of decent folk, then flee back to the safety of the verge of Court. Safe from the law there. To be mildly chastised at most.

A most uncomfortable position for a Lord Mayor, the aldermen and all their men: to maintain a safe, orderly city when courtiers behave like common rogues and common rogues imagine themselves to be the very models of chivalry.

It is not mere whisper of rumor that feeds offense. The city has plenty of bastards of the Court. Pimps and procurers are packs of hounds seeking out young women (even wives!) to corrupt in the service of the Court. And ladies of Court drink like the men, appear in public with their breasts more revealed than protected by the thinnest, sheerest of lawn, and have their own pimps and places for assignation with lusty lads of the city. And if he will pay the price, a common citizen can have such a fine lady flat as a flounder beneath him. But will risk pox as much as if he took his pleasure from a sixpence whore.

Well, pox will take them all soon enough.

Paying the price is all. A man can have knighthood or baronet for a price, it's true. But not thereby gain acceptance or respect at Court. To the courtier, though he may not have a clay pot to piss in, a bought title will gain a citizen nothing but contempt.

But worst of all is the violence of these men of Court. Their murderous duels with each other are bad enough. And most curious since the King hates such things and speaks out against them again and again. But a common citizen has no recourse, being considered unfit by law to defend himself or to duel for his honor with a courtier. The man from Court can strike and beat and ridicule the citizen with impunity on his own grounds. In the city he will hire a pack of ruffians to beat or murder a citizen.

Since there is no recourse to justice—even the old Star Chamber is now strangely turned against the commoner—the watch of the wards have been instructed to make no fine distinctions. Many a gentleman from Court has lately been well cudgeled. And if he will fight with weapons, he must take his chances like any other man.

The Court meanwhile has so taken up the habits of cutpurses and thieves that there is more safety in the darkest places of the city than in Court. Such stealing goes on that the King himself is not secure. He has lost so much plate, that except for the rarest occasions he has ordered the use of pewter service.

[659]

Of course they blame this upon the Londoners. Admitting, thereby, that rogues can move among them and go unnoticed.

It may be as well, after all, that King and Court will be absent from this Lord Mayor's Day. Only last year, in early November, Sebastian Harvey's predecessor, honest George Bolles, the draper, undertook to entertain the Knights of the Bath at Drapers' Hall. He might as well have invited a pack of Turks or Blackamoors. There was to be a feast and a play for their pleasure. But they were insolent and unruly, drunk and devoted to the cause of seducing good wives. Sir Edward Sackville locked himself in a chamber with a woman and the sheriffs had to be called to break down the door. Whereupon these noble guests took offense and left the hall without waiting for the feast. They chose instead to gather at The Mitre on Fleet Street, where there were so many disorders the watch had to be called out.

No, Sebastian Harvey's disappointment at the absence of the King on this day is balanced by some sense of relief.

But to order an execution upon this day!

That's offense to the honor of London. A day before or a day after and no matter, but the King has chosen this day.

Meaning?

Far be it from Sir Sebastian Harvey to imagine he can comprehend the motives of a king, especially a Scotsman. But if Sebastian will ask Sebastian (and so he does), one will reply to the other: that though no man may presume to fathom the mind of a king, it appears to one humble subject, loyal and true to be sure, that the King is repaying the gentlemen of London for what the King deems an insolent slight. Matter of the riot at the Spanish Ambassador's dwelling in springtime of this year. Rumor was that one of Gondomar's men had ridden his horse over and killed a London child. And not so much as deigned to

[660]

pause. True or false, it was a plausible rumor, and it was occasion for unruly Londoners to throw a shiver of fear into the Spaniards, to terrify the hated Gondomar.

On top of which—believe it or not, Sebastian, it is true—this Gondomar, once his safety was secure and he had changed his Spanish breeches, having no doubt pissed himself like a hanging man, rushed to the King and did not ask, but *demanded* all the culprits be sent to Spain for trial and punishment.

Which the King could not do and Gondomar knew it.

By laws and customs of England, the culprits were tried in London and by men of London. And, as any reasonable man might expect, their judgment was lenient. Only a few poor snakes of no consequence, troublemakers already, were found guilty. And they were punished lightly, considering the offense.

Therefore, Sebastian, the King will now bite his thumb at London and make a jest, cruel as it is, out of your Lord Mayor's Day.

Ah, says the other Sebastian, you cannot mean it. For surely the King has more wisdom than you or I. It would be presumptuous to imagine a king to be a man like ourselves.

Indeed? he answers. Perhaps you are right, good Sebastian. Perhaps . . . Can you keep a secret? Can you check and bridle your tongue and never repeat what I say? For our lives could depend on that.

Is it treason?

It is sometimes called that. Some might make it to our disadvantage if they overheard.

I had better not listen. . . .

Must you always be a coward? We must trust each other, Sebastian. We must come, after all these years and ere we die, to trust each other a little.

[661]

Well, then, say on, Sebastian. But, mind you, whisper.

Whispering then: I say, sir, there are many good men in London, neither kings nor noblemen, men of the Guilds I say, who have more wisdom in the fat of their arse than rests in the head of James I.

Shame!

Nay, I speak truth. Have they saddled themselves with unbearable debts? Would they give up their goods and their friends and followers upon the gamble of the good will of a mortal enemy? A common English tinker has more wisdom and more wit than that. . . .

Which meditation is interrupted by that same donkey-arse lad as before, a frightening apparition carrying a flaming pitch torch which could light up this room in one flaming moment, burn house to ashes and memory and probably half of London as well.

"I could not find a candle," he shouts. "But this here should give the barber enough light to see by."

The barber . . . Thank God . . . !

He is deeply grateful for this barber-surgeon who has risen up so early to attend to him.

He explains the nature of his indisposition to the barber.

The fellow prescribes a cup of sack and a few drops of a cordial. While Sir Sebastian drinks the medicinal cup, the barber rouses some servants, arranges for a fire and candles; for he must see to prepare the Lord Mayor. And he makes ready for the clipping, razoring, and singeing to be done.

Holding a looking glass, Sebastian Harvey feels somewhat better than the man reflected there.

Sebastian in the looking glass is a skeptical fellow. Then let him stay there, as in a painting, in his place while the barber makes the true Sebastian handsome.

He would tell the looking glass Sebastian that. But no confidences. Cannot trust the dour face with confidences. Least of all . . . a confidence of confidence. For he is the one who, wrinkling his brow, tells true Sir Sebastian for the first time the truth that there is bound to be confusion about the sheriffs of London and Middlesex this morning.

Knowing nothing of their plans, he doesn't know what to do. Can only do nothing and pray for the best.

He reproaches himself for not thinking of this before. His head, in response, begins to ache again. He groans.

"Sir?" asks the barber.

"Good sir," Sir Sebastian says. "If you carry a heading ax in your chest, you have my permission to use it."

The barber laughs.

"Have another medicinal cup," he says. "The pain will leave you anon."

"But I shall be drunk as a Scotch lord before I've even broken fast."

"Better drunk, sir," the barber says, "than so hurt you look for an executioner to cure you."

6

All in shades of green, the ancient color for faith and for hunts-
men too since Adam first eased his sweating brow by killing for
table, in fine materials and all green shades, save for the gloss of
the boots, the suede and lace of gloves, leather of saddle, reins
and bridle, shine of steel, brass, silver, and a few jewels winking
at the orange of flaming torches; all tricked out in green as if
decked in leaves of silk and satin and lawn, all green against
leather and glinting bits of metal and polished stones, capped
in green felt of broad brim, featherless, seated straight in the
saddle, seeming indeed a more proud and commanding figure
than ever in robes upon a throne; here green and leather and
flecks of metal lit by fat torches of servants and touched by the
cold light of morning stars, proud horseman, straight-backed
and easy on saddle, here is the most high and mighty prince,
James, by the grace of God, King of England, Scotland, Ireland,
France, Defender of the Faith, etc.

"Behold him!" cries a thin high reedy voice, like a talking
bird's. "Make way for the sovereign of the centaurs!"

"Curb your insolent tongue, you leprous pigmy, or, by God, you shall ride horseback too."

"Where shall I go riding?"

"You will ride to London backwards and talk to the tail of a swayback, gallfoot sleepy nag and be answered by continual loud farts."

"That will be sweet music to my ears after your sackbut blasts."

"You molting magpie, you shall not hear the music of your horse's bowels, though you will sniff out the sense and drift of her argument well enough and your eyes will smart and weep."

"How is it I shall know the perfume of the horse and weep to prove it, and yet hear not?"

"How can you hear without ears? We shall have your dirty ears in our purse."

"Better my dirty ears, Your Majesty, than the stale air of an empty purse."

"Go to, you poor fool, before we find another to take your place."

"No matter there, Your Majesty. For you can replace me with any man alive."

"Meaning?"

"Meaning in the Kingdom of Fools all men are one and the same, cut from the same cloth, beggar and lord alike."

"And the King?"

"'Tis said that in the country of the blind the one-eyed man shall be the King."

"And who shall be King in the Kingdom of Fools?"

"Some say the greatest fool of all, but they be fools who say so."

"What say you, Archy?"

"I give them the lie. If that were so, Your Majesty, Archy Armstrong would be King. There is no justice in this wicked world. In the Kingdom of Fools, he with half wit shall reign."

The King laughs out loud and attendant courtiers follow his example.

"By St. George, you will ride to London at the horse's tail for your impudence. Nothing else shall satisfy."

"Nor satisfy poor Archy more in this amazing year. For he that rides at the horse's tail is better than a bishop."

"How say you so?"

"Why, Sire, it seems every bishopric in England hath learned the jadish trick to cast all riders."

"Then be silent, or I might make you a bishop."

"Mercy on me, dread Sovereign! Whip me and hang me in chains, but spare me that cruelty."

"Bring me my cup," the King calls out. "We shall drink the health of Archy Armstrong, Archbishop of Fools."

James, mounted and waiting to begin the morning's hunt, makes merry with his jester. He is wide awake. He seems to those close around him to be most cheerful, a man who has slept untroubled.

His sleepy-eyed companions, though they shiver in the cold and though their bowels grumble discontent, smile and laugh at the proper times. And they are grateful the King is merry. A good chase and a clean kill will divert him. Though they may be sore in their saddles and dressed in English mud by dinner, that's a small price of discomfort measured against the King in a foul humor.

The King has his cup, already tasted by a guard, holds it to sniff the aroma while servants pass among the riders bearing cups of spirits. The King sniffs the scent of distilled warmth, then sips eagerly, slopping some drops on his green doublet.

"Drink up and drink deep!" he cries out. "For we have a far piece to ride before we break fast."

Voices call out health and long life of the King as they drink.

Cold and clear in the autumn country, barren and bare, under the infinite treasury of stars.

Horses shifting with weight of riders, snorting, breathing ghosts. Servants in livery holding pitch torches high while others move among the riders filling cups.

And now shuffling and growls, belling and yapping, here out of the dark come the King's hounds and the King's Huntsman, Henry Halfhide. He, too, a green man like the King, though clad in coarser stuff.

The King brightens to greet him.

"I think we are the only two here who are wide awake," he exclaims. "And, for paradox, the Huntsman and the King are the only two present who can swear to a day's hard labor yesterday and light sleeping too."

The huntsman bows and waits for a further sign or word from the King.

The King would be happy if he were as cheerful as he seems to be. If he could have a brain as empty as his purse. Thinking nothing but the joy of riding and the hunt. And perhaps once they are riding and the dawn comes on he will be purged of troubles. Perhaps the strong spirits he drinks will silence all inner voices and disperse unruly doubts.

By midmorning Walter Ralegh will be accounted for. Though it is not Ralegh or his fate that troubles the King most. No,

[667]

there are things, larger and more uncertain. And beyond them something nameless, close to dread.

Dread sovereign racked by dread as if by chills and fever. Though he smiles and makes merry with jester and huntsman, though the prospect of good sport pleases him well, the King is afraid of something he cannot name. Something from a dream he cannot remember.

Better to think on something palpable and near to fear.

His Queen, ill since springtime, lies at Oatlands, dying. She withers away like a cut flower. Pitiful and foolish, ever merciful and, in her pleas, making no distinctions between common thief and the fallen great, she has joined with others in petitioning for the life of Walter Ralegh.

This is not her first letter concerning the matter. She has been writing, pleading and cajoling, trying different courses. And no wonder. She has always liked Sir Walter and his wife. And the clever Fox, never hesitant to take advantage, has cultivated Queen Anne. Even to the writing of poems to her. Which must flatter, but are a waste of time. Good lady, she has neither the taste for poetry (except as a sort of music for a masque) or the power of attention to read closely. Of course, it is foolish that she would be flattered by a poem from Ralegh or anyone else. But he's old enough to be amused at his own annoyance, to understand how she can be pleased by a poem, whatever its merit or faults, from such a man. For many reasons, mostly wrong reasons, but woman's reasons, and she is too old to change her ways now.

She has written many times about Ralegh. And he has read each letter.

But this most recent petition baffles him. It seems to contain some knowledge he has not imagined she possessed.

[668]

He did not, could not last night read all the letters which had come to him. But, out of duty and lest he should be more ashamed, he read her latest. In her own hand. Weak and faint as her health. Weak in reasoning and rhetoric as ever, health or no. But strong in sincerity. Poor woman, she can have no more reason, no more mind than God gave her. And she who had good health, if not great beauty, can keep health and strength no longer than God intends. Yet it seems that as the body fails, the light of her spirit grows clearer. As if fever and suffering and pain may have served to refine her.

Once she could reach him with wiles and arguments, and now she can wound him, not with woman-cunning or persuasion, but by the clean stroke of purity of spirit. Which is outside the realm of reason.

How to explain the strange discontent, the wince, wound and shame of, yes, God forgive him, envy?

The words of a woman poor in health and, most curious, rich as an emperor in spirit, she who loved dancing and masques, fine clothes, trinkets and baubles, laughter and the games of children, wound him to the quick. As if, yes, she were in spirit male and had transformed his soul to female. With every thrust, then, his teeth on edge from groaning. As if, to a female soul, the road to bliss were paved with stones of pain.

Thus in her pain, he suffers most.

And all his naked failings measured against the glass of . . . what? not her successes, for she has succeeded in nothing much and cannot even embrace Death gracefully. . . . All his naked failings as man, husband, king, and ruler, measured against the simplicity of her spirit.

Late last night James Hay came to his bedchamber. Hay having ridden like a madman, or like James Hay when he has a

[669]

mind to ride hard and fast, alone from Westminster to report upon the hearing at King's Bench.

James Hay, once a handsome favorite in Scotland, now favorite no more; but made a nobleman, he has proved most noble, and time has proved him constant in loyalty. Never a proper pupil, indeed to the King, his teacher, intractable, for his spine of character was already formed, he is a surprising pride to the King, a source of gladness at heart. For if he could not teach and shape him, he could not by errors corrupt him, as he has done Robert Carr. And if Hay could not ever have learned with the quickness of George Villiers, James Hay had less to learn. He was not made to learn these things at all. Rather to serve and, in service, to teach others, even the King, by example.

Now he has become a lord and his youth has gone, but not his loyalty, his harsh honesty, his Scots wisdom.

If he made nothing out of James Hay—even titles and rewards cannot change him for better or worse—he can take credit for choosing him wisely from the crowd.

Hay, muddy from his ride and indifferent to the King's fastidious concern for such things (why, after all this time, should he and the King play the game of strangers?), was admitted to his chamber as the King in his bed was rereading and pondering the petition of the Queen. So the King put the question to him straight, as he could not and never would to Steenie, who hovered nearby, tall and handsome in white. Do they not, behind his back, call Steenie "the King's white mule"?

The King handed the letter to James Hay and asked him not what the words meant, which any fool could cipher, but what it was that could cause him to feel a great sadness, close to dread.

And Hay, still too vain, even in vanity constant, to carry his own spectacles, had to borrow the King's to read it.

This pleased the King and let him smile.

"It is said that a cordial of Ralegh's making has rallied her somewhat," Hay said, even before he commenced to read.

"No nonsense of cordials and chemicals," the King said. "Read the letter and tell me how it is I can translate it into such discontent."

"The words are plain enough."

"I take the words at their meaning."

"The Queen has no guile."

"Still, sir, I would have you translate it for me."

"I am a plain man, Your Majesty."

"I know what you are. Tell me what it is she says to me."

"You are asking me to be a prophet."

"Be my Daniel, then. Tell me the truth—if you are not afraid."

Flushing with Scots anger, Hay read the Queen's letter to himself, the King's spectacles slipping down the bridge of his nose, his lips moving with each word. Straight through, eyes moving left to right, line by line behind glass and not stumbling or backtracking, until he finished. Then folded the letter and removed the spectacles and returned them both to the King's hand.

"Well, what is the woman trying to tell me?"

"I think she is trying to tell you that you shall find more felicity if you shrink your ambition."

"You are more cryptic than she is. Speak plain."

"You ask me to make light of obscure matters, to speak of feelings she cannot name. And to find words for my own feelings."

"I ask, nay I demand, out of love and loyalty, nothing less than that."

Hay cleared his throat and looked directly into the King's

[671]

eyes. The King unblinking, observing indeed that the beauty of James Hay's eyes, sad as a hound's, had not vanished.

"From the edge of her grave, which in her pain and fever she has peered into, your wife speaks out of love. Speaks of love and charity. She chastises you, Sire, and thus you feel the shame she intends. She tells you that you have wandered from the true path and are lost. And the pity of it, for she loves and pities you, is you have erred and strayed in the name of a great good dream. She says your dream is an illusion."

"Speak more and more particular."

"Ah, that's the burden of her message to you. She says you have sacrificed felicity and with it your humanity for a general love. And in so doing you have lost the power to love anything."

"What in God's name is that supposed to mean?" the King snapped, feeling a flush of anger and striving to suppress it.

"Meaning, Sire, you shall live better and die well by simple acts of mercy and particular love, that you shall be more blessed by these common things than if you should succeed in bringing a peace to the world for a thousand years. Which, Sire, she has seen in her vision of the grave, you shall not accomplish."

"She is ill, it is true. In her illness she imagines death. But she has not yet seen it."

"It seems to the Queen that she has," Hay answered.

"And you, James, what do you say?"

"It is not for me to say, not to speak of feelings, but to act out of reason and to advise, when need be, in matters of policy."

"You have always thought well of Ralegh. . . ."

"Not always," Hay interrupted, and ignoring the King's frown: "Let us be truthful on both sides. I changed my opinion of the man at Winchester all those years ago."

[672]

"Changed to a contrary opinion and have not changed it since."

"I have not found occasion to."

"None of his offenses, his tricks and jests and stratagems have so much as chipped the pedestal of your certainty."

"I do not make sculpture of my opinions. When I have reason to change my mind, I shall speak out."

"I do not doubt it," the King said. "You learned the trick of plain speaking when you were a young dog. It is too late to amend it now."

"We are older," Hay said. "It is too late to amend many things."

"Very well, James. I shall not badger you more. Except . . . You will speak, you say, on policy. I call on you to do so now."

"Your Majesty," Hay said with a sigh, "you are so set in your policy that nothing I can say will alter it."

"Christ's bloody wounds! No man dares presume to read me like a book. If he does, he deceives himself. I say to you, James Hay, that you are together with my Queen in this. Both of you would rather serve a fox than your King."

In his anger the King had closed his eyes. Opened them to find James Hay kneeling by the bed. His head bowed. His jaw tight and his neck above the limp, sweat-stained, mud-flecked ruff, as red as a fresh-boiled lobster.

"If it pleases Your Majesty, believe that," he said, not looking up.

The King swallowed spit and sat up, swung around to put his hand lightly on James Hay's shoulder.

"Tell me what I must do," he said softly.

Hay not moving to look up again.

[673]

"Go and find the prophet Daniel. Perhaps he will answer you."

"Begone, then!" the King cried out. "Go and be damned. But I warn you. Beware the next time you come to the lion's den."

And Hay bowed himself out of the chamber.

The King controlled tears until the door was shut and bolted. Then turned his face to the pillow and wept.

Thank God for Steenie's gentle hand on his back. Otherwise he might have wept all night long like a child. Like himself as a child. . . .

"He was most uncivil," Steenie said.

He turned over. Allowed Steenie to prop some pillows behind him, accepted a handkerchief to dab at his eyes and blow his nose. Feeling much relieved. Not so much by these attentions as by the purgative of tears.

"Bless you, boy," the King said.

"It is blessing enough to be with you," Steenie answered.

He looked into the young man's unlined, open, handsome face, the luster of his eyes. Too young, too beautiful for guile yet. Guile's a game for him. His duplicity is innocence. He could hope the young man would live long and do great things.

"He should never have so presumed upon friendship," Steenie was saying.

The King stiffened slightly.

"Do not, even out of love, be critical of James Hay," he said. "He speaks truth and that's the rarest thing in this world."

"I meant no offense. I only wished to say . . ."

The King thinking: *For God's sake not another quarrel tonight.* Then smiling on the boy.

[674]

"Nor I," said James. "Only that you can learn something from James Hay. Learn to tell a true and loyal servant."

"Then I shall strive to be like him."

The King laughed. And the young man frowned slightly, puzzled.

"Spare me that," he said. "One is enough."

Then added, touching the smooth cheek of the young man gently with the tips of his fingers. "He was never, even in his best days, half so handsome as you."

"He has beautiful eyes," Steenie said.

"Ha! You noticed that, did you? You are becoming more observant day by day. Which pleases me. But, Steenie, pray do not be captivated by a pair of eyes."

"How can I? I am your captive. Now and always. . . ."

Now in the morning on horseback he would make a peace with his old friend.

"Hay!" he calls out, turning into torchlight, seeking a sign from the dark. "James Hay?" Then by his title: "Doncaster? Who has see Doncaster?"

There is no answer from courtiers and servants. They turn their heads to look for him too.

"Where can he be now?" the King calls out.

Into the silence breaks a reedy voice.

"Why, since he is not here, there can be but two places for him."

"Where, then, poor snake?"

"Perhaps he has gone to his grave and reward. For 'tis all the fashion for the great ones this year."

True, true enough. This has been a year of death. Bishops have dropped from place like overripe fruit. But there are al-

ways more bishops. But God knows the lords of England have been dying as if a noble title were a listing on the plaguey bill. Four gone in October alone: Lord St. John of Bletso, Lord Rooper, the Lord Delaware dead in Virginia, and the Lord Clifton, who took his foolish life with a little penknife. A war could do no worse. . . .

"Dead? You say *dead?*" the King hears himself asking in a cracked voice.

No answer. Courtiers and servants are silent. They look everywhere except at the King.

"Answer me, Archy, or in God's name I will cut your tongue like a crow!"

Anger restores the tone of his voice. Anger's the best purge of fear.

"Nay, Sire, he is not dead."

"Where then, fool? You said he might be in two places."

"It was a poor jest. Blame it upon the spirits I have drunk."

"Let me judge the merit of the jest."

"My Lord Doncaster was up and gone toward London while the Court slept."

"Why?"

"There are two possible causes. Perhaps he has gone to celebrate Lord Mayor's Day and drink free claret from the conduits, being a true Scotsman and troubled by the waste."

The King manages a grim smile.

"And the other?"

"Even a good Scotsman may lose his wits if he tarries too long in the Kingdom of Fools. 'Tis said there shall be a showing of the head of John the Baptist in Westminster Yard. And he, the poor fool, does believe it."

"Let him believe it and be damned!" the King says.

[676]

And now in control of warring factions of feeling, he can force a loud laugh and indulge himself in the pleasure of hearing it echoed by false and flattering courtiers. Which false laughter spares him from any shame at his own.

"A cup of spirits for my jester," he says. "And . . ."

Turning to the huntsman all in green.

"Your Majesty?"

"Kennel up the dogs. There will be no sport today," the King tells him. Then, to the others, studious in impassivity. "Prepare yourselves for a journey. We shall go to the Queen."

Someone gasps in surprise, but not at what he has said. That gasp is echoed and all, servants and courtiers, huntsman and jester, clear in torchlight or hidden, look to the sky.

All but the King. Who knows what they have seen. The long bright sputtering arc, like a rocket, of a dying star falling across the sky. He need not look up to see it. It has been a year of omens.

Oh, it is true, to be King among fools a man needs only half wit. . . .

Jerks reins, digs spurs, lashes flank with whip. And the horse leaps and away he gallops toward the stables, alone for once, startled others coming behind him in shouts and confusion. Let them chase and catch him if they can.

The wind bathes him and he feels his lips form a grin. As if he himself were the horse gripping the cold harsh bit, biting the snaffle, wincing from the sting of the spurs.

Part Eight

For in that we foreknow that the sun will rise and set, that all men born in the world shall die again, that after winter spring will come, after the spring, summer and harvest, and that according to the several seeds that we sow, we shall reap several sorts of grain, yet is not our foreknowledge the cause of this or any of these. Neither does the knowledge in us bend or constrain the sun to set, or men to die.

RALEGH—*History of the World*

Beginning of the second day.

More than these last are up and about, and many preparing the
affairs of the day to be. In all of England only a few will be
still sleeping and dreaming; for all must live for the hours of the
day, whether sunlit or twilight-shadowed from sunrise to sunset by autumnal weather. To live by day they rise, light candles
and torches, begin tasks and chores, breakfast, and await the
dawn.

Last hour before dawn. Time for the crowing of cocks. And
time for wandering ghosts to break obdurate silence and speak,
if ever, before they are harried back to the cramped space of the
grave.

All who are awake have the common future of this day to
share. And even now the mysterious cipher of the day, of their
future time, of all future time to the ending of time, is written,
not in some ledger, not in a magic mirror, not in the entrails of
sacrificial beasts or the omens of stars and birds, but in hearts
and bones, in all and every part of the book of the natural

[681]

world. And, though the future is written there and some of the living, wise or simple, know it to be so, there is not one man alive, not the wisest, who can read a word of the cipher of the future and translate it.

Some study the stars, conjunctions, oppositions, dominance, and submission within the twelve signs of the zodiac; the shape and shadows of the moon; the color of the rising and setting sun; or the wandering of planets, brightness or diminution of most distant stars.

Some, who are scholars of light, will study the tints of candlelight, lamp, and lantern, firelight in its flaring and dying away. Some listen for the screech of the night-hunting owl, the reedy music of ravens, bass notes of bullfrogs, cry of crickets, muttering of parrots in their cages. Some look to the elder tree, where Judas hanged himself and thus, oddly, sanctified. Study the mushroom or the trembling aspen. Have both ears alert for the sound of a prowling gib-cat; just as in May and early summer there are folk who will ask the cuckoo the secret questions and then count the answering cries to know the number of years they shall have for living.

All these ways and many more of seeking the signs of the future. And since every man alive must wonder, whether or not he has hopes and wishes, all men are seeking to find where fortune and necessity may lead them next. Adam was the first of these seekers, and no doubt the last man will be last.

All are seeking, have and will so long as they live, and none will find it until it arrives.

In adversity now, in strict and simplified condition, Walter Ralegh is spared from this common expense of spirit. And what was once a young soldier's way, to live most keenly here and now by chosen deferral of the future, has remained his own.

Long since he concluded that Fortune (that fantasy of men) is not a subject of foreknowledge. If so, Providence, which is no fantasy, is beyond powers of reason or imagination to comprehend. Why would God be so careless as to cloak his enigma in the sounds of a few birds, in the actions of stars or the habits of common plants? Since no man since Adam has understood these holy mysteries, then only the most ignorant or vain, in this age of iron, can assume himself to be chosen and gifted above all mankind to know. The wisest know only this—that the mystery is there, written on everything and in the hearts and bones of the living. From Ralegh, who can imagine only an alternative, single and profoundly simple—he will live or he will die this morning—to the King of England, who believes it is his duty to imagine something of the future of his kingdom into times beyond any imagining.

And yet there is not one soul in all of England or the world who can at this moment, between the last of the night and the beginning of the day, picture the future. For the future is always, as the dead Queen could have told them, stranger than all dreaming and imagination.

If, as many awake, living and breathing this morning believe, ghosts of the dead possess the vision of what will be, being bodiless as dreamers who are lifted above demarcations of time, now is time for them to speak their news, before cockcrow sends them to narrow beds of clay and cold stone.

But the dead have nothing to say to the living.

Perhaps because they have found no language the living can comprehend.

Perhaps because, out of an enormous weariness, they wish to spare the living any diminution of the doubts and fears which are the privilege of the living.

Perhaps because the dead do not know or, anyway, turn away from all vision of the future lest they, too, must bear the inevitable crippling sorrow of ancient gods, prophets, and seers, being already freighted with a sad cargo of memories, of the things undone which they ought to have done, of those things done which they ought not to have done, the sum of which must seem, in the strict cells of clay and stone where they wait for the Day of Judgment, the true accounting of their lives.

This day ghosts will go to ground and keep silence, as always.

Still, in this final hour between old night and the new day, between dreaming and waking, a time outside the music of living time, the secrets of the future are there, just as the forgotten past blooms briefly again.

In this kingdom the beginning and the end lies with the King. Though not so much as he hopes and wishes.

Begin and end with James, the King.

His alternative, as he can conceive it, is as simple as Ralegh's.

The Spanish Match. Either he will succeed and it will follow. Or all this will come to nothing.

Beyond which he cannot imagine worse.

Nor can imagine whether success or failure will prove well or ill. Or whether decisions he has made and must make will prove to be wise or foolish. Cannot imagine if, either way, wise or foolish, he will live to know or whether or not his subjects will take the results (success or failure) as wise or foolish, and praise or blame him, living or dead, for his choices.

Beyond the imagining of the King are some truths:

that, after a long life of fear of violent death, he will die safe

[684]

in bed, unwounded, and with all the cloudy questions, which plague him, remaining unanswered;

that this death by nature will be worse by far than violent wounds, will be long, exquisitely painful, and ineffably sad;

that it will be Charles, his son and heir, who will one day die violently and more so than James has ever feared or imagined for himself, his own fear being transmuted into the fate of his son's blood and bone;

but that when that day will come the son will triumph over the father's fears, dying with no fear and dying well;

that young Carew Ralegh will be Charles' friend, and faithful too, to the end, just as Carew will be friend and companion to the son of Robert Cecil;

that an awkward boy, one whom the King has never so much as heard of, one Richard Brandon, who, in the course of practice of the vocation he is this morning seeking to learn, will be the instrument to end his dreams and the life of Charles;

that after that day and time (sooner than anyone, king or fool, can imagine) England will change her nature and, though changing again and again ever after, will never be the same nation again;

that his lifelong labor for peace, for the blessed name of peacemaker, will in his lifetime come to nothing and Charles, the son, and Buckingham, favorite and pupil, will make war and disastrously; and likewise igniting fires of a full century of war and devastation on the Continent;

that soon enough Charles and Buckingham, called Steenie, will bury him twice over, first in metaphor and truth while he lives, as he had feared Prince Henry would, never finding cause to fear Charles or Steenie enough; then literally, though after any time when living or dying will matter to James;

[685]

that, soonest, Queen Anne will be dead and that in her absence he will have much time to come to know what value, what service she had been to him when he did not know it;

that, to compound irony, another of his deep fears will prove to have been premonition, though not for himself but for Steenie, who will die in agony from an assassin's knife, just so;

that pupil and protege, this handsome Steenie, will prove too perfect in his studies, learning everything—including, it may be, the art of poison—too well, but not learning what virtues James could have taught;

that thus this pupil, like Carr, will become a figure sculpted by the King, but one whose perfection will be to be a living parody of the King's best intentions;

these and many more things, all sharp turnings against him, sharper than blades, the King could even now imagine as contingencies and spare himself and his progeny and projects the consequences of, if he dared to look deep enough into himself, dared to set free imagination wholly to face the future he loves and lusts for, both himself and the future meeting in the naked embrace of lovers; but will not; and so, for a time, since there is neither hope nor amendment possible, is spared the horrid vision of his future stripped of all finery, wigless, without paint and perfume, until there is no remedy but to bear it;

that least of all can he conceive the destiny of Walter Ralegh, whose future lies now most firmly in the King's hands and is conceivable; that Walter Ralegh, who has squandered his future many times over and should for certain be bankrupt for all future time;

that it will be, in times beyond imagining, Ralegh's spirit and name which will be summoned up in memory by many who will know him not well, if at all; and that many of these, honoring the name and spirit of a stranger, will find inspiration to actions which would have appalled him.

Nor can Ralegh, though a student of the ironies of time and capable as any man of comprehending the turns and counter-turns of future time, imagine the satirical ending of his own chronicle, as for example:

that many, indeed most of his schemes will truly come to pass, though in different form than he imagined or intended, so that he will come in time to seem a kind of prophet, child of the future he renounced;

that strangers and countrymen will take his spent memory and recreate it as they wish and need, sometimes into a heroic emblem, blindly admired; sometimes equally distorted and de-faced, made into a bloody-minded, deceitful, conniving, ruth-lessly ambitious rogue, a sign and symbol of a mad brutal age of scheming, himself the chief schemer among a crowd of mur-derers, vagabonds, and knaves;

that of all his writings, the outward and visible expense of his feeling and thought, it will be the poems which will live longest, at the last to be read by schoolboys just as he once read the tags and remnants of the ancients, and that his greatest labor, the *History,* will live for a brief time, flourish, then vanish into dusty places;

that Sherbourne, though lost for good to himself or his line, will endure, be preserved, a monument at the last, not to the Digby's, who will keep and preserve it, but to himself;

that even his name will change, becoming most commonly known and spelled in the one fashion which, among half a hun-dred variations he used, he never once employed.

Many things happen between the cup and the lip.

Nor can any of the others whose lives and fortunes for yesterday and this day impinge upon the life and fortune of Walter Ralegh, imagine the separate futures which wait upon them already.

Each at this moment dividing night from dawn is, no matter how surrounded by kith and kin, friends and servants, alone with his store of memory and the secret ciphers which make a record of it, and with the present of clear, cold, starlit time.

Each is clothed in garments of his own concerns. They pass each other, strangers in a strange land, without seeing. Or are like ships on open sea at night, each with a lone lantern burning high on the poop. Not ships passing each other or on a crossing course, but each, unknown to the other, sailing the same course, riding the same wind, sailing for the same unknown destination. . . .

Sir Lewis Stukely, Vice-Admiral of Devon, already revenged for injustice (real or imaginary) inflicted by his kinsman, enriched for his service to the King and soon to be richer. He will move to receive the blessings of the Lord Admiral, then, he thinks, to take the *Destiny*, furniture, fittings, and cargo.

Will not believe his ears (this morning, no later) when he hears Lord Howard of Nottingham, who should be too old to summon up more than a weary shrug: "Thou base fellow! Thou, the scorn and contempt of men! How dare you presume to come into my presence!"

Stukely will not have the *Destiny* or any part of it.

Three fourths of all that vessel's value is already marked for Bess Ralegh, in payment for her investment in the venture; and she will have it though many others will remain unpaid.

Yet, fleeing wrath and public disgrace, the Lord Admiral's voice striking him like a knotty cudgel, and assuming that to be the worst he could imagine, Stukely will be wrong. It will not be the worst.

Within a few months, he will find himself out of favor with every man in England. Will have the King's reply to his complaint ringing his head more roundly than the Lord Admiral's words.

"I cannot hang every man who speaks ill of you," the King will tell him. "There are not enough trees in this kingdom."

And shortly enough he'll be penniless, a pauper and felon in the Tower, charged and punished for counterfeiting. And false or true (whether a portion of his payment was made in clipped coin to ensnare him or he was so reduced and rash to clip coins himself) no one will care, and no one will ever know.

Still young, he will die a madman on the Isle of Lundy within two years.

Sir Thomas Wilson, undaunted, will have the wisdom of past experience confirmed again. He will find himself out of favor and out of purse for his service. Lucky to keep body and soul together, neither sadder nor wiser. Of the books, papers, maps, instruments, etc., he desires, some few will indeed go to the King, but none will pass through Wilson's hands.

He will live to see Lord Lieutenant Apsley, his bad fortunes ended, marry off his daughters well.

Sir Hugh Hammersley will have some present fears come true, but he could take heart if he imagined that, come what may, he will be both colonel and president of the London Artillery, will be most influential in days ahead. And it will be he who holds this office upon the erection and opening of Artillery Garden in 1622. All in due time, in 1627 he will be the Lord Mayor of London as well.

Sir Sebastian Harvey will be led a merry chase. While he swears his oath in Westminster Hall, the winds will turn again, and weather will turn with the wind. Cold rains will blow away much of the joy of the procession, will wet and stain and soak a wealth of finery and expensive robes, including his own.

Yet for all this, Harvey will have his day to remember. A day which will be remembered.

Within the year, seeking a wife with good dowry for Buckingham's brother, Kit Villiers, the King will select a young daughter of Harvey for this honor.

But neither threats nor bribes by the King of England will budge the stout ironmonger from refusal. Nor a Star Chamber fine of 2,000 pounds exacted for some old error new-discovered. At last the King of England will be forced to summon Harvey and his wife to Court and into the royal presence, before the assembled Court, and, letting the beams of royal light shine upon them, the King shall plead a mighty persuasive case.

To which Sir Sebastian Harvey will have the extreme pleasure, in the presence of all that company, of replying with an unbudging, unequivocal *no*. . . .

The marriage will not take place.

Less than a fortnight Robert Tounson will be able to write an account of his part in the events of this coming morning to his friend, Sir John Isham; and he will confidently conclude: "That was all the news a week ago, but it is now blown over. . . ."

And the Dean will be rewarded with the Bishopric of Salisbury, and for a price within his means. But before he is even properly settled in that seat of eminence, Tounson will be dead of smallpox.

George Abbot, Archbishop of Canterbury, stiff and gloomy man, leaning ever more strongly toward the Puritans, often tactless and sometimes cruel, yet ever courageous and unflinching, will remain the man he is. In and out of favor he will hold his office until he dies in 1633.

He will remain consistent against both Spain and the Catholics and a nettle to the King. And will not lose the gratitude of the King for having first found and brought forward George Villiers.

He will continue, one by one, to lose old friends and allies at Court—first the late Prince Henry, then Winwood, Queen Anne, Coke, Bacon, and even Buckingham will turn against him. He has tested the King to the quick by his arguments against the royal prerogative and most especially for his actions

[691]

against the Countess of Essex when she sought a simple divorce in order to marry Robert Carr; by being outspoken in arguments against the Spanish Match; by encouraging the Princess Elizabeth (at enormous expense and soon enough to cost greater grief) to marry Frederick, Elector of the Palatinate. For (at least it is widely believed) advising Ralegh to make open war with Spain on his last voyage; for resisting already the growing power and influence of his own creature—Buckingham.

He will endure. Even the embarrassment of being briefly stripped of his office and powers by Charles I in 1627.

Above all will endure the one event he cannot possibly imagine. Will endure true sorrow, shame, mortification, even after July 21, 1621. When, while visiting Lord Zouch at Bramshill, on a fine day of hunting together with a noble company, the Archbishop will aim his crossbow at a stag, and his bolt will kill the gamekeeper, Peter Hawkins. He will then retire to an almshouse, but find himself saved from loss of office by the vote of Lancelot Andrewes, together with the benefit of an apt old precedent uncovered by Sir Edward Coke.

And thereafter for the rest of his days the Archbishop of Canterbury will fast and pray one Tuesday every month to do penance for the death of Peter Hawkins.

Among all the lawyers and judges it will be, ironically, Sir Edward Coke who fares best, though often in danger and threatened.

Old, he will remain a leader in the Commons, his spirit unchecked by twenty-six weeks and five days of strict imprisonment in the Tower, following the Parliament of '21. He will be as strong and unyielding as ever in debate during the Parliament of '24. And likewise no less a presence in '28, under Charles I;

by which time he will be known as a kind of king himself and will be called *Monarcha Juris.*

And after that, in his last years will come to write the *Reports* and *Institutes,* which, by recovering the English law of the past, will create English law for all time to come.

And though old and feeble and much alone, he will be so feared by King Charles that, at the last, while he lies quietly dying at the age of eighty-two, having outlived both friends and enemies, the King's men will urgently ransack his library, notes, and papers, searching for words and precedents which they, by then, will fear more than cannons and hostile armies.

And living long, Coke will see how the fortunes of such as Francis Bacon and Henry Yelverton turn and change by the spin of the wheel. . . .

Will witness Francis Bacon utterly overthrown in 1621. Impeached by Parliament for taking of bribes and gifts; sentenced to a fine of forty thousand pounds and to imprisonment in the Tower at the King's pleasure and "to be ever incapable of holding any office, place, or employment in the state or commonwealth," and never "to sit in Parliament nor to come within the verge of the Court"; and to be spared by only two votes, one of these cast by his archenemy, Buckingham, from being publicly degraded and deprived of all of his titles.

It will be the King's pleasure to keep Francis Bacon in the Tower for three days, then to release him in a gesture as much of indifference as mercy.

And Bacon will give up beautiful York House to Steenie. Whose motto *Fidei Coticula Crux* will grace the arch at the water gate.

His fine will be reduced, and he will live quietly at Gorhambury for five more years, where he will have leisure to finish the writing of his own works.

Will die of a sudden illness in 1626, dying at Arundel House on Easter Sunday.

And will die, to no man's surprise, at least twenty thousand pounds in debt.

Sir Henry Yelverton has something to learn of the whims of fortune. He will soon lose his office of Attorney General. Will, upon advice and urging of Francis Bacon, be tried before Star Chamber, fined and imprisoned. And after that his tongue, never silver, will denounce Buckingham by name. And that slip of tongue will increase his woes.

But later still, King Charles will soften and will appoint him to the bench as a judge of common pleas.

Coke, outliving both of them, will see all this and much more, neither health nor spirit broken until his time of death. Will become, ironically, the long-living proof of King James' judgment of him: "Throw this man where you will, and still he lands on his legs."

Of the nobility, those who have come to be present witnesses to whatever the King wills for Walter Ralegh . . .

Henry de Vere, quick-tempered, restless, bold, and unlucky. Within a short time he will be sent twice to the Tower for public, incautious remarks about Buckingham. Will be badly beaten and injured in a fray with some men of the London Watch.

Then, forsaking quarrels, wagers, whoring, and drinking, he

will seek honor in the service of Frederick of Palatine. And he will die in that service in 1625, not of wounds, but a fever.

Lord Compton, First Earl of Northampton, still at this moment counted one of the wealthiest men in England, will spend and give away most of that wealth before he dies (1630), to be remembered chiefly as a great drunkard.

Baron Sheffield will live longer, long enough to join with the Parliament against King Charles and to fight against the Royalists.

Two of these lords will continue to serve King and country as long and as well as they are able.

James Hay will do good service on many diplomatic missions. He will change neither his views nor his general policies. He will never abjure his lavish taste for fine things or his singular pride. Nor will he ever find a means to pay his debts. In 1619 he will marry the daughter of the wizard Earl of Northumberland, who is still confined in the Tower. And it will be Hay who secures the Earl's final release, softening the old man's rage of disapproval of the marriage.

Through difficult times as in halcyon days James Hay will be a faithful servant to the King, perhaps more than most, for he will serve out of love and loyalty and without any loss of honor or infidelity of conscience.

Thomas Howard, Earl of Arundel will soon witness the final downfall and disgrace of all his Howard kin. Even the Lord

[695]

Admiral will be forced to resign to be replaced by Buckingham, when the full scandal of the decay of the King's Navy is known.

Arundel, once outcast, will find himself last of that family in power.

Attendance and diplomacy—the King's progress to Scotland, the journey of Princess Elizabeth to Heidelberg—are his special skills. He will continue to serve the King with unflagging loyalty.

The King will send Arundel to York House to take back the seal when Lord Chancellor Bacon falls.

Under Charles I he will be lodged in the Tower on account of the marriage of his son. But then will be restored to both power and favor to act as mediator between the King and Parliament in 1628. And he will be sent as special ambassador to Ferdinand II of Austria. Though he has never been a soldier, he will be sent as a general against the Scots in 1638.

Late in the reign of James, at a time when the King, asleep at Whitehall, will be frightened nearly out of his wits (some prankster scholars at Gray's Inn fire off a cannon in the middle of the night, and the King awakens crying "Treason! Treason!"), it will be Arundel alone who races to protect the King with his sword drawn against whatever may come. And the King will be for once most grateful for an unsheathed blade in loyal hands.

Later, deeply disenchanted with Court, he will take occasion to join the escort of Henrietta Maria and Mary to the Continent. And then he will go into an exile at Padua.

Still, when the fortunes of the Royalists are at lowest ebb, he will contribute thirty-five thousand pounds to their cause. With the result that after their defeat, all his estates and possessions in England will be lost.

And so he will die poor in Italy.

To be remembered and honored chiefly for the wonders of his collections of works of art. Which wonders will be scattered and lost when his estates are seized.

There is yet another man, of no mean distinction in his own country, absent in flesh, but here in spirit—Don Diego Sarmiento de Acuna, Count of Gondomar. He is in Spain and most pleased with the success of his labors. For five amazing years, by many ways and means, by a subtle potion of outrage, arrogance, and a twilight wit, by threats and promises, more promises and deft delays, he has kept England neutral and immobilized, at peace with Spain and seeking to preserve that peace. And this at a time when England could be most dangerous.

His chief stratagem has been the Spanish Match. The notion is preposterous to Spain, but Gondomar has beguiled the English King. And now has returned home in triumph. The fate of Ralegh (whether he now lives or dies is of no consequence) stands as eloquent testimony to Gondomar's achievement.

But back to England Gondomar must go, in March of 1620, to renew the negotiations for the Spanish Match.

He will find, in so short a time, the King is older, lonely, feeling the ruins of time. At first the King will seem happy to welcome back an old friend and adversary. Will find the King, ignoring the feelings of his subjects, still eager to wager everything for the sake of peace, still believing the dream of the Spanish Match.

Gondomar will again succeed (and this his most marvelous success) in holding England in check through the King. The King will stand firm though Court, Parliament, and the people rage against the duplicities of Spain.

[697]

He will reach such power as to persuade the King of England to dissolve a Parliament.

And then, riding a crest of accomplishment, having done these things for his own King, country, and faith, in April of 1622 Gondomar will go home to Spain for good, in sweetest triumph, to be replaced by a new ambassador to England.

There will be a new King, Philip IV, in Spain, with new men all around him. And the Count of Olivares, Chief Minister, will find no reason to reward Gondomar or even to repay him for his expenses.

And when, finally, the old dream of the Spanish Match dies in England, Gondomar will discover that in Spain the clever policy which has served Spain so well, and stripped him of his wealth, will have become, through the tricks of time, too much associated with his name. Failure, coming last, will outweigh all his work and success.

In disgrace and dire need, this proud man will taste a deeper shame than he knows of. He will be given the privilege of sending his son to England to beg for some succor in the memory of the father at the Court of King Charles.

Gondomar will die in poverty.

The lives of each of these could demonstrate that behind the whimsical turnings of the wheel of Fortune, is some pattern. It is in part the working out of the character of each and all. But more, it is, in sum, the mysterious wedding of that character to what is unknown and unknowable.

All who listen for the owl, count cries of the cuckoo, stare at toadstool and trembling aspen are fools. Yet their study is altogether reasonable. Their folly is in the hope that the world would answer their questions if it could.

Faith begins with the certainty that the world will not answer.

Faith is the understanding that past, present. and future can be possessed by the imagination, but only in a coinage of questions.

Wisdom is, then, the knowledge that if any of these men, from King to hangman's son, could, by signs and portents, come to imagine part of the truth of the future, he could not believe it.

To believe would be to be turned to stone or into swine, as in the old myths. And he would no longer be able to live as a man, not able to feel, and therefore unable to care.

To be a man alive, awake or asleep, darkness or daylight, is to feel and to care.

Best, then, that none of the living can read the ciphers of the future.

Which are vanishing with the rising of the sun.

Part Nine

And this is my eternall plea,
To him that made Heauen, Earth, and Sea,
Seeing my flesh must die so soone,
And want a head to dine next noone,
Iust at the stroke when my vaines start and spred
Set on my soule an euerlasting head.

RALEGH—*The passionate mans Pilgrimage*

1

The walk from the dean's yard of Westminster to the gatehouse is a short one, a few brisk moments for the Dean. Yet at the entrance he pauses to catch his breath. Feeling as if he has come to the end of a long journey, even as the day and his duties are about to begin. A deep weariness without cause or reason.

While an acolyte holds a looking glass and a linkboy stands near with torchlight, he examines his appearance, straightens his clothing. The torchlight gives his flesh the color of the heart of a Spanish orange.

Bishop of Salisbury. . . . That magnificent cathedral with its high central tower, topped by the soaring miracle of a spire. Its spacious old cloisters, the equal of those at Wells and more perfect, better situated. No seat finer for him to imagine. And there with power and authority, his piety can manifest itself in good works, can be practical and expedient.

He must do his duty in this matter and give satisfaction, true. Must minister unto the condemned man, test him and

[703]

his faith, and when it is over, one way or the other, make his judgment known. Therein is the crux. His judgment of the Christian faith of Walter Ralegh, which has been questioned before, must be . . . satisfactory. To contrary factions. And no man knows this better than Ralegh, so adroit at the craft of concealment.

In short time the Dean must somehow strip away disguise and subterfuge and come to judgment.

Satisfied with his appearance, he sends the linkboys and all but the prebend and one acolyte back to the Abbey. He greets the porter, who leads him up the stairway to the chamber.

Entering, Dean Tounson is surprised to find the chamber lit and Walter Ralegh dressed, a servant brushing and combing his hair.

Fully dressed, elegant in a hair-colored doublet of fine satin, black taffeta breeches in the new style, black wrought waistcoat, embroidered, silk stockings of ash color. And a neat small starched snowy ruff band at the neck. The very image, despite his somber shades of black and gray, of the courtier.

The Dean suppresses a smile. Those who have imagined the Fox will appear today like the pitiful wretch who came before King's Bench yesterday have guessed wrong.

"Good morning to you," Ralegh says. "Let us proceed promptly with prayers and communion. A good breakfast is waiting for us."

"I think it would be wise to talk a little together before prayers and the sacrament."

"What subject do you propose?"

"Your faith, sir, and your present state of spiritual health."

"Well," he says lightly enough, "that is easily disposed.

[704]

My faith is as firm set as the Pole Star. And, thanks be to God, my spirit is in far better health than the flesh and bones it inhabits. I can only wish this morning finds you feeling as well as I do."

"You are extraordinarily . . . *bold*."

"Nay, merely cheerful. I have been taught and I have always believed that a Christian should be of good cheer, especially at the last."

"Let us speak more of your beliefs," the Dean says.

Ralegh calls for chairs, two joint stools placed near the fire. Servants, acolyte, and prebend move away from the voices of the two.

DEAN

It is my duty to encourage you to fear death for the sake of your soul.

RALEGH

My flesh fears death. My soul . . . Death is contemptible to my soul. My soul trusts God. My skin and bones depend upon such courage as can be mustered in this world. My soul rejoices.

DEAN

I have never heard any doubt your courage.

RALEGH

Before you were born I ceased to dance to the pipes of other men's opinion. I do not know whether they think well or ill of me.

DEAN

Is that not a kind of pride?

RALEGH

Should a man be ashamed of his own flesh and blood? The Fathers have taught us that we are each wed to our bodies while we live. We should love them, without either pride or shame.

DEAN

Then you conceive that courage is a quality of flesh?

RALEGH

I am not such an old fool as that. Flesh knows fear. There is always fear in the flesh for itself.

DEAN

Then it follows that courage to master fear comes from God.

RALEGH

So does the fear. All things come from God.

DEAN

You persist in skeptical opinions.

RALEGH

I may be allowed to doubt without denying. I have seen savage men, Godless men—though some professed and called themselves Christians and others in innocence did not—I have seen men who lacked every virtue except courage. I think, too, of the courage of creatures—the hunter and the hunted. I have seen boarhounds, not blessed with immortal souls, who could summon up courage a saint could envy.

DEAN

Then your cheerful manner may be more like the stoic courage of the pagans than a flower of Christian faith.

There are many who still recall the rumors of atheism. There are ecclesiastics who recall the record and the unresolved investigation in Whitgift's time. If, then, Ralegh should die with courage today, something may yet be salvaged for the crown by ascribing his behavior to another cause: to the false courage of the pagans.

And if he wavers and trembles, that can be ascribed to the absence of faith.

DEAN

There have been Christian martyrs and saints who trembled in fear at the face of death.

RALEGH

It is well that they should.

DEAN

Why do you say that?

RALEGH

To be a saint is the highest calling, the highest order of mankind beneath the angels. And martyred saints are highest of all.

DEAN

And so?

RALEGH

As St. Paul has taught, their doubts must exceed our own by at least as much as their merits. Think on it. What a burden they must bear! For they desire their poor flesh to serve them well enough to overcome doubt and to be worthy in the eyes of God. I am dazzled with admiration for martyred saints. But I do not envy their deaths. That glory, that tribulation, is beyond common envy.

DEAN

Now, as to yourself . . .

RALEGH

I am a sinner. A yeoman in the fields of this world. Yet, sir, I am as true and sure in my belief as any. For I must believe in the mercy of God or else turn to dust. I owe one death to God. The price is the same, paid now or later. I have faith in God's mercy and therefore I shall summon up all the courage I can. To bear witness to that faith.

DEAN

And still you fear to die.

RALEGH

I have seen death's faces many times. All are fearful to behold. Reason tells me that this death is swift and sure. Easier to bear than a long siege of chills and fever or infirmity or death in battle, all unprepared. Reason tells me I am fortunate to die in this way. There are other deaths which would test my faith to the quick.

DEAN

I must ask you outright what faith you hold, what religion.

Walter Ralegh smiles and shrugs. In shrugging he opens both palms and holds them out before him while he speaks.

RALEGH

I shall die as I have lived, in the only faith I have known, the faith professed by the Church of England. And I hope and pray to have my sins washed away by the most precious blood of our Savior Jesus Christ.

Amen. . . .

The Dean has prayed with dying men before. Some were men
of courage. Some were terribly afraid. None was as important
as this one. All more simple to read.

Ralegh is a devious and subtle man of this world, skilled in
the world's crafts of seeming what he wishes.

He may know something which the Dean does not. May
be calm in confidence that he will not die today. Which would
be well enough unless his confidence is ill founded. In which
case the Dean, all ambitions, offices, bishoprics aside, will fail
in the simplest duty of a minister of the Gospel. By trusting
him, judging him to be firm in faith, he will fail to prepare
him for death. And thus will have a heavy burden on his conscience.

Besides which Ralegh may be playing a stage part so that the
Dean will report him to have died a good Christian. And in
that report the Dean could ruin his future. Or not ruin it. He
cannot know what it is he must say. Fallible and human, no
saint himself, and therefore as much as this man dependent
entirely upon the mercy of God, he would tell them whatever
it is they want to hear. If only he knew.

But he does not know, cannot conceive what is true or false
in the man. And cannot conceive whether true or false report
is what is expected of him.

RALEGH
You are full of wonder and doubts. Consider that every man
is at least two men as long as he lives and breathes. All men
see and judge the outward man. But no man can know without doubt the inner, invisible man. He remains a mystery.

[709]

I say, good Dean, I am as troubled as you are. I must do what I can, then, and act in faith toward myself. I must believe that I believe, and then pray God to help my unbelief.

Strange reversal, to be ministered unto by the man he should be teaching. He might be nettled by pride. But the Dean, listening to the words, has not been hearing them so much as thinking on the picture of Ralegh's open hands. Now folded, tight and calm in his lap, they were, when he smiled and shrugged and held them, palm-upward, long-fingered, level, they were steady and strangely beautiful. Those hands and fingers were graceful, steady, perfectly relaxed, not a tremble. Not even the trembling of age. He saw then not a vain old man in courtier's finery, not the lined face still haunted with remnants of beauty ruined, not the small bright, half-hooded eyes, not any of this, but a pair of hands, as if a portrait had been done in this fashion, the essence of all his being, past, present and to be, distilled, abstracted, disembodied, becoming at last a pair of slender-fingered, open-palmed, eloquent hands, those hands tranquil and gentle. Not soft, but gentle. A gentleness which startles him as the low voice in a Westcountry accent says words he hears clear enough.

Words to be believed or not believed.

To deny those hands would be to deny everything. Not only the unseen, which must be always inferred, but the first beginning of all knowledge and inference—the report of his senses.

Dean or Bishop, good fortune or bad, he must trust himself that much, be faithful to his version of this world even if he doubts it.

"Let not your heart be troubled," the Dean says, feeling a weight lifted from his own heart as he says those ancient words.

And he knows he has chosen. That he will tell the truth in his report. That he will report his judgment and stand by it.

Still there remain a few things which he knows he must inquire into, if only as ritual formality.

DEAN

You are still regarded by some to be the chief instrument in the death of the Earl of Essex in the Queen's time.

RALEGH

The instrument in the death of Essex was a common English heading ax.

DEAN

Have you anything to confess in that matter?

RALEGH

Essex was fetched off by a trick. But it was none of my doing. At the time I had no knowledge of it. I confess I was sorry to see him die, but he died well and in justice.

DEAN

And so there is justice in your death.

RALEGH

With this difference. I am an innocent man.

Dean Tounson starts a little from his settled composure. Looks closely, past Ralegh's smile, to the heavy-lidded eyes. In which he can read nothing at all.

The question of justice, guilt or innocence, pertains to Caesar not to God. The Dean of Westminster must render unto Caesar, the King, that much. Though he may choose to believe the

[711]

truth of Ralegh's faith, he cannot permit Ralegh to die professing an injustice rendered in Caesar's world.

DEAN

Do you doubt the justice of the King?

RALEGH

I do not question the justice of the law or the King. But if
I must die, I will do so with the knowledge in my heart that
I am innocent.

DEAN

You contradict yourself.

RALEGH

Come, sir, if my heart tells me I am innocent, why should I
preserve that secret? I could deceive you easy enough, Dean
Tounson, if I had a mind to. And I think you know it, too.
But I am not so foolish as to imagine I can deceive God, from
whom no secrets are hid.

DEAN

When you speak from the scaffold . . .

RALEGH

I shall not question the justice of the King. But neither will I
acknowledge a guilt I do not feel.

DEAN

I trust for your sake . . .

RALEGH

. . . and your own . . .

DEAN

I trust you will be circumspect.

[712]

RALEGH

By the grace of God and with faith in his love and favor, I
hope to die well this morning, if I can. If I must die. . . .
You came here to minister to me. You have chastised me for
my cheerfulness and seeming courage. You have questioned my
faith. . . .

DEAN

I must do my duty.

RALEGH

I do not doubt you. But I remind you of the Gospel you
preach. No man who loves God and fears Him can die in
cheerfulness and with courage except he is certain of God's
love. There may be others who can make an outward show, but
these are husks. They feel no joy within.

DEAN

And do you truly feel joy?

RALEGH

My flesh is frail and shrinks from death, and I confess my spirit
is weak and heavy. And yet, good sir, the thought of God's
love and mercy is so light and glad within me that I can forgive
my flesh and rebuke my doubtful spirit. Joy is the yoke of a
Christian, lighter to bear than an April breeze. I praise God
and thank Him for the gift of joy.

DEAN

I humbly ask your pardon, sir.

RALEGH

Let us contend no more. We are both Christians, and you are
God's servant. Let us proceed with the holy sacrament.

[713]

Dr. Robert Tounson, Dean of Westminster, nods and rises from his chair. He turns to beckon to his acolyte. Turning back, he sees Walter Ralegh kneeling before him, head down, hands clasped together.

Taking up his *Book of Common Prayer*, the Dean finds the place, puts on his spectacles to read, though he knows it by heart and has never before in public used reading spectacles.

Servants have brought a small table. The prebend spreads a white linen cloth over it. Nodding, Dean Tounson stands before the table, facing the kneeling man, and begins to read.

"Our Father, which art in heaven, Hallowed be Thy Name. Thy Kingdom come. Thy will be done . . ."

When he has taken the communion Ralegh will rise, seeming more blithe than before. He will eat like a farmer with a long morning's labor ahead, or a man at an inn facing a journey on the open road. And as the day's sunlight begins to stream through the windows and the servants snuff out the candles, he will call for a pipe and smoke it.

Leaving the Dean of Westminster to wonder how he shall retell this last gesture.

All the world knows how much the King hates the habit of tobacco.

Eight o'clock and the bell of the hall tolling to mark the hour.

Morning of Thursday, 29 October. Lord Mayor's Day in London.

A morning bright and cold. Surprisingly chilly brightness. A clear sky with a few wan white clouds, far sails seen from atop a tall mast, running with fair wind.

Here below no wind. Only gusts of breeze now and again sweeping Old Palace Yard. Lifting and teasing a scattering of sodden leaves. Rippling and wrinkling pools of water standing from the rain.

Sun painting the wall and the western gatehouse. Panes of the supper chamber gilded in high polish of sunlight. Extravagant clear light lavishly painting and polishing the wall and gatehouse and splashing over the high wall into narrow Tothill Street.

Tothill Street, where people come to crowd into Old Palace Yard. A rainbow crowd in holiday finery. Nudged and directed by yeomen and men in the livery of the sheriffs. Going in a slither through the gate and past the gatehouse. Like a many-colored garden snake sliding home. Home not to blackness, but to clear sudden space of Old Palace Yard. Spilling inward, falling loose in that space under a wide sky. Rolling free from this side of the wall like a broken string of beads.

Behind them, huge, Westminster Abbey. Before them, across the yard to the east, the hulk of the old palace, crumbling towers, roof and gable joined by the long line of Westminster Hall.

From Tothill Street, sunlight leaping the wall and splashing them with light and shade, they press on foot in their holiday finery.

A few of the better sort, high and proud, on horseback. Edging through the crowd.

And coming from the east also. Coming by boat and wherry to land amid shouts of Southwark watermen struggling for space, place to leave off their fares.

Stepping careful to shore from rocking and tip of boats. Sunlight blazing on Thames behind them, river afire and blinding.

Stepping careful to shore, to mount the flight of stairs and enter by the river gate, thence across a space and toward the line of houses and outbuildings facing the river. Where windows blossom with the clothing of strangers who watch from window, from doorway, and some upon rooftops. Gate, walk, Abbey, hall, and palace humble them. They come in procession like pilgrims. Noise from river and bankside, noise and voices dwindling and dying behind them. Entering the yard from the east, humbled. To walk slower while voices soften to whispers.

Tothill Street a humming beehive. Cries of vendors, beggars, and all such. Voices pitched loud to be heard. And noise of voices rising as they make through the gate. Once within the

[716]

yard, facing the quiet slow walkers from the river, they, too, fall to whispering.

All moving, from east and west, toward the high scaffold and the barriers. Barriers unseen because of press of the crowd, but marked by glint of halberd, partizan, and pike of the yeomen of the Guard and the sheriffs' men.

Entering from east or west they look first toward the scaffold. Where the headsman and a boy stand waiting. Then glance toward the gatehouse, seeing nothing there but a blinding shower of gold. Gatehouse, like the river, is all afire.

From this blinding gold, out of this pyre and into the chill and beneath an enormity of wide blue sky where a few clouds fill their sails with high winds, he must come.

He is tardy for this appointment.

Many who feared they were late, now smile, thinking already the Lord Mayor's barge and the procession of barges will be mustering in London and soon coming to this place.

If he delays further, if he speaks and prays long, two shows will become one pageant.

The King in his wisdom may have arranged it so. A theater for his benevolent mercy. In which event the throng will toss hats high and cheer his name.

Or—and *think* but say nothing of this to friend or neighbor —this King will fuse an alloy of wisdom and folly. Coinage of fool's gold . . .

The upper chamber of the gatehouse is crowded now. Ralegh's servants, servants of the porter of the gatehouse, Dean Tounson and his acolytes, a yeoman of the Guard, one of the sheriffs of London and Middlesex, a portly, fidgety gentleman, and some of his servants.

Odors of beef, bread, beer, cheese, and wine upon the trestle table still. Of woodsmoke and tobacco. Scents of perfume and pomander. Smell of human sweat.

Sweatless, the man has his hair combed and brushed a final time.

Above a ground bass of muted voices in the room, crackle of fire, creak of boots and harness, whispers of cloth, above muted counterpoint, the voice of Robert Tounson is clear. He stands by Ralegh, near as a shadow, reading from Romans.

"Christ rising again from the dead now dieth not. Death from henceforth hath no power over him. For in that he dieth, he died but once to put away sin. But in that he liveth, he liveth unto God. And so likewise count yourselves as dead unto sin, but count yourselves as living unto God, the Father, through Jesus Christ, Our Lord."

"Amen," says Ralegh. "Now I shall have my gown and cover."

A servant assists him into his long gown, all velvet, black and sleek as a raven's coat.

Another comes with the hat, high-crowned, wide-brimmed, black felt brightened by a single peacock's feather. And with the hat, a silk nightcap, black, though wrought in subtle stitchery of gold and silver.

He eyes the nightcap doubtfully.

"Is it so cold as that?"

"Aye, sir. It is cold as a key outdoors."

"And only a dead mouse feels no cold."

"So the saying goes, sir."

The clock strikes eight across the yard, rattles panes and echoes in the room.

The sheriff winces at each stroke.

"Be not alarmed, Mr. Sheriff," Ralegh tells him when the clock has struck the hour. "I am almost ready now."

He nods to the servant who fits the nightcap to his head, then places the hat, not square on his head, but at a slight tilt over the right eye and the brim in front turned down at the edge. Someone holds a looking glass and Ralegh nods approval, then adjusts the angle of the hat himself.

Tounson still reading: "Hear my prayer, O Lord, and let my crying come unto Thee. Hide not Thy face from me in the time of my trouble; incline Thine ear unto me when I call. . . ."

"Very well, Mr. Sheriff, I am as ready as I shall ever be."

The sheriff sighs with relief. There is a movement toward the door and the sheriff moves to take his place with the Dean and Ralegh.

"Where is your fellow?" Ralegh asks the sheriff.

"God knows, not I."

"Perhaps it is too cold for him this morning."

"Aye," the sheriff mutters. "An ass will be cold even at the summer solstice."

Going toward the door now at last. To go down and outside. At the open door Ralegh halts.

"Wait! I shall wear my ring also." Turns to the sheriff, whose cloudy face is wet with sweat. "It was given to me by our late Queen. And I should wear it now."

A moment while servants search for the ring. Silence except for the sheriff's deep breathing. Then Ralegh holds out his right hand for a servant to slip the ring upon his finger.

"Now then, Mr. Sheriff, mop your brow, and let us be about our business."

Down the steep rickety stairway one at a time. Ralegh stepping slow and careful so as not to trip on the hem of his gown.

Bouquet of staring faces clustered around the entrance of the house. From which he plucks one or two he knows. The porter offers him a bowl of strong wine.

"Here, sir, it is the custom."

He takes the pewter bowl, looks at the color of the wine. Raises it and drinks deep. Drinks again and offers it to the Dean. Who shakes his head and continues to read.

The sheriff shrugs and accepts the bowl.

"How do you like the mixture?" the porter asks Ralegh.

"As the fellow said who was drinking a St. Giles' bowl on his way to Tyburn, it is a good drink indeed, if a man might tarry with it."

Yeoman of the Guard laughs out loud. And then others are laughing.

It is to laughter, then, he steps through the doorway. Laughter behind him, cold clear air greeting him, cold air and sunlight. And a single shout is echoed and becomes a roar in the crowd. Like fire sudden catching in dry twigs.

Stands a moment outside the door, as laughter fades behind him. Waiting for the sheriff to take his place. Tounson still mumbling, now from the Psalms. Stands a moment, smiling faintly, breathing deep of the air, squinting into the sun and an arras of faces.

Then as the sheriff stumbles to a place beside him, the smile is gone. He stretches, stands full height, tall above all around him, head and hat high, bobbing like a little boat amid the crowd all around him.

Walks slowly forward, eyes ahead toward the rude stage, where a man and a boy wait for him. Walks slowly, therefore need not display his limp, while the yeoman and sheriff's men struggle to make a path.

The shouting dwindles. Lightly he rests one hand on the Dean. For he has forgotten his cane. Lowers eyes from the scaffold to close faces nearby. And sees with a start a wizened face. A bald, wrinkled head. A very old man. Who must have been a man when he himself would have been a boy.

How do they manage to live so long?

He stops and faces the man.

"Good sir," he says. "Why have you come here this morning?"

A portrait of death would have such a face. But the limner would be deceived. See, the old eyes are clear. This oak is still a green one. Not death by any means. Rather the tenacious patient triumph of life. May he live long and die in peace and quiet. . . .

"What is it you want, sir?" Ralegh asks him again.

"Nothing, sir, but to be here to see you. And to pray God have mercy on your soul."

"I thank you for your prayers."

Ralegh removes his hat. Then the nightcap, which he places upon the old man's head.

"Wear this to cover your naked head," Ralegh tells him. "For you have more need of it than I."

Moves on then, holding his hat in his hand.

Up to the edge of the scaffold and the rude stairway to mount it. Looks up. Huge and shadowy against the sun behind him, the headsman stands, hands clasped behind his back, nodding patiently.

Ralegh grips Tounson's arm more tightly now. The sheriff slips a hand below his elbow. And they mount the stairs to stand above the crowd—a field of weeds and flowers swaying. A giddy sight. Or is it his breath is short now? Or does the fever and ague come again?

From the river, from London, carried upon random puffs of breeze, the peal of many bells. Announcing the Lord Mayor's Day.

He looks the headsman eye to eye. Squat and sturdy, a solid stump of a man, heavy-footed and -legged, thick-waisted, broad-backed, neck of a bulldog, head upon bulked sloping shoulders. And the hands? Cutting his eyes away from the other's to see them. Large, leathery, calloused, thick-wristed, horn-knuckled. Yet calm and passive. And in that passivity, oddly gentle.

Back to the eyes and face. A plain homely common English face. Work of a country stone carver. Weathered, lined, crumbled a little by time. But withal an honest, gentle face. A trusty face. The eyes unblinking. Passive and calm. Matching the hands in tranquillity . . .

Breeze blowing brisk, tugging at his velvet gown.

Turns from the man to see the scaffold and its accommodations. Neat and clean. Buckets of water and brushes. Basket of fresh straw. Beside which a boy with awkward large hands seems to shrink and wish to be small. As if—as boys think—every eye were upon *him,* judging him. The boy does not look at him. Clasps his hands tight to keep them still, looks down at the straw in the basket.

Ralegh looks to see what he has not yet wished to. A low curved block of hard wood, sanded smooth and paid with a fresh even coat of stain. If final pillows must be wood, this one looks decent enough, adequate. Beside it, flat upon the heavy timbers of the scaffold, is the heading ax. Winking in the light. No fleck of rust on head or edge. Kept with care, polished and honed fine.

Beside the ax there is a small shiny red leather bag. Modestly embossed, Ralegh's own coat of arms . . .

[722]

Red leather bag, his arms in gold. Companion to the other bag, the one he imagines, stolen by Sir Judas Stukely to carry his gold. The red leather bag sent by Bess, then. Her presence here with him as if she had sent him a hothouse rose. Not to be stained or spoiled by any blood. And he knows, without wishing to look, that beyond the edge of the crowd in the cool shadows, itself a shadow with black curtains drawn, a coach is waiting to carry this red bag home. Not Bess behind the curtains. She promised, and that promise was exacted because she could not, must not bear this any more than in mind's eye she bears it now and for as long as she shall live. Not Bess, but some servant, and no doubt a woman. For this is the duty of women. And which of the women will this be? Why, of course, her cousin Mary, who came with her last night (long ago) by proxy to be the image of youth and now to age into the image of herself. Mary, alone behind the curtains of the black coach, praying for his life now if for no other reason than that she may not have to carry the weight of that red leather bag in her lap. Praying that when she bounces homeward in the coach, the bag shall lie empty and limp beside her.

And he grateful for her prayers whatever her motive may be.

Smiles at that and turns to look again into the eyes of the headsman. Who has not moved a muscle or, it would seem, blinked an eyelid.

Drums and a trumpet call. Tounson's voice. The sheriff beside him, facing the crowd and raising his hands for quiet.

Ralegh touches the hand of the headsman.

"Are you not Mr. Gregory Brandon?"

"Aye, sir."

His hand heavy and warm, not flinching from touch.

"I should have known you, but it has been much time."

[723]

"The years go at a gallop, sir."

"And is that boy yonder your son?"

With his free hand Brandon motions toward the boy, calls softly.

"Come make your manners to the gentleman."

The sheriff with arms raised still and the crowd beginning to quiet. The boy comes shuffling, head down, shy.

"This is my son, Richard."

"A fine lad who favors his father."

Ralegh touches the boy, and the boy, startled, raises his head, wide-eyed.

"Your father is a good and honest man," he says. "I pray you shall favor him in character as you do in appearance."

The boy drops his eyes again.

"Bless you, boy," Ralegh says, slipping a ring from his fingers and placing it in the palm of the boy's hand.

The boy clasps the ring in a tight claw, a white-knuckled fist. Steps back to his place.

"Pardon the lad, sir. It is new to him."

"I have a son myself, Mr. Brandon. I know . . ."

Now the sheriff's voice, breaking with hoarseness in the first words so he must clear his throat and commence again. He begins to read the sentence of execution.

Walter Ralegh places his hat on his head, squarely this time and pulled down almost to the ears against the breeze. Turns slowly, tall, to face the crowd.

Breeze is dying away. The crowd stands listening as the sheriff strains to raise his voice and be heard, reading from the document.

His head unmoving, but eyes shadowed by the low brim of his hat, Ralegh glances upward toward the windows of the old palace. Sees color, fine clothing of courtiers and ladies, and the white of faces there. The upturned faces near him are flushed and tanned in sun and chill.

The sheriff reads, holding the document now close to his nose, now at arm's length. Poor fellow has need of spectacles. Perhaps he has forgotten them. . . .

Finished, he turns to face Ralegh. Moves closer.

"It is bitter cold, sir. Would you wish to warm yourself by a fire before you speak? My men can kindle a blaze at the foot of the scaffold."

"I thank you, but I fear it would aggravate my ague, Mr. Sheriff, and cause me to tremble and shiver. Besides which, I doubt my legs would freely mount this scaffold a second time. One climbing is sufficient."

"An' it please you," the sheriff answers. "Have you some words to say?"

"A few words. A few . . ."

Producing from beneath folds of his gown a sheaf of papers, thick, crawling with many words. The sheriff startled by the bulk of it.

"Patience," Ralegh whispers. "I shall not read it all."

Steps forward to the edge of the scaffold, gripping the papers, to read.

It is very quiet now. So quiet that a mother's shushing of a child far at the edges of the crowd is loud. Still, he has never been blessed with much voice.

"My honorable good lords, and you, the rest of my friends who have come to see me die. . . ."

Lowers the papers.

"For two days I have suffered two fits of ague. Yesterday morn I was taken from my bed in the midst of a fit of fever

[725]

to stand before King's Bench. It has left me much weakened. Whether or no I shall escape it this morning, I cannot tell. Chills and fever come and go as they will, forbearing no time or place or occasion. I pray God to spare me from it this one last time. And I implore you all, out of honest love and charity, that if you shall mark any disability in my voice or seeming sadness and dejection of countenance, you shall impute it to the disorder of my body and not to any dismay of mind or shrinking of the soul. . . .".

Raising the papers to begin again.

"Honorable lords and friends, I offer my thanks to Almighty God that He hath vouchsafed me to die in daylight and in the presence of such an honorable assembly and not alone in the darkness."

Looking up again toward the windows where the great ones, the greatest here today, lean far out from high chambers and apartments to catch his words. Cupping his hands to call out, as if at sea.

"I will seek to strain my voice," he calls. "For I would willingly have all your honors hear me."

The crowd turning their necks to follow his glance. Silent staring at the windows. A moment of hesitant silence before one up there with a deep clear voice replies.

"Nay, sir. We shall rather come down to you and come upon the scaffold."

Faces vanish from the windows. Crowd buzzes and hums. Gregory Brandon, who has slipped from the scaffold unnoticed, returns from his cart bearing a small stool for Ralegh to sit on while he waits. Ralegh nods and sits.

Tounson stands aside, clasping his heavy Bible.

The sheriff looks in the direction of the river gate. He is as sad-faced as a basset hound.

"Pray, be of good cheer," Ralegh tells him. "At worst the Lord Mayor can join us as a witness."

"My orders were most strict," the sheriff says.

"Well," says Ralegh, "it is a difficult time for both of us. Let us try to make the best of it."

A noise and ripple in the crowd reveal the lords and nobles coming across the yard toward the scaffold. Ralegh watches their passage until he can see their faces clearly. Arundel, Oxford, Northampton, the Lord Sheffield, and others of distinction and lesser rank.

Also, though out of the crowd itself and not from the palace, comes James Hay, his clothes water-stained, mud-spattered. His face and beard dirty, lined and pouched from lack of sleep. But his head high, himself in one sense the proudest of them all.

"Ah, Mr. Sheriff, these are the nobility. We must wait upon them, if that is their will."

"I know, I know," the sheriff groans.

When they reach the scaffold Ralegh rises to greet them. As if he were host. As if he welcomed them into his chambers. Presents them to the sheriff, to Dean Tounson and to Mr. Gregory Brandon.

At last, after all courtesy and amenity, with these men grouped about him, he faces the assembly and begins to read his speech again.

"As I have said already, I thank God most heartily that He has brought me out of the darkness into daylight to die. He would not suffer me to die in the dark prison of the Tower. And I offer thanks to the Almighty that I seem now upon this morning to have been so far spared my fever and

[727]

chills. I prayed that I might be spared. And I believe that prayer has been answered."

True, his color is good now and his voice is clear enough as, reading quickly, he summarizes the case and the suspicions of King and Council against him. Then he denies all the charges and suspicions, raising his voice to call upon God to be his witness.

"For any man to call upon God as his witness to a falsehood, at any time, is a most grievous sin. And for a man at the time of his death to do so is far more grievous and impious. Such a man can have no hope of salvation. And so, knowing that within this hour I shall hope to see God in His Kingdom, I call upon God to witness the truth of my words. And if I do not speak true, O God, let me never enter into Thy Kingdom."

Next denies further plot or disloyalty against the King in word or deed at any time. Unequivocal denial. Adding:

"Nay, I will protest even further. I say here that never in my life did I harbor any evil or disloyal thought against the King. Not in my most secret heart.

"It is not for me to flatter the King or any of the kings of this world. For I am now the humble subject of Death. And soon I shall appear before the great tribunal of the King of Kings, our Sovereign in heaven.

"If I speak falsely, let the Lord blot out my name from the Book of Life."

Pauses and eyes them all. Then confesses, briefly, to some faults in this affair. That he did, indeed, out of fear for his life, seek to escape. That also he did dissemble and pretend sickness in Salisbury to gain time.

"But I hope this was no sin. I recall from Holy Scripture that David, a king himself and a man after God's own heart, did for the safety of his life make himself a fool. He let his spittle fall upon his ragged beard and he, as wise as Solomon after him, went upon all fours like a beast. Yet it has not been imputed as a sin of David to do so.

"I intend no ill against His Majesty. I intended only to prolong my time and, hopefully, to gain the ear of the King, in hope also of some compassion, some commiseration from him.

"But I now forgive all those who spoke against me then, just as I likewise do forgive Sir Lewis Stukely with all my heart for the wrongs he has done me. For I have received the sacrament this morning from Dr. Tounson here beside me. Receiving the holy sacrament, I have forgiven all men, even as I ask God to forgive me. Still, in love and charity to my fellowmen, I am bound to caution against him and such as he is.

"Touching, then, upon my kinsman, Sir Lewis Stukely . . ."

A slow itemized account of the dealings and double-dealings of Sir Judas. Nonetheless confused, knotty, perplexing. Yet himself, Ralegh, so clear and open and evidently generous that all the shadows and doubts fall upon Stukely. And pausing there, allowing the picture of his shadowy kinsman to sink from view while he shuffles his papers and notes, as if searching for something, seeking some sign of remembrance. A moment for the listeners to shift their weight, to cough and clear throats. To be fully conscious, living bodies again.

He looks up at them from the papers and smiles.

"Well, I have gone thus far," he says. "Bear with me patiently. A little more, only a little more and I shall be done."

Still, more still than any time before, faces upturned, they become a field of eyes and ears again.

"It was told to the King that I did not return freely to England, but was brought back here by mutineers. . . ."

And now, in the form of a story, his version of what took place. Much' the opposite of all report. How he was kept close prisoner in his cabin by mutineers. How they had forced him to take an oath, or be cast into the sea, that he would never bring them home to England. How "by wine, gifts, and fair words" he managed to divide them against each other and took command again. How he agreed to pardon those who would serve him and bring them safely home, if they wished. Those who feared England he would leave in the south of Ireland. And so he did.

"There was some report, also," he continues, "that I never meant to go to Guiana at all. That there was no mine. That I sought only my liberty. Which, it would seem, I lacked the wit to keep. . . ."

Here he smiles broadly and invites laughter. And there is some laughter from the crowd.

"It was my full intent to go for gold for the benefit of His Majesty and myself, for those who sailed with me . . ."

Turning suddenly to the Earl of Arundel, but speaking for all to hear.

"My lord, you yourself were in the gallery of my ship at my departure. And I remember how you took me by the hand and said you had but one request to make of me. Which request was that, whether I had a bone voyage or a bad one, I should return to England. And, my lord, I promised you in faith that I would do so."

Arundel of the clear loud voice replies, nodding, to Ralegh and for the crowd.

"So you did," Arundel says. "It is true. Those were our last words before you sailed."

Swift then, point by point, to scotch reports and rumors concerning his last voyage to Guiana. All trivial, each point. Of interest and import to his hearers only in that they should seem significant to Ralegh at this urgent hour.

That he intended to leave his men in Guiana. Not so.

That he had stinted them of fresh water. Not so. Though some, unaccustomed to the sea, may have been quite thirsty on that voyage.

That he carried sixteen thousand pieces of gold with him secretly. Not so. He considered himself most fortunate to have one hundred pounds for divers purchases.

Here he stops speaking. Lowers his head, as if in a deep study. Moments pass slowly.

The sheriff steps forward. Nervously, touches his arm.

"I will borrow but a little more of your time, Mr. Sheriff. I shall not detain you very long."

A muttering from the crowd. The sheriff steps back, behind the shield of the nobility.

And just so, in metaphor, does Walter Ralegh himself, though literally alone and unmoving on the stage of the plain scaffold, alone and tall in velvet from chin to toes, his white hair and white beard pale against the lean sunburned face, alone at the edge of the scaffold, though standing against a background of the nobility, not new men but young men with old and ancient titles and names, just as the sheriff steps out of view, so Walter Ralegh (more graceful to be sure, a step as light as a dancer's) in one step dismisses trivial present time, like a magician with a wand of words, banishes the present to reappear in and from the past, a younger past, himself sharing and partaking of that youth, summoning out of memory a glory which has been lost forever and, being lost, is now valued as priceless, calling up ghostly figures dancing to a music of which even the echoes have faded to the absolute purity of silence.

Or so it would seem, must seem, does so seem to those here standing to hear his soft voice and Westcountry accent for the last time; thus so attentive, so still, that it is as if he had turned them into stone; a man speaking to a field of stones. A man in the wilderness addressing sun-struck, sun-dazzled stones with naked words, words of the heart itself. The stones not passive, though still and quiet, but sentient. Though unmoving, able to be moved by words. Totally attentive, drinking his words. As a man with a black, chapped, salty, thirst-ridden mouth might kneel by a spring and cup the cold, light-dancing clarity of water in both hands. . . .

They see him, true, tall, and unmoving. See all that is to be seen. Yet already like the chorus in an English play, he has painted scene after scene more palpable than anything they see. So that, at last, they sway as to a spell, hearing words but seeing most with mind's eye.

As if in afterthought, as if in haste against the power of the present, which is being measured and signaled and tolled by bells in London, and those bells growing louder and clearer to mark a slow progress on the Thames, as if in afterthought (thus all the more urgent for its apparent inspiration), he calls upon one fading memory from the past.

"I shall speak somewhat of my lord, the Earl of Essex."

Breath caught and held, the stones listen. His voice over-mastering the sounds of bells. Accompanied not by bells and distant trumpets of the present but by ghostly music.

"The imputation has been laid upon me that I was the persecutor of my lord of Essex. It has been said that I rejoiced in his death. It has been told that when the Earl of Essex stood upon the old scaffold in the shadows of the Tower, I stood in a high window over against him and puffed out tobacco smoke in rude defiance of him.

"God is my witness that I shed tears for him when he died. As I hope and pray to look God in the face hereafter, I swear that my lord of Essex did not see my face at the time of his death. For I was far off in the Armory. I saw him, but he did not see me.

"It is true that I was of another faction, a contrary faction to his own. But I take the same God for my witness that I had no hand in his death. Nor did I bear my lord of Essex any ill affection. I always believed it would have been better that his life had been preserved.

"After his death I got the hatred of many of those who had wished me well before in better days. And those who set me against him afterwards did set themselves against me. They became my greatest enemies.

"My soul hath many times grieved that I was not nearer to my lord of Essex when he died. Because, as I was to understand afterwards, at his death he asked for me by name and desired that we should be reconciled."

There it stands, the death of Essex acted out again in theater of memory. Ending at last in reconciliation. Across a wide gulf of years Essex offers his hand to Walter Ralegh. They shake hands and embrace upon that scaffold and upon this one, being one and the same now just as the green and shadowy Yard of the Tower becomes one with the space of Old Palace Yard; and, dizzy from turning and turning in time, his hearers can believe they are in both times and both places.

He is no longer alone upon a scaffold with a few living lords of the land—but stands in the company of all the great men dead and gone, friends and enemies alike. They are all here, next in the crowd, though invisible, as the men at each elbow. And the scaffold is huge, crowded with familiar and forgotten faces drawn larger than life.

It is as if he had already stepped aside from skin and bones, not content to wait upon the brutal parting of head from body, stepped out of flesh to become not alone, but one of a multitude stitched in many colors into the texture of an arras. An arras more brilliant than all flags, rich and intricate as English springtime.

Has already departed them and this scene, stepping out of time into the memory of springtime. And over that springtime rules, rejoicing, beautiful as once she had been, herself a springtime of jewels, clad in richest and strangest of leaves and flowers, Elizabeth, Queen of England then and now and still for as long as there is England. The Queen whose name has not been mentioned once here because she need not be named to be honored.

It is in her honor he and the Earl of Essex shake hands and embrace, reconciled at last. And thus they die together. And their deaths becoming a sort of allegory. As if in old armor they only pretended to die. A play or pageant for the tiltyard . . .

Excepting some act of mercy from the King, he must die in the present. Yet has made that truth, that present, almost inconsequential. A mere symbolic act, no more. Death or life, rigor or clemency, no matter. For he has already lightly stepped out of time and his aging, dying body to become a member of the evergreen court of history.

Giving life or death, the King of England cannot change that.

[734]

All that remains is to lead his body by the hand, as one might lead a blind man, to cross a road.

"And now I pray and entreat you all that you will join with me in prayer to that great God of heaven, whom I have most grievously offended while I lived. For I am a man who is full of vanity and I have lived a sinful life in such callings as have been most inducing to it. For I have been a soldier, a sailor, and a courtier, and these are courses of wickedness and vice. And the temptations of the least of these are able to overthrow a good mind and a good man.

"I ask you to join with me in prayer that God, who alone is the author of all mercy and forgiveness, will forgive me, and that he will receive me into everlasting life.

"And so I take my leave of you, making my peace with God."

With a slow deliberate gesture he removes his hat and bows his head. Light breeze ruffles his hair.

The sheriff moves forward to make the proclamation that all men should now leave the scaffold, as is the custom. But as he does so Ralegh, still bowed in prayer, gives him the hat he holds. The sheriff looks at the hat, glances at the line of great men, their heads bowed, and lowers his head also.

Upon that cue, all in the crowd bow their heads. And some few kneel.

A dog barks. A baby cries. From Thames the thunder of cannon and the hives of bells becoming louder.

"Amen," says Walter Ralegh.

Then moves to the edge of the scaffold to bid farewell to the lords and gentlemen.

"I have a long journey to go," he tells them. "Therefore I must take my leave."

[735]

One by one, they file down the steps to stand at the foot looking up at him.

Turns and, taking a black purse from beneath his gown, gives money to the sheriff. Who is awkwardly holding the hat behind his back.

Mr. Gregory Brandon steps close.

"Permit me to assist you with your clothing."

Like a servant, the executioner assists him as he removes the gown.

A little gasp from some in the crowd who remember the sudden scarlet shirt of Essex. But Walter Ralegh, ever exact, is dressed for mourning in black and gray. Except, as some can see and others will see, his black velvet slippers are brightened with red rosettes. As if with two tiny drops of blood.

Off comes the white ruff band and the doublet.

"Take these," he tells Mr. Brandon. "And have my purse. It is thin enough, but perhaps it may serve you."

"I thank you."

Brandon folds doublet and ruff neatly, giving them and the purse to his son. The gown he folds and places near the red leather bag. He will wrap the gown around the bag before he gives it to Lady Ralegh's messenger.

And now he picks up the heading ax and takes a wide-footed stance by the block.

"A moment, Mr. Brandon, if you please. May I see the ax?"

Brandon blinks, surprised. Does not move.

"I prithee, let me see it. Do you think I am afraid of it?"

Brandon does not offer him the ax, but he does release it as Ralegh takes it from his hands.

Hefts it with a tight smile. Turns toward where the sheriff stands, face like a flounder, close to Dr. Tounson.

Tounson, spectacled, bent close to his Bible, reading.

"The Lord is my shepherd and therefore can I lack nothing. He shall feed me in a green pasture. . . ."

Ralegh, facing the sheriff, runs his thumb along the edge of the ax.

"Mr. Sheriff, this is sharp medicine. But it is a sound cure for all diseases."

The sheriff's face seems to melt like a plate of butter left too close to fire. He looks away.

Ralegh turns again to Gregory Brandon and returns the ax to him. Sees that Brandon has removed his own cloak to spread it out for Ralegh to lie upon.

"Mr. Brandon, after I put my head upon your block, I should like one moment of prayer. When I am done, I shall stretch forth my hands and you may strike."

A swift look around. The old stone buildings, surf of faces all around, the dark-boned, wind-plucked trees. And sees the black carriage waiting.

The sky grayer, the sunlight fading behind high clouds. And high, blank scraps of paper (*all our speeches, all our words*), a few gulls circle and soar.

Brandon kneels before him. Ralegh lays both hands on his shoulders and, nodding, whispers his pardon and forgiveness.

Bells are pealing in Westminster. From the landing and the arched gate a roll of drums. Trumpets sounding.

Brandon rising. Ralegh kneeling down, stiff-jointed.

Commotion of cries and voices nearby the scaffold. The sheriff mumbling something.

Ralegh looking up into Brandon's eyes, questioning.

Brandon bending beside him, placing one hand, calm heavy hand, light on Ralegh's shoulder, whispering in his ear.

[737]

"It is customary, sir, to lie down with the head facing east toward the rising sun."

Ralegh shaking his head.

"So long as the heart is right, it is no matter which way the head lies."

"But you will see the shadow of the ax and flinch."

"Do you think if I fear not the ax itself, I shall be frightened by a shadow? No, Mr. Brandon, I shall not flinch."

Brandon, still bending, spreading and smoothing his cloak for Ralegh to lie upon.

Ralegh easing forward on the cloak, lying full length, lowering his head, resting his neck on the cool, smooth, waxed hardwood of the curved block. Seeing, before he closes his eyes, the towering shadow of a man with an ax, the shadow of himself, his head and breeze-ruffled hair, a stain against the raw timber. Closing his eyes.

Yea though I walk through the valley of the shadow of death, I will fear no evil for thou art with me . . .

Hearing Brandon's breathing, steady, louder than all drums and bells and trumpets at the landing.

. . . thy rod and thy staff they comfort me. . . .

Sudden then stretching forth arms full length. Rings on his fingers flashing with light.

Nothing.

Thou preparest a table before me . . .

Nothing.

Sweat in his eyes.

. . . in the presence of mine enemies . . .

Calling out to the huge shadow. A voice accustomed to the habit of command.

"What doest thou fear? Strike, man, strike!"

The ax is bright in dwindling sunlight. Flashes high before it falls.

Higher by far a lone gull banks and circles on the darkening air. Then flies away to vanish over the Thames.